Margaret Pemberton was born in Bradford but has lived in London for many years. Married with five children, she is the author of many successful novels including the bestselling *The Flower Garden*, *Lion of Languedoc*, and *Never Leave Me*. Her most recent novel, *A Multitude of Sins*, is also available in Corgi paperback.

Also by Margaret Pemberton

A MULTITUDE OF SINS

and published by Corgi Books

# WHITE CHRISTMAS IN SAIGON

## Margaret Pemberton

**CORGI BOOKS**

WHITE CHRISTMAS IN SAIGON
A CORGI BOOK 0 552 13093 1

Originally published in Great Britain by Bantam Press
a division of Transworld Publishers Ltd

PRINTING HISTORY
Bantam Press edition published 1990
Corgi edition published 1990

This book is set in 10/11 pt Plantin

Corgi Books are published by Transworld Publishers Ltd., 61–63 Uxbridge Road, Ealing, London W5 5SA, in Australia by Transworld Publishers (Australia) Pty. Ltd., 15–23 Helles Avenue, Moorebank, NSW 2170, and in New Zealand by Transworld Publishers (N.Z.) Ltd., Cnr. Moselle and Waipareira Avenues, Henderson, Auckland.

Printed and bound in Great Britain by
Cox & Wyman Ltd, Reading

# ACKNOWLEDGEMENTS

Many people gave assistance to me during the writing of this book, but my deepest debt is to Ms Carolyn Nichols, Bantam Books, New York. Her enthusiasm and encouragement gave me the courage to embark on a subject that would otherwise have daunted me. For two years she gave unstintingly of her valuable advice and time, sharing with me her personal library and her deep interest in all things Vietnamese.

My thanks and acknowledgements are also due to the following: the staff of the American Embassy, London; the Beverly Hills Hotel, Los Angeles; the California State Division of Veteran Affairs; the Caravelle Hotel, Ho Chi Minh City; the Colindale Newspaper Library, London; the Foreign Languages Publishing House, Hanoi; the Imperial War Museum, London; the Jefferson Hotel, Washington; Travis Air Base Information Center, California; the Thang Loi Hotel, Hanoi; the War Museum, Hanoi.

I owe special thanks to Madame Dai, Bibliothèque Restaurant, Ho Chi Minh City; Diethelm Travel, Bangkok; Mr Geoffrey Hann, Hann Overland Travel, London; Dr Bich Nguyen, London; Mr Richard Pugh, the British Epilepsy Association, Leeds; Mr Robert Radcliff, Hutchinson, Kansas; Mr Richard Tomlin, London; Vietnam Tourism, Hanoi; Mr Ron Wilson, Civil Aviation Authority, London.

Also, my sincere thanks to Mrs Diane Pearson, of Transworld Publishers, London, and my literary agent, Miss Carol Smith, London, for their friendship and never-failing support.

Vietnam
1954–1975

Tinh Tuc

NORTH
VIETNAM

CHINA

Dienbienphu

Hanoi

Haipong
Thai Binh

LAOS

Golf of
Tonkin

Dong Hoi

← 17th PARALLEL
DEMARCATION LINE

Hue

Danang

THAILAND

Quang Ngai

CAMBODIA

Pleiku

SOUTH VIETNAM

Fish Hook

PHNOM PENH

Cu Chi

Nha Trang

Saigon

Van Binh

Ca Mau Peninsula

U Minh Forest

Names underlined represent fictitious places
© Richard Tomlin

For Marian W., without whom, quite literally, this book would never have been written.

For the friends I made while travelling in Vietnam:

> Anne Convery
> Ling and Mike Clatterbuck
> Debbie and Jim Fallows
> Genevieve and Guy Caufriez
> Franz Pitzal
> Jean Marc Studemann
> Steve Turley

In the words of General Giap, they were truly 'unforgettable days'.

And last but not least, for my husband, Mike, as always.

One watches things that make one sick at heart.
This is the law: no gain without a loss,
And heaven hurts fair women for sheer spite.

                              Nguyen Du
                              (1765–1820)

# PROLOGUE

The day was cold, the sky leaden, full of the sombreness of November. The three women had arrived in Washington separately, on different days during the preceding week. Now they stood, arms linked, on the corner of 7th Street and Constitution Avenue, about to march in one of the most moving and unorthodox parades the city had ever seen.

'Who is up front?' Gabrielle Ryan shouted in a heavy French accent to her companions. All around them people were greeting one another and calling out, struggling to be heard above the deafening sound of a military band gustily playing *The Girl I Left Behind Me*.

'General Westmoreland!' Abbra Ellis shouted back, glossy black hair skimming her shoulders, her cherry-red wool coat glowing like a jewel in the dull afternoon light.

'You bet he is!' an army veteran in faded fatigues and a boonie hat responded as he squeezed past them. 'The President sure as hell isn't!'

'Is that true?' Serena Anderson's voice was disbelieving. 'Isn't the President leading the procession?'

Abbra shook her head. 'No,' she said, her eyes dark. 'None of those who should be here are here. Not the Vice President, not the Secretary of State, not Richard Nixon, not Henry Kissinger. Only Westmoreland.' She slipped her hand into Serena's and gave it a tight squeeze. 'Nothing really changes, Serena. You should know that.'

Serena, tall and elegant and stunningly beautiful, nodded. Twenty-four hours earlier she had been working with the refugees in the Nong Samet refugee camp in Hong Kong. Now here she was in Washington again and, as Abbra had said, despite the parade and the reason for it, nothing had really changed. Not where it mattered. Not on Capitol Hill.

'We're moving!' Gabrielle cried as the crowd around them began to edge forward into the avenue and the strains of *The Girl I Left Behind Me* were replaced by a thunderous rendering of *God Bless America*.

'This is it!' a long-haired, bearded middle-aged man in jeans shouted exultantly. 'Jesus Christ! I've waited nine years for this!'

A lump rose high in Abbra's throat. She, too, had waited nine years. As they turned into the broad sweep of the avenue, she looked around her, laughter and tears vying for expression. She had been in many marches but never one as ragtag yet as splendid as this one.

General Westmoreland, silver-haired and wearing a trench coat, had led it off over two hours earlier, marching alongside a group of veterans from Alabama. Other veterans had followed, marching under the name of their state: New York, Montana, Maryland, Kansas. Some men wore battle fatigues. Some were resplendent in full dress uniform. Some marched, some walked, some hobbled with the aid of canes. Others pushed themselves along in wheelchairs, or were pushed by a buddy or a wife, a son or a daughter.

As the contingent from each state passed, the crowd lining the pavements called out its name and clapped and cheered. The last state represented in the parade was Wyoming; Abbra and Serena and Gabrielle marched along in the centre of the crowd following the delegation, and Abbra felt tears sting her cheeks. The men around her had been too busy reuniting to have marched off under the name of their state. Some sported flags; others carried bottles of beer; many walked, arms around each other's shoulders, some laughed exuberantly, cracking jokes with their companions; others wept. They had come together to remember their shared past and to honour their dead, and the occasion had turned into

10

an emotional homecoming that had been long denied them.

The three women walked among the men, their arms linked, feeling natural. On this day, 13 November, 1982, they belonged in the parade, just as the men around them belonged. They, too, had paid their dues. Abbra, in the centre, hugged her friends' arms, looking first at Serena and then at Gabrielle.

Serena's fragile-boned face was pale, her mouth set firm. Despite the bitter wind she wore no coat. She wore her grey flannel slacks, white cashmere turtleneck, and black velvet blazer with cool, understated English elegance. Her blonde hair was pulled away from her face, coiled in a loose knot at the nape of her neck, revealing clearly the thin white scar that ran from high on her temple to the corner of her left eye which marred her otherwise flawless beauty. Another woman might have cut her hair into bangs and a bob, disguising it. It was typical of Serena that she had done no such thing, wearing her hair as she had always worn it.

Gabrielle was typically fully protected against physical discomfort. Her snakeskin boots were high, teeteringly heeled to compensate for her diminutive height. A pale champagne suede coat was belted at her waist, a huge lynx collar soft against her face, a matching hat tilted rakishly on top of impossibly red hair. Looking across at her, Abbra could see that tears were glittering on her lashes. She hugged her friend's arm tighter and Gabrielle turned towards her, flashing her a dazzling smile, saying, 'It is all right, *chérie*. I was remembering. That is all.'

They were reaching the long end of the avenue. To the left of them was the Lincoln Memorial; a little farther away was the Jefferson Memorial. And now, as they crowded down on to a leafy, two-acre site, the memorial they had honoured with their parade, and which was to be dedicated, came into view.

Abbra caught her breath. This was why the three of them had returned to Washington. She from San Francisco;

11

Gabrielle from Paris; Serena from Hong Kong. The memorial, two huge, tapering walls of shiny black granite forming a wide V and bearing 57,939 names, was simple and elegant and dignified, everything that the war in which the men had died was not. For the memorial had been erected by veterans of one of the ugliest wars that had ever taken place. The war in Vietnam.

Al Keller, national commander of the American Legion, addressed the packed throng stretching far back along Constitution Avenue. 'Today we dedicate a memorial to a generation of Americans who fought a lonely battle,' he began ringingly.

Abbra's eyes were not on him but on the wall. The names had been engraved in chronological order of death, beginning with army major Dale R. Buis, who had been killed on 8 July, 1959, and culminating with air force second lieutenant Richard Vane Geer, who had died on 15 May, 1975. So many names, so much heartbreak.

The crowd was packed with women, many, like herself, in their late thirties, teenage children alongside them. Others were much older, their faces harrowed with lines of grief and loss, their husbands at their sides, their mouths grim as they surveyed the huge black wall bearing the names of their sons.

*Curtis Richard, Titus Epps, Dan Stuber, Richard H. Davies*

Abbra's throat tightened as she looked at them, remembering the other marches that had taken place in Washington, the demonstrations and speeches protesting the very death of the men now immortalized.

*Glenn Rethington, Richard Salmond, Robert G. Drapp*

She remembered the doors of the Justice Department being barricaded against them, the injured who had lain helplessly on the ground as the police had broken up the demonstrations with water from hoses and with tear gas; and she remembered the singing and the chanting and the folk songs.

12

*Gerald Aadland, Craig Reska, Perry Mitchell*

Thirteen years before to the month, at the antiwar March Against Death, the demonstrators had recited, one at a time, the names of the 40,000 Americans who had been killed up to then. The past Wednesday morning, in a chapel at Washington's National Cathedral, the bleak recitation had begun again, and she had been one of those taking part. It had been almost more than she could bear.

A letter from the Secretary of Defense, Caspar Weinberger, was read; Wayne Newton sang; General Westmoreland spoke. The cold stung their cheeks and she felt Serena shiver.

'We are here to remember the suffering and endurance of those who fought in Southeast Asia . . .'

Abbra slipped her hands into Serena's and Gabrielle's.

'We suffered, and we endured as well,' she said passionately, her eyes fiercely bright, and all of a sudden it was as if she had finally reached the end of a long, lonely journey. 'Hell! We did more than that!' She was filled with overwhelming emotion. 'We survived, goddammit! We survived!'

# CHAPTER ONE

'But it's going to be a perfectly respectable party, Mom,' Abbra Daley protested, half amused and half exasperated by her mother's low opinion of her friends and her social life. 'Nearly everyone there will be from Stanford and—'

'And the others?' her mother interrupted crisply as she began to take heavy silver cutlery from a velvet-lined mahogany box. 'The ones who will be there and who aren't from your University? Will that offensive young man you are so obsessed with be there?'

Abbra pushed a fall of silky shoulder-length hair away from her face. 'No,' she said, her eyes clouding slightly, her amusement waning. 'He won't be there.'

Her mother put the silver she had selected to one side and closed the box. 'How can you be so sure? Beatniks don't have to be invited to a party to attend it, do they? They just turn up and make a nuisance of themselves.'

'Jerry is in New York,' Abbra said briefly, keeping a tight rein on her impatience. 'An underground newspaper there is interested in publishing some of his poems and—'

Her mother gave an unladylike snort. 'Poems! Anything that young man writes will be gutter trash. How a girl of your upbringing can be so taken with such an unsavoury specimen I can't begin to imagine. Nor do I understand why his kind finds it so necessary to flock like lemmings to San Francisco. Why can't they stay in their hometowns?'

It wasn't a question that she expected an answer to. She carried the silver across to the large dining table, smoothing an imaginary crease from the hand-made lace tablecloth, every line of her body registering outrage.

15

'Who is coming to dinner?' Abbra asked, realizing that the subject had to be turned away from Jerry. And quickly.

'Tom Ellis is visiting from New York. His son is going to be here as well. And the Parkers.'

Abbra tried to look interested, but it was difficult. Colonel Tom Ellis was an old family friend with a distinguished war record not only in the Second World War but in Korea as well. His conversation – all his conversation, Abbra recalled – centred around things military. His wife had been her mother's childhood friend, and though she had died tragically of cancer shortly after her younger son's birth, the friendship between her parents and the colonel had continued.

'Which son?' she asked, taking a handful of silver and beginning to lay it.

'Older one of course!' her mother said, her tone of voice indicating that the fact should have been self-evident. 'I would hardly invite a *football* player as a dinner guest, would I? The Parkers would think I had taken leave of my senses!'

Sam Parker was an eminent neurologist, as was Abbra's father.

'What's so socially acceptable about the older son's career?' Abbra asked, amusement at her mother's snobbishness restoring her good humour.

'Lewis is an army officer.' Her mother examined a silver candelabrum carefully to make sure that the maid had cleaned it to her satisfaction. 'West Point. Surely you remember that your father and I attended his graduation?'

Abbra shook her head. She had met the colonel on numerous occasions but had only a shadowy recollection of seeing Lewis when she was eight or nine. He had been a teenager in an army cadet uniform, and because she had expected someone her own age she had been intensely disappointed, and too shy to exchange more than half a dozen words with him.

16

'Tell me about the younger brother,' she said as her mother handed her a clean cloth with which to polish already sparkling wineglasses. 'Is he really a football player?'

Her mother nodded, stepping back from the immaculately laid table and regarding it critically. 'Unfortunately, yes. He's causing his father a great deal of anxiety. If you're here when Tom arrives, I would appreciate it if you wouldn't mention Scott's name.'

Abbra didn't have the slightest intention of being there when the dinner guests arrived. She said again, as she had at the beginning of the conversation, 'Since my car is being serviced, can I borrow yours to go to the party tonight? I promise I won't be back too late.'

Her mother's eyes held hers. 'Do you promise that Jerry Littler will *not* be there?'

'Mom, I'm *eighteen* for goodness' sake!' Abbra said, unable to hold back her impatience any longer. 'This kind of cross-examination is ridiculous!'

'No, it isn't. If I had been more vigilant a few months ago, you would never have become acquainted with a beatnik. Now, for the last time. Will the person I am referring to be there?'

Abbra closed her eyes and prayed for strength. 'No,' she said when she could at last trust herself to speak. 'I've told you. He's in New York.'

'Then you can borrow the car on one condition: Lewis picks you up at midnight.'

Abbra stared at her incredulously. 'You can't mean that, Mom! It's absurd! It's, it's—' She struggled for a word that would do justice to it – 'It's *humiliating*.'

'No, it isn't.' Having laid and decorated the dining table to her satisfaction, Mrs Daley now turned her attention towards the flower arrangements. Both were tasks that she never delegated. 'It's sensible,' she continued, removing a Lalique vase from a display cabinet. 'Lewis won't mind, not in the least, and I'll be able to enjoy the evening with an easy mind. Now, do you think I should use

17

this vase for the roses, or would they look better in the Tiffany?'

Abbra drew in a deep, steadying breath. There were times when her mother's overprotectiveness had to be challenged, but the present issue was too trivial to be one of them. It was also farcical.

'The Tiffany,' she said, her good humour returning.

Her mother caught the new inflection in her voice and looked across at her, a vase in either hand. 'I don't see what's so funny,' she said reprovingly. 'You should be glad that you have parents who care about you.'

'I am,' Abbra said as contritely as her amusement would allow. She made a strategic retreat towards the door before adding mischievously, 'But isn't it just my bad luck that the never-do-anything-wrong older brother is your dinner guest this evening? Being picked up by the football-playing black sheep of the family would have been much more fun!'

The party was being held in a house high on Telegraph Hill. From the bare windows a thousand lights could be seen glittering along the Embarcadero and Fisherman's Wharf.

'Crowded as hell, isn't it?' a friend from her English class at Stanford shouted to Abbra.

Before she could answer, the music changed from the Beach Boys to the Supremes. Abbra merely nodded. It was so crowded it was almost impossible to move. Her cornflower-blue mini-skirt was twisted and riding too high on her thighs. Her shining black hair held away from her face with two heavy tortoiseshell combs was damp with perspiration. 'I hardly know anyone,' she shouted to her friend.

A blond giant moved skilfully between them and grinned down on her. 'I'm your hostess's brother's buddy,' he said, steering her towards a set of French doors. 'Let's go on to the terrace. There should be room to dance there.'

There was. The Supremes gave way to the Beatles, to the Stones, to Sonny and Cher.

18

'. . . And so I go to LA next week to try out for the Rams.'

'I got you Babe,' Sonny and Cher sang out. 'I got you babe.'

'You mean you're going to be a football player?' Abbra asked, grateful for the cooling night breeze that was blowing in from the Bay.

'You bet your sweet life I am. If Scott Ellis can make it professionally, I sure as hell can make it.'

She stopped dancing. 'Scott Ellis?' she said incredulously. 'You did say *Scott Ellis*?'

He nodded. 'He's my buddy. He's here somewhere.' From his advantageous height he scanned the heads of the other dancers. 'There he is, over near the doorway.'

Abbra turned to look. The figure he was pointing to had his back toward them and was surrounded by a bevy of admiring girls. He was tall, easily six feet three or four, with magnificently broad shoulders and a thatch of sun-bleached hair.

'Oh boy!' she said, her voice thick with laughter, feeling no twinge of destiny, no intimation of fate. 'My mother is never going to believe this! I wonder if his father knows he's here in San Francisco? If his brother knows?'

The giant shrugged uncomprehendingly. 'Why should anyone know?' he asked as they began to dance again, this time to the Kinks. 'Scott doesn't have to check in with anyone. He never has. He never will.'

When *Set Me Free* came to an end, she declined another dance with a smile and a shake of her head, knowing that if she stayed any longer, he would consider her his personal property. She didn't seek out Scott Ellis. He had enough adoring females around him without another one swelling the ranks. Instead, she danced with her friend's brother, and then with some of the guys from Stanford, and then with her friend's brother again.

'Someone's come to get you!' a classmate shouted across to her.

Abbra glanced down at her watch, said an exasperated 'damn' beneath her breath, and began to ease her way through the crowd and out of the room.

'Abbra?' He was twenty-eight or twenty-nine and bore no resemblance at all to the slightly awkward teenager she remembered. He was in uniform, and beneath the porch light lieutenant's pips gleamed dully.

She nodded, stepping out on to the porch, saying with an apologetic smile, 'I'm sorry about this. I'm afraid there are times when my mother behaves as if I were twelve years old!'

'It's no trouble.' His voice was deep-timbred. 'Your mother said for you to leave her car here. She'll have her chauffeur pick it up in the morning.'

There was no easy affability about him. His mouth was intimidatingly uncompromising, and he was obviously a man who smiled neither easily nor often. Yet she was suddenly sure that she was going to like him. Beneath his peaked cap his hair was thick and curly, and his face was hard-boned and abrasively masculine. He wasn't tall, not nearly as tall as the blond giant she had danced with, but he was toughly built and held himself well, with a muscular coordination that spoke of hard training and perfect physical fitness.

'I suppose you're wondering why my mother didn't ask her chauffeur to pick me up this evening,' she said with friendly ease as they began to walk down the lamplit drive towards his car. 'He *could* have, but you see, if the party had proved to be wild, she wouldn't be able to rely on him to inform her. She thinks you'll be braver.'

'And was it wild?'

There was the merest touch of a smile at the corners of his mouth.

'No. Just the opposite.' She suddenly remembered Scott. 'Your brother was there. Probably still is.'

His car was a two-seater MG. 'That doesn't prove that the party was respectable,' he said dryly, opening the door for her. 'More the opposite.'

20

She giggled, glad that a sense of humour lurked beneath his somewhat forbidding manner. 'Don't you want to go back to the party and say hi to him?'

'No.' He flinched slightly as someone in the house turned the volume on the record player up. 'Parties are Scott's scene, not mine.'

Her amusement deepened. She believed him. It was impossible to imagine him at a party like the one she had just left. He was far too staid and serious-minded to let his hair down dancing to the Beach Boys.

'I love parties,' she said as he slipped into the seat beside her and slid the MG into gear, 'and I hate leaving them just when they're catching their second breath.'

'We could go back if you want.'

He was a man who rarely acted on impulse, and his suggestion surprised him almost as much as it surprised her. He swung the MG out of the drive and into the street, wondering why he had made it. The answer wasn't hard to find. From the instant she had stepped from the lighted hall on to the porch he had been attracted to her. Because he found her radiant wholesomeness, and her vibrancy and vitality, immensely appealing.

She was staring at him. 'But you don't like parties,' she protested, uncertain about whether or not he was joking. 'And I thought you promised my mother to have me home before the clock strikes twelve and I turn into a pumpkin.'

'I promised to pick you up,' he said, the breeze from the Bay tugging at their hair. 'I didn't say anything at all about the time I would get you home. What do you want to do? Go back to the party or go for a hamburger?'

There was an almost overpowering quality about him that she was beginning to find very interesting.

'A hamburger,' she said, knowing that if they returned to the party, he would immediately become the centre of female attention and she would lose the opportunity to get to know him better.

He drove down to a hamburger joint on the Embarcadero and they sat at a table overlooking the ink-black Bay.

'Your mother tells me you're at Stanford,' he said when he had given the waitress their order. 'What's your major?'

She suppressed a grin. This was a little like being taken out by a diligent uncle. 'I haven't decided yet. Political science perhaps, or literature.' She remembered her dim memory of Lewis as a teenager in an army cadet uniform. 'Have you always been decisive about what you want to do?' she asked curiously. 'Have you always wanted to be in the military?'

'Always. We're a military family. Apart from Scott, that is. All Scott's ever wanted to do is kick a ball around a field.'

The disapproval in his tone was so intense that Abbra had to struggle to keep her eyebrows from arching in reaction. 'I've never been friends with anyone from a military family,' she said, discounting his father, who was her parents' friend, not hers. 'Is it as restricted and dutiful a way of life as it sounds?'

'No,' he said firmly, and she could see tiny flecks of gold in the brown of his eyes. 'It's fun.'

The waitress delivered their hamburgers and french fries and Cokes. He waited until she had gone and then said, 'I guess you know that my father was a battalion commander in the Second World War?'

Abbra nodded, wishing she had paid more attention whenever the conversation at home had included Colonel Ellis.

'When the war was over he continued to serve in Europe and we were posted to twelve or thirteen different countries. I loved every minute of it and I knew at a very early age what it was that I wanted to do when I grew up. Later, when we returned to the States, I went to West Point and Scott went to Michigan State. It took my father quite a while to adjust to the idea that Scott wasn't going to follow in his footsteps as well.'

'But you did. That must have pleased him.'

Lewis's hard-boned face softened slightly. 'It did. When I graduated from West Point he was as pleased as hell.'

He was silent for a moment. A deeply reserved man, he couldn't remember the last time he had spoken with such ease about himself. Aware that Mrs Daley had cast him in the role of an older brother, and not wanting to abuse her trust, he asked hesitantly, 'I'm on three days leave at the moment. Could we meet again and spend the day in Sausalito or Carmel?'

Her first reaction was pleasure at the inherent flattery in his question. All her previous dates had been with young men close to her own age. Lewis was worlds removed from them. Tough and mature and sophisticated. Then she remembered Jerry.

'I'd like to,' she said truthfully, 'but it's a little awkward.'

'You mean that you're already dating somebody?'

'Not *exactly*.' She folded her arms on the table and leaned slightly on them, her hair falling forwards softly at either side of her face. 'But I do have a kind of an understanding with someone.'

'Tell me,' he said, already determined that whatever kind of understanding it was, it wasn't one that was going to stand in his way.

'Jerry is a poet.' Her eyes took on an impassioned glow. 'At the moment he is in New York, but he'll be coming back to San Francisco and when he does . . .' She couldn't finish the sentence as she would have liked to because she and Jerry hadn't made any commitments. Instead, she gave an expressive lift of her shoulders, intimating that no more need be said, that when he returned they would be together.

'Poets are pretty unconventional,' Lewis said, giving no indication that he already knew all about Jerry Littler.

Her mother had told him at dinner how distressed she was by Abbra's infatuation with him. How Littler wasn't a legitimate poet but a long-haired, work-shy beatnik who attached himself like a parasite to anyone foolish enough to fund him.

23

'He isn't going to hit the roof simply because you have a day out with a family friend,' Lewis continued, determined that Littler was never again going to surface in Abbra's life. 'I'll pick you up at ten tomorrow morning and we'll go to the beach.'

'Do you always make people's decisions for them?' She tried to sound indignant but was too pleased to pull it off.

He rose to his feet, knowing that if he didn't take her home soon her mother would no more allow her to spend the day with him than she would allow her to spend the day with Jerry Littler. 'Always,' he said, flashing her a smile that completely transformed his serious face. 'It's my military training.'

'Well, I have to admit that I'm surprised by this turn of events,' her mother said doubtfully when Abbra told her the next morning that she was going out with Lewis for the day. 'I approve of Lewis, of course, but he *is* ten years older than you—'

'It isn't a date, Mom,' Abbra said. 'He's on leave and I have nothing else planned for today, and so we're going to the beach together. As friends. There's no romance in the air, so please don't behave towards Lewis as if there were.'

'Nevertheless it would be extremely *suitable*,' her mother said musingly. 'Military weddings are so attractive, and Lewis is obviously destined to become a colonel, perhaps even a general.'

From beyond the front door there came the sound of a car drawing to a halt.

'Well, I am not destined to become an army wife,' Abbra said deflatingly. 'Lewis is a conformist. He's simply not my type.' It was true. Although he was undeniably attractive, he was also staid and predictable. Unlike Jerry.

She didn't wait for him to ring the doorbell because she didn't want her mother to waylay him. She hurried out of the house, her hair swinging glossily, her fashionably short lemon sundress revealing long, suntanned legs. Although it was true that he was not her type, she knew that she was his.

She had seen it in his eyes the previous night, and she saw it now as she strode across the gravel towards him.

He wasn't in uniform and he looked different, far more relaxed. His cream-coloured slacks were snug on his hips and his short-sleeved cotton shirt was open at the throat, revealing a hint of tightly curling, crisp dark hair.

'I've brought a picnic,' he said, sliding the MG into gear.

She was just about to say how impressed she was when she saw bruising on his right temple that had not been obvious the previous evening. 'What on earth did you do to your head?' she asked, staring at a painful-looking swollen place an inch or two into his hairline. 'Walk into a door?'

He gave a sheepish grin, 'I got thwacked on the head a few days ago on a training manoeuvre.'

'It looks nasty.' She was suddenly very much her father's daughter. 'What did your medic say about it?'

'You don't run to a medic with every little bump and bruise,' he said, amused and more than a little pleased by her concern. 'The last thing a career soldier needs is a long medical record.'

She frowned slightly. She could understand that. Peak physical fitness was obviously the first requisite for a soldier. Nevertheless, she knew enough about neurology to appreciate that any head injury, however slight, justified medical attention.

'Your commanding officer should have *ordered* you to go to a medic.'

He smiled. 'My commanding officer hadn't the slightest idea that I'd been hit,' he said, dismissing the subject and pressing his foot down harder on the accelerator, heading south, toward Carmel.

They spent the morning strolling along Main Street, browsing in the little shops and boutiques, pausing at a café to sip margaritas, walking barefoot along the beach.

'Let's drive out of town and picnic up on the cliffs,' he suggested as they began to walk back to the car.

She nodded agreeably, happy in his company, enjoying herself hugely.

'What are you going to do with this bachelor's degree of yours when you get it,' he asked suddenly.

She knew very well what she wanted to do, but she had never told anyone. Not even Jerry. *Especially* Jerry.

She said now, unselfconsciously, 'I want to write.'

'You mean you want to be a journalist?'

'No.' A wide smile curved her mouth, dimpling her cheeks. 'I want to write fiction.'

His brows rose slightly. 'Wouldn't journalism be more sensible?' he asked, opening the car door for her.

Her smile deepened. It was impossible to imagine Lewis doing anything that wasn't sensible. 'It would, but I don't want to be sensible. I want to be a novelist.'

He began to laugh but she didn't mind. She began to laugh with him. 'I want to be a world-famous, best-selling, *superstar* novelist!'

They were still laughing when he parked the MG high on the cliffs and retrieved the picnic basket from the backseat.

'What have you got in there?' she asked, the ocean breeze blowing her hair around her face as they walked over the springy turf.

'Thinly-sliced ham and melon and roast chicken,' he said, setting the basket down and sitting cross-legged beside it. 'And peaches and strawberries and watermelon.' He pulled her down beside him. 'And French bread and whipped butter and pastries . . .'

She was on her knees, sitting back on her heels. He forgot about the picnic. Just looking at her high-cheekboned face and her wide-set blue, heavily lashed eyes, brought a lump into his throat. She was very beautiful. The most beautiful girl he had ever seen. But he couldn't tell her so. Not so soon. She didn't yet feel about him as he was beginning to feel about her, and to say anything now would jeopardize the intimacy developing between them.

'I have another weekend leave at the end of the month,' he said lightly, lifting a bottle of Chablis from the basket. 'Why don't we do this again? We could go to Sausalito or to the zoo.'

'Let's go to the zoo.' She helped herself to a slice of melon. 'I haven't been there for years. Not since I was a child.'

He smiled. She made it sound as if her childhood were light-years behind her.

He raised his glass towards hers. 'To the zoo,' he said, suddenly so sure that they were on the verge of a very special and precious relationship, that he had to resist the temptation of leaping to his feet and whooping out loud.

'Where are you stationed?' Abbra asked three weeks later as they strolled past the koala bear enclosure.

'Fort Bragg, North Carolina.'

She halted in stunned surprise, staring at him. 'But I thought you were stationed somewhere near San Francisco. Do you mean you've come all the way from North Carolina just so that we could go to the zoo?'

'I came all the way from North Carolina to have a pleasant weekend away from school.'

'School?' she asked curiously, beginning to walk along beside him once again. 'If you're a lieutenant, what are you doing in school again? I don't understand.'

'I'm at Fort Bragg, at the Special Warfare School, taking courses in counterinsurgency, counterguerrilla operations, and military assistance operations with foreign governments.'

This time she not only stood still. The blood drained from her face. 'You mean you're going to Vietnam?'

'I hope so,' he said with dry humour, 'or the months I've spent studying Vietnamese history and customs and language will be a waste!'

'But I thought only marines were going out there. To guard the air bases.'

27

In February there had been a devastating Viet Cong attack on a US base near South Vietnamese Army headquarters at Pleiku. American special forces and military advisers had been billeted at the camp, and eight of them had died and a little over a hundred and twenty others had been wounded. Almost immediately President Johnson had ordered retaliatory air strikes against the north. Abbra remembered clearly the disbelief she had felt at his action when she had seen the newspaper headlines. A month later American marines had splashed ashore at Da Nang to guard the nearby airfield from Viet Cong attack. They had been the first US combat troops to land on the Asian mainland since the Korean conflict.

'But they won't be the last,' her father had said grimly. 'There's going to be no backing down now. We're committed whether we like it or not.'

'What will you be doing out there?' she asked, not sure that she really wanted to know.

'I'm going to be a military adviser to the South Vietnamese Army.'

'So you will be helping the Vietnamese fight their own war?'

'What a nice, simplistic way of putting it. Yes, Abbra, when it comes down to the bottom line, that is what I'll be doing.'

It was as they were leaving the zoo that she thought she must have inadvertently said something that had shocked him, just as much as his conversation about Vietnam had shocked her.

He stopped short suddenly, his eyes blank, as if in stunned surprise.

She turned towards him questioningly. 'What is it? What did I say?'

For a second she thought he wasn't going to answer her, and then he said vaguely, 'I'm sorry . . . just a minute . . .' He raised his hand as if to ward her off.

He looked a little as if he were going to faint. She frowned, stepping towards him, saying in sudden deep concern, 'Lewis! What is it? Are you sick?'

'No . . .' He still didn't move, although the colour had begun to come back into his face. He shook his head as if to clear it. 'That was the damnedest thing.' There was a park bench a few yards away from them and he walked across to it, sitting down, beginning to laugh a little. 'Hell! I suddenly felt as if I'd gone down the biggest roller-coaster in the world!'

'You mean you were dizzy?' She sat beside him, trying to keep the alarm out of her voice.

'Yes. No.' He seemed to have completely recovered. He gave her a slightly abashed grin. '*Giddy* would be a better word. Nothing was going round and round. I just felt as if I'd fallen a hundred floors in an elevator.' He rose to his feet. 'Come on. If we don't leave soon, we'll be locked in for the night with the animals.'

As they began to walk back towards the car, she said curiously, 'Has that ever happened to you before, Lewis?'

'No.' This time his grin was genuinely carefree. 'It must have been the shrimp rolls at lunch.'

She was silent for a minute, and then she said hesitantly, 'You don't think it might have something to do with the blow you received to your head last month?'

His grin vanished. He stared at her. 'No, I don't. That's a ridiculous suggestion.'

'Not really. Daddy has patients who—'

'I had a reaction to something I ate. That's all.'

There was such finality in his voice that she didn't finish the sentence she had begun. She was probably being imaginative anyway. To say anything more to him before she had spoken to her father was pointless.

'Who are we talking about?' Abbra's father asked.

She shrugged vaguely. 'Just a friend. She got hit on the head a few weeks ago and never had it checked out.'

'And what did you say happened to her in class? Did she have a momentary loss of consciousness?'

29

'Not exactly. It was more as if she just didn't know where she was for a second. She said afterwards that she felt as if she had fallen a hundred floors in an elevator.'

'It sounds as if she might be suffering from focal epilepsy. It's quite common when there's been a blow to the head. It results in an underlying structural abnormality being revealed. Natural resistance to epileptic activity is lowered, and mild seizures can occur. Tell her not to worry too much, but it goes without saying that she should report what happened to her doctor at the earliest opportunity.'

'If it *was* a mild epileptic seizure, would she have more and would they be harmful enough that her choice of career might be affected?'

'If what she suffered was a mild epileptic seizure triggered by the injury she received, then it is more than likely that there will be another. There are no hard and fast rules where epilepsy is concerned. And, of course, if that is what it is, then her choice of career may be circumscribed.'

'She wants to go into the army,' Abbra said, her hands behind her back, her fingers crossed.

Her father picked up a copy of the *Chronicle* and shook it open, saying with finality, 'If she has become subject to epileptic seizures she is highly unlikely to be accepted into any profession requiring a stringent physical. Suggest to her that she become a schoolteacher instead.'

Even though she knew Lewis would not want the subject raised again, she was determined that the next time he flew out to see her, she would do so. Incredibly, because of what happened within minutes of their meeting again, she forgot all about her intention and the subject was never broached.

He had taken hold of her hand, drawing her toward him, and before she could protest, his arms had slid around her and he had lowered his head to hers, kissing her lovingly.

In the first brief second, as his lips touched hers, her every instinct was to push him gently away, and to say that though she was fond of him, she didn't want their easygoing friendship to develop into anything more. She didn't. It was a very pleasant kiss. The nicest she had ever received. Instead of pushing him away her arms slid up and around his neck, her mouth parting softly and warmly beneath his.

'But there is still Jerry,' she had said afterwards, not wanting to be guilty of leading him into believing that what was happening between them was serious.

He had shrugged dismissively and she had been unable to see the expression in his dark eyes. 'Jerry is in New York,' he had said, and neither of them had mentioned him again.

In June there were newspaper reports of battalion after battalion of South Vietnamese troops being defeated by the Viet Cong, and Lewis's phone calls to her, and letters, were full of impatience because he still hadn't received orders to leave for Saigon.

It was while he was on the telephone, telling her how President Johnson was going to have to send more combat troops to Vietnam, that she knew he was experiencing another giddy spell.

He broke off speaking in the middle of a sentence.

'Lewis?' she had said. 'Lewis?'

'Yes. Just a minute . . .'

His voice had the same disoriented quality about it that she had noticed at the zoo.

'Lewis!' she had said again, her voice sharp with anxiety. 'Lewis! Are you all right?'

'Yes.' There had been a moment's hesitation, and she knew that he was lying. There was a note in his voice she had never heard before, a note that seemed incredible in a man so tough and supremely confident. A note of fear.

She said with utter certainty, 'You've just had another giddy spell.'

'Wait a minute, Abbra . . .' He sounded as if he were gathering his wits with difficulty. After a little while he said, 'I'm okay now. I was just a little light-headed for a second.'

31

She said carefully, not wanting to arouse the same chill response in him that she had aroused the last time she had tried to talk to him about it, 'When it happened before, at the zoo, were you tired afterwards?'

'Yes,' he said, and at the relief in his voice she knew he was assuming she thought his momentary disorientation was merely due to overtiredness.

She said gently, disillusioning him, 'I spoke to Daddy about what happened. I told him it had happened to a university friend. He thinks the giddiness and momentary loss of awareness may be a mild form of epilepsy known as focal epilepsy. And all epilepsy sufferers feel the need to sleep after an attack.'

'Epilepsy?' First there was disbelief in his voice, then anger. '*Epilepsy?* You can't be serious. You can't suggest I'm suffering from *epilepsy*! Christ, Abbra! That's the most ridiculous thing I've ever heard! I'm damned glad you didn't mention my name to your father! A malicious rumour like that could end my career!'

'Not if medical tests proved it *was* only a rumour.'

'There's no need for medical tests! I was a little disorientated for a couple of seconds. I didn't fall down on the ground in a fit, frothing at the mouth and swallowing my tongue!'

'That's grand mal. I never suggested you were suffering from grand mal. All I'm suggesting is that the blow you received on your head has done more damage than you were aware of. Some epileptic seizures are so slight that it's even hard for the sufferer to realize what it is they are experiencing.'

'I couldn't care less whether they know or not! *I* wasn't experiencing a seizure! I've passed medical test after medical test, and for your information, I am one hundred per cent physically fit!'

'Go for a complete physical,' she said softly, refusing to give in. 'Then we need never mention it again because there will be no doubt, one way or the other.'

32

'There's no doubt now!' he said, obviously furious, and hung up on her.

Abbra was sure Lewis would never telephone her or see her again. She was intensely unhappy. Over the last few months he had become a part of her life. She tried to stop thinking about him and to think about Jerry instead. The rumour at Stanford was that he was on his way back to San Francisco. Once she saw Jerry again, she would stop missing Lewis. Lewis had been too old for her anyway. Too endearingly old-fashioned.

It was a Sunday morning, three weeks later, when the telephone calls came. The first had been from Jerry. He had laconically said that he was back in town and at his old apartment in North Beach. He was tied up all day, but if she wanted to see him tomorrow, it was fine by him.

The next telephone call, minutes later, was from Lewis.

'You were right,' he said briefly, his voice oddly flat. 'I've been to a doctor. A neurologist. I have a hairline fracture of the skull, and the blow evidently reduced my resistance to epileptic seizures. What I'm actually suffering from is something called temporal lobe epilepsy, which I think is the same sort of epilepsy your father was referring to. There are a wide range of symptoms that can be experienced and the brief, momentary loss of awareness I've suffered from a time or two, along with that almost pleasant giddy sensation, is the way that I experience it. It may develop and I may, in the future, suffer a full-scale epileptic attack. On the other hand, I may never notice a damn thing wrong with me, ever again.'

'And the army?' she said fearfully. 'What did the doctor say about your career in the army?'

'He didn't know about it. However many army physicals I undergo, I'm unlikely to have a brain scan. And without a brain scan no one can know that there's anything wrong with me. And there isn't really anything wrong. I haven't had another attack, and I personally doubt if I ever will have another.'

'So you're not going to give your army medical officer a copy of the neurologist's report?'

'No.'

'But, Lewis—'

His voice was no longer flat. It was so overwrought it was nearly out of control. 'For Christ's sake, Abbra! The word epilepsy on my army records would finish me! I'd be desk-bound for the rest of my career! And why? Because very occasionally I feel as if I've come down a roller coaster? No one is ever going to know about this, Abbra. No one! Not ever!'

'Okay.' She didn't know why, but she had begun to cry. 'I'm so sorry about it all, Lewis.'

'Yes. I know.' His voice had softened. He sounded unutterably weary. 'I have a two-day pass, and I have some other news for you as well. I'll see you this evening. We'll go to a movie.'

'A movie would be lovely.'

She had put the telephone receiver back on its rest. She knew that what he was doing was very wrong, but she couldn't think any less of him for doing it. The army was his passion and his life. He always had wanted to be a soldier. She couldn't even begin to imagine him as anything else. And he was right about the epilepsy. Once on his army medical record it would never come off, no matter how mild the form he was suffering from, no matter if he never, ever suffered from another attack again.

He would be here this evening. She would see him then. And though Jerry had said he was tied up all day and couldn't see her until tomorrow, she was going to ignore what he'd told her. After all, she hadn't seen him for nearly six months, so she certainly wasn't going to wait another six hours. She was going to drive over and see him right away.

Half an hour later she parked her Oldsmobile in the street outside his apartment. The apartment was over a liquor store and she ran up the stairs, excitement mounting in her till she could hardly bear it. She had missed Jerry. He was so talented, so outrageous, such wonderful fun. She could smell the sickly

34

sweet aroma of marijuana and was uncaring. Jerry was a poet. All poets smoked pot. And pot was harmless. Nothing more than a stiff drink.

The door at the top of the uncarpeted stairs was closed. She gave only the briefest of knocks before opening it, a wide smile on her face, saying sunnily, 'Hi, Jerry! I thought I'd surprise you!'

He didn't look remotely surprised. Only vastly amused. He was laying naked on unclean, dishevelled sheets. The girl beside him, eyebrows raised in surprise, was naked also. As was their sweat-sheened male and obviously mutual friend.

It was the girl who was smoking marijuana. Jerry was snorting coke. Abbra had never seen the white powder before, but she knew what it was.

She stood for a moment, almost too dazed to react, all the anticipated pleasure draining from her. There was a time when she might have thought this kind of a scene was fun, hip. No longer. The semen-stained sheets, and the tangled, perspiring bodies made her feel nauseated. She didn't want any part of this. She didn't want to be even remotely connected to such people.

She turned on her heel, uncaring of the shouts of laughter that followed her down the stairs.

She was crying when she reached the Oldsmobile. Not because she knew that she was never going to see Jerry again, but because she was so ashamed of her own foolishness. How could she not have seen him as her mother had so clearly seen him? As Lewis would no doubt have seen him. How could she have been so stupid for so long? So blind?

She rammed her car key into the ignition, slamming the Oldsmobile into gear. She didn't want to go home. Not yet. Not until it was evening and Lewis would be there.

She drove north, stopping the car in deserted countryside to walk. Walking always calmed her and it calmed her now. She was glad that she had driven down to North Beach so unexpectedly. Glad that she had seen what she had seen. She felt suddenly much more mature, more sure of who she was and of what she wanted in life. As dusk fell she returned to her car, driving back to San Francisco, happy and eager to see Lewis again.

He pulled in the driveway only seconds ahead of her. She was out of her car even before he was, running towards him. 'Oh, Lewis! I'm so glad to see you!' she cried, hurling herself into his welcoming arms.

He held her very close, sensing a momentous change in her. 'What is it?' he demanded gently, and then intuitively, 'Is it Jerry? Have you seen Jerry?'

She nodded, lifting her head to his, her arms still tightly around his waist. 'Yes, and Jerry doesn't matter anymore. I didn't realize it until today, but he never has mattered.'

'I'm going to 'Nam,' he said, not letting go of her. 'I leave at the end of next week. Will you marry me before I go?'

'Oh, yes, Lewis!' She began to laugh and cry simultaneously. 'Yes! Yes! Yes!'

# CHAPTER TWO

Serena Blyth-Templeton woke at dawn to the sound of an army of men hammering tent pegs into the ground to make gigantic marquees. She groaned and rolled over pulling a pillow over her head. It was the longest day of summer. The day Bedingham was to play host to the Rolling Stones, the Animals, a dozen lesser-known bands, and God alone knew how many thousands and thousands of fans.

'Oh hell, oh shit,' she said loudly. 'I shouldn't have driven home last night! I should have stayed in town!'

But she hadn't stayed at her family's town house in Chelsea; she had driven home through the English countryside, intoxicated on champagne and high on marijuana, and the fates had been kind to her, as they always were, and she'd had no accidents and no police cars had come screaming after her. Serena didn't know whether this was a relief or a disappointment. Life was so boring, and a night in a cell sounded as if it might have a certain piquancy about it. It would certainly stir up her father, which was always fun, and it might even impress Lance.

Her twin brother had become obsessed with everything extremely left wing. If it was anti establishment, anti his father, anti his privileged upbringing and expensive education, then Lance was fervently in favour of it. The latest object of his contempt was the police, though Serena privately doubted that Lance had ever had anything to do with them apart from cursing them when they politely asked him to remove his Aston-Martin from the double yellow lines outside the house in Cheyne Walk. Nevertheless, for the past two months Lance had denounced all policemen, even their friendly local police, as 'fascist pigs', to his mother's bewilderment and his father's irritation.

The hammering continued relentlessly, the goosedown pillow no defence against it. With a groan of despair Serena flung it to one side and with an obscene lack of a hangover, sprang agilely from the bed. It was a day she had been looking forward to for months, though wild horses wouldn't have made her admit it. To do so would have been uncool. She had decided early on in the planning of the concert that the only acceptable reaction to Mick Jagger's presence and performance at Bedingham was to assume an attitude of sophisticated indifference. After all, she wasn't a groupie, queuing all night for the privilege of seeing Mick at a distance of five hundred yards. She was Lady Serena Blyth-Templeton, and as such Jagger was surely *her* guest, just as much as he was her father's.

With long, easy strides she crossed to the window and pulled back the curtains. The green sward that fronted Bedingham and stretched away gently uphill into a three-mile-long avenue of elms was nearly invisible beneath a stage swarming with technicians and groaning under the weight of expensive sound equipment. Seating around the stage was still being erected, though the punters, as Serena's father always referred to those members of the public who paid for the privilege of visiting Bedingham would, for the most part, either sit on the grass or stand.

Serena smiled. Despite her indifference to almost anything and everything, she loved Bedingham passionately. It had been in her family ever since the sixteenth century when Matthew Blyth, an adventurer, had been rewarded by Henry VIII for dubious services rendered, and been given permission to acquire and domesticate the dissolved abbey of Bedingham in Cambridgeshire. He had done so with zest, transforming Bedingham into a house fit for royalty.

Under Mary's reign, when upstart Anglicans were out of favour, Bedingham had suffered and lost the major part of its more glittering trappings, but under Queen Elizabeth I, favour had been restored and more land acquired. Through a satisfactory marriage alliance Blythes became Blyth-Templetons. Under Charles I, the Blyth-Templetons being royalist, Bedingham suffered a minor setback, but after the accession of Charles II, its star entered its zenith. The family was ennobled, an east and west wing were added, and the elaborate formal gardens around the house conceived and executed.

Under the boring rule of the Hanoverians, Bedingham had lost a little of its grandeur, declining to play host to a royal family undeserving of it. Under Queen Victoria it had continued to flourish. A long library had been added to the house, and more avenues and follies added to the grounds. Only in the last century had true difficulties arisen, and these, being financial, Serena's grandfather had sensibly solved by marrying the only daughter of an American railway king of Swedish descent.

Serena patted the ancient stone sill of the mullioned window. After playing host to Tudors, Stuarts, Saxe-Coburgs, and Edward VII, Bedingham was now going to play host to the Rolling Stones. 'You've seen a lot,' she said affectionately to the ivy-covered bricks and mortar, 'but in four hundred years you won't ever have seen anything quite like this!'

There was a perfunctory knock at the door, and without waiting to be asked to enter, her brother strolled into the bedroom, his thumbs hooked into the pockets of his jeans, his hair shoulder-length. 'Hell of a lot of noise, isn't there?' he asked cheerfully. 'The old man is going to open the gates at eight to relieve the pressure building up in the village. Apparently the local roads are already jammed. Hundreds of those coming to the concert camped in surrounding fields last night. I don't suppose we'll be at all popular with our farmers.'

Serena shrugged, indifferent to the wrath of the farmers who tenanted Bedingham land. 'What time does the concert get under way?'

'Ten o'clock, but what you really mean is what time does Jagger arrive?' Lance flung himself facedown on the rumpled bed and rested his chin in his hands. 'Two o'clock, supposedly. Until then, the fans have to be content with lesser mortals.'

'He is staying on, isn't he?' Serena asked, turning away from the window and rummaging in the drawer of a George III mahogany chest for a pair of jeans and a T-shirt. 'I mean, he is coming to the ball?'

'He's been invited and the word is that he's accepted, but I can't quite see it, can you?' Lance asked, grinning at her speculatively as she pulled the jeans on beneath the discreet cover of her nightgown. Ever since she had returned home on vacation from her Swiss finishing school, she had been at pains to let him know how shockingly sexually experienced and liberated she had become. It amused him that her sexual liberation didn't extend to himself and that, where he was concerned, proper sisterly modesty was still the order of the day.

Serena, aware of his amusement and knowing very well what had caused it, pulled her nightdress defiantly over her head, her breasts gloriously naked as she reached for her T-shirt with a studied lack of hurry, not bothering to keep her back towards him. 'Why shouldn't he accept?' she asked. 'HRH has accepted, hasn't he?'

A flare of shock, like an electric current, had run through him. Her breasts were small and high, her nipples so pale as to be almost invisible. They needed biting into to gain colour. He found the mere idea cripplingly erotic. 'Yes,' he said, wondering why incest had never entered his thoughts before. 'Prince Charles is coming.'

The ball that was to follow the concert was to be the kind of ball that Bedingham was accustomed to. Dress would be formal, the young bloods of England's oldest families would be in attendance, a carefully selected sprinkling of stage and screen stars were invited to add glamour to the evening.

Serena pulled her T-shirt down over her head. Wondering why he had never before realized the strength of his sexual feelings for his sister, Lance said, 'Why you should think Charles's presence guarantees a fun evening, I can't imagine.' Lance's views of the Windsors were on a par with his ancestors' views of the Hanoverians. They were bores and he could well do without them.

Serena surveyed her reflection in a walnut-framed cheval glass. 'I like Charles,' she said unexpectedly. 'He might be a stuffed shirt, but he's a sincere stuffed shirt.'

Lance temporarily forgot the fascinating path down which his thoughts were taking him and rolled over on to his back, shouting with laughter. 'Oh, God, Serry! Don't tell me you have ambitions in that direction! I couldn't bear it! Queen Serena! What a hoot!'

'I think I would make a very good queen,' Serena said, sweeping up her long, pale gold mane of hair and piling it experimentally on top of her head. 'A tiara would suit me.'

'Bollocks!' Lance said disrespectfully, 'the days of Blyth-Templetons fawning to royalty are over, thank God. What we need in the family now is some good, unadulterated, revolutionary blood!'

Serena let her hair fall back down to her shoulders. She adored Lance and always had. He was the most important person in her life, but he bored her when he got on his political soapbox. She frowned slightly as she searched in the bottom of her French armoire for a pair of white leather high-heeled boots. Perhaps it wasn't so much boredom as resentment. Until his political involvement with the far left, they had always been in complete agreement about everything.

As children they had often been left for long periods in the care of nannies and au pairs and housekeepers while their parents had cruised the Mediterranean, skied in Switzerland, or shot grouse in the Scottish Highlands. They had been totally dependent on each other for companionship

41

and affection and had grown up with the unswerving attitude that it was the two of them against the rest of the world. The unity that had been forged between them as children was still the most important thing in their lives, and Serena had tried hard to share his left wing passions. She had failed. Politics, even revolutionary politics, bored her.

She found the boots and pulled them on. Except for politics they had always been alike in everything. Both of them were tall and slender, light-skinned and blond-haired. In Lance this had resulted in a certain air of effeminacy, and Serena often thought that one of the reasons for his radical left wing views was that he thought they gave him a harder, more macho image.

There was nothing pale and washed out about the combination of Serena's Nordic and Anglo-Saxon beauty. There was strength as well as delicacy in her fine-boned features, and the Swiss sun had given her skin a luminous honey-gold tone. Her eyes were grey, wide-set, dark-lashed, their smoky depths alight with fiery recklessness. When she moved she did so with utter assurance, carrying her tall, superbly proportioned body with the arrogance and ease of a dancer or athlete.

She lifted the two dresses that had been hanging on the front of her armoire, and that she had moved in her search for her boots, back into position. Both were white. One bore a Mary Quant label and was so minuscule as to border on the indecent; the other bore a Norman Hartnell label and was of heavy satin, ankle-length, and encrusted with thousands of tiny seed pearls. The Mary Quant was the dress she intended to wear for the concert; the Norman Hartnell was the gown she was to wear for the ball. She looked at the dresses in happy anticipation, knowing that they said a lot about her. They were at opposite ends of the fashion spectrum, yet she thought them equally wonderful. She liked extremes. It was safe, middle-of-the-road moderation that she couldn't stand.

'Our house guests, the Andersons, arrived while you were living it up in town last night,' Lance said, wondering if Serena would be disturbed if she knew the way his thoughts were turning, or if she perhaps shared his agonizingly erotic fantasy. 'Pathetically small-town America despite their millions and their boast of being one of Boston's oldest families.'

Since Lance had spent the last few months denouncing America and Americans with the same arbitrary passion he mustered to denounce the British police force, his verdict on their house guests was not surprising.

'Where does their money come from?' Serena asked with interest.

The American ability to rise from pauper to millionaire in a single generation fascinated her. Their own great-grandfather had been a penniless Swedish immigrant when he had arrived in America, yet when he had died he had left his daughter a fortune so large that Bedingham and they were still thriving on it.

'Banking,' Lance replied. He shrugged, then sat up on the bed, swinging his legs to the floor. 'But the family fortune is bolstered by whisky. The grandfather picked up a whisky franchise in Scotland during the last days of prohibition. When prohibition conveniently ended, he became a millionaire overnight.'

'He was taking a risk,' Serena said, pulling a comb through her slick-straight hair. 'What if prohibition hadn't ended? What would he have done with his whisky franchise then?'

'He was in politics,' Lance said dryly. 'He *knew* prohibition was going to end.'

Serena gave a deep-throated chuckle. 'I think I would have liked the grandfather. What is the grandson like?'

Lance shrugged again, suddenly sure that Serena would also like the grandson. He didn't like the idea. 'He went to Choate, he's at Princeton now and he thinks England is an anachronism.'

'If he's at Princeton, he can't be *that* dumb,' Serena said, tossing her comb down on to the Lalique tray on her dressing-table, 'and if he thinks England an anachronism, I would have thought you would have been in total agreement with him. After all, you're the one who wants to bring the country to its knees and revolution to the streets!'

'Maybe so, but I don't need a bloody American to help me do it!' he said, throwing a pillow at her.

Serena sidestepped the pillow with ease. 'Come on, brother mine,' she said, striding towards the door, her breasts pushing tantalizingly against the thin cotton of her T-shirt. 'Let's make sure Bedingham is ready for its day of glory.'

That Bedingham would be among the first buildings to be put to the torch if Lance and his fellow revolutionaries ever had their way was something never mentioned between them. When Lance was with his left wing friends, he always and loudly disowned Bedingham, vowing that when his father died, he wouldn't accept his hereditary title, and that for all he cared, the house could be reduced to a pile of rubble. It was a statement he never made in front of Serena. He knew how much and how deeply she felt about Bedingham. It was a measure of how deep his feelings were for her that he never talked rashly of Bedingham's future in her presence. They walked down the sweeping staircase, through the large inner hall and then through the entrance hall, its floor tiles emblazoned with the Blyth-Templeton family motto and crest. Even though the concert was not due to start for two hours, they could hear music.

'The music is coming from transistor radios,' Lance said as they stepped out on to the stone steps of the south entrance. 'My God! Look at the crowd pouring down from the gates! What is it going to be like when things really get under way?'

'It's going to be fabulous!' Serena said, her eyes shining as she ran down the steps towards the gravel dividing the house from the lawns fronting it.

The gates that her father had opened at eight o'clock were so far distant they couldn't be seen, but the first of the fans to stream through them were already making their way down through the avenue of elms, towards the lawns and the stage.

*She Loves You* was blaring out from a score of transistor radios, and Roy Orbison blared from dozens more on a different station.

'Hey, want a joint?' the first of the invaders to reach the front of the house, a long-haired individual wearing an Afghan coat and a multicoloured headband, shouted across to her.

'I'd love one!' Serena responded enthusiastically, accepting the sweet-smelling marijuana and drawing deeply on it while Lance looked at her, not knowing whether to be amused or annoyed. 'Wouldn't breakfast be more suitable?' he asked. 'It's barely the crack of dawn.'

Serena sucked down another lungful of smoke. 'It may be more sensible, Lance, but it will also be boring and I'm going to do *nothing* today which is boring. Today all I'm going to do is have fun, fun, *fun!*'

At ten o'clock her father announced that the concert was to begin – but he did so, Serena thought, with the air of a drowning man bereft of all help.

Masses of singing, shouting, dancing bodies covered the lawns surrounding the stage, and the grassy hill and avenue beyond. There was tight security around the house. Uniformed police were at every entrance, and there were large No Admittance signs on all the doors. Her father, after his dazed declaration that Bedingham's pop festival was officially under way, had reeled into the house, unable to believe that his simple project for bringing in extra income could have turned into such a monster. Never in a million years had he expected so many thousands of young people to throng to Bedingham. He couldn't even begin to imagine where they had all come from. And never had he imagined that music could be so excruciatingly, so shatteringly, *loud*.

45

'It's unbelievable!' he said weakly to Serena as they passed on the stairs. 'A sea of unwashed, half-naked humanity stretching as far as the eye can see.'

'It's a hot day,' she said practically, 'and if the new class of punters is beginning to get you down, just think of all the lovely lolly they're bringing in.'

Her father already had. It was his only consolation.

'But the grounds,' he moaned, clinging to the banister. 'There won't be a blade of grass surviving by the time it's over!'

She patted his arm. 'Bedingham survived the Civil War,' she said comfortingly, 'and it will survive the Stones. Stop worrying, Daddy. Enjoy yourself.'

'Serena!' he called out after her as she continued buoyantly on her way. 'Our house guests! Are you taking care of them?'

'Haven't even seen them,' Serena responded, not halting in her march for the door. 'I should have a whisky if I were you, Daddy,' she added over her shoulder. 'It will steady the nerves.'

Her father groaned and turned toward his study. Serena's was the first sensible suggestion anyone had made since the debacle had begun.

As Serena ran lightly down the sweeping stone steps of the south entrance, past the policeman on duty, she had a bird's eye view of the rear of the stage. It was packed with sound equipment and back-up musicians, and one of them, a tall, languid-looking man about her age was so striking-looking he attracted and held her attention despite the press of people around him.

He was standing at the very edge of the rear of the stage, leaning nonchalantly against an amplifier, his thumbs hooked into the pockets of his jeans, one foot crossed over the other at the ankle.

His negligent stance, and his air of bored indifference in the midst of such fevered excitement, reminded her of

Lance, though that was as far as the similarity went. The musician's hair was blue-black, falling low across his brow, and despite his slender build, there was a sense of power under restraint about him, an animal-like magnetism that Lance conspicuously lacked.

The Animals had just bounded on to the front of the stage; the roar of applause and shouting and stamping was deafening. As Eric Burden's raw, unmistakable voice gave vent to the first line of *House of the Rising Sun*, Serena smiled to herself.

The musician might not be a famous name, but he obviously had other more than compensating qualities. And Serena saw no reason why she shouldn't enjoy them. By the time she had reached the rear of the stage, Burden was reaching the last erotic, skin-tingling stanza of his song.

'I'm Serena Blyth-Templeton,' she shouted to the stewards who blocked her way. 'Let me through!'

They responded to the authority in her voice almost immediately, but even so, by the time she squeezed around to the edge of the stage, her quarry had disappeared.

'There was a musician here a few minutes ago,' she shouted over the roar of applause to a still-perspiring member of the band who had preceded the Animals. 'Do you know where he went?'

'Haven't a clue, love,' he said, looking her up and down appreciatively. 'Will I do instead?'

Beneath his stage makeup he had blemishes and there was a whiff of stale alcohol on his breath. 'No,' she said, softening the blow with a grin. 'I'm sorry, but you won't.'

He shrugged and laughed, and as Burden began to sing *Don't Let Me Be Misunderstood* she philosophically abandoned her search and moved to the front of the stage, squeezing into the centre of the crush, dancing on the spot to the sound of the music, cheering until she was hoarse when the song came to an end.

As morning edged into afternoon, the heat became almost unbearable. 'I thought it was supposed to rain every day in

47

England,' a powerfully built Australian yelled to her as they stood, arms around each other's waists, swaying to the beat of the music.

'It usually does!' she shouted back. 'But sometimes, just sometimes, we actually have a summer! This is it!'

Some girls had dispensed with their T-shirts altogether, dancing bare-breasted, shrieking with laughter as the occasional cooling bottle of beer was poured over them. Serena was tempted to take off the Quant mini-dress she had changed into just before the start of the concert. If she had been anywhere else, she would have done so. Only respect for Bedingham restrained her.

When the announcement came over the loudspeakers that the Rolling Stones had arrived and would be appearing in approximately twenty minutes, a roar went up and the chant 'We want Mick' began to surge through the vast crowd.

Serena extricated herself from the sweaty hold of the Australian. She needed the bathroom and she had no intention of forcing her way to one of the many portable facilities that had been parked on the grounds. As the female group onstage pounded into a blistering rendition of *Then He Kissed Me*, she pushed and shoved her way out of the throng, running towards the house. She ducked beneath the barriers that had been erected, saying breathlessly to the policeman who ran towards her, 'I'm Serena Blyth-Templeton! I live here.'

The policeman recognized her and lifted the last barrier to allow her through. She ran up the south entrance steps and hammered on the enormous double doors there. The butler ascertained it was a member of the family and not a member of the mob and opened the door. Serena ran past him, saying between gasps for air, 'Thanks, Herricot. Super fun, isn't it?'

The butler didn't demean himself by agreeing with her. Instead, he speedily relocked and bolted the doors and retreated to an inner sanctum where he could

48

lengthen his odds of survival by placing cushions against his ears.

Serena took the steps of the great staircase two at a time. She was dripping with perspiration and she wanted to have a quick, cold shower before she returned to the fray. Even in the house the music was deafening. From her bedroom window she had a spectacular view of the sloping hillside and the avenue of elms, every inch of space packed with dancing, clapping, cheering, applauding fans. Banners were being waved, some emblazoned with 'We love Mick', others with 'Peace not war', and 'Americans out'.

She giggled as she stepped out of her dress and danced, hips swinging, into her bathroom, hoping that the visiting Andersons wouldn't imagine the banners were personally for them. American involvement in Vietnam had been escalating all summer, and so had the protests against it. Today, at least, Lance was surrounded by thousands of political sympathizers.

She stood, face upturned beneath the shower, the water turned on full blast. For once life wasn't boring. She was blissfully high on a combination of alcohol and generously shared joints. In another few minutes Mick Jagger would be onstage. Later, there would be the ball, and Jagger would be there. She would meet him, and who knew what would happen after she did?

She stepped out of the shower, treading dismissively over the discarded white mini, yanking another dress from her armoire, this time a lemon-coloured one, equally short. To the best of her knowledge, the idea of a Bedingham pop festival was the first and only idea that her forty-six-year-old father had ever had. It had been stunningly well worth the wait. There were television cameras recording the event, BBC interviewers roaming through the crowd, and the festival was already being spoken of as if it were an established annual event. As it would be.

'This year the Stones, next year the Beatles!' she said zestfully to the house in general, striding out of the bedroom, slamming the door behind her.

As she hurried down the main staircase, a door in the inner hall below her opened and a tall, dark stranger walked nonchalantly out of the salon and towards the door leading to the drawing room.

'What the devil do you think you're doing?' she shouted indignantly, beginning to run down the remaining stairs towards him. 'The house is closed to visitors! Didn't you see the signs? The barriers?'

He turned unhurriedly, one hand on the knob of the living room door. 'I would have had to be blind not to have seen them,' he said dryly.

She stopped suddenly on the bottom step, her heart beginning to slam. She knew she had been right about his overpowering masculinity when she had seen him from a distance. Now, close up, his sexuality rushed over her in waves. 'The house is closed to visitors,' she repeated, walking towards him.

His eyes weren't dark like his hair; they were a hot electric blue, and there was charm as well as insolence in the lines of his long, mobile mouth.

'I'm not a visitor,' he said, his eyes moving from her hair to her face, to her breasts, to her legs and back again with brazen appreciation.

The minute he spoke she knew that he was American, but an American with a very generous dash of the Celt. His tall, lean build, and his colouring, were those of a certain type of Irishman and, like them, he had a whippy look to him that said he would be an ugly customer in a fight – and something else about him made Serena believe he wouldn't need much of an excuse to join any fight.

'I know damn well you're not a visitor!' She wanted to sink her teeth into his neck, to lick the perspiration from his skin, to see if he looked as magnificent naked as he did in his open-necked white shirt and his tight-fitting blue

50

jeans. 'You're a musician. I saw you earlier, on the rear of the stage. Now, will you please leave the house? As I have already said, it is not open today to visitors.'

She had walked right up to him, with every intention of physically knocking his hand away from the drawing room doorknob. When he left, she would go with him. She wasn't about to lose him again. But she would be damned to hell before she allowed anyone, even this excessively handsome man, to have the run of Bedingham.

'I am not a visitor,' he said again, leaning back against the door and folding his arms negligently across his chest. 'And I'm certainly not a musician.'

'Then who the devil are you?' she demanded. Suddenly her eyes widened and her voice choked with laughter, she said, 'Oh, hell! Don't tell me! I know! You're an Anderson!'

'And you're a Templeton,' he said, eyes gleaming with answering laughter and with something else, something she knew was naked in her own eyes: unconcealed, instant sexual desire.

'A Blyth-Templeton,' she corrected him, her eyes moving over him with the same blatant appreciation he was showing. At five feet ten, she was nearly as tall as he. Slowly her eyes roved back towards his face, over the bulge in his crotch, the olive flesh tones of his neck and throat, the attractively self-deprecating quirk at the corners of his mouth. Their eyes met and held, and excitement raged through her. This wasn't going to be just good! This was going to be sensational!

'What is it?' he asked. 'Sabrina? Sophie? Selina? I can't remember.'

'Serena. And you?'

'Kyle.'

She nodded. She had been right about the Celtic blood. 'I thought you were supposed to be old Boston, not Boston Irish,' she said, so close to him that she could feel the warmth of his breath on her cheek.

'Our family is like yours,' he answered her, white teeth flashing in a dazzling, down-slanting smile. 'We turn a blind eye – when it suits us.'

She laughed throatily. 'And would it suit you now?' she asked, one hand on her hip, the line of her thigh knowingly provocative.

He grinned. It was very rare for him to meet a girl tall enough to face him eye to eye, and rarer still to be so flagrantly propositioned by one as beautiful. She had come down the broad, sweeping staircase towards him with all the speed and grace of a panther. His grin deepened. With her long mane of gold hair, and her honey-gold skin, she wasn't a panther, she was a puma. Sleek and supple, and wonderfully predatory.

'Why not?' he said, easing himself casually away from the door. 'How about a guided tour?'

Outside, the screams and shouts had reached cataclysmic proportions as the Stones belted out the opening bars of *It's All Over Now* and Mick Jagger leapt onstage.

Serena's smile widened. Incredibly she no longer gave a damn about Jagger. 'Come this way,' she said, opening the drawing room door with a flourish. 'It will be my pleasure.'

This room was Bedingham's formal drawing room, used only for receptions and soirées. An eighteenth-century Blyth-Templeton, eager for a room that would serve as a grand reception room for county balls, theatricals, concerts, and other entertainments, had commissioned the leading architect of the day and asked him to create one. He had done so by removing several internal walls and ceilings and the rooms above them, creating a grandiose room that rose the whole height of the house, culminating in a wide skylight dome, ecclesiastical in splendour.

Kyle whistled through his teeth. 'Is the whole house as old as this?'

'This isn't old,' Serena said in amusement, walking across to the white marble and ormolu chimney breast and standing with her back to the sheet of mirror that rose above it, one foot on the fender as Kyle looked around him. 'This room was added in the 1770s, which is late in Bedingham's lifetime. The house was originally built around the remains of a dissolved abbey in 1532.'

'Okay,' Kyle said as she led the way out of the room and through a door in the far corner to an adjoining room. 'I'm impressed. What room is this?'

'It's known as the Red Room because of the colour of the walls. We use it as the family dining room.'

Unlike the drawing room, which had been light and airy, the walls covered in panels of yellow silk, the carpet a dove grey bordered in blue and gold, the Red Room's walls and ceilings were painted a deep Pompeian red. The room was dark and oppressive.

'It isn't a colour I'd like to live with myself,' he said with blunt frankness.

Serena laughed. 'It wasn't our choice either. It was painted like this in Queen Victoria's reign and hasn't been altered since.'

Kyle shook his head in disbelief. 'My mother has the house painted every year. She'd have a stroke at the thought of eating in a room that hadn't been changed in over a hundred!'

'Oh, we refurbish it a little every now and then,' Serena said, laughing and watching him, wondering where she would take him for the culmination of their tour. Her bedroom or a guest bedroom? She walked across to one of the windows looking out over the north lawns. 'Do you see that yew tree? The one nearest the house? It was already fully grown when Henry VIII gave Matthew Blyth permission to domesticate the abbey. Wood from that tree provided bows for the weapons of the yeomen of England. That is how old Bedingham is.'

He looked across at her curiously. 'You really love this place, don't you?'

She turned away from him, the deafening sound of the concert a little more muted now that they were on the north side of the house. 'Of course,' she said simply. 'It's magnificent. Let me show you upstairs.'

They left the room by an opposite door, climbing the back stairs and coming out in a long gallery, the walls ornately decorated with plaster garlands of fruit and flowers and laurel wreaths.

'I know where we are again,' Kyle said as from outside the thunderous beat of *Little Red Rooster* was replaced by *Not Fade Away*. 'My room is the little yellow room, just off the first landing.'

Serena ignored the guest rooms. They weren't splendid enough as a setting for what was about to take place. Only one room was splendid enough.

'This is the Queen's Room,' she said, throwing open a door and entering a large sun-filled room with a four-poster state bed standing in the centre on a small dais. 'So called because Queen Elizabeth I is reputed to have slept here, and Queen Anne in 1712 most certainly slept here.'

There was a central canopy, the corona carved with Prince of Wales feathers. The bedposts were painted white and gold and the netted hangings were backed by crimson brocade edged with thick braid and a deep knotted fringe, and held at the corners by elaborate tassels.

'It's impressive, but a little small,' Kyle said, standing at the side of the bed, one hand resting on a white and gold post.

'When Queen Anne slept here, she slept alone,' Serena said, her tongue moistening her lips as she stood at the opposite side of the bed, barely four feet away from him, wanting him so much that she could barely stand.

'Poor Anne.' His glossy blue-black hair was low over his brows, his Celtic blue eyes holding hers. 'Has anyone slept in it since?'

The dark, rich throb of his voice sent shivers down her spine.

'Queen Victoria,' she said, her vulva engorged and aching. 'And one or two lesser notables.'

'But no one recently?'

Her voice was hoarse, her eyes burning. 'No one in living memory,' she said, wondering how long it would take them to scramble out of their clothes, wondering if the state bed was strong enough for the punishment it was about to receive. To a roar of applause that could be heard a county away, *Not Fade Away* merged into *I Wanna Be Your Man*.

The light in his eyes was devilish. 'Then let's rectify the situation,' he said, his hands on his belt, his buckle already half undone.

Without a further word of encouragement, without his even laying a finger on her, she pulled off her boots and unzipped her dress, sliding it off her shoulders in feverish haste, kicking it away from her, wrenching her panties down with trembling fingers.

He threw his jeans and shirt away from him, whistling low. 'I knew you'd look fantastic naked,' he said thickly, 'but you look even better than I'd imagined!' Without wasting any more time on words, he reached across the bed for her, pulling her down on it, rolling her beneath him.

Her nails clawed his back, her legs opening wide. She needed no preliminaries, no soft words or caresses. She had been ready for him ever since she had faced him at the foot of the staircase. 'Now!' she demanded fiercely, twining her legs around him, her body straining toward his in primeval need. '*Now, you bastard! Now!*'

His mouth came down hard on hers, and the moment that he mounted her, he entered her, plunging deeply and unhesitatingly into her hot, sweet centre. Outside, Mick Jagger blasted into *Come On*, fifty thousand fans screamed and shouted, the ancient bed shook and shuddered, and as Kyle's sperm shot into her like hot gold,

55

Serena reached a climax that left her almost senseless.

For long minutes neither of them even attempted to move or speak. His heart slammed thuddingly against hers, beads of perspiration running down his neck and shoulders.

'That . . .' he said at last, easing himself away from her and rolling over on to his back, '. . . was quite . . . remarkable.'

Serena let out a long, deep, satisfied sigh, and opened her eyes. 'I knew it would be,' she said composedly. 'I knew the minute I saw you, on the rear of the stage.'

He turned over on his side, resting his weight on his elbow. 'That's quite an ability,' he said, grinning down at her. 'If you could put it in a bottle and market it, you'd make a fortune!'

She giggled and then stretched languorously. 'Before we make love again, I need a drink and a smoke. Stay here and conserve your energy and I'll go on a foraging expedition.'

'If you're intent on making love again in anything like the same fashion as last time, make sure whatever you bring back is strong,' he said teasingly.

She sat up and leaned over him, kissing him full on the mouth, her sheet of pale gold hair swinging down like a curtain around them. 'I will,' she said, her eyes dancing as she drew her mouth away from his. 'Because I am. Again and again and again and again.'

He groaned in mock defeat, and she laughed springing from the bed and stepping back into her lemon mini-dress, saying, 'I'll be back in five minutes. Don't move.'

'I couldn't,' Kyle said, the hot afternoon sun spilling through the leaded windows on to his hard, lean body. 'I doubt I'll ever move again!'

'You will,' she promised, swinging from the room as Jagger launched into *The Last Time*.

Kyle grinned. He knew he would. His zest and vigour were more than equal to hers. He just didn't see why she should take anything for granted.

By the time she returned, he was already hardening again at the mere thought of her. She was like some magnificent amazon. Beautifully proportioned, totally uninhibited.

'Where did you learn to make love in such a hurry?' he asked as she moved a couple of Staffordshire figurines from a rosewood side table to make room for two bottles of Margaux and two glasses.

'I wasn't in a hurry,' she said impishly, taking off her dress and tossing a joint across to him. 'If I'd been in a hurry, I would have made love to you on the steps of the great staircase!'

He laughed, watching her as she poured out the wine, the tousle of her pubic hair a rich wheat-gold. 'Hurry or not, it was still pretty experienced.' He lit the joint, inhaling deeply. 'How old are you?'

'Eighteen,' she said, walking across to the bed, a full glass of wine in either hand. 'And you?'

'Nineteen.' He didn't want to talk about himself; he wanted to talk about her. 'Where did the expertise come from? Rollicking with the yokels in local hay-stacks?'

'Certainly not. The expertise is from an *extremely* exclusive Swiss finishing school.'

He arched an eyebrow. 'I thought they were for perfecting French and learning how to play hostess to ambassadors.'

'They are also for learning how to ski,' she said as if explaining everything.

White teeth flashed in a grin. 'Okay. I give up. What has learning to ski to do with sex?'

She laughed huskily at his innocence. 'Skiing itself has nothing to do with it, but oh, those Swiss skiing instructors! Those wonderful, handsome, athletic, adventurous, sex-mad, *virile* Swiss skiing instructors!'

'If Swiss skiing instructors are responsible for the mind-bending experience of a few minutes ago, then I raise my glass to them,' Kyle said, lifting his glass of Margaux high. When he put it down again he said, the mere tone of his voice making her damp with longing, 'Finish your wine. It's my turn to surprise you.'

She did. And he did. 'Oh,' she gasped, her eyes widening, the sensation in her solar plexus like a bomb that had been detonated. 'Oh! *Oh! Oh!*'

They didn't talk again for a long time. Outside, Mick Jagger was succeeded by Peter and Gordon, and after them Gerry and the Pacemakers.

In the Queen's Bedroom, all through the long afternoon, Serena and Kyle made love with the zestful, undiminished appetite of two healthy young animals. He made love to her slowly, withdrawing whenever she neared satisfaction, teasing and arousing her until she screamed at him to come to a conclusion. He made love to her with his tongue alone, not allowing her to reach out and touch him, forcing her to remain completely and excruciatingly passive. By the time they lay exhausted, sheened with sweat, the ornate brocade covers of the bed half falling on the floor, the sun was sinking in the sky and both bottles of Margaux were empty.

'What is the *wildest* thing you've ever done, Kyle?' she asked, her head on his chest as the sweet smell of marijuana surrounded them.

Kyle squinted up at the canopy above him, and the carvings of the Prince of Wales feathers. 'Making love on a bed Queen Elizabeth I and Queen Anne slept in while Mick Jagger and a score of other pop groups sing a mere fifty yards away comes pretty near to heading the list,' he said dryly.

Serena moved her lips languorously over the smooth, sun-kissed flesh beneath his cheek. 'But what else have you done that is *really* wild?'

He frowned, his head so light with alcohol and marijuana that he could scarcely think straight. 'I once flew

58

my uncle's Piper Twin Comanche under the Brooklyn Bridge.'

She giggled and he carefully killed the cherry in his joint and even more carefully placed it on the table at the side of the bed. 'What about you? Or are your escapades so wild as to be beyond belief?'

'I don't think so,' she said modestly. 'On the last night of term, the school's head girl crept into my bed. She's German and built like a Valkyrie.' She giggled again, moving her hand lower down his abdomen. 'That was pretty wild.'

Kyle would have liked to ask for more details, but he was having difficulty coordinating what he wanted to say with what he was able to say.

'I wish we could do something wild, something really wild, together,' Serena said, bending her head to his penis, her tongue circling it in long, lazy strokes.

'You mean, like *both* of us going to bed with your German friend?' Kyle asked, wondering who the fool had been who had said that English girls were frigid.

Serena paused in her ministrations. 'No, silly. Something momentous and far-reaching and totally, totally shocking.'

'We could always elope,' he said, wondering if he was physically capable of making love one more time, and if he was, whether he could capture a place in the *Guinness Book of World Records*.

'Eloping isn't shocking,' she murmured, straddling him, holding his penis with one hand and moving herself teasingly and tormentingly back and forth over its engorged tip.

'Believe you me, as far as my parents are concerned, it is,' he said, wondering how long he could bear the pleasure before having to take action. 'In fact, I can't think of anything that would shock them more!'

She slipped the head of his penis into the mouth of her vagina. 'You're quite right,' she said, her voice high and slurred from wine and marijuana. 'My parents would be shocked to death. It would cause the most frightful fuss.'

She sank down on him, closing her eyes in ecstasy. 'So why don't we do it? Why don't we elope?'

Kyle tightened his arms around her, deftly rolling her beneath him. 'Because I don't know any blacksmiths,' he said reasonably, driving deep inside her in an agony of relief.

She laughed, twining her legs around him, suddenly sure that she loved him and that she would always love him. 'Silly,' she said, her diction very slurred now. 'Marriages at Gretna Green over the blacksmith's anvil haven't been legal for years and years.'

'Then why do people elope there?' He gasped, his eyes tightly closed, an expression of intense concentration, almost of agony, furrowing his features.

'Because . . .' Serena struggled for breath. 'Because . . . you can be married in Scotland without parental consent as long as you're over sixteen.'

'I'm over sixteen,' he said unnecessarily, knowing that his climax was going to be the most shattering he had ever experienced. 'Let's forget the ball this evening. Let's go to Scotland instead.'

'I'd love to,' she panted, lifting her legs over his shoulders. 'Oh, Kyle! Oh, God! *Oh, Kyle!*'

# CHAPTER THREE

Gabrielle Mercador sat completely immobile, the late afternoon sun streaming through the skylight on to her semi-naked body. One hand was resting on a small table at her right-hand side, and her chin was propped on her other hand while her large, luminous eyes gazed soulfully into the distance.

'That is enough,' said the heavily built, bearded Frenchman standing a few yards in front of her, wiping his brush on a rag and surveying the painting on the easel before him with satisfaction. 'We are nearly there, *ma petite*. Another three or four sessions and it will be complete.'

Gabrielle happily snapped out of her pose and soulful expression and stretched catlike. 'Good,' she said, not bothering to walk across to survey the result of the three-hour sitting. 'Do you want me back the same time tomorrow, Philippe?'

He nodded, still studying his handiwork. 'Yes, but it is a pity you cannot come in the morning, *ma petite*. The light is so much better. There is a softness about afternoon light that is not compatible with what I am trying to achieve.'

Gabrielle gave a small Gallic shrug of her shoulders as she crossed the studio towards her pile of clothes. '*C'est impossible*,' she said as she reached for her brassiere. 'I am still sitting for Léon Durras in the mornings.'

'Bah!' Philippe uttered expressively, at last looking away from his painting and towards her. 'Durras has never done any decent work, and he's too old to begin doing so now!'

The corners of Gabrielle's generous mouth quirked in amusement. She sat regularly for over a dozen artists and was used to their jealous backbiting and bickering. For a

61

moment she was tempted to remind Philippe of Léon's recent excellently reviewed exhibition but decided against it. Such provocation would result in a harangue from Philippe that could last half an hour, and she hadn't the time to spare to listen to it.

'Tomorrow afternoon, then,' she said, zipping herself into a short, straight black skirt and pulling a thin sizzling pink cotton top down over full, lush breasts.

'Unless that bastard Durras falls down dead, and then I'll see you in the morning,' Philippe said sourly.

Gabrielle grinned. Twenty years before, just after the liberation of Paris, Philippe's wife had been Léon's mistress. It was an insult Philippe had never forgotten, or forgiven.

She slipped her feet into perilously high stiletto-heeled shoes and picked up her straw shopping bag.

'Are you singing at the Black Cat this evening?' Philippe asked suddenly as she walked across to the spiral staircase that led down from the studio to the ground floor and the street.

She paused, one hand on the metal handrail. 'Yes,' she said coquettishly, 'are you coming?'

He forgot the bad temper that her sitting for Léon Durras had aroused. 'I might,' he said with a grin.

She laughed. 'Then I will see you there,' she said, blowing him a kiss and going carefully down the awkward stairs into the street. Philippe was easily old enough to be her father, and in all the years she had been modelling for him, he had never made an indecent suggestion to her, but he liked to flirt. It made him feel good. And flirting was such second nature to Gabrielle that she wasn't even aware when she was doing it.

She swung out of the darkened vestibule and into the sunlit street, a petite, buoyant figure with a shock of squeaky clean titian curls, laughter-filled green-gilt eyes, and a wide, generous mouth. Her mother was Vietnamese, her father

62

French, and from her mother she had inherited cheekbones that were Asian and high, like those of a Tartar princess, and a short, straight, perfectly shaped nose. From her father she had inherited a firm chin, an earthy sexuality, and the hard-headed common sense that is every Frenchwoman's birthright. No one knew where her remarkable hair colouring had come from. It was as individualistic, as unique as everything else about her.

'Good afternoon, *chérie*,' the aged flower seller on the corner of the rue de Clignancourt and the boulevard Rochechoart called out to her as she swung past, her capacious straw shopping bag over her shoulder, her bottom bouncing tantalizingly beneath her tight, brief skirt.

'Good afternoon, Helena! It is a lovely day, is it not?'

Helena cackled toothlessly. The little Mercador was always so full of *joie de vivre* that just seeing her made the greyest day seem bright.

'*Oui!*' she shouted back jauntily as Gabrielle brought the Montmartre traffic to a halt by stepping out into the street, crossing over towards the place d'Angers. 'It is when you are young, *chérie!*'

Gabrielle grinned and raised a hand to show old Helena that she had heard, and then she walked across the place and into the avenue Trudaine, humming beneath her breath. She would sing *Fever* tonight at the club, and *Lover Man* and *Fly Me to the Moon*, and it was about time she gave *I Gotta Right to Sing the Blues* a public airing. She had been rehearsing it for weeks now and thought that at last she had personalized it and made it her own.

'Good afternoon, Gabrielle!' the local butcher called out to her as she walked exuberantly past his window.

Gabrielle gave him a wide, dazzling smile and threw him a kiss.

'Good afternoon, Gabrielle!' the old woman selling papers at the corner of the avenue Trudaine and the rue Rodier, said to her. 'How is your mother? Your father?'

'They are both well, thank you, Madame Castries,' Gabrielle replied sunnily, taking a newspaper and tucking it into her bag.

'That is good,' Madame Castries said with a pleased nod of her head. The little Mercador wasn't like some eighteen- and nineteen-year-olds. She looked after her parents. It was a pity that there were not more girls like her.

Gabrielle went into the bakery and bought two loaves of bread, chatting to the baker about his wife's health and the progress his children were making at school. In the maze of streets that lay to the south of Sacré-Coeur, there wasn't a man, woman, or child who didn't know her and didn't greet her with pleasure.

She had lived in Montmartre since she was eight years old. Since the French had been defeated at Dien Bien Phu and her father had circumspectly decided that it was time he and his family left Saigon for good. Her mother had never settled comfortably in Paris, which was so vastly different from Vietnam. The climate was cold and damp instead of hot and humid. Her father, too, though France was his homeland, had never been able to come to terms with the difference in life-style between Saigon and Montmartre. Only Gabrielle, after the first few bewildered days, had adjusted, as happy in the narrow, cobbled streets of Montmartre as she had been in the wide tree-lined boulevards she had left behind her.

She crossed the road to number fourteen. A passing *gendarme* winked at her and told her he would be at the club that evening. A young man on a motor scooter called out to her that he had seen Léon Durras' latest canvas and that, thanks to her, Durras had created a masterpiece. Gabrielle paused at the door that led up to her parents' top floor flat, laughing and shouting back that she was glad he thought so.

Beside her, on the wall, was a bird cage with two canaries in it. As the motor scooter zipped away, Gabrielle put her hand into the bottom of her straw bag and withdrew some birdseed.

'There, *mes petits*,' she said, tossing it into the cage. 'Enjoy your supper.'

The canaries belonged to old Madame Garine, who lived in the ground floor flat. When Gabrielle had first arrived in Paris, only the canaries in their little cage had been familiar to her. In Saigon every house had its cage of brightly fluttering birds, and in those first strange, lonely days, Madame Garine's canaries had been a great comfort.

She stepped into the lobby and hurried up the dark stone steps, a rueful smile on her lips. Her father had promised her mother and her, when they left their large sun-filled house in Saigon, that they would live just as comfortably in Paris. They had not. In Saigon there had been servants and easy luxury. In Montmartre there was only a small flat and penny-pinching economy. Her mother, lonely without her Vietnamese family and friends, had begun to stay more and more indoors so that now, ten years later, she very rarely ventured out. It was Gabrielle who shopped, Gabrielle who brought the gossip of the streets to the dining table, Gabrielle who insured that there was still laughter and gaiety in the Mercador household.

Her father, Étienne, had left his home in a small provincial French town for Saigon in 1932. He had had only a moderate education and could see no great future for himself in France. The colonies promised richer pickings. A family friend, already in Saigon, saw to it that there was work waiting for him when he arrived, and for eight years he was happily and profitably employed as a civil servant in a French government department. In 1938, enjoying the rank and life-style of a senior department head, he married Duong Quynh Vanh, a Roman Catholic Annamite of good family. When war broke out in Europe a year later, it made little difference to Étienne and Vanh Mercador. Étienne continued to enjoy the respect and prestige of his government position, and Vanh continued to enjoy the lazy leisurely life-style of a French colonial wife. And then, in 1940, the Japanese swept south.

The French administration in Vietnam was crushed, the French interned as the Japanese surged onwards, driving the British from Malaya, the Dutch from Indonesia, and the United States from the Philippines.

Étienne gritted his teeth, proclaimed himself a supporter of the French government in Vichy, and escaped internment by the skin of his teeth. Vanh's brother, Dinh, moved north, seeing in the Japanese invasion of his country hope for a future Vietnam free of *all* invaders. The Japanese would be defeated eventually by the Allies. When they were, Dinh was determined that his country would no longer be governed by the likes of his brother-in-law. Vietnam would become independent and free.

In the North, a middle-aged freedom fighter, Ho Chi Minh, was consolidating nationalist groups under one banner, fighting a guerrilla war against both the Japanese and the French. Dinh said good-bye to his family in the south and went north, on foot, to join him.

When the war ended and the Japanese left, Étienne had looked forward to a period of increased prosperity. But his brother-in-law's belief that native Vietnamese could force the French out was naive. The French had governed the country for a hundred years and, now that the war with the Japanese was over, they intended to govern it for another hundred.

Vanh had kept her thoughts to herself. She loved her husband, and she loved the French way of life. She had been educated in French convents, and she enjoyed the ease and luxury of her husband's French salary. Yet, like her brother, she wanted to see her country independent. As life after the war began slowly to return to normal, she comforted herself with the belief that the French would allow the Vietnamese a greater say in the governing of the country, and in the fact that she was, at last, pregnant.

In 1945 and '46, the French reasserted their authority over Vietnam, but only with difficulty. In the North, Ho Chi Minh proclaimed a provisional Vietnamese government in Hanoi, and in the south, Britain came to France's aid, subduing bitter protests and bloody street fighting, and imposing French rule yet again.

As a child in Saigon, Gabrielle was happily unaware of the tensions surrounding her. The family home was in the avenue Foch, a wide, tree-lined, flower-filled boulevard. She had a Vietnamese nanny to look after her, a monkey for a pet, and a garden crammed with tuberoses and orchids and gardenias to play in.

Fighting continued from 1946 until 1954 when the French met with the forces of General Giap, Ho Chi Minh's right hand man, at a small village on the Lao border, called Dien Bien Phu. All the previous bloody engagements had been running guerrilla battles, in which the Viet Minh had the advantage. At Dien Bien Phu, the French, with superior air power and superior weapons, and fighting the kind of battle that they were accustomed to, were confident that they could thrash the Viet Minh once and for all.

Shortly after French troops were airlifted in to the floor of the steep valley, General Giap moved thirty-three infantry battalions, six artillery regiments, and a regiment of engineers toward Dien Bien Phu. In a tremendous feat of muscle power, soldiers, coolies and cadres dragged artillery to the tops of the surrounding mountains. From then on, the incredulous French were under constant blistering attack. A howitzer was positioned within range of the French air strip, cutting off flights in and out of the valley and making it almost impossible for them to receive supplies or to evacuate their wounded. Almost from the beginning the French were in a state of siege.

Seven horrific weeks later, in a sea of blood and mud and vomit, the Viet Minh's red flag went up over the French command bunker. The French had been defeated; colonial rule in Vietnam was at an end, and an international conference was set up in Geneva to plan the country's future.

Whatever that future was, as a minor French civil servant, Étienne knew that his good fortune had run out. He packed his bags and returned to the land of his birth with his wife and child. And the three had long since settled in Paris.

Gabrielle climbed the last few steps and opened the door of the apartment. From the kitchen there came the appetizing aroma of shredded pork and rice vermicelli, for her mother still cooked the traditional Vietnamese dishes.

'Hello, *Maman*. Is Papa home?' she asked, putting her straw bag on the kitchen table and removing the two loaves of bread and the newspaper.

'No, he is playing *boules*,' her mother said, kissing her cheek.

When they had first returned from Saigon, her father had been devastated to discover that his government would not employ him. He had found work as a manager of a local garment factory and then the factory had closed. For the past two years he had not worked at all.

Gabrielle looked down at the table. There was a letter from her aunt. Her mother, diminutive and fragile in Vietnamese traditional dress, sat down at the kitchen table, a doubtful frown creasing her brow.

'Nhu says that so many Americans have arrived in Saigon in the last few months, it is as if they are taking over the country. That instead of being a French colony, Vietnam is becoming an American colony.'

Nhu was her mother's sister in Saigon, from whom letters were received regularly.

'Nhu is being ridiculous,' Gabrielle said briskly.

She loved her pretty, decorative mother dearly, but intelligence and a grasp of current affairs were not her strong points. 'Without American aid, the Viet Cong would be victorious and Nhu would be living under a Communist regime. She doesn't want that, does she?'

'No,' her mother said uncertainly. 'But Dinh believes it is the only way and that communism under Ho will not be as bad as we fear.'

68

Gabrielle sighed. 'It will still be communism,' she said impatiently. Her mother's trouble was that she wanted to be loyal to all the people that she loved. Whenever she was reminded of Dinh, the dearly loved brother she had not seen for nearly twenty-five years, she wondered if the Communist threat was not as terrible as her sister said it was.

On a dark evening in 1963 he had knocked at Nhu's door and had stayed until the early hours of the morning. It was the only time that any of his family had seen him since he had walked north so many years before. He was now a colonel with the North Vietnamese forces. He had come south on an undercover mission for General Giap. The General intended to infiltrate large numbers of his forces into the south and he wanted the situation in the south assessed before he committed them. Together with a dozen military specialists and a handful of civilian cadres, Dinh had trekked down a jungle trail that threaded its way through southern Laos and north-eastern Cambodia, into the highlands of South Vietnam.

'But how can they sweep south now that the Americans are helping us?' her mother had asked him bewilderedly. 'The North Vietnamese are peasants. They cannot fight America!'

Now she said, still bewildered, 'It is so hard to understand what is happening at home when we are so far away.'

Saigon was still home to her mother, though neither of them knew if she would ever see it again.

Gabrielle finished her glass of kir. 'I want to go over my repertoire for this evening, *Maman*. I don't want anything to eat before I go. Save me something for when I come home.'

Her mother nodded. Gabrielle had been singing in Montmartre nightclubs for over two years now, but it had been two weeks since her last engagement and she had been carefully putting together a whole new selection of songs.

Gabrielle went to her tiny bedroom and picked up her guitar. When she sang in the clubs she sang to piano accompaniment, but there was no room in her parents' flat for a piano, and even if there had been, there was no money for one.

Painstakingly she went over all the songs that she intended to sing. Her musical style was very strongly her own. Although she often sang songs that internationally known stars had made famous, she had the ability to take the most well-known lyric and transform it so that her audience felt as if they were hearing it for the first time.

The club circuit was highly competitive, and though she was not aware of it, her growing success was due to the perfect match between her voice and her personality. She had a husky, knowing voice, with a sensual chuckle deep inside it, the kind of voice that announces its owner loves not always wisely, but too well, and who doesn't give a damn one way or the other. Though she'd become popular singing standard love songs by Irving Berlin, Cole Porter, and Lerner and Loewe, she had begun to write her own songs: committed, passionate love songs that sent tingles down the spines of her audience.

Satisfied with the selection she had made, she bathed in the apartment's ancient, iron-framed bathtub and dressed for the evening's performance.

The fresh skirt that she stepped into was a little longer than her previous one had been, but was still black. The sweater she wore was also black, long-sleeved, and fell low over her hips, the neck high and straight, every inch covered in a mesh of tiny, glittering sequins.

She slipped her feet into high-heeled black suede pumps, and dropped her list of songs and the accompanying music into a small black shoulder bag.

'Au 'voir Maman! Au 'voir, Papa!' she called out as she walked out of her bedroom and towards the apartment's front door.

'Au 'voir, chérie!' her parents called after her from the kitchen, where they were eating their evening meal. 'Good luck!'

Gabrielle closed the door and started down the three flights of stone steps that led to the street. Her parents always wished her luck, and her mother often waited up until the early hours of the morning so that she could make her an omelette and coffee when she returned home, but nothing Gabrielle could do would persuade them to come and watch one of her performances.

She hurried down the last of the steps and walked quickly through the lobby and out into the spangling blue dusk. They never said so, but she knew it was because no matter where she appeared, striptease artistes invariably preceded and followed her act. Girls who took off their clothes before men were, in her parents' eyes, little more than women of the streets, and they did not wish to be reminded of how closely their daughter worked with them.

The dome of the Sacré-Coeur was pale against the evening sky as she hurried past it, towards the Black Cat. She wondered if Philippe would keep his word and visit the club that evening. She doubted it. He would be immersed in work, already making sketches and drawings for whatever his next project was even though his present painting was incomplete.

'Good evening, Gabrielle,' the porter at the Black Cat said to her as she hurried down the steps into the club. 'You're early this evening.'

'I want to run through a couple of songs with Michel,' she said, flashing him a smile that made the bulge in his crotch harden. He knew that his employer had tried hard to persuade her to remove her clothes as she sang; regrettably he'd been unsuccessful. It was a pity. It was a sight he would have given a year's salary to see.

Gabrielle greeted Henri, the barman, as he busily polished glasses. 'Is Michel here yet?' she asked, sitting down on one of the high stools.

Henri paused in what he was doing and poured her an anisette. 'He's in the dressing room, trying to persuade Paulette to sleep with him.'

71

Gabrielle laughed. Michel was her pianist, a tall, thin, bespectacled youth who could play the piano like an angel, but who enjoyed a spectacular lack of success with women.

'I'll go and rescue her,' she said, draining her glass and pushing it back across the bar toward him.

Henri removed it with a grin. 'It is not Paulette who needs rescuing so much as it is Michel who needs helping!' When she laughed, he added, 'It's nice to have you back, Gabrielle. The last couple of singers have been long-haired beatniks who looked as if they never washed. At least tonight, with you and Paulette on the bill, the club will be full.'

It wasn't hard to fill the Black Cat. Even when packed to capacity the large below-street-level room held only seventy people, and then the tables and chairs were squeezed so closely around the tiny stage that Paulette often complained that she could feel the audience's breath on her flesh.

That evening Paulette performed to a boisterously appreciative audience, coming offstage with the perspiration breaking through her makeup. '*Mon Dieu*, Gabrielle. I should have listened to my mother and become a schoolteacher! It would have been an easier life!'

'You wouldn't have liked it,' Gabrielle said impishly. 'It would have been far too boring!'

When the applause for Paulette began to fade, Michel began to play her introductory music. She waited for a moment, judging her timing, and then walked out on to the stage.

Gavin Ryan was no expert on nightclub singers, especially singers who sang in clubs as small and sleazy as the Black Cat, but he had known the first time he had seen her, nearly three weeks before, that the audience's response to her was unusual.

Singers in Montmartre clubs were given far less attention than the strippers. When the strippers had departed and the singer came on, it was generally the signal for the audience to turn its attention to the bar and order another round of drinks while they discussed the merits or faults of the last stripper.

Gabrielle was different. When she came onstage, she commanded the audience's attention even before she began to sing. After the excess of flesh that had preceded her, and that the patrons were accustomed to, her black skirt and glittering black high-necked, long-sleeved sweater were as stark and uncompromising as a nun's habit, the spicy red flame of her hair almost indecent by contrast.

She made none of the usual efforts to woo her audience with flirtatious words and smiles before she began to sing. Instead, as Michel played the first few bars of her opening song, she stood perfectly still, insolently indifferent to them, and when she sang, it was as though she were singing for herself and herself alone.

Gavin put down his glass of cheap champagne. He had seen her twice before, in a different club, and was as riveted by her now as he had been then. She had the most extraordinary face, both sensuously feline and appealingly, childishly gamine, and there was the merest hint of duskiness in her complexion, as if she were of mixed blood, Moroccan, perhaps, or Algerian.

The fellow Australian he was sitting with the first time they had seen her had said to him, 'I agree with you that she's amazing-looking and that she has a terrific singing voice, but I wouldn't go near her if I were you, cobber. They're all on the game, the lot of them. No telling what you might catch.'

Gavin rather reluctantly agreed with him. At twenty-three, he'd bummed his way from Brisbane halfway round the world, and miraculously caught nothing worse than influenza in India. The hostesses in the club were certainly prostitutes. He had already spurned two very definite propositions. It was a pity though. There was something mesmerizing about Gabrielle Mercador. She had the rare capacity to be completely still, and yet to command unwavering attention. When she sang, the emotion in her voice was naked, raising goose pimples on his flesh. Her opening song was followed by one he had never heard before, then she sang *La demoiselle élue*, by Debussy, and then the most evocative rendering of *Fever* that he had ever heard.

When she walked off the stage to enthusiastic applause he felt a devastating sense of loss. Telling himself he was a fool, he rose to his feet. As he did, a young black girl strutted on to the stage dressed in thigh-high black boots, white satin shorts, and a revealing scarlet bolero. He turned away, uninterested, squeezing his way through the crowded room towards the bar.

The bar was deserted. Every back was turned toward it as the black girl divested herself of her bolero, throwing it wide and high into the audience to thunderous wolf whistles and shouts of crude encouragement.

'A beer,' Gavin said to Henri, wondering if he was going to have enough sense and willpower to resist coming to see Gabrielle Mercador the following evening.

He wasn't aware of her approach. One minute he was deep in thought, the next he heard a husky, enticing voice asking the barman for an anisette with water.

He turned his head swiftly, eyes widening in disbelief. She was standing next to him, so near that he could smell her perfume. Her makeup was heavier than he had expected, but almost immediately he realized that that was because of the strong spotlight under which she sang.

'Excuse me,' he said in halting French before he could lose his nerve. 'But could I have the pleasure of buying your drink?'

'*Non, merci.*' Her response was automatic. She never socialized with the patrons. They were nearly always sweaty and lustful and drinking too much.

She hadn't looked at him when he had spoken to her, but now, as she turned to move away, she did so, and she hesitated. He wasn't the usual sort of patron. He was young and clean-cut, with a mop of shaggy, sun-gold hair. His disappointment was obviously so sincere that she said impulsively, trying to soften the blow she had dealt him, 'I'm sorry, but I never drink with the patrons.'

Gavin was nonplussed. In all the other clubs that he had been into, *all* the girls – singers, strippers, and hostesses – touted for laughingly expensive bottles of champagne.

'I'm sorry too,' he said, not wanting her to walk away from him. 'Couldn't you make an exception? Just this once?'

He had strongly marked brows bleached blond by the sun like his hair, and his eyes were a deep, warm grey.

'Yes,' she said, breaking one of her cardinal rules. 'A lemonade please.'

He quirked an eyebrow. 'Not another anisette?'

She laughed. 'No, I have to perform again in half an hour.'

'I saw you last week at the Columbo,' he said, searching for the correct French words with difficulty. 'I thought you were sensational. That's why I came here tonight. I wanted to see you again.'

'Oh, how nice!' Her pleasure was genuine. There was nothing hard or artificial about her. Prostitute or not, she was the nicest girl he had ever met. He cleared his throat.

He was far from sexually inexperienced, but he had never before attempted to do what he was going to do now.

'Are you, er, available later on?'

A small frown creased her brow. '*Pardon?* I'm sorry. I don't understand.'

'Could I see you later on, after the show?'

He wondered if his French was totally incomprehensible to her and put his hand inside his breast pocket, withdrawing his wallet, hoping to indicate that he knew what the situation was.

Her eyes widened as she looked at his wallet and realized what he was trying to ask her. If it had been anyone else, she would have walked away indignantly, but he looked so uncomfortable and so agonized that instead of being insulted she began to giggle.

He flushed scarlet, not knowing what he had done or said to make himself ridiculous.

'I'm sorry,' she said, still giggling. 'It's just that you have made a mistake. I am a singer. That is all. Only a singer.'

Relief swamped him, and he didn't care that he had made a first-class fool of himself.

'I'm glad,' he said, grinning. 'My name is Gavin Ryan, and I still want to take you out after the show.'

'I am not sure,' Gabrielle said truthfully. 'I will make up my mind later. Where are you from? New Zealand? Australia?'

'Australia,' he said, wondering how he could have been such a fool and determining to sock his friend on the jaw the next time he saw him.

'And what are you doing in Paris?' she asked as the black girl finally divested herself of her last article of clothing to wild applause.

'I've just gotten myself a job as a reporter with a press agency. What I really want to do is to go out to Vietnam and cover events there, but the agency has a rule that you have to work for three years in one of the European offices before being assigned as a war correspondent.'

Gabrielle's eyebrows rose slightly. 'And what do you know about Vietnam?' she asked teasingly.

'I know there are some big stories brewing there,' he said, loving the way she spoke. 'And there's going to be one hell of a lot of action now that the Americans are beginning to fight.'

A three-piece band had begun to play, and couples were starting to cram the tiny dance floor. She put her glass of lemonade down on the bar. 'I have to go now,' she said regretfully. 'I am onstage again in ten minutes. Good-bye, Mr Ryan, it has been nice talking to you.'

'But I thought you said I could see you after the show?' His alarm at the prospect of losing her was so naked that she burst out laughing again.

'I said that I would *think* about it,' she said reprovingly.

'And have you?'

His anxiety and urgency were so raw that she couldn't resist teasing him just a little longer.

'I will let you know, when I sing,' she said, moving away from him. 'My first song will be my answer.'

He watched as she moved away from him and then ordered himself another beer. If her song was a refusal, he would come back tomorrow night, and the night after, and the night after that. He would come back every night until she agreed to see him. Until he could talk to her in clean air, and not in a smoke-filled cavern packed with a lecherous audience totally unworthy of her.

When she walked out onstage, his chest physically hurt. She stood for a moment, perfectly poised, effortlessly in command of her audience, her spicy red curls burning like a candle flame. The pianist began to play and a tiny smile quirked the corners of her mouth as she turned towards the bar where he was standing and began to sing, *I'll Be Seeing You*.

He had his answer. His grin was so wide it split his face. He wanted to shout a loud 'hooray'; to push to the front of the stage and seize her and hug her until she was breathless.

'A bottle of champagne,' he said to Henri. 'A genuine one!'

When the last notes of the song died away, she began to sing Irving Berlin's *Always*. Though neither of them could possibly have guessed it, it was a song that was appropriate for the long, agony-filled years that lay ahead.

# CHAPTER FOUR

Abbra had never been happier. Lewis was given a special two-day pass and they were married in the military chapel at Fort Bragg. The only thing marring the day was the absence of Scott. He was at football training camp and was unable to be best man though he had sent his congratulations and his apologies. A friend of Lewis's, who had been his classmate at West Point, was best man.

After the wedding her parents returned to San Francisco, and after her one-night honeymoon Abbra had followed them by train.

It was a strange feeling, becoming a married woman with so little warning. A married woman whose husband was, in twenty-four hours time, going overseas to fight in Vietnam.

Once she was back home the feeling of strangeness increased. Outwardly her life was the same. She still lived with her parents in Pacific Heights; she still attended college. Yet inwardly she'd changed. She no longer had any interest in parties or dances. They were for girls who were on the lookout for men, and she was no longer looking; she was married to Lewis and she had no desire to behave as if she were still single.

She began to see less and less of her close friends. After the first heady pleasure of showing off her wedding ring and receiving her friends' squeals of congratulations, she found that she had very little to say to them. The endless talk about who was dating whom was no longer fascinating, and they were not interested in the things that preoccupied her: the military situation in Southeast Asia and her fears for Lewis's safety.

As September merged into October, she wondered if returning to San Francisco had been a mistake. If she had moved into quarters on an army base, then at least she would have had other married women to talk to, women who would understand her position and who perhaps also had husbands serving overseas. As it was, she felt oddly isolated and increasingly lonely. After six months in Vietnam, Lewis would have five days leave. He had already written to her and suggested they spend his leave together in Hawaii. There was hardly a waking moment when she wasn't thinking about it, looking forward to it, but there was another three months before the dream would become reality, and the three months stretched ahead of her as if they were three hundred.

On the second Thursday in October a ring at the front door put an end to her growing worries. She was in her bedroom, writing the daily portion of her weekly letter to Lewis, when her mother knocked and entered, saying in a voice that indicated she wasn't very pleased by the event, 'You have a visitor, Abbra. Scott.'

Abbra put her pen down immediately, rising to her feet in happy anticipation.

'I appreciate the fact that as he is now your brother-in-law a certain courtesy is due him, but I don't approve of him, Abbra. He is so unlike Lewis. Why any well-educated young man should opt out of his responsibilities in the way that Scott has done is completely beyond me. With all his opportunities he should have become a lawyer or a stockbroker. Or followed his father and Lewis into the army.'

'Playing professional football *isn't* opting out of responsibilities, Mom,' Abbra said patiently, sliding the half-written letter into the top drawer of her desk. 'It's a career, just like any other career, and it's a tough and competitive one.'

Her mother shook her head, unconvinced. 'I'm sorry, Abbra, but I can't possibly agree with you. Professional football players are not the sort of people that we would normally mix with.'

'Well, we're mixing with one now, so everyone had better start getting used to the idea!' Abbra said with asperity. 'Where is he? In the living room?'

Her mother nodded, her lips tightening. Even though she had approved of Lewis, she had not approved of the indecently quick wedding. It had not been at all the kind of wedding she had pictured for her daughter. And now this. A football player in her house. She didn't like it, and she had no intention of allowing it to become a regular event.

Abbra ran quickly down the stairs, hoping that her father wasn't being as cold to Scott as her mother had obviously been. When she went into the living room and found him standing by the window in an otherwise empty room, her reaction was one of relief.

'Hello,' she said with a welcoming smile. 'I'm Abbra.'

Scott had been looking out over the bay and turned quickly, shocked amazement flaring in his eyes. He strode to meet her, suppressing his emotion almost immediately. 'I'm glad to meet you, Abbra,' he said, taking her hand. 'Sorry I wasn't able to make the wedding. It was my first training camp and there was no way I could break loose, even for a day.'

'It's all right,' she said truthfully, 'I understood.'

He grinned down at her. 'That's good. My father certainly didn't. When I was injured in the first game of the season, he said it was God's punishment for my putting training before family commitments!'

Her eyes darkened with concern. 'I'm sorry. I didn't know you had been injured. What happened? What did you do?' As she asked, she wondered why he'd looked shocked when she walked into the room. What had he been expecting? Someone far more glamorous and sophisticated? He had known she was still at college. Surely he couldn't have expected her to be much older?

'I made a seventy-five-yard touchdown interception which won the game, but I was hit after the whistle and the ligaments in my ankle were badly torn. I've been having physical therapy on them now for six weeks, and it will take another three or four weeks before I can play again.'

He was taller than Lewis, six feet three or perhaps six feet four, and he was as powerfully built as the genial giant she had been dancing with the night she had met Lewis. Scott's hair was nearly as blond as the genial giant's had been. It grew low into the nape of his neck, a rich barley-gold, and thick and curly.

'So while I'm resting up and having treatment on it, I thought I'd catch up on my family obligations.' He grinned again. 'Which in this case means getting to know my new sister-in-law. I wondered if you'd have an early dinner with me, to help the process along?'

'I'd love to!' she said immediately. It was deeply important to Abbra that she get on well with Lewis's family. Though she had met his father as a child, the wedding was their first real opportunity to talk. She'd liked him and been fairly sure that the feeling was mutual. Now she had a chance to get to know Scott and she would also, at long last, be able to talk to someone about Lewis.

'I'll just put some shoes on and let my mother know I'm going out,' she said.

Incredibly, he hadn't realized she was barefoot. He and Lewis were so dissimilar in taste and temperament that he had never in a million years imagined Lewis would have married any girl he, Scott, thought halfway passable. When Abbra had walked gaily into the room in jeans and an open-neck cotton shirt, glossy dark hair swinging silkily around a square-jawed, high-cheekboned face, he had been so stunned that he could hardly speak. He had known that she was still at college, but had never for a moment imagined she would be so young and glowingly vital.

He looked down at her feet. They were narrow and well-shaped, the nails painted a pale, pearly pink. He wanted to

tell her not to put on anything too stylish in the hope that
after they ate they would be able to go down to the beach
and walk. Almost as soon as the thought entered his head
he cursed himself for a fool. He was taking her out for a
meal, but it wasn't a date. It couldn't end on the beach or
anywhere even remotely similar. She was his sister-in-law,
not a prospective girlfriend, and the sooner he realized it,
the better.

Her mother was crossing the hall as they left the
house. He said good-bye with friendly politeness, and she
responded with chilly formality.

'Was it something I said?' he said half jokingly to Abbra
as they walked across the gravel drive towards a gleaming
new Ford Mustang.

When she had left the room for her shoes, she had also
changed out of her jeans and cotton shirt, and was now
wearing a turquoise skirt that swirled around her legs, a
pale mauve silk shirt, and high-heeled, delicately strapped
sandals. Her eyes, as they met his, were agonizingly apologetic.

'I'm sorry, Scott. It's just that my mother doesn't
approve of professional football players. She's convinced
that all they do is hang around bars and get into drunken
fights.'

He opened the car door, the grin back on his face.

'It could be your mother is right,' he teased.

She gurgled with laughter, the sound carrying back to the
house. In the luxuriously furnished living room, Mrs Daley
sat down on a sofa, her back straight, her lips tight. When
her husband came home she was going to have a very serious
talk with him. Scott Ellis was nowhere near as socially
acceptable as Lewis and, brother-in-law or not, she didn't
like his free and easy attitude toward Abbra. This initial
excursion could not be allowed to develop into a habit. If it
did, goodness only knew what the gossips would make of it.

It was early evening and the light was soft over the Bay
and the bridge and the cliffs beyond. Scott drove down

Broadway, leaving the opulence of Pacific Heights behind him, manoeuvring deftly through the Chinatown traffic and on to Columbus Avenue toward her favourite Italian restaurant.

'Hi,' one of Luigi's chefs called out to her from the open-plan kitchen. 'Long time no see!'

'I've been busy getting married,' Abbra responded as Scott ignored the formality of the booths and led the way to the counter, where they could sit and eat and watch the chefs as they worked. She held up the third finger of her left hand so the chef could see her gleaming new wedding ring.

'Congratulations,' he said, beaming at both of them, and then, to Scott, 'you're a lucky guy.'

Scott's eyes danced in amusement and Abbra flushed rosily, saying quickly, 'This isn't my husband. My husband is serving overseas. This is Scott Ellis, my brother-in-law.'

The chef paused in what he was doing and looked at Scott with fresh interest. 'Say, aren't you the guy who was injured scoring during the Rams' season opener?'

Scott nodded, and admitted modestly that he was.

The chef shook his head sympathetically. 'That was pretty bad luck. I saw the game on TV. It was a pretty mean late tackle. The guy should have been suspended. I wish to God you were playing for the 49ers. We could use you!'

Scott accepted the compliment with easy grace and returned his attention to Abbra. 'I'm glad to see that you don't talk about football *all* the time,' she said teasingly as they ate perfectly cooked fettuccine with a delicious white sauce, and talked about books and writers, discovering a shared passion for Dashiell Hammett.

'Did Lewis tell you I did?' he asked, topping up her glass of burgundy.

There was something in his voice that reminded her that Lewis had been disapproving of Scott's choice of career. The flush that had touched her cheeks when the chef had mistaken him for her husband edged back. 'No, of course

83

not,' she said, uncomfortably aware that if Lewis hadn't actually said so, he had certainly hinted at it. 'It's just that I imagined professional football players would talk about football and nothing else.'

'Well, this one doesn't,' he said good-naturedly, knowing that she was being tactful and that Lewis had most certainly been speaking disparagingly about him. 'The problem is, when I'm with Lewis, I don't know what the hell else to talk about!'

She stared at him, wondering if he was joking, and then realized with amazement that he wasn't. 'But how can you not have anything to talk to him about?' she asked bewilderedly. 'He's your brother!'

He grinned. 'And you're an only child, right?'

She nodded.

'Believe me, Abbra, being a sibling doesn't automatically mean that you have everything in common. Most brothers that I know have very different interests. Where Lewis and I are concerned, the differences are pretty big. Dad has lived his life for the army. He loves it passionately and I don't think it ever occurred to him that Lewis and I wouldn't follow in his footsteps. With Lewis he was lucky. As a child all Lewis wanted to do was play soldiers. Me? I was sick to death of soldiers and army life. All I wanted to do was play football, and that's exactly what I've done. I don't have any regrets, but it hasn't exactly brought me and Lewis very close.'

'You make it sound as if you're not even friends.' Her voice was heavy with disappointment.

He resisted the urge to cover her hand comfortingly with his. 'In a lot of ways we're not. We don't hang around together and we never have. But what we have is deeper than friendship, so don't worry about us, Abbra. We're brothers. We annoy and infuriate each other, but when it comes to the bottom line, we care about each other more than we care about anyone else. And that's all that matters.'

84

'Doesn't he write to you from Vietnam?' she asked, her dismay ebbing.

'I had a brief note from him at the end of July, shortly after he arrived. He sounded as if he was in his element, though how anyone could actually *enjoy* living out in the jungle and facing sniper fire twenty-four hours a day, I can't imagine.'

As soon as he said it he regretted it. Her face had paled, her eyes darkening until they were a deep-drowned purple. 'Did he tell you that he was under constant sniper fire?'

He shook his head. 'No, don't worry, Abbra. That's just my own idea of what life out there must be like. He told me he was serving as an adviser to a Vietnamese infantry battalion, but to tell the truth, I don't have an idea of what that means.'

Zabaglione had followed the pasta and wine, and coffee had followed the zabaglione.

'He's part of a five-man American advisory team,' Abbra said, her voice warming as she was at last able to talk about the subject closest to her heart. 'It's composed of a captain, a first lieutenant, and three non-commissioned officers.'

'And Lewis is the first lieutenant?' Scott asked, already knowing the answer to his question.

'Yes.' There was such quiet pride in her voice that his heart felt as if it were being squeezed tight. 'They are operating in the southernmost part of Vietnam, in the Ca Mau peninsula. Lewis says that the Vietnamese battalion commander has been fighting the Communists for over six years, and that several of the other Vietnamese officers have been fighting for just as long.'

'And before that they were fighting the French,' Scott said, sliding his coffee cup away from him and signalling for another. 'It isn't worth thinking about, is it?'

'No,' she agreed, bleakly trying to imagine what it must be like for Lewis, rarely seeing another American apart from the four in his team; spending days, sometimes weeks at a time hunting through the U Minh or Nam Can forests for reinforced Viet Cong regiments; never knowing when they would stumble into an ambush or meet with enemy fire.

He saw the troubled expression in her eyes, and this time he did reach out and comfortingly cover her hand with his. 'Don't worry about him, Abbra. Lewis is a professional soldier. This is what he's been trained for; he's looked forward to it his whole life.'

She stared at him, appalled. 'He isn't *enjoying* it out there! He couldn't be! No one could!'

'Well, perhaps *enjoying* is the wrong word,' Scott said, not truly believing that it was. 'I guess I should have said that he would be satisfied that he was doing the job he was trained for and doing it well.'

'Yes,' she said slowly. 'The area where he's operating is one that the Viet Cong have been trying hard to control for several years. He told me that hundreds of teachers and village chiefs had been assassinated for refusing to cooperate with them. If the area is more stable now that he and his Vietnamese battalion are operating there, and if the people in the villages are suffering less, then he *will* be gaining satisfaction from what he's doing.'

Scott wasn't sure whether the area would be more stable or not, but obviously thinking that it would be was the only way Abbra could come to terms with Lewis being there. He wondered how she would get along with the wives of Lewis's fellow officers, and remembering the wives of his father's fellow officers felt a surge of pity for her. He couldn't imagine her as a typical army wife, her only interest her husband's career, living for him and through him, with no real interests or life of her own.

'We'd better go,' he said gently. 'Your mother will think I've run off with you.' It was nearly ten-thirty and they had been talking for over three hours.

She rose regretfully. It had been the nicest evening she could remember since parting from Lewis.

'Are you going back to Los Angeles tonight?' she asked, wondering when she would see him again.

He shook his head. 'I'm not really supposed to be driving at all, not until the physical therapist gives me the all-clear. I've arranged to stay over at a friend's house and then I'll drive leisurely back to L.A. tomorrow morning ready for my afternoon appointment with the therapist.'

She nodded understandingly, saying nothing as they walked out into the street, but he noticed that her shoulders were drooping very slightly and it occurred to him that she had enjoyed the evening just as much as he had. None of Lewis's friends or their wives were living in San Francisco, and he couldn't imagine that her mother encouraged much conversation about Lewis, or about anything else that interested her.

'I'm coming up again next weekend,' he said casually. 'It would be nice if you could take pity on me again and have dinner with me. Being a semi-cripple, I'm not exactly in great social demand at the moment.'

It was a lie. As an up-and-coming star with the Rams, his social life had never been more hectic and his injury had made not the slightest bit of difference to that part of his life.

Her face lit up, and he slid his arm around her shoulders, hugging her tight. He had driven to San Francisco on a duty visit to meet a sister-in-law he had expected to have nothing in common with. Instead, he had found a woman he knew was going to be a great friend and that he loved as family already.

Abbra happily accepted the crushing hug in the manner that it was given. She had never had any brothers or sisters, and she was overjoyed at the immediate closeness that had sprung up between her and Scott.

'We nearly met once before, on the night that I first met Lewis.' Her face softened, her eyes glowing as she remembered. 'It was at a party given by a friend of mine in San Francisco at the end of May. Her brother had invited lots of his friends, and you were among them. I danced with

87

another friend of yours. He pointed you out to me because he was telling me how he hoped to be drafted by the Rams, and of how you had already signed with them.'

They were at the car now, and he had released her shoulders, and was staring down at her. 'You mean we were both in the same room and I didn't notice you?' he said incredulously. 'It isn't possible!'

She laughed affectionately. 'Oh, but it is. You were surrounded by admiring females.'

He continued to look down at her, still puzzled. 'I don't remember Lewis being at any party that I was at. In fact, come to think of it, I can't remember Lewis being at *any* party.'

He opened the door for her and she slid into the seat. 'I'm surprised he didn't tell you. He was on leave and had had dinner with my parents. He came to pick me up.'

He quickly came around the car and eased himself behind the steering wheel. 'And he never came in and joined the party?'

She shook her head and he could smell the faint lingering perfume of her shampoo. 'No. We left together and went out for a hamburger and a Coke.'

He sat in the dark car, not moving as the enormity of her words sank in. Then he switched on the engine and slammed it into gear. Jesus. He'd been as near as *that* to meeting her first; to asking her out; to falling in love with her.

'What's the matter?' she asked in concern as he slewed out of Columbus Avenue and into Broadway, his brows drawn together in a savage frown. 'Have I said something to upset you?' She couldn't, for the life of her, think what it could have been.

'No.' He looked towards her, forcing the frown away, giving her a lighthearted grin that was far from what he was feeling. 'I was just thinking how the course of our lives can be altered by small acts. Entering or not entering a room; being somewhere five minutes early or five minutes late. That sort of thing.'

She nodded. 'I know. I go cold with fright when I think

88

of how I might have refused to let my mother send Lewis instead of our driver, and how, if I had, I would never have met Lewis.'

It hadn't been exactly what he was thinking, but he could scarcely tell her that. He drove her home, still appalled at his instant reaction to knowing that they had been in the same room together before she had met Lewis. If he had seen her, would he have noticed her? The answer was a thundering yes. And would he have asked her out on a date? He couldn't imagine himself meeting her and not asking. But would he have fallen in love with her? That was a question he couldn't answer.

He had never in his life been seriously in love, and he didn't expect he ever would be. Long-standing commitments were not his style. Lewis was the one who was always serious about any emotional involvement he might enter into, and it was typical of Lewis that after meeting Abbra and falling in love with her, he had seen marriage as the next logical step. Scott had enough self-awareness to know that if it had been him, he would never in a million years have thought of anything other than having an intensely passionate and enjoyable love affair.

As he swung the car into her parents' drive, he smiled ruefully. He hated to admit it, but Abbra had been far better off falling in love with Lewis than she would have been falling in love with him. The smile deepened into a self-deprecating grin. Hell, how had he the arrogance to even imagine that she *would* have fallen in love with him? He was a football player, and in the world that Abbra and her parents inhabited, a football player came pretty low in the potential-husband stakes.

'Why are you smiling?' she asked curiously as he braked to a halt.

He laughed, wondering what on earth she would say if he told her. 'I was just thinking how damned lucky Lewis is to have you as a wife,' he said tactfully, 'and of how damned lucky I am to have you as a sister-in-law.'

He walked around and opened the car door, resisting the

urge to kiss her on the cheek. 'I won't come into the house with you. I have a feeling your mother has seen enough of me for one day.'

She stepped out of the car, the night breeze blowing her hair softly across her face. 'And I'll see you next week?'

He nodded. 'I'll pick you up about seven. We'll go somewhere a little more upbeat than Luigi's. The Golden Eagle or the Kichihei. Somewhere that Lewis will approve of.'

As she walked away from him into the house, she wondered if, subconsciously, he often tried to do things that would gain Lewis's approval. Perhaps, when Lewis's tour of duty in Vietnam was over, they could go together and see Scott play. She was sure Lewis had never done so, and she knew that though he wouldn't admit it, Scott would be as pleased as hell to know his elder brother was cheering him on.

Although it was after eleven by the time she reached her room, she didn't immediately begin to get ready for bed. Instead, she sat down at her desk, taking her half-finished letter to Lewis out of the drawer. She wanted to tell him all about Scott's visit and, as usual when a pen was in her hands, she became unaware of time, and it was well after midnight before she eased her chair away from the desk.

Talking to Scott about Lewis had somehow made Lewis seem much nearer. The three months until she'd see him again no longer seemed like three hundred, but more like thirty. She undressed and slipped on her nightdress. The following week, when she'd see Scott again, would make the time seem even closer. With a happy smile she climbed into bed and turned off the light, closing her eyes, imagining that Lewis was with her, holding her, loving her.

'But you can't possibly intend to go out with him again!' her mother said, horrified. 'You're a married woman, Abbra! You can't still go out with young men as if you were single!'

'I'm not, Mom,' Abbra said, quickly losing her patience. 'Scott is my *brother-in-law*, not a date. There's a whole world of difference.'

Mrs Daley was not sure that there was, but she could hardly say so without sounding crude. Her husband had not agreed that Abbra's friendship with Scott Ellis was undesirable, and to her dismay Abbra had gone out with him again. The following week he had driven up to San Francisco and they had gone to the zoo and on a ferry ride, and for a fish supper at Sausalito.

'I really don't like it,' she had said to her husband. 'How do we know that Lewis will approve of all the time Abbra is spending with his brother? I was under the distinct impression that Lewis did not think very highly of Scott!'

'He doesn't think very highly of Scott's choice of career,' her husband corrected her. 'Their father told me that. But I'm sure it's just Scott's age. I'm sure he'll come around.'

Mrs Daley pursed her lips. There was nothing for her to do but make sure that Abbra continued to be aware of her disapproval, and to hope that the day would never come when her nameless fears would take on substance.


In November, Scott was pronounced fit and was in the roster to play in a home game against the Cleveland Browns.

'Why don't you drive down and watch the game?' he suggested to Abbra. 'You could be the first member of my family to see me play.'

'I'll be there,' she promised. Lewis had written to her, telling her how pleased he was that she and Scott had become friends, and in his last letter he had teasingly asked if she was now a fan and attended games.

Her mother had shaken her head in disbelief when Abbra had told her of her plans. 'You are going to get yourself a reputation for being one of those girls who follow football players from city to city!'

'Oh, Mom! You're being ridiculous,' Abbra said in affectionate irritation. 'Everyone knows that Scott is my brother-in-law. No one is going to think that I'm a fan who has latched on to him!'

'They will,' her mother insisted. 'And almost as bad is the amount of time you're spending away from your school work. You have exams to think about and you should be home studying, not driving down to Los Angeles to watch the Rams play the Browns!'

Abbra sighed, feeling a twinge of guilt. She hadn't told her parents yet, but she had already made up her mind to leave college at the end of the semester. She would be leaving when Lewis returned anyway, and college was no longer what she wanted. She wanted to write, and she had already begun, showing Scott her first tentative stories, encouraged by his enthusiasm.

'You should send them off to one of the women's magazines,' he had said when he had read them. 'They're much better than most of the stuff they publish.'

She had laughed. 'And when was the last time you read any stories in a woman's magazine, Scott Ellis?' she asked teasingly.

He had grinned, his wide-set eyes and thick curly hair reminding her of a painting she had seen of a medieval Medici princeling. 'Perhaps it wasn't very recently,' he admitted, unabashed, 'but I'm damned sure that what you've written is worthy of publication, and they certainly won't be published if all you do is put them away in a drawer. The British Special Air Service has a motto, "Who dares, wins". Remember that and send them off. Nothing ventured, nothing gained, and all that jazz.'

She had laughed again and told him that he was an idiot, but a few weeks later, when she had gone over the stories for the twentieth time, she plucked up her nerve and sent one of them to the fiction editor of a leading women's magazine.

Despite her mother's continued disapproval, she drove down to Los Angeles to watch the Rams play the Browns and enjoyed herself thoroughly. It was the first time she had seen Scott in his own environment, and she was surprised by the amount of attention he attracted from fans and the media.

'You've been playing for the Rams only a few weeks. How come you're such a big star?' she asked teasingly.

'I don't know,' he replied with his easy, self-mocking grin. 'It must be the way I comb my hair!'

She had laughed, but the time that she spent with him when he was Scott Ellis, professional football player, only increased her deep affection for him. He had such an open and honest air that she knew no amount of flattery would corrupt him. Despite his media appeal and his veritable army of fans, there was a total lack of pretence or show about him. He was, quite simply, always himself. And even though he was far more of an extrovert than Lewis, underneath his easygoing affability there was the same kind of attractive solidity and inner strength.

At the end of the month, when the team was playing in Denver, he asked her if she would like to fly out and watch the game with the team wives and girlfriends. She had already met and made friends with quite a few of them, and when one of the girls suggested that she share a room with her, there seemed to be no reason why she shouldn't go.

'A *weekend*?' her mother had shrieked. 'It's absolutely impossible! Totally unthinkable!'

This time even her father agreed.

'I'm a married woman, Daddy,' she said, knowing that her mistake had been in returning home after her marriage as if she were still a schoolgirl. 'I'll be with other women I know and with my brother-in-law. Morally and physically I shall be utterly safe, and there is no reason at all why I shouldn't go.'

Her father was not swayed by her argument, and only a timely telephone call from her father-in-law prevented her from either having to cancel her plans or face an all-out fight with her parents.

'It's Colonel Ellis,' her mother said, the telephone receiver in her hand, a hint of respect in her voice. 'He wants to speak to you, Abbra.'

Ever since the wedding her father-in-law had courteously telephoned her once a month. Usually he merely asked her how she was; if she had heard from Lewis; and reminded her that she was welcome to spend a few days in New York at the family home whenever she felt like doing so. This time he was telephoning to say that he had business in Pueblo, so he was going to drive to nearby Denver to watch the Rams play the Broncos. He had spoken to Scott to tell him he would be there, and Scott had told him that she was also going. He was telephoning to tell her he was looking forward to seeing her.

From then on she knew that the battle was won. After she had finished speaking to him, he spoke with her father. Abbra heard her father agreeing with the colonel that it was a pity he and her mother couldn't accompany Abbra for the weekend and make a real reunion of it, but that they would, no doubt, meet up again next year to celebrate Lewis's return home.

Her father-in-law's attitude toward the President's buildup of forces in Vietnam was predictably enthusiastic.

'It's the only way to show those bas—' He corrected himself quickly. ' – To show the Communists that we mean business,' he said as they ate dinner in a small restaurant he had taken them to after the game. 'Leave them to their own devices and they'll be swarming up Waikiki Beach before we've had time to blink!'

'Isn't that a little bit of an exaggeration?' Scott asked idly, spearing a forkful of broccoli. 'The Communist aim is to unite North and South Vietnam under Ho Chi Minh, not invade America.'

Abbra saw an angry flush stain her father-in-law's neck and knew that he was controlling his temper only with difficulty. 'The Communist aim is world domination!' he said, forcefully, leaning across the table toward his son and stabbing his finger on the tablecloth to emphasize his point. 'If Vietnam falls to the Communists, then the entire region, the whole of Southeast Asia, will collapse too, and when that happens, the United States will find itself surrendering the Pacific and having to defend our own shores!'

'And if we continue to send in more troops, and the conflict continues to escalate, then the end of the road is going to be the direct intervention of China and nuclear war,' Scott said, provoking his father even more.

The colonel's nostrils flared, the red flush staining and spreading. 'How the hell have you become such an expert on what will or will not happen?' he bellowed, oblivious of Abbra and the other diners. 'You haven't been to West Point! You're a ball player, not a general!'

'I'm just giving my opinion,' Scott said tightly.

His father was about to say that his opinion wasn't worth a shit, when he became aware of Abbra's agonized expression and of other diners turning their heads towards their table with prurient curiosity.

He clamped his mouth tight shut, took a deep, steadying breath, and then gave Abbra an apologetic smile. 'I'm sorry, Abbra. I should have warned you that my opinions and Scott's differ widely. But the lessons from the Second World War are too easily forgotten. If we and our allies had moved earlier than we did to stop the Nazis, then that war could have been averted. The same rules apply to the Communists. We need a strong display of muscle to make sure that they know we mean business. Then, and only then, will they back down and allow the South its freedom.'

He glared coldly at Scott as he spoke, daring him to contradict. Scott, tempted almost past endurance, resisted the urge for Abbra's sake. He knew she had been thrilled that at last his father had attended a game and watched him play. And that the flare of disagreement which had erupted between them had distressed her.

'Okay,' he said, suppressing his irritation and forcing a smile. '*Pax*. Let's talk about something a little less emotive. Let's talk about the Rams' chances next week when they play the Chicago Bears.'

The conversation turned to smoother waters, and the evening had ended amicably but from then on Abbra was aware of the great difference between Scott's uneasy relationship with his father, and Lewis's relationship with him.

In December, President Johnson announced that the bombing of North Vietnam would be halted on Christmas morning for an indefinite period. In the first week of January she received a letter from Lewis describing a Christmas Day dinner of locally caught duck embellished with *nuoc mam* sauce, and an afternoon spent treating the village children to candy from his SP rations, and in the same week Scott decked a fellow player in the dressing room for making off-colour remarks about his relationship with her.

It was an ugly incident and one she was not aware of. It had been a home game against the Chargers and the Rams had lost miserably. Tempers had been short in the locker room and someone had savagely made an accusation that there was too much partying going on between games and not enough hard training.

One of the veteran players on the team, who had been receiving bad coverage in the press with veiled hints that he had peaked and was now past his prime, had looked viciously across at Scott and said loudly, 'That goes *especially* for guys who can only get it up with their brothers' wives. What do the two of you do every night, Ellis? Pray that some accommodating Viet Cong puts a hole in big brother?'

Scott's fist sent him flying backwards even before the word *brother* was out of his mouth. The brawl that followed was the worst to take place in a locker room that anyone could remember.

When they had finally been separated, and when their furious coach had warned them that if there was a repetition of the incident, both of them would be suspended for a week without pay, Scott had stormed into the club bar, where Abbra was waiting for him, saying tersely to her, 'Come on, we're leaving.'

'What on earth is the matter? What's happened to your face? What . . . ?'

'Come on,' he had repeated taking her by the arm and steering her towards the door. In another few seconds the club room would be full of differing reports of what had happened, but all the reports would be unanimous on what the remark was that had triggered the fight. It made him sick just to remember it, and the thought of her overhearing it made him feel murderous. 'I had a disagreement with another player in the locker room,' he said to her when they were safely outside. 'It was no big deal, but I don't want to find myself drinking with him this evening. Let's go to Yesterdays for a beer and a sandwich.'

He had been so obviously reluctant to talk about the incident that she hadn't asked any further questions. At the end of the week she was flying out to Hawaii to join Lewis, and she could scarcely think of or talk about anything else.

'Hawaii's going to be a big change for him after Vietnam,' Scott said, driving downtown, the filthy words of his fellow player ringing in his ears.

Abbra had begun to tell him that it wouldn't be quite so bad as perhaps they imagined, because Lewis had already enjoyed a three-day rest and recuperation break at Vung Tau, an in-country beach resort, but Scott was no longer listening to her. In the three months since he had met her, he hadn't looked up any of his old girlfriends, and he hadn't once dated any new ones. In fact, incredibly, for the last four months he had been totally celibate. It was quite a thought, and so was the reason for it.

She was talking happily about the presents she had bought for Lewis and jealousy, hot and hard, twisted his gut. He hadn't been dating because he had been happier with Abbra than he could possibly be with anyone else. He hadn't been screwing around because the only girl he wanted to screw was Abbra. His brother's wife. His hands tightened on the steering wheel until the knuckles were white. Jesus. Why hadn't he seen the truth before? Why had it taken the ugly words of a teammate, jealous of his prowess on the field, to make him see the blindingly obvious? And now that he had

# CHAPTER FIVE

For the next forty-eight hours Lewis filled every one of Abbra's waking thoughts. On the morning that she was to fly out to meet him she could hardly breathe for physical excitement.

'There's some mail for you, darling,' her mother said as they sat at breakfast. 'I've left it on the hall table.'

'Thanks, Mom.' Abbra pushed a plate of barely touched scrambled eggs away from her and rose to her feet, her voice breathless.

'I have to leave now, or I'll miss the eight-thirty airport bus.'

'They run every fifteen minutes,' her father said in fond amusement. 'Why not let me or our driver give you a lift out to the airport? What's so special about travelling there by bus?'

'Nothing, Daddy.' She slipped her arm around his neck and kissed him on the cheek. 'It's just easy, that's all.'

'And it's just another little gesture of independence,' her mother said, the distress behind the pleasantly uttered words unmistakable.

Abbra refused to respond and to be drawn into another tense conversation with her mother about the way she was leading her life. These conversations had become increasingly frequent. She knew that the real cause was that her mother was unable to accept that Abbra was no longer a child. She hadn't anticipated the change in her that marriage would bring. The wedding had been too sudden for her mother to be able to truly adjust to it, and not for the first time Abbra wished that Lewis hadn't been sent overseas immediately after their marriage. If only they'd been able to start their married life together in America. The transition, then, from a daughter to a daughter who was also a wife would have been more clearly marked and one her mother could have coped with.

'Come on, then,' her father said, picking up her suitcase. 'It's eight-fifteen now. If you want to catch the eight-thirty bus, we'll have to move.'

'Bye, Mom.' Abbra kissed her mother's cheek, following her father out into the hall, grabbing the mail from the hall table as she did so and stuffing it into her shoulder bag.

It would take an hour to get to the airport and to check in. The flight to Honolulu would take approximately another five and a half hours, and the connecting flight between Honolulu on Oahu and Lihue on Kauai, where she was to meet Lewis, would take another twenty or thirty minutes. Seven hours. In seven hours time they would be together again. It still seemed to her too wonderful to be true.

Her father dropped her off at the bus terminal at the corner of O'Farrell and Taylor streets near Union Square, and kissed her good-bye.

'Give Lewis my best,' he said, taking her suitcase out of the Cadillac's boot. 'And tell him to make sure he comes home all in one piece in six months.'

'I will,' she promised fervently. The thought that at this very moment Lewis was no longer in danger on Vietnamese soil, but was winging his way across the Pacific in a Boeing 707 was exhilarating. For the next five days no bullets would mow him down; no bombs would blow him up. He would be deliciously safe, safe, *safe*.

She stepped on to the already full bus. She was on her way. Every minute that passed was one that was bringing them closer together. His flight from Saigon was due to land in Honolulu three hours before hers, and he was going to fly straight on to Lihue and would be waiting for her when she arrived.

As she checked her baggage in at the airport she was almost sure that some of the other women travelling on her flight were also army wives. One or two of them seemed to know

100

each other, and she wished she had the nerve to approach them and to ask if they were joining husbands on leave. Too shy to do so, she bought herself a paperback book and glanced down at her wristwatch. Only six hours to go. Lewis's flight would now be two thirds over. At this very moment he would be thinking about her as she was thinking about him.

'Soon, my love,' she whispered to herself as her flight was called. 'Soon!'

All through the flight the book lay unopened on her lap. Their reunion would be the first they had ever had as husband and wife. She wondered if such reunions were something she would eventually get used to and become blasé about, and smiled at her idiocy. How could she ever become blasé about meeting Lewis? It wasn't possible. Even if they were married for fifty years, she would still feel the same hungry excitement at the prospect of meeting him again after an absence, whether the absence was one of days, or one of months, as it was now.

As the plane flew high over the searing blue of the Pacific, she looked frequently down at her wristwatch. Five hours. Four hours. Mentally she was with Lewis as his flight landed at Honolulu and as he transferred to his Kauai flight. She couldn't even begin to imagine what Hawaii would seem like to him after the horrors he had been living with.

His letters home, though scrupulously regular and reassuringly loving, had told her very little about his actual day-to-day existence. She knew only what she had told Scott. That he was part of a five-man advisory team assigned to an ARVN battalion; that they operated in the Ca Mau peninsula, rarely seeing other South Vietnamese units; and that most of their time was spent in hunting down the Viet Cong regiments that used the Nam Can and U Minh forests as a base.

One of the things she was most looking forward to was hearing about his experiences. She wanted to know what his life in Vietnam was like, every possible detail. She wanted to share it mentally and be a part of it. His reticence on paper had

101

disappointed her at first but then she had realized that putting emotions down on paper didn't come as easily to most people as it did to her. Lewis was obviously one of those. When they were together, and when at last they could talk, it would be different. Then there would be no reticence, only a total union of their hearts and minds.

The pilot's voice came over the intercom with matter-of-fact prosaicness. 'In ten minutes we will be landing at Honolulu Airport. I hope that you have had a pleasant flight and that you will fly with us again. Thank you.'

Excitement spiralled through her. In about an hour, she would be in Lewis's arms. The 707 dipped to the right, circling in to land, and far beneath her she could see Pearl Harbor and the silver-tawny flanks of Diamond Head and the great golden curve that was Waikiki Beach.

'Have a pleasant stay,' the stewardess said, smiling at her as she stepped out into brilliant sunshine and balmy heat.

A Hawaiian band was at the edge of the runway playing traditional music. Hula girls, laden with flowered leis, stepped smilingly forward to greet them, laughingly placing the leis around their necks.

As Abbra felt the flower petals brush her skin, and as she inhaled their perfume, happiness struck through her so pure and hard that she could barely contain it. Lewis had served over half his tour of duty in Vietnam and he had not been injured. In another six months time she would be meeting him again, and when she did, it would be for a far longer reunion. From then on their married life together would truly start. They would have a home on an army base and she would be what she longed to be – a fullfledged army wife.

She had a ten-minute walk before reaching the terminal for the interconnecting island flights and the small plane that was to take her to Kauai. For the hundredth time she looked down at her watch. In half an hour's time she would be with him. He would already be at Lihue waiting for her, she thought as she boarded. As the plane gathered speed and left the ground, she clenched her fingers into the palms of her hands, hardly able to bear the joyous anticipation flooding through her.

Abbra stepped out into the brilliant sunshine, her eyes feverishly scanning the low, white airport buildings. The only waiting figures were some distance away, and none of them was in army uniform. For one terrible, terrifying moment, as she descended the steps, she thought that he wasn't there. That something had gone horribly wrong; that his flight had been delayed; that perhaps he hadn't even left Saigon. Or even that his leave had been cancelled. And then she saw him, broad-shouldered and auburn-haired, dressed in white flannels and a light blue cotton shirt and loafers.

'Lewis!' she cried, oblivious to the crush of passengers round her. '*Lewis!*'

She was running towards him, her arms wide. A waist-high barrier separated arriving passengers from those who had come to meet them, but she didn't notice it. She raced towards him, entering his arms.

'Oh, Lewis!' she gasped joyously. 'Oh, darling, *darling*.'

His mouth came down hard on hers, and the months of separation slid away from her as if they had never existed.

'Oh, God, I missed you!' he groaned, burying his head in her hair, holding her so close to him that she thought her ribs would crack. 'You wouldn't believe how much I've missed you, Abbra!'

'Oh, but I would,' she said fiercely, raising her face to his. 'Because I've missed you every single minute of every single day!'

The grin that only she could conjure from him split his face. 'Then let's make up for lost time.' He relaxed his hold and took her hand in his. 'And the first thing is for you to come to this side of the damned barrier!'

With their hands still tightly clasped they walked the length of the barrier, and when she rounded it he folded her against him once again, oblivious to the indulgent glances of the people around them.

'I thought today would never come,' he said huskily when at last he lifted his head from hers. 'I knew I loved you when I married you, Abbra. But only now do I know how very, very much.'

She raised her hand, touching his face gently with the tips of her fingers, all the love she felt for him shining in her eyes. 'I love you with all my heart,' she said softly. 'I couldn't live if you didn't love me, Lewis. I wouldn't know how.'

He hugged her against him again, his throat so tight he was robbed of speech, and then, sliding his arm around her waist, he led her out to where her luggage was waiting.

'Where are we staying?' she asked as they stepped out of the airport toward the waiting line of orange taxicabs. 'In a hotel or an apartment?'

'An apartment.' Sudden doubt flared through his eyes. 'That's okay, isn't it? If you'd prefer a hotel, I can always cancel the apartment.'

'No.' She shook her head firmly. 'An apartment will be wonderful.'

It would be a place of their own, even if it was for only a few days. She didn't want them to spend their time together in the impersonal atmosphere of a hotel. The scent from the flowers around her neck, as Lewis gave the taxi driver the address of their Poipu Beach apartment, was as thick as smoke in the sunlight, the heat beating up from the ground in waves. Their fingers were still intertwined, and she gave his hand a squeeze, hardly able to believe that after all the long months of waiting, he was, at last, beside her.

'Happy, sweetheart?' he asked as he opened the rear door of the taxi for her.

'Oh, yes!' She was so happy that it hurt. He slid into the seat beside her, and she looked across at him. He had changed in the six months they had been apart. He had lost a little weight. Her heart twisted in her breast. If he had lost weight, it was not surprising. The surprise was that he had not lost far more.

'Were there many fellow officers with you on your flights?' she asked, hugging his arm. 'There were quite a few women on my flight to Honolulu, and I'm sure they were army wives flying out to join their husbands.'

'A couple,' he said, covering her hand with his. 'Not many. Taipei and Bangkok are more popular destinations than Hawaii.'

'But why?' Her brow creased in bewilderment. 'Hawaii is at least *American*. I would have thought they would far rather spend their R&R on American soil than in Taipei or Bangkok!'

'Taipei and Bangkok are closer to 'Nam, and I guess most of the men don't want to be hassled with a long flight.'

'But it's not closer for their wives!' she protested.

He grinned. 'Not many wives fly out to share R&R. You're in the minority, Mrs Ellis.'

'But why not? I don't understand. I couldn't bear to think of you on leave and so near home and not being with you.'

There was no way he could explain to her that for most men serving in 'Nam, R&R was an opportunity for a week-long orgy of screwing and drinking, and that the last thing they wanted was a wife. Instead, he said 'Hawaii isn't close to home for most wives. From New York, which is where Des Cawthorn's wife comes from, for instance, Hawaii is as far away as Italy and Switzerland.'

'Who is Des Cawthorn?' she asked with avid interest, wondering if he was perhaps a member of Lewis's team.

'A fellow officer who was on my flight,' he said, shrugging dismissively. He had no desire to talk about Cawthorn, or the way other officers spent their leaves. 'Do you see that mountain over there?' he asked, changing the subject as their taxicab hurtled across the southeast corner of the island. 'That's Mount Waialeale, and believe it or not, it's the wettest place on earth.'

'You're kidding,' she said disbelievingly. 'In *Hawaii*?'

He nodded, the naturally hard line of his mouth softened by a smile. 'I know because all I had to read while I was waiting for your plane were tourist brochures. It rains an average 500 inches a year; that's a lot of rain!'

105

'As long as it doesn't rain on the beach, I don't care,' she said, resting her cheek against his sturdy shoulder, savouring the sight, sound, and cologne-fresh smell of him.

It was still only mid-afternoon when they reached their apartment, and though the beach shimmered and shone only yards away, neither of them was even remotely tempted by it.

'The beach can wait,' Lewis said in a voice that expected no contradictions and received none. He deposited the luggage in the cane-furnished living room and turned towards her, his eyes so hot and dark she could barely tell iris from pupil.

For one sudden spellbinding moment she felt actually shy, and then his arms closed around her and her shyness vanished. In one easy movement he lifted her off her feet, carrying her into the sun-dappled bedroom as if she were a new bride.

'It's been so long,' he said hoarsely, lowering her to the bed, his mouth on her hair and her eyelids and the corners of her lips, his fingers gently and purposefully undoing the little pearl buttons on her blouse. 'I love you, Abbra. Only you. Forever.'

Her arms were around his neck, her body seeming to melt boneless into his. 'Ah, Lewis,' she whispered, shivering in pleasure as his hands found her flesh and touched and explored. 'I love you . . . I love you . . . I love you . . .'

He slid her arms out of her blouse and her breasts were pale in the sunlight that spilled across the bed, the nipples silkily rosy. With powerful yet careful hands he lifted her up beneath him, sliding her skirt down, his fingers brushing lightly over the wisp of cream lace that encased the dark spring of her pubic hair.

'Please love me,' she whispered, breathless and panting, shocked by the shameless depth of her hunger and need. 'Now, Lewis! Oh, please! Quickly!'

The slow deliberation of his lovemaking was one of the things that most aroused and excited her. Even now, when they had been separated for six long months, he did not take her in haste. He shed his clothing, drawing her towards him, revelling in the sight of her nakedness and then, when she thought she couldn't endure another moment of waiting, he rolled across her, closing his mouth over hers, reaching for her body with his hands.

The next morning they hired a jeep and set off toward the Hanalei Valley. The roadsides and fields were a mass of colour. Poinsettias bloomed wild in scarlet profusion; Judas trees lifted their clouds of scented flowers the colour of purple daphne; bougainvillea ran riot, blossoms of magenta and pink and foaming cream vying for supremacy.

'Oh, it's wonderful,' Abbra sighed, leaning close to Lewis as he circled her shoulder with one arm, driving the jeep with single-handed expertise. 'I never want to leave. Never.'

At Nawili wili they parked the jeep and swam in a tiny cove to the north of the bay; and at Kapaa they paused again, strolling the streets, admiring the wooden nineteenth-century buildings and the balconies that bellied out over the shop fronts, crammed with terra-cotta pots of narcissus and iris.

'Where to now?' Lewis asked. 'Another beach? Lunch somewhere? Or a walk out on one of the headlands?'

His heart seemed to leap in his chest as he looked down at her. She was wearing a white silk blouse, open at the throat, a red cotton skirt that swirled around her legs just short of her knees, and delicate sandals so insubstantial he wondered how she could possibly walk in them. Her hair was a little longer than it had been on their wedding day. It skimmed her shoulders glossily, pushed away from her face with delicately carved ivory combs.

'Has anyone ever told you that you're the most beautiful woman in the world?' he asked, wishing that he hadn't suggested the beach or a walk, but bed.

'No.' Her eyes danced with happiness. 'I don't think they have, Lieutenant.'

'Then let me rectify the omission.' He put his hands around her waist, swinging her up into the jeep. 'You, Abbra Ellis, are without doubt the most beautiful woman in the whole wide world!'

'Why, thank you,' she laughed, kissing the tip of his nose. 'I was hoping you would think so!'

'Abbra . . .' His voice had deepened and he was about to suggest that they drive straight back to the apartment, but before he could she said, 'I think I'd prefer a walk out on one of the headlands, to the beach or to lunch. Where have we to go? Kilauea Point or Makeheuna Point?'

Makeheuna Point was back the way they had come, and only a few short miles from Poipu Beach. 'Makeheuna,' he said unhesitatingly, knowing that from there they could very quickly get back to the apartment and bed.

Not until they were out on the Point, the grass rough beneath their feet, an indigo sea creaming at the base of sandstone cliffs, did she say at last, 'Tell me everything you couldn't tell me in your letters, Lewis.'

He looked down at her, an eyebrow quirking. 'Such as?'

Her arm was around his waist, her head leaning against his shoulder. 'You know what I mean.' Her voice was low and soft and full of love.

He hadn't the faintest idea. He sat down on the coarse grass and pulled her down beside him. 'You're not worrying about my fidelity, are you?' His brows pulled together in sudden concern. 'Because if you are, there's no need.'

She stared at him in astonishment. It had no more occurred to her that he would be unfaithful than it had that she would be unfaithful to him. 'No, of course not,' she said indignantly. 'I'm talking about your life in Vietnam. What it is that you're doing. What it's like for you living with the ARVN, under constant fear of enemy attack?'

The rare grin that other people seldom saw creased his hard-boned face. 'You sound like a newspaper reporter,' he teased, pulling her so that her back was resting against his chest. 'I've told you what I'm doing. I'm a military

108

adviser to an ARVN battalion. What more can I possibly tell you?'

She pulled free of his arms, turning to face him, sitting back on her heels. His reply was so unexpected, so staggeringly unlike anything she had even remotely imagined, she could only say unsteadily, 'You are kidding, Lewis, aren't you?'

He shook his head, his brows pulling together again slightly. 'No, I'm not, Abbra. There's very little else to tell you. Most of our time is spent out on patrol, hunting down Viet Cong. It's hot and it's wet and the insects are hell. What more can you possibly want to know?'

'But I want to know everything! I want to know how it feels to march for hour after hour through flooded paddy fields; I want to know what it's like to be surrounded by South Vietnamese – any one of whom could be Viet Cong; I want to know how it feels when you go into battle or are ambushed, knowing that any moment you might be killed!'

He stared at her as though she had taken leave of her senses. 'But for God's sake, why?' There was more than just bewilderment in his voice. There was revulsion.

Despite the midday heat she felt suddenly chilled. Surely he understood? How could he *not* understand? She was seized with the crazy notion that she was talking to a stranger. A stranger who was being polite, but who had no insight into her heart and mind.

'Because I love you!' she said desperately, leaning towards him and taking his hands in hers, holding them tight. 'Because I want to share *everything* with you! I want to share your experiences in Vietnam so that while you are there I can feel closer to you!'

His rising irritation ebbed. She was still scarcely more than a child and had no idea how ghoulish her request had sounded. He drew her towards him, saying gently, 'Vietnam is a million miles from anything you could ever imagine, Abbra. There's no way that I can share my experiences there with you. Hell, I wouldn't want to, even if I could!'

'But what about your fellow officers? The ones in the ARVN? Can't you tell me a little something about them?' she asked, unable to believe that he meant what he said.

He sighed, running a hand through the close-cropped curly thickness of his hair. 'Okay,' he said at last, humouring her with deep reluctance. 'My fellow officers in the ARVN have been fighting nearly all their lives. First the French, now the Communists. Trung, our battalion commander, fought under General Giap at Dien Bien Phu, and over the years he must have been wounded more times than he, or anyone else, can count.'

'I thought General Giap was a Communist?' she interrupted, confused.

'He is. He's Ho Chi Minh's right-hand man. But when the Vietnamese were trying to free themselves from colonial rule, Communists and non-Communists fought together. After the French conceded defeat, Trung crossed to the government side. He hadn't fought to free himself of French domination in order to exchange it for life under the Communists. Many of the men in the battalion have a similar history. It's the experience of the older officers, under Giap, that makes them so tenacious in battle.'

She was silent for a moment, wondering how it must feel for them to be fighting against a general they had once fought for and who, if the tone of Lewis's voice was anything to go by, they still admired.

'Have there been many battles?' she asked apprehensively, at last bringing the subject around to the one that preoccupied her.

'A few,' he said, the grin back on his face as he rose to his feet and stretched down a hand towards her. 'Those are the best times, when the adrenaline begins to surge . . .'

She stumbled as he drew her to her feet, her eyes wide and horrified. Her earlier shock at his amazement that she would want to know about his life in Vietnam was nothing to the shock she felt now. She felt as if a huge weight were on her chest, crushing her.

'—but for most of the time it's just tedious monotony,' he continued, assuming the horror in her dark eyes to be fear for his safety. 'Most of our time is spent in arduous day-long searches for Viet Cong we never locate. We find their campfires, but ninety times out of a hundred we don't find them. They vanish. God alone knows where.' Her hand was in his, and they were walking back to the jeep. 'Happier now?' he asked, smiling down at her, feeling that he had indulged her enough.

She opened her mouth and tried to tell him that she had never felt less happy in her life; that she couldn't believe that his reaction to battle, and to death and killing, were so many light-years removed from her own. As her gaze met his, the words died in her throat and she felt dizzy, as if an abyss were opening at her feet and yawning wide. He was a professional soldier. His attitude to war was never going to be the same as hers. Her horror at his words, if he knew of them, would only drive a wedge between them. The feeling of perfect unity, so important to her, would be lost forever.

'Yes,' she lied, her voice little more than a croak. She forced a smile. 'Yes, of course.'

They had driven back to the apartment and made violent love, but that night, as she lay sleepless in the circle of his arms, his words repeated themselves time and time again. 'Those are the best times, when the adrenaline begins to surge . . .'

Scott had been right after all. In some way that she couldn't possibly understand, Lewis was *enjoying* his time in Vietnam. It was as if the war between North and South Vietnam, in a country half a world away from his home, was *his* war, just as the Second World War had been his father's war. She closed her eyes and tried to sleep, but sleep was a long time in coming, and when it did come, her dreams were disturbed and restless and full of horrifying imagery.

They didn't talk about Vietnam again. The next morning, when he woke her by kissing her gently on the mouth, she

111

forced all visions of him as a soldier and in uniform to the farthest corner of her brain. The adjustment she knew she would have to make could not be made now. It would have to be made when she was back in San Francisco. Now was the time for loving and closeness. She had to forget about Vietnam, as Lewis was apparently forgetting about it. All that mattered was that they were together and that they loved each other and always would love each other. Not until the day before the end of his leave did reality intrude upon them again.

They had driven up to Waimen Canyon for the day and were walking back to where they had parked the jeep when an open-topped Chevrolet pulled up near them with a screech of tyres and a chunkily built man, his hair as closely cropped as Lewis's, vaulted out of the car, yelling 'Whoa, Lew! So this is where you're hiding! I thought you'd be on Waikiki, soaking up the sun!'

There was a pretty Hawaiian girl in the Chevrolet's passenger seat, but though her smile was friendly, she made no attempt to walk across and join them. Her dress was low-cut and clinging, her nails, as they drummed idly on the Chevrolet's door, vividly scarlet.

'Abbra, I'd like you to meet Des Cawthorn,' Lewis was saying, and Abbra could tell from the underlying tautness in his voice that he was annoyed by the accidental meeting. 'Des spent two months on our team at the end of the year. Since then he's been sitting pretty at staff headquarters in Saigon.'

'*No one* sits pretty in Saigon,' Des Cawthorn said cheerfully, shaking Abbra's hand. 'Relax for just a minute and some damned terrorist will lob a bomb through the window. How are you enjoying Hawaii, Mrs Ellis?'

Abbra didn't know if he was joking about the bombs in Saigon or not. She hoped he was. She had spent the last few months praying that Lewis would be transferred to a desk job at staff headquarters.

'I think it's wonderful,' she said truthfully, her eyes drawn against their will back to his waiting companion, a sudden frown marring her brow.

Des saw the direction of her thoughts and had the grace to look slightly abashed. 'Well, I guess I'll be getting along and let the two of you enjoy your last day together,' he said, taking a step or two backwards. 'Nice meeting you, Mrs Ellis. See you on the plane in the morning, Lew.' With a grin and wink he turned on his heel, striding back towards the Chevy. As he slid behind the wheel, the Hawaiian girl circled his neck with her arm and Abbra said uncertainly, 'That was the Des Cawthorn who flew with you from Saigon, wasn't it?'

Lewis nodded, turning and walking in the direction of their jeep. She hurried after him, slipping her hand into his. 'Didn't you say that he was married?'

'Yes, his wife is a high school principal in Pittsburgh.'

'But that *wasn't* his wife, was it?' she persisted, distressed.

'No,' he said tersely, wishing fervently that the encounter had never taken place.

She climbed into the jeep silently, and then said in a small, bewildered voice, 'Is that why so many men choose Taipei and Bangkok? Because of the girls and . . . and things?'

He sighed, running a hand through his tight, short curls. 'I guess so, Abbra. It's hard to explain, but five days isn't long enough for most men to unwind from 'Nam. They have to use girls and booze and dope. The way they spend their leave is as far removed from their real lives as the rest of their time in 'Nam is.'

She wanted to say to him that if he would only *talk* about Vietnam to her, then she might very well understand. And she wanted to ask him if he, too, sometimes sought release in girls and booze and dope. The words remained strangled in her throat, but he saw the agony in her eyes and took her hands in his, saying fiercely, 'For Christ's sake, Abbra! I'm not Des Cawthorn! I'm not a grunt in 'Nam against my will! I'm a professional soldier, carrying out a job I've been trained for! I don't need to seek oblivion in sex or drink or drugs, and if I did, I sure as hell wouldn't choose to find it with a whore!'

His voice was raw, his gold-flecked eyes dark with urgency. 'I love you, Abbra. Don't you understand that? Don't

113

you know what it means? I don't want other women, and I don't make love to them. There's only you, Abbra. Only you. Always.'

Tears of shame for even allowing such thoughts to enter her head glittered on her eyelashes. 'I'm sorry,' she whispered contritely. 'I didn't really believe . . . it was just seeing Des Cawthorn with his Hawaiian girl . . . Knowing that his wife was probably missing him and longing to be with him just as much as I missed and longed to be with you. I know you're not like him, Lewis. You're honourable and true and I will never doubt you again. Not for a moment.'

Gently he wiped the tears away from her face. 'That's good,' he said huskily. 'Let's cut this trip to the canyon short and go back to the apartment.'

She nodded, too full of emotion to speak without bursting into tears.

He rammed the jeep into gear, speeding away from the canyon, on to the route south. She hugged his arm, leaning against him, terrifyingly aware of how little time was left to them. When she remembered how she had allowed his remarks about battle to come between them, the shame she felt at having even imagined he would be unfaithful to her deepened. What did it matter how he felt when he was in battle? How could she possibly understand something so removed from her own experience? What mattered was that he loved her in a way few women were fortunate enough to be loved. She was lucky. Lucky. And she would never allow anything to come between them ever again.

The sun was still high in the sky when they returned to their apartment, but they closed the shutters and retired to bed, showing each other in every way they knew how, just how much they loved each other, and how much they would miss each other during the coming six months.

When she awoke among the crumpled sheets, the knowledge that time had nearly run out on them engulfed her and filled

114

her with a panic she could scarcely control. For the first time she understood why some wives preferred not to have a reunion until their husbands' time in Vietnam was completely over. To have been together again, only to be parted so swiftly, was almost unbearable. He turned toward her, opening his eyes sleepily, and she fought down the panic, afraid that he would see it and that it would spoil their remaining few hours.

Right from the start they had agreed that she would not drive with him to the airport to see him off on his flight back to Saigon. Her own flight did not leave until six hours later, and she was going to tidy up the apartment, return the key, and hire a taxi for her own trip to Lihue. Not until then was she even going to admit to herself that their idyll was at an end. She was going to imagine that he was leaving on a fishing trip, a golf trip. Anything that would allow her to enjoy every second of their time together.

She made a special breakfast of papaya and mangoes, smoked salmon and scrambled eggs, champagne and freshly squeezed orange juice.

'Abbra,' he said thickly, stretching a hand out to her across the flower-decked table, and for a moment the tears she was holding in check nearly overwhelmed her.

'No,' she said, smiling fiercely, 'please don't say it, Lewis! Please don't say anything! Please let's pretend for just a little longer.'

It wasn't until she was searching her shoulder bag for her flight ticket that she found the unopened envelopes she had scooped up so hurriedly from the hall table the morning she had left San Francisco.

'What are those?' he asked teasingly, circling her waist with his arms. 'Letters from admirers? Movie offers from Hollywood?'

She laughed, leaning back against him, grateful for the fleeting sensation of normality that the unopened mail had given. 'Whatever they are, I hope they aren't important. I've been carrying them around all week.'

115

The first letter was from a book club; the second was from an aunt in Nebraska; the third was a letter of acceptance from the fiction editor of the magazine to which she had sent her short story so many months before.

She stared down at it incredulously. 'Oh, my goodness! I've done it! I'm going to be published! Oh, Lewis!' She twisted around in his arms, hugging him tight. 'I can't believe it! I'm an author! Isn't it great?'

Still holding her with one arm, he took the letter from her. 'What on earth did you write that they would want to publish?' he asked, amusement in his voice. She was about to say that she had written about an army wife, apart from her husband, but in a moment of blinding revelation, as instantaneous as Paul's on the road to Damascus, realized if she did so, his reaction would be horror, not pride.

'I wrote a . . . a love story,' she said weakly, disappointment rushing so hard on the heels of elation that she felt physically light-headed.

'Just as long as no one knows about it,' he said easily, pulling her towards him again, his mouth hot and sweet against her temples.

She swallowed, unable to think clearly. Surely other people would know of it? Surely her name would be beneath the title in the magazine? Surely he *wanted* other people to know of it? To admire her? Damn it. *She* wanted other people to know of it! She said fiercely, 'It was a very *well-written* love story, Lewis. Otherwise the magazine that I sent it to wouldn't publish it. They have millions of subscribers and . . .'

His amusement deepened at her indignation. 'Okay, okay,' he said, conciliating, rocking her against him. 'I didn't mean to sound insulting. It's just that as an army wife you have to be a little careful, Abbra.'

'But why on earth . . .' she began, and then she remembered the precious minutes ticking away, and horror at how near they were to spending them arguing stopped her short.

116

'Yes?' He tilted her face towards him, his warm brown eyes alight with the love he felt for her.

'Nothing,' she whispered. 'Oh, hold me, Lewis! Tell me that nothing is going to go wrong between us. Not ever!'

'Nothing will ever go wrong between us, sweetheart,' he said, his voice so full of certainty that her fears died as quickly as they had arisen. For a long time he held her against him, feeling the slamming of her heart against his, the softness of her hair against his cheek. At last, his voice suspiciously hoarse, he said gently, 'It's ten-thirty, Abbra. I have to go.'

The floor seemed to tip and tilt beneath her feet. She took a deep, steadying breath, reminding herself that she was an army wife; that partings such as these were a part of their life together; that the last thing he needed was for her to be upset.

'Yes,' she said unsteadily. 'Please go quickly. Please go quickly and stay safe.'

He kissed her one last time, hard and hungrily, and then he turned on his heel, striding from the room, slamming the door behind him.

She stood where he had left her, listening as he pulled away from the front of the apartment, listening as the sound faded into the distance.

He had gone. The coming six months would pass just as the previous six months had passed. All she had to do was endure them.

'I love you, Lewis,' she whispered aloud. 'Oh, God, I love you so much!' And then, forgetting all about her determination to be brave, she flung herself facedown on the crumpled sheets of the bed and cried.

# CHAPTER SIX

'You're what?' Serena's father said incredulously, lowering his shotgun to his side.

The last remains of the debris from the concert had been removed finally and for the first time since the event had taken place, he was enjoying a morning walk in his grounds, his two aging cocker spaniels at his heels.

'We're married,' Serena said composedly. She held out her hand for his inspection and the plain narrow wedding ring, all they had been able to purchase in their haste, glittered corroboratingly.

'You're *what*?' her father repeated, staring disbelievingly first at Serena and then at Kyle, who he couldn't quite place, and then back at Serena again.

'We're married,' Serena repeated obligingly. 'It was all rather sudden, Daddy, and—'

'You're *what*?'

Kyle sighed. Serena had been adamant that it was up to her to break the news to her father, but it was obvious that she wasn't doing a very good job of it, or his new father-in-law was stone deaf. 'We're married, sir,' he said, his careless stance and the rather bored tone of his voice taking away any respect there might have been in the word *sir*.

'The devil you are!' the earl spluttered, the dogs looking mournfully up at him, aggrieved at the interruption to their walk. 'What sort of silly statement is that? Married indeed! Take your cock-and-bull stories somewhere else and leave me in peace!'

This time it was Serena's turn to sigh. Her father really was an ass at times. 'We're married,' she said for the fourth time. 'Married as in Darby and Joan, trouble and strife . . .'

'Marriages are made in heaven,' suggested Kyle helpfully.

'Marry in haste, repent at leisure,' Serena finished, a little insensitively.

'If this is a new parlour game, now is neither the time nor the place for it!' her father said.

They were standing on the crown of the hill looking down toward the house. It had taken Serena and Kyle a good ten minutes from the point where they had parked the car to walk up through the avenue of elms and waylay him, and in Kyle's opinion it had been a wasted exercise.

'For the love of God,' Kyle muttered beneath his breath, and then, louder, 'Serena and I were married yesterday. If you don't choose to believe us, there's nothing we can do about it. We've told you, and as far as I'm concerned, that's where our responsibility ends.'

The earl glared at him, his hand tightening on his shotgun, and Kyle backed away a foot or two. 'How dare you, you insolent young pup! You've no business on my land! Remove yourself immediately!'

'Kyle is a house guest, Daddy,' Serena said with admirable patience. 'He's Royd Anderson's son. They've been staying with us since the end of last month, remember?'

Her father peered at Kyle, vaguely recognized him, and slackened his hold on the shotgun. 'So he is. Stupid of me. Now, whatever it is you want, leave it to later, there's a good girl. I haven't had a day of peace since that wretched concert. Men were still moving litter at six o'clock yesterday morning, and some damn fool of a fellow has been on the telephone all morning insisting the event has to be repeated next year!'

Kyle turned toward Serena and said in weary disbelief, 'We're wasting our time. You've told him four times, I've told him twice.'

'Told me what?' the earl asked with absentminded interest, wondering if they had perhaps interrupted him on his walk because they wanted to join him. Americans often liked a little shooting, and the Anderson boy looked

119

as if he might be handy with a gun. He wasn't dressed for it though. A button-down shirt and tight jeans and crepe-soled suede shoes. Serena was no better. Her minidress barely skimmed her bottom, and her thigh-high white boots had heels on them that made walking over rough ground virtually impossible.

'Wellingtons,' he said forthrightly. 'Much more sensible.'

Kyle raised his eyes to heaven, wondering if insanity ran in the family and if perhaps marrying Serena in haste, without a medical check beforehand, had been wise.

'We haven't come to help you decimate the local wildlife,' Serena said, long practice enabling her to follow her father's often tortured thought processes. 'We've come to tell you that we've been away for a few days. In Scotland.'

'Hadn't missed you,' her father said truthfully. 'Were you here for the concert? Shocking row. Couldn't hear myself think. Shall never have another.'

Serena refused to be deflected into talking about the concert. 'We went to Scotland to get married,' she persisted, speaking slowly and clearly, as if to a child. Her father continued to stare at her in blank incomprehension, and she abandoned patience, saying exasperatedly, 'For Christ's sake, Daddy! We *eloped*!'

'You *what*?' he expostulated for the fourth time, understanding at last beginning to dawn. 'You can't be married! You're too young. Need consent.'

'That's why we eloped,' Serena said with remarkable restraint. 'You don't need consent in Scotland, Daddy. Not if you're over sixteen.'

She held her left hand out towards him again. He looked down at the shining new wedding ring and said with commendable brevity, 'Your mother won't like it. There's going to be a devil of a fuss.' He peered long and hard at Kyle, and then said with brutal candour, 'Come to think of it, I don't like it much either. Needs some thinking about.' And he turned on his heel, stalking away. The spaniels spoiled the effect somewhat. They had fallen asleep and he had to return for them, prodding them awake with the butt of his shotgun.

'I suppose it could have been worse,' Kyle said as he and Serena began to walk back towards the house.

'Oh, yes, and it will be! Poor daddy. He really did make hard work of it, didn't he? I wonder what conclusion he will come to after his walk and his think?'

'God only knows.' At the prospect of Serena's father thinking, Kyle's imagination failed him. For the past four days he had been permanently high on alcohol or marijuana or both, and he was finding his present sobriety something of a strain.

'Who do we tell next?' he asked, determined that whoever it was, he would fortify himself with a joint or a stiff whisky beforehand.

'What about your father? He's the one who holds the purse strings, isn't he? Might as well find out if you're to be cut off without a dollar to your name,' Serena suggested.

'If I am, I shall divorce you,' he threatened in perfect seriousness.

Serena grinned and pushed her long mane of pale gold hair away from her face. 'Don't worry. If you and your money are parted, I shall *beg* for a divorce!'

The earl's reaction to news of the marriage was mild in comparison with Kyle's father's. 'Of all the stupid, crass, *inane* things to have done!' he thundered. 'We're *guests* here, for Christ's sake! Don't you realize he's a peer of the realm? How many millions of . . .'

He was about to ask how many million dollars the whole fiasco was going to cost, before it was over, in alimony and settlements, when the peer in question ambled into the room. He bit the words back with difficulty, contenting himself with a strangled 'You need horsewhipping, for Christ's sake!'

Kyle stood nonchalantly in the centre of the yellow-walled room, his hands in the pockets of his jeans, Serena at his side. His father, mindful of his host's presence, sucked in his breath. 'Just answer me one question,' he demanded unsteadily, 'in the name of God, *why?*'

Kyle shrugged. 'It seemed like a good idea at the time,' he said truthfully, a lock of blue-black hair falling Byronically low across his brow.

His father choked, Serena giggled, and the earl said in obvious puzzlement, 'There's half a dozen newspaper reporters at the gates, clamouring for admittance. Wouldn't be fobbed off. Said they knew the story of the elopement was genuine. Said someone had telephoned them anonymously from here with the news.'

Royd Anderson suppressed a groan and tried to look as baffled by the information as the bearer of it. He knew damned well who had leaked the news to the press, sabotaging any hopes of a quiet annulment. His wife had stared at him for only the briefest of seconds after he had broken the news to her, then said unequivocally, 'Good, it couldn't be better.'

'What do you mean, it couldn't be better?' he had yelled. 'Don't you realize what this marriage is going to cost us? This isn't a marriage that is going to *last*! This is a joke! You can bet your life both of them were stoned out of their minds when they said "I will" or "I do" or whatever the hell it was that they said. When it comes to the divorce, and the Blyth-Templeton lawyers get to work, they'll be talking in seven-digit telephone numbers! Christ!' He ran his hand through his thick thatch of grizzled hair. 'The only reason for that awful pop concert was to get some cash to fill the family coffers! By marrying Kyle, that girl has set herself up financially for the rest of her life! And on *my* money, goddammit!'

'You're being extremely shortsighted!' his wife had said with composure. 'Think of the social advantages. Serena's name has been linked romantically with that of Prince Charles. She could probably have been the future queen of England if she'd put her mind to it.'

'The future king of England could probably have afforded the divorce! I can't!'

They were in their bedroom and she was sitting at the dressing table. Until now she had been talking to his reflection in the mirror, but now she turned to face him, saying chidingly, 'You're being ridiculous, Royd. Look at things sensibly for a minute. The way Kyle has been behaving these past two years, he could have eloped with a barfly, a two-bit actress, a flagrant fortune hunter . . .'

'She *is* a fortune hunter!'

'But she's *not* a two-bit actress! She is *Lady* Serena. She is the only daughter of one of England's oldest and most respected aristocratic families. The Blyth-Templetons can trace their family tree right back to Henry VIII. Think of the social contacts we will gain. Serena is still close friends with Prince Charles. He will attend the wedding, he will probably be godfather to their first child . . .'

'Have you completely lost your mind? The wedding is over! In the past! History!'

'*That* wedding may be over,' his wife agreed, undeterred, 'but the *real* wedding is still to come. I believe St Margaret's, Westminster, is the church for high society weddings. We shall have to hire a couple of private planes to ensure that our side of the family is represented. *The Boston Globe* and the society editors of *The Washington Post* and *The New York Times* will have to be informed.'

Royd chewed his bottom lip. 'You really think this could be to our advantage?' he asked, frowning.

'Of *course* it is!' She rose to her feet, crossing the room toward him, removing a speck of fluff from the shoulder of his jacket. 'Think of some of the girls Kyle *might* have eloped with. Think of the *prestige* of him marrying a girl whose name has been romantically linked with that of England's future king. Think of the social advantages of our being related by marriage to leading members of the British aristocracy. The only thing is, we mustn't seem *too* pleased by it. We don't want the Blyth-Templetons thinking that we *planned*

123

it. They must be absolutely furious. By marrying Kyle, Serena has ruined any hopes they might have had where Prince Charles was concerned. They are probably scheming how to have it speedily annulled right this very moment.'

Royd had muttered darkly that he wouldn't blame them if they were, and had marched off in the direction of the yellow room, where he had been informed that the newlyweds were awaiting him. He still hadn't spoken to Kyle face-to-face. News of the wedding had been telephoned to him earlier in the day, when he had been enjoying a lavish business lunch in London. He had promptly abandoned his steak tartare and driven back to Bedingham at high speed.

His host had greeted him and had unhappily confirmed that their respective children had, indeed, eloped to Gretna Green and had now returned to Bedingham as man and wife.

Royd still couldn't believe it. Kyle was suicidally hot-headed, but for him to get *married*, and at *nineteen*, made no sense whatsoever. He had already discounted the fact that Serena might be pregnant. Hell, they'd been in England only three weeks! Even if Kyle had knocked her up the moment he had met her, she still couldn't know if she was pregnant or not. Besides, he was damned sure that neither Kyle nor Serena possessed a shred of the kind of responsibility that might have prompted a quick marriage if she had been.

His anger, which had been white hot, had ebbed a little since his conversation with his wife. She had been right. There *were* advantages to the marriage. As he strode along the long portrait-lined corridor and down the main staircase, his remaining fury was tempered by embarrassment. Kyle was a *guest* at Bedingham, for Christ's sake, and as a guest he had transgressed every rule in the book. He slammed into the drawing room, intending to give his son the lecture of his life, only to be stopped dead in his tracks by his host walking in on them.

'Newspaper reporters are a bloody tenacious breed,' the earl was saying glumly. 'Won't leave until they get a story.

One of them even had the effrontery to ask if he could come in and take a photograph of the happy couple!'

'Well, he can't!' Kyle snapped, his amusement at the consternation he and Serena had caused beginning to wane.

His father-in-law eyed him unlovingly. He couldn't imagine what Serena saw in him. He looked more Irish than American. All quick temper and damn-your-eyes. 'It's not what I would have wanted,' he said with unhappy bluntness, 'but now that it's happened, there's nothing to do but live with it.'

Royd, once he was sure that it was the marriage that was being referred to and not the presence of the newspaper reporters, breathed an infinitesimal sigh of relief. Now that news of the elopement had been leaked to the press, any steps his host might have taken in order to terminate the marriage would have been seen only as an insult to Kyle and to himself. 'How did Serena's mother take the news?' he asked in awkward concern.

He had been friends with the earl for nearly five years, ever since they had been guests on a Mediterranean yachting cruise hosted by a mutual friend, but he still found it difficult to think of the countess by her Christian name, and virtually impossible to address her by it. To address her by her title, when he was her guest, went against his democratic principles. So 'Serena's mother' helped him get around the situation.

The earl pondered the question. He was physically unable to tell a lie, and he was dimly aware that to tell the truth might be a little tactless. 'Emotionally,' he said at last, rather pleased with his choice of word. 'She took the news very emotionally.'

The stark truth was that his wife had shocked him by being, not outraged at the news, but overjoyed. 'Oh, it's a *wonderful* marriage! How clever of Serena! There will have to be another wedding, of course. A proper one at Bedingham. We'll have the reception out of doors on the front lawn, with a few marquees in case of rain.'

'Can't see what you're so pleased about,' he had protested, baffled. 'The child is only eighteen. The whole affair is damned ridiculous.'

'No, it isn't,' his wife had said practically. 'The Andersons are one of Boston's oldest families *and* they are extremely wealthy. As the only son, Kyle will eventually inherit. I couldn't be more pleased at the way things have worked out if I'd arranged it all myself.'

'Well, *I'm* not pleased,' he said stubbornly. 'If there's going to be a proper wedding at Bedingham, it means there will be caterers all over the place and hundreds of people littering the grounds with their vile cocktail sticks and cherry stones. It will be nearly as bad as the concert and I'm not having another of those, no matter *how* financially successful you say that it was!'

He said now, reluctantly, 'There'll have to be another wedding, of course. Families present. All that sort of thing.'

Kyle groaned and Serena looked across at him in amusement. 'It's beginning to get a teeny bit boring, isn't it? Shall we drive up to London and celebrate our nuptials with champagne at the Ritz?'

'No! I've just driven all night from Scotland! I'm sure as hell not going to drive all the way to London!' the groom said unequivocally.

The earl waited with interest for his daughter's reply. When Serena suggested doing something, she was accustomed to people falling in with her plans. It became obvious, almost immediately, that she had no intention of having them thwarted now.

'Then I'll go by myself,' she said, unperturbed, holding out her hand for the car keys.

The earl's interest deepened. Kyle's father held his breath. The groom was being faced with an ultimatum, and both of them knew it. The groom knew it, too, and was blissfully indifferent.

126

'She's getting low on gasoline,' he said, speaking of Serena's Porsche as if it were a ship at sea and sliding his hand into his hip pocket for the car keys. 'You'd better put some in at the first gas station you come to.'

'Thanks,' Serena said coolly, taking the keys from him. 'See you. Bye,' she added and turning on her heel, she strode nonchalantly from the room.

The earl was aware of a grudging surge of respect for his new son-in-law. He had called Serena's bluff and seemed unconcerned about the outcome. Perhaps there was more to him than he had first thought. 'Have a whisky,' he said to him companionably. 'Devilish long drive, Scotland to Bedingham. Wouldn't fancy it myself.'

Royd was unable to share the earl's apparent calm at the turn events had taken. Before he had even spoken to Kyle he had been ninety-nine per cent certain that the marriage hadn't a hope in hell of surviving. Now he was a hundred per cent sure, and he knew who was going to have to foot the bill. He glared in impotent fury at his son, unable to gain even the slightest grain of comfort from the fact that his soon to be ex-daughter-in-law was also the ex-close friend of the future king of England.

Serena was surprised at the depth of her disappointment as she drove at high speed past the gaggle of reporters at the gates. Damn Kyle. If he hadn't wanted to drive, he could at least have been happy for *her* to drive! The news of their elopement would soon be in all the national papers, and being in town with him, receiving the congratulations of all her friends and endlessly celebrating would have been fun. As would a continuation of the glorious, almost nonstop sex they had been enjoying. She swung out of Bedingham Village and on to the main road south, pressing her foot down hard on the accelerator. Damn Kyle. Damn him, damn him, damn him!

As far as the press were concerned, her arrival in London, and her presence at the more exclusive discos and nightclubs without her spouse only served to elevate a minor society story into a major one. 'Runaway Lady Serena Parties Without Groom' was one headline and 'Anderson Heir Stays Home While Bride Cavorts' was another. Serena did not care. The elopement, and her subsequent discarding of her groom, had only added lustre to her already wild and reckless reputation.

On her first night in town, after a party at Annabel's that had gone on until dawn, she had been escorted back to the Chelsea house by a long-standing male friend, and had shocked both him and herself by saying on the doorstep, a note of surprise in her voice, 'You can't stay the night, Toby. I'm a married lady now. Adultery after forty-eight hours of wedded bliss is a little steep, even for me.'

'But I thought the elopement was just a joke,' Toby Langton-Green protested, piqued.

'Well, it was,' Serena said, her thought processes slightly dulled by the amount of champagne that she had consumed. 'But it's not a *complete* joke, if you see what I mean.'

'Dashed if I do,' Toby said, swaying unsteadily on his feet. 'Not as if the fellow would know, is it?'

'No,' Serena agreed. 'But *I* would know.'

Toby hiccuped, not relishing the thought of a drive back to his own bed in Hampstead. 'And does that matter?'

'Yes,' Serena said, intrigued at the discovery. 'I'm afraid it does, Toby. Strange, isn't it?'

'Bloody peculiar,' Toby agreed. 'If I can't sleep in the marriage bed, or what will be the marriage bed if the groom ever deigns to put in an appearance, can I at least sleep on the sofa?'

'Yes.' She yawned. 'But don't wake me when you leave, Toby. I haven't slept for forty-eight hours, and I won't want to get out of bed until the end of the week.'

She staggered exhaustedly across the threshold, heading unhesitatingly for the bedroom. Toby remained in the minuscule living room for a minute or two, eyeing the sofa with reluctance. It really did look damned uncomfortable. He removed his evening jacket, extricating his arms from

128

the sleeves with difficulty, and went in search of Serena. The very least she could do was to loan him a pillow for the night. She lay on the bed, facedown and fully clothed, snoring softly, and he was able to flop thankfully down next to her without her giving any protest.

Serena remained in town all week. The newspapers continued to avidly follow the story of her elopement, fuelled not only by her own fevered partygoing, but by that of her groom's.

Twenty-four hours after Serena had driven away from Bedingham, Kyle had also left his father-in-law's roof, whether amicably or not, the press were unable to decide. They had scrambled into cars and followed him, certain that he was driving to London in order to reclaim his erring bride. They were wrong.

His destination was not Chelsea but the Dorchester, where two of his cousins and a mutual friend from college had just checked in. Within hours the groom and his cronies were out on the town, painting it red. For five newsworthy nights, Serena could be found dancing with Toby Langton-Green or a dozen other old admirers at Annabel's and the Cromwellian, and Kyle could be found squiring any one of a number of debutantes to the Claremont and to Ronnie Scott's. Flocks of photographers followed in both their wakes, eager for the moment when the paths of bride and groom would cross. Against impossible odds, they did not do so.

Serena and her entourage would abandon the hexagonal-sided dance floor at Annabel's for the slightly larger one at The 400 only to miss a full-scale confrontation with Kyle and his cronies by seconds as they boisterously left The 400 for the Ad Lib.

Media interest mounted when the earl announced that following the elopement and civil wedding of his daughter and Mr Kyle Anderson of Boston, a church wedding was

129

to take place at Bedingham's fourteenth-century parish church.

Serena read the news with interest. There were times when she had to admire her father. To have made such an announcement, and gone ahead with all the plans necessary for such a wedding – when she and Kyle were hitting the headlines daily and separately – showed breathtaking aplomb. She wondered if arrangements for her wedding dress and her bridesmaids' were also being made in her absence. And if Kyle was as bemused by the situation as she was.

At the thought of Kyle, her bemusement vanished. That morning the William Hickey column had published a photograph of him dancing with one of her old school chums at The Darkroom. She had been there herself earlier in the evening, with Toby, and was not sure if her fury was because she had been cheated out of confronting him, and freezingly ignoring him, or of confronting him and being rapturously reunited with him. One thing was certain. *She* wasn't going to be the one to contact him! *He* would have to contact her!

He didn't do so, and the date of the wedding drew closer. When his cousins returned to the States, Kyle returned with them, and while his parents remained at Bedingham, announcing that they would not be returning to Boston until after the wedding ceremony, Kyle was photographed wining and dining young women in New York.

Serena didn't know whether to be amused or outraged. The date was set, and it had not been an easy wedding to arrange. The bishop, whom her father had approached for permission, had agreed that a church wedding was desirable even though a civil ceremony had already been conducted. He was not so sympathetic, however, when it came to his attention that the bride and groom were no longer on speaking terms and not even on the same side of the Atlantic. It had taken all her father's considerable charm to persuade the bishop to allow the second ceremony to take place.

'Don't worry about your dress, darling,' her mother had said to her airily over the telephone. 'Mary has all your measurements and is going ahead with the most *wonderful* design. . . .'

'Mary?' Serena had asked, mystified.

'Quant. Sweet girl. I've invited her and her husband to the wedding, of course, and Mr Jagger and the Animal man.'

By Animal man, Serena assumed her mother was referring to Eric Burden. 'What about the groom?' she asked, intrigued. 'Have you invited him as well? And has he accepted?'

'I'm not sure I like your sense of humour, darling,' her mother had replied crisply. 'Of course Kyle will be there. How could he not be?'

'Very easily. According to this morning's newspapers, he's still in New York.'

'New York isn't far away these days.' Her mother's voice was bland. 'Why, even Socialists go there for holidays now.'

At the mention of Socialists, Serena was reminded of Lance. She hadn't seen him since the day of the concert and was missing his companionship and acerbic remarks almost as much as she was missing Kyle's lovemaking. 'Where's Lance?' she asked, a small frown furrowing her brow. 'Is he back at Bedingham yet?'

Lance had removed himself from Bedingham the weekend that she and Kyle had eloped, informing his mother that he was about to take part in an antiwar vigil outside the American Embassy. Serena had watched the television news attentively, but though the demonstration had been reported at length, she had seen no sign of Lance's distinctively tall, slender figure and silky pale hair.

'No, darling,' her mother said without apparent concern. 'These demonstrations of his go on for weeks sometimes. Was Kyle hoping he would be best man?'

131

'Kyle and Lance barely know each other,' Serena responded dryly. 'And I'm quite sure that Lance is the last person on earth Kyle would invite to be his best man. *If* Kyle is going to turn up at the church, and *if* he's had the forethought to ask someone to be his best man, both of which events I think highly unlikely, then he will ask one of his innumerable cousins or a buddy from Princeton.'

When she had replaced the telephone receiver on its rest she had gazed long and hard in a nearby mirror. Kyle could easily have got in touch with her if he had wanted to. The address of her mother's Chelsea house was hardly a secret, nor was the telephone number.

She tilted her head thoughtfully. Neither, of course, was the address and telephone number of the Dorchester, which was where Kyle had been staying until his departure for the States. *She* could have got in touch with *him* if she had wanted to. And she was honest enough to admit that she *had* wanted to. After all, it wasn't as if they had quarrelled bitterly. The few days they had spent together had been unbelievably wonderful. Yet she hadn't telephoned the Dorchester, and now the wedding that had been arranged for them was only three days away.

The frown that had creased her brow when she had been talking to her mother deepened. An army of Blyth-Templetons was due to descend on Bedingham in droves; flocks of Andersons were about to depart from Boston at any moment aboard a private plane chartered by her father-in-law. And she still hadn't decided what she herself was going to do.

Was she going to be there? Was she going to walk down the aisle on her father's arm, in her Mary Quant wedding dress? And if she was, would Kyle be there at the altar, waiting for her? The newspapers were already running bets on the outcome, and the odds were heavily against either her or Kyle being at the church for what was being termed the nonwedding of the year.

132

She turned away from the mirror abruptly. If only Lance hadn't left in such an annoying way, then she would at least have had someone to share the ridiculousness of the situation with. As it was, there were times when she was beginning to find it extremely boring.

Moodily she turned on the bath taps and emptied half a bottle of Chanel No. 5 into the steaming water. But she wasn't bored with Kyle. If the truth were known, she was missing him dreadfully.

When there were only twenty-four hours to go before the ceremony, her father finally telephoned her with what he seemed to regard as a minor query. 'Wondered if you'd seen Kyle lately?' he asked pleasantly. 'His parents haven't. They're at Bedingham again. Until the wedding.'

'There isn't going to be a wedding, Daddy. Or, rather, there isn't going to be *another* wedding. One's obviously quite enough.'

'Poppycock. Has to be another wedding. Your mother wouldn't like it if there wasn't. You should be here by now. Rehearsal at the church and all that sort of thing. I'll tell your mother that you are on your way. Don't want her getting into a state over everything. Kyle's mother isn't being much of a help. She was quite hysterical at breakfast. Has some fool notion young Kyle is going to make a mess of everything.'

'Well, he probably is,' Serena said, wondering how on earth she could have let such a farcical situation arise. 'He's obviously not going to be there, and neither am I.'

'Don't be a silly girl,' her father said lovingly. 'Wouldn't be cricket if you didn't turn up. Bad for the family name and all that,' and he severed the connection, leaving her standing there, the telephone receiver in her hand, tears glittering on her eyelashes.

There were no signs of tears when Toby Langton-Green picked her up that evening in his MG.

'The papers are doing you proud,' he said, dropping a copy of the *Evening Standard*. 'The latest odds on a

133

complete debacle at the church tomorrow are fifty to one. If only one of you turned up, I'd stand to win a quite tidy little sum. I don't suppose you're thinking of doing so, are you?' he asked hopefully.

Serena glared at him. 'Don't be an ass, Toby. Do I look like a bride on the eve of her wedding?' She was wearing over-the-knee derring-do snakeskin boots and a shocking pink, breathtakingly short minidress, the material glittering and shimmering and clinging to her curves as though it were a second skin.

'No,' he said frankly, putting the MG into gear and pulling away from the curb. 'Can't say you do.'

He turned into the King's Road, heading west toward Chiswick. 'I thought we were going for drinks at the Peppermint Lounge and then on to White's?'

'We are.' Toby was elegant in a lace-frilled evening shirt and blue velvet dinner jacket. 'But there's a party I'd like to drop in on for a few minutes.'

Serena looked across at him doubtfully. Toby was looking extremely pleased with himself. As if he knew something that she didn't know and it amused him.

'If you've arranged for newsmen to be there, so that you can hit tomorrow's headlines as "The Man who Escorted the Bride who Never Was" then you're going to be very disappointed, Toby. I'm not playing.'

'Of course you're not, dear girl,' Toby said understandingly, patting her knee as he rounded Fulham Palace Road. 'Wouldn't dream of it. Nasty things, reporters. Avoid 'em like the plague myself.'

The party was in a towering block of luxury flats overlooking the Thames.

'Toby!' squealed their hostess, pushing through the crush to greet them. 'Serena, *darling!*'

Serena stared beyond her to where Kyle was lounging against a far wall, one foot crossed over the other at the ankle, a whisky glass in his hand. Their eyes met as streamers flew and champagne corks popped. 'Toby!' Serena admonished. But she was elated as the corners of Kyle's mouth twitched and broke into a dazzling grin. 'Toby! You *devil*!'

'Had to do something, old girl,' he said, his grin nearly as wide as Kyle's. 'Stand to make a tidy sum if one of you turns up tomorrow. If you both turn up, I stand to make a bloody fortune!'

Kyle eased himself carelessly away from the wall and crossed the room towards her. 'Long time no see,' he said affably, reaching out for her with a strong hand and drawing her close. 'Don't we have a date somewhere tomorrow?'

'Oh, you bastard!' she sobbed, her arms sliding around him, her body fitting in perfect familiarity against his. 'You unbelievable, impossible, evil-natured, *wonderful* bastard!'

As far as media attention went, it was without doubt the wedding of the year. The elopement and then the bizarre separation and subsequent behaviour of the bride and groom had aroused prurient interest. The presence of pop stars such as Mick Jagger and Eric Burden, and personalities such as Mary Quant, insured that there was a full complement of reporters and photographers present when the bride and her father arrived at Bedingham's ancient ivy-covered church.

Her dress was of white lace, miniskirted and daringly low-necked. Instead of the usual white satin pumps, she wore knee-high white kid boots, and her veil was the length of her dress, billowing around her and held in place by a single, lush white Bedingham rose.

She was followed down the aisle by two of her friends from finishing school, who had been delighted by the countess's suggestion that they would surprise Serena by being her bridesmaids, and their dresses, too, in lemon silk, were knee-skimmingly short.

The only blight on the ceremony was the mysterious absence of the bride's twin brother.

'I don't understand it,' Serena said, turning to her mother as they posed for photographs before leaving the church for the reception. 'Where on earth can he be? Do you think we should report him to the police as missing?'

'Oh, I don't think Lance would like that at all,' her mother said. 'You know how he feels about the police.'

Serena knew how Lance felt, but she was becoming so worried that she was beginning not to care.

'It's been four weeks,' she said to Kyle as they were driven the short distance back to the house in her father's Silver Shadow Rolls-Royce. 'He's *never* disappeared for so long at a stretch before. Not even when he was taking part in the vigil outside South Africa House.'

'For goodness sake, forget about him,' Kyle said equably. 'He's not a child. The only people who could be excused for worrying about him are your parents, and neither of them seem even faintly upset.'

'Neither of my parents are what you might call obsess-ively *caring*,' Serena said, twisting her new diamond-encrusted wedding ring around her finger. It lay snugly next to the cheap, shiny ring she had originally been married with and which she had adamantly refused to remove. 'In fact, they can't even be described as normal.'

For once Kyle agreed with her. 'But whereas Lance would know they wouldn't be worrying about him, he would certainly know that *I* would be worrying.'

Kyle looked across at her, one eyebrow rising slightly. It wasn't the first time he had noticed the throb of emotion in her voice whenever she spoke of her brother. He had met him only briefly, when he and his parents had first arrived at Bedingham, and he hadn't been overly impressed. There was something weak, almost effeminate about Lance Blyth-Templeton, and from what he had heard of his political affiliations, he doubted if they would ever have much in common.

'He's probably at Bedingham,' he said, not caring much whether he was or he wasn't. 'The wedding was a bit of a free-for-all. You can't blame him for skipping it.'

136

The reception was already under way as their Rolls slid to a halt outside the south entrance. Eric Burden performed a rendition of *House of the Rising Sun* without the benefit of his group, Mick Jagger sang *Come On*, and Kyle and Serena, remembering the circumstances under which they had previously heard him sing it, exchanged hot looks and then burst into shouts of uncontrollable laughter. When old Herricot eased himself through the crush to her side and whispered to her that Master Lance had arrived and was in the old nursery and wanting to have a few words with her, Serena's happiness was complete.

'Lance has arrived,' she said exuberantly to Kyle. 'I'm just going to find out where he's been. I won't be five minutes.'

She had hurried off, still in her wedding dress and veil, and Kyle had frowned in annoyance and then had his attention taken by an Anderson aunt, eager to give him her congratulations.

Serena rushed into the room that had been the nursery. He was standing with his back towards her, staring down on to the grounds and the giant marquee and the milling guests.

'Lance!' she cried joyfully, running towards him. 'Where on *earth* have you been?'

He spun toward her, his face a white, contorted mask.

'You bitch!' he snarled, seizing her wrist. 'You stupid, *whoring* little bitch!' And raising his free hand, he slapped her open-palmed across her face with all the force he was capable of.

# CHAPTER SEVEN

Gavin wanted his date with Gabrielle to be special. He didn't want to sit with her in a smoke-filled bar. He wanted a whole day with her, and he wanted the day to be spent far away from Montmartre's steeply narrow streets and shabby nightclubs.

'I'll pick you up at ten on Monday,' he said to her when she told him that Monday was her first day off.

'Ça va,' she said agreeably, hiding the disappointment she felt. 'Okay. But I am not singing anywhere on Monday. I could meet you a little earlier if you wish.'

He had chuckled and hugged her, aware that for the first time he had met a woman who not only filled him with raging desire, but who also aroused in him the laughing affection that he had previously reserved only for his younger sisters. He was well aware that it was a lethal combination.

'Ten in the morning,' he said, grinning down at her. Even in her stiletto-heeled shoes she still barely reached his shoulder.

She groaned, affecting horror at the thought of facing the day at such an ungodly hour, but her eyes were sparkling and he knew that she was pleased.

'We'll go to Versailles or Fontainebleau or Chartres,' he said, not really caring where they went, just as long as they were together and away from the pimps and prostitutes who thronged the area around the Black Cat.

They went to Fontainebleau. He had bought a battered old Citroën the second week after he had arrived in Paris, and as he swung out of Montmartre and on to the many-laned boulevard périphérique, Gabrielle noted with amusement that he drove with the panache of a native Parisian, blissfully unintimidated by the suicidally inclined drivers hurtling along on either side of them.

The leather of the Citroën seats was cracked and disintegrating and reeked of Gauloises and stale perfume. Gabrielle settled herself comfortably in the front passenger seat, aware that her own distinctive perfume was already mingling with the exotic odour left by past occupants.

Gavin headed south for Fontainebleau via the small town of Évry, and the villages of Fleury-en-Bière and Barbizon. The day was already hot, only the merest wisp of cirrus trailing across the brassy blue bowl of the sky as they skimmed down the white, tree-lined roads.

They lunched in Fontainebleau at a small hotel of the same name, and it wasn't until the wine had been poured and the first course served that he asked the question he had been longing to ask from the moment he had first set eyes on her. 'What nationality are you, Gabrielle?'

'French,' she said, and then, knowing that she hadn't answered the question he had been trying to ask, she added, 'But though I'm a French citizen, I'm only half French. My mother is Vietnamese.'

He had expected her to say that she was French-Moroccan or French-Algerian. He stared at her, his sunbleached brows rising comically. 'No wonder you asked me what I knew about Vietnam when I said that I was eager to be sent there.' He looked touchingly discomfited. 'Do you know the country? Have you been there?'

'I was born there,' she said, taking a sip of her wine. 'It was my home until I was eight.'

Mentally, he figured out that she'd left the country shortly after Dien Bien Phu. He looked slightly disappointed. 'Then you were too young to have any real memories of it. I don't suppose you know any more about the situation out there than anyone else does,' he said regretfully, about to abandon the subject.

Gabrielle laid down her fork and leaned her elbows on the table, clasping her hands and resting her chin on them. 'No,' she said slowly. 'No, I was not too young.'

The years rolled away; the memories were so vivid that she could almost hear the clicking of Mah-Jongg tiles; see the wide, lush avenues and the white stuccoed house with the many verandas that had been her home; smell the aroma of exotic spices, the fragrance of carefully tended tuberoses and gardenias, the dark, pungent scents of the encroaching bush. Homesickness, harsh and raw, swept over her. She had known, ever since he had told her he wanted to be sent to Vietnam to cover the war, where their conversation would inevitably lead. What she hadn't known was the depth of longing such a conversation would unleash.

She had been looking beyond him, her eyes unfocused, registering nothing of her present surroundings, seeing only the past. Now she gave her head a tiny shake, the sun that streamed through the restaurant's windows gilding her spicy red curls a burnished gold.

'My mother's family still lives in Saigon, and they write to us regularly.' She paused for a moment. She had never spoken to anyone before of her Vietnamese aunt, and her uncles and cousins. Now she heard herself saying prosaically. 'And one of my uncles, my mother's youngest brother, is Viet Cong.'

If she had said that her uncle was Ho Chi Minh, Gavin could not have looked more stunned. He blinked and said unsteadily, 'And are you in touch with him as well?'

'No.' She paused again and speared a button mushroom with her fork. 'But my aunt is. Irregularly.'

Gavin signalled the waiter over and ordered a beer. He had been enjoying the wine, but if he wanted to think clearly, and assess what Gabrielle's information might mean to him once he was in Vietnam, he needed the familiarity of a beer to help the process along.

'How irregularly?' he asked when his beer had been poured and he had taken a fortifying drink.

'He left home in 1940 to join the Communists in Hanoi. For twenty-five years no one heard anything from him and then, two years ago, he visited my mother's oldest sister, Nhu, who is living in Saigon.' She paused again. Her uncle Dinh's activities were something she and her mother never discussed with anyone, not even her father.

Her eyes met Gavin's across the white tablecloth. She had known him for only three short days, and out of that time had spent only a few hours in his company, yet she knew instinctively that he would never betray her trust. 'He had come south on an undercover mission for General Giap. . . .'

'*Giap!*' At the mention of the man who had led the Viet Minh forces to victory at Dien Bien Phu, every journalistic nerve that Gavin possessed screamed to life.

Gabrielle nodded. 'He is now a colonel in the North Vietnamese Army, though Nhu said that he did not look like a colonel. He and his men had travelled every inch of the way south on foot, trekking through Laos and northeastern Cambodia and entering the South through the highlands. Nhu said that she scarcely recognized him, he had changed so much.'

Gavin's breathing had become light and shallow. 'And why had he come south?' he asked, already seeing the headlines such a story would make.

She tilted her head slightly to one side. 'General Giap wanted to infiltrate large numbers of his men into the south, and he wanted the situation assessed first, by someone he trusted.'

Gavin let out his breath slowly. The story she had told him, if corroborated by names and dates, would sell like hotcakes to *Time* or *Newsweek* or *Le Monde*. But if any of those magazines did publish the story, Gabrielle's family in Saigon would suffer. Nhu, and Nhu's children, would be considered Viet Cong. He would have his story and they would face interrogation and possibly even death. He wondered if Gabrielle realized how grave the consequences of trusting him could be.

'You know what could happen if I sell this story, don't you, Gaby?'

It was the first time he had affectionately shortened her name.

She nodded, her eyes holding his steadily. 'But you will not sell it, will you, Gavin?'

They had been speaking in English, and her heavy accent, as she pronounced his name, sent shivers of pleasure down his spine. He reached across the table for her hands, trapping them in his. 'No,' he said huskily, knowing what her act of trust symbolized for them. 'No, I shall never write anything that could harm you or your family. Not ever.'

'That is good, *mon ami*,' she whispered softly, and from that moment on both of them knew that they were going to be lovers for life.

They spent the afternoon hand in hand, wandering the great gardens of the palace of Fontainebleau.

'Why did you leave Australia?' she asked as they stood in the Jardin de Diana before the bronze statue of the goddess.

The crowds of sightseers who had crowded the gardens at the weekend had now gone. Only a few stray tourists remained, cameras slung over their shoulders, guidebooks in hand.

As a middle-aged American couple approached, intent on photographing the fountain-figure of Diana, Gavin gently steered Gabrielle away, walking in the direction of the old moat that rounded the north wing of the palace.

'Restlessness,' he said with a grin. 'I was eighteen when I left and it seemed to me that London was where

142

everything was happening, and London was where I wanted to be.' His grin deepened. 'I still haven't got there!'

Gabrielle gave a little Gallic shrug. 'There is only La Manche to cross. It is only a narrow ribbon of water. You could be in London by this evening if you truly wanted to be.'

'It isn't so easy,' he said without regret. 'Somewhere on the way between Brisbane and Paris, I discovered I really wanted to be a war correspondent. Landing my job at the press bureau is a major step toward that goal. I don't want to hurt my chances by whining for a transfer to London when things are going so well here.'

'*Je comprends*,' Gabrielle said as they rounded the north wing and began to stroll, their arms around each other's waists, towards the formal garden known as the parterre. 'I understand.'

It was now mid-afternoon and behind them the sun-steeped stone of the palace glowed like gold, heat coming out of the ground in waves.

'And then there is also the question of a certain nightclub singer,' he said, pausing beside an ornamental pond and turning her around to face him. 'She may not go with me if I go to England.'

Gabrielle looked up into his boyish, almost vulnerable face. He was not at all the sort of man she had envisaged herself falling in love with. He was ridiculously young, only four years older than herself, and she doubted if he owned much more than the clothes he had on and the battered old Citroën that had brought them to Fontainebleau.

A smile tugged at the corners of her mouth. She knew that she was not being sensible and French. She was, instead, succumbing to a sense of destiny that was wholly Vietnamese.

'I think your nightclub singer may very well go with you wherever you want her to, *chéri*,' she said, and sliding her arms up and around his neck, she raised herself on to her toes and pressed her mouth softly, yet ardently, against his.

His response was immediate. His arms tightened around her and his mouth opened, his tongue sliding deeply and fully past hers.

The hair on the nape of his neck was crisp against her palms, his body hard and urgent as he pressed her into him.

'Let's go back to the town,' he rasped hoarsely, 'and see if the hotel has a room for the night.'

Gabrielle gave a deep-throated chuckle. She knew very well that they would have, as she had prudently reserved one while he had been paying the bill for their lunch. '*Bien*,' she said, agreeing. She was happy for him to think that he was taking the initiative and knowing that as the patron was a Frenchman, her secret would be safe.

It was like being in bed with a good-natured and over-eager young bear, Gabrielle reflected as Gavin collapsed, exhausted, beside her. She ruffled his tousled hair with her hand. Whatever sexual experience he had gained on the long trip from Brisbane to Paris, it had been neither expert nor profound. In her widely experienced past she had met men who had a lot to learn, but she had never before met one who had everything to learn.

Gavin heaved himself up on to one elbow. 'Are you all right?' he asked, looking down into her dazed, disbelieving face, the concern in his voice indicating that he believed his enthusiastic and criminally swift act of copulation had caused the earth to move for her, and that she was still in the throes of recovery.

'*Oui*,' said Gabrielle lovingly, wondering which was the best way to handle a rather delicate situation. 'That was—' She paused, searching for a word that would do the experience justice. 'That was *incroyable, mon amour*.' She pulled him down towards her, the corners of her wide, generous

144

mouth quirking into a smile. 'As it is still only six o'clock, let us have a little sleep and then, afterwards . . .' She settled his head comfortably on her breast. 'Afterwards I will explain something to you, *chéri*.'

The task of explaining was a deeply enjoyable one, and one that was carried out with such skill that Gavin was happily convinced that most of what he had learned was his own idea.

Gabrielle surveyed the vast double bed and its crumpled sheets late the next afternoon and gave a little sigh. 'Things will not be so easy to arrange when we are back in Paris, *mon amour*,' she said regretfully, leaning back against the pillows. Her previous lovers had either been artists with their own studios or businessmen with their own apartments. Gavin shared decidedly basic accommodation in Montmartre with three fellow Australians.

'Do you always have Monday night off?' he asked her, an edge of panic in his voice as she glanced at the wristwatch that lay on the bedside table and then slid reluctantly from the bed.

She nodded, knowing very well the direction his thoughts were taking. Before he could suggest that they stay every Monday night at the hotel, she said apologetically, reaching for the wisp of black lace that served her as a bra, 'But I cannot stay away from home all night, every Monday night, *chéri*. My parents would worry.'

For a moment he wondered if she was teasing him and then, with a mixture of amusement and incredulity, realized that she was telling him the simple truth. 'But you're a *nightclub* singer!' he protested, laughing despite his disappointment.

'But a nightclub singer with a *very* protective *maman* and *papa*,' she said, laughing with him as she fastened her bra and reached for her panties.

He watched her in rapt fascination, intrigued by the combination of wanton and innocent that coexisted so happily in her sunny, uncomplicated nature.

145

'Then we'll drive out here every Monday morning and spend the day in bed,' he said, solving the problem with devastating ease. 'And in the evening, after a leisurely early dinner in the hotel restaurant, I will return you at a dutifully early hour to *Maman* and *Papa*.'

'*Bien*,' she said, her eyes dancing as she stepped into her skirt, 'but next Monday I think we will have to forgo our dinner in the restaurant, *chéri*.'

'Why?' His face fell. He didn't want to forgo one minute of the time they would have together.

She pulled her sweater down over full, lush breasts. 'Because we shall be dining *en famille, mon amour*,' and then, in case he had not understood her, she said with unmistakable clarity, 'We shall be having dinner with my parents. *Tu comprends?*'

'*Je comprends*,' Gavin said with a broad grin and in an execrable French accent. She hadn't said so, but he was fairly sure that the invitation was a rare honour and one that very few of her previous boyfriends, if any, had received.

That there had been previous boyfriends – a lot of them – he did not doubt. Even taking into account an inborn capacity for sexual enjoyment, her expertise and virtuosity could have been gained only through practice. Strangely enough, the knowledge did not disturb him. Whatever the number of her previous lovers, there was something so pure and unsullied about her, something so joyous and generous, it made them unimportant. What mattered were the qualities he knew he could stake his life on. Her honesty and her loyalty and her greatness of heart. And for him, that was more than enough.

He had been correct to assume that few previous boyfriends had ever found themselves sitting at the Mercador dining table. In actual fact, none had.

Her mother had stared at her, her eyes widening, when Gabrielle had told her that she had invited Gavin to dine with them the following Monday.

146

'But who is this . . . this Gavin?' she had asked apprehensively. 'Is he a new artist you are sitting for, *chérie*? Is he—' She had hesitated, her apprehension deepening. 'Is he a . . . a gentleman you have met at the club?'

'Strictly speaking, I suppose that he is,' Gabrielle replied truthfully, 'but he isn't remotely like the usual kind of patron. He's Australian,' she added as if Gavin's nationality explained all.

Her mother sat down weakly. She had envisaged all kinds of horrors. An impoverished artist, a married businessman, the middle-aged patron of one of the clubs, but at least all her imaginings had been Frenchmen. An Australian was so foreign to her as to be almost beyond belief.

'You will like him, *Maman*,' Gabrielle said confidently. 'He is one of life's innocents.'

'*C'est impossible*,' her mother said faintly, imagination failing her altogether.

When Gavin entered the small top floor apartment, Gabrielle's father regarded him dubiously. He had never had any dealings with Australians, and had never wished to. To him they were a breed stranger even than Americans, and that was saying a lot.

'*Bonsoir*,' he said stiffly, making no attempt to speak in his extremely creditable English.

'Would you like a drink?' Gabrielle asked, helpfully speaking in English. 'A kir?'

'A kir would be fine,' Gavin lied, thirsting for the fortifying alcohol content of a beer. Gabrielle, knowing very well that a kir was the last thing on earth Gavin would normally choose to drink, grinned and disappeared into the kitchen, leaving him to his fate.

'*Êtes-vous à Paris longtemps?*' Gabrielle's mother asked, good manners overcoming her prejudice at his nationality.

'*Deux ou trois mois*,' he replied manfully, deciding that if French was to be the name of the game, the sooner he launched himself into it, the better.

147

Both Mercadors flinched at his accent. 'Perhaps—' Gabrielle's father said when he had recovered his power of speech, ' – perhaps it would be better if we spoke English.'

'That's fine by me,' Gavin said with disarming relief. 'French is a great language, but it can be a little tricky.' A slight smile twitched at the corners of Vanh Mercador's mouth. Gabrielle had been right. There was something innocent and charmingly vulnerable about the open-faced young man she had brought home.

She had thought that all Australians were enormously tall and powerfully built with loud voices and intimidatingly rough manners. The young man before her, though far taller than Gabrielle, was still only five foot eight or nine, and was slim and supple in a crisp white shirt and close-fitting blue jeans. Only his hair, bleached gold by the sun, seemed to her typically Australian, but he did not wear it cropped short, as she had imagined Australians wore their hair. Instead, it was long, as if he were a student, dark blond curls twisting indecently low on the nape of his neck.

'Gabrielle tells me that you are a journalist,' she said haltingly, her English only a little better than his French, 'and that you wish to go to Vietnam?'

Gavin saw a slight frown crease Mr Mercador's forehead and realized that the subject was not one that he encouraged. It was, however, a subject that dominated the evening.

'And will your country, too, become involved in Vietnam, as the Americans have become involved?' Étienne asked him as Gabrielle cleared away the soup plates and her mother placed a large, steaming casserole dish in the centre of the table.

'Southeast Asia is our neck of the woods,' Gavin said, and Gabrielle, seeing the look of mystification on her father's face, interrupted, saying, 'Gavin means that Southeast Asia is geographically very close to Australia, Papa.'

Her father nodded comprehendingly. 'And?' he prompted Gavin.

148

'And anything that happens there is automatically of great interest to us.'

'Will Australia be sending troops to Vietnam, as America has?' Vanh Mercador asked, presiding over the dinner table in a traditional silk *ao dai*, the pastel-coloured costume fitting tight from throat to hip, the side-split skirt billowing softly over loose black trousers.

'Last year the Australian government introduced a form of national service,' Gavin said, wondering from where Gabrielle had inherited her startling titian hair. 'It isn't a blanket call-up, it's a selective system in which those who have birthdays on certain randomly drawn dates are required to make themselves available for two years national service. The service was for both the defence of Australia and military purposes beyond Australia.'

The casserole was beef accompanied by mushrooms and freshly made noodles.

'Which will be Vietnam,' Étienne said prophetically, spearing a mushroom with his fork. 'But what the French failed to achieve in Vietnam, no amount of Americans or Australians will be able to achieve.'

Gavin was just about to say that the situation wasn't quite the same, as neither America nor Australia had colonial intentions toward Vietnam, but Gabrielle gave him a warning little shake of her head. 'Perhaps you could tell me what it was like living in Saigon in the thirties and forties,' he said instead. 'I'd be grateful for any background information that you can give me.'

Étienne, when the casserole and the dessert that had followed it had been removed, was only too happy to oblige.

By the end of the evening no remnant of his original hostility towards Gavin remained. True, he was an Australian, which was a pity, but he was also presentable and intelligent and it was better that Gabrielle had brought an Australian home than one of the pimps or the con men who abounded in the area.

★ ★ ★

The Monday evening dinners *en famille* became a weekly event. Gavin swiftly discovered that where Vietnam was concerned, the tenor of the conversation was far different when Gabrielle's father was not present. Vanh would reminisce about her childhood home in Hue, unwittingly revealing her deep homesickness.

'When you go to Saigon, you must visit my sister, Nhu,' she said repeatedly, her eyes overly bright. 'You must try to persuade her to leave Vietnam and to settle near us, in Paris.'

He had promised faithfully, but he had begun to wonder if he was ever going to step foot on Vietnamese soil.

All through the summer he had bombarded his superiors with requests that he be sent to Saigon to cover the war. The reply was always the same: he was too junior a member of the staff to be sent on such a coveted assignment. Journalists were required to work for at least three years in the head office before aspiring to become correspondents.

Without Gabrielle he knew he would have succumbed to frustration and restlessness, and that he would have abandoned his ambition and moved on. To America perhaps, or to Canada. As it was, he remained in Paris, becoming as familiar with the narrow cobbled streets of Montmartre as Gabrielle was. Every flower vendor and paper seller knew him by name, as did every barman and doorman. The prostitutes knew him, too, cheekily soliciting him whenever Gabrielle was not at his side. Gavin's reply was always an amused grin and a shake of his head, his amusement caused by the knowledge that if he had ever accepted an offer, the girl in question would have immediately withdrawn it, and indignantly reported his faithlessness to Gabrielle.

It was October and he was at his desk, reading a report that had just come in from Stockholm, where a large meeting had been held protesting against American policy in Vietnam.

'Looks like it's your lucky day,' his immediate boss said as he strolled into the office. 'The agency's manager for Asia is in the building and he wants to see you.'

150

Gavin had given a quick thanks to heaven, and had taken the stairs leading to the executive offices two at a time.

'If Vietnam is what you want, Vietnam is what you've got,' a laconic Englishman said to him, the top two buttons of his shirt undone and the knot of his tie pulled loose. 'You'll be in Singapore for a few weeks first, until we get your visa sorted out. After that I'd like to see some real reporting from you. I don't want you to just sit on a hill and watch a battle and then report what the Americans say has happened at it. I want you to ignore the Follies and find out what is *really* happening.'

'The Follies?' Gavin asked, wondering if he was being given a caution against the nightclubs and bars of Saigon.

'The Americans give a press conference every afternoon at five, at the United States Public Affairs Office. It's known as the Five O'Clock Follies. You'll soon find out why.'

'Yes, sir,' Gavin said exuberantly, hardly able to contain the excitement surging along his veins. 'And thank you!'

The Englishman looked at him pityingly. 'Don't thank me now,' he said dourly. 'Thank me when you get back. If you still want to. Which you won't,' and he reached for one of the box files on his desk, indicating that the interview was over.

Gabrielle tilted her head slightly to one side. 'Are you quite sure?' she asked.

The elderly doctor rested his clasped hands on the surface of the mahogany desk that lay between them. 'But certainly. There can be no mistake.'

A small smile touched the corners of Gabrielle's mouth. 'Thank you, Doctor,' she said, rising to her feet.

His brows drew together in a concerned frown. 'And what are you going to do about it?' he asked bluntly.

Gabrielle's smile deepened. 'Why, nothing. Nothing at all.' And with a happy, husky laugh she walked out of his office and down the narrow, winding stairs that led to the street.

She had arranged to meet Gavin at a sidewalk café on the corner of the rue des Martyrs and the rue le Tac, and she quickened her step, not wanting to be late. The October sun was still warm, and she raised her face towards it, her own reaction to the doctor's news so immediate and uncomplicated that it did not occur to her to wonder if Gavin's reaction would be different.

She turned into the rue le Tac and with a leap of joy saw that he was sitting at one of the café tables, waiting for her. There was a cup of coffee on the checked cloth in front of him and a folded newspaper.

'Gavin!' she called out, breaking into a run. 'Gavin!'

He turned his head towards her, rising instantly to his feet, a welcoming grin splitting his face.

'I have some great news!' he said buoyantly as she hurtled into his arms and he hugged her close.

Her eyes laughed up into his. '*Alors, chéri!* I too, have news *incroyable!*'

'Then ladies first,' he said gallantly, reluctantly releasing his hold of her and pulling out one of the cane chairs so that she could sit at the table.

She waited until he had sat down beside her and took his hands, imprisoning them in hers, her eyes shining. 'Are you sure that you do not want to tell me your good news first?'

He laughed and kissed the tip of her nose. 'My news will wait,' he said, exercising superhuman restraint, his head whirling with the hundred and one things he had to do, the arrangements he had to make. 'What do you have to tell me, Gaby?'

She leaned forward and kissed him full on the lips and then, as she drew her mouth lovingly away from his, she said softly, 'I'm having a baby, *mon amour*. Isn't that the most wonderful news you can imagine?'

# CHAPTER EIGHT

Abbra had a window seat on the flight back to San Francisco, and she sat gazing down into the shimmering blue haze of the Pacific. Her reunion with Lewis had been wonderful. The memory of their lovemaking warmed her like a glowing fire and would, she knew, continue to warm her through the months of waiting that lay ahead. And yet . . . And yet . . .

Far below her the blue haze eddied into shades of aquamarine and jade. A small frown creased her brow and her dark-lashed eyes were sombre. She knew very well what it was that was troubling her, and she also knew that she could no longer put off confronting it. Her husband was a complete stranger. The man who had said of battle that those were the best times, when the adrenaline begins to surge, had not been a man she had even remotely known. Neither had the man who couldn't understand her desire to know of the life he led when he was away from her. Yet that man, that stranger, was the man she loved and the man she had pledged to share her life with.

The public address system hummed into life and the captain informed them that they were approaching the California coastline and would shortly be landing at San Francisco International Airport. She fastened her seat belt, aware that there were no easy answers. They were married and they loved each other, yet they had not lived together in the day-to-day intimacy of husband and wife. When they did, then they would learn to understand each other. The prospect reassured her, and her frown cleared and a small smile touched the corners of her mouth. In a little less than six months time they would be together again and their married life would truly begin.

'I love you, Lewis,' she whispered as the tone of the engines changed and the plane prepared to land. 'Just come safely home to me. That's all that matters.'

When she walked out into the arrival area, the first thing she saw was Scott's tall, powerful figure. Her eyes lit up and her smile deepened as she began to walk quickly towards him, the skirt of her white linen suit skimming her knees, her long, suntanned legs seemingly endless.

The breath slammed hard in Scott's chest. Ever since he had said good-bye to her he had been determined that he would not drive up from Los Angeles to meet her when she returned. But all his resolutions had been in vain. He had procrastinated to the last possible moment, trying to convince himself that he was not going to weaken, and had then been obliged to drive like a maniac up Highway One, praying that he wouldn't be stopped by a vigilant patrolman.

Now, seeing her stride gaily towards him, her smoke-black hair falling glossily to her shoulders, her pansy-dark eyes dancing with innocent pleasure at the sight of him, he knew he had been a fool to think he could stay away.

'It's good to have you back,' he said, making sure that there was only affection in his voice as he took her luggage and kissed her with light brotherliness on the temple.

'If only Lewis had been able to come back with me, then I could truthfully say that it's nice to be back,' she said, smiling up at him in a manner that nearly undid him.

Abruptly he began to forge a way through the press of people around them towards an exit. God in heaven, but it was even worse than he had imagined it would be. He had known that meeting her again, after admitting to himself his feelings for her were not in the least brotherly, but flagrantly carnal, would be difficult. But he had not expected it to be near impossible. He had imagined he would be able to simulate the easy camaraderie that had always existed

154

between them, and she would be unaware of any difference in their relationship. Now he was not so sure. The urge to drop her luggage to the ground and to seize her, crush her against him, was almost more than he could endure. Beads of perspiration broke out on his forehead. Hell, it was even worse than making a twenty-five-yard touchdown with only ten seconds left to play.

'How was Lewis?' he asked, struggling to keep his eyes ahead of him, terrified of what would happen to his willpower if he looked down into her face.

'He was fine,' she said, and though the words were studiedly casual, there was so much love in her voice that he felt his shoulder and arm muscles harden into knots. 'He hasn't even had a stomach ache.'

'That's good,' Scott said, leading the way out of the airport terminal into brilliant sunshine. 'So what is he doing over there?'

They were approaching his car, and it was a second or two before he realized that his question was causing her some difficulty.

'Oh, he's still serving as part of a five-man advisory team,' she said at last, her voice so oddly vague that he swivelled his head towards her, his eyebrows rising.

A slight touch of colour flushed her cheeks, and she didn't hold his glance; instead, she walked away from him and towards the car. 'He's still in the Ca Mau peninsula,' she said, opening the car door. 'I imagine he'll be there until his tour of duty is over.'

'Yes,' Scott agreed, wondering what on earth was troubling her. 'Sure.' He slid into the seat next to her, turning the key in the ignition, gunning the engine into life. 'You'd think that as his second six months is voluntary, they'd post him somewhere a little easier. Saigon, for instance.'

They were driving out of the airport and on to the motorway. Abbra looked across at him, puzzled. 'What on earth do you mean, voluntary?'

155

'Well, combat officers usually do only a six-month stint in 'Nam. Lewis must have angled for this second six months. He wouldn't have been given it if he hadn't.' He looked across at her, about to say that it was typical of Lewis to be such a glutton for punishment, and then he saw the expression on her face. His hands slid on the wheel, the car swerving as he said in stunned incredulity, 'But you must have known, Abbra! He must have told you! Christ, I thought *everyone* knew combat officers served only six-month stints!'

'No.' The word was strangled in her throat. She looked deathly pale. 'I hadn't known. . . . I didn't realize . . .' She saw the way he was looking at her and forced an unsteady smile. 'Lewis is a military adviser. Perhaps that doesn't come under the classification of being a combat officer. But if it does, you're right, it *is* typical of him to go the extra mile.'

Her eyes were overly bright and her voice was tremulous. For one terrible moment he thought she was going to cry.

'Abbra . . .' he began, slowing the car down, reaching out to her with his right hand.

'Don't,' she said thickly, pushing his hand away. 'I'm all right and I think you're wrong, Scott. I don't think he volunteered for this second six months of duty. It's obligatory, I'm sure of it.'

Scott said nothing. There was nothing he could say. Even if it hadn't been obligatory, Lewis would have volunteered for it, and both of them knew it.

There was a letter waiting for her when she arrived home. It was from the editor who had accepted her short story, and it suggested that, as she apparently had no literary agent, she might like to contact one. Three names were listed, but one, Patti Maine, was located in Los Angeles. As Abbra stared down at the address, the shocked sense of betrayal she had been feeling at Lewis's act of deceit eased. She had another focus for her thoughts now, and she found shelter in it. Without even pausing to unpack her

156

suitcase, she telephoned Patti Maine's number and asked the secretary who answered it if she could please speak to Miss Maine.

'Who is calling?' a crisp voice asked, and as she gave her name Abbra accepted the fact that she was unlikely to be connected and that she would have to introduce herself by letter.

'Patti Maine speaking,' an unexpectedly young voice said, 'I was hoping you would give me a call, Abbra. Bernadette Lawler wrote me, telling me that she had given you my number.'

Abbra was so taken by surprise at Patti Maine accepting her call, and at being addressed by her first name that for a second she could only say, 'Oh,' and then, gathering her scattered wits, she said with a rush, 'it's very kind of you to speak to me.'

'It isn't kindness at all,' Patti Maine said dismissively. 'If Bernadette's hunch about your work is correct, and Bernadette's hunches usually are, then it's you who will be doing me a favour, not the other way round. When can you come and see me?'

'Tomorrow,' Abbra said instantly, and then apologized for her foolishness. 'I'm sorry, I wasn't thinking. You're obviously very busy. I can come and see you whenever it is convenient for you.'

'You're right, I am very busy,' Patti Maine said briskly, 'but as it happens, my lunch date for tomorrow has just cancelled. If you get to the office by twelve-thirty, we can have a chat and then go on to the Beverly Wilshire. It means I won't have to cancel the table.'

Abbra felt disorientated. 'Thank you,' she said breathlessly. 'Thank you very much. I look forward to seeing you. Thank you. Good-bye.' By the time she had uttered her last thank you she was speaking into thin air.

'That's terrific!' Scott said when she telephoned him with the news. He had driven straight back to Los Angeles after dropping her off at her home, his thoughts and emotions in turmoil.

He couldn't go on seeing her. It would lead to disaster. Sooner or later, he was bound to reveal his true feelings for her and at the thought of her horrified reaction when he did so, he felt sick. There was only one sensible course of action to take, and he had already taken it. He had a date for that evening and the following one.

'Patti Maine is a big name,' he said, his pulse rate increasing at the mere sound of her voice. 'Hell, even I've heard of her! Your lady editor in New York has certainly done you a big favour, sweetheart.'

The minute he uttered the endearment he could have bitten his tongue, but she seemed not to notice it, saying nervously, 'We're having lunch at the Beverly Wilshire. I haven't a clue what I should wear. Do you think my white linen suit will be okay? Or should I wear something more sophisticated? Like black?'

'Good God, no!' he said, laughing. 'Wear the white linen. You look sensational in it.' It was true, and he found some relief in being able to tell her so in a way that would cause her no unease.

'What will she want to talk to me about?' There was a note of panic in her voice. 'I've only written a few short stories!'

'One of which a leading women's magazine is about to publish,' he finished for her. 'Don't be so modest, Abbra. Your editor wouldn't be introducing you to an agent of Patti Maine's stature if she weren't sure you had something to offer. Enjoy the lunch and don't worry. Patti Maine will do the talking. All you have to do is tell her what she wants to know and be your bright natural self.'

'I'll try,' she said, feeling slightly reassured. 'I think our lunch will be over by three. Probably long before if Miss Maine discovers I'm not the literary sensation she expected! Can you meet me around three-fifteen, or three-thirty? Or will you be at practice?'

'It might be a little difficult,' he said resolutely. 'I have a date tomorrow.'

'Oh!' Abbra was momentarily taken aback. For a highly eligible bachelor, Scott rarely dated. In fact, she couldn't remember his ever having dated all the months she had known him.

'That's great,' she said a trifle uncertainly. 'She must be very special.'

'Oh, she is,' Scott agreed, unable to remember what the woman looked like. Underneath Abbra's congratulations, he could sense her disappointment. She had been looking forward to telling him everything about her meeting with Patti Maine. He wasn't picking up his date until seven o'clock. There was no reason why he couldn't see Abbra first. No reason except that he would be breaking his hard-won resolution even before he had had a chance to put it into practice.

'I'll meet you at three-fifteen,' he said, despising himself for his weakness. 'In the Polo Lounge.'

It was their usual rendezvous whenever she came down to see him.

'Are you sure it won't make things difficult for you?' There was sisterly concern in her voice.

He grinned wryly. 'No,' he said, knowing that every time he met her it made things more difficult than she could possibly imagine. 'See you tomorrow, Abbra. Drive safe.'

She had worn her linen suit, white kid sling-back shoes, and small pearl stud earrings. Patti Maine's office was in a lux-ury apartment block just off Highland Avenue. The walls of the entrance hall were pale magnolia, the ankle-deep carpet was magnolia, and pale, creamy out-of-season magnolias were massed in a tall cut-glass vase. A smiling secretary ushered Abbra through a large, similarly decorated room that obviously served as an office, and into a smaller, even more luxuriously furnished inner sanctum. 'Mrs Ellis,' she announced, discreetly withdrawing.

The woman who rose from the small satinwood desk to greet Abbra was slightly older than her voice had indicated, but not much. 'Hello, Abbra. I'm very pleased to meet you,' she said with a wide, easy smile. Her hair was blond and fashionably bouffant, her short skirt was of pale champagne suede, her shirt blouse was of barley-coloured silk, the top two buttons left provocatively undone. 'What will you have to drink? White wine? A spritzer?'

'A white wine, please,' Abbra said, immediately responding to Patti's straightforward friendliness.

Patti gestured her toward a deep-seated cream sofa and poured out two glasses of ice-cold Chablis. 'Now,' she said, handing Abbra her drink and perching on the arm of a nearby chair, 'tell me all about yourself.'

Abbra had never been to a psychiatrist, but she imagined that the experience would be very similar to the one she was now undergoing.

'I'm nineteen, I live in San Francisco, and I'm married to an army officer who is serving overseas in Vietnam.'

Patti Maine cocked her head slightly to one side. 'And you write . . .' It wasn't a question, simply a statement of fact.

'Yes,' Abbra said, her confidence growing. 'I write.' She hesitated a moment and then added, 'I've brought some of my short stories with me. I left the box in my car—'

'They're probably very good, but they're not what I want from you. Nor do I want the kind of thing that you submitted to Bernadette.'

'Then what *do* you want from me?' Abbra asked, beginning to rise to her feet, not at all surprised and sure that there had been a big misunderstanding.

Patti motioned her to sit down again. 'I want something different from you. Something I have a gut feeling about. Something I feel sure you can do.' She paused for a moment and then said as if it were the most reasonable thing in the world, 'I want you to write a book.'

160

Abbra stared at her and Patti laughed. 'You write, don't you? Why not go for the big one? A book that could become a best seller.'

'But I wouldn't know what to write about!' Abbra protested, wondering if Patti was a little unbalanced, or if, perhaps, it was she herself who was unbalanced and imagining the whole conversation.

Patti put down her glass and rose to her feet. 'That,' she replied calmly, 'is a minor problem and one that we are going to resolve over lunch.'

As they picked leisurely at their salads, Patti asked Abbra to tell her all about her childhood and her upbringing.

'No,' she agreed as the waiter poured wine for them, 'I quite agree with you, there's nothing in your personal history that would serve as a springboard for a novel. What about your husband? How did you meet him? What sort of a man is he?'

'Oh, there's nothing there,' Abbra said quickly, so quickly that Patti Maine's intelligent eyes flared with interest. 'I wouldn't want to use anything in my private life as a basis for a novel.' She paused, her eyes suddenly becoming unfocused, seeing something that wasn't visible. 'But there is something . . .'

'Yes?' Patti prompted her, recognizing the creative light in Abbra's eyes.

'I just came back from Hawaii,' Abbra said, 'and something happened while I was there. Something that I can't quite put out of my mind.'

She took a sip of wine and then began to tell Patti about her meeting with Des Cawthorn.

For the next two weeks Abbra barely moved away from her desk. She wrote and rewrote, and as she did so, the characters she was creating took on shape and substance, developing a life of their own. There were times when she stared down in surprise at what she had just written, amazed at how one idea sparked off another, and at how her originally simple story line was taking on twists and turns she had never thought possible. Her novel even had a title now: *A Woman Alone*.

Scott had enjoyed his date with Rosalie Bryansten. She had been as unblushingly eager to share his bed as he had been eager to have her share it, and he had found the sexual release of their lovemaking cataclysmic. He was not a man to whom celibacy came easily, and for the first time he realized the incredible strain he had been living under. It was a strain he was determined that he would not subject himself to again. His belief that he could live without seeing or hearing from Abbra lasted all of ten days. By the time the end of the second week was drawing near, he ached for her.

'We're playing the Chargers on Saturday,' he said to her on the telephone. 'Why don't you fly down to San Diego? We could drive back to San Francisco on Sunday and stop by Carmel.'

Abbra was about to ask whether the woman he had dated the previous week would be going down to watch the game as well, and if so, whether a sister-in-law might be an awkward third. She decided against it. For some reason she found it hard to speak to him about the unknown woman he was presumably still dating.

'I don't think I can, Scott,' she said a little wistfully. 'I still haven't finished the outline for the book, though it's taking shape far better than I ever thought possible.'

'It will take shape even better when you've had a rest for a couple of days,' Scott said encouragingly. 'Make a reservation for an early Saturday-morning flight to San Diego, and I'll meet you there.'

Abbra felt herself weaken. It would be fun to watch Scott play and to spend the Sunday with him and talk to him about the book. 'Okay.' She laughed. 'You win.'

Scott was exuberant. 'Great! It's going to be a hard game.

162

The Chargers have always been tough on defence, and we're going to need all the support we can get!'

It had been a happy, carefree weekend. The Rams had won and Abbra had been blissfully unaware of the speculative expressions in Scott's teammates' eyes as they asked about Rosalie.

'Rosalie?' she had asked Scott.

'The girl I've been dating.' His voice was casually dismissive and he did not mention her again.

After the game they had gone out on the town with a crowd of Scott's fellow players and their wives and girlfriends, staying overnight in primly proper separate rooms at the Ramada Inn. The next morning, instead of flying back, Scott had rented a car and they had driven via San Clemente towards Carmel.

'The first place Lewis and I ever went together was Carmel,' Abbra said as the car sped into the little town's outskirts.

Scott grunted noncommittally, but when they reached the turnoff for the main street and the beach, he continued straight on.

She looked towards him, surprised. 'You've missed the exit, Scott.'

'No, I haven't.' His voice was light and easy, betraying none of the dark emotions that he was battling with. 'There's a restaurant near Sausalito that I've been meaning to take you to for a long time.'

She suppressed her disappointment. Perhaps, after all, it was best that they didn't go to Carmel. Memories of Lewis would be so strong that they would be nearly impossible for her to bear.

Scott had looked tense and drawn for the past five days and she wondered if his new girlfriend was causing him problems. She said suddenly, caring for him so much that it was a physical pain, 'Are you happy, Scott? Is there anything troubling you?'

He looked down at her, a smile she didn't understand crooking the corner of his mouth. 'I'm fine, Abbra, just fine,' he said thickly, and she had not pursued the subject. But she had not believed him.

By the end of February her synopsis was finished. She placed the twenty cleanly typed pages into a manilla envelope and addressed it to Patti Maine in a bold, firm hand. 'Please like it, Patti,' she whispered to herself as she drove down to the post office. 'Please God, let Patti like it!'

Lewis's letters to her, since his return, had been slightly more informative than his earlier ones, but not much. He had been given another assignment, still in the deep south of the country, but this time a little nearer to the Cambodian border. Although he was still part of the five-man American advisory team, the team was no longer working with a large South Vietnamese infantry battalion. Instead, they had been posted to a small village, Van Binh. Their task was to assist the villagers with rural development projects and to help the villagers protect Van Binh, and the surrounding villages, from the Communists.

*And these people need all the help they can get,* Lewis had written to her. *The area south of Saigon is so heavily infiltrated by Viet Cong that as far as the government troops are concerned, it's practically a no-go area. A situation we intended to change!*

There was a postscript, written in a hurried scrawl. *My commanding officer has been taken ill and flown out. For the moment I'm in temporary command. Long may it last!*

The situation was the same at the end of March, when his next letter reached her. *The local district chief is a fine man, doing a very difficult job as best he can. Together I think we can make Van Binh and the surrounding villages secure from both Viet Cong infiltration and Viet Cong aggression.*

It was obvious that he was relishing his new responsibilities. *As a co van truong, senior adviser to district chief, I'm in a position to make requests to Saigon for school supplies and building and agricultural development assistance, and you can bet your life I'm taking advantage of the opportunity.*

The letters cheered her up. Although she knew that his primary task was to flush out the Viet Cong operating in his area, he very rarely mentioned them, and never described any encounters with them. Instead, his letters continued to be full of heady exhilaration at being in a position to help the people he had begun to identify with.

All through spring and early summer the letters continued, and she took great comfort from them, happy to think of him as a benefactor, winning hearts and minds. Not wanting to think of him as a warrior.

# CHAPTER NINE

For a moment after Lance struck her Serena was too stunned to react. She staggered backwards under the force of the blow, her eyes wide, her mouth open, gasping in disbelief and pain.

'An American, for Christ's sake! *You have to throw yourself away on a stupid, fucking AMERICAN!* ' His face was scarcely recognizable, twisted with revulsion.

'But, Lance . . .' She had regained her balance and she stepped towards him, ugly scarlet weals rising across her face.

'*Christ, don't you understand?*' His voice was a sob. '*It was just beginning for us, Serry, and now it's all over!* '

Bewilderment overrode her anguish. 'What was just beginning? What is all over, Lance?'

'*This, for Christ's sake!* ' and he seized her shoulders, his fingers bruising her flesh, his head swooping down to hers, kissing her open-mouthed with demented violence.

Serena could taste blood on her lips. Vainly she twisted her head, trying to free her mouth of his invading tongue, trying to speak to him, to reason with him. But Lance was beyond reason. Serena was the most important creature in the world to him, and he knew that he had lost her for good. She would leave Bedingham, leave England. She would live in a country he hated with a man he had hated on sight. And his sexual desire for her, previously properly held in check and causing him only bemusement, was now unleashed and out of control. There could be no going back now. And he had no wish to go back.

'Serry! Darling!' His hands were on the white silk of her wedding dress; her veil billowed around them.

'Lance! Please!'

He was deaf to the horror in her voice. She was his. She had always been his. There had always been just the two of them. He and Serena against the world. His mouth silenced her protests, his hands slid down from her shoulders, cupping her breasts, squeezing and kneading.

She raised her hands to his hair, grasping its silky fineness, pulling his head savagely backwards, freeing her mouth. 'No, Lance! This is crazy! No! Please!'

She tried to wrench away from him and he flung her back against a wall, panting for breath as the petals from the rose in her hair scattered around his head and shoulders. *'You feel the same way!'* he shouted. *'We've always felt the same way!'*

'Lance! Listen to me—'

His hands seized the delicate white silk and ripped it wide, exposing her small, high, brassiered breasts and the ugly marks on her shoulders where his fingers had dug into her flesh.

'Christ, Serry! We must have been mad not to have realized long ago!' he sobbed, bending his head to her rosy nipples, sucking and biting in an agony of need.

'This is insane, Lance!' Her voice was strangled with conflicting emotions. Lascivious desire was raging through her, as was horror and anguish. Small beads of blood were dripping from her mouth on to her torn dress, spreading and staining. 'Please stop, Lance,' she begged. *'Please!'*

However erotic the experience, it was one that she wished to bring to an end. She couldn't become her brother's lover. It would be an act that would irrevocably drive them apart. 'Lance, *please!*' Her voice was no longer panic-stricken but was calm and loving, deeply urgent.

Her dress slithered down to her hips and he groaned, sliding down on to his knees, still crushing her toward him, his face pressed against the soft flesh of her stomach, his mouth only centimetres above her brief panties and the springy blond bush of her pubic hair.

167

'Oh, Christ, Serry, I need you!' He was crying now, his tears damp against her skin. Relief surged through her. It had come to an end. She knew by the agonized defeat in his voice that he had come to his senses, that he would not take her by force.

'I love you, Serry. I've always loved you,' he said thickly, his arms still around her, his mouth hot against her naked flesh.

'And I love you,' Serena said softly. 'I shall never feel as close to anyone else. Not ever.' And she stroked his hair gently, knowing that in a moment he would release her, and that in another few seconds they would be laughing shakily at the Greek drama of their passions.

It never occurred to Kyle that he should knock at the nursery door before entering. It wasn't a bedroom, for God's sake. Annoyed by the length of her absence, not wishing to continue standing alone in the yellow drawing room, receiving guests on her behalf, he had excused himself and had asked Herricot where the hell she was. The butler, not accustomed to being spoken to in such a direct manner, had frigidly replied that Lady Serena was in the old nursery and had reluctantly given him the directions so that he could join her there.

As he strode along the upper corridor he heard Serena's voice cry out loudly, *'Lance! Please!'* and then, as he approached the nursery door, he heard, quite unmistakably, Lance Blyth-Templeton saying in an agonized voice, 'I love you, Serry! I've always loved you!'

He froze, one hand on the doorknob, pausing just long enough to hear Serena's reply, and then, without a second's hesitation, he flung open the door, striding into the room, horrified at the scene that met his eyes.

Serena was half naked, her dress lying in a white pool around her feet, her veil still billowing around her. Blyth-Templeton was on his knees before her, clasping her toward him, his face pressed ardently against the white lace of her brief panties. Serena was cradling his head, looking down at him with an expression of unmistakable love, tears of anguish streaking her face.

Not for one fraction of a second did Kyle believe that her tears were those of distress for Lance's obvious sexual advances toward her. He had heard no words of protest, had heard only their mutual confessions of love for each other. And one glance at the wanton intimacy of their embrace left him in no doubt as to the context in which the words had been spoken.

The depth of his revulsion stunned him. He had thought himself way out, liberated, wild. Now, faced with a wife who really *was* way out and wild, his reaction was one of traditional moral outrage.

'Jesus!' he said, his nostrils flaring, the colour draining from his face. 'Jesus *God!*'

Serena turned her head swiftly toward him, her eyes flying wide with alarm. 'Kyle! Please! You don't understand!'

Lance was still on his knees, his arms holding her tight, uncaring of Kyle's presence.

'I sure as hell do understand! If I'd had any brains I would have understood a damned lot sooner! I knew there was something wrong about the relationship between you two! I heard it in your voice every time you spoke his name!' White lines etched his mouth, and a nerve jumped convulsively at the corner of his jaw. 'But I never imagined . . .' His hands had balled into fists. He wanted to kill the bastard, and he wanted to kill Serena too. The marriage service in Bedingham's village church had affected him more deeply than he had ever thought possible. Hell, he had been *happy* to be marrying her again! He had meant the vows he had exchanged with her! But she hadn't meant them. For Serena it had been just another joke, another outrageous experience to add to her long list of outrageous experiences.

'You're being ridiculous!' Serena snapped, her voice edged with panic. She tried to pull herself free of Lance's grasp, but Lance was laughing now, clinging to her as if he never, ever, meant to let her go.

'No! I'm through being ridiculous,' he said savagely, knowing that he couldn't physically assault Blyth-Templeton, that he couldn't bear to have any physical contact with him, not even a blow. 'I'll tell my lawyers to start divorce proceedings immediately!' Unable to bear the sight of Serena's nakedness and Lance's hands on her flesh a moment longer, Kyle slammed the door.

'*Kyle!*' Serena's voice was an anguished shriek. She seized Lance's hands, struggling to break their hold, but Lance was laughing uproariously, hugging her to him, saying jubilantly, 'Let him go! You're free, Serry! Your marriage was a practical joke. Nothing more.'

'*Let me go, Lance!*' she shouted desperately. 'For God's sake . . .' She struck out at him with a white-booted foot and he fell sideways, a look of astonishment on his face. Free of his hands, she snatched at her wedding dress, lifting it up and around her hips, struggling to slip her arms into the sleeves of the tattered bodice as she ran for the door. The corridor was empty. Hysteria rose up inside her. He would go. He had meant every word he had said. He would go, and this time he would not return. 'Oh shit, oh fuck, oh hell!' she sobbed, racing for the stairs.

As she reached them, the chatter and laughter of the wedding guests rose to meet her. There were photographers. Journalists. To race down there, her dress savagely torn and half off her shoulders, would cause a sensation that she, and Bedingham, would never live down. She hesitated only a second.

In another few seconds Kyle would be driving away from her at a criminal hundred miles an hour. There wasn't time for her to go to her room and change her dress; to put on a wrap; to make herself decent. 'Oh, damn you, Lance!' she sobbed, beginning to run down the stairs.

It was her father-in-law who averted a further scandal. Aware that both the bride and groom had deserted their guests, he had walked angrily out of the yellow drawing room in search of them. As he paused in the marble-floored entrance hall to speak to Herricot and to ask if the butler knew where they were, Kyle came leaping down the grand staircase, taking the steps two at a time, his eyes blazing like live coals, his face ashen.

'What the hell . . .' his father began as Kyle forced his way through the wedding guests milling in the entrance, sprinting for the doors and the flight of stone steps leading down to the drive.

Herricot closed his eyes, rallying his strength. There would be worse to come, he was sure of it.

Royd Anderson was just about to set off in pursuit of his son when he heard the sound of Serena's running feet. He turned his head swiftly back in the direction of the staircase and sucked in his breath on a gasp of horror. The bride was hurtling down the stairs towards him, the bodice of her wedding gown ripped, her breasts, in their delicate white lace, half-cup brassiere, exposed.

He heard a cry of incredulity from first one guest and then another, and before every head was turned upward, he sprang for the stairs, racing up them, shielding her from view.

'Let me pass!' Serena shrieked, beginning to push him desperately out of her way.

There was no time for reason. No time for anything but swift restraining action. His fist shot out so swiftly that even Herricot wasn't sure if he had seen right. What he did see, and what the vast majority of guests with a view of the proceedings saw, was the bride crumple and her father-in-law sweep her up into his arms.

'Mrs Anderson has fainted!' he shouted back over his shoulder to the reluctantly admiring Herricot. 'Ask if there is a doctor among the guests, and if not, please telephone for one.'

Herricot's position at the foot of the stairs hadn't been quite as advantageous as Mr Anderson's had been, but he had received the distinct impression, before Mr Anderson had shielded her so masterfully from view, that the bride's clothing had been in a state of alarming disorder. He had also received the impression that Mr Anderson would prefer it if a doctor were not found too speedily. Not, in fact, until the bride could be made presentable.

Kyle never returned to Bedingham. He did exactly what Serena had known he would do. He vaulted into his father's car and drove like a maniac back to London. Four hours later, still glittery eyed and ashen-faced, he was aboard a plane bound for Boston, Massachusetts.

Lance was only a half hour later in following him down the London-Cambridge road. Serena's demented dash in pursuit of Kyle had brought him numbly to his senses. Both his parents and Anderson's would demand an explanation for the abrupt collapse of the marriage, and the disappearance of the groom. There would also be Serry's torn and bloodstained gown to explain away, and the weals on her face and the bruises on her shoulders and breasts.

He didn't for one moment imagine that Serry would tell them the truth, but he was damned sure that Anderson would. He would telephone his father, or his lawyers would make contact. Whichever method he used, Lance knew that he and Serry would be accused of having an incestuous relationship, and that there was a more than likely chance that the accusation would be believed. He had tried to speak to Serena and had failed. A doctor was with her, their parents and Royd Anderson were with her. In a very short while old Herricot would be questioned, and when he was, it would be quickly discovered that Serena had left the yellow drawing room to meet him. Lance had no intention of still being at Bedingham when that moment arrived.

He packed a suitcase swiftly and hurried out of the house, amused to realize that the guests were still apparently unaware of the bride and groom's absence. The giant marquee was still packed with laughing, chattering relations, a band was playing, champagne-laden waitresses were circulating among the groups strolling the lawns, and every inch of carefully maintained grass was covered in a pastel-pink drift of confetti.

Lance gave the scene one last, hate-filled look and then hoisted his suitcase into the rear of his MG. He drove off without a backward glance.

When the doctor arrived, Royd Anderson had persuaded him to sedate Serena heavily. He didn't know what the hell had happened between her and Kyle, but he was determined to try to find out a few hard facts before she gave out any story that would discredit his son or his family. As it was, when she regained consciousness, she steadfastly refused to say anything. Her mother pleaded with her, certain that Kyle Anderson had raped and beaten her. Her father tried to reason with her. Royd, when he finally managed to speak to her alone, flagrantly threatened her. All to no avail. Whatever had happened between her and Kyle remained a mystery, a mystery that wasn't cleared up when, three days later, Kyle telephoned his father from the States.

'I'm at Fort Dix,' he said blandly.

'You're *where*?'

'Fort Dix, New Jersey. It's an army base.'

'I know what the fuck it is!' his father shouted. 'What I want to know is what the fuck are *you* doing there?'

'I've applied to be a pilot candidate in the army. I'm here for basic training, then I go to Fort Polk for a month of advanced infantry training . . .'

'Like hell you do!' Royd thundered. 'What about Princeton? What about your marriage? What about . . .'

'After Fort Polk I'll be sent to Fort Wolters for four months of primary flight training,' Kyle continued, unperturbed.

'No you won't!' The veins in Royd's neck stood out in knots. 'If you want to go into the army, you go in the right way!'

'Which is?' Kyle sounded amused.

'Christ, you're an Anderson! You know damn well which way you go into the army. You go through West Point!'

'No. I'm going in the fastest, easiest way I can, and that means the warrant officer aviation programme.'

Royd felt sick. There were beads of sweat on his forehead and his heart was pumping crazily. 'You can't,' he repeated helplessly. 'That programme is nothing more than a conveyor belt for Vietnam!'

'By the time my training is finished, 'Nam will be old hat.'

'No, it won't be, and you know it!' In his anger and terror Royd had almost forgotten Serena and the fiasco of the marriage. Now he said suddenly, 'What the hell happened here, Kyle? That crazy wife of yours isn't talking. Her brother has taken off again, no one knows the hell where. Her mother's distraught, and old Blyth-Templeton is even more vague and confused than ever.'

There was a slight pause at the other end of the telephone, and then Kyle said tightly, 'She'll be served with divorce papers. That's all anyone needs to know.'

'*Like hell it is!*' Royd bellowed, dollar signs spiralling crazily through his head. 'I want to know *exactly* what happened, exactly what I'm—'

'Bye, Dad,' Kyle said, a rare note of affection in his voice. Then the line went dead.

Royd looked at Serena with loathing. From the moment she had woken from her sedated sleep, she had shown no visible sign of distress, only an icy calm. She faced him now, pale gold hair hanging waterfall straight down her back, the skirt of her minidress barely skimming her buttocks, her fashionable thigh-high boots giving her the appearance of a female Gulliver.

'He joined the army, goddamn you! He's at Fort Dix.'

174

For a second he had the pleasure of seeing utter horror flash through her eyes and then she was utterly composed again, saying coolly, 'I can imagine Kyle as a lot of things, but not as a run-of-the-mill soldier.'

'He won't be a run-of-the-mill soldier,' Royd snarled. 'He's training to be a helicopter pilot.'

Serena returned his glare with composure, tilting her head slightly to one side. 'Yes,' she said thoughtfully, 'it's easier to imagine him as a pilot. He'll enjoy it.'

'He won't damned well enjoy it when he's flying under fire in 'Nam! If he's killed, you'll be responsible! If he comes back with two stumps for legs, you'll be the one to blame!' He saw her flinch and continued viciously. 'He wouldn't be there if you hadn't driven him away! He'd be on his honeymoon, for Christ's sake! He's done this because of you! What the hell happened between the two of you? It was all lovey-dovey when you were receiving the guests. I know *when* the shit hit the fan! I just want to know *why*.'

'The shit hit the fan, as you so graphically put it, when your dumb-brained son put two and two together and came up with a hundred and five.' Despite her outwardly cool appearance, her voice was unsteady and Royd looked at her in astonishment. She looked as if she were about to burst into tears.

'You mean there was a misunderstanding? You mean the whole thing could blow over?' His voice was incredulous.

'Yes, there was a misunderstanding, and no, it won't blow over,' she said, her voice once again under tight control.

'What about the divorce?' he asked bluntly. 'Are you going to contest it?'

He saw her eyes widen fractionally, their smoked-crystal depths darkening. 'No,' she said after a slight pause. 'No, I don't suppose so.'

The fleeting compassion he had felt for her when her voice had trembled vanished. 'You can forget any ideas of a huge settlement,' he said savagely.

She held his gaze steadily, looking vaguely surprised. 'I hadn't thought about the money,' she said truthfully, 'but you've no need to worry. I don't want any.'

Royd sucked in his breath and then turned on his heel, striding away from her. He had no intention of ever seeing her again. He was leaving Bedingham, leaving England. He could not communicate with a woman who said she didn't want any money. Especially one who obviously meant what she said.

Serena was deeply relieved when the Andersons finally left Bedingham. The day after they did, her mother flew down to join friends at Cowes, and her father took off for Scotland, a mound of fishing gear in the rear of his Land-Rover. At long last she had Bedingham to herself, and it offered her a measure of comfort.

That she needed comfort came as a surprise. Their elopement had, after all, been nothing more than a ridiculous joke. But the wedding at Bedingham hadn't been a joke. It had been a profoundly moving experience. And she was sure that she was not alone in that feeling. Though he hadn't said so, she was almost certain that Kyle had been as deeply affected by it as she had been. And now, thanks to Lance's idiocy, it was all over.

She stayed at Bedingham until the end of August and then, when her mother returned from Cowes and her father returned from Scotland, she drove with uncharacteristic soberness back to London. There seemed no fun left in her life now that Kyle had gone. Toby and her host of other friends no longer amused her. By the end of September she had come to the startling conclusion that she was so bored there was nothing to do but look for a job.

'Rupert Carrington is looking for someone to manage his antique shop in Kensington,' Toby said to her helpfully. 'Why not give him a call?'

'I don't know the first thing about antiques.'

176

'Rubbish, darling,' Toby said, amused. 'You live among antiques at Bedingham. A knowledge of them must be in your blood and in your bones.'

Serena nodded thoughtfully. He was probably right. She certainly didn't know much about anything else, and her only other option would be a boutique.

'Right,' she said purposefully, 'selling antiques has to be a more intelligent proposition than selling clothes. I'll give him a call.'

Her call was successful. Rupert's only stipulations were that she should be known by her maiden name and title. As Lady Serena Blyth-Templeton she would, he explained, have decidely more clout where clients were concerned than she would have as plain Mrs Anderson.

By Christmas Serena's life had settled into a moderately satisfactory pattern. She worked three, sometimes four days a week in Rupert's exclusive antique shop, her newfound interest in what she was doing prompting her to enrol in a Sotheby's 'Works of Art' course. She lived her private life as though she were still single, dining with well-born escorts at the Ritz and the Savoy, and dancing until the small hours at Regine's and Annabel's.

Annabel's was her favourite nightspot, and she began to go there with Rupert, sharing late suppers with him, never much before midnight, and always ending with a dish of the club's famous marmalade icecream and a glass of exquisitely sweet Château d'Yquem.

But behind her laughter she was not the same person she had been before her marriage. There were times when Toby caught a look of pensiveness in her eyes. Certainly the old Serena would never have taken her job with Rupert seriously, and not even Rupert had expected her to remain once the initial novelty of being a working girl had worn off.

Her reunion with Lance had been surprisingly easy. He had strolled carelessly into the Chelsea house, his hands in his jeans pockets, his negligent stance and the way he held

177

himself reminding her so much of Kyle that her throat had ached.

'Sorry for being such a stupid fucker,' he had said with a sheepish grin. 'I was a bit over the top, wasn't I? Am I forgiven?'

'Oh, Lance, you *are* a fool!' she had said, walking quickly toward him and hugging him tight, too relieved that everything was once again normal between them to feel angry or bitter.

At the start of the New Year the long-expected divorce papers were served on her, and she was intrigued to discover that the grounds on which Kyle was seeking the divorce were desertion on her part. There was no mention of adultery. No mention of incest. The papers only needed her signature, but she stared down at them for several minutes and then put them, unsigned, in her bureau drawer.

Through February and March she didn't hear a word from Kyle or his lawyers. It was as if he were too involved in his new life to pay enough attention to free himself from her.

'Where is he now?' she had asked her father. 'Still at that revolting-sounding training camp?'

The earl, who was still in contact with Royd, said, 'No, he's just finished his primary flight training at Fort Wolter and now he's at a place called Rucker, or Pucker, or something similar, in Alabama. He'll be there for another three months.'

'And after that he'll go to Vietnam?'

'Yes,' her father replied, looking at her over the top of his glasses in a way that made her deeply uncomfortable. 'After that he'll be in Vietnam.'

At the end of March, 4,400 protestors marched in New York City in an antiwar demonstration. In April Lance was arrested when a demonstration outside the American Embassy in London had broken up in wild disorder. In May he was arrested again. The war had become impossible to ignore. It dominated the front pages of both national and regional newspapers, and every evening the television news was full of scenes of bombing and carnage, carnage that Kyle would soon be experiencing firsthand. At the beginning of June, Serena told Rupert, 'I think I may take off for a week or two. You'll be able to manage if I do, won't you?'

Rupert raised an eyebrow slightly. He rarely set foot in the shop now. Serena handled both sales and buying with such cool panache that he'd left the shop completely to her. They had also begun to sleep together on an increasingly regular basis, and he wondered if she would invite him to accompany her wherever it was she intended to go.

'Yes, sweetie,' he said, and then, as the expected invitation wasn't forthcoming, he added, 'Where will you go? France? Italy?'

'Alabama,' Serena said, enjoying his look of stunned surprise. 'To attend to some unfinished business.'

She booked herself into a hotel in Daleville, which was the closest town to the army base. She had brought the divorce papers with her, signed. If he refused to see her, then she would mail them to his lawyers. But she hoped passionately that he would not refuse.

Contacting Kyle had been difficult. The first morning she had telephoned the base and asked to speak to Mr Kyle Anderson.

'This is the army, ma'am,' a voice had said dryly. 'We have lieutenants and warrant officers, but we don't have misters.'

'Well, he'll hardly be a lieutenant,' Serena said tightly, 'he joined the army only ten months ago.'

'Then it wouldn't be likely, ma'am, would it? May I ask if you are a wife or a girlfriend?'

'Wife,' Serena said succinctly.

It took over half an hour before she was finally told that Warrant Officer Anderson had been contacted and another

179

ten minutes before she heard his voice on the other end of the line.

Shock rippled through her. She had thought herself completely in control of the situation, but at the sound of his voice she knew that where Kyle was concerned, she would never be completely in control.

'Hello there, Warrant Officer,' she said, adopting an exaggeratedly careless tone in order to mask the nervousness she was feeling. 'I was just passing through Alabama and wondered if you'd like to help me break my journey.'

There was a long silence at the other end of the line, during which she died a thousand deaths. Then, to her overwhelming relief, he said, a slight hint of amusement in his voice, 'No one passes through Alabama on their way to anywhere. What are you doing here?'

'I've told you, I'm just passing through.'

'On the week I'm due to leave for 'Nam? A bit coincidental, don't you think?'

Serena felt suddenly sick. 'I didn't know you were due to leave so soon. When do you go?'

'Thursday.'

'Oh!' She gripped the telephone receiver tightly. Today was Monday, or was it Tuesday? She wasn't sure. Transatlantic flights always confused her timewise. 'Does that mean you won't be able to see me?'

This time the silence at the other end of the telephone stretched out. 'I hadn't planned on seeing you ever again,' he said at last. This time there was no amusement in his voice.

'Nor me you,' Serena snapped. 'But 'Nam is 'Nam, and a wife is a wife, and I rather fancied the idea of bidding the warrior good-bye. With your shield or on it, and all that.'

'You mean that the thought of my perhaps not coming back would be a sexual turn-on for you?' he asked with lazy curiosity.

'No! That isn't what I meant at all!' She was so indignant that her pose of careless indifference slipped, and before she could stop herself she was saying, 'I've missed you, goddammit! I want to sleep with you again!'

'Then why didn't you say so?' This time all the old amusement was back, and though she couldn't see him she knew that his eyes were full of laughter and that his mouth was crooked in a smile. 'You called just as I was about to leave camp on a twenty-four-hour pass. Where do you suggest we spend it?'

'Here,' Serena said promptly. 'In bed.'

'Where's here?'

'The Daleview Motel.'

'Okay,' he said with military efficiency. 'I'll be there in forty minutes.'

He was with her in thirty-five. When she opened the door of her room she gasped, her eyes widening. He was in uniform, warrant officer bars and silver wings emblazoning his immaculately cut jacket, his cap worn at a rakish angle. 'Kyle! My God! You look incredible!' She wanted him so much she could barely stand.

Hot, electric-blue eyes met hers, the lazy grin that turned her heart over touching the corners of his mouth. 'You're looking pretty good yourself,' he said, and as he moved forwards to enter the room she stepped towards him, her arms slipping up and around his neck.

His arms closed around her, both the rift and the hideous reason for it temporarily forgotten. God, but she was beautiful he thought. He had forgotten how beautiful. She reminded him of a picture he had seen in a gallery somewhere. It had been of Diana the Huntress, and she had been tall and beautifully boned and splendidly half naked with a look of fearless, wanton daring in her eyes. It was a look he had never seen in the eyes of a flesh and blood woman. Until he had met Serena.

His hands slid down, cupping her buttocks, pressing her in against the rocklike bulge in his pants. She had more style in her little finger than other women had in their entire bodies, and he wasn't going to forgo the pleasure of this unexpected reunion, no matter how loud the voice of common sense yelled that he should.

'Oh, Kyle, I've missed you!' Her voice was low and husky, breaking with need. 'I've missed the sight and smell and the taste of you!'

'How the hell do I smell? You make me sound like a hog,' he said as he lifted her off her feet, striding towards the large double bed in the room.

She giggled throatily, her mouth on his neck, her tongue licking and tasting. 'You smell of soap and sun-ripened lemons and newly baked bread, and you taste . . . Oh, God!' Her teeth gently bit his flesh. 'You taste *wonderful*!'

'Let me taste you,' he said thickly, lowering her to the bed, pushing her brief skirt waist high.

She trembled in delicious anticipation, closing her eyes, winding her fingers through the black silkiness of his hair. She had been faithless scores of times over the past ten months but never once had she experienced the total abandonment that Kyle aroused in her. He confounded her with desire. Convulsed her. Crucified her.

'I love you, Kyle,' she whispered in shocked acceptance of the truth. 'Love you! Love you! Love you!'

Afterwards, their bodies slaked and sheened with sweat, he leaned against the pillows and said, as if their love-making had not taken place, 'Have you signed the divorce papers yet?'

She had been lying beside him, her head resting on the taut flatness of his stomach, her arm flung across his hips. She moved slowly, pushing herself into a sitting position, her hair spilling down over her firm, high breasts. 'No,' she said, 'but I will if you want me to.'

He was looking at her through half-closed lids, remembering. 'Yes,' he said. 'I think it would be best, don't you?'

She pushed her hair back over her shoulder and said hesitantly, 'You were wrong in what you thought, Kyle.

There has never been anything unnatural in my relationship with Lance. What you walked in on was an isolated occurrence. And one that I was not a willing partner to.'

He swung his legs from the bed, walking in splendid nakedness to his discarded jacket, searching in the pockets for cigarettes and a lighter. It was a subject he had vowed not to raise. He had seen what he had seen and he had no desire to have his feelings of revulsion reawakened by useless protestations of innocence. He found his cigarettes and tossed one across to her. 'You weren't exactly crying "Rape" or "Help me!" were you?'

'No, but I had been crying out for him to stop,' Serena said, the throb of truth in her voice. 'And he had stopped. He had come to his senses and he was desperately sorry and ashamed of what had happened and I was comforting him. That was when you walked in on us.'

'Christ! How could you comfort a pervert?' Kyle spat out, lighting his cigarette and drawing hard on it. 'He's your brother, for Christ's sake! How could you even bear to let him touch you after what he had done and tried to do?'

Serena's eyes held his, crystal clear and utterly without guile. 'Because I love him. Not in the way that you assumed. I love him because up till then he'd been the most important person in my life. I love him because in some way that I can't explain there's something vulnerable about him, something that arouses my protective instincts. He doesn't like you and he never will, and he was shocked and distressed by our marriage. What happened between us in the nursery was as much a storm of anger on his part as it was forbidden passion. He apologized to me the very next time he saw me. It was a crazy incident that has been forgotten. I'd like it to be forgotten between us as well.'

Evening sunlight seeped through the drapes into the room. Her fragile-boned, beautiful face was sombre, her hair tumbling down to her waist like a golden, silken curtain. He wanted to believe her. Hell, he almost *did* believe her.

'If you're telling me the truth, why didn't you write me, telephone me, get in touch with me?'

'Would you have listened to me if I had?'

'No,' he said honestly. 'No, I wouldn't.'

'But you believe me now?'

Her eyes held his in perfect steadiness. 'Yes,' he said slowly. 'Yes, I believe you.'

A wide smile curved her mouth. 'Then put your cigarette out,' she said, sliding voluptuously down the pillows on to her back, one leg bent at the knee, the other sprawling wide, 'and come and make up for a stupidly wasted ten months!'

He had done as she had bid, and divorce had not been mentioned again. Four days later, as she sat aboard a plane, bracing herself for takeoff, she opened her handbag in search of a mint and found instead the divorce papers in their battered envelope.

She took them out of her bag, looking at them as the plane screamed down the runway and began to climb.

Kyle would be aboard a troop carrier heading west toward Vietnam. She pressed the tips of two fingers to her mouth, blowing a small, loving kiss in the direction that she fondly imagined the Pacific to lie, and then she tore the envelope in half and in half again and again, letting the small pieces of paper flutter down on to her lap like so many pieces of confetti.

# CHAPTER TEN

For a long time Gavin could only stare into Gabrielle's radiant, glowing face.

'A baby?' he said at last, desperately playing for time. Christ. What was he going to say to her? What in hell was he going to do?

'*Oui, mon amour*.' She slid her hand into his, squeezing it tight. 'I have had my suspicions for a few weeks now, but I am so irregular and I have felt so well. However . . .' She shrugged, grinning impishly. 'Today I thought I would make quite sure.'

'And there's no doubt?'

'No, none at all.' She drew away from him a little, looking at him curiously, aware for the first time that his reaction was not quite what she had expected. 'What is the matter, Gavin? You are not annoyed, are you?' The joy in her eyes had died, and her kittenlike face was suddenly wary. 'You do not wish me to get rid of it, do you, *mon amour*?' she asked, tilting her head a little to one side, the October sun gilding her sumptuous curls.

'No!' His reply was so outraged and emphatic that her eyes lit with laughter again. '*Très bien*,' she said, a husky chuckle deep in her voice. 'Because I would not have done so, even if you had wanted me to. So . . . as you have no objection to me having our baby, perhaps you would tell me why you are looking so unhappy about news that I thought would delight you?'

'I *am* delighted,' he said, wishing that he could take her in his arms and pull her on to his knee. 'Except—' he hesitated awkwardly – 'except I have news as well.'

185

'Oh!' She looked into his face and then slowly leaned back in her cane chair. '*Je comprends*. I understand. You are to go to Saigon?'

He nodded. 'Almost immediately.' He leaned across the metal-topped table, taking both her hands in his. 'Gaby, I . . .'

He wanted to tell her that her news changed everything. That he would no longer be going. But he couldn't. Vietnam was too important. As a journalist he was sickened by reading reports of fighting that had been filed by newsmen who had never left the comparative safety of Saigon, newsmen who did little more than repeat, verbatim, whatever statements were issued to them by the American command.

He wanted to do more. He wanted to get out into the countryside and to report on what he himself saw. He wanted to report the war from the Vietnamese standpoint as well as from the American. He wanted to discover for himself if the American view – that the war was essentially a conflict between Vietnamese and Vietnamese and that America was merely coming to the aid of a democratic government fighting to hold off the forces of communism – was accurate.

The letters he had seen from Nhu to Gabrielle's mother had made him doubt the American argument. If the South Vietnamese government was a democracy, then it was not what he, or many other westerners, would recognize as a democracy. And if westerners were being misled about the true nature of the South Vietnamese government, then what other deceptions were being perpetrated? Whatever they were, he wanted the chance to discover them for himself. And to make them public.

'Gaby, I . . .' he began again, his eyes agonized.

She leaned toward him, silencing him with a kiss. 'I know, *mon amour*,' she said gently as she drew her mouth away from his. 'You must go.' Her eyes were bright with intensity. 'And I want you to go. Talking about Vietnam with you these past few months has made me realize how

186

very Vietnamese *I* am. When I think of home, I think of Saigon, not Montmartre. When I think of my relations, I think of Aunt Nhu and Dinh and my Vietnamese cousins, not of the distant members of my father's family who never visit us or ask us to visit them.'

Grateful for her understanding, love for her swept over him like a tidal wave. For a brief, crazy second he was tempted to tell her that wild horses couldn't drag him from her side, and then she said, her voice unexpectedly fierce, 'Go to Vietnam for me, Gavin. Visit Nhu. Find out if what we are reading in the newspapers and seeing on the television is truth or propaganda. Write about things as they are, not as the Americans would like us to believe they are.'

'There's one thing we must do before I go,' he said, knowing now that he would go. She looked at him questioningly, and he was amazed that the idea had never occurred to him before.

'We have to get married,' he said, enjoying the look of astonishment on her face.

'But it is not necessary, *mon amour*,' she protested. 'Just because there is going to be a baby does not mean that—'

'It is very necessary,' he said firmly, rising to his feet and pulling her up. 'And not because of the baby.' He drew her into his arms, oblivious of the waiter who had come out to clear their table and of the indulgent glances of passersby. 'It's necessary because I love you, Gaby,' he said thickly. 'Because I could never live with anyone else. Because I want you to be my wife.'

She laughed up at him. 'I have never thought of myself as a wife,' she said teasingly but with truth. 'But if you think I'll make a good wife . . .'

'You'll make a wonderful wife,' he said hoarsely, lowering his head to hers, kissing her passionately.

There was not enough time to arrange a church wedding. Gavin was to leave for Saigon on the following Friday and only with extreme difficulty was a wedding arranged at all.

187

The bride wore a simple, hastily bought cream satin dress. It was demurely mid-calf length with short cap sleeves and a satin jacket to match. She wore cream stiletto-heel satin pumps and carried a small bouquet of mixed roses – Gloire de Dijon and pale, flushed Ophelias and tiny, pink-budded Michelle Meillands. There were no guests; her parents served as witnesses and after the ceremony the small wedding party repaired to La Closérie des Lilas in the boulevard Montparnasse for a celebratory champagne lunch.

When they were leaving the restaurant, disaster struck. Gavin, happily intoxicated, turned round to speak to his father-in-law, who was walking a yard or so behind him, lost his footing, and fell awkwardly down the short flight of steps leading to the street.

Gabrielle's first reaction was to burst into laughter, and then she saw his face whiten and tense against the pain, and the ugly angle of his leg as it lay buckled beneath him.

'Gavin! What have you done? Are you all right?' She ran down the steps, kneeling at his side. '*Merde alors!*' she muttered, pressing her gloved hand to her mouth, seeing only too clearly what he had done and knowing that his leg was either fractured or broken. She turned to her father, who was hurrying down the steps toward them. 'An ambulance, Papa! Quickly!'

Turning her head back to Gavin, she saw that the whiteness of his face and the tight, clenched lines of his mouth were occasioned as much by fury as by pain.

'Of all the stupid, fucking *idiotic* things to have done!' he said as she slid her arms comfortingly around him. 'There'll be no Vietnam now! Not with a stupid, fucking broken leg!'

Despite the anguish she felt for his disappointment, she had to repress a smile. It was so unlike Gavin to swear, and his Australian accent, usually so faint that it was mistaken for American or Canadian, was now comically pronounced. 'There will be, *chéri*.' There was such fierce confidence in

188

her voice that despite his pain and disappointment he gave a shadow of a grin.

'Maybe,' he said, wondering who the agency would send in his place. How long would his leg take to heal? And would the agency still consider him as a war correspondent when it was?

'Do you think you can brush some of this confetti out of my hair before the ambulance arrives?' he gasped as the maître d'hôtel and a couple of waiters ran out of the restaurant towards them, uttering cries of concern. 'There'll be so many bad jokes if people realize it's my wedding day.'

She lovingly did as he asked, knowing that as she was still wearing her cream satin wedding dress, everyone would know that it was his wedding day even if she removed every speck of confetti from his hair.

'*Je m'excuse*,' she whispered to him as the ambulance screeched to a halt and her father and the maître d'hôtel shooed away the curious group of onlookers. 'I am so sorry, *mon amour*.'

He clenched his hands and his jaw against the pain as the ambulance driver lifted him on to a stretcher. 'Phone the office,' he said to her tightly. 'Speak to Marsden. Tell him what an ass I've been.'

She carried out his instructions and listened first to an expletive even more colourful than Gavin's had been, and then to a hasty apology. 'How long is he going to be laid up?' Marsden had asked her.

'I don't know,' she said truthfully. 'Perhaps five to six weeks. It might be much longer.'

It was two months.

Gavin devoted most of the time to learning Vietnamese, insisting that when his mother-in-law visited him in the hospital, she speak to him only in her native tongue. In the few days prior to their wedding neither he nor Gabrielle had seen any point in looking for a place of their own, and there seemed no reason to do so now, not until Gavin was

189

discharged from the hospital and knew what the future held for him.

In November, a US airborne division crushed three North Vietnamese regiments in the Ia Drang Valley. Though the engagement cost the Communists nearly two thousand men, and was regarded as a victory by General Westmoreland, more than three hundred Americans died, the majority of them in a single ambush.

'Does this mean that the Americans have gained the upper hand, that the end may be in sight?' Vanh asked bewilderedly. Gavin, still hospitalized, and with his leg in a cast held in traction, shook his head.

'No. No matter how much Westmoreland insists that it was a victory, American parents won't consider it one, not with an entire company of American boys virtually decimated.' His voice was cynical. 'The ratio of a couple of thousand to three hundred might seem to be in America's favour, but American parents aren't going to equate their boys' lives to those of the enemy. The end isn't in sight yet, Vanh.'

He wasn't the only one who thought so. Later that month, Robert McNamara, President Johnson's Defense Secretary, a man who had previously been firmly optimistic about America's role in Vietnam, visited Saigon and was visibly shaken by what he found. The North Vietnamese had begun to infiltrate the south, there was no sign of them halting, or of General Westmoreland being able to curb them. 'The war is going to be a long one,' McNamara bleakly told the reporters covering his visit. 'There is no guarantee of US military success,' and, even more bleakly, he admitted that US troops killed in action were expected to be in excess of a thousand a month.

In December, Marsden promised Gavin that he could expect to be sent to Saigon in June or July, when the reporter who had gone in his place returned.

Cheered by this news, Gavin applied himself to his study of Vietnamese with fresh enthusiasm. He was discharged from the hospital at the beginning of December, returning on crutches to the Mercador apartment, and whenever his father-in-law was absent, he and Vanh and Gabrielle spoke nothing but Vietnamese. His accent was nearly as execrable as his French one, but Vanh assured him that this did not matter. He could now make himself understood in her native language and he could read and write it with passable fluency.

'Which is more than the majority of reporters stationed there can do,' Gabrielle said with satisfaction.

Her stomach had begun to round now, and she was no longer sitting for any artists. She was still singing, though, and Gavin would walk with her to whichever club she was appearing in. He still couldn't walk without a cane, and his persistently heavy limp worried him far more than he dared admit. If he was not one hundred per cent fit by the summer, he knew that the agency would not send him to Vietnam.

At Christmas there had been a faint flicker of hope that the war might end in a negotiated peace. President Johnson had announced a halt to the bombing of the North, a halt that began on Christmas morning. Although the war on the ground continued with as much ferocity as ever, the bombing freeze lasted thirty-seven days. President Johnson sent emissaries to more than forty countries, trying to assure them he was willing to come to terms with the Communists.

The Communists remained unconvinced. A Radio Hanoi broadcast denounced the bombing halt as 'a trick' and said no political settlement was possible until the Johnson administration halted the air raids 'unconditionally and for good'. They did not. On 31 January the bombing raids over the North resumed, and hope for a negotiated peace died. In response, anti-war demonstrations in America and Europe increased in both number and participants.

'Have you been given a firm departure date for Saigon?' Gabrielle asked Gavin one evening as he walked her through the cobbled streets towards the club where she was to sing.

His editor had said June or July and it was now the end of March.

He shook his head, his shock of dark gold hair tumbling low over his brow. 'No.' His arm tightened around her shoulders. He knew what she was thinking. The baby had become more active, disturbing not only her sleep but, as he held her close in his arms at night, his as well. The birth no longer seemed an abstract event. The baby was already a little person who was somehow manifesting his own personality. It was due the second or third week of June, and Gavin desperately wanted to be there when it was born.

In April he was told officially that he was to fly out to Vietnam on 1 June. Relief and dismay hit him in equal amounts. Relief that though he still had a pronounced limp, he had not been replaced, and dismay that he would not be with Gaby for the baby's birth. He knew he would not see his son or daughter for a year, or perhaps even eighteen months.

'Never mind, *chéri*,' Gabrielle said, gallantly hiding her own fierce disappointment. 'We will still be here when you return. And babies are not very interesting creatures. All they do is sleep and eat.'

Her careless dismissal did not deceive him in the slightest. He hugged her tight, determining to speak to Marsden to request that his departure be delayed by at least a month. Gabrielle, sensing his thoughts, pulled away from him, looking up at him with an unusually serious light in her eyes. '*Non, chéri*,' she said firmly, 'you must not do what you are thinking of. They might very well change their minds and send someone else. You have been given the opportunity, and you must take it. *C'est compris?*'

'*Oui*,' he had said, knowing that his French always amused her. '*Je comprends*.' He had pulled her gently against him, kissing her hairline, her temples, the corners of her eyes. '*Je t'adore, ma chérie*,' he had said huskily, lowering his mouth to hers. '*Je t'adore*.'

By May the situation in Southeast Asia was worse than it had ever been. The continual heavy bombing raids over the North had failed to quell the resistance of the North or to bring the North Vietnamese to the conference table.

US Defense Secretary Robert McNamara reported that despite the efforts of American troops patrolling the border areas, North Vietnamese were infiltrating the South at a rate of four thousand five hundred men a month, three times the 1965 level. Because of the savage fighting taking place in the border areas, Vietnam's neighbours, Laos and Cambodia, were finding themselves increasingly in the firing line. Even more ominously, China's border territory was being threatened. The war was escalating.

'It does not help that America has no real understanding of Vietnam or the Vietnamese,' Gabrielle had said bitterly. 'Look at this report in today's *Le Monde*. We are not Vietnamese, we are gooks. That is not just American terminology for the North Vietnamese. It is the way they speak of the South Vietnamese as well. How can there be success when the Americans speak with so little respect of the people they are fighting with and for?'

The most recent letter from Nhu was equally disconcerting. 'The present government no longer has the support that America would like to believe it has,' Nhu had written to Gabrielle. 'Premier Ky may seem to be popular, but his popularity does not run deep. The Buddhists hate him and are doing everything possible to remove him from power.'

She was right. French newspapers were full of reports of fighting in Da Nang and Hue between troops loyal to Ky and other South Vietnamese troops loyal to the Buddhists.

'It is crazy,' Gabrielle had said disbelievingly. 'Not only is the South fighting a war with the North, it's beginning to fight a war against itself as well!'

As Gavin packed his capacious nylon bag, there were reports of Buddhist parades, hunger strikes, and other demonstrations taking place in the city, demonstrations that degenerated into riots as government troops ruthlessly dispersed them with tear gas and bayonets.

Gabrielle wrapped her arms around her now-enormous stomach, despising herself for her sudden cow-hearted desire to plead with Gavin not to go. 'If he is brave enough to go, then I must be brave enough to allow him to go,' she scolded herself. She decided not to read any more newspapers or listen to the radio news broadcasts until Gavin boarded his plane.

The day before his flight he drove her down to Fontainebleau for a last, sentimental lunch at the Hôtel Fontainebleau.

'Take care of yourself, Gaby,' he said, his grey eyes dark with anxiety as their dessert plates were cleared away and the coffee cups were placed on the table.

She nodded and then winced, sucking in her breath sharply. It wasn't the first time that she had seemed to be in discomfort, and he said in deepening concern, 'What is it, sweetheart? Heartburn again?'

'No, I do not think so, *chéri*.'

He took her hand across the table and squeezed it tight. 'I wish to God I could stay with you and be here when the baby comes.'

Gabrielle winced again, and when the spasm of pain had passed, she gave him a small, satisfied smile. 'I think that you are about to have your wish, *mon amour*.'

He stared at her, a comprehension dawning, his eyes widening in disbelief and horror. 'But you can't . . . It isn't due for another two or three weeks . . . We're over an hour's drive from Paris.'

'That doesn't matter, silly,' she said, rising to her feet with difficulty. 'Babies don't come so quickly. Not first babies anyway. We have plenty of time.'

He pushed his chair away from the table, grabbing his jacket. 'Let's go now! Quickly! Can you walk to the car?' He ran his hand distractedly through his hair. Christ! His flight left in seventeen hours. What if the baby hadn't been born by then? He couldn't leave her in the middle of childbirth. It wasn't humanly possible.

The waiter was hurrying toward them and Gavin grabbed a handful of notes from his pocket. 'We have to leave,' he said, thrusting the notes into the waiter's hand, uncounted. 'My wife has been taken ill . . . The baby is coming.'

Gabrielle was grasping the back of the dining chair, her knuckles white.

'Ready, sweetheart?' he asked, sliding his arm around her.

'Yes,' she said as he began to lead her from the room, and then, almost immediately, she stopped, leaning her weight against him. 'No.' She sucked in a deep breath, her hands splayed across the hard, swollen magnificence of her stomach. Her eyes met his, bright with laughter and nervous anticipation. 'I was wrong when I said that first babies don't come quickly, *chéri*. This baby is. It is coming very quickly.' A spasm of pain crossed her face, so intense that he did not need to ask if she was sure.

'Oh God!' he said, looking round wildly for the waiter. 'Oh hell!'

The waiter's eyes were nearly as alarmed as his own. 'A chair, monsieur!' he said, thrusting one of the dining chairs toward Gavin, presumably for Gabrielle's use. 'I will get the proprietor!'

'Get a doctor, for Christ's sake!' Gavin shouted as the laughter left Gabrielle's eyes and she gasped in pain, her face ashen.

The waiter fled and Gabrielle panted. 'My waters have broken. I'm all wet. Can you help me up the stairs? To our usual room?'

He nodded, praying that the room was unoccupied; that a doctor could be found in time; that the baby would be healthy; that Gabrielle would be safe.

They were nearly at the top of the stairs by the time the proprietor came running up to them. He took one look at the size of Gabrielle's stomach and at her face, and squeezed past them, running ahead and flinging open the door of the room they had so often reserved in the past.

'A doctor has been called! Is there anything I can do? Hot water? Extra blankets?'

Gavin looked at him helplessly. He knew that hot water and blankets were customarily called for whenever a birth was imminent but he hadn't the faintest idea why, or what they were used for, and there was already a wash basin and water in the room and plenty of blankets on the carefully made bed. 'Yes. No. I don't know,' he said as Gabrielle seized the doorjamb and leaned heavily against it, sucking in short, sharp breaths.

'Lean your weight on me, Gaby,' he said urgently. 'Let me help you to the bed.'

She did as he said, and to his amazement gave a little giggle. 'Oh, *chérie*! I should have known that I would not have a boring, routine labour!' She broke off, sitting on the edge of the bed, once again panting deeply. When the pain had passed, he lifted her legs on to the bed and she said with impish amusement, 'Do your realize that this is the bed where we first made love, *chérie*? It is possibly even the bed where the baby was conceived. It feels very right that it should be born here.' She broke off again, closing her eyes and clenching her fists.

'Tell me what to do, Gaby,' he said urgently, wondering where the hell the proprietor had fled to; where the doctor was; where anybody was.

'Oh!' She gave a low, deep cry, twisting her head sharply to one side. When she could speak again she gasped, 'Take my panties off for me, *chéri*. Put towels on the bed. The baby is coming. I can feel it!'

He stared down at her, panic racing through him. 'It can't! The doctor isn't here . . .'

She gave a deep, anguished grunt of pain. The sound was primeval and unmistakable: a sound he had never heard before. 'Oh God,' he whispered, knowing that his child was about to be born. The panic faded. Suddenly he felt calm and perfectly in control. Babies that came as speedily as this one was weren't babies who would experience any difficulties at birth. It was going to be all right. It was going to be more than all right. It was going to be wonderful.

'Breathe deeply, Gaby,' he instructed as he pulled her panties down and removed her stockings and garter belt. 'Breathe deeply. The baby is coming! I can see it!'

Her legs were wide, her knees drawn high. There was a sheen of sweat on her face, a look of total, intense concentration.

'Don't push anymore!' Gavin commanded as he saw the crown of the baby's head pulsing inside her vagina. 'Don't push! Pant!'

He didn't know where his knowledge came from. But it didn't matter. All that mattered was that he knew that he was right.

'Try to relax, Gaby!' he urged, squatting down at the end of the bed. Nothing mattered in the whole world but what was taking place between her legs, the awe-inspiring, unbelievable miracle of that pulsing head covered with gleaming dark-gold hair.

Gabrielle gave another deep, primitive groan of pain. She felt as if she were being torn apart, as if the baby were splitting her wide open, wrenching her impossibly wide. 'No!' she cried, and then, as the head crowned, she screamed.

Gavin didn't hear her. He had no sense for anything except the child he was easing into the world. The baby's head was in his hands now, warm and damp. There was a pause. Nothing happened. Gabrielle was silent, panting for breath.

'I think it's time to push again,' he said, not lifting his gaze from the dark gold head he held with infinite care. 'Push for the shoulders to come out, Gaby. But don't push too hard. Gently. Gently.'

The pressure was building up in her again, and nothing in the world could have prevented her from pushing. She

197

was bathed in sweat, almost mesmerized by pain, but above everything she was exultant. The baby was nearly born. It was nearly over. Her sense of triumph was ecstatic. Every muscle in her body bore down. There was a great rush of water between her legs, a slithering sensation and then an overwhelming nothingness. The rock-hard bulge that had been splitting her in two was no longer there. She was free of pain, free of the child that had inhabited her body for nine long months.

'Oh, God,' she sobbed, trying to push herself up against the pillows, trying to see. 'Is it all right? Why doesn't it cry, Gavin? Why doesn't it cry?'

He wasn't listening to her. He was carefully and gently wiping mucus away from the baby's nose and mouth. The umbilical cord was thick and blue, unbelievably knotted. Still the baby didn't cry, and he blew gently on its face. There was a little shudder from the slippery wet body in his hands, and then a little cry.

'Oh, God,' she sobbed again, this time in relief. 'Is it all right? Is it a boy? Is it a girl? Oh, let me hold it, Gavin, please let me hold it!'

For the first time since the baby's head had begun to crown, he looked towards her. 'It's a boy,' he said with a wide, triumphant grin. 'It's a boy, Gaby, and he's perfect!'

There was nothing to wrap the baby in, and he placed it in her eager arms, the wrinkled red flesh still smeared with blood and mucus, the umbilical cord springing from its tummy, its eyes closed, its tiny hands balled into fists as it squalled lustily.

'What do I do now?' he asked, grinning down at them both, tears of joy and relief streaming his face. 'Do I cut the umbilical cord? Tie it off?'

'No,' Gabrielle said firmly. 'You have been magnificent, *mon amour*, but there is no need for you to do anything else. The doctor will be here soon. The only thing I need is something to wrap the baby in so that he does not catch cold.'

He handed her one of the hotel's towels, and together they wrapped it gently around their son. He stopped crying as they did so, snuffling a little and pursing his mouth hungrily.

'This is what he wants,' Gabrielle said with deep satisfaction, baring her breasts and lifting the baby toward them. She guided a nipple into the hungry little mouth and the baby immediately began to suck.

'Clever little thing, isn't he?' Gavin said in wonder.

Gabrielle laughed, her eyes shining joyously as they met his. 'I think the afterbirth is coming away,' she said. 'Have another towel ready. Where is that doctor? It must be hours since he was called.'

Gavin crossed to the wash basin for another towel and looked down at his wristwatch. 'It isn't,' he said, his voice full of disbelief. 'It's only been twenty minutes.'

Gabrielle looked lovingly down at her suckling son. 'What are we going to call him?' They had thought of several names, some French, some Australian, even some Vietnamese, and decided on none of them.

'Whatever you want to call him,' Gavin said, returning to the bed with the towel and spreading it beneath her.

'Then I would like to call him after you, and after my father, and, if you do not mind, after my mother's brother and her father.'

'I don't mind,' he said truthfully, 'but Gavin Étienne Dinh is going to be quite a mouthful. What name will we use?'

'Gavin,' she said unhesitantly. '*Mon petit* Gavin.'

There came the sound of footsteps hurrying up the stairs.

'The doctor,' Gavin said with relief. He looked at his watch again. 'I'm going to have to leave you both in another few hours,' he said awkwardly.

'I know.' Her spicy red curls were tousled and damp with sweat. Except for a smudge of mascara below her eyes, no makeup remained on her face. She looked unbelievably beautiful.

'I love you, Gaby,' he said, knowing that as long as he lived, he would never forget how she looked at that moment, cradling their newborn son. He would remember *always*.

There was a peremptory knock at the door and the doctor strode into the room. Sixteen hours later, as Gabrielle lay in the small, sun-filled bedroom at Fontainebleau, their son in a hastily acquired crib at her side, Gavin sat aboard an Air France 707, flying up and over Paris, heading for Saigon.

# CHAPTER ELEVEN

Lewis had several distinct advantages over the majority of his peers serving in Vietnam. He was there because he wanted to be, not because he had been drafted. And he believed that America's presence in Vietnam was both justified and honourable.

In Lewis's eyes, any country fighting for freedom against the threat of Communist domination deserved financial and military assistance. After serving six months he no longer believed that South Vietnam was the shining democracy that America's propaganda machine liked to depict, but he was damned sure that dictatorial and repressive and full of faults as it was, it was still a hell of a lot better than the government in the North.

Unlike Hanoi, whose avowed aim was the invasion of the South, Saigon had never announced any intention of invading the North, nor had it tried to impose its system of government on to an unwilling people.

In his six months in the peninsula he had witnessed enough acts of barbarism perpetrated by the Viet Cong and the North Vietnamese Army to know exactly why he and his countrymen were in Vietnam. They were there because the South Vietnam government had invited and welcomed them there; they were there because they were helping the South Vietnamese fight for their freedom; and they were there to stem the expansion of world communism.

Besides the advantage of total commitment, he also had other, less obvious advantages. Unlike many of the conscripts, he did at least know where Vietnam was, geographically. He also had a good understanding of the country's history and customs and language. Even rarer, he didn't loathe the country on sight; he didn't regard South Vietnamese civilians with contempt; and he didn't despise the South Vietnamese who fought at his side.

He knew he was lucky. The majority of the Army of the Republic of South Vietnam was poorly trained and poorly motivated. His fellow officers' bitter complaint that the ARVN did not want American help in fighting, but wanted them to fight the war *for* them, was often justified.

His own experience as a military adviser had been a good one. His first assignment had been with the 21st ARVN Division. By the time his six months with them had come to an end, and he had gone on leave in Hawaii, he had nothing but respect for both the South Vietnamese officers of the battalion and the men. They were hard, dedicated fighters it had been a privilege to serve with. On his return from leave, he had learned that he was not returning to the 21st, but instead was being assigned to a MAT team in An Xuyen province.

MAT was short for Mobile Advisory Team. Each of South Vietnam's forty-two provinces had a large American advisory team assigned to it, and, as each province was divided up into several districts, each of these teams was assigned several smaller MAT teams. The teams were based in remote hamlets and villages, and the men assigned to them lived alongside the villagers and rarely came into contact with other army personnel – Vietnamese or American.

Lewis had been specifically trained for this type of environment and he adapted rapidly. He was promoted to the rank of captain and posted to Van Binh as team leader and district senior adviser. His wide-ranging responsibilities for the welfare and military security of the villages and hamlets in his district sat easily on him.

The village where his team was based was deep in the delta, as far south as it was possible to go in Vietnam. The whole area was crisscrossed with canals and ditches, the water gleaming glossily against the dark green foliage of reeds and vines and waist-high elephant grass.

Lewis was glad that his assignment was not the usual GI troop duty. Here in Van Binh he was the most senior officer. There was no one he had to ask permission of before his orders could be implemented. With his four fellow Americans, and with the help of the local Popular Forces platoons, forces made up of trained and armed local villagers, he was able to wage his own private war against the Viet Cong units who used the area as their sanctuary.

Lewis and his men found themselves up against more than just Viet Cong. Although An Xuyen province was eighty miles from the Cambodian border, the North Vietnamese Army regiments operating out of Cambodian sanctuaries used the Delta's vast network of canals to their advantage.

Nearly all the patrols and ambush operations that Lewis and his men undertook were carried out in or on water. Water dominated their lives, although the rainy season, with its nightmare of ceaseless rain and ankle-deep mud, and its attendant miseries of mildewed clothing, damp bedding, sodden cigarettes, foot rot and a dozen other forms of fungicidal infection were now behind them. Lewis came to hate the long hours spent negotiating the canals by sampan, but he never, unlike some of the men under his command, prayed for a posting to Saigon. He had spent three weeks in Saigon at the beginning of his tour of duty, and he had no desire to spend even another hour there.

One of his lecturers at West Point, a man who had spent many years in Vietnam, both before and after the defeat of the French, had told him how beautiful Saigon was, likening it to an elegant French provincial town. By July '66, when Lewis arrived in Saigon, all traces of elegance were fast disappearing.

Tu Do Street, the main thoroughfare that had reminded Lewis's lecturer of a boulevard in Avignon, was now littered with blatantly seedy girlie bars and brothels and massage parlours. American dollars flooded the city, bringing instant wealth to some, and increasing the poverty of others. The number of prostitutes in the city doubled and then quadrupled as girls flocked in from outlying villages, eager for a share of American wealth.

It was the sight of these girls more than anything else that sickened Lewis. The city-born whores were easy to ignore. They were like whores anywhere, tough and professional and more than capable of taking care of themselves. But the eager young girls swarming in from the countryside, lured by the knowledge that a prostitute in Saigon could now make more in a week than her father could in a year, were a different matter. Their delicate-boned faces were still innocent and fresh, their eyes full of nervous appeal as they solicited outside the restaurants and bars and the Continental Palace Hotel and the Majestic and the Caravelle.

Lewis had been approached repeatedly, and each time had vehemently told the girl in question to pack her bags and hightail it back to her village. The only response had been a look of blank bewilderment and then a repeated honeyed request that he take advantage of the services she was offering. After half a dozen such encounters, he had stopped trying, knowing that nothing he could say or do would make the slightest bit of difference.

Whenever he saw one of his fellow countrymen taking advantages of prostitutes' services, Lewis was disgusted. The massage parlours and clubs in Tu Do Street were full of Americans. In some clubs, such as The Sporting Bar and La Bohème, dope as well as sex was freely for sale, and the air was thick with Cambodian red marijuana as fourteen- and fifteen-year-olds draped themselves, topless, around the necks of relaxing servicemen.

Despite the other problems in the countryside, the atmosphere of mercenary depravity was blessedly absent. The village girls dressed and behaved with traditional modesty; there were no small boys busily trying to sell the sexual services of their still smaller sisters and though Lewis knew no one should be trusted absolutely, since there was a great deal of Viet Cong infiltration in the area, he found the village men both courteous and helpful.

Most of the residents were farmers or fishermen. They grew rice in the paddy fields that surrounded the village and they caught fish in the many canals. Apart from this they had very little. There was no running water in the village, no electricity, no sewerage; none of the things that Lewis and his men had always taken for granted. As an adviser it was part of Lewis's responsibility to help the people with development projects. Aid was available, if only people knew how to apply for it. As all the villagers were virtually illiterate, no one had.

Within hours of his arrival Lewis had requested medical aid and educational aid and had asked for everything that there was the faintest hope of getting.

His assistant team leader was a young Texan who was as eager as he was to improve the primitive conditions.

Apart from Lieutenant Grainger there were three northerners in his team. His light weapons specialist, Sergeant Drayton, was from New York State, and his heavy weapons specialist, Sergeant Pennington, and the team medic, Master Sergeant Duxbery, were both from Massachusetts.

As a team they worked well together. The only short-time man, with an eye on his flight home, was Drayton, but even he was committed.

It was while he was with Drayton in the palm-thatched hut that served as their team house that he heard the shouts and screams that introduced him to Tam.

'What the devil's going on out there, *Trung uy*?' he snapped, looking up from the map he had been studying and addressing Drayton by his Vietnamese rank, as was customary.

'Christ knows,' Drayton said, hoping to God they hadn't been hit, and striding quickly towards the open doorway.

There was no smoke and no sign of an explosion. The ruckus was coming from the perimeter of the village, some one hundred yards away from the fortified team house and the huts that served as troop barracks. 'It's nothing, *Dai uy*,' he said, turning back to Lewis with relief. 'Just a local disagreement.'

The screaming had continued, unmistakably female, and furious and raging rather than being full of fear or pain. Village life was as full of marital discord as any American army base for marrieds, but the village women were usually too indoctrinated by the Buddhist precepts of female docility and obedience to protest too strenuously at mistreatment.

'For Christ's sake, can't someone shut that woman up?' he said bad-temperedly, throwing down the pen he had been marking the map with and striding across to the doorway to join Drayton.

'I think some of them are trying to bring her up here, *Dai uy*, and some of them are trying to hustle her into one of the village huts,' Drayton said, leaning against the bamboo frame of the doorway and watching with amused interest.

'I don't want her in here,' Lewis said decisively, knowing that once the villagers milled into the team house there was no telling when he would be rid of them. The agitated group was beginning to move slowly toward them, despite the furiously resisting girl in its midst and the several dissenters viciously tugging her in the opposite direction.

'Looks like someone's wife has been up to a bit of no good,' Drayton said, taking a box of matches and a pack of Camels out of his pocket and settling himself to enjoy the entertainment.

'We're here to fight a war, goddammit, not act as marriage counsellors!' Lewis abandoned all hope of finishing the job he had in hand until the fighting, kicking, and screaming group had been dispersed. 'Come on.' He began to walk across the beaten earth to the approaching melee. 'Let's settle this fracas with a little American common sense.'

Drayton sighed and ground his freshly lit cigarette out under his rubber-soled sandals. They had been up half the night hoping to ambush a squad of Viet Cong rumoured to be bringing supplies in to the local units. Lewis was now mapping out the site for an ambush that he hoped would be more successful.

As soon as the quarrelling villagers saw the two Americans they halted in their tracks, still holding on tightly to the kicking, screaming girl.

Lewis strode up to them. He was wearing only a pair of black pyjama pants and rubber sandals, as he had found the loose cotton clothing that the villagers wore was more comfortable and practical than standard army issue.

'What the hell is going on here, *Em?*' he asked the village headman, addressing him as a brother and a good friend.

The village headman looked unusually nervous. 'This girl crazy, *Dai uy*. That is why we bring her to you. So that you know we do not sympathize with her, or help her. That there are no more crazy girls in our village.'

A slight frown creased Lewis's brow. He had anticipated a marital or parental dispute. The nervous expression in the old man's eyes indicated that there was more to the disturbance than he had originally thought.

Immediately after the old man had spoken, a storm of protest had broken out from the men still trying to tug the protesting girl in the opposite direction. Yes, the girl was crazy, they confirmed, but she didn't need to be brought before the *Co Van*. She needed only a whipping.

Lewis raised his voice over the conflicting shouts, demanding that the girl's father step forward. A man even older than the village headman reluctantly did so, dragging the girl behind him.

'Is this your daughter?' Lewis demanded. The girl was now on the beaten ground, still struggling to free herself of her father's grasp, and of the dozens of other pairs of hands helpfully restraining her.

'Yes, *Dai uy*.' The old man looked as nervous as the headman, and there was something else in his eyes as well. Fear.

He looked swiftly from the girl's father to the headman. In the months he had been in Van Binh he had forged a good relationship with the old man, a relationship that he believed had been founded on guarded mutual trust.

'Why is this girl crazy, *Em*? Why does she need to be whipped?' There was steel in his voice, and the conflicting shouts from the men around them died down. Everyone was waiting and listening. Only the girl seemed unaware of the new tension, continuing to kick and struggle against her captors.

'This girl's brother-in-law is a Viet Cong, *Dai uy*,' the old headman said at last, reluctantly. 'He is not from Van Binh. He is nothing to do with Van Binh. The girl's sister has shamed her family and has run off to join her husband in the jungle. This girl, who is crazy in the head, was trying to follow her.'

Lewis understood the villagers' agitation. Their village was designated as one that was free from Viet Cong control. As such it received special privileges. If it was suspected that there was a Viet Cong infrastructure at work, life would become more difficult for both the villagers and the team.

'Truly, *Dai uy*,' the headman said, his eyes pleading for Lewis to believe him. 'The girl's brother-in-law is not from Van Binh. No one in Van Binh knows him. He sent message to his wife and his wife go into the jungle to join him. No one knows where. Even this stupid girl does not know where.'

Lewis's instincts were to believe him, but he had no intention of relying on instinct alone. There was a good deal of questioning to be done before the matter was closed, but he had no intention of conducting questioning out in the open on the village perimeter.

'You take the girl, *Dai uy*,' the headman continued. 'You punish her. Then you know that our village does not sympathize with Cong.'

Lewis had no intention of doing any such thing. For the first time he turned his attention to the panting, breathless girl. Despite the tangled mat of hair half covering her face, he was surprised to see that she was far younger than he had anticipated, fifteen or sixteen.

'Let her father punish her,' he said, determined to keep the incident on a domestic level if possible.

There was a general murmur of relief from the crowd of interested villagers, and the girl's father beamed toothlessly at him. 'That is what I say in the beginning, *Dai uy*,' he said with a look of defiance towards the headman.

His daughter didn't share in the general relief. Still with her rump on the beaten earth, her knees bent and her bare feet planted firmly in the dust, she glared up at Lewis, her delicate-boned face filthy, her sloe eyes sparking venomously. Then, to the horror of the bystanders, she spat at him.

Lewis's jaw hardened fractionally, and then he gave a nod of dismissal to the headman and turned, striding back towards the team house. Sergeant Drayton remained just long enough to see the girl's father clump her energetically around the head and then, as she was dragged off to her family hut, this time with the full support of the headman, he turned and followed Lewis.

'You shouldn't have let her get away with it, *Dai uy*,' he said, referring to her contemptuous spit. 'Not responding to such an insult will be seen by the villagers as a weakness.'

'Did you get a close look at her?' Lewis asked wearily, hoping to God that there weren't more village women in contact with lovers or husbands who were Viet Cong. 'She's little more than a child.'

'Not in Vietnamese eyes,' Drayton said truthfully. 'Under all that dirt and that mat of hair she was quite a looker. The only wonder is that she isn't married and hauling a couple of kids around with her.'

Lewis grunted, knowing that Drayton was right. She had probably been of marriageable age in Vietnamese eyes for over a year. 'Tell the headman and the girl's father that I want to see them both.' He still believed that his indifferent reaction to her gesture had been the only one possible; any other reaction would simply have made matters worse.

Drayton left again, and spotted Pennington, who was returning to camp after a training session with one of the Popular Forces units. 'Hey, Pennington,' he said, when he reached the other man, 'looks as if Charlie is more welcome in Van Binh that we thought.'

'What the shit is that supposed to mean?' Pennington said after him as Drayton continued to stride away toward the village.

'It means that one of the local belles has a VC for a husband,' Drayton yelled back, turning his head around but not bothering to halt. 'And she wasn't alone in thinking he was the local hero. Her sister wanted to follow the pair of them into the jungle and share in the action as well!'

Richard Pennington stared after him and then shrugged and continued on his way to the team house. It wouldn't have surprised him if the whole damn village was Cong. The villagers smiled, agreed with everything that was said to them, took every dollar that was offered, and left him with the uncomfortable sensation that none of their real feelings had been revealed. Whoever had coined the word *inscrutable* for Orientals hadn't been exaggerating. They were so damned inscrutable that most of the time, at least for a boy from rural Massachusetts, they were incomprehensible.

By the time Lewis finished questioning the headman and the girl's father, he was nearly a hundred per cent convinced that the girl's marriage to a Viet Cong was an isolated instance.

That night he took Sergeant Drayton and Sergeant Pennington and five of the village men out on another attempt to ambush the Viet Cong supply squad rumoured to be trying to make its way through their area.

Lewis was almost certain he'd picked the correct trail, and for seven long, tedious, damp hours they lay in wait at a strategic point along it, tortured by leeches, ants, mosquitoes, and a hundred and one other nameless tormentors, and by the constant drip, drip, drip of the tropical moisture seeping down from the foliage above them.

It wasn't until the first hint of grey touched the night sky, that Lewis began to think that another night's efforts had proved fruitless. Then he heard faint sounds of stealthy movement coming down the track toward them.

'*Cong lai!*' one of the village militiamen whispered urgently. 'The Communists are coming!'

Lewis nodded, pressing his cheek against the stock of his M-16, his finger tightening around the trigger. There was no need for him to give any orders. Each man knew exactly what to do and when to do it. It was going to be a textbook operation.

The slightly built, black-pyjama-clad figures took on shadowy shape and substance. Lewis could hear their laboured breathing, smell their body odours. His excitement grew to fever pitch, he could hear his own heartbeat slamming, could feel his pulse racing. It was an exultancy that he could never in a million years have explained to Abbra, an exultancy that would only increase if the unsuspecting Cong engaged them in a fierce firefight.

'Any minute now, you bastards!' he whispered to himself. 'Any minute now!'

The first of the Cong was now nearly level with him, and he hoped to God that he had judged the positioning of Drayton, Pennington, and the militiamen correctly. If he had, then by now all the Cong trudging in their leader's wake would be in a rifle sight. If he hadn't, then when he opened fire, and the others followed suit, they would come under answering fire from Viet Cong at the rear of the column. He took a deep breath. The barely visible, dark-clad figure leading the column was now abreast of him. Zero hour had arrived.

'Okay, Charlie,' he thought as he positioned the M-16's sight on to the leader's chest. 'It's bye-bye world time.'

His finger tightened on the trigger, and the instant his own volley of shots blasted the man into eternity, Pennington and Drayton and the militiamen opened up on his followers.

It was all over in under a minute. A short and bloody operation that wiped out the unsuspecting Cong while resulting in no injuries to themselves.

'For fuck's sake, *Dai uy*! They really walked into that one!' Richard Pennington whooped triumphantly as they speedily searched the pockets and packs of the dead Cong. 'Bam! Bam! Bam! One after the other. Not even one round of retaliatory fire! Grainger is going to shit himself with envy when he hears about it!'

Lewis grinned, still on an adrenaline high as he sifted through the packs of provisions that the Cong had been carrying. Pennington was right. It had been a dream of an operation.

'He sure as hell is,' he said, knowing that his lieutenant was going to be apoplectic with fury at having missed out on such a trouble-free confrontation.

Fatigue was beginning to set in as the nervous energy of the long wait and the resulting action began to ebb. He distributed the supplies among his men and then ordered them to head back to Van Binh, assigning himself the task of bringing up the rear. There was a slight chance that they hadn't accounted for all the Viet Cong in the supply squad. A chance that, tired and triumphant, they could come under unexpected sniper fire. And if they did, Lewis wanted to be in the position to handle it.

He slept the next day until noon. During the afternoon he made out his report on the night's action, and it never occurred to him to wonder what had happened to the girl who had caused the disturbance the previous day.

During the next two days he sent out a platoon of local men, under Lieutenant Grainger's command, to make a thorough sweep of the area where the ambush had taken place, while he supervised a full-scale medical check of the women and children in the village that his medic, Master Sergeant Duxbery, had been planning.

The operation met with great success. Women and children from nearby villages swelled the ranks of Van Binh's population, all of them queuing patiently in the sweltering heat until it was their turn for Duxbery to examine them.

It was only as Duxbery was coming towards the end of his task that Lewis remembered the kicking, screaming girl who had put the village's loyalty to the South Vietnamese government in doubt.

'Was the sister of the Viet Cong bride a genuine head case?' he asked, not really believing for a moment that she had been, but idly curious.

Duxbery sat in one of the bamboo and thatch village houses that he had turned into a temporary clinic. He looked up at Lewis, his eyes red-rimmed and tired. 'What was the name?' he asked, pulling a sheaf of paper towards him.

'Tam. Nguyen Van Tam.'

Duxbery looked through his list of names and shook his head. 'She's not down here, and the only women still to be seen are the ones who are too old or too sick to make it to the clinic. She wasn't sick, was she?'

Lewis remembered the girl's fierce and energetic struggles. 'No, she wasn't sick,' he said, his brows drawing together as inner alarm bells began to ring furiously. Had he been too complacent about the incident? Too quick to believe that the girl didn't know the whereabouts of her sister and her brother-in-law? The thought that there might be more than one village girl with knowledge of the local Viet Cong's whereabouts, and who was more than willing to keep slipping away from the village with information for them, was not a pleasant one. Still frowning, he strode quickly out of the makeshift clinic and went in search of the headman.

The headman was beamingly reassuring. 'The girl is still in the village. How could she run away when neither

213

she nor anyone else knows where the local Viet Cong camps are?'

'If she's in the village, why didn't she attend the medical inspection?' Lewis demanded.

'She is still being punished, of course.'

'Let me see her,' Lewis demanded suspiciously, no longer trusting a word that was being said to him.

The headman nodded obligingly, leading the way down the single village street toward one of the closely packed bamboo and thatch houses that backed out on to a canal.

'She is there, *Dai uy*,' he said with flourish of pride, indicating a darkened doorway. 'Her father punish her very, very good.'

Lewis bent his head down to enter the house, and was almost immediately overcome by the stench of stale sweat and vomit. A middle-aged female figure sitting just inside the doorway rose with a cry of alarm as he entered.

'It all right,' Lewis heard the headman saying to her as she fled outside, 'the *dai uy* just wants to see how your foolish daughter has been punished.'

The interior of the hut was so dark that for a few seconds Lewis could see nothing. When his eyes adjusted to the dim light he saw only too well, and what he saw he didn't believe.

The girl was lying, half-naked, on the floor, her wrists manacled together with bamboo and secured to a stake driven in the ground. But it wasn't the sight of her bound wrists that filled him with horror. It was the blood-encrusted weals that scored her back and buttocks.

'Jesus!' he spat out, sucking in his breath and striding quickly across to her. She was barely conscious. Her lips were dried and cracked and he could see no sign of a water jar.

*'Can you hear me?* ' *he asked urgently.* '*Can you speak?*'

A swollen eyelid flickered open. The tangled mat of her hair was even thicker now, stiff with dried sweat and flecks of blood.

'*Di di mau*,' she whispered hoarsely. Added to Lewis's feelings of horror and revulsion and concern, was a tug of amused admiration. Loosely translated, what she had said was, 'Get the hell out of here.' It was a strong language for any rural Vietnamese girl, and unheard of language for anyone to be using to an American who was not only a *dai uy*, but a *co van* possessing life-and-death powers.

'I'm going to take you to the *bac-si*,' he said, taking a knife from his belt and slicing through the bamboo. *Bac-si* was the Vietnamese word for doctor and the title that the villagers gave to Master Sergeant Duxbery. The girl closed her eyes again, muttering a word that was barely intelligible but which Lewis was certain was grossly insulting.

Arranging the scrap of dirty blanket that covered her as strategically as possible, he lifted her up in his arms, carrying her out into the fierce sunlight.

When he emerged, the expression on the headman's face changed from one of beaming complacency to one of alarmed concern.

'What is the matter, *Dai uy*?' he asked anxiously. 'Why do you look so angry?'

'Did you know what had been done to her?' Lewis asked, white-lipped. 'Was it on your orders?'

'No, no, *Dai uy*.' The headman hurried at his side as Lewis made his way up the village street toward the hut where Master Sergeant Duxbery was seeing the last of his patients. 'Your orders. The girl was to be punished by her father. You said so.'

Lewis swore viciously. 'For Christ's sake! I didn't mean she was to be beaten to death!'

The headman gave a slight shrug. The *dai uy* had chosen not to punish the girl himself. No one could be blamed if the girl's father had punished her in a way that displeased the *dai uy*. It was the *dai uy*'s fault. He should have carried out the punishment himself.

'Bring her father to me!' Lewis ordered, hating himself for not foreseeing what would happen; hating the primitiveness of the society that allowed such things to happen; hating, for the first time since he had set foot in it, the whole damned fucking country.

'You found her,' Jim Duxbery said unnecessarily as Lewis entered the hut. He eyed the savage whip marks on the girl's back as Lewis laid her as gently as he could on the table. 'It appears that parental discipline is a little heavy-handed in these parts,' he said dryly, reaching for a bottle of hydrogen peroxide.

'You're fucking right it is!'

Jim Duxbery looked across at Lewis with interest. Ellis was that rarest of breeds, a professional soldier who very rarely resorted to foul language.

He saturated a swab with the peroxide and said briefly, 'This is going to sting like the devil, but it's the only antiseptic I have.'

As the peroxide touched her flesh, beginning to bubble, the girl let out an agonized cry, her eyes flying open.

'It's to stop the cuts on your back from becoming infected,' Lewis said to her, taking hold of her hands and gripping them hard. 'Hold on to me. It won't hurt for long.'

For a minute he thought she was going to drag her hands contemptuously from his grasp, and then Duxbery began to swab the weals in earnest and she moaned, digging her nails into his palms.

'When this is over, I want you to come up to the team house,' Lewis said to her in Vietnamese. 'I want you to be our cleaning girl.'

Jim Duxbery looked at him, his eyebrows rising slightly. They already had a cleaning woman. She wasn't a day under fifty and her teeth were blackened with betelnut. It had long been a source of contention with the team that Ellis had hired such a crone when there were lots of pretty village girls that he could have chosen.

'No,' the girl whispered hoarsely, shaking her head vehemently.

Lewis dismissed her refusal. 'It wasn't a request, it was an order,' he said brusquely. He knew that if she came up to the team house every day, no one would dare to lift a hand to her.

'No!' Vainly the girl tried to pull her hands free of Lewis's comforting grasp. 'No, no, never!'

Lewis swore. He was sure that if he returned her to her home, another beating, this time to punish her for attracting the *dai uy*'s attention in such a way, would soon follow.

He explained all this to her, but her only response was a sullen silence and a firm shake of her head.

'She won't come,' Jim Duxbery said, cleaning the last of the hideous blood-encrusted cuts. 'If gentle docility is a natural characteristic of Vietnamese women, then this girl is the most uncharacteristic Vietnamese girl I've ever met.'

'She'll come,' Lewis said grimly. As the peroxide bottle was put away and Jim began to apply salve to the festering weals, the girl determinedly pulled her hands free of his.

Reluctantly, he did not restrain her. There was something about her that intrigued him, something that attracted him as he had been instantly attracted to Abbra. He wondered if it was because, in some curious way that he couldn't define, she reminded him of Abbra. As soon as the thought came into his head, he dismissed it as ridiculous. How could she remind him of Abbra? She was an illiterate, dirty Vietnamese peasant. And yet there was something about her . . . the defiant tilt of her jaw and the uncompromising light in her eyes.

'*Dai uy*.' It was the first time she had addressed him with any semblance of politeness. She had pushed herself up on one elbow, facing him, her dark eyes suddenly speculative. '*Dai uy*, I will come to the team house as a cleaning girl on one condition.'

It was going to be money, of course. A spurt of disappointment surged through him. For some insane reason

217

he had been sure that the girl, despite her obvious hatred toward Americans, was not mercenary.

'What is the condition?' he asked, wearily taking a pack of Winstons from the pocket of his tiger-stripe fatigues. 'That you teach me English,' she said. As her eyes fearlessly met his, he knew what it was about her that reminded him of Abbra. She was not only vital and strong-willed. She was also, beneath the grime of sweat and dried tears, exceptionally beautiful.

He knew damned well why she wanted him to teach her English. She would be of great value to the Cong if she could serve them as an interpreter.

'*Khong xau*,' he said, determining to so successfully win her heart and mind for the South Vietnamese government that she would forget all ideas of running away and joining the Cong. 'Okay. No sweat.'

He grinned suddenly. Not only was it going to be easy. It was also going to be fun.

# CHAPTER TWELVE

Kyle was on the longest, most mind-bending high he had ever experienced. It was better than alcohol, better than drugs, better than sex. It was combat high, and after six weeks in 'Nam he was drunk on it.

He had been assigned to a company of the Assault Helicopter Battalion, 1st Cavalry Division (Airmobile). Their base was on the perimeter of the Central Highlands, where there had been heavy fighting ever since the vicious Ia Drang Valley battle, six months before.

For the first two weeks he flew only routine flights, ferrying commanding officers to neighbouring units in Pleiku and Qui Nhon. Nothing he saw or experienced made him sorry he'd volunteered. The countryside was lush and dramatic, dense jungle interspersed with soaring, gleaming ridges of rock. He loved skimming low over them, clearing them with only feet to spare, flying the Huey over the jungle canopy with the same measured recklessness with which he had driven his Ferrari.

The women were another reason for signing up. They were all beauties, slender and fragile-boned and, according to his buddies who had been in 'Nam for a while, universally willing. Regrettably, he had not put the truth of their statements to the test. Saigon, with its bars and clubs, was 260 miles away to the south, and though some lucky bastards had been detailed to fly down there on administration flights, and had enjoyed overnight stays there, Kyle had pulled nothing more exotic than quick, celibate daytime trips to Pleiku and Qui Nhon.

On his third week in-country he had his first taste of flying troops in to a landing zone. He and Chuck Wilson, his copilot, were to fly to Yan Len in formation with sixteen other Hueys and four gunships. When they had dropped the troops at the scheduled landing zone, they were to fly back to a cold landing zone some distance away and stand by until radio contact instructed them to make a pickup.

'It's going to be a walkover,' the experienced Chuck said nonchalantly.

Kyle grinned, a flicker of excitement twisting deep in his gut. He didn't want it to be a walkover. He wanted it to be adrenaline-packed hassle. After all, that was what he was here for. To walk on the wild side and to live dangerously. Anything else just plain sucked.

The early morning sun was fierce in his eyes, sweat already staining his fatigues as the signal to crank up was given. He slipped on his sunglasses and clicked on the intercom.

'Ready?' he asked the crew chief and the gunner, and on receiving their affirmatives he rolled the throttle open. The starter motor whined, the rotor blades began to accelerate, and then the turbine caught. Slowly Kyle pulled the collective up, and the heavily burdened Huey rose, climbing laboriously above tree level as it closed up in formation with the other three ships in the squad.

The elation he experienced at being airborne surged through him. Flying in close formation, he would have no opportunity to do any of the acrobatics that he loved, flying fast and close to the ground with only a couple of feet between the treads and the treetops, or executing wild, ship-shaking U-turns that terrified whoever he was flying with half to death, but there would be compensations.

Although Chuck had predicted the mission would be a walkover, it was more than likely that they would meet with enemy fire when approaching the landing zone. And it would be Kyle's first time. His heart began to race, his nerve ends tingled with anticipation. For the first time since he had been in 'Nam, he found himself thinking of Serena. It was a crazy time to be thinking of anyone or anything besides the job at hand, but he knew why she had suddenly sprung into his thoughts. Her heedless, reckless nature would have responded to the dangers of 'Nam just as hungrily as his own.

He grinned to himself as they neared the landing zone, and he slowed the Huey down from 100 knots to 80 knots so the gunships could fly ahead. Hell, but she would have made a great chopper jock. She was certainly a great lay. It was even possible, when his tour of duty was over and if she didn't send back the divorce papers, she would make a great wife.

White smoke streamed behind the gunships ahead of them as they peppered the landing zone with flex gun and rocket fire. He hoped she wouldn't return the divorce papers. The fun they had together was too mind-blowing to be thrown away. His grin deepened. Christ, if he wasn't careful, he would be metamorphosing into an adoring husband!

'Close up,' Chuck said tersely over the intercom, breaking into his thoughts.

Kyle acknowledged, closing the distance between the Huey and the gunships, and dropped lower.

'Clear to use gun doors! Clear to use gun doors!' his flight leader radioed from the leading Huey.

As the Huey lost height, the rotor pitch changed and the noise deepened to an ear-splitting whine. They were only three hundred feet from the ground now, and a bare quarter of a mile from the landing zone. Kyle felt his stomach muscles tighten. The landing zone was hot. There was enemy fire as well as the blasting fire from the gunships.

'When do our gunners get the okay to fire?' he yelled across to his twenty-three-year-old senior.

'Now ought to be about the right time,' he said laconically, flicking on his intercom.

They were only a hundred yards from the landing zone. Kyle could see the gunners in the Hueys ahead of him, blasting down into thick bush. He wondered how the hell they

221

could see what they were firing at. Rockets were pounding the ground, shooting earth scores of feet into the air. The white smoke from the gunships was barely discernible now among the swirling coloured smoke that identified the centre of the landing zone, and the dense black and grey plumes of artillery and rocket fire.

'It's a hot LZ, guys,' Chuck said unnecessarily over the intercom to the troops about to disembark, and then, to the door gunners, 'fire at will.'

Kyle's hands were slippery with sweat on the control stick. The pilots of the Hueys ahead of him were reporting that they were taking enemy fire. He knew it hadn't been expected. The operation had changed character. They were flying into enemy fire, and he didn't envy the troops about to disembark one little bit.

They were losing height rapidly now, the tail rotor spinning just a few yards from the ground. Chuck's hands joined his on the control stick, army regulations in case one of them was hit. The door gunners behind them were giving it all they'd got, the noise from their guns deafening, the reverberation decidedly disconcerting.

'Jeez!' Kyle exclaimed beneath his breath, the blood hammering in his temples as bullets smashed into the Huey's airframe. He began to decelerate rapidly, the Huey's nose rising steeply to slow its forward motion. As he hovered some three feet from the ground, about to land vertically, the troops began to leap to the ground, racing for cover, firing as they went.

Sniper fire was raining in on them, a pilot in one of the other Hueys was hit, and the last of the troops had sprung to mother earth before the skids had even made contact with it. Fear and exhilaration, equally mixed, surged through Kyle's veins. This was reality. This was the big time. At any second the ground fire could blast the Plexiglas chin bubble under the Huey's nose, or destroy the instrument panel or slam into his own unprotected body, winging him on his way to eternity.

Over the intercom the order came for him to go. He didn't need telling twice. The other choppers around him were all dipping their noses in unison as they picked up airspeed, the gunships still darting and swooping above them as they gave covering fire. The downdraft from the rotors riffled the tall grass beneath them; the air was heavy with the smell of cordite, thick with smoke.

The Huey gained height, whirring up above the tree line, the door gunners still blasting away into the bush beneath them. Kyle pressed back on the control stick and began to climb to cruising height and the chatter, chatter, chatter of the guns ceased.

It was over. They were flying to a standoff position and they hadn't been hit. He hadn't screwed up. Wilson hadn't had to take over.

He did so now. 'I got it,' he said over the intercom and then, dryly, 'I told you it would be a walkover.'

Kyle clicked off his intercom and let out an exultant whoop. It hadn't been a walkover, but it had been the most mind-blowing few minutes of his life. He was drenched with sweat, bathed in it. He clicked on his intercom again, so keyed up with adrenaline that he couldn't wait for the moment when they flew back in. 'For a walkover, it was pretty hip,' he said with a grin.

Chuck banked to the left to keep in formation and shot him a pitying look. 'You won't think so in another few weeks,' he prophesied darkly, 'not after you've flown a few dust-off missions.'

'How did the medical rescue missions get the name dust off?' Kyle asked curiously.

'Rumour has it that it was the call sign of one of the first medevac pilots to be killed,' Chuck replied, levelling out and cruising at twelve hundred feet, high enough to be out of the way of any stray ground fire but low enough for a quick descent to the cold landing zone they were fast approaching – where they were to laager, or stand by.

223

They didn't have to wait long before they received a radio call instructing them to return and pick up. This time Chuck took the controls, Kyle assisting him when tracer fire streamed past them and the Hueys descended to the landing zone, door gunners firing like a swarm of predatory dragonflies.

It was hairier picking the troops up than it had been disgorging them. This time the Huey had to make a firm landing, its rotor blades beating the air as men raced across the clearing to scramble aboard.

Kyle could see one running figure fall, and then another, both of them hauled to their feet by their companions and half dragged, half carried to the Huey's open doors.

Over the radio came the order to power up, and Chuck rotated the throttle, watching the gauges, then the order came to lift off, and as Kyle watched a black-pyjama-clad figure burst from the bush, racing towards them, a grenade in his hand, the order came to go.

As they did so, picking up airspeed, one of the door gunners hit the figure running in their wake. There was a violent explosion, a billow of dust, and then the Huey swung up and over the trees edging the clearing, and the black-pyjama-clad figure was no longer discernible. All he could see were scraps of black cloth blowing in the downdraft.

During the next few weeks such missions became routine though not all of them were into hot landing zones. Many were straightforward drop and extraction missions, as unexacting as a courier or an administration flight. Others were not so pleasant.

The first time he had had to fly back to base with a load of bloodstained canvas body bags aboard he had nearly puked. Unseen arms and legs poked stiffly and grotesquely at their coverings. Even worse were the bags that looked half empty. Just a trunk being delivered back to base for shipment home. He remembered the army's proud boast that any man wounded would be hospitalized, by chopper, within twenty minutes, and the promise that serious injuries would be flown to Japan within twelve hours. He gagged at the stench rising from the bags. The army had forgotten to add that any man killed would be home in a week.

A month after his arrival he finally drew a coveted three-day stopover in Saigon. It was a maintenance trip and he was to fly his Huey down to Tan Son Nhut air base so that it could be overhauled at the big depot there. His copilot was Chuck Wilson.

'Seems like the army doesn't want you out of my sight, Anderson,' he had said with affected weariness.

Kyle had grinned. He liked Chuck Wilson. He had a sophisticated, laid-back, world-weary attitude to the war that he himself liked to assume. At twenty-three Chuck was the old man of the outfit, a possessor of three Purple Hearts, and on his second tour of duty. Kyle couldn't help wondering what he had been like before 'Nam. When he had been young.

'Maybe they figure you're too old to totter around the big city by yourself,' he said, itching to be in the Huey's cockpit, winging his way south.

'And maybe they figure that you're not going to live too long unless you start treating your seniors with a little more respect,' Chuck said, cuffing his ear.

The flight down to Saigon was great. The country they were flying over was mainly Viet Cong territory, so they flew high, at a cool five thousand feet.

'What made you up for another tour of duty?' Kyle asked curiously over the intercom as the coast flashed into view and they neared the city.

He knew that Chuck must have volunteered. With three Purple Hearts, he never had to serve in 'Nam again.

A faint smile tugged at the corners of Chuck's mouth. He had wondered when Kyle would ask. 'Because if you're sane, you hate the 'Nam with every single cell that's in your body, and if you're insane, you get hooked on it.'

They were over the city now, and it looked as if it was going to live up to all the names it had been given in the past. Pearl of the East. Paris of the Orient. It lay beneath them, a panorama of long, wide avenues flanked by tamarind and lime trees; spacious, lushly green parks, delicate, pink-stuccoed houses; the Saigon River winding its way sensuously through its centre.

Chuck's smile broadened. 'I got hooked.'

Kyle began to decelerate as they approached Tan Son Nhut and the rotor pitch changed, the noise deepening as they lost airspeed. 'I know,' he yelled back, the Huey responding beneath his hands as smoothly as pure silk. 'I'm hooked as well!'

'There's a word for it,' Chuck said, and this time he wasn't smiling. The tone of his voice made the hair on the nape of Kyle's neck stand on end. 'It's psychotic.'

From the ground Saigon was not the flawlessly elegant city it had appeared from the air. It was still possible to see how graciously French it had once been, before the hundreds of bars and clubs and strip-joints had opened. But the freshness and charm it had once possessed had been destroyed forever.

'You're the one who knows his way around,' Kyle said exuberantly, relishing the sensation of being let loose after a month's captivity. 'Where do we hit first?'

They had left the Huey at the maintenance base and hopped a cab to the central square, two blocks down Tu Do Street. 'We check into somewhere decent,' Chuck said, paying the driver off and leading the way across the square. 'Somewhere with hot baths, clean beds, and a decent bar.'

'And that is?'

'Here.'

They were outside the four-storeyed European splendour of the Continental Hotel.

Kyle gave a whistle of appreciation. He liked the way Chuck did things. It was the way he had always done things himself.

'Isn't this where Graham Greene is supposed to have written *The Quiet American*?'

226

'The very place,' Chuck said as they strolled across the lobby to the reception desk. 'He wrote it on the terrace, and there's always a hyped-up journalist sitting there, reading it.'

The room they were given was enormous. 'How come we get the VIP treatment?' he asked, impressed.

'The proprietor is a personal friend,' Chuck said, strolling across to the windows and looking down into the square. 'And for a friend he'll always find a room, even if it means throwing someone else out!'

Kyle began to take off his sweat-soaked shirt, making a beeline for the shower. 'Give me five minutes and then I want a tour of Tu Do from beginning to end!' he shouted, turning the water on full blast.

It was a tour that was still only half completed nine hours later, when the city's curfew forcibly curtailed it. First they had descended on the bars. In the Sporting Bar, packed with Green Berets, Kyle had become happily drunk. In the Bluebird he had been delighted to find that ready-rolled joints were easily available, being dispensed on demand from a jar beneath the counter.

Weaving their way out of the Bluebird, they had made their way to La Bohème, where the girls paraded in see-through dresses and descended on them like a flock of vultures, taking their hands and thrusting them strategically down their dresses and up their dresses, cooing, 'You buy me Saigon tea?'

Kyle had grinned. If Saigon tea was what it took to get on even friendlier terms with the ladies of the town, then he was quite prepared to buy it until it ran out of their ears.

'I think this is where we split for half an hour,' Chuck had said with a wink, a golden-skinned beauty draped around his neck.

Kyle had been only too happy to agree. His only sexual outlet since he had arrived in the country six weeks earlier had been the near orgasm he experienced when flying the Huey fast and low in and out of combat zones. 'Come on,

227

baby,' he said to the girl who had claimed him by the simple and effective expedient of clutching his balls. 'You've got a customer. Lead the way.'

Half an hour later he and Chuck had staggered into the nearby Melody for a reviving bourbon.

'This is a journalists' bar,' Chuck had said, heaving himself on to a bar stool. 'It's a good place to come if you don't want to be harangued by Green Berets telling you how they could win the war single-handed if it wasn't for the ARVN.'

'Lucky journalists,' Kyle said, looking around him. The girls were prettier and fresher-looking than the girls in La Bohème, and he was beginning to wish that he had saved his strength.

'Stop crying into your bourbon,' Chuck said, reading his mind. 'We'll call back here later on. After we've eaten.'

It was dark now and Tu Do was packed with off-duty servicemen looking for a little recreation. Neon lights glittered out the names of the bars and clubs. Denver, Cincinnati, Arc en Ciel, Maximos, La Pagoda, Joe Marcel's, Bong Lai, Chicago. The music reverberating out of the ultraviolet-lit depths was a pulsating cacophony of Jimi Hendrix, James Brown, Wilson Pickett, and the Temptations.

They dined at the Blue Diamond, ordering sweet and sour pork and drinking more bourbon. Afterwards they strolled unsteadily across to the Maximos, avoiding the heavily congested traffic with difficulty. It seemed to Kyle that every South Vietnamese in the country was the proud owner of a Honda or a Yamaha or a 50cc Suzuki, and that all were intent on mowing down anyone or anything that got in their way. Cabs fought for road space, horns blaring. Jeeps blasted their way through, seeming to care even less for the rules of the road than the cyclo riders. There was not the slightest attempt to control traffic. It was every man for himself, and the devil take the hindmost.

The next morning Kyle couldn't remember whether they

228

had returned to the Melody or not. Chuck assured him that they had, and that they had bought enough Saigon tea to float a tanker.

They breakfasted at the Continental, huge ceiling fans creaking noisily above their heads, the heat already oppressive.

'Well, we hit half of Tu Do Street pretty thoroughly last night,' Chuck said, drinking his third cup of black coffee. 'What does the little tourist boy want to do today?'

'Hit the other half.'

Even at eleven in the morning Tu Do was crammed with streetwalkers, pimps, children selling cigarettes, and trucks and jeeps and a thousand bikes.

'Christ!' Kyle yelled, leaping to safety as a little four-door Renault taxicab nearly mowed him down. 'I was told this city was the Avignon of the East! Avignon, my ass! It's more like New York City when there's a subway strike!'

They had begun drinking in the Sporting Bar. 'These guys are a gas,' Chuck had said, referring to the Green Berets. 'To hear them talk, you'd think they were God's own!'

The ceiling fans above the bar were more efficient than the ones at the Continental, and Kyle began to feel relatively comfortable. It was impossible to feel cool. That morning sweat began to darken his fatigues before he had even finished putting them on, and he had long ago vowed that no matter how bleak a Boston winter, he would never crave the sun again. He downed his third beer, his sense of well-being increasing.

'You guys Air Cav?' a powerfully built Green Beret asked, peering at the horse patch on Kyle's fatigues.

Kyle nodded, draining his glass.

'What's the matter with you guys, don't you have no bar of your own to go to?' the Green Beret grumbled.

Kyle grinned. 'If we do, I haven't found it yet.'

229

The Green Beret belched. 'Jeez. You a new guy? How many days you got left in 'Nam? Three fifty-eight? Three fifty-seven?'

'Three twenty-three,' Kyle said, unperturbed.

'Jeez,' the Green Beret repeated sympathetically. 'Your poor mother. I'm short. I've got nineteen days left. Nineteen and then I'm on that big silver bird back to the world!'

'Air Cav,' the guy sitting next to them said derisively. 'What do the fucking Air Cav know. You two chopper jocks?'

Kyle nodded while Chuck continued to drink his beer as if no conversation were taking place.

'What the hell! Fly in, fly out. Hot showers at night, clean sheets, orange juice, Coke, and American apple pie. What the fuck do you guys know about sleeping in the jungle with a million bugs for weeks on end, about having your feet in paddy fields so long they begin to rot, about not being able to take a step without wondering if you're going to set off a booby trap that will blow your legs in front of your face, or a hole in your chest they could drive a truck through. What the fuck' – he was yelling now – 'do you guys know about fighting a cocksucking war?'

Kyle didn't answer. Watching from the Huey as he offloaded troops into jungle scores of miles from the nearest base camp, knowing that they were setting off on patrols into Viet Cong territory that would possibly last for days on end, he had often wondered the same thing.

His war bore no relation to their war. His war was flying hundreds of thousands of dollars of steel and Plexiglas with all the skill and recklessness and panache of a First World War flying ace. It was the sexiest thing he had ever experienced. To Kyle, a Huey was the last word in glamour. He loved to see them flocking back to base like great, silk-black birds of prey. He loved their speed, their manoeuvrability, their sheer, goddammed eroticism. Chuck answered the savage questioner for him.

'I know that statistically one in five of us is going to end up dead,' he said conversationally, still hunched over his drink and not bothering to turn his head.

There was a slight, ominous silence. Although neither Chuck nor Kyle were built on the bull-like lines of the men on either side of them, they both possessed the air of dudes who, in Green Beret parlance, definitely had their shit together.

'Let's give the guys a break,' the first Green Beret said magnanimously, too hot to want to brawl with the Air Cav. 'What are you drinking? Jeez. Why don't we make a party of it?'

They did so, spilling drunkenly out from the Sporting Club two hours later, arms around each other's shoulders as if they'd all been buddies since first grade.

'How about a little fem-i-nine company?' The Green Beret who had initially been belligerent was now as friendly as a pussycat.

'I need to stop by the International and pick up some more dough.' His buddy hiccuped. He turned unsteadily towards Chuck and Kyle. 'You staying at the International too? The officers' club at the International serves the best rare sirloin and baked potatoes with sour cream this side of the Brooklyn Bridge.'

Kyle had long ago guessed that the Continental's fading splendour catered mainly to journalists and civilians, and that staying there wasn't normal for US military personnel. 'Sure,' he said agreeably, 'wouldn't think of bunking down anywhere else.'

By the time they reached the International, Kyle was so affected by the numberless beers and bourbons he had drunk that he could hardly stand. He staggered past the military police at the door, wishing to God that the jerk they were with would hurry up and pocket his dough so that they could hit the street again and find themselves some girls.

The guys back at camp had been right when they said that all Vietnamese girls were more than willing. Christ,

231

he'd enjoyed himself last night almost as much as he had with Serena.

There was a girl behind the desk in the lobby. The prettiest, sweetest girl he'd ever seen in his life. Jet-black hair flowed straight down her back. Her sloe eyes were thick-lashed and lustrous, her nose as cute as a kitten's, her mouth smiling and inviting. She wasn't wearing one of the short, ill-fitting miniskirts that the girls he had seen the previous night had worn. She wore the most feminine dress he had ever laid eyes on. It was a high-necked ankle-length tunic slit to the waist over loose silk pantaloons. There wasn't an inch of flesh showing, and yet it was a hundred times more arousing than the see-through dresses that the girls had worn in the La Bohème.

'Oh, boy,' he said beneath his breath to Chuck. 'Am I going to get me some of that!'

Chuck said something back to him, but Kyle wasn't listening. He was already weaving his way to the desk and the smiling vision beckoning him onwards.

'Shaigon tea?' he queried leeringly, leaning his weight on the desk as the room spun around him. 'How much Shaigon tea for a nice, friendly fuck?'

He was too drunk to see that the smile had frozen on her face and that her eyes had filled with sudden alarm. He reached out for her, grasping hold of her arm and pulling her toward him. 'You wanna feel my dick?' he asked, remembering the free-for-all there had been for such a privilege in La Bohème. 'You wanna feel a real, big, hard American dick?'

Chuck and his newfound buddies, hooting with laughter, reached him seconds before the military police did.

'Come on, lover boy,' Chuck said as the three of them hauled him away from the desk and began to drag him in the direction of the doors. 'If you want to get your rocks off, you're going to have to learn to do it in the right place!'

They found so many other places during the rest of the day that Kyle was unsure how many of them were

232

right and how many were wrong. One thing he was sure of, though, and that was that none of them contained the dream in flowing traditional dress who had smiled so sweetly at him.

When he awoke next morning in his room at the Continental he was suffering from the worst hangover of his life.

'Can't take the pace?' Chuck asked teasingly as Kyle groped his way into the bathroom and vomited into the toilet.

It was fifteen minutes before he returned, white-faced, to the bedroom. 'It must have been the dope we were given at the Bluebird,' he said weakly. 'It must have been spiked.'

'Spiked, my ass,' Chuck said. 'You were just out of your league, that's all.' He began to laugh as he slicked his short fair hair down in front of a smoky mirror. 'Christ, you should have heard yourself with the receptionist at the International. "Shaigon tea? How much Shaigon tea for a nice, friendly fuck?"'

Kyle groaned and reached for his pants. 'Don't tell me any more. I don't think I want to remember.'

Chuck, freshly showered and dressed in clean fatigues, leaned against the bathroom door, arms crossed, watching pityingly as Kyle struggled to zip up his pants.

'You were damned lucky not to find yourself in the caring custody of the military police,' he said, grinning. 'There's an army of street-walkers in Tu Do, and you have to proposition the one dink who is definitely out of bounds.' He shook his head in mock despair. 'Christ, don't they teach you guys anything at Princeton?'

Memory was filtering back into Kyle's brain. He pulled on his shirt and said slowly, 'Was that the girl in the long flowing tunic and pants?'

'An *ao dai*,' Chuck said patiently. 'The long flowing silk tunic and pants are called *ao dai*s. They're Vietnamese traditional dress.'

233

Kyle was remembering more than the *ao dai*; he was remembering silk-black hair and soft, gentle eyes, and a sweet, captivating smile. 'Who did you say she was? What did you say I said to her?' he asked, tucking his shirt into his pants. 'I wasn't rude to her, was I?'

Chuck hooted with laughter. 'Depends on what you privileged Princeton guys call rude. How does, "You wanna feel a big, hard American dick," grab you?'

Kyle's lean-angled face tightened. 'Are you shitting me? Is that really what I said?'

'That's really what you said, lover boy. Didn't seem to impress the lady though. Seemed it was an offer she had no trouble refusing.'

He was still laughing, but Kyle felt even sicker than he had twenty minutes earlier. Christ, had he really said those things? And to a girl who he now remembered clearly had looked as shy and as innocent as a Raphael Madonna.

'Come on,' Chuck said impatiently, dismissing the episode. 'We have only two hours before we have to report to the maintenance depot. Let's get a decent breakfast before we leave.'

Kyle slipped a pack of Winstons into his shirt pocket. 'You go on. I think I ought to make my way over to the International to apologize. Who did you say she was again? The receptionist?'

Chuck nodded. 'But don't bother with any apologies,' he said as they walked out of the room and into the corridor. 'She may be the receptionist, but she's still only a dink. What happened was no big deal, just the sort of thing girls like her have to get used to.'

They walked down the broad sweep of stairs to the Continental's restaurant, the most attractive feature of the hotel. There was only a carved stone fence between the restaurant and the main street. If passersby saw anyone they recognized dining, they were able to stop and exchange a few words.

234

Kyle drank his first cup of coffee quickly and then rose to his feet. 'I'm going to split for five minutes,' he said as Chuck looked up at him in surprise. 'I'll be back before you've finished eating.'

Chuck had no time to ask him where the hell he was going as he walked quickly away. He wanted to talk to the girl at the International. He wanted to see her smile again.

When she saw him stride into the lobby, the smile she had been wearing for some departing servicemen died. She took a prudent step or two backward, away from the desk, so that he could not grab hold of her again.

At first Kyle was relieved. She was just as beautiful in the cold light of sobriety as she was when he was drunk. He hadn't made an ass of himself over a girl who wasn't worth it.

'Do you remember me?' he asked, suddenly feeling awkward, as if he were fourteen again and propositioning his first date.

She nodded, remaining a good two feet away from him, her dark eyes wary.

'I was drunk as a skunk,' he said without preamble. 'I understand I said some pretty unforgivable things to you. I've come to say that I'm sorry.'

The expresssion in her eyes had changed from wariness to bewilderment. She hadn't spoken, and he wondered if she understood what he was saying. 'I'm sorry,' he said again, enunciating the words slowly. 'I . . . was . . . drunk . . .'

'. . . as a skunk,' she finished for him, sloe eyes dancing with laughter.

He grinned, no longer feeling awkward. 'And I'm sorry.'

A slight flush of colour had touched her pale amber cheeks, and she lowered her eyes from his, saying a little shyly, 'That is all right. I accept your apology.'

Kyle hesitated. He wanted to see her again but was suddenly aware that he had no idea what sort of approach would be acceptable. She was a respectable South Vietnamese

235

girl and he realized with something of a shock that he knew nothing at all about her culture, of what freedoms she enjoyed or didn't enjoy.

'I'm flying back to my base today,' he said, wishing that she would look up again so that he could hold her eyes with his. 'I don't know when I'll be back in Saigon, but when I am, will you have dinner with me?'

She had begun to shake her head, and he said with fierce urgency, 'You can bring along a chaperone if you like. I just want to make amends for my rude behaviour. Have dinner with you. Talk.'

This time her silk-dark head rose and her eyes met his, the laughter dancing in them once again. 'You would not mind my elder sister coming with me?'

He shook his head. 'No.' Hell, he didn't care if she brought Ho Chi Minh with her. He just wanted to see her again.

'Then yes, I will have dinner with you the next time you are in Saigon,' she said as a marine walked up to the desk and asked for his room key.

There were more marines entering the lobby, and as she turned toward them, he said with sudden panic, 'I don't know your name!'

'Trinh,' she said, her voice so lilting that it sounded like a note of music.

He grinned. 'Mine is Kyle.' As the marines descended on the desk, clamouring for attention, he reluctantly turned on his heel, striding buoyantly back out into the searingly hot street.

Three days later the war changed forever for Kyle. He and Chuck had been detailed to fly a search-and-destroy patrol to a village some twenty miles north of their base. There were three other Hueys flying with them, each carrying a full complement of men. Five minutes after they had lifted off, an order came for them to make to an alternative landing zone and to stand by.

'What's the matter?' Kyle had asked Chuck over the intercom. 'Is the original LZ too hot?'

Chuck had shrugged. 'You tell me,' he said disinterestedly.

For four tedious hours they blistered beneath the heat at a landing zone without shade and with no supplies except those they had with them. Chuck settled himself in the Huey's cockpit and managed, with great difficulty, to fall asleep. Most of the men were just sitting miserably in the small amount of shade that the Hueys gave, talking. Kyle was playing poker with a fellow Bostonian who had been in the country even less time than himself.

'Three weeks,' Ricky Skeffington said slightly defensively. 'But don't call me a damned cherry. I hate being called a damned cherry!'

He was a well-built, personable boy with a thatch of bright red hair, a host of freckles, and a cheeky grin that Kyle had liked right away.

For a while, as they played, they talked about football. Ricky had been selected for a draft pick. When his tour of duty was over, he hoped to play pro ball. They talked about the New York Giants and the New England Patriots and what their respective chances were for the next season.

Suddenly Ricky changed the subject. 'A little bird told me you went to Princeton,' he said as he dealt with the flair of a riverboat gambler.

Kyle nodded. Princeton seemed so far in his past that he could barely remember it.

'Okay,' Ricky said, now that he had established Kyle's credentials. 'I did only one year in college, but you're an educated guy. You tell me if it's true what some guy in training camp told me. That the French overran Vietnam and that in the last war America supported Ho Chi Minh against the Japanese?'

Kyle studied his hand and threw away two cards. 'It's true that Vietnam was a French colony and it's also true that America supported Ho Chi Minh in his fight against

237

the Japanese.' He grinned. 'Hell, the Japs were our enemy too, you know.'

'Yeah, but this guy in training camp said that when the war was over, the Viets didn't want the French back. He said that the British helped the French to regain control and that they did so with American consent.'

Kyle nodded. 'That's more or less what happened.'

'And then what?' Ricky continued doggedly.

'The Vietnamese eventually defeated the French, and it was agreed in Geneva that the country would be temporarily divided at the seventeenth parallel. The idea was that after a year or so, elections would be held for the government of a reunified Vietnam. But the head of the South Vietnamese government was Ngo Dinh Diem, and because he was afraid that an election would put Ho Chi Minh into power, he refused to allow any elections to be held.'

Ricky stared at him in disbelief. 'Jesus H. Christ!' he said at last. 'Someone should tell the fuckers in Washington what the hell's been going on here and get us the hell out! If the South Vietnamese want to vote a Communist government into power, let them. They probably won't like it when they get it, but I sure as hell won't be losing any sleep over it!'

Kyle grinned, amused by the passionate outrage in Ricky's voice. 'Me either,' he said. 'It's your throw, buddy.'

By the time radio instructions were received detailing them to continue to the original landing zone, Ricky had lost his first month's pay.

'I'll get it back, you bastard, next time we meet,' he said good-naturedly as he began to walk toward the Huey's open door. 'I was just lulling you into a sense of false security this time, that's all.'

Kyle had grinned, pulling on his flight helmet and pocketing the bucks. It was okay with him if Ricky wanted to lose a month's pay every time they met. Hell, he was doing him a favour. If he lost all his money at cards. he wouldn't have any to spend on booze and whores!

When they flew into the original landing zone, it was cold and they were given no explanation for their four-hour standoff.

'Have fun!' Kyle yelled to Ricky as he leapt to the ground with his companions. 'Good luck!'

Over the roar of the rotor blades Ricky acknowledged the good wishes, raising his M-16 high into the air and grinning broadly before turning and following his platoon leader into the bush.

They were still in the air, returning to base, when the intercom clicked and they were ordered to fly the hell back. A member of the platoon had been killed and two injured by a Bouncing Betty. Kyle had flinched. Bouncing Bettys were bastards. Land mines that were triggered off by a careless step, and which, when triggered, jumped four or five feet before exploding, spraying down and out, bringing apocalypse not to the guy who had triggered it, but to those ahead of him or behind him.

'They need a dust off, not us,' Chuck had yelled into the intercom. 'We don't have a medic!'

'You're only a minute away from them, and there's a medic with the platoon. He'll fly back with you to the nearest field hospital. Now, git!'

'I hope that fucker Ricky is okay,' Kyle said as they began to bank steeply. 'Did I tell you he's going to play for the Patriots when his tour is over?'

Men were running towards them, carrying the injured in ponchos. Before their skids touched the ground, Kyle caught a glimpse of bright red hair. 'Jesus,' he muttered fiercely. 'Don't let it be him! Don't let it be him!'

As Chuck landed the Huey, Kyle leapt to the ground, running towards the first of the injured men. The bright red hair was plastered dark with blood. His pants had either been blasted off him or had been torn off him by the medic. One leg had been ripped from its socket, leaving a bloody and twitching stump, and where his balls and penis should have been there was nothing but scraps of torn and twisted flesh.

His eyes were wide and frantic as they met Kyle's. 'My legs!' he screamed, stretching his hands out towards him. 'Dear Christ, my legs!'

Kyle was retching, tears pouring down his face as he helped to lift Ricky aboard the Huey.

'Don't leave me!' Ricky screamed at him, and then there was a hideous gurgling sound and his head fell back, blood gushing from his nose and his mouth.

Kyle remembered nothing of the desperate flight to the field hospital. He knew that Ricky was dead, and though the other injured man was still alive, he neither knew what his injuries were nor cared.

For the first time since he had been in 'Nam, the war had reached out and touched him. It had become real. Ricky's blood smeared his hands and his fatigues. There was a scrap of skin on his sleeve. He had been going to play for the Patriots. He was going to be a pro football player. He had promised to win back the money Kyle had won from him the next time they met.

As they lost height and began to descend toward the field hospital, Kyle began to shake. A thousand years ago a numbnut kid with his brain and his body had thought that war was glamorous. He didn't think so now. As the Huey came in to land he leaned out over the ground skimming beneath him and vomited. If he lived to be a hundred, so help him, he would never think so again.

# CHAPTER THIRTEEN

Gavin's emotions were still torn when he landed at Tan Son Nhut airport, countless hours later. He was coiled as tight as a spring with nervous energy and anticipation for the job that lay ahead of him, though he was agonized at leaving Gabrielle behind when she needed him. Most of all he was devastated by the knowledge that he wouldn't see his newborn son again for months, possibly even a year.

A grin of exhilaration touched his mouth as he thought of *le petit* Gavin. It had never occurred to him that when the baby was born it would dive into the world complete with its own little personality, a personality so individual and engaging that Gavin was certain he would be able to single him out even if he were in a room with a score of other, equally newborn babies. He was going to miss *le petit* Gavin. He was going to miss him almost as much as he was going to miss Gabrielle.

A blast of hot air hit his face as he stepped from the plane, so scorching in intensity that it temporarily robbed him of breath. He looked out over a vista of sandbags and barbed wire to where military airplanes shimmered and danced in the heat. There were big-bellied C-130 transports, Phantoms, Air Force 707s, and helicopters and beyond them were long, low buildings that he presumed were also military. After over a year of waiting, he was actually here in Vietnam. He walked down the flight stairs, carrying his only piece of luggage, a nylon zip-up bag, over his shoulder, pinching himself to make sure that he was not dreaming.

The sandbags and barbed wire gave the airport a look of security, but Gavin knew that only two months before the Viet Cong had launched a daring and devastating attack here.

Gavin walked quickly towards the elderly Vietnamese man holding up a sign with the name Gavin Ryan written on it. The heat was suffocating and moist, and in the few seconds since he had left the airplane's airconditioned interior, he had perspired so much that his shirt was damp beneath the armpits. He followed the Vietnamese across the tarmac towards a battered old Renault, wondering how on earth he was going to survive his cab ride.

The news bureau offices were in Tu Do Street, only a short walk from the Continental, where he intended to stay.

'But no one there now,' the driver said to him, vying for road space amid a battalion of bicycles and pedicabs and tri-Lambrettas. 'Siesta time. When sun so hot, no one works.'

Gavin was relieved to hear it. At least it indicated that the heat wasn't always so stultifying. 'Then would you mind dropping me off at the Continental?' he asked as they sped over a narrow bridge, narrowly missing a group of labourers in black pyjamas and women carrying water on coolie poles.

The driver nodded, entering the city's broad, tree-lined streets. 'Behind those trees is Le Cercle Sportif,' he said informatively. 'Very nice club for Europeans. Very exclusive.' He veered left, the sea of bicycles surrounding them as dense as ever. 'This is Tu Do Street.'

Gavin could see the large red-brick Catholic cathedral that marked its beginning, and, several blocks down on his right-hand side, he could glimpse the gleam of the Saigon River, where it ended.

In front of him, in the square itself, was the shabby grandeur of the Continental, and on the other corner of the square was the taller, more modern façade of the Caravelle Hotel.

'Thanks,' Gavin said as he opened the Renault's door and stepped into the street. He reached for his wallet, but the man shook his head.

'No. The bureau pay me to pick you up. No money, thank you.'

Gavin grinned and hoisted his bag on to his shoulder.

When the sun had lost its ferocity, Gavin walked the short distance from the hotel to the newspaper's office. The bureau chief, Paul Dulles, was a middle-aged and rather elegant Frenchman, and though he was politely welcoming, Gavin sensed that he was dubious about having a suspiciously young-looking twenty-four-year-old Australian on his staff.

'—and so all news is centred on the Buddhists' demands that Premier Ky resign and that a civilian government be elected into power,' he said, thawing a little when he discovered that Gavin's French, though uniquely accented, was fluent enough for them to converse.

He perched on the corner of his desk, one foot swinging negligently. 'It's a lulu of a situation. Ky triggered it off by dismissing one of his former buddies, General Nguyen Chanh Thi. Thi always enjoyed the support of the Buddhists, and within days of his dismissal outraged Buddhists were streaming into the streets of Da Nang and Hue, demanding that Ky resign and that the country return to a civilian government.'

He paused, reaching out for a nearby bottle of Scotch, lifting it queryingly towards Gavin. 'Will join me? There are glasses in the cupboard behind you.'

Gavin did as he was asked, amused to discover that the glasses in question were hand-cut crystal, not the chipped all-purpose glasses usually to be found in bureau offices.

'And it wasn't only Buddhists who took to the streets,' Paul continued, sipping his whisky. 'Government troops who had been under Thi's command joined them. It began to look as if the South was on the verge of civil war, with one half of the South Vietnamese army fighting the other half, and the Buddhist faction growing increasingly hostile towards the Americans.'

His foot continued to swing languidly, revealing striking purple socks. 'Ky dispatched two thousand troops to Da Nang and successfully quelled it, but in the process hundreds of rebel troops and countless Buddhists and civilians were killed. Now he needs to bring Hue to heel. When you've got yourself accredited, I'd like you to go up there. The Buddhist leader is Tri Quang, he's a *bonze*, which is the same thing as being a priest. I'd like to know what sort of a government it is that he wants, and who he would like to see leading it.'

'How do I get to Hue?' Gavin asked.

'With great difficulty!' Paul said with a flash of humour. 'Normally, once you're accredited, you travel by army helicopter. At the moment the Americans are steering clear of Da Nang and Hue, so you'll have to either drive up there or go by local bus.'

Gavin grinned. It was obvious what the setup was going to be. Paul would stay snugly in Saigon while he, Gavin, covered all the assignments in the less comfortable parts of the country. He didn't mind. It was the less comfortable parts of the country that he was interested in.

'Come on,' Paul said, slipping from the desk. 'Let's get you accredited. Until we've done that, you can't go anywhere. Have you got a couple of spare passport photographs with you?'

Gavin nodded, and the two men strolled out into the still-strong sunlight. The square, and the street leading off it, were as crowded and as noisy as they had been when Gavin had arrived.

Paul led the way into JUSPAO, the Joint United States Public Affairs Office. 'All American military announcements are made here,' he said. 'At eight o'clock every morning they put out a three- or four-page press statement, and every afternoon at five they hold a full press conference.'

'The Five O'Clock Follies?' Gavin asked, remembering what he had been told in Paris.

Paul's lopsided grin was in evidence again. 'You've heard about them?' he asked. 'Whenever you're in Saigon, it will be your responsibility to cover them. If a big story breaks, don't waste time by hurrying back to the office with it. Phone it through. In this game, seconds count.'

They walked into one of the countless offices, and a tough-looking marine gunnery sergeant thrust a couple of forms towards them. Minutes later, after handing over his passport photographs, Gavin possessed a little plastic-coated accreditation card that confirmed he was a member of the Vietnam press corps and that his priority for travel aboard US military aircraft was equivalent to that of an American major.

'Phew!' Gavin whistled as they walked back through the maze of corridors to the entrance. 'That's quite impressive, isn't it? I hadn't reckoned on becoming a major overnight!'

'It's nothing,' Paul said dismissively. 'They give journalists the rank of major in case they're captured by the Viet Cong.'

'Why? What difference will being a major make?'

'Very little, I imagine,' Paul said dryly. 'But it is fondly presumed that officers will be treated with more respect than enlisted men. However, as the Viet Cong will also presume that an officer will be in possession of officer-level information, I find it a little disconcerting. Their methods for making people talk are not very refined. Especially if the poor bugger in question has no information to give!'

Gavin grimaced. 'No, it wouldn't be very nice,' he agreed, 'but I wouldn't have thought there was much risk of a journalist being taken prisoner. Surely the only prisoners being taken are pilots who are shot down during bombing raids over the North?'

Paul gave a Gallic shrug of his shoulders. 'They are most at risk, I agree, but American intelligence is pretty sure that some men who are listed as missing in action are being kept prisoner in the U-Minh forest, and in the border areas between South Vietnam and Cambodia and Laos.'

'Where is the U-Minh forest?' Gavin asked curiously as they strolled down a small side street and back into Tu Do Street.

'It's a godforsaken, snake-ridden, Viet Cong-controlled tract of land deep in the Delta, where the Saigon military don't venture,' Paul said, waving his hand in greeting as a pretty European girl on a Lambretta called out his name.

'And do you think it's true?' Gavin persisted, intrigued. 'Do you think men are being held prisoner there?'

Again Paul shrugged. 'Who knows? There are certainly enough pilots being held in the North. We received reports of two more who were shot down last month and who have been classified as POWs, a Lieutenant Robert Peel and a Major Lawrence Guarino.'

Gavin was silent for a few minutes as they walked along the crowded street, past sidewalk cafés, where tables and chairs were shaded from the sun by gaily striped awnings. 'It's against the rules of the Geneva Convention,' he said at last.

Paul turned towards him, his brows rising high. '*Merde*! I had no idea you were a lawyer as well as a journalist.'

'I'm not,' Gavin said with a grin. 'I just have a talent for remembering odd nuggets of information. According to Article Nineteen of the Geneva Convention, prisoners of war may not be held in combat zones. And even if the Saigon military don't venture into the U Minh, it's still slap in the middle of a combat zone, isn't it?'

'I take it you've done quite a bit of boning up on the situation out here?' Paul said, leading the way into a café that was blessedly quiet.

'A little.' Gavin grinned as he thought of the long hours of conversation about Vietnam with Gabrielle and Vanh. He patted his shirt's breast pocket and the piece of paper with Nhu's address on crackled reassuringly. Vanh had insisted

246

that he visit Nhu immediately after he arrived in Saigon, and Gavin had promised that he would do so. However, now that he was here, he felt oddly reluctant to keep his promise.

Even though he had been in the city only a few hours, he realized there was very little fraternization between the Europeans living in the city and the Vietnamese – except for encounters between the bar girls and the soldiers, and between the shoeshine boys and taxidrivers and waiters and their clients. Any visit he made to a non-European part of the city would be glaringly conspicuous and one that might make things difficult for Nhu.

Paul had ordered two beers and Gavin picked up his ice-cold glass, drinking gratefully. He would postpone his visit to Nhu until his return from Hue. By then he would have a better feel for things.

Later that evening he met the other two members of the news bureau's staff. Lestor McDermott was a tall, bespectacled French-Canadian, slightly older than himself, and Jimmy Giddings was an American of unknown age who had been covering wars before either of his colleagues had been born.

'The difficulty with being a news-agency reporter in a war like this,' Jimmy Giddings said to him as the four men sat over drinks on the terrace at the Continental, 'is that ninety-nine per cent of the time we're tied to reporting announcements. That is what the powers-that-be want, goddamn them. They don't want opinions and they don't want anything that deviates from what other news agencies are printing.'

'Surely it's different for out-of-town assignments? Situations that we report firsthand?'

Jimmy shook his head cynically. 'If you're thinking that you can trip off to Hue and file a report describing what you've seen there, and then have that report printed verbatim in the newspapers the bureau feeds, you're in for a big disappointment. Only the big guys, guys with regular by-lines in *The New York Times* and the *Washington Post* and the *Daily Telegraph* can get away with having what they write treated as holy writ. We lesser mortals have to suffer having firsthand reports emasculated and reworded by our respective world-desk editors.'

'Depressing, huh?' Lestor said to Gavin with a wink. 'But I wouldn't worry about it if I were you. Rolling out of bed each day to attend the Follies is far more comfortable than trawling the countryside, risking your life for a scoop that some pencil-wielding bastard on the world desk will reduce to three lines.'

They all laughed, and Paul, noticing the ring that Gavin wore, asked about his wife.

Gavin had no desire to talk about Gabrielle to men who did not know her and who would not be able to even begin to imagine how wonderful she was. What would their response have been if he'd told them she was half Vietnamese? And that her uncle was a major in the North Vietnamese Army?

Gavin strode into the bureau's office, walking briskly across to Paul's desk. He'd bought khakis, helmet and canteen for himself that morning at the marketplace.

'I'm just about ready to leave,' he said as Paul looked up from the nightlead he was editing. 'I bumped into the Vietnamese who picked me up at the airport. He was able to get hold of a Mini-Moke for me, so I'm driving to Hue.'

Paul nodded, as if the acquisition of a Moke was so commonplace that it was unworthy of comment.

'Do you know the man?' Gavin continued. 'He's volunteered to go with me. Is he safe?'

'As a driver, no. In any other city in the world he would not even be given a licence. However, if you mean is he safe from a security point of view, then the answer is unequivocally yes. Just don't let him drive. And Gavin . . .' He looked up again as another thought struck him.

'Remember you have to be patient when you're telephoning copy back to the office. The American military radiophones link into the old French telephone system, and you have to be connected from exchange to exchange all the way down the country. If you're unlucky, it can take up to two hours.'

'Thanks,' Gavin said dryly, hoping a delay filing copy would be the worst of his problems.

The name of his companion, sitting happily beside him as he drove out of Saigon was Tran Ngoc Huong.

'But all Vietnamese first names, last name,' he said helpfully. 'So my name Huong.'

Gavin nodded. He already knew most of the information that Huong gave him as they drove north in the searing heat of late morning, but he listened patiently, impressed by the fluency of Huong's self-taught English.

Although Hue was less than 500 miles from Saigon, it took them four days to reach it on roads congested with troops and refugees. They arrived to find a city in chaos. Government troops had cut off all essential food supplies in an effort to starve the Buddhists into submission. Rumours about what had happened, or had not happened, when the troops had stormed Da Nang, were rife. On 26 May a group of students and young workers burned down the USIS library; on 31 May they burned the US Consulate.

In the midst of all the mayhem, the mayor of Hue, Lieutenant Colonel Pham Van Khoa, declared that he was no longer going to give the Buddhists his support and moved out of the city, taking the thousand troops under his command with him.

On 8 June, when government troops finally entered Hue, the only resistance they encountered was of unarmed civilians. It was a resistance that was soon put down. By the time Gavin returned with Huong to Saigon three weeks later, he had seen Buddhist students forming human road-blocks across the avenues leading into the city, only to be mown down by machine-gun fire. During his stay he had seen women and children brutally manhandled; he had witnessed, in sick disbelief, an aged Buddhist nun burn herself alive before one of the city's central pagodas.

Even though he hadn't managed to interview Tri Quang, who was on a hunger strike, he knew he had achieved a great deal. He had entered Hue under almost impossible conditions, and he had filed copy under atrocious ones. He was so tired he could barely stand, and so hungry that he would have eaten whatever was put in front of him, however dubious. Above all, he was deeply satisfied. He hadn't liked what he had seen in Hue, but he had coped.

As he parked the Moke in front of the bureau's office in Tu Do Street, and as Huong bade him good-bye, he determined that the first thing he would do, after bathing and eating and sleeping, would be to contact Nhu.

Five minutes later he discovered that the initiative had been taken from him. Her message lay on his desk. She would meet him at seven that evening, on the terrace of the Continental.

# CHAPTER FOURTEEN

Abbra didn't wait for Patti Maine to approve or disapprove of the finished synopsis. The mere act of writing it, of creating the character that had, until then, existed only nebulously in her head, had opened the floodgates of her imagination. She wrote with total, single-minded concentration for eight, and sometimes nine hours a day; she felt as if she'd discovered a whole new world, a world so magical, so absorbing, she didn't want to relinquish it even for a few days. By the time she received Patti's encouraging letter telling her that the synopsis was better than she had hoped and that she now wanted the first three chapters so she could sell the idea to a publisher, Abbra had already completed her second chapter.

'But surely you can take a break for just one weekend?' Scott asked her when he made his regular Thursday night telephone call.

It was the off season now, and Rosalie Bryansten had long ago been relegated to the position of an ex-girlfriend. She had had several successors, all of whose reigns had been equally brief. There was only one person Scott wanted to be with, and that was Abbra.

'I'd like to come down to L.A. for the weekend,' Abbra said truthfully. Scott had tickets for a film premiere, and she knew that if she went she would enjoy herself hugely. 'But I'm just two pages into chapter three, and it's going so well I hate the thought of setting it aside, even for a couple of days.'

Scott was in a telephone booth at the Beverly Hills. He bit his lip, trying hard to curb his disappointment. He had made a pact with himself. Even though he did not have enough willpower to stick to his resolution of never seeing her again, he had promised himself that he would never force the issue. If he tried to override her protestations, he would be doing exactly that.

'Okay,' he said with an easy indifference he was far from feeling. 'We'll make it another time. When chapter three is safely under your belt.'

She gave a little laugh, relief and disappointment inextricably mixed. 'I'll look forward to it,' she said sincerely. 'I'm scared to death about what will happen when chapter three is finished. Patti is sure that she will be able to get a contract on the strength of the synopsis and first three chapters, but what if she can't? What if no one is interested?'

'Patti Maine is a professional,' Scott said, wishing that he could reassure her with more than words. 'If she thinks a publisher will be interested in buying the book, then you can bet your life that they will.'

'But not even Patti has seen the first two chapters yet. What if they don't live up to her expectations?' she asked, a note of panic creeping into her voice.

Scott chuckled, visualizing the expression on her face, her violet-blue eyes dark with self-doubt. 'You're too hard on yourself,' he said, hoping that she would interpret the love in his voice as brotherly affection. 'You had exactly the same worries over the synopsis. And they were groundless. The book is going to be great. Just try to relax and enjoy yourself while you're writing it.'

She giggled, her doubts fading as they always did in the face of Scott's boundless confidence. 'Okay, professor, I'll do exactly as you say, and I *am* enjoying myself. More than I've ever enjoyed anything before in my life. The minute I sit at the typewriter, and my eyes focus on the paper in front of me, my brain shuts out the rest of the world. I feel like Alice must have felt when she fell through the looking-glass. I just tumble into another world and the hours fly by and it's absolutely terrific.'

Scott's smile faded. He knew that she wasn't exaggerating. Over the last few months she had gained confidence in her talent and she now placed it first, before everything, which was fine by him because he loved and understood her and knew how important her writing was to her. But would it be okay with Lewis? Would Lewis understand, when there were army functions to attend, when she asked if she could be excused because she was in the middle of a chapter? From what he knew of his older brother, Scott doubted it very much.

'Have you written to Lewis about the book yet?' he asked casually, pretty sure that she hadn't.

The pause before she answered was so brief that no one but himself would have been aware of it.

'No.' Her voice was vaguely dismissive. 'I'm going to wait and see if anything comes of it before I do that.'

Scott leaned against the wall of the booth, his sun-bleached eyebrows drawing together in a frown. She had never even hinted that she was anything but deliriously happy and deeply in love with Lewis. Yet she wasn't sharing with him the most important thing that had ever happened to her. He wondered if she was aware that in all likelihood Lewis would disapprove of her writing. And if she was, he wondered what on earth she intended to do when Lewis came home.

It took her a month to finish the third chapter. The original draft had been finished in less than two weeks, but the prospect of mailing it off to Patti and hearing her reaction was so terrifying she wrote and rewrote until she was dizzy.

'Make a copy of it before you send it off,' Scott advised her when she telephoned him with the news that it was finally ready. 'And once you've sent it off, try to forget about it for a few days.' He hesitated for a moment and then said tentatively, 'There's going to be a march this coming weekend in New York. I'm going to fly out there to take part. Would you like to come and keep me company?'

She had no need to ask what the march was for. At Christmas, when President Johnson had ordered a halt to the bombing raids over North Vietnam, there had been a faint glimmer of hope that the war might end through a negotiated peace. That hope had died at the end of January when American jet bombers once again flew north. All through February and March there had hardly been a week when an antiwar demonstration had not taken place in some major American city.

'No,' she said quietly but without the least hesitation. 'You know that I can't, Scott.'

Alone in the apartment he had rented for the summer in Santa Monica, Scott shook his head in despair. The war in Vietnam, and the rights and wrongs of America's participation in it, was the only subject they did not agree on. Scott knew damn well what Abbra's true feelings were about the war. He also knew that if it hadn't been for her marriage to Lewis, and her loyalty to him, she would have participated in any and every peace demonstration. The previous year she had been first in line when students from her college marched in sympathy with the civil rights marchers in Selma. But where Vietnam was concerned, he knew she couldn't be true to her own instincts and judgement.

While antiwar demonstrators protested against the war in Washington, New York, and on campuses across the country, Lewis was risking his life daily and hourly in the cause they derided. For Abbra to march with them would be, for her, the most flagrant act of disloyalty toward Lewis imaginable.

'Then I shall march alone,' he said wryly.

She giggled. 'Hardly. The *Washington Post* predicts there'll be a big turnout.'

Four days later, the morning after the march, she saw that the *Washington Post* had been correct. Protestors jammed the streets of New York, and there was a photograph on one of the inner pages of a young, blond-haired English boy being hauled away by police, a placard declaring 'Johnson for Ex-President' and 'Where Is Lee Harvey Oswald Now That We Really Need Him?' still clutched in his hand. His name was Lance Blyth-Templeton and there was a further photograph of him being escorted to John F. Kennedy International Airport for deportation to England.

She sighed and pushed a silky-dark strand of hair away from her face. It had been two days since she had sent the first three chapters of her novel to Patti. It would be at least a week, possibly longer, before Patti read them and passed judgement on them, and until she did so Abbra knew that she wouldn't be able to concentrate on anything.

During her most recent writing binge, she had been so immersed in her imaginary world that she hadn't read the newspapers. Now she read the *Washington Post* and the *Los Angeles Times* avidly. Both papers were full of reports of the Buddhist demonstrations taking place in Hue and Da Nang and culminating in grisly photographic coverage of a Buddhist nun immolating herself in the market square in Da Nang.

Lewis's letters did not mention the Buddhist campaign to oust Premier Ky. His initial enthusiasm at being a *co van truong*, and of being in a position to help the living standards of the villagers for the better, continued. At the end of April he wrote to her that a village girl who had been badly mistreated by her family was now working for him as a hooch-maid. 'Her name is Tam,' he wrote in a large, enviably neat hand, 'and she is so quick. I've been teaching her English and in only a few weeks she's become practically colloquial in it!'

It was the kind of letter that Abbra liked to receive. It made no mention of ambushes and search-and-destroy operations and death and killing, and she was able to imagine Lewis as more of a Peace Corps worker, helping the people to improve their harsh living conditions, than as a soldier.

It was several weeks before she received her long awaited telephone call from Patti.

'I'm sorry to have kept you waiting so long, Abbra,' she said cheerily. Abbra's knuckles clutched the receiver so tightly they were white. 'I've been in London and flew back only five days ago. While I was there I showed your synopsis to a publishing friend and he was very interested. He said that if the opening chapters lived up to the promise of the synopsis then he wanted to have first refusal.'

'And do they?' Abbra's voice was a croak.

'The chapters are wonderful!' Patti said, her throaty voice full of laughter at Abbra's barely concealed anxiety. 'Although first novels are usually difficult to place, I'm sure we won't have a problem finding a publisher. I'm sending copies to my London friend immediately, and also to a New York publisher who is building up a new list and who has expressed an interest.'

Abbra leaned her head weakly against the wall. It was all happening just as Patti had said. A publisher was already interested in her novel and it wasn't even finished yet.

'Are you still there?' Patti asked.

Abbra laughed. 'Yes. I'm just trying to believe that all this is actually happening. How long do you think it will be before you hear from the publisher in London?'

'It could be a week, and it could be four,' Patti said practically. 'Leave all the worrying about publishers and contracts to me. Your job, Abbra, is to write the book and to make sure that the remaining twenty or twenty-five chapters are as good as the first three.'

For the next six weeks she didn't see Scott. She didn't see anyone. To her mother's increasing irritation, she stayed almost permanently in her bedroom, her fingers flying over the typewriter keys as she transferred the vivid images in her head on to paper.

'I'm glad it's going so well,' Scott said to her when he made his usual Thursday night call. 'How many chapters have you finished now?'

'Seven?'

'Which is how many pages?'

'A hundred and forty.'

He whistled. 'So you're a third of the way there?'

When she had discussed the book with him in the early stages, she had told him that she thought it would run to about four hundred pages.

'I'm not sure. The more I write, the more I seem to want to write. I think it's going to be longer than I first anticipated. Do you think it will matter?'

She had already signed a contract with the British publisher who had been interested in the synopsis, and a deal had been made with a New York publishing house. The book was going to be published in hardback in Great Britain and in paperback in the United States.

'I don't think so, not unless it's going to be several hundred pages longer than you first projected. Is it in any shape for me to see yet?'

So far she had shown him everything that she had written. The synopsis. The opening chapters.

'Yes.' She wanted Scott to read what she had written. His remarks were always on target and his boundless enthusiasm bolstered her spirits. 'I would have sent the last few chapters down to you, but I've been so busy writing that I haven't had time to have them copied.'

'Never mind mailing them down,' Scott said firmly. 'Bring them down. It's my birthday on Saturday, and Dad is flying in for a celebration dinner. I've reserved a table at the Polo Lounge for three.'

She could tell by the tone of his voice that to try to refuse would be pointless, and besides, she didn't want to refuse.

'I'll be there,' she promised. 'I'll drive down and stay at the Jamaica Bay.'

The Jamaica Bay, where Abbra had stayed on previous trips to L.A., was on Admiralty Way, just off Marina del Rey and though only four minutes from L.A.X., its beach was superb.

'Okay. I'll pick you up about six and we'll have drinks before meeting up with Dad.'

The days when he would have tried to persuade her to stay at his apartment rather than at a hotel were long gone. That type of arrangement would have been pure torture.

'What do you think?' she asked nervously when he'd finished the last page.

For the past hour he hadn't spoken. They were sitting at table one in the Polo Lounge, and while she had toyed with Pacific bay shrimp and sipped at a glass of Pinot Chardonnay, Scott had been reading the new chapters.

He laid the typewritten pages down on the table and looked across at her, a broad grin on his face. 'I think you're a very clever lady, Mrs Ellis. If you're not careful you're going to be such a huge success that you'll be able to live permanently in the Beverly Hills Hotel!'

She leaned back against the banquette, laughing with relief.

'Do you really think it's good? I've become so involved in the life of the woman I'm writing about that there are times when I feel as if I am her! The next few chapters are set in Boston, and so I'm going there for a few days to walk in her footsteps, so to speak.'

'It sounds like fun.' He hadn't planned anything important for the next few weeks. He could easily fit in a trip to Boston. And if he did, the gossips would have had a field day. He was well aware that his close relationship with his sister-in-law was being commented on, and he lived in dread that the prurient speculation would come to Abbra's attention. He knew her well enough to know gossip might cause her to see far less of him.

He said with forced lightness, overcoming the temptation of Boston with difficulty, 'You haven't wished me a happy birthday yet.'

Her eyes flew wide, a look of horror crossing her face. 'Scott! I'm so sorry! I was so keyed up about your reaction to the book that I completely forgot!'

He sighed in exaggerated disappointment, shaking his head of curly blond hair in mock despair. 'I don't know, Abbra. I act as a Svengali to you, advising you on every single word you write; I wine and dine you at the most prestigious watering hole in the entire damned country, and what do I get for my pains? Not even a birthday card!'

She had begun to laugh. When she was with Scott, she was always laughing. 'Idiot,' she said affectionately. 'Not only have I brought you a card, I've also brought you a present.'

She reached down into her handbag, which was tucked discreetly beneath the table, and withdrew a card and small gold-wrapped box tied with scarlet ribbon and topped with a scarlet bow.

'Happy birthday,' she said in the soft, low-modulated voice that he loved so much. 'I hope you like them.'

If she had bought him nothing but a ten-cent stick of gum, he would have treasured it for the rest of his life.

The card was a reproduction of Renoir's 'Luncheon of the Boating Party' from the Phillips Collection in the Washington Gallery, and she had signed it simply 'Abbra'. The small box contained a pair of gold, black-faced cameo cuff links.

He kept his head low over the box for a few seconds, knowing that the expression in his eyes was too revealing. When at last he raised his head and looked across at her, his hazel eyes were light and laughing, totally carefree.

'Thank you very much, sister-in-law mine,' he said, resisting the temptation to lean across and kiss her. 'From now on I'll be able to shoot my cuffs with style and panache.'

Style and panache were such an inherent part of his personality that she laughed, her cheeks dimpling. 'I'm glad you like them,' she said, turning her head as her father-in-law's tall shadow fell over them.

'Abbra my dear. You look well. How is Lewis liking his new role as a *co van truong*?' he asked, sitting down next to her. 'Is he making the most of it?'

She nodded. 'Yes. It's given him an opportunity to improve the living standards of the villagers who are living under his jurisdiction.'

Her father-in-law raised his eyebrows. 'He's there to root out Viet Cong, my dear,' he said baldly, 'not play at being a welfare officer.'

Scott raised a hand protestingly. 'No Vietnam,' he said good-naturedly but with steely firmness. 'This is a birthday celebration. *My* birthday celebration, and I don't want it ruined with controversy.'

'There's no controversy between Abbra and myself,' his father said with asperity. 'She understands what the war is about and why Lewis is out there. Which is a damned sight more than those fools who took part in that antiwar demonstration in New York.'

Scott's jawline had tightened and he leaned across the table toward his father, his body taut with tension.

'Listen to me for a moment, Dad. I was—'

Abbra interrupted him with feverish haste. 'You'd better get ready to blow out some candles, Scott. There's a cart heading this way with a cake on it.'

Scott's eyes widened in stunned disbelief.

'Happy birthday, sir,' the waiter said, wheeling the cart to the side of their table.

The cake was iced in lemon, decorated by the figure of a football player wearing a Rams shirt emblazoned with Scott's number, and surrounded by flickering candles.

'Who the devil . . .' he began, forgetting the fight he was just about to have with his father.

'Everyone should have a cake on their birthday,' Abbra said, wondering for a fleeting moment if she had misjudged his reaction to her surprise.

He began to laugh, taking hold of her hand and squeezing it tight. 'I might have guessed! Hell, I haven't had a birthday cake since I was eight years old!'

'Are you going to blow the candles out, sir?' the waiter asked.

'You have to make a wish,' Abbra reminded him.

He had reluctantly removed his hand from hers, and for a brief moment the smile on his face was rueful. He sure as hell couldn't wish for what he really wanted.

'Come on,' Abbra urged him, laughing. 'You have to blow them all out at once, remember.'

He took a deep breath, blowing them out with ease, not wishing for the thing he really wanted, Abbra's presence at his side as his wife. Instead, he wished that she would be with him on his next birthday, and his next and his next and his next.

'Would your wife like a slice of cake now?' the waiter was asking.

Scott stared at him, momentarily shaken at how the innocent query had dovetailed with his private thoughts.

Abbra had flushed rosily. It was an understandable mistake. She had ordered the cake in her own name, and her name was, after all, Ellis. But she found the assumption that she was Scott's wife strangely disconcerting.

Only Colonel Ellis seemed unperturbed by the waiter's error. 'Mrs Ellis is the wife of my older son, who is serving in Vietnam,' he said, oblivious to the sudden strain on Scott's face. 'Do you want a slice of cake now, Abbra, or when we've finished dinner?'

'When we've finished dinner,' she said, the flush in her cheeks dying slowly.

'I'm sorry, madam,' the waiter said. 'I'm very sorry, sir.'

261

As he made his apologies and wheeled the trolley and cake away, she tried to catch Scott's eye, wanting to laugh with him over the waiter's mistake, knowing that once they had joked about it, she would feel more comfortable.

'What a silly mistake for anyone to have made,' Scott said lightly, picking up the leather-bound menu. 'As if I could be so lucky!' And though his voice was light and careless, he didn't laugh, and his eyes didn't meet hers, and her uneasiness was a long time in dying.

Abbra flew to Boston. She had written to Lewis about her plans for visiting the East Coast in her regular weekly letter to him, but not the reason behind her trip. She would do that later, she promised herself, when her book was finished. She had two hundred pages finished now, and the book had become such a vital part of her life that she couldn't imagine how she had existed in her non-writing days.

As she strolled the streets, walking in the footsteps of Maddie, her heroine, it was as if Maddie were walking at her side, as if she actually existed. There were times when, if Scott had been with her, she knew she would have been saying, 'That's the corner of the Common where Maddie met Rory' and 'That's the restaurant where she learned about her son's illness.' It was a strange, beguiling sensation, visiting scenes where events conjured in her imagination had taken place, and where now, as she visited them, it seemed as though they actually had taken place.

'Did you travel to Boston by yourself?' Patti asked her as they lunched in an elegant French restaurant near her office, celebrating the news that Abbra's British publisher was delighted with the first two hundred pages of the novel.

Abbra nodded. 'Yes. I thought that having someone with me would be a distraction, though there were dozens of times when I wanted to show Scott places I had written about.'

Patti laid down her fork and leaned back in her chair. When she had asked if Abbra had travelled to Boston alone, Patti had been wondering if Abbra had taken her mother with her, or a female friend. She hadn't imagined for a moment that she might have taken her brother-in-law.

She asked, intrigued, 'Do you and Scott often take trips together?'

'No,' Abbra said guilelessly, spearing a button mushroom with her fork, two shiny wings of night-black hair swinging forward slightly and brushing her cheeks. 'Not unless you count flying to places like Denver and San Diego to watch him play.'

'But you think he would have enjoyed the Boston trip?' Patti prompted.

Abbra took a sip of her wine and smiled. 'Yes. I think Maddie has become as real to him as she is to me.'

Lunch could wait, Patti decided. She had been curious before about Abbra's relationship with the fabled Scott Ellis. Now she was determined that her curiosity would be satisfied.

'And what about Lewis?' she asked. 'Is Maddie real to him too?'

Abbra pushed her plate away and leaned back in her chair, but with none of Patti's sense of leisured ease. 'No,' she said with a slight frown. 'I can't really share the book with Lewis. He has so much on his mind in Vietnam. It would seem—' She hesitated, and then said reluctantly, 'It would seem trivial somehow to be writing to him about a novel.'

Patti's brows rose slightly. 'But it isn't trivial to you, is it?'

'No.' Abbra flashed her a vivid, wide smile. 'It's the most important thing that's ever happened to me. Apart from my marrying Lewis, of course.'

'Of course,' Patti agreed a trifle dryly, her curiosity far from slaked. 'Are Scott and Lewis very much alike? Is that why you spend so much time with Scott? Because it's like being with Lewis?'

Abbra burst into laughter. 'Good heavens, no! They're nothing alike! Lewis is very much a military man. Very correct and precise. Scott is just the opposite, very happy-go-lucky and devil-may-care. I doubt Lewis has ever been to a football game in his life, and Scott's whole existence is focused on the game. I can't truthfully think of any one thing they have in common.'

Patti rested her elbow on the arms of her chair and steepled her fingers together, lowering her chin. Far from being cleared up, the mystery was deepening. 'Then I'm sorry, Abbra,' she said with her usual directness. 'But I really don't know why you and Scott spend so much time together.'

Abbra stared at her. 'But it's very clear,' she said at last, struggling to come to terms with the fact that Patti obviously thought it was strange. 'I mean, we're family. He's my brother-in-law. It's only natural that I go and watch him play, isn't it?'

Patti tilted her head slightly to one side, her blond bouffant hairdo resembling a halo. 'Scott used to be a regular item in the gossip column,' she said musingly. 'Wherever he went, there was always a gorgeous model or movie star clinging to his arm. These last six months there's been no one.' She paused and then said, her voice carefully free of insinuating intonation. 'Apart from yourself, of course.'

Abbra's face had gone white. 'Is that how it looks?' she asked at last, her voice taut. 'As if there were something . . . not quite right about our relationship?'

Patti felt a twinge of remorse. She hadn't meant to distress Abbra, just discover exactly what sort of relationship she had with Scott. But if Abbra was unaware of the speculation the two of them were arousing, then she didn't really regret bringing the subject out into the open. It was inevitable that someday, someone would ask, and it was better that the question come from her rather than from a prying journalist.

Abbra had risen to her feet, her hands shaking slightly as she picked up her clutch bag. 'I think I'd better go now, Patti. It's been a lovely lunch, and I'm more excited than I can say about the British deal but I've got a lot of work still to do on the book and I think I should get back to San Francisco and start it.'

Patti nodded. She knew why Abbra was cutting and running, but if it had never occurred to Abbra before that her relationship with Scott was one that was likely to cause gossip, then maybe it was good that she had been made aware of it, and that she give it some thought.

'If you want to talk to me about anything, please don't hesitate to call,' she said, rising to her feet, and kissing Abbra affectionately on the cheek.

Abbra forced a small smile. 'Thanks, Patti. I'll remember. Bye.'

She walked quickly from the restaurant, attracting admiring glances from a group of businessmen at a nearby table. She had driven down to Los Angeles the previous afternoon, and had booked into the Jamaica Bay for two nights. After her lunch with Patti she planned to so some shopping and then, at five o'clock, she had arranged to meet Scott at the Fine Arts Museum. From there they had planned to go to the movies or the theatre.

She flagged down a taxi outside the restaurant and asked to be taken, not to Rodeo Drive and the shops, but back to her hotel. She couldn't see Scott. Not now. She sat in the back of the taxi, her knuckles white.

She had met Patti Maine only a half dozen times, but she knew her well enough to know that she didn't speak carelessly. If Patti thought there was something wrong about her relationship with Scott, and had had the honesty to tell her so, then other people must be thinking so too. She remembered the waiter at the Polo Lounge and the innocent mistake that he had made. Major football stars were always targets for gossip, and the press loved nothing better than to insure that the gossip reached as wide an audience as possible. The mere thought of a story insinuating that Scott had abandoned all his previous girlfriends in order to escort his sister-in-law around town made Abbra feel physically ill. No one who knew them would believe the insinuations for a moment, but they would still distress her father-in-law and her own parents.

She stepped out of the taxi at the Jamaica Bay and hurried through the lobby to her room. All sorts of things were suddenly making sense. The speculative expression in some of Scott's teammates' eyes and the quickly suppressed laughter whenever she and Scott joined them for drinks or a meal.

She threw her jacket and her clutch bag on to the bed and reached for the telephone, asking for an outside line. And there had been that odd incident, months ago now, when Scott had been involved in a fight. It had been so unlike him; he was so easygoing and even-tempered. Scott had said merely that the guy he had decked had said something to which he had taken exception. With sudden certainty she now knew what that something had been.

She dialled his number, her fingers still trembling. They couldn't continue seeing each other as they had been doing. Sooner or later a gossip columnist would get hold of the story and milk it for all it was worth. He wouldn't care. She knew that. But she cared *for* him. She didn't want to see ugly speculations being printed about him.

'Scott Ellis's office,' the woman from his service answered.

Her breath was tight in her throat. For a second she was tempted to put the receiver down and to try again later, and then she knew that if she waited, her resolution would fail.

'It's Abbra,' she said, forcing her voice to be steady. 'Please tell Scott I've decided not to stay overnight in L.A. After having lunch with my agent I realized how much work I have to do on the book and I've decided to go away for a while so that I can concentrate.'

266

As the woman thanked her and hung up, Abbra closed her eyes tight. She wouldn't be seeing him again. Perhaps not for months. There were a hundred and one things she wanted to say to him. She wanted to tell him about the British book deal. She wanted to show him the chapter she had finished writing on Friday.

She wanted, quite simply, to be with him.

The realization was cataclysmic. She stood, still holding the telephone receiver in her hand, staring blindly in front of her. When had it happened? In the name of God, how had it happened?

Clumsily she replaced the telephone receiver.

'Oh, God,' she whispered, not moving, standing as immobile as a pillar of salt. 'Oh, dear, dear God!' And then her tears began to fall, sliding down her cheeks, splashing unrestrainedly on to her hands and her dress.

# CHAPTER FIFTEEN

To Serena's surprise Rupert was waiting for her at Heathrow when she landed.

'In the message you left on my answering machine, you said you would be in the shop on Tuesday morning, so I assumed you would be flying back today.'

'But how did you know which flight I would be on?' she asked as he kissed her chastely on the temple and swung her Louis Vuitton suitcase from the trolley she had been pushing.

'It wasn't exactly a masterpiece of detective work,' he said in his habitual amused drawl. 'Flights aren't pouring in from Alabama on the hour, every hour. This was the only flight you could possibly be on, assuming, of course, that you hadn't fled the wilds of Alabama for the more civilized fleshpots of Los Angeles or New York.'

Despite her fatigue after the long flight, she giggled and tucked her hand affectionately through the crook of his arm. 'It could have been a temptation,' she said dryly. 'Fort Rucker, Alabama, isn't the most alluring place in the world.'

'Fort where?' Rupert asked in deepening amusement as they stepped out of the arrivals bay and into brilliant sunshine.

'Fort Rucker.'

When she saw him waiting to greet her, she had made an instant decision. She wasn't in love with him, not in the way she was in love with Kyle, but over the last few months he had been enormous fun, both as an employer and a lover. It would be a year before she would see Kyle again, and she saw no reason why Rupert shouldn't continue to be enormous fun. And why he shouldn't also become a friend.

'Would it be impertinent of me to ask why anyone in their right mind would wish to leave London and the delights of Annabel's and Regine's, for a place that sounds as if it's straight out of a Civil War novel?'

They had reached his Lagonda and he tossed her suitcase into the boot, opening the front passenger seat door for her, regarding her quizzically.

Serena stepped into the car, leaning her head comfortably back against the luxurious headrest. It seemed that in her absence Rupert had also come to some decisions about their relationship. Until then he hadn't asked any questions about her private life. He knew about her elopement and the subsequent razzmatazz that had attended her wedding, but he had never questioned her about Kyle and their subsequent, immediate separation. Now, it seemed, he too wanted to take on the role of a friend, in whom confidences could be safely placed.

'Fort Rucker is a US Army Advanced Helicopter Training School.'

Rupert, who had driven the Lagonda smoothly out of the airport parking lot and on to the A4, nearly drove off the side of the road.

A smile curved Serena's mouth. 'Don't worry, Rupert. I'm not thinking of becoming a female air ace. I went there to see Kyle.'

He looked across at her, one eyebrow rising slightly. 'I hadn't realized the two of you were even on speaking terms.'

Serena's smile deepened. 'We haven't been. Which is why I flew to Alabama. I wanted to rectify the situation.'

He was silent for a minute or two, driving at high speed towards the outskirts of Hounslow. 'And did you succeed?' he asked at last, a slight note of tension creeping into his upper-class drawl.

'Oh, yes,' she said, knowing quite well the direction his thoughts were going and enjoying his probing. 'As reunions go, it was definitely eight point nine on the Richter scale.' Her smile faded and she said in sudden seriousness, 'Joking apart, Rupert, it really was the most wonderful reunion. I'm in love with Kyle, heaven only knows why, but I am.'

'And so no divorce?' he asked, keeping his eyes on the road ahead of him.

'No divorce.'

'And no more friendly nights in my company at Annabel's or Regine's?' he asked, taking the turn off for Kew.

'Kyle is going to Vietnam,' she said, a shadow darkening her eyes. 'He's going to be there for a year and I don't imagine for one instant that he's going to spend that year in a state of celibate faithfulness. It wouldn't be in his nature.'

He had turned his head swiftly towards her when she had said the word *Vietnam*, shock flaring across his face. Now he said curiously, 'And is it in yours?'

She pushed a heavy fall of pale blond hair away from her face and over her shoulder. 'No,' she said, unabashed. 'I can't see what difference my going to bed with you makes to my relationship with Kyle. In fact, it's probably beneficial. After all, a steady relationship with one person has to be far preferable than a year-long succession of one-night stands, hasn't it?'

'It's one way of looking at it,' he agreed, both amused at her unsentimental practicality and disturbed by the thought of Kyle Anderson, flying out to South Vietnam and God only knew what kind of a fate.

'It's the way Kyle would look at it,' Serena said with such conviction that he found himself partially believing her. As they sped past the entrance to Kew Gardens, she changed the subject. 'Has Lance got himself into any more scrapes while I've been away?'

'Not that I am aware of.' There was an undertone of indifference in Rupert's voice. At thirty-two, he felt himself too old to be in sympathy with the students who regularly massed outside the American Embassy in Grosvenor Square, chanting antiwar slogans and generally making a confounded nuisance of themselves. If he had any politics at all, they veered towards the right, and he had very little patience with Lance or his revolutionary pretensions.

He turned into King's Road and looked across at her curiously. 'How does Lance feel about having an American for a brother-in-law, especially one who is a member of the armed services?'

She turned her head quickly away from him, before he could see the anguish that had sprung into her eyes. 'He doesn't like it,' she said briefly, with a slight dismissive shrug of her shoulders, as if his not liking it was unimportant. 'You could hardly expect him to, could you?'

'I don't suppose so,' he said easily, heading towards Serena's family home in Cheyne Walk, well aware of the distress his careless question had aroused, and unpleasantly shocked by it. Serena wasn't the kind of girl to become distressed without genuine cause, and he could only imagine that Lance's reaction had been extreme.

'There are a couple of important house sales taking place in Kent this weekend,' he said, making a left-hand turn into an exclusive mews. He drew up before a glossily painted white door flanked by bay trees in terra-cotta pots and by tubs of geraniums and lobelia and trailing pansies. 'Why don't we both go? We can stay at the Grand at Eastbourne and make a weekend of it.'

'That would be nice,' she said, stepping out of the car, her eyes meeting his, her voice once more perfectly under control. 'What kind of sales are they? Georgian? Regency?'

'Georgian. Primarily glass and silver. There should be some interesting bargains to be had.'

He swung her suitcase out of the boot and decided not to invite himself in for a drink. She'd had a long flight, and signs of strain and tiredness were beginning to shadow her eyes.

'Don't bother coming in tomorrow,' he said as she searched in her clutch bag for her key. 'Stay in bed all day and have a good rest. Wednesday will be soon enough to be back at the battle stations.'

As she fitted her key into the lock she turned towards him with an affectionate smile. 'I might just do that, Rupert. Are you coming in for coffee or a drink of something a little stronger?'

He shook his head. 'No,' he said, and knew that she was relieved. 'I've things to do, people to see. Remember to pack a sensible pair of flat shoes as well as glad rags for our Kent and Sussex trip.'

'Flat shoes?' she asked, laughing despite the strain that thoughts of Lance had aroused. 'What on earth do I need a pair of flat shoes for? I don't think I even possess a pair!'

'Then you should,' Rupert said practically, gunning the Lagonda's engine into life. 'A walk over Beachy Head before breakfast on Sunday morning is an obligatory part of a weekend in Eastbourne.' He leaned his head out of the window as the car began to pull away. 'And bring a scarf as well!' he called out. 'It can be devilish windy, even in June!'

She raised a hand, waving good-bye, and then stepped into the house with her suitcase, closing the door behind her.

*Lance*. Incredibly, all the time she had been with Kyle, she hadn't given him a single thought. Leaving the suitcase in the tiny hall, she walked through into the sun-filled living room. She hadn't even asked Rupert if Lance had been telephoning the shop, asking where she was. If he had, and if Rupert had told him that she had gone to Alabama, then he would have known why she had gone there. And he would be prepared for the news she was about to break to him.

And if he hadn't telephoned the shop? If he was unaware that she had even left the country? She moved slowly across the room toward the telephone. Then he wouldn't have the slightest inkling that a reunion between herself and Kyle was even a possibility. He, and her parents, and all her friends, believed that her marriage was dead, and that it was only a question of time before a divorce buried it once and for all. The information that her marriage was far from dead, that it was, instead, very much alive and kicking, would devastate Lance, and might destroy the closeness that had been reforged between them. It wasn't the kind of news that could be broken over the telephone, and she didn't even try.

'Would you like to come over for a drink tonight?' she asked, chewing the corner of her lip as she waited for his reply.

'You sound suspiciously formal,' he said cautiously. 'What is this? An invitation to meet a new, godawful boyfriend?'

'No.' She kept her voice light despite her deepening apprehension. 'I've been away for a few days and I'm tired, and I fancy an evening at home. With family.'

By family, Lance correctly assumed that she meant only the two of them.

'Okay,' he said agreeably. 'I'll be there in about an hour and a half, but I shan't be able to stay for very long. I have a meeting to go to at eight.'

She said good-bye to him and walked tiredly upstairs to run herself a bath, wondering whether the purpose of his meeting was the planning of yet another anti-Vietnam war demonstration.

An hour later, feeling marginally refreshed, she switched on the television in order to catch the early evening news. It was dominated, as usual, by the events in Vietnam. Two weeks before, unmoved and uninterested, she would have quickly changed channels. Now, knowing that Kyle was going there, she watched avidly.

There was a clip of film showing helicopters flying through heavy ground fire on an operation named Nathan Hale. According to the news, it was being fought by the 101st Airborne and 1st Cavalry Divisions. She wasn't sure, but she thought Kyle had said he was going to be with the 1st Cav. The idea bothered her even though she knew he hadn't arrived yet. She poured herself a gin and tonic, wincing as one of the helicopters took a direct hit. The film clip ended. The reporter announced in a monotone that Hanoi had rejected the new American proposal for peace talks, and was reiterating its demand that an unconditional bombing halt precede any negotiations.

Premier Ky's jaunty image flashed on to the screen, and the newscaster informed viewers that after smashing antigovernment resistance in Saigon, Hue, and other major cities, Premier Ky had applied for conciliation and forgiveness for the 'misunderstandings of the war'.

There was then a short piece of film from Paris, where students were rioting, followed by a brief news item about the Beatles.

She moved away from the television to pour herself another drink, grateful that at least there hadn't been a report of any antiwar demonstrations with protestors being hauled away by the police. Her father still hadn't recovered from the ignominy of Lance's very public deportation from America.

The next programme was an inane game show, and she turned the television off, wishing passionately for the hundredth time that Lance were not so left wing in his views, and so virulently anti-American. She was just about to wander into the kitchen and make herself a sandwich when she heard the unmistakable sound of his MG turning into the mews.

She hadn't bothered to dress, and she pulled the tie belt on her white terry bathrobe a little tighter around her waist, smiling wryly to herself as it occurred to her that she was metaphorically girding up her loins.

'My God! You really *aren't* going anywhere tonight, are you?' he said in amazement as he walked into the room, a bottle of Kahlua in one hand. 'I bought this with me just in case you had nothing else for the vodka but the revolting tonic water you pour in your gin.'

He looked, as he always looked to Serena, heartachingly young, as if he were years her junior and not her twin. His arms seemed to be too long for his jacket, though it had been tailored in Savile Row. With loving amusement Serena reflected that Lance never allowed his left-wing views to deny him the luxuries he had always taken for granted. His wrists protruded from his sleeves bonily, with all the awkwardness of a young adolescent's. Even though his hair was obligatorily shoulder-length, it still didn't look quite as reactionarily unkempt as he no doubt wished it to. Silky-straight and blond, like her own, it served only to make him look more feminine and more touchingly vulnerable.

'You said you'd been away for a few days. Where did you go? Paris? Rome?' Without waiting for an answer, he strolled across to the rosewood cocktail cabinet and poured himself a large vodka. 'I know exactly how you spend your year, and it doesn't include being away in June, when it's the Derby and Ascot and Wimbledon.'

'What does it include?' Serena asked, intrigued, glad of the opportunity to delay breaking her news to him.

He splashed some Kahlua into his vodka, added a generous amount of ice, and said with a grin, 'January in the sun in Cape Town, to the shame of your politically unaware heart. Skiing in Europe in February and March. Home to an English spring at Bedingham in April. Monaco and the Grand Prix in early May, and then on to St Tropez for the last two weeks of the month. June in England for the aforementioned Derby and Ascot and Wimbledon and, also, as you're a cricket fan, the first and second Tests. A week in Ibiza to break up July, then back to England and Bedingham in August for the beginning of grouse shooting on the glorious twelfth. September is a month-long house party in St Tropez, October starts in Paris for the Arc de Triomphe and ends in New York, and in November you hare off to the West Indies, coming home to Bedingham, of course, for Christmas.'

'Idiot,' she said, perching on the arm of the sofa. 'I haven't been to the Arc de Triomphe in years.'

'The rest of it is pretty accurate though,' he said with a grin. 'Or it was until this year and your sudden, inexplicable decision to work for Rupert.'

His brows were raised questioningly. She knew he wanted to know if she was sleeping with Rupert and she decided not to satisfy his curiosity. It would only make what she was going to say to him even more complicated.

'I haven't been to Rome, or Paris,' she said carefully. 'I've been to Alabama.'

'Alabama?' There was blank incomprehension in his eyes. She realized with something of a shock that he knew nothing of Kyle's whereabouts, or what he had been doing for the past ten months.

'There is a United States Army Advanced Helicopter Training School in Alabama,' she said, trying to keep her voice light and easy. 'Since we never talk about Kyle I hadn't realized that you didn't know he had spent nearly all of last year training to be an army helicopter pilot.'

'Training to be a *what*? Christ! I thought he was at fucking Princeton!'

'It shows how long it is since you've spoken to Daddy. I thought he would have told you months ago about Kyle joining the army.'

'Why should anyone in our family talk about Kyle Anderson? Or give a fuck about whatever it is that he's doing? He's history, for Christ's sake! A past event! I didn't think we were even going to celebrate the divorce when it comes through, because doing so would be to acknowledge his existence!'

Her eyes held his. 'Kyle is not a past event,' she said quietly.

He slammed his drink down so hard, vodka and Kahlua splashed on to the cocktail cabinet's rosewood surface. 'No, by God! I don't suppose he is! Not if you've been flying to bloody Alabama to see him!'

They hadn't had a row since the ghastly scene on her wedding day. She said, keeping her voice steady with difficulty, 'I'm in love with Kyle, Lance. It's something you're going to have to accept . . .'

'I bloody well do not have to accept it!' he shouted, spittle gathered at the corners of his mouth, his fists clenched, his pale face contorted with anger.

He had faced her with exactly the same expression in his voice and eyes when he had been seven and she had ridden his brand new bicycle into Bedingham's lake, and when he had been fifteen and their parents had decreed that she could holiday with friends in the Caribbean, but that he must stay home because his school report had been poor.

In both instances they had fought fiercely, but it had been over within an hour. She had waded waist-deep into the lake, retrieving the bicycle herself, much to her mother's horror. And she had told her parents that if Lance wasn't allowed to go to the Caribbean, then she wasn't going either. And she hadn't. She had spent the holiday in question at Bedingham, with Lance.

She ran a hand through her hair, pushing it away from her face. 'Please be reasonable, Lance. You don't have to speak to Kyle. You don't have to see him. All you have to do is to accept that he's the person I'm married to and . . .'

'An American army pilot!' he spat out. 'No doubt he joined the bloody army so that he could go to Vietnam and burn babies and rape underage girls and murder old women and bomb the North!'

The tight rein that Serena had been exercising over her patience snapped. 'Don't be so utterly ridiculous!' she flared, jumping to her feet and marching across to the cocktail cabinet. 'I don't know about the babies and the underage girls and the old women, but I do know that he won't be bombing the North! He's flying a helicopter, for Christ's sake! Not a B-52 bomber!'

She poured more tonic into her glass, her hand shaking, appalled at her intense reaction to the hideous images

Lance's words had conjured up. Until her reunion with Kyle, she had barely given Vietnam a thought. Now she found herself unable to think of anything else. He would be there soon. Shortly he would be a part of the savagery. When protestors marched through the streets of London and Washington with placards declaring 'Don't turn our sons into killers', it was Kyle, and young men like him, that they were referring to.

Lance was so stunned that she knew the difference between a helicopter and a bomber that he temporarily forgot his rage, and the reason for it. 'It's not only B-52s that are flying over the North, they have F-8 Crusaders and F-2 Phantoms and E-2 radar planes as well. All the poor bloody North Vietnamese have is a handful of MiG fighters.'

For a brief second, thinking of the atrocities that were no doubt taking place in Vietnam, and which might reach out and touch Kyle, Serena had been stunned to find herself near tears. She despised easy emotionalism and she checked herself instantly, telling herself that her transatlantic flight had left her more tired than she had previously supposed.

'Let's call a truce, Lance,' she said wearily. 'If I can forgive you for your demonstrations and marches, and for the unpleasant press attention you attract to yourself, surely you can forgive me for marrying and staying married to Kyle?'

'But your marrying *anyone* is so bloody pointless!' The white heat of his anger had died and his voice was thick with misery and jealous frustration. 'You're not exactly in need of financial protection, are you? And what other reason is there for any woman to marry?'

His bewilderment was so genuine that despite her fatigue there was laughter in her voice. 'Darling brother mine, I can think of one or two reasons, but I doubt if you would regard them as being rational ones.'

'That's your whole bloody trouble,' he said petulantly. 'You never *are* rational! You never think about anything seriously and neither does Kyle bloody Anderson. He's gone out there, quite willing to kill and maim, and I don't suppose he knows any more about Vietnam, or the Vietnamese struggle for liberation, than you do.'

'No,' Serena said agreeably, too relieved that Lance was now being merely sulky, and that they were no longer on the verge of an appalling fight to take exception to his assumption that Kyle would be killing and maiming with impunity. 'I don't suppose he does.'

The last of Lance's anger ebbed away and only irritation remained. 'I don't know how anyone so bright can be so ignorant,' he said.

She grinned. 'I presume you are referring to me, and not Kyle?'

He snorted with derision at the thought of saying anything complimentary, however obliquely, about Kyle.

'Well,' she said, changing the subject, 'at least I don't get myself arrested, brother mine. How many times have you been taken into custody this year for disturbing the peace? Six? Seven times?'

It had been seven times, but the next time a Blyth-Templeton found themselves in the middle of controversy, and consequently in the gossip columns of the nation's newspapers, it wasn't Lance who stood there. It was Serena.

She had spent the evening at Annabel's with a party of friends. Toby had been there, and since they hadn't seen each other for quite a while, the champagne had flowed and they had danced on the small, dark dance floor until the early hours of the morning. When the brutal noise of hard rock changed to a slower, smoochier rhythm, she inebriatedly announced that she had had enough, and that she was going home. Alone.

Toby, more than a little drunk himself, knew by now that when she said alone, she meant alone, and he made no attempt to follow her.

As she stepped out of the foyer, two middle-aged men in evening dress alighted from a taxi cab and walked towards the nightclub's entrance.

'Did you hear the late night news?' one of them was asking the other. 'Hanoi Radio has apparently reported that several captured US pilots have been paraded through the city in front of angry crowds.'

'The Americans won't like that,' the other said grimly. 'Too humiliating by half.'

There was a short laugh and then, as the doorman opened the door to them, the words, 'Poor buggers, whoever they are.'

The taxi had moved off, and she stood on the pavement, making no attempt to flag one down. *Airmen*. She presumed they had been referring to bomber pilots shot down over the North and captured.

There had been a photograph of one such airman in one of the leading Sunday newspapers a week or so earlier. He had been brought by his captors to stand on what looked to be a small, bare stage, before members of the world press sympathetic to the North Vietnamese cause. His head had been shaved and was lowered, his eyes blinkingly shying away from the fierce light of flashbulbs as he confessed to being a Yankee imperialist aggressor and a war criminal.

Thinking of the conditions under which he was no doubt being imprisoned, and under which his confessions had presumably been extracted, Serena had thought that perhaps his eyes would have shied away from any light. Even daylight.

He had been wearing ill-fitting, coarsely woven prison garments and sandals cut from old rubber tyres. His hands had been shackled behind his back and he had looked so prematurely old and stooped, so utterly alone and so abject, her throat had tightened with rage and pity.

Now, as she thought of the young American pilots being paraded through the Hanoi streets so they could be jeered and spat upon, her rage and pity returned tenfold. Kyle could so easily be one of those men, might one day be one of them. She pulled her white mink jacket closer around her shoulders and, abandoning the idea of a taxi, began to walk down Charles Street towards Hyde Park Corner.

In the two months that Kyle had been in Vietnam she had received only two letters. She hadn't been surprised. It was impossible to imagine Kyle as a letter writer, and she herself had written only a couple of times more often. She knew where he was based and had gone to the trouble of looking the area up on a map. She knew the type of missions that he was assigned, and she knew that nearly all of them entailed flying over countryside held by the Viet Cong.

She hadn't yet heard of a helicoper pilot captured and taken north to the infamous prison known as the Hanoi Hilton. But it could happen. And at the thought of Kyle being subjected not only to physical torture but to public humiliation as well, her hands clenched until the knuckles showed white.

It was early August and the night air was warm and balmy. She crossed Hyde Park Corner, which was ethereally quiet apart from a few stray taxicabs, and began to walk down Upper Belgravia towards King's Road. About forty-five minutes later, as she crossed King's Road and entered Chelsea, a crowd of drunken teenagers spilled from a nearby club, chanting riotously, 'Americans out of Vietnam!' and 'Ho-Ho-Ho Chi Minh!'

As they stumbled past Serena, one of them fell against her. '*Ho-Ho-Ho Chi Minh!*' he yelled into her face.

It was the last straw. All the fear and rage and pity that was burning deep inside her broke free. 'To hell with your bloody Ho Chi Minh!' she shouted back at him, raising her ivory-clasped evening bag and hitting him violently across the face.

The boy staggered backward, falling into the street, and as he did so, and as Serena began to viciously kick out at one of his friends who was trying to seize hold of her, a police car sped into the street, screaming to a halt.

281

Serena was oblivious. One of the boys had pulled her mink jacket off her shoulders and was trampling on it as he vainly tried to ward off the blows she was raining on him with her evening bag.

'Bastard!' she shrieked at him, her fury at the damage that was being done to her jacket increasing the fury that she felt at their anti-American slogans.

When the two officers intervened, trying to separate the pair of them, Serena hit out at them as viciously as she had hit the boy who was still on his hands and knees in the gutter. The ivory clasp of her evening bag caught one of the officers at the corner of one eye. Blood poured from the cut. Seconds later she was ignominiously bundled into the rear of the police car, still struggling violently.

Her appearance next morning at the Magistrate's Court charged with being drunk and disorderly and having assaulted a member of Her Majesty's Police Force did not go unnoticed by the daily press. By the time the afternoon editions hit the streets, they all contained photographs of Serena, still wearing her knee-skimming, sequin-encrusted, Mary Quant evening dress, a rather grubby white mink jacket slung nonchalantly around her shoulders.

Rupert had bailed her out, ignoring with admirable élan the reporters and photographers who jostled them on their walk from the Magistrate's Court to his waiting Lagonda. As they drove into Cheyne Walk, there was an enterprising photographer waiting for them on her doorstep.

Serena stepped out from the Lagonda, sweeping past him, disdaining to shield her face from the flashbulb that went off uncomfortably near her eyes. Her telephone was already ringing, and she knew with wry humour who would be on the other end of the line.

'Well, at least I don't get myself arrested!' Lance said mincingly, mimicking the words she had used to him the night she had told him that she and Kyle had been reunited. He chortled gleefully. 'You have now, sister mine, you have now! Welcome to the club!'

# CHAPTER SIXTEEN

Ten days after the baby's birth, Gabrielle wrapped him snugly in a shawl given to her by the Hôtel Fontainebleau's proprietor's wife, and returned to Paris by public transportation. She felt fit and happy and full of optimism. Gavin was fulfilling the ambition that had brought him to Europe, and in doing so, he was fulfilling her own ambition, an ambition which, until she had met him, she had not even suspected: the deep, burning desire to identify more closely with the country of her birth; to strengthen the links between herself and her Vietnamese aunt and uncle and cousins; to become, after living for more than ten years in France, more Vietnamese than French.

Her father met her at the Gare de Lyon. He pulled the shawl gently away from *le petit* Gavin's face and his own aged and sombre face creased into a smile.

'He looks wonderful, *ma chère*. Every inch a Frenchman.'

Gabrielle smiled and retucked the soft wool of the shawl once more around *le petit* Gavin's head. Her son was only one quarter French, and she did not think that he would ever look archetypically French. His hair was the wrong colour, for one thing. Like Gavin's, it was a warm honey-gold, but there were hints of auburn among the gold and she knew that as he grew older, the auburn would deepen into a glossy, spicy red.

'*Maman* is thrilled,' her father said, guiding her protectively through the crowds entering and leaving the station. 'She has a crib all ready, and she has ironed and aired all the baby clothes you and she have been so busy sewing and knitting this past few months.'

He had flagged down a taxi and was holding the door open for her. 'The christening is all arranged too,' he said as she stepped inside and sank back against a cracked leather seat reeking of Gauloises. 'I spoke to Father Gerald two days ago, and Gavin Étienne Dinh is to be christened on the first Sunday of next month.'

The taxicab slewed out of the boulevard Diderot and into the avenue Daumesnil. 'It is a pity that his father will not be able to attend the ceremony,' her father said as the taxi swerved violently to avoid a pack of cyclists. 'But . . . ' He shrugged philosophically. 'He is an Australian, and I do not suppose that christenings are as important to Australians as they are to us French.'

Gavin was not a Catholic, and though she knew that he would not mind *le petit* Gavin being baptized a Catholic, she knew that for once her father was right. It was not a ceremony that would have any great meaning for him. She wondered where he was at that precise moment, if he was still in Saigon, or if he had moved north to Hue, or Da Nang. She wondered if he had made contact with Nhu. And she wondered how long it would be before his first letter would reach her.

'Michel came to the house yesterday morning,' her father said as the taxi checked, and then ground to a reluctant halt behind a bus. 'He said he had something very important to talk to you about, and asked that you get in touch with him as soon as possible.'

'Michel?' Gabrielle hadn't given a thought to her young pianist the whole time she had been at Fontainebleau. 'But we had no engagements. We haven't had for nearly two months.'

Gavin had insisted that she accept no offers of work in her last weeks of pregnancy, or for several weeks after the baby was born. Michel had been understanding. He was too good a pianist to be adversely affected by her decision. There were always vocalists looking for good accompanists, and if he didn't wish to form another partnership, however temporary, then there were always clubs who would be only too happy to hire him for his talent alone. And Gabrielle, after years of performing, was glad for the small self-indulgent break.

The taxi driver, running out of patience, accelerated and overtook the bus with a bare three centimetres to spare.

Her father steadied himself with the hand strap and then said with another of his habitual shrugs, 'He didn't say what it was that he wanted to talk to you about, *ma chère*. But he did seem extremely anxious. He wanted to know where you were so that he could telephone you, but your mother refused to allow me to give him the name of the hotel. She insisted that you needed rest and that today would be quite soon enough for you to be disturbed.'

At the thought of her fragile, gentle mother laying the law down with such unaccustomed fierceness, Gabrielle smiled. No doubt that same fierceness would also be extended to herself, once she arrived home. She knew that her mother would not want her to return to work, either modelling or singing, but would want her to stay home all day, to be company for her. And she knew that she was completely incapable of doing any such thing for an extended period of time. Eventually, the desire to perform, to sing for others, would lead her back to the clubs.

'Philippe also stopped me in the street, asking after you,' her father said as the taxicab swerved across the place d'Angers and into the avenue Trudaire. 'I told him that the baby had been born and he said to give you his congratulations and to tell you that he has work for you if you want it.'

Gabrielle made no comment. It was nice to know that at least one of the artists who had always so regularly commissioned her was prepared to use her again, even after *le petit* Gavin's birth and the inevitable changes that had taken place to her figure. But she had done less and less modelling in the months that had followed her marriage to Gavin, and now it seemed as if modelling was very much a part of her past.

The taxicab bumped over the Montmartre cobbles and then skidded to a halt outside the shabby entrance to their apartment. She stepped out of the cab into the warm July sunlight and was greeted by the sound of Madame Garine's canaries trilling loudly.

'I'm sorry, *mes petits*,' she said affectionately as she walked past their cage. 'But I have no birdseed with me. I'll bring some down for you in a little while.'

As they entered the lobby she could hear, three floors above them, the door of their apartment open and then the sound of her mother's footsteps hurrying down the stone stairs towards them.

'Gabrielle? Gabrielle? Is that you?'

Gabrielle hurried up the stairs to her mother, *le petit* Gavin stirring restlessly in her arms, his fist pressing against his mouth as he sought hungrily for food.

'*Oh!*' Her mother paused for a moment, overcome with emotion as she rounded the second landing and came face-to-face with Gabrielle and her grandson. 'Oh!' she said again, this time much more softly, running down the last few steps that separated them, the ankle-length tunic of her *ao dai*, split to the waist over loose silk trousers, floating diaphanously around her. Very, very gently she lifted *le petit* Gavin from Gabrielle's arms. 'Oh!' she said for a third and last time, and this time her voice was unimaginably tender. 'Isn't he absolutely beautiful?'

There were tears of joy in her eyes as she looked down at her now wide-awake grandson. Gabrielle kissed her mother lovingly on her cheek and then, putting a hand beneath her arm in order to steady her, she began to lead her back up the stairs towards the apartment.

'And have you plenty of milk, *ma chère*?' her mother asked concerned, a little while later as Gabrielle sat on the sofa, her blouse undone to the waist, *le petit* Gavin at her breast.

'I have enough milk for a score of babies, *Maman*,' Gabrielle said with unabashed truthfulness.

There was a knock at the door, and her father went to answer it.

'That is good, *ma chère*,' her mother began to say, 'beca'ise . . .'

'Philippe would like a word with you, Gabrielle,' her father said, coming back into the room, Philippe at his heels.

Her mother rose agitatedly to her feet, appalled at her husband inviting a man into the room when Gabrielle was breastfeeding. Gabrielle smiled up at Philippe, completely unperturbed. 'Have you come to congratulate me, Philippe? Or to try to coerce me to sit for you?' she teased.

'Both,' he said, grinning through his beard and sitting his massive figure down in a chair opposite her. 'And I want you to sit for me exactly as you are sitting now. With the baby at your breast, your body lush and ripe and utterly superb.'

Her mother's eyes widened in disbelief. '*Di!*' she said to him furiously, lapsing into Vietnamese, as she always did on the rare occasions when she was overcome by anger. '*Di! Di!*'

Philippe was totally baffled. 'What is the matter?' he asked, rising perplexedly to his feet. 'Have I done something to offend you, Madame? Have I perhaps said something?' If he had, he couldn't for the life of him imagine what on earth it could have been.

Only the anguish in her mother's voice prevented Gabrielle from succumbing to helpless laughter. With great difficulty she suppressed it. 'It's all right, *Maman*,' she said in Vietnamese, 'Philippe is leaving now,' and then, to Philippe, '*Maman* mistook something you said, Philippe.'

Before he could ask what it had been, she rose to her feet, crossing the room toward him and beginning to walk with him to the door. 'I'm not sure that I want to do any more modelling, Philippe, at least not for a little while.'

287

'You will be a great loss to me, *ma petite*,' he said in his deep rumbling voice, pausing in the doorway and looking down at her with genuine regret. 'Promise me one thing. Promise me that if you will not model for me, you will not model for anyone else. Especially that bastard Léon Durras.'

The laughter she had been suppressing with such difficulty burst free. 'I promise.' She stood on tiptoe and kissed him on his bearded cheek.

'And the singing?' he asked quizzically, deeply pleased. 'Will I still be able to hear you sing at the Black Cat?'

'I'm not sure,' she said, suddenly thoughtful. 'I shall still sing. I shall always sing. But for some reason that I do not understand, I do not think that I will ever sing again at the Black Cat.'

'You must be telepathic,' Michel said an hour later as she told him about Philippe's visit. He sat across from Gabrielle. 'I've been frantically trying to get in touch with you since yesterday morning to tell you that you've got the chance to do something really different.'

Gabrielle sat in the old, comfortable armchair that dwarfed her, but that had been barely big enough for Philippe. Although she was dressed in a loose black cotton top and a black leather miniskirt, she glowed with colour. Her sumptuous red hair had grown longer in the months she had been pregnant, and tumbled around her face in a riot of untamed waves and springing curls. Her green cat eyes danced with happiness. Her suntanned legs and feet were naked, her toenails painted the same vibrant glossy pink as the nails on her fingers.

'And what is that, *chéri*?' she asked affectionately, curling her legs beneath her with restless energy.

Michel grinned at her. Though he was absolutely bewitched by her, he had known from the instant he had met her that his feelings would never be reciprocated. He had learned not to mind. Instead of being her partner in a love affair, he was her musical partner, and he was her friend. And as musical partnerships and friendships often lasted for a lifetime, whereas love affairs seldom did, he had come to terms with the situation. 'Rock and roll,' he said, enjoying the look of incredulity that crossed her face. 'Good old-fashioned, beat-dominated rock and roll.'

She began to laugh so helplessly she could hardly speak. 'I'm a nightclub singer, Michel,' she protested at last, her voice still full of giggles at his idiocy. 'I sing slow, melodic stuff. Torch songs. Committed, passionate love songs. I couldn't become Brenda Lee or Connie Stevens if I tried.'

Michel reached out towards the plate of cookies that her mother had brought in. Like all Gabrielle's friends, he seldom visited her at home, but when he did, Vanh always went out of her way to make him feel welcome. She found his bespectacled, intellectual appearance reassuring. He seemed to her more like a student or a young schoolmaster than a musician.

'No one would want you to,' he said, grinning. 'You're far too sexy to be a teenybopper's delight, and an imitative Miss Lee or Miss Stevens isn't at all what Radford has in mind.'

'Radford?' she asked, intrigued despite the fact that rock and roll was not her style.

He finished eating his cookie and leaned towards her, his hands clasped loosely between his knees, his eyes alight with enthusiasm. 'Radford James. He's an American. Black, talented, and very, very ambitious.'

She began to laugh again. 'So what is new, *chéri*?' she asked, leaning over the crib at the side of her chair and tucking the blankets more securely around her sleeping son. 'What is so special about this particular talented, ambitious American?'

'What is special about him is the sound he has come up with,' Michel said in a voice that was so unequivocal that Gabrielle raised her eyebrows slightly. As a musician,

Michel was a perfectionist, and he was not impressed easily.

'He had some success with an all-male, all-black group in America in 1964, but they were too like a hundred other groups for them to make any real impression. When the music scene moved to London he followed it, playing the clubs, and at the end of the year he formed a new band. Instrumentally they're great. A hard-edged mixture of black soul and honest-to-goodness rock. More Rolling Stones than Beatles. What he needs now is a lead vocalist. Someone with blatant sex appeal and with the raw-edged quality to their voice that whips up an audience's emotions. He thought he'd found someone. A girl from Liverpool who, like Lennon and Jagger, sounds black when she sings. They played bottom of the bill on a tour in February, and stole the show. Since then they've picked up a record contract and done a month-long tour of the States. Next month they're booked to appear at what is going to be the biggest open-air pop festival ever held in France.'

'And?' Gabrielle prompted impatiently, wondering when he was going to come to the point.

'*And* their lead singer has walked out on them. She's married a South African businessman and returned with him to Johannesburg. Radford needs a female singer. Urgently. A female singer who isn't imitative of any other singer at present on the pop scene. I think that what he needs is you.'

She shook her head, the sun streaming through the window behind her highlighting her titian hair with gold. 'No,' she said, wondering why she found such a ridiculous idea tempting. 'My style is too individualistic for me ever to become a pop singer, Michel.'

'You're wrong!' His voice was vehement. 'I know this could be a turning point for you, Gabrielle! I can feel it in my blood and in my bones! The band is already on the verge of becoming as big as the Stones, or the Beatles or Bob Dylan!

290

When you meet Radford, you'll know why I feel so certain that he's going to be a major star. And when you hear the music, I know you'll want to be a part of it.'

His eyes were so intense, his voice so certain, the laughter that had been rising in her throat died away. To her surprise, she heard herself saying, 'All right, Michel. All right. If you feel so passionately about this American, then I will meet him.'

His grin split his face. 'I knew you would! I knew it was a challenge you wouldn't be able to resist!'

She tilted her head to one side, looking at him curiously. 'Why is this so important to you?' she asked, puzzled. 'After all, if Radford likes my voice, and if I begin to sing with his band, then we will not be working together anymore. And we have worked well together, *chéri*, haven't we?'

She wasn't flirting with him. It was a plain statement of fact.

His grin died and his eyes behind his thick-lensed glasses were embarrassed. 'Yes,' he said awkwardly. 'We have worked well together, Gabrielle. We will still work well together, for I will still arrange the music for the songs that you compose. Only now I shall have another satisfaction as well.'

A flush of colour touched his cheeks, and he paused for so long that Gabrielle thought he was never going to find the courage to finish what he had begun to say. At last he said, the colour in his face deepening, 'I shall know in the years ahead that it was because you trusted me and acted on my advice that you became a star. And you *will* become a star, Gabrielle. You will become a world-famous star. It is impossible for you to be anything else.'

Gabrielle doubted that Radford James would be interested in hiring her as his lead vocalist. Though part of her success came from her effortlessly erotic stage presence, it was her ability to sing love songs in a husky, knowing voice that made her unique.

291

'So why go?' Vanh asked bewilderedly. 'There is no need for you to earn money. Gavin has arranged for part of his salary to be paid direct to you, has he not?'

Gabrielle nodded, laying *le petit* Gavin in a Moses basket. 'Yes.' The money that Gavin had arranged to be transferred from his salary to her had been the source of their only argument. In Gabrielle's opinion, the amount was far too much. Gavin had insisted that it wasn't, that he would be living almost exclusively on expenses in Saigon and therefore wouldn't need the greater half of his salary. And that she would.

'Then I don't understand,' Vanh repeated. She was seated at the kitchen table and she looked across the room at Gabrielle forlornly. 'I thought that you would not be working any longer, *ma chère*, that we would be at home together with *le petit* Gavin.'

Gabrielle knew very well that that was what her mother had been hoping for, and she had always known that she would have to disappoint her.

'I cannot stay at home all day, every day, *Maman*,' she said gently. 'It isn't good that you do so. You should go for a walk every afternoon. Pass a few words with Madame Castries. Visit Madame Garine. Make some friends.'

Her mother gave a shrug of her shoulders that was almost Gallic, saying a trifle sulkily, 'In Saigon it was easy, *ma chère*. We had so many friends – educated, wealthy people. People who respected us. Now, when Papa has no position . . .'

'You must forget the way that we lived in Saigon, *Maman*,' Gabrielle said firmly. 'Madame Castries and Madame Garine are neither wealthy nor educated, but they would be good friends to you if you would allow them to be.' Michel's car horn tooted loudly. 'Do you promise me that you will try?' she said, walking across to the door and opening it, pausing for a moment. 'That you will go for a walk and buy a paper from Madame Castries and pass the time of day with her? And that you will knock on Madame

Garine's door and ask her if she would like to come upstairs and share a pot of coffee with you.'

Michel's car horn tooted again, this time more insistently, and Vanh said reluctantly, 'All right, *ma chère*. For your sake, I will try.'

Gabrielle gave her a dazzling smile, blew her a kiss, and with the Moses basket and its precious cargo in one hand, hurried down the stone stairs.

The room Radford James and his band were using for rehearsals was above a bistro in one of the streets in the maze around the place de la Bastille. Michel's ancient Citroën coughed and spluttered down the rue de Rivoli, nearly coming to grief with a sleek Mercedes at the corner of the rue de Sévigné.

'What makes you so sure that Radford James will even listen to me?' she asked, turning towards the backseat to make sure that the Moses basket was safe.

The driver of the Mercedes was still hurling verbal abuse in their wake. Michel ignored him, saying complacently, 'Because he has already heard you sing.'

'When? Where?' she exclaimed indignantly. 'You never told me!'

A grin split his angular, almost adolescent features. 'He heard you the night of your last performance at the Black Cat.' He swerved into the rue de Birague, a cloud of exhaust fumes in his wake. 'There's something else I haven't told you.'

'And what is that?' There was a dangerous gleam in her eye. His voice was so sheepish, she knew that whatever it was, she wasn't going to like it.

He drew to a halt outside a bistro, the sound of rock music blasting the street from the upper windows. 'He has copies of all the songs you've written,' he said, making a speedy exit from the car.

'*Merde!*' she flared furiously, opening her own door, and then the rear door, hoisting the basket from the backseat. 'How dare you, Michel! That really is awful of you! Really—'

She broke off, forgetting her incensed indignation as the music hit her ears in a wall of sound. '*Tiens!*' she said in stunned amazement. 'How many musicians are in this rock band? Fifty?'

Michel laughed, leading the way inside and up a flight of bare wooden stairs. 'Seven at the moment. Three guitars, two bass, two pianos.'

*A Fool in Love* merged into *Nowhere to Run*. At the top of the stairs they crossed a small landing and walked into a large room, bare except for the musicians and their instruments and a black woman in a red leather minidress, singing the *Nowhere to Run* number in a voice that was a passably good imitation of Martha Reeves's.

'Fine, baby. Great,' a voice said dismissively. 'That's all for now, I'll be in touch.'

The woman looked as though she were going to argue the point, and then, as he turned away from her and toward Gabrielle and Michel, decided against it, shrugging a jacket around her shoulders and walking quickly from the room, flashing Gabrielle a look of frustrated fury as she did so.

'Well,' Radford James said uncaringly, standing with his fingers splayed on his hips in a gesture that would have been effeminate in a man less sinfully masculine. 'You're actually *here*, baby!' White teeth flashed the broadest smile that she had ever seen.

He was tall and loose-limbed, broad shoulders tapering down to a lean waist, the narrowness of his hips erotically emphasized by the tightness of faded blue denim. He was younger than she had anticipated, twenty-two or twenty-three, and his skin was so dark and smooth that there was almost a sheen to it.

She was flooded with a sense of immediate rapport, as if meeting for the first time someone she had always known.

294

'Yes, I'm actually here,' she said, laughter bubbling up in her throat as she put the Moses basket down and walked towards him.

He was the most beautiful man she had ever seen, and she knew that the rapport blazing between them was inextricably mixed with instant, almost overwhelming sexual attraction. If they had met a year earlier, she knew she would have had no hesitation in tumbling into his bed. But they hadn't met a year earlier, and she was married to Gavin, and the only bed she was ever going to tumble into was his.

Radford took hold of her hands, laughing down at her, his eyes telling her everything she already knew. 'Honey, when I saw you onstage I knew you were only a little-bitty thing, but hell, offstage you ain't no bigger than a minute!'

Gabrielle gave a throaty chuckle. She was wearing stiletto-high heels that added at least four inches to her height. She resisted the temptation to step out of them, and also the temptation to tell him that though she was petite, she had a big voice. He would find that out soon enough. As would Michel.

A smile quirked her mouth as Radford began to lead her towards the nearest piano. The songs she sang in the clubs never required her to give her voice full rein. She didn't know if the next few minutes were going to be a surprise for Radford, but she knew that they were going to be a shock for Michel.

'What would you like me to sing?' she asked, knowing that whatever it was, she would be able to do it just the way he wanted to hear it.

He looked down at her, an eyebrow rising slightly at her buoyant confidence. 'You know that this is a real long shot, don't you? I mean, I want a *big* voice as well as one packed with emotion. I *know* you have the emotion. But we're not a small-club band, and I don't want a small-club singing voice.'

'You're not going to get one,' Gabrielle said with sudden gentleness, knowing that he was nervous because he so desperately wanted her voice to be right.

Something unspoken, almost atavistic, passed between them. 'Okay,' he said softly. 'Okay, girl. We'll give it a try with one of your own songs. I've kept the structure and the basic melody, but you're going to find the treatment a hell of a lot different. Sit tight while we play it through and then, when you're ready, come in with the vocal.'

She stood by the side of the piano, and from the moment they played the opening riff she knew that Michel had been right. The sound was sensational. Blues oriented and gritty. And it was a sound that was backing *her* song. She looked across at Michel and flashed him a wide smile, trying to dispel the tension she knew he was feeling. It was going to be okay. Her nerve endings tingled with anticipation. It was going to be more than okay. It was going to be the start of a whole new career.

She stood very still for the few seconds before they began to play the song through for the second time and then, as the opening riff, honed razor sharp, hit the air, she launched herself away from the piano, dancing to the centre of the room, the sound tearing out of her.

She never had to ask if she was good. The roar of applause from the band and from Radford and Michel, when the last note had been played, told her everything.

'Girl, you can sing,' Radford whooped exultantly, whipping them straight into *Peaches 'n' Cream* and then *I'm Ready for Love*, song following song, some of them songs she had written herself and that Radford had already worked on with his band, some of them classic oldies. Only when *le petit* Gavin, overwhelmed by hunger, began to cry lustily, did the session come to an end.

'I guess that's it for today, baby,' Radford said as she wiped the perspiration from her face and lifted her crying son into her arms. 'How does it feel to be a queen of rock?'

'It feels great.' Her face was radiant, her heart still slamming against her chest, her pulse racing, perspiration trickling down her neck and her back.

He flashed her a dazzling, down-slanting smile. 'Wait till you give the same kind of performance under lights, honeychild. Then you'll *know*/where it's at!'

She had undone her sweat-soaked shirt and the baby was nuzzling at her breast. He had never before met anyone like her. She was so petite, so guileless, so effortlessly sexy. And she wasn't about to take their mutual, almost crucifying attraction for each other to its logical conclusion. Her apologetic refusal to the unspoken question he had asked within seconds of meeting her was clear and unmistakable in her eyes.

He wondered why. He didn't believe for a moment that she was the kind of lady who would allow a husband and a child to hamper her natural inclinations. Not unless she wanted them to. And if she wanted them to, then it meant she had to be simply crazy in love. He wondered who her husband was, that he commanded faithfulness from a lady whose sexual appetite was, he was sure, as uninhibited and as wide-ranging as his own.


The open-air concert was to be held on the last Saturday of the month. For the next two weeks they met daily in the room above the bistro, Michel taking on the role of baby-sitter and audience as Radford had Gabrielle and the band rehearse numbers over and over, constantly altering the material, and improvising and discarding.

'That's *very* close,' he would say sometimes when they were all near to dropping with exhaustion. 'That's very close, but it's not quite it. Let's try it again.'


'You know that if this comes off, the record contract is in the bag, don't you?' Michel asked her, dangling *le petit* Gavin on his knee as Gabrielle nervously gathered together the dress she was going to wear, and her white leather stage boots, and her makeup.

'Yes.' She couldn't allow herself to think about the record contract. All she could think of was the concert. In two hours she would make her debut as a rock singer. And at least two of the songs she had written would get a massive hearing.

'I haven't forgotten anything, have I, *chéri*?' she asked, looking around the apartment, the dress and boots in one hand, her makeup bag in the other.

'No.' He was almost as nervous as she was. The concert wasn't just any old pop concert. It was going to be televised. It was going to reach an audience of millions. The cream of British and American rock groups had travelled to France especially to participate. The very best groups that France possessed had hustled to be with them on the bill.

'*Ça va*. Then I'm ready,' she said, her sumptuous red hair framing her face in an untamed riot of waves and curls.

Her mother came into the room, startled as always by Michel's easy, confident handling of her grandson. 'There is a letter for you, *ma chère*. It is from Saigon. And it is not from Nhu.'

'*Mon Dieu!*' Gabrielle did the impossible. She forgot about the concert, opening the envelope with trembling fingers, reading Gavin's untidy scrawl with a fast-beating heart.

'—and so I'm back from Da Nang now, and I think the Buddhists are going to run out of steam,' he had written toward the end of his letter. 'Nhu thinks they never had a chance since they can't offer any alternative political leadership. Your aunt Nhu is quite a girl! Very vital and very positive. She's taken me under her wing, and from now on life looks as if it's going to be very interesting indeed—' He ended by saying that he missed her like the very devil, and he sent her all his love.

'Good news?' Michel asked, his nervousness increasing. If it was bad news, he would never forgive her mother for

298

having handed her the letter two hours before the most important concert of her life.

'Yes.' She held the letter close to her breasts for a moment, fighting an upsurge of tears. God, but she loved him! And she missed him!

'Then we'd better be going,' he said, lifting *le petit* Gavin up against his shoulder with one hand and picking up the Moses basket with the other.

She nodded agreement, blinking hard. Gavin would be horrified if he knew that she was missing him enough to cry from sheer longing. After all, *she* had encouraged him to leave her and go to Vietnam. By being there he was fulfilling her ambitions as well as his.

She smiled at her idiocy, the unshed tears clinging shimmeringly on her lashes. 'Yes, let's go, *mon brave*,' she said, walking quickly across to the door and leading the way down the stairs and into the street.

They did not perform until the second half of the concert, and afterwards Gabrielle never could remember any of the prestigious American and British rock groups who preceded them. All she remembered was Radford saying to her, his eyes glittering like agates, 'This is it, baby! We're on!'

The opening riff boomed out over giant speakers. *Da-da-da-da-dum! Da-da-da-da-dum!* She crossed her fingers on both hands, threw a prayer up to heaven, and whirled onstage after him, mercurial dynamite in a black leather minidress and knee-high, stiletto-heeled boots.

The audience was with her from the very first moment. '*Do you love me?*' she belted out as the music stormed over them in a great majestic rock 'n' roll roar. '*Do you want me?*' As she danced downstage towards them, her hair burning red in the sunlight, her hips grinding, her feet stamping the rhythm, twenty thousand voices roared out assent.

They played their four scheduled numbers and the crowd howled for more, whistling and screaming, refusing to be pacified until they launched into yet another number.

'Okay!' Radford yelled to the band from his piano stool. 'Let's give them *Lover Man*.'

It was one of the songs that she had written, and Radford's arrangement of it was more blues than rock. Triumph and elation surged through her as she stood for a moment, suddenly still, gaining control of her breathing, and by the sheer force of her personality bringing the audience into a new mood with her.

'*Lover man, where have you gone?*' she sang, suddenly vulnerable, heart-stoppingly female, deliberately unleashing the touching, broken-edged quality in her voice that she had always used in the clubs to such staggering effect.

For a rock group it had been a daring choice to close with, and it was a sensation. As the last chord died away, the audience erupted in a storm of applause, shouting and screaming and stamping their feet. She could see Michel, offstage, whooping in exultation, and Radford, only yards away from her, punching the air with his fists.

The band was centre-stage with her, hugging her and waving and shouting compliments back to the audience.

It was an incredible moment, a moment she knew she would never forget. And then Michel lifted *le petit* Gavin from his Moses basket, holding him so that he could see her, and she knew that if only Gavin could have been there, too, it would have been more than incredible. It would have been the most wonderful moment of her life.

# CHAPTER SEVENTEEN

Life for Lewis, through May and June of 1966, was much the same as it had been since his arrival. Despite the constant stress and danger, there was a routine to his days that gave them structure and that even, on occasion, became monotonous. Day after day was passed with the same activities – patrolling the surrounding canal-infested countryside; ambushing any Viet Cong forces that were detected and could be flushed out; training the local Vietnamese militia units; administering civil operations such as medical programmes and agricultural projects as well as military operations. Lewis's only relaxations were sleeping and eating. And army rations, supplemented by local produce, left a lot to be desired.

Sleeping was even less of a pleasure. Mosquitoes, and a dozen other bugs that Lewis was unable to name, made nights a torment. Despite heavy spraying of insecticide inside the net covering his bunk, and lavish applications of insect repellent on his skin, some mosquitoes always survived, crawling into his hair and settling on his arms and chest to feed from convenient capillaries.

Tam's laconic indifference to the blood-sucking pests never ceased to amuse him. She would swat them away, barely pausing in whatever task she was doing.

His team's euphoria at having Tam in the house, washing dishes and laundering and cleaning and sweeping, was short-lived. They had looked forward to flirting with her and teasing her, and they were sorely disappointed. Unlike most of the village girls, whose eyes were always full of mischief, and who laughed and smiled at the slightest opportunity, Tam was inscrutable. She did her work with

301

flawless efficiency, scraping dried mud from the floors and from their boots, scouring the cooking pots until they shined, sewing up tears in fatigues. But she did it all with an attitude of barely veiled contempt, never speaking to the men unless it was absolutely necessary, and then only in a voice so ice cool and impersonal that they soon gave up any idea of thawing her into amiability.

Far from sharing his men's disappointment, Lewis was relieved by Tam's aloofness. A stunningly pretty seventeen- or eighteen-year-old in the team house and its precincts for six or seven hours a day could have been a sure-fire recipe for trouble. As it was, after the first few days, when the novelty of her presence had worn off, Lewis knew that he could relax. Even his optimistically persistent assistant team leader, Lieutenant Grainger, had given up trying to elicit a friendly response from her. If there were going to be any repercussions from having her as their cleaning girl, they were not going to be the sexual ones he had feared.

The only person she ever spoke to at length was himself, and he knew that she did so only in order to practise her English. She was a model pupil, listening avidly, never having to be told twice, returning each day with the previous day's grammar and vocabulary committed to memory, only her pronunciation being a little uncertain.

'By the time I leave Vietnam, your English will be good enough for you to apply for a job as an interpreter with the Americans,' he said to her one morning in late July as they came to the end of her daily lesson.

She looked across at him, and her eyes, normally devoid of expression, were curious. 'You cannot believe that I would do such a thing,' she said in charmingly laboured English.

He pushed his chair away from the rough wood table and walked across to the coolbox for a vacuum bottle of drinking water.

'Why not?' he asked mildly. In the three months that she had been working at the team house, it was the first time

302

their conversation had approached being personal. A tingle of triumph ran down his spine. If he could get her to talk about herself, then he might also be able to get her to listen to advice she badly needed, advice which, if he had given it previously, he knew she would have contemptuously spurned.

He returned to the table with the vacuum jug and two plastic beakers and she said, her eyes holding his, her curiosity touched with defiance, 'I am not learning English in order that I can help the Americans.'

He poured water into the beakers and handed her one of them, swatting away an insect that had landed on his arm. 'I know.'

A hint of a flush touched her tawny skin. 'You do not know. You cannot know.'

He ran a hand through his thickly curling hair. 'I do know,' he said again quietly. 'I know that you asked for English lessons so that you would be able to help the Viet Cong. I have always known that.'

In her eyes, curiosity and defiance had been replaced by stunned amazement. 'And yet you still taught me?'

He nodded, her incredulity and bewilderment arousing a wave of tenderness in him.

She frowned, and for a moment he thought she was going to retreat into her customary pose of careless indifference, and then she said, her voice troubled, 'I am sorry, *Dai uy*, but I do not understand.'

It was the first time that, addressing him by his title, she had not given the words a sarcastic edge. A slight smile touched the hard line of his mouth. If she wasn't careful, she would soon find herself treating him as a friend.

'No, I know that you don't, Tam,' he said gently, relieved that she was at last lowering the barriers that she had erected between them. He rested his folded arms on the table, leaning toward her slightly. 'Let me try to explain.'

\* \* \*

'I do not believe you,' she said flatly when he told her of the atrocities committed by the Viet Cong against village chiefs who refused to cooperate with them. 'None of those things have happened here, in Van Binh.'

'Only because there is an American presence in Van Binh,' he said dryly.

'I still do not believe you.' Her hands were clenched tightly in her lap. 'The Viet Cong are freedom fighters. They are fighting for a free Vietnam.'

'They're fighting for a *Communist* Vietnam,' Lewis said, feeling his patience beginning to slip away from him. 'And if that's what you want, let me tell you that when you get it, you won't like it at all!'

'Why should you care?' she asked with a flare of her old spirit. '*You* are not Vietnamese! What is it to you what we Vietnamese do? If you want so much to be in Vietnam, just wait a little while and perhaps in your next reincarnation you will be born Vietnamese!'

She looked so pretty, her almond eyes sparking angrily, her waist-length black hair shimmering down her back, that his impatience died and he burst into rare laughter.

'There could be worse fates,' he said as Lieutenant Grainger walked into the team house, looking quizzically at them both.

For the first time since he had known her, Lewis saw a small grin edge the corner of her mouth. 'Perhaps, but not, I think, for an American,' she said naughtily, and with a gleam of laughter in her eye, she rose from her rickety wooden chair, and ignoring Lieutenant Grainger completely, she swept out of the team house, walking with eye-riveting grace across the compound to her washtub and her laundry.

'What was all that about?' Lieutenant Grainger asked, dragging his gaze away from her. 'Is the ice maiden beginning to thaw at last?'

'Maybe,' Lewis said noncommittally, irrationally annoyed by his assistant team leader's remark and his tone of voice.

If Tam was beginning to thaw, it sure as hell wouldn't be in Grainger's direction. 'It's about time we set off for Tay Phong. Are the district chief and his cronies here yet?'

Tay Phong was the village farthest from Van Binh in his area. It was in a particularly vulnerable position, dangerously close to the network of waterways that the Cong used to smuggle supplies from the Cambodian border to their units. Lewis had a good relationship with Tay Phong's village chief that he wanted to maintain. If Tay Phong underwent a change of loyalty, becoming sympathetic to the Viet Cong, then he had no chance of ever again intercepting the supply convoys.

'Hoan is on his way up here now,' Grainger said, referring to the district chief who was to travel to Tay Phong with them. He picked up his M-16, turning back toward the door, wondering what the hell pretty Tam had done or said to have provoked such unaccustomed laughter from his sober-sided captain.

Lewis strapped on his .45 service automatic and followed him. The sun seemed unusually bright, and he blinked his eyes uncomfortably as he strode across the compound to meet Hoan and the two members of his staff who always travelled with him.

'Chào, Dai uy,' the elderly district chief said cheerily.

'Chào, Em,' Lewis responded. His relationship with Hoan was a good one. He was a rare creature, a district chief who was unbribable and incorruptible. Today, however, Lewis knew that Hoan regarded himself as being off duty because he was going with them to Tay Phong only because he had a brother living there. The visit, made in the comfort of a water taxi, would give him the chance for a family chat.

As they walked down towards the village and the battered construction that served as a pier, Lewis turned his head, looking back at the compound. Tam had paused in her laundering and was standing, watching him. He grinned, pleased at the rapport that had suddenly sprung up between

305

them, wishing he could have stayed in the team house, talking to her, rather than travel with Grainger and Hoan to Tay Phong.

The water taxi was a small engine-powered boat with a sheltered passenger compartment and was the common means of transportation from one village to the next. As Lewis stepped aboard, he was aware that he had the beginnings of a headache.

He sat beneath the shade, wishing yet again that he hadn't arranged to have a discussion with Tay Phong's village chief and to inspect its local militia platoon. He had a letter from Abbra tucked into the breast pocket of his tiger-stripe fatigues and he withdrew it, reading it yet again, his strong, hard-boned face softening slightly as he did.

She didn't appear to be seeing so much of Scott now that the football season was over. He didn't mind about that too much. He didn't want her getting so hooked on the game that she would want him to accompany her once he returned home. They would have better things to do than sit in the stands and cheer Scott on.

His smile deepened. The birthday party at the Polo Lounge sounded like fun. It was nice to think of them all there together, Abbra and Scott and his father, being a real family. He wondered whose idea it had been to have candles and a miniature football player on the cake and guessed that it had been Abbra's.

There wasn't too much else in her letter. She had been to Boston for a few days and waxed lyrical about the squirrels on the Common and the sun shining on the golden dome of the State House, and the winding old streets on Beacon Hill. He couldn't imagine why she had chosen the East Coast and Boston for a vacation when she could quite easily have driven down to Monterey or Carmel or even Mexico.

His head was beginning to throb, and he refolded the letter and put it back in his pocket, shivering slightly. There wasn't long to go now before he would be back home with her, and when he was, they would vacation together.

Mexico would be a good choice. They could go to Acapulco and Oaxaca.

'Looks like we're going to be in for an uncomfortable ride, *Dai uy*,' Grainger said to him glumly as the water taxi approached the next village along the canal bank.

Lewis squinted into the fierce sunlight. There was a small crowd waiting at the makeshift dock. Black-garbed elderly women with baskets of farm produce, and farmers, cages of live hens at their feet. He groaned. Travelling with the villagers on a local water taxi was always a hardship, but today it would be unbearable.

His head was throbbing viciously and his limbs had begun to ache. If he had been back home in California he would have thought he was coming down with the flu, and he would have taken a couple of aspirin and shrugged it off. In Vietnam the solution wasn't as simple. He could be suffering from anything, goddammit, and he had no access to any medication until they returned to Van Binh.

The water taxi glided to a halt and the chattering villagers loaded themselves aboard. He squeezed himself into a position from which he could keep a careful eye on the canal bank, knowing that Grainger would be doing the same on the other side of the boat. They never had come under sniper fire while travelling by water taxi, but there was always a first time.

He was beginning to feel nauseated, and determined that once in Tay Phong, his visit would be brief. He would inspect the militia, have a word with the village chief, and then he would go back to the team house and dose himself with aspirin and try to sleep off whatever it was he was coming down with.

'Are you okay, *Dai uy*?' Grainger called across from the far side of the boat, looking at him anxiously.

Lewis gave a brief nod. He was far from okay, but there was no point in whining about it to Grainger.

After a journey that seemed interminable, the water taxi glided to a halt in Tay Phong. Every muscle Lewis possessed ached as he climbed from the boat and began to walk towards the main street, Grainger, Hoan, and his cronies in his wake.

Tay Phong was like every other village in the province. There was one main street, hemmed in by shops and small houses made of grass and thatch. On one side the houses faced out over the canal, and a few sampans were tied up to wooden stilt pilings. Halfway down the street was the market square and a few more buildings: a Catholic church, a schoolhouse, both made of masonry blocks.

A pig careered across their path, a stream of children running noisily in its wake as they made their way to the village office, where the village chief was waiting to meet them.

'*Chào! Chào! Co van!*' the chief said buoyantly, greeting Lewis by his title of adviser and pouring out glasses of the local homemade firewater.

Lewis took the proferred glass reluctantly. Good manners demanded he drink it, and he did so in one swallow, certain it would either kill him or cure him.

'I have information, *Co van,*' the village chief said when the formalities of drinking the *ba si de* were over. He leaned towards Lewis over a table even more battered than the one in the team house. 'A supply unit is due to come into the area, a big one.'

Lights were dancing on the periphery of Lewis's vision, and he had to clamp his hands on his knees to prevent them from quivering. 'Are you sure it's coming this far south?' he asked, struggling to concentrate.

Usually it was only the offshoots of the big supply units that penetrated this far south. A main supply unit would be too big for his team and the local militia units to manage. They would need a backup force. Perhaps even a Special Forces 'A' team.

The village chief nodded his head vigorously. 'Yes, *Co van,*' he said emphatically. 'My informant is a member of the Viet Cong infrastructure who has discovered that his superior officer has been sleeping with his wife. The officer will be accompanying the supply unit and it is for revenge that he has come to me with information.'

'When he says a big supply unit, how big does he mean?'

It was common knowledge that there were at least two North Vietnamese Army regiments operating from just across the Cambodian border. The nearest province to them was Kien Phong, and in only one night's travelling the Cong, supplied from Cambodia with medicines and money and ammunition, could be deep in the province. From there, smaller units spread the supplies via boat and the labyrinthine canal network into the provinces of An Giang and Sa Dec, and as far south as their own province.

'Very big,' the village chief confirmed. 'The supplies are going to be brought in, not by the local Cong, but by the NVA themselves.'

Lewis groaned. He was feeling like death; all he wanted to do was to crawl into his bunk and pull a blanket over his head, and the chief was telling him that they were on the verge of a massive confrontation with North Vietnamese troops. 'When?' he croaked, aware that both Lieutenant Grainger and Hoan were looking across at him anxiously, knowing that there was something wrong with him.

'Four nights. Maybe five nights. My informant will come back to me and will tell me their route and checkpoints.'

'Okay.' Lewis rose to his feet, staggering as he did so. 'Let's go and inspect the militia.'

'Do you think you should?' Grainger said to him urgently, *sotto voce*. 'You're burning up. We should get you the hell back to camp.'

'Fifteen more minutes isn't going to make any damn difference, and if we're about to face the NVA, it would be nice to know that Tay Phong's militia is prepared.'

With Hoan at his side, Lewis inspected the troops, warning the platoon commander to be in a state of readiness over the next few days, and then, barely able to see for the raging pain in his head, and barely able to walk because of

309

cramps in his legs and his feet, he struggled back to Tay Phong's crumbling jetty.

'For Christ's sake, *Dai uy*, what the hell are you coming down with?' Grainger demanded, terrified that he was going to have to call in a chopper to whisk Lewis to the nearest field hospital, and that in Lewis's absence the responsibility for organizing the ambush of the NVA units was going to fall on to his shoulders.

Lewis didn't answer. He couldn't. He was dimly aware that they had boarded a water taxi, and that it was mercifully free of the live farm produce that had accompanied them on their earlier journey. He was pretty certain he hadn't been poisoned. He knew damn well that he hadn't been in contact with any punji sticks, or any other poisoned booby trap that the Viet Cong were so adept at laying.

He tried to think what he had eaten in the last twenty-four hours, but his brain wouldn't function. Rats? Had he eaten any rat lately? Rat meat was a local staple and one that Sergeant Drayton often used in order to supplement their C rations. Chopped and cooked Chinese style with beans and flavoured with the *nuoc mam* sauce that accompanied every Vietnamese dish, it was surprisingly palatable. But Drayton hadn't served any for over a week, Lewis was sure of it.

By the time the water taxi bumped gently against the canal side in Van Binh, he was leaning over the side of the boat, retching his heart out.

Very slowly, taking all of Lewis's weight on himself, Lieutenant Grainger began to half carry and half drag him back towards the team house.

Lewis knew that he was throwing up, and he knew that someone was holding a bucket for him, was murmuring words of comfort, but he didn't know who it was. As the unknown person removed the bucket and handed him a cloth to wipe his mouth with, and then a cup of water, he thought perhaps that it was his mother. His mother had always been gentle and understanding when, as a child, he had been ill.

He rolled back into his bunk, aware that someone was tucking a blanket in around him. He felt a fall of silken hair touch his face, and despite his abject misery, he tried to smile. Abbra. It was Abbra, of course.

'Thanks, sweetheart,' he mumbled gratefully, squeezing her hand before sliding once more into unconsciousness.

She didn't leave him, and in his brief moments of lucidity he knew that she was there, sponging his face and his chest, holding a cup of water to his mouth, re-covering him with the blankets he feverishly tossed aside.

'Love you,' he said as lights and colours whirled about him. 'You're a wonderful girl, sweetheart. The very best.'

It was morning when the fever broke. He lay, looking up at the base of the bunk above him, trying to work out where the hell he was. Turning his head slightly, he could see the wooden-floored, sparsely furnished room and a girl who was not Abbra sitting cross-legged on a mat, sewing up a tear in a pair of tiger-stripe fatigues. Vietnam. He was in Vietnam and Abbra was over eight thousand miles away.

'Welcome back to the world of the living, *Dai uy*,' Lieutenant Grainger said with a grin, handing him a cup of coffee. 'You had me pretty worried for a while.'

'Not half as worried as I was,' Lewis said dryly, easing himself up and resting his weight on one elbow as he sipped gratefully at the coffee. 'How much time did I lose?'

'Eighteen hours. The fever broke at about three in the morning. Since then you've been sleeping like a baby.'

From the far side of the team house Tam was watching him as she sewed. There was a strange expression in her eyes, a look almost of apprehension. He dimly remembered the gentle touch of feminine hands sponging his face and chest, holding cups of water to his mouth, even, dear God, holding a bucket for him as he vomited. He looked across at her, feeling grateful and more than a little embarrassed. He couldn't say anything to her in front of Grainger, not

311

the things that he wanted to say, but as their eyes held he gave her an affectionate and appreciative smile.

The effect was amazing. Her apprehension vanished, replaced by an expression of overwhelming relief – and shy familiarity.

Later, after she had left the team house and he had dressed, he had walked across the compound to where she was laying freshly laundered fatigues out in the sun to dry.

'I'm sorry you had to play nurse,' he said, acutely aware of the soft curve of her breasts and the slender line of her hips beneath her cheap cotton *ao dai*.

She paused in her task, looking laughingly across at him, the familiarity in her eyes no longer so shy. 'I did not mind, *Dai uy*,' she said, her voice full of naughty mischief. 'You were not half so fearsome when you were helpless!'

It was no way for a cleaning girl to talk to a *co van* and a *dai uy*, but he did not reprimand her. As far as he was concerned, she had earned the right to speak to him as a friend, and he was enjoying their easygoing camaraderie.

In the days that followed, the lighthearted teasing of their new friendship did not take place when Grainger or Drayton or Duxbery or Pennington were within earshot. On those occasions she spoke to him with cool respect, and then only when necessary. But at other times, when he was teaching her English, or when Lieutenant Grainger was out on patrol with Sergeant Drayton and Sergeant Pennington, and Lewis was engaged with administrative work, then she would ask him about America, laughing with delighted incredulity at whatever he told her, and in more serious moments he would talk to her about her own country, educating her about the true nature of the Viet Cong, and what would happen in the South if they and their North Vietnamese masters were successful in their ambitions.

312

Tam had at first doubted, but gradually her disbelief had begun to fade. After all, if the *dai uy* said these things were true, then they must be true. The *dai uy* was clever, far cleverer than her sister and her brother-in-law.

By the time Lewis and his team and the local militia, supplemented by the militia of other villages in the area and by a Special Forces squad, left camp to intercept the NVA supply team, Tam had given Lewis her complete trust and loyalty.

It was dusk when the men filed out of the compound, making their way down to the canal and the waiting patrol boats that had been requisitioned from the navy especially for the night's operation. She watched them board the boats, and then walked back into the team house, making sure the mosquito netting was down around Lewis's bunk, that his second pair of boots were clean and mud-free, that there was clean clothing for him to change into when he returned. As she lifted the jacket of his green jungle fatigues, a photograph fell out of an unbuttoned breast pocket.

She picked it up and looked at it. It wasn't the first time she had seen it. It was a photograph that the *dai uy* almost always carried with him, but though she had caught glimpses of it previously, she had never before been able to study it at length. She knew who it was of, of course. The *dai uy*'s wife.

She looked down at the photograph jealously. She had thought that all American women were fair-haired, but the girl in the photograph had hair as glossily black as her own. And the *dai uy* had married her. He must have thought her very beautiful, which meant that he liked long black hair, and her own hair was far longer than the American girl's, and even more night-black. She slipped the photograph back into the *dai uy*'s pocket feeling immensely cheered. At least she knew now that she was physically attractive to him. And over the last few days, that had become very, very important to her.

\* \* \*

Lewis boarded the head patrol boat, grateful for the special equipment. A possible confrontation with North Vietnamese Army forces was a very different ball game from a skirmish with the local Viet Cong, and the local Viet Cong were bad enough. He ordered one of the Vietnamese to squat in the bow and to keep a sharp lookout over the tall reeds that choked the canal banks. He laid his M-16 across his knees and mentally reviewed his strategy, hoping to God that he wasn't going to find any flaws in it now.

The branch canal that the informant had told them the NVA were going to use was one he was unfamiliar with, and he had had to trust his local militia commander's knowledge of the area to determine the best point to stage an ambush.

'Here, *Dai uy*,' the young commander of Van Binh forces had said unequivocally. 'There is an intersection here with a main waterway. If we diverge here,' – his finger had stubbed at the map spread out on Lewis's desk – 'then we can converge on them from both sides.'

Lewis had nodded in agreement. It seemed an ideal point for an ambush. The only problem was that the NVA were well aware of every vulnerable position on the routes that they used, and they might be prepared for them. There was another worry too, one which he had discussed far into the night with the other members of his team. Their informant might not be an informant at all. He could very well be giving them false information in order to lure them into a trap.

'In other words, we might very well find ourselves ambushed by superior forces before we have the chance to lay our own trap,' Sergeant Drayton had said dryly, as he cleaned his Colt .45 automatic. 'Not a very nice thought, is it?'

It wasn't, but Lewis had decided that it was a risk they would have to take. If worse came to worst, they would be able to summon air power. The patrol boats were radio linked to a USS aircraft carrier a mile out in the South

China Sea, and helicopter gunships could be dispatched from the carrier's deck the instant they were asked for. It was a comforting thought, but he was fiercely hoping that such action wouldn't be necessary. He wanted the ambush to be as trouble free and as textbook an operation as their last ambush had been.

It was dark now, and the moon was full and high as the boats chugged softly down the waterway, deeper and deeper into what Lieutenant Grainger termed 'Indian country', country where the Viet Cong had complete control, country where they could expect, at any moment, to come under heavy enemy fire.

As they turned off the main waterway on to narrower, less-used canals, the undergrowth from the banks reached out towards them, low-lying branches flicking them with damp, insect-infested leaves.

'Christ, I hate this damned country!' Sergeant Drayton whispered viciously as he swatted at a party of ants that were scurrying down the neck of his fatigues.

Lewis could cope with the ants, it was the leeches he hated. No matter what kind of operation they had been engaged in, when they returned to the team house, they would be covered with leeches. Burning them off with the end of a lighted cigarette was the most effective way to remove them, but out in the country it wasn't always possible to light a cigarette and then their unwelcome and painful travelling companions just had to be endured.

As time passed they began to move slower and slower, hampered by the water vines and reeds that choked the little-used channels.

Lieutenant Grainger looked across at him anxiously. 'How are we for time, *Dai uy*?'

'We have a little.'

They hadn't much and they both knew it. If they weren't in position at the intersection before midnight, then they ran the very real risk of running straight into the oncoming convoy of boats. And the kind of firefight that would ensue would be anything but text-book.

The Vietnamese militia commander crept towards him. 'We're nearly there, *Dai uy*,' he whispered.

Lewis nodded, signalling for all engines to be cut. As they glided over the fetid black water, he strained his ears for the sound of any other movement. Nothing.

'Here we go, *Trung uy*,' he said quietly to Lieutenant Grainger. 'Let's hope to God it isn't a setup.'

It wasn't. With swift expertise he was able to string his troops out along both sides of the canal bank. The navy patrol boats were heavily armed and he had the .30-calibre machine gun that each boat carried offloaded and mounted in ambush position, to increase their firepower.

He flicked on his PRC-25, his portable receiver-transmitter that he was never without, transmitting softly to the commander of the local militia platoon that was on his left flank, checking for problems. The answer was negative and he called in Lieutenant Grainger who was with a platoon from Van Binh on the other side of the canal. 'Lima, this is Foxtrot, over.'

'Foxtrot, this is Lima,' Grainger's voice said, so quietly he could barely hear it. 'Go ahead.'

'This is Foxtrot . . . Have you any problems? Over?'

'This is Lima. Negative. Over.'

They were all in position. The patrol boats, with their deck-mounted mortars, were discreetly out of sight several yards down the main waterway from the intersection. There was nothing for them to do now but settle among the soggy wetness of chest high reeds and wait.

As Lewis crouched in acute discomfort in the darkness, he was sure that he wasn't alone in hoping that their information was wrong, that if and when a convoy appeared, it would be Viet Cong, not NVA. If it was the NVA, then they were going to be in for a vicious battle. The North Vietnamese were outstanding soldiers, never giving way and never retreating. If the same tenaciousness and discipline could be bred in the soldiers of the ARVN, then Lewis felt quite sure that South Vietnam would have been more than capable of fighting its own battle, without American aid. But for some reason, in many units of the ARVN, tenaciousness and motivation were conspicuous only by their absence.

The radio crackled. 'Foxtrot, Lima, over.'

'Lima, this is Foxtrot,' he whispered into his hand mike. 'Over.'

'This is Lima. We have lights approaching. Over.'

The canal network was so labyrinthine that sampans travelling in a convoy at night habitually travelled with a small single light in the bows so that they could easily follow one another and not become lost.

'This is Pelican. How many lights? Over.'

There was the faint possibility that the sampans were being manned by fishermen. And if they were, the last thing he wanted to do was to come up on them with .30-calibre machine guns and deck-mounted mortars.

'This is Lima. A whole string of them. Eight or nine. Maybe a dozen. Over.'

Lewis muttered an obscenity beneath his breath. A dozen sampans in convoy were not local fishermen. All his units were on the one radio frequency, and he knew that all had heard his conversation with Grainger.

'This is Foxtrot to all units,' he whispered tersely. 'Stand by to attack. Over.'

Ambushing a fleet of sampans wasn't the straightforward task that ambushing an unprepared foot patrol was. Lewis knew that the NVA's first reaction would be to leap into the canal and to make for the banks in order to have the advantage of fighting on solid ground. Once that happened, it would be close fighting of the very worst kind, and he wanted to avoid it by decimating them with machine-gun fire before they even had a chance to hurl themselves overboard.

But it was an impossible ambition. The sampans were too far apart for them to be able to open fire on all of them

317

simultaneously. It seemed to Lewis that even before he gave the signal for all units to blast the boats with everything they had, they were under answering fire. Nothing went as planned. The patrol boats were slow in moving out of their hiding place in the main waterway to give them support; the NVA from the tail boats were in the water and on the banks, raking them with fire from AK-47's even before the answering fire from the lead boats had been silenced.

Almost from the word go he knew that the operation was a debacle. Despite the explosive, savage spray from the .30-calibre machine guns and the ceaseless roar of fire from M-16's, the North Vietnamese kept hurtling towards them, Kalashnikovs at their hips, firing as they came. He knew he could expect no help from Grainger. Over the PRC-25, Grainger had yelled that he and his platoon were under heavy attack and were already being forced to fall back.

Lewis cursed the moon, so full and bright that it gave them virtually no cover. As he let rip with his M-16 at the crack North Vietnamese troops bearing down on them, Drayton leapt to his side, attaching a fresh belt to the flapping tail of his ammunition and then reloading his own M-16 and firing off another clip as the NVA steadfastly advanced.

As a fresh surge of troops from the sampans made the bank, Lewis hurtled past Drayton, racing towards them, a hand grenade, pin out, in his fist, his arm cocked as he threw and then dived for cover.

'*That got the motherfuckers!*' he could hear Drayton yelling exuberantly.

Lewis's first instinct, when he knew there were only eight or a dozen boats in the convoy, was that there was no need to call in air support. Now it was a decision he bitterly regretted. By not calling in the helicopter gunships right from the beginning, precious time, and lives, had been lost. He had called for them the minute he had realized the size of the operation they were involved in, but there was still no sign of them.

'Come on, come on!' he muttered viciously between his teeth. For nearly two minutes he had been unable to make contact with Grainger. It could be Grainger had simply become separated from his PRC-25. Or it could be that Grainger was dead.

By now they were receiving the support they needed from the patrol boats. Mortar fire was deluging the sampans and silencing all returning fire from that direction. The main remaining danger was from the North Vietnamese who were on the water-logged banks, spraying everything that moved with AK-47 fire. If they once got away from the bank and spread out, they'd never be able to get the bastards.

'*Don't let them get away from the bank!*' he yelled across to Drayton. As he raced forward, firing as he ran, he could see one of the Vietnamese from Van Binh local militia, standing, feet apart, machine-gunning from the waist. '*Move!*' he shouted across to him. '*Let's get the bastards!*'

One minute the darkness was so full of fireballs and smoke and screams and shouted obscenities that he was both blinded and deafened, and the next there was silence.

He had been flat on his stomach, half submerged in water, firing, firing, firing at the remaining North Vietnamese. He raised himself up on one knee, looking around cautiously. From a distance of a mere three yards a wounded North Vietnamese was struggling to lift an AK-47 into a firing position.

'Oh, no, you don't, sonny boy!' Lewis said between clenched teeth. He lifted his M-16 with speed and unloaded six rounds into the North Vietnamese's chest. The moon was bright enough for him to see the expression of horror on the soldier's face, and then his body sagged, collapsing in a sea of blood.

The silence was broken by the pounding of approaching helicopter rotors. They were arriving and they were too late. They no longer needed two gunships, they needed a dust off.

Of the twenty-four men who had set off from Van Binh, six were dead and four were injured. Even before Lewis had splashed across to the canal's far bank, he had known that Lieutenant Grainger was dead. All the men he had designated to that position were dead, their M-16s still in their hands, their faces toward the enemy.

He was well trained enough, and well adjusted enough, not to consume himself with guilt. He had planned the operation to the best of his ability, and in his superiors' eyes it would be considered a success. An American and five South Vietnamese had died, but so had two dozen crack North Vietnamese troops. And a convoy of supplies for the Viet Cong had been thwarted. But Grainger's death weighed heavily on him.

'I am sorry about Lieutenant Grainger,' Tam said to him with touching sincerity, and then she added fiercely, 'But if it was fate that an American must die, then I am glad that it was Lieutenant Grainger, *Dai uy*, and that it was not you!'

Despite Tam doing her best to cheer him, Lewis brooded miserably over Grainger's death. Grainger had been short, like himself, with only a few weeks to go before his tour of duty was over. And now he was dead. As each day passed, Lewis could feel himself becoming more taciturn and more sombre. And for the first time he found himself counting the days until he would shake the soil of Vietnam from his boots for good.

Ten days after Lieutenant Grainger's death a report came in that a handful of North Vietnamese troops were holed up in a remote village. Whether they were troops who had escaped from the fight that had taken place on the canal bank, or they were fresh troops who had perhaps brought in a replacement convoy of supplies, he had no way of knowing. Either way, he had no reason to think that hunting them down would be any different from a score of previous such operations.

It was Tam who was filled with sudden, dreadful pre-monition.

'Do not go, *Dai uy*,' she said urgently.

He had smiled at her affectionately and told her not to be a silly girl, but she had persisted in pleading with him, and in the end he had said a little curtly, 'That's enough, Tam, you're behaving as if I'm your husband or your father!'

She had stared at him as if he had slapped her, and then had said quietly, 'Not my father, *Dai uy*.'

He had been putting maps into his map case. Very slowly he finished what he was doing, the blood drumming in his ears. Surely she had not said what he thought she had said. And if she had, surely she had not meant it to sound the way that it had sounded. His own remark had been stupid enough. He couldn't for the life of him imagine why he had said the word *husband*. What he had meant to say was that she was fussing around him as though he were a member of her family, a brother or a father. And instead he had said husband. One look at her face, and the expression in her eyes was enough to tell him that she had meant exactly what she had inferred.

He was appalled, appalled not by the emotion he could read so clearly in her eyes, but by his own, immediate, answering response to it.

'I'm going, Tam,' he said as indifferently as he could manage. Dear God in heaven! Why hadn't he had the sense to see where their easygoing familiarity would lead? She would have to stop working for them. She couldn't continue to clean the team house, not now that he had admitted to himself how very much she attracted him.

There was a half-written letter to Abbra on his desk, and he slid it into a drawer. Abbra. He had never imagined that he could be unfaithful to her, but he knew that for one swift instant he had been unfaithful to her in spirit. He would not be so again. Much as he would miss Tam, and he would miss her dreadfully, their close relationship would have to come to an end.

It was as if she had read every word that he was thinking. 'I am sorry, *Dai uy*,' she had said, her eyes holding his steadily. And then, with devastating candour she had added simply, 'But I love you.'

'You can't love me!' His voice had been choked. Sweet Christ, but how had he got himself into such a mess? The last thing on earth he wanted was to hurt her, and if he had set out deliberately to hurt her, he couldn't have been more successful. 'We'll talk later, Tam,' he said, knowing that Duxbery and Drayton were waiting for him in the compound.

She had said nothing, but her eyes had said everything – that she knew what it was he was going to say to her, that she wouldn't be able to be his cleaning girl anymore, that he was never going to love her and take her back to America with him. In silent agony she watched him as he strode out of the team house and across the compound towards Sergeant Duxbery and Sergeant Drayton.

He didn't look back. Together the three of them began to walk down towards the village, where the local troops were waiting, and as they did so, Tam began to search feverishly through the breast pockets of Lewis's spare fatigues. The photograph wasn't there. She couldn't tear it up or burn it. Hot tears stung the backs of her eyes. She hadn't wanted to fall in love with him. She had hated him and had been determined to continue hating him. But he wasn't a man it was possible to hate. And now she loved him.

The faint put-put of engines could be heard, and she ran across to the door, hoping for one last glimpse of him. Because he had been wearing the same blue beret as his South Vietnamese troops, she couldn't distinguish him. She leaned against the jamb of the door, pressing her hands hard against her stomach in an effort to quell the dreadful presentiment of disaster that was churning there.

The village where the NVA were rumoured to be hiding out showed no signs of them. Lewis was relieved. In his present

322

disturbed state of mind the last thing he wanted was another confrontation with North Vietnamese. He ordered his men to search the surrounding paddy fields and dykes to make sure that the area was clean, and then ordered a return to Van Binh.

It was as their boats emerged from the narrower branch canal that served the village that the North Vietnamese struck. It was as neat an act of revenge as he had ever seen. In exactly the same way as they had ambushed the North Vietnamese, the North Vietnamese now ambushed them, raking them with blistering machine-gun fire from both banks, and sealing off the canal with a flotilla of sampans that he was sure were mined.

Duxbery was hit almost immediately, screaming out in pain and clutching at his chest. Lewis leapt towards him, and as he did so a bullet hit him in the shoulder, lifting him from his feet. He was aware of pandemonium breaking out all around him and of Duxbery staring up at him with dead eyes, and then, shouting for the South Vietnamese to do likewise, he threw himself over the side of the boat, striking out for the thick, concealing vegetation that lined the bank. Bullets plummeted into the water and he took a deep breath, struggling to dive deep. Chokingly thick vines and reeds foiled him. His lungs were bursting, and when he at last broke surface, it was to find a North Vietnamese standing waist-deep in the water, pointing an AK-47 at him. The North Vietnamese grinned. '*Lai! Lai!*' he barked, gesturing with the machine gun for Lewis to wade out of the canal ahead of him. '*Move! Move!*'

# CHAPTER EIGHTEEN

For the next two months Kyle tried every trick in the book to pull a trip to Saigon.

'You've already pulled one three-day R and R trip to the big city,' his operations officer said sourly when Kyle demanded to know when the hell he was going to be listed to fly a ship down to the Tan Son Nhut air base. 'If you don't quit carping, the next time you see it will be when you're on your way out of this goddamned country – for good!'

'For Christ's sake, forget her,' Chuck said in exasperation. 'There's free tail all over this country and you want to make life hard for yourself by paying court to a chaperoned virgin! It makes no sense.'

Kyle knew it wasn't sensible, but despite his drunken visits with Chuck to the ladies of the nearest town, returning to Saigon and seeing Trinh again had become an obsession.

'What about the little lady back home?' Chuck asked as they flew troopers up to a landing zone that was reported to be cold.

Kyle grinned. Chuck's phrase was completely inappropriate for Serena. 'The *little lady* back home is a five-foot-ten blonde who is so wild herself she would make your hair curl!'

This time it was Chuck's turn to grin. 'She sounds like fun,' he said, flaring steeply to slow the Huey ready for landing.

'She is.'

His voice was so unequivocal that Chuck raised his eyebrows. He had Kyle marked down as a lot of things, but a devoted husband was not one of them. If he had been wrong, then the five-foot-ten blonde must be quite a girl. Kyle was the least likely devoted husband he'd ever seen.

For several days they ferried troopers into cold landing zones, spent hours laagering in wait for them, and then flew in to pick them up.

'For chrissakes, this is boring,' a fellow pilot said to Kyle as they sweated under a hot sun, waiting for the signal to crank up.

Kyle was in complete agreement. The tedium of waiting around for hours on end was far worse than the adrenaline-filled fear and excitement of flying into a battle zone.

'Look at this shit,' his companion said disgustedly, his finger stabbing at the magazine he was reading. 'Antiwar protesters marching on the White House. What kind of Americans are those? Why the hell aren't they marching in protest against Ho Chi Minh? And look at this fuckin' photograph here! This one was taken in England! England for chrissakes! What do the fuckin' English know about anything!'

Kyle looked across at the photograph with idle curiosity. A group of antiwar protesters had marched on the American Embassy in Grosvenor Square and had refused to disperse peacefully. Fighting had broken out and several protesters had been arrested. There was a vivid photograph of one protester, banner still in hand, as police manhandled him into a Black Maria.

'Here, let me have a look at that!' he said suddenly, his interest quickening. He took hold of the magazine and then let out a whoop of disgust. 'Would you *look* at that! That moron is my brother-in-law, for Christ's sake!'

Chuck, who had been lying in the shade beside his Huey with a paperback covering his face, now removed it and opened one eye.

'No joke? That guy in the photo is your brother-in-law?'

'No joke,' Kyle said grimly. 'Christ. Given the choice, I think I'd rather shoot him than a gook! Have you seen his banner? "Long live Ho Chi Minh." I'd like to drop the prick into the middle of a battle zone being overrun by Cong and see if he'd still sing the same fucking song!'

Chuck sat up and reached across for the magazine, looking at it with interest. Lance's hippie-length blond hair and slightly effeminate features could be seen clearly. Underneath the photograph, in small print, it read, 'Viscount Blyth-Templeton being removed by police after leading a party of antiwar protesters with a petition to the American Embassy.' Chuck didn't know very much about English aristocracy, but he figured that if Lance Blyth-Templeton was a viscount, then his sister, Kyle's wife, must be a lady or a viscountess or something.

He grinned. A five-foot-ten blonde, wild English viscountess must be quite something. Maybe he'd keep in touch with Kyle when their time in 'Nam was over. She was one lady he sure as hell would like to meet.

'Just *one* maintenance R and R trip to Saigon,' Kyle said pleadingly to his operations officer.

'What's the matter with you, Anderson? Aren't the women up here good enough for you?' his operations officer said bad-temperedly. 'Why the fuck should I give a three-day trip to Saigon to a warrant officer when I have captains lining up for the pleasure?'

'Because I've been flying my ass off for two months, that's why!' Kyle retorted furiously.

'Everyone flies their ass off. You aren't the only one banging Lady Luck and walking away in the morning without so much as a thank you, ma'am.'

'Look, this is real important to me. Just one three-day maintenance trip to Saigon.'

'Only if you say please,' his operations officer said without the least change in the tone of his voice or his facial expression.

For a second Kyle didn't register what he had said. 'I'll do anything. I'll . . .' The words finally penetrated his brain. 'Please! Please! Pretty please!' he yelled exultantly, throwing his helmet into the air.

'Don't go overboard,' his operations officer said with a glimmer of good humour. 'It isn't all good news.'

'What's the bad?' Kyle asked, not caring.

'I'm scheduling you to go with Wilson,' his operations officer said, shaking his head in despair at his soft heart.

'And who am I supposed to drink and whore with while you pay court to little Miss Goody Two-Shoes?' Chuck said, disgruntled.

'Drop in at the Sporting Bar and fall in with some Green Berets,' Kyle said, opening his mail.

He had been surprised at how often Serena was writing to him. She wisely didn't mention Lance, but she made him chuckle with her anecdotes of a visit to a country house and contents sale with Rupert.

'For a wild woman, your lady at home is pretty good at putting pen to paper,' Chuck said, sifting through his own mail and then throwing it to one side in disgust.

'She's probably high on the novelty of it,' Kyle said with a carelessness he didn't truly feel.

After their previous year of separation, when they hadn't been in communication at all, he hadn't expected her to write. Nor had he expected that if she did, he would feel so appreciative. His own letters back to her were far less frequent, consisting of hastily scrawled postcards written whenever he was drunk enough to be maudlingly reminiscent.

Kyle was well aware of the daredevil reputation he had carved out for himself. Both he and Chuck were regarded as halfway to being crazy because of the risks they took. Whenever anyone called him crazy to his face, he simply grinned and agreed with them. Of course he was crazy. Hell, he wouldn't be there if he weren't!

'Those poor fuckers we're leaving behind wouldn't think you were quite so hip if they knew how you intend spending your three days R and R,' Chuck said dryly over the intercom as they cruised south towards Tan Son Nhut at one thousand five hundred feet. 'For Christ's sake, what is it with you? Have you never met a woman who was off limits before?'

'Nope,' Kyle replied, unperturbed. 'To tell you the truth, I don't think I have!'

Saigon shimmered in the heat below them, and he felt his stomach muscles tightening in nervous anticipation. Would she still be at the International? Would she remember him? If she remembered him, would she still agree to go out on a date with him?

'I swear to God I can smell that town from here,' Chuck said as they began to decelerate ready for landing. 'Swamp and mildew, stale perfume, exhaust fumes, and *nuoc mam*.'

'And sex,' Kyle said with a grin. 'Don't forget the sex.'

Chuck gave a snort of agreement. 'That town is so steeped in sex it reeks of it! And you, numbnut, are going to spend your time there holding hands, as if you were a bashful teenager!'

He didn't even bother to check in with Chuck at the Continental. Instead, he made his way straight to the International, bounding up the steps and into the lobby, his heart in his mouth.

She was there. For one instant, as she looked towards him, not recognizing him, her smile was polite and impersonal, and then it widened, recognition flooding her eyes.

'I'm back,' he said unnecessarily. 'We have a date, remember?'

His fatigues were still soaked with the sweat from his flight, a lock of dark hair fell untidily across his brow, and his electric-blue eyes were hot and determined.

A dimple touched the corner of her mouth beguilingly. 'It is not quite so simple,' she said, an undertone of laughter

328

in her voice. 'You must meet my sister first and meet with her approval.'

'Lead me to her!' His grin was splitting his face. He felt as Alexander must have felt after conquering Persia.

Her amusement deepened. All Americans were crazy, but this one was certainly crazier than most. 'This evening, when I have finished work, then I will talk to her and ask her if she will meet you.'

Her last sentence had brought an uncomfortable element of doubt into the situation. 'Where would she enjoy dining most?' he asked, feeling that if a time and place were decided upon, a successful outcome was just a little bit likelier. 'The restaurant at the Continental? The Caravelle?'

'I think perhaps the Continental,' she said, wondering why, after eighteen months of being solicited by nearly every American who had crossed the International's lobby, she was now capitulating to this tall, lean, criminally young helicopter pilot with the reckless eyes.

'I'll book a table for seven-thirty.' It was a ridiculously early hour to be eating in Saigon, but he didn't care. He just wanted to be in her company, and if that meant being in her sister's company as well, then it was a small price to pay.

'I can't talk any longer,' she said softly as a boisterous party of European construction engineers entered the lobby.

He nodded, understanding at once. If she was overheard, or seen, talking to him with such familiarity, then the International's patrons would assume she was available and she would be overwhelmed by amorous advances.

'Right,' he said briefly. 'Bye.'

'*Chào*,' she said, the dimple in her cheek still in evidence.

As he strode past the engineers and out into the street he decided that it was time he came to grips with the Vietnamese language. Why on earth did the Viets use the word *chào* to both say hello and good-bye? It didn't make sense. For all he knew, they probably used the same word for other opposites, like stop and go, and friend and enemy. If they did, it was no wonder the

329

American High Command had difficulties in understanding them!

'How was Miss Goody Two-Shoes?' Chuck asked him when he walked into their room at the Continental.

'Okay,' Kyle said, good-naturedly noncommittal.

Chuck had already showered and changed into jeans and a T-shirt, ready to hit the streets. He finished combing his close-cropped light brown hair, tucking the comb into his hip pocket, saying in amusement, 'So that's the way the cookie crumbles, is it? Miss Goody Two-Shoes really is a serious item and not a fit subject for bawdy speculation?'

'You got it.' Kyle stripped off his sweat-soaked shirt.

Chuck shook his head in mystification. 'Okay,' he said at last. 'If that's the way it is, buddy, then even though I'll never understand it, I promise I won't give you a hassle. As far as I'm concerned, Miss Goody Two-Shoes is your wife, your sister, your mother, and the Virgin Mary all rolled into one, and will receive all due respect.'

'Then start off by referring to her by her name,' Kyle said, pulling off his trousers and throwing them in Chuck's direction.

Chuck dodged the trousers. 'And that is?'

'Trinh, and for your information, it means pure and virtuous.'

'How do you know?' Chuck was intrigued. 'Did she tell you that?'

Kyle walked into the bathroom and turned on the shower. 'No,' he yelled over the sound of the gushing water. 'There was a Vietnamese interpreter in camp the other day and I asked him!'

Chuck stared towards the open bathroom door. Kyle was really taking this thing seriously, far too seriously for his liking. After all, what the hell could come of it? Kyle was married. The girl was probably a Buddhist or a Confucian and even if Kyle got a divorce, there would be no way that her family would allow her to marry him. In his book, for Kyle to embark on such a relationship was absolutely pointless.

330

He shrugged his shoulders. It wasn't his business. He was Kyle's buddy, not his keeper. And he was wasting precious time. The bars and brothels were waiting.

'If you want to catch up with me, I'll be in La Bohème or The Sporting Bar,' he yelled, striding out of the room, knowing that he wouldn't be without a companion for very long.

There was a whole long afternoon to while away before he was due to meet Trinh and her sister, and for once Kyle was perplexed as to how he should spend his time. He couldn't do any heavy drinking. If he reeked of alcohol when he met her sister, then he would very probably never manage to date Trinh ever again. And he couldn't whore. Or could he?

He mentally debated the point while he towelled himself dry and changed into crisp, clean fatigues. After all, Trinh would never know, and if he didn't get himself some sex in before their date, then he certainly wouldn't get any during. He chuckled as he zipped up his pants. He was in grave danger of achieving the impossible. A three-day celibate R and R in Sin City. If word of it ever got around, his reputation would be shot to pieces.

As he walked through the lobby he ran into a Vietnamese wedding party making their way towards the Continental's tiny interior garden. The garden, with its mass of frangipani blossom and potted palms and gaily coloured turquoise china elephants was a great favourite with local photographers.

He stood watching them. The groom was almost as slightly built as his bride, and they were holding hands, laughing across at each other, their hair and shoulders thick with flower petals. The bride was dressed in red, not white, and her friends twittered around her, as pretty as butterflies in their floating, pastel *ao dai*s. For a few brief minutes they surrounded him and then they were gone, crowding ebulliently into the little garden.

He strolled out into the street. He was beginning to find the South Vietnamese a very attractive people. He wished

331

to hell he had been taught more about their way of life and their customs when he had been at helicopter school. All he could remember was learning to call them dinks and slopes and gooks. His knuckles tightened fractionally. Anyone he heard referring to Trinh as a dink would very speedily regret it.

He paused for a moment before turning into La Bohème. Tu Do was massed with bicycles and cycles as it always was, but the cars honking for a passageway were American and driven by Americans. The dudes mobbing the pavement and dodging the street traffic were American. Neon signs advertised American brand names; Coke, Winstons, Levi's. The music blaring from American transistors was American music: James Brown, Wilson Pickett, The Temptations.

It was as if a monstrous wedge of downtown Los Angeles had been grafted on to the coast of Southeast Asia. And the Vietnamese smilingly serviced the invasion. They shined shoes and waited tables and cooked food and washed laundry and provided sex. For the first time Kyle wondered about the thoughts behind those smiles. He wondered what Trinh thought of the Americans in her city. He wondered what she thought of him.

'Saigon tea? You buy me Saigon tea?' a lady of the house said, curling herself around him.

Kyle slapped two dollars into her palm to keep her quiet, and looked around for Chuck.

'You number one,' his newfound friend said, winding her arms around his neck and rubbing herself seductively up against him.

Chuck was at the bar with a couple of marines, all of them with girls on their knees. All he had to do was walk across and join in the fun. He looked down at the girl, whose hand was now roving speculatively over the bulge in his crotch. She was very pretty, with fine, doll-like features and hair shimmering loosely down her back to her waist.

'You buy me another Saigon tea?' she asked winningly.

Kyle grinned down at her and then, surprising himself almost as much as he surprised the girl, he said, 'No. Today I seem to be right out of money for Saigon teas.'

The expression on the girl's face changed from one of winsomeness to one of incredulity and then disgust.

'You number-one cheap Charlie!' she flared indignantly, removing herself from him with all speed. 'You suck-suck!'

From the bar Chuck caught sight of him, shouting across for him to join them. Kyle raised a hand in acknowledgement and then shook his head. 'Not this time, buddy,' he yelled back over the deafening sound of Wilson Pickett's 'Mustang Sally'. 'See you later, back at the Continental.'

For the rest of the long, hot afternoon he kept out of trouble, restricting himself to a couple of beers. After that he turned to coffee, sitting beneath the awning of a sidewalk café, watching the world go by and spurning all offers of female companionship. When he finally made his way back to the Continental, he saw Chuck and his companions stagger from a bar and half fall, laughing and uproariously drunk, into another.

He grinned to himself. It was a strange sensation being sober and celibate in a city so swingingly sinful. It was certainly an afternoon he would remember. Hell, it was an afternoon in Saigon so stainlessly pure, he would be able to tell his grandchildren about it!

He was glad that he had suggested they meet early. By 7:40 p.m. as a waiter led Trinh and her sister across to his table on the Continental's terrace, the surrounding tables were already beginning to fill.

He had been waiting for them for twenty minutes in an agony of impatience. For the past ten minutes he had been certain that they were not going to come, and then he had seen them, sumptuously dressed in silken *ao dais*, walking with head-turning grace in the waiter's wake.

As he rose to his feet his mouth was dry. He felt like a kid on his first date.

'My sister, Mai,' Trinh was saying to him. 'Mai, Kyle . . .'

'Anderson,' he finished for her quickly, knowing that she still didn't know his surname, as he, incredibly, did not know hers.

'I am very pleased to meet you, Mr Anderson,' she said with cool formality.

'Just call me Kyle.' As they sat down, Kyle wondered if he had made a crass mistake. Perhaps such an invitation to a lady he had only just been introduced to was considered ill bred in polite Vietnamese circles. And he was certain that Trinh and her sister belonged to very polite circles indeed. As they had entered the hotel, and before the waiter had led them across the terrace, he had seen the proprietor bowing to them from the waist, greeting them warmly, an honour conferred on very few of the Continental's guests.

He ordered a bottle of chilled vin blanc cassis, and tried to redeem his thoughtless crassness.

'I'm very pleased to meet you, Miss . . . ' He could have bitten off his tongue. He still didn't know her surname. 'Mai,' he said quickly, aware that Trinh was all too aware of his discomfiture and that she was having great difficulty in suppressing her giggles.

'I am very pleased to meet you too,' Mai said, her English charmingly touched with an unmistakable French accent. 'Our family has many Western friends, but they are not—' She paused, her sloe-dark eyes holding his. 'They are not army personnel. You understand what I am saying, Mr Anderson?'

He understood perfectly. He looked across at Trinh, as beautiful as an exotic flower in her silk *ao dai*, her eyes laughing into his, and then he turned once more towards her sister.

'I know very little of Vietnamese customs and manners,' he said truthfully. 'But I do know that I want to see Trinh again. I understand the kind of girl she is, and the kind of

334

family that she comes from, and that you are concerned for her reputation.' He cleared his throat, wondering what Serena's reaction would be if she could see and hear him. Would she throw the nearest available object at his head, or would she burst into shouts of disbelieving laughter? 'If you allow me to see her, I promise you that she will come to no harm . . . that I won't take unfair advantage . . .' He was floundering and he knew it. He had never had these intentions before in his life, much less tried to articulate them.

'As our parents are dead, I am the head of our family,' Mai said, coming to his aid and looking too charmingly fragile to be the head of anything. 'If you wish to see Trinh, then you may do so, Mr Anderson, providing she is adequately chaperoned.'

'By yourself?' Kyle asked, relieved that the inquisition, such as it was, appeared to be over.

Mai nodded, smiling a little shyly, and he was suddenly aware that she, too, was relieved that the business of the evening was over. 'Great,' he said, reflecting in amusement that if the sister's positions had been reversed, Trinh would have made a far sterner interrogator. 'Now that that's taken care of, let's eat.'

They started off with *canh chua* soup, a delicate mixture of shrimp and bean sprouts and pineapple and celery, and Trinh told him a little of her family history. 'We are a very old family in Saigon,' she said, sipping at her wine from a long-stemmed glass. 'My father was a mandarin and an adviser to Bao Dai, the last emperor.'

He listened, intrigued, discovering that she was neither Buddhist nor Confucian, but Roman Catholic, and that she had been educated in French schools in Saigon and had spent two years in Paris, at the Sorbonne.

As rice and finely chopped, tender beef wrapped in grape leaves followed the soup, he was aware that they were receiving several curious glances from the other diners. The majority of them were Americans from the embassy and the

335

aid agencies, eked out by a handful of portly Vietnamese businessmen dressed Western-style. He knew very well what they were all thinking. Were Mai and Trinh high-class hookers? And if they weren't, what the hell was he doing squiring them around?

He was grateful when a fair-haired man about his own age walked across to a nearby table, escorting a Vietnamese companion who looked even more respectable than Mai and Trinh. She was, surprisingly, easily in her late thirties, and perhaps even in her early forties.

He looked across at them speculatively, wondering about their relationship. The guy didn't look to be army, his hair was far too long, and he didn't look to be American. He was deeply suntanned, and even though he was young, there was a web of fine lines around his eyes, as if he were accustomed to screwing his eyes up to look into the sun. As soon as he spoke, asking for the wine list, Kyle knew he had been right about him. He was an Australian.

'. . . where were you born in America?' Mai was asking him.

'Boston,' he said, dismissing the Australian from his mind, and wondering when he was going to be able to surreptitiously hold Trinh's hand.

'Well?' Chuck asked blearily the next morning as he dragged himself into the world of the living. 'Has the novelty of being a monk worn off yet?'

In the nearby twin bed Kyle rolled on to his back, resting his head on his hands. It was a very pertinent question. He had been able to hold Trinh's hand only briefly, when he had handed her into the taxicab that Mai had insisted they go home in, alone. That had been the full extent of the physical contact between them. Smiles across a table and a hot, urgent handhold. He thought of Trinh's delicate, flawless face and her laughing dark eyes, and his stomach turned a somersault as if he were going down a roller coaster.

'No,' he said, wondering for the first time where

their relationship could possibly go. What it would lead to. 'No, I seem to be turning into a pretty damned good monk!'

Chuck groaned and pulled the sheet up over his head. 'Later,' was all Kyle could indistinctly hear. 'Tell me all about Miss Goody Trinh Two-Shoes, later.'

He did better than that. At lunchtime, in the lobby of the International he introduced Chuck to her.

Chuck was impressed. She was certainly something, every inch a lady but with that naughty light of laughter in her eyes that every Vietnamese woman he had ever met seemed to have been born with. All the same, if he were Kyle, he knew where his preference would lie. And that would be with the five-foot-ten, wild aristocratic blonde, in swinging London.

When they returned to camp, Kyle put his mind to the serious task of sorting out regular time in Saigon. Vietnam was a land that ran on bribes and corruption, and he saw no reason why he shouldn't sink to those depths himself, if they would get him what he wanted.

'You're an Anderson of the Anderson banking family?' his operations officer asked him, suddenly acutely attentive.

Kyle nodded.

'You're not shitting me, are you? Because if you are . . .'

'I'm not shitting you,' Kyle said, amused at how easy it was all going to be. 'All I want to do is to come to an arrangement.'

'Oh, I think we can do that all right,' his operations op said, grinning broadly, 'Yes, I certainly think we'll be able to do that all right. For a price.'

The price was astronomically high, but as far as Kyle was concerned, it was worth it. Before the month was out he was seeing Trinh at least two weekends out of every four. Mai still accompanied them on what Trinh termed their 'official' dates. But there were other times, snatched moments when she escaped from the hotel desk and they were able to be alone together. Sometimes they would walk through the back streets behind Tu Do, down to the river; sometimes they would walk in the park that backed on to the Presidential Palace gardens; sometimes they would sit drinking coffee in Broddards, a café that catered to Vietnamese rather than Americans. The idyll lasted until September, until Trinh said that she couldn't see him on his next free day because it was the anniversary of her mother's death and she was going to spend the day with Mai.

Kyle now knew enough of Vietnamese tradition and custom to realize that it would be useless to argue with her. Even though she was a Catholic and not a Buddhist, as a Vietnamese, ancestor worship was in her blood and her bones.

Now that he was beginning to understand a little of what made the Vietnamese tick, he was constantly exasperated by how ignorant his fellow Americans were about them. The Strategic Hamlet programme was a case in point. Under Diem, and with American approval and American aid, peasants had been forcibly removed from their villages and farms and transferred to new 'fortified' villages, villages which, in theory, the Viet Cong would be unable to penetrate.

In regions such as the Mekong Delta, where the peasants did not live in concentrated settlements but in farmhouses strung out along the edges of the dykes, this involved taking them from the land that had been their father's and their father's father's, and no new allotment of land was given to them. The peasants, far from being grateful for their new 'safe' villages, resented the government and the Americans who funded the government. And this was all because they didn't understand that the plots of land, where their ancestors were buried, were sacred to the Vietnamese.

Some Vietnamese were removed from their land so that it could be defoliated with Agent Orange and made a wilderness in which nothing, not even Viet Cong, could survive. These vast areas were turned into 'free fire zones', where anything moving would be a legitimate target for American forces. Because of this, huge numbers of needless refugees were created. And the peasants' resentment was exploited ruthlessly by the Viet Cong.

If Chuck had been with him on the Saturday he was in Saigon and Trinh was unable to see him, then he might very well never have become drunk, might very well never have gone to her house to wait for her. As it was, he had a whole day to while away, with no prospect of even seeing her in the evening. He began drowning his sorrows at ten in the morning in the Sporting Bar, finding companionship among the Green Berets. By twelve he was in the most doubtful of all areas in Saigon, in Canh Hoi, behind the docks. Here, the only Americans to be found were black and the only ladies were dark-skinned Khmers.

It wasn't the first time he had been unfaithful to Trinh. He had been seeing her now for three months and he had had to find sexual release somewhere. But it was the first time he had so bitterly resented making love to a nameless whore, when the only woman he wanted to make love to was Trinh.

By five o'clock, back in the relatively respectable area of Tu Do Street, he sat broodingly over a beer in La Pagoda, the only bar that he knew where there were no girls to solicit the clients. If Trinh had not refused to see him, when it had cost him an arm and a leg to wangle the flight down, then the incident with the Khmer girl would never have taken place. By the time it was five-thirty he had convinced himself that Trinh was entirely to blame, that she wasn't appreciative of the lengths he had gone to in order to see her so regularly, that she was treating him shabbily, and he didn't deserve it.

He peered blearily at his Rolex. Five forty-five. Trinh and Mai were visiting her mother's grave, but wherever it was, surely they would be back by now. Surely there was no reason why she couldn't see him that evening.

He hauled himself to his feet. She would see him that evening. It was about time she and Mai understood the lengths he had to go to in order to fly south so regularly. Christ. He was paying enough out in bribes to fund the fucking war! And because it was the anniversary of her mother's death she wouldn't even see him.

'This shit,' he said to himself as he staggered out into the street in search of a taxicab, 'hash got to shtop.'

He knew where she lived, though Mai had seen to it with gentle firmness that he had never been invited inside. 'Avenue Charnier,' he said to the impassive-faced taxi driver, enunciating clearly with difficulty. 'The house with the orange walls.'

It had once been a very elegant house, but it was now beginning to show signs of decay. Not for the first time he wondered about Trinh and Mai's finances. They had obviously inherited money when their parents had died, but he had a sneaking suspicion that it wasn't very much and that only careful husbandry enabled them to continue living in their family home.

Swaying slightly, he paid the taxi driver. If they wanted money, then they could have it. He began to make his way unsteadily towards a white-painted front door flanked by verandahs. But they wouldn't ask for money. Not in a million years. Hell. They didn't even know that in Western terms he was rich, rich, rich. He hiccuped and jangled the bell. They would know when he told them about the bribes he was paying in order to fly down so regularly. He could hear the sounds of footsteps approaching the other side of the door. Light, feminine footsteps. Perhaps then Mai would cease her vigilance. Perhaps, at long last, he and Trinh could have a normal, loving relationship.

She swung the door open and stared at him, a mixture of pleasure and bewilderment and slight apprehension in her eyes.

'Kyle . . . what are you doing here? Why . . .'

'Need to talk to you,' he said abruptly, reeling past her and into the house.

If she made any attempt to prevent him, he was unaware of it. The house had the same air of faded gentility on the inside as it did on the outside. The teak floors were highly polished, but the French period furnishings, heavy with ormolu and filigree decoration, were shabby and well worn. Through an open door he saw a family ancestral altar with candles flickering before it and he realized, a little sheepishly, that he had disturbed her at prayer.

'Where's Mai?' he asked, looking around. 'Want to talk to Mai as well.'

He had had enough dates *à trois*. It was time they all had a good talk, time he made it clear that three months of being chaperoned was all he was going to take. There were going to be some changes made.

'Mai is still at the family burial ground. I felt ill. I had a headache and a temperature and so I came home early, alone.'

He rocked back on his heels, looking at her in concern. She did look a little unwell. There was a suspicious flush of colour in her golden cheeks, and he pressed the back of his hand against her forehead.

'Flu,' he said knowledgeably. 'You're probably coming down with flu.' It was only then, as he looked down at her in tender concern, that her words penetrated his drink-fumed brain. 'You mean Mai ishn't here? No one ish here? Jusht you and me?'

'You're drunk,' she said gently, taking hold of his arm and trying to steer him towards the now-closed door.

He resisted, standing his ground. He wanted to talk to her, didn't he? He wanted to tell her that he'd had enough of chaste kisses and infantile handholds. Christ. He was a chopper jock, a warrior, a war hawk who flew into battle with only Plexiglas, and tinfoil between him and the Apocalypse. His sex began to throb and harden. Three months he'd

341

waited for her – three months on which on any given day he'd stood a crucifying chance of it being his last. He wasn't going to wait any longer. Only a dickhead would wait any longer.

'C'me here,' he said huskily, pulling her towards him. 'Love you, Trinh. Love you so much I'm dying by inches for you.'

At his touch she had started to tremble slightly, trying to pull away from him. He held her easily, lowering his head to hers, kissing her with pent-up hunger. Her hair slithered voluptuously over the backs of his hands. He could feel her small, high breasts beneath her silken *ao dai* soft against his chest.

'Oh, God,' he muttered hoarsely as unbridled passion roared through his loins. 'I've waited so long, Trinh. It's been cruel of you to make me wait so long!'

He knew she was struggling against him, and her struggles only inflamed him further. His hands were clumsy on the unfamiliar *ao dai*, but beneath the long, floating slit skirt he found the band of her silken pantaloons and began to pull them down roughly, his hands hot on the warm, smooth flesh of her buttocks.

'*No, Kyle! Stop! Please stop!*' she was crying frantically, squirming against him in a manner that nearly had him shooting sperm before he had even entered her.

There were no rugs on the floor, no cushions. As he pushed her down beneath him, subduing her with his weight, the shiny teak floor bruised his knees and grazed his elbows. Her fists were drumming vainly on his back, but he had his belt unbuckled, his fly unzipped. She loved him. He knew she loved him. She'd waited for this just as hungrily and as frustratedly as he had waited.

'Love you,' he said again as he pinned her wrists to the floor above her head with one hand and guided his dick toward the warm, moist mouth of her vagina with the other. He forged deep inside her, feeling as if he were going to die with pleasure. '*Oh, Christ, Trinh!*' he gasped convulsively. '*Oh, Christ!*'

It was not going to be a long ride home. He was too drunk. But it was going to be the most meaningful ride of his life. He felt her nails scoring his back, heard her give a cry that sounded as if it had been torn from her heart, and then hot gold was shooting through him, his face contorting in a rictus of ecstatic agony as he cried out in primeval urgency, '*Oh, yes. Trinh! Yes! Yes! Yes!*'

It was a long time before he became aware of her tears sliding slowly against his shoulders. He had collapsed on top of her in drunken and exhausted fulfilment, losing consciousness. It was only as she tried to free herself of his crushing weight that his eyelids flickered open and he raised himself up on his elbows, looking down at her.

Her eyes were wide and dark, full of nameless horror. 'Trinh?' He eased his weight away from her, appalled by the sight of her tear-streaked face. 'Trinh! Don't cry! There's no need to cry!'

She sat up slowly, as if in great pain, and then pushed herself across the floor away from him, still in a sitting position, her silken trousers crumpled around her ankles. 'You have spoiled everything,' she whispered, her voice breaking in an agony of grief. 'I will never be able to see you again. Never.'

'No!' Dimly he was aware that he had ruined everything, that all the time he had been making love to her she had been fighting him every inch of the way. 'No, Trinh.' He was no longer drunk. He had never felt so sober in his life. He zipped up his trousers, buckling his belt, his hand shaking slightly as he did so. Christ, but he had been every kind of a fool. She was the most precious thing in the world to him, and he had treated her as if she were a two-bit whore from Tu Do Street.

He reached out a hand to touch her, but she shrank away from him, and he dropped it to his side knowing that the next few minutes were going to be the most important of his life.

'I love you, Trinh,' he said urgently, kneeling on one knee before her, feeling as if he were trying to regain the trust of a small, frightened wild animal. 'I love you and I want to marry you.'

It was true. He did want to marry her. She needed him as a husband in a way that Serena had never needed him and never would need him. And unless he was her husband, she would never be able to leave Vietnam and enter America with him when his year of duty was over.

Behind them, in the shaded house, the candle flames before her family altar flickered and flamed. He looked towards them, conscious of the solemnity of the vow he was making.

'I'm going to marry you, Trinh,' he said, taking hold of her hands and drawing her toward him. 'It may take a little time for the paperwork to be in order . . .'

How long would it take him to get a divorce now that he really wanted one? Would he have to start all over again? Would his previous divorce petition be held in his favour or be held against him? He didn't know, but he did know that he was not going to allow obstacles to stand in his way.

The first thing he would do when he arrived back in camp was write to Serena, explaining to her what Trinh's position would be if he had to leave 'Nam without being able to marry her. Perhaps, with Serena's cooperation, he could get a Mexican divorce. He would get his father's lawyers on it. They would be able to work something out. They would have to. 'We're going to be married and you're going to come to America with me, and it's going to be all right,' he said, loving her so much that he felt as if his heart were about to burst.

'And Mai?' she asked tremulously. 'What about Mai? I cannot leave her here on her own.'

He grinned. There was an old joke, marry an Oriental, and you become financially responsible for her entire family. It seemed to be true. 'And Mai as well,' he said, wondering what the hell his father was going to say when he arrived home

344

in Boston with not only one Vietnamese girl as a souvenir of war, but two.

He wrote to Serena the morning after he returned to camp. Chuck watched him, sporting a headband of ragged cloth that gave him a piratical air as he studiously cleaned his Smith & Wesson .38. 'You're wasting your time,' he said as they sat together on his bunk. 'You won't get a divorce before you have to leave 'Nam. Even if you did, the army sure as hell isn't going to be ecstatic about you marrying a Viet. They'll make it damn near impossible.'

Kyle ignored him. *I'll always be glad that you flew out to Alabama before I left for 'Nam*, he was writing, resting the notepad on Chuck's locker. *What we've had between us is something I wouldn't have missed for the world, and something I will never forget. But I have to be able to marry Trinh. I have to be able to protect her. If you knew what life was like out here, Serry, you would understand.*

Strangely enough, he was sure that she would. Rich, spoiled and headstrong as she was, she was also uncompromisingly fair and if, when the recriminations were over, she could bring herself to be a friend to Trinh, then she would be the best friend that Trinh could ever hope to have.

'Put away the pen, Anderson, and forget about writing the great American novel,' his operations officer said sarcastically, striding towards him. 'We have a hot one. A reconnaissance squad needs picking up from the border.'

Chuck slipped his Smith & Wesson into its holster, grateful for some action. 'How near the border?' he asked.

'A half a mile,' the operations officer said, grinning. 'On Charlie's side.'

Kyle slipped the unfinished letter into the top drawer of Chuck's locker. 'You're not still pairing me with that dumb-shit cherry, are you?' he asked, referring to the company's latest new arrival who had been flying with him all week.

'You're flying with that dumb-shit cherry until he's right-seat qualified and as skilled as you in air-assault operations,' the operations officer said mercilessly, turning on his heel and striding away in the direction of the operations tent.

All through the briefing, as the operations officer gave them frequencies and ship numbers and suspected enemy locations, Kyle's attention kept drifting back to his letter to Serena. He would finish it the minute he got back to camp. With luck she would receive it before the end of the week.

'Okay,' the operations officer said at last, satisfied. 'That's it. Let's go.'

As he walked across to his ship, the cherry in his wake, he checked his gear. Pistol, flak jacket, maps. Helmet. He took hold of the base of his helmet, spreading it slightly and pulling it over his head. He would have to write a letter to his father, too, if he wanted his help in speeding up the lawyers.

He grimaced as he opened the Huey's door, putting one foot on the skid and hoisting himself into his high-back seat. That letter would be even harder than his letter to Serena. He clicked the lever that anchored his shoulder straps to his wide lap belt, wondering how difficult it would be to take Trinh out of Vietnam and into the States if he wasn't married to her. Would she be able to enter on a visitor's visa? And if so, for how long?

He squeezed the radio trigger switch on his cyclic to the first click and said through his phones to his nervous copilot. 'Okay?'

The new arrival nodded. Kyle gave him a thumbs-up sign and rolled the throttle open to the indent starting position, squeezing the trigger switch on his collective. As the rotor blades began to turn, he wondered if perhaps it would be easiest to fly Trinh to England or to Sweden. She would surely be able to enter Sweden without any difficulty, and stay there, as a visitor, until they could marry.

He checked the gauge and nosed the Huey forward with a gentle push of the cyclic. But to make those kind of arrangements, he would have to level with Trinh and tell her that he was already married, and that he definitely didn't want to have to do.

Chuck was first pilot in the ship in front of him, and as it climbed up over the trees at the edge of the camp, Kyle followed him, holding his speed down until they, and the accompanying ships, were all in formation.

Despite the trickiness of the area they were flying into, they met with no ground fire. They flew north, over mountainous terrain, to a border area where Cambodia and Vietnam and Laos merged. Even when they located the reconnaissance party, they ran into no difficulties. It was a much smaller party than they had anticipated, and all the men boarded the first couple of ships, leaving Kyle and Chuck unloaded. It was only as they were preparing to take off, angry at being called out unnecessarily, that hell broke loose. The firing was so unexpected, so ferociously intense, that even Kyle lost his cool for a moment, muttering a frantic 'Holy Christ!' as his flight commander yelled over the radio. '*Go! Go! Go!*'

Kyle didn't need telling twice. He was being machine-gunned from what seemed to be every direction at once, and he knew as the Huey lifted off the ground that they were taking hits.

'*C'me on, baby! C'me on!*' he said savagely beneath his breath.

The Huey cleared the tree line. Over the radio he could hear shouted reports of other ships being hit. A steady stream of tracers flew towards him. He swore viciously. Some bastard had him in his sights and was concentrating entirely on him. He banked hard to the left, trying to lose the tracer fire, and almost immediately, as more bullets slammed into the tail rotors, he began to oscillate, losing control.

'*Skyhawk three! We're hit and going down!*' was the last terse, furious message Chuck heard over the radio as the Huey tumbled brokenly from the sky, crashing down into the jungle canopy.

# CHAPTER NINETEEN

Gavin stared at Nhu across the candlelit table on the Continental's terrace. 'You mean your brother is in the South again?' he asked, careful to keep his voice low despite his incredulity. 'Here? In Saigon?'

Her eyes went quickly to the other tables around them. No one was paying them any attention. The young American who had been looking curiously in their direction when they had first arrived, was now deep in conversation with his two Vietnamese companions. She said very quietly, 'Not in Saigon. But nearby.'

Gavin's mind raced furiously. According to Gabrielle, her mother's brother was a full-fledged North Vietnamese Army colonel. If he could meet him, talk to him, then he would learn more about the war in five minutes than he would in a year of attending official American press conferences and ambiguously worded briefings.

'I want to meet him,' he said, laying down his fork and sipping a glass of water. 'Can you arrange it, Nhu?'

She didn't answer him for several seconds, and when she did, her voice was unsteady, betraying the agitation that lay beneath her veneer of unruffled composure. 'Yes,' she said, so quietly he could barely hear her. 'That is why I am here.'

Her reply was so unexpected that his hand shook and water spilled as he set his glass back down on the table. 'I'm sorry,' he said, wondering if he had misheard her. 'I don't understand . . .'

Her eyes were troubled. 'Neither do I, but I have shown Dinh the letters Vanh sent to me in which she says you can be trusted. And he wants to talk to you.'

Sheer elation sang down Gavin's spine. He had hoped that his family-by-marriage in Saigon would prove helpful to him as a reporter, but he had never envisaged a coup such as this. Gabrielle had said that when Dinh had come south in 1963, it had been on the express orders of General Giap. And Giap was Ho Chi Minh's right-hand man, the architect of the French defeat at Dien Bien Phu. He wondered what on earth Vanh had put in her letters that such a man would trust him, sight unseen.

He said hesitantly, knowing he would never forgive himself if his confession ruined his chances of a meeting, yet knowing he would never be able to live with himself if Gabrielle's uncle were to risk capture and death under the mistaken impression that he was meeting a fellow Communist, 'I sympathize with the North, Nhu. I think the American bombing campaign against northern towns and the killing of large numbers of innocent civilians is morally indefensible. But I am not a Communist.'

'Neither am I,' she said, a slight smile touching her mouth. 'I am a nationalist, and I support Ho. Although he is a Communist, I believe that he is also, first and foremost, a nationalist and a patriot.'

A waiter approached and she fell silent. When he had refilled her glass and moved away a safe distance, she continued quietly. 'And as a patriot I believe he will always place Vietnam's interest above that of personal ideology.'

It was a popular view. From everything he had read about Nguyen That Thanh, born seventy-six years ago in the village of Kim Lie, some 300 kilometres south of Hanoi, and known to the world by the alias Ho Chi Minh, Gavin thought that it was probably also correct.

'Are there any arrangements for me to meet your brother, Nhu?'

'I haven't yet been told. I had to meet you first and—' she blushed slightly, looking much younger than her thirty-two years – 'and make my own judgement about you.'

He grinned, knowing that trust had sprung up between them immediately and that her judgement would be favourable.

The waiter approached again, removing plates and asking if they were ready for coffee. Gavin said that they were, and when the waiter was once again out of earshot he said curiously, 'I must confess I was surprised when you suggested we meet here, Nhu. Isn't it a very conspicuous rendezvous? Aren't we liable to attract attention?'

Her smile deepened. 'Have you never read that great story "The Purloined Letter" by Edgar Allan Poe?'

He shook his head, bemused at the unexpected range of her literary knowledge. Reading his thoughts, she said, unoffended, 'You forget that I was educated at a French school, Gavin. American literature was part of our syllabus in my last year.'

'It was part of mine as well,' he said, his eyes crinkling at the corners. 'But somehow or other we seem to have overlooked Mr Poe. Tell me about his purloined letter. What does it have to do with us meeting here, at the Continental?'

The waiter came and served coffee. The terrace where they were sitting overlooked the plaza surrounding the old opera house, and as the hour grew later, the always-chaotic traffic intensified. Young Vietnamese pimps on souped-up scooters and Honda 50s zipped between Citroëns and Renaults as they transported their charges from rendezvous to rendezvous. The girls sat behind them, some in miniskirts so short it was doubtful if they were wearing anything below the waist at all, some in gossamer-light *ao dais*, their split skirts fluttering like streamers in their wake, and all with exotically painted faces.

She said, 'The letter was searched for in vain. Under carpets, beneath mattresses. But because it was known to have been hidden, no one thought of looking in the most obvious place.'

'Which was?' he asked, wishing that Gabrielle were with him to enjoy the company of her delightful aunt.

Her eyes sparkled mischievously, reminding him so much of Gabrielle that a pang of longing stabbed through him, so sharp he had to physically prevent himself from crying out. 'In the card rack,' she said, gurgling with laughter. 'And the Continental is our card rack. Meeting openly like this, in front of all Saigon, will arouse far less suspicion than meeting furtively.'

They had drunk their coffee and then he had walked her down the steps leading to the plaza and had flagged down a battered blue and yellow taxicab for her.

'I will contact you,' she had promised, and then her eyes had become dark and urgent. 'But please remember, Gavin. Tell no one of who it is you are going to meet.'

He needed no reminding. Enormous trust was being placed in him and he had no intention of betraying it. 'I won't,' he said gravely. 'Good night, Nhu.'

She stepped into the taxi, and as it began to draw away she leaned toward the open window, once again smiling, calling out teasingly, 'I did not think an Australian nephew by marriage would be at all a nice thing to have, but I was wrong! Welcome to our family, Gavin!'

He waved, grinning with pleasure, and then turned and walked slowly back into the hotel. Despite the success of his trip to Hue, he was still very much a new boy at the press bureau and he had no idea if Paul Dulles would be cooperative about his disappearing on a story he was unable to even talk about.

He had a nightcap in the bar and decided that he would say nothing to Paul for the moment. There would be time enough to worry about Paul's cooperation when Nhu made contact, and that might not be for days, or even weeks. He slid from the bar stool and made his way to bed, wondering what Gabrielle was doing at that very moment, whether she was thinking of him – if she was missing him as painfully as he was missing her. ★ ★ ★

The next afternoon Paul sent him with Jimmy Giddings to JUSPAO, the Joint United States Public Affairs Office.

'It pains me to admit it,' Jimmy said, munching on a hamburger that was serving as a late lunch, 'but these biased announcements issued by the American command are almost the only source of our news. Investigative trips like yours to Hue are rarer than you might think.'

They turned into the JUSPAO building, passing an armed marine at the door. Above the entrance was a framed portrait of a smiling President Johnson. 'That guy sure has a lot to answer for,' Jimmy said as they began to walk through a maze of windowless corridors. 'He got America into this damned mess, but Christ knows how he's going to get her out of it.'

Corridor led into corridor, and just as Gavin was beginning to wonder if they were ever going to end, they came to a small theatre crowded with newsmen.

'Here we go,' Jimmy said, finding a space against the rear wall and settling himself comfortably against it. 'The cheapest, most entertaining show in town.'

There was a chuckle of agreeing laughter from the reporters standing nearest to them, and then the noise level in the room died down a little as an American colonel strode across the stage to a lectern. Behind him was a large-scale map of Vietnam, liberally highlighted in blue and pink, and on a board by his side were pinned half a dozen statistical charts.

'The blue bits on the map are areas controlled by US and allied forces, the pink bits are the areas controlled by the Cong,' Jimmy whispered as the colonel wished them all good afternoon and a soldier in front of the stage activated a large reel-to-reel tape recorder.

'What are the white bits?' Gavin whispered back.

Jimmy began to chew on a piece of gum. 'The white bits are so-called "movement areas", all moving towards being blue bits if you believe what the man up there is going to tell you. Personally, I don't.'

Gavin listened to a recap of the Buddhist disturbances in Hue, the descriptions of the horror that he had himself witnessed sanitized by specialist lingo. The reports of engagements between American troops and Viet Cong were treated in the same disorienting manner. Accidental civilian deaths were 'friendly casualties', Americans killed in action were referred to only by the letters KIA, and figures that looked horrendous to Gavin were described as being 'light'. There was a sheet on which was estimated the weekly kill ratio, the number of Viet Cong killed per American, the conclusion seeming to be that no matter the number of American dead, if numerically there were more Viet Cong dead, then the war was being won.

'How do they know that the figures for Viet Cong dead are correct?' he whispered to Jimmy. 'I thought the VC tried to recover their dead whenever possible?'

Jimmy looked across at him pityingly. 'They do,' he said, transferring his chewing gum from the left side of his mouth to the right. 'But whenever a platoon has engaged the enemy, the officer in command is asked how many Cong they hit. He doesn't have to have the bodies to back up his figures. He just has to think of a number and double it.'

'You mean the Viet Cong dead figures are estimates, and only the American figures are for real?'

'If you get any sharper, you'll cut yourself,' Jimmy said with good-natured sarcasm.

' – American aircraft bombed targets close to Hanoi and Haiphong yesterday,' the colonel continued, 'destroying an estimated fifty percent of the North's fuel supply—'

'If we can't rely on what we're being told, why do we come?' Gavin demanded, sotto voce.

'Because it's easy,' Jimmy said, his tone indicating that it was a fact even a three-year-old would have grasped. 'And because only the military know what's been happening all around the country, each and every day. They may tell us only what they want us to know, but at least we get some sort of a coherent picture. You could spend weeks hitching

353

helicopters with the troops, but you won't necessarily get any clearer a view of what the hell is happening.'

Gavin's mouth set in a tight, firm line. Jimmy, middle-aged and war weary, had settled for relying on the information being given out by the American military, but it didn't mean that *he* had to. The sooner he could hop aboard a helicopter with the troops, the better he would like it.

Two days later he got his chance. 'How would you like to cover the making of a free fire zone?' Paul asked as he strolled into the office. 'As the answer is obviously yes, get yourself down to the air base. There's a party of marines on their way to a place called Cam Lai. They're expecting you.'

It was his first time in an army helicopter. A big, black marine grinned at him and handed him a helmet and a flak jacket. 'Don't worry, man, this ain't no heavy situation, just a safe little hop, a pleasant afternoon out in the boonies.'

Gavin looked around at the other marines seated on the floor of the wide-bellied Chinook. From the bored expressions on their faces, he figured he'd been told the truth.

The village they were flown into was made up of thatched-roof huts and paddyfields.

'Come on men!' the officer shouted as the marines began to bundle out of the helicopter into the stifling mid-morning heat. 'Let's git it on and over with!'

The first thing that Gavin heard above the roar of the rotor blades was the sound of desperate sobbing. Women were milling bewilderedly in the mud-baked streets, babies on their hips as they struggled with boxes and baskets of pitiful possessions.

The leading marine was already shouting to them to make their way toward the waiting Chinook, jerking his rifle to emphasize his words.

'How long have these people had to prepare to leave their homes?' Gavin shouted to the officer over the sound of the still-pulsating rotors.

'They were leafleted at nine this mornin',' the marine said, taking out a cigarette and lighting it as his men began to search the huts, ejecting wailing toddlers and terrified old people at rifle point.

'Christ!' Gavin felt as if he were in a lunatic asylum. 'It's only eleven now! How the hell do you expect them to be ready to abandon homes they've lived in for generations in just two hours?'

'Aw, they ain't got much stuff,' the officer said complacently.

Gavin wondered what would happen to his press accreditation if he socked an officer on the jaw on his first trip out in the field. One of the women, nearly dwarfed by a bundle of household belongings, tottered and fell as she was herded towards them. None of the marines made any move to help her to her feet.

'These are our *allies*, for Christ's sake!' Gavin yelled at the disinterested marines as he ran forward, taking hold of the woman's arm and helping her ease herself up from the dirt. 'We're supposed to be winning their hearts and minds, not terrifying the life out of them!'

The officer strolled threateningly towards him. 'You're goin' to make yourself very unpopular playin' the boy scout,' he said as the woman hurriedly picked up her bundle, clutching it close to her chest. 'Seems to me you should be askin' yourself why there's no able-bodied men in this here village. And the answer is, because they're probably all VC. If they are, then it'll be a pleasure to burn their village to the ground, and if they ain't, then I reckon they should be pretty glad to be goin' to a camp where they'll be protected 'gainst the VC.'

There was nothing Gavin could do. He stood impotently, white-lipped with rage, as the crying, protesting villagers were herded aboard the Chinook. God alone knew where they were being taken. The officer had said a camp. Wherever it was, it wasn't home and it never would be. Home was the village where their fathers had been

355

born, and their father's father, and their father's father's father.

'We've got a problem, sir!' one of the marines yelled out, running up to them. 'There's an old man no one can move! Says his family shrine is here and he has to stay and tend it!'

'Assholes,' the officer said succinctly. 'Tell him this is goin' to be a free fire zone, and after today, anythin' movin' here will be regarded as VC and shot. Got that?'

'Yes sir,' the marine said unhappily. 'I've already told him that, sir, and he says he won't come. He says it's his duty to stay with the graves of his people. That if we want to move him, we'll have to kill him first.'

For one terrible moment Gavin thought the officer was going to give a laconic order for the old man to be shot. Instead, he said irritably. 'Okay. Leave him. We're behind schedule. Zippo the huts and let's be off.'

As the last of the villagers crowded aboard the Chinook, some with baskets of squawking hens, a couple of them with pigs in their arms, none of them knowing where they were going or what was to become of them, the marines set fire to the straw-thatched huts.

The smoke billowed thickly up into the hot, humid air. Aboard the Chinook the sobbing gave way to despairing whimpers and then to passive, helpless silence. Gavin climbed aboard and joined them, sick at heart. The old man had run off limping towards the paddy fields and, presumably, his family burial ground. Gavin knew that he wouldn't survive there for long. In a free fire zone nothing, man or beast, survived for very long.

'So you didn't like what you saw?' Paul said to him later at the bureau office.

'I didn't *understand* what I saw!' Gavin exploded savagely. 'Those people are our *allies*! America is supposedly in Vietnam to help and protect them! Can you imagine American or British generals in occupied France or Italy during the Second World War, ordering the herding of whole communities away from their homes to live in what can be described only as concentration camp conditions so that free fire zones could be created? The answer is that you can't, and if you want to know what the difference is, then I'll tell you! The difference, conscious or unconscious, is racial. If those Vietnamese I saw being ordered on to that Chinook at gunpoint and against their will had been white civilians, then the operation would have been carried out with a damned sight more civility!'

Paul leaned back in his chair, one leg crossed over the other, his foot tapping the air and revealing a flash of a startling emerald sock. 'I thought you said the officer in charge was black?'

'I did. For all I know, the majority of black servicemen may have more empathy with the Vietnamese than their white counterparts, but the one I came across today didn't.'

His rage was so white-hot, so naive, that Paul suppressed a cynical smile. He could vaguely remember reacting the same way himself when he had first arrived, but that had been over a year ago. Since then, in order to survive, he had learned the art of remaining aloof from the insanity surrounding him. It was an art Gavin would no doubt learn too, in time.

'There are always two points of view to every argument,' he said, reaching for a glass and a bottle and pouring himself two fingers of whiskey. 'From the American military point of view, creating free fire zones makes sense.' He raised a hand to silence Gavin. 'Once the villages in a Viet Cong-infested area have been destroyed, and their inhabitants removed to a safe place, then the Viet Cong have nothing and no one to shelter them. They become clearly identifiable targets. And they can be attacked without the lives of innocent civilians being put at risk.'

357

'If they are still there to attack!' Gavin snorted derisively. 'Which they won't be! And while they scarper off to new pastures, we destroy homes and communities and create hundreds of thousands of refugees. And that's another point!' He ran his hand through his hair. 'Why the hell are they referred to as refugees? They're *not* refugees, and calling them that distorts the truth of this situation. They're evacuees, and that's what they should be called!'

'That could be the beginning of the end,' Paul said dryly. 'Before you know where you are, even enemy WBLCs would be given their right name.'

'WBLCs?'

'Waterborne logistics craft.'

'What the hell are they?'

'Sampans,' Paul said with a grin. 'Come on, let's go to the Continental for a drink. I want to know why you described the camp the villagers were transferred to as a concentration camp.'

*It was a planned shantytown,* Gavin wrote later that day to Gabrielle, *miles from anywhere, with no paddy fields for the villagers to farm, and no trees for shade. All the surrounding ground had been bulldozed flat so that there was no vegetation to give cover to any Viet Cong. To keep the Viet Cong away, the tin-roofed houses were surrounded by barbed wire and watchtowers. The place was dirty, dusty, and utterly soulless. The refugees already living there were sullen and resentful, and who can blame them? If they weren't Viet Cong sympathizers before they were uprooted from their land, then they must surely be Viet Cong sympathizers now. But the Americans can't see it. This morning's operation was described officially as being a great success, the 'removal of several score villagers from a place of insecurity to a place of safety'.*

In his last letter, he had written about his meeting with Nhu, and had only hinted that he might meet Dinh, saying that he was 'looking forward to meeting the rest of her family quite soon'. Now he wrote: *I love you and I miss you, and I'm beginning to love this country too, or at least the un-Americanized bits! Tu Do Street has to be seen to be believed! It's like the worst parts of Las Vegas and Los Angeles all rolled into one and the clubs make the Black Cat seem a model of respectability!*

The rest of Gavin's week was spent covering the routine briefings at the Follies. US airforce and navy jets had begun a major campaign to wipe out fuel installations in the Hanoi-Haiphong area, and the briefings were even longer than normal, the hundred or so journalists in attendance asking a lot of questions about the escalation of the war.

He was alone in the bureau office, typing, when the door opened and to his utter astonishment Nhu stepped a trifle uncertainly into the room.

'Is it all right if I come in?' she asked hesitantly, looking around and seeing with relief that he was alone.

'But of course!' He was on his feet, pulling a chair away from one of the other desks so that she could sit down.

She shook her head when he motioned her to sit. 'No. I am not staying, Gavin. I have come to tell you that the time is now. Dinh has sent someone to escort you to him.'

'When? Now? This very minute?'

She nodded.

'But I can't, Nhu!' he protested. 'I have to finish my article, tell my bureau chief—'

'That is precisely what Dinh does not want you to do,' she said gently. 'You are to leave now, without speaking to anyone either here or at the Continental.'

Through the screen door of thick, inch-square wire meshing, he could see a small Renault, a Vietnamese at the wheel.

'I can't possibly, Nhu! To disappear without a word would arouse far more problems than it would solve!'

'You are to leave a note, which I am to make sure your bureau chief receives,' Nhu said, unperturbed. 'And you are not to return to the Continental for a change of clothes. A change of clothes has already been arranged for you.'

He gazed around him helplessly. His half-finished article protruding from his typewriter read: *China has reacted by calling the bombing of the fuel installations in the Hanoi-Haiphong areas, 'barbarous and wanton acts that have further freed us from any bounds of restrictions in helping North Vietnam'*. For the life of him, he couldn't remember what he had planned to type next.

'You must write your note now,' Nhu said. 'The messenger Dinh has sent will not wait for you more than a few minutes.'

Gavin groaned. He had no choice but to write a note to Paul and disappear in the waiting Renault, but he was well aware that it was an action that could cost him his job.

'How long will I be away, Nhu?' he asked, reaching for a sheet of typing paper.

'I do not know. Three or four days. Perhaps a week.'

He scrawled: *Paul. Something huge has come up. Will explain all when I return, possibly end of week. Gavin.*

He propped it on Paul's desk, praying that when he returned it would be such a big story that forgiveness would be automatic, and followed Nhu out into the street.

'I am not going with you,' she said as the Renault's driver indicated to him that he should sit in the rear of the car. 'I am to stay here and make sure that your note is found and read.' She hesitated and then said, her voice trembling slightly, 'When you see my brother, tell him that I miss him.'

He nodded, stepping into the Renault's stiflingly hot interior.

The car sped out of the city through Cholon, the Chinese quarter, the driver remaining uncommunicably silent. Since he knew it would be a waste of time to ask where they were going or how long the trip would take, Gavin did neither. He sat back, looking out of the window at paddyfields and swamps and canals, wondering if they were on the road that ran northwest from Saigon to Phnom Penh in Cambodia, and how far they could possibly go before being stopped and questioned by the police or the military.

Some ten or eleven kilometres from Saigon they careened into a small village looking much the same as the other villages they had driven through. This time, however, they turned off the road, bumping and swaying into a dusty alley between closely packed thatched-roof houses built of bamboo and corrugated iron.

'Are we here?' Gavin asked in Vietnamese. It was the first time he had spoken, and the driver's eyes flew wide at the shock of being spoken to by a round-eye in his own language.

'I return to Saigon,' he said uninformatively as two black-pyjama-clad figures emerged from the nearest house, Soviet Kalashnikov AK-47 rifles in their hands.

The men began to walk towards the car and Gavin, suspecting that he was not going to be a passenger on his companion's return trip, opened the rear door and stepped out into the blistering midday heat. He didn't wait for the men to approach but took the initiative, walking confidently towards them.

'Chào,' he said, smiling tentatively and shaking their hands firmly.

'You are Mr Gavin Ryan?' one of them asked in Vietnamese.

Gavin nodded.

'Your press accreditation card, please.'

Gavin removed his card from his shirt pocket, and handed it to him. The man, in his black pyjamas and sandals made out of discarded truck tyres, scrutinized it as carefully as if he were a civil servant in a government office.

'Thank you,' he said, handing the card back to Gavin. 'Please follow me.'

Gavin hesitated for a fraction of a second. Behind him the Renault's engine revved into life, in front of him the door of the nearest thatched-roof house opened, revealing an intimidatingly dark interior. The man who hadn't yet spoken to him walked across to the Renault, exchanged a few words with the driver, and then the Renault began to back out of the alley, raising a cloud of dense dust.

Gavin turned and watched it for a moment. Then he followed the man who had been speaking to him into the house.

It took his eyes several seconds to adjust to the gloom. When they did so, he looked round him in astonishment. He had expected to find Dinh in the room. There was no one, just a few functional articles, a sleeping pallet, a table, two chairs, a grate for a fire, and a few cooking pots.

The Vietnamese handed him the suitcase that had been removed from the rear of the car. 'Are you armed? Have you a gun? A knife?' he asked.

Gavin shook his head and the man ran his hands swiftly and efficiently over him.

'Good,' he said, satisfied. 'You are to come with us, Comrade Ryan. This way, please.'

The Vietnamese who had so far remained silent kicked the cooking pots away from the grate with his foot and then squatted down, plunging his hand into the middle of a pile of cold ashes.

Gavin watched, mystified, and then his mystification changed to disbelief as the Vietnamese pulled hard, lifting open a small wooden trapdoor. As the man eased himself into the opening, dropping feetfirst out of sight, his companion turned to Gavin.

'This way,' he said again, and Gavin was almost sure there was a gleam of relish in his eyes as he motioned him forwards.

If he had been as chunkily built as Jimmy Giddings, or as big-boned as Lestor McDermott, his adventure would have ended there, before it had begun, because there would have been no way Jimmy or Lestor could have eased themselves down through the narrow opening. As it was, he was almost as slight as the Vietnamese and with a last longing look toward the open door of the house and sunlight, he lowered himself into the claustrophobic darkness.

The shaft dropped into a tunnel, not high enough to walk in, but large and wide enough to wriggle along. It did not run straight. It zig-zagged, and every now and then there would be a cavity hollowed out in the tunnel's side, just deep enough for a human body to squeeze into. Sweat was pouring into his eyes and his breathing was harsh and rasping. He wondered how on earth the tunnel was ventilated, where it lead, and then, after about thirty-five to forty yards, they came to a second trapdoor which opened on to another shaft, which led deeper into the earth.

When he had entered the tunnel he had imagined that it led, after a few yards, to an underground hiding place. He never imagined that it would be so long and complex. There was bamboo lining the tunnel roof now, and they kept coming to intersections where other tunnels led off blackly.

Something scurried past his face, and he hit out blindly with his hands, barely controlling his panic. Had it been a spider? He hated spiders and he knew that in the tropics all spiders were likely to be poisonous. He was trembling violently, barely able to control his rising panic. It would be over soon. It couldn't go on for much longer. They would reach their destination. There would be light and air.

And the return? He wouldn't think about returning, only about arriving without disgracing himself by betraying his claustrophobia and his fear of whatever insect life was present but unseen.

Just when he thought he could continue no longer, faint light permeated the darkness and the Vietnamese in front of him scrambled from his belly on to his feet, standing upright.

Two seconds later Gavin was gratefully doing the same thing. He stared around him. The light was not daylight. It was the light of an improvised oil lamp, an old medicine bottle with a wick in it, and he was not in a shaft leading upward, as he had hoped, but in a chamber large enough to hold ten or twelve people. At a makeshift desk a Vietnamese wearing the green uniform of the North Vietnamese Army sat writing. The two black-clad Vietnamese waited respectfully for him to look up from his work. When he did so, he said only, 'Colonel Duong is waiting for you, Comrades.'

With every muscle in his body aching from the effort of his crawl, and his skin drenched with perspiration, Gavin followed his Vietnamese companions across the chamber and into another tunnel, this time one that was high enough to walk in upright. There was a dull rumble and the ground shook above them, a scattering of earth falling on to their heads. 'It is the big monkeys,' the Vietnamese who had done all the earlier talking, said to him. 'They are bombing the Boi Loi Woods.'

By big monkeys, Gavin assumed that his companion referred to the Americans. He wondered if Australians were also referred to in the same derogatory manner.

The chamber they walked into was as big as the previous one, but more comfortably furnished. There was a large table made out of packing cases and planks of wood, around which stood three men, all in North Vietnamese Army uniforms and all looking down at a large scale map. There were other boxes stacked against the wall which appeared to be serving as filing cabinets. And there was a hammock in one corner, and a smaller table on which was a lamp made out of an old menthol bottle, a dagger, a rifle, and a rice bag.

The men looked up, and the smallest of them, the one standing centrally and facing Gavin, said, 'I am Colonel Duong Quynh Dinh. Welcome to the tunnels of Cu Chi, Comrade Ryan.'

'I'm very pleased to be here,' Gavin said, trying to suppress his feeling of being entombed and to inject a note of sincerity into his voice.

Gabrielle's uncle looked far older than his forty-two years – the lean, wiry figure with not an ounce of excess flesh on his bones and a taut, heavily lined face seemed nearer to fifty-two.

He moved from behind the desk, walking up to Gavin, standing in front of him and holding his eyes for what seemed an eternity.

'I am told that you are a journalist and that your sympathies are with us, Comrade?' he said at last.

Gavin nodded. If Dinh was under the impression that he was a committed Communist, now did not seem the time or the place to enlighten him.

'And that you are my nephew-in-law?'

Gavin felt a tremor of relief. By publicly acknowledging the family connection, Dinh was giving him credentials in the eyes of the other North Vietnamese.

'Yes.' He unbuttoned his shirt pocket. 'I have brought two photographs for you, Colonel. One of them is Gabrielle and myself on our wedding day, the other is of your sister, Vanh.'

Dinh took them, looking down at them for a long time. Gavin knew that Dinh had not seen Vanh for several years, and that he had never seen Gabrielle.

'It is a long time since I have seen some members of my family,' Dinh said to him, taking a small notebook from his pocket and slipping the two photographs between the leaves. 'It is a hard price to pay for victory, but it is a price that I and my fellow comrades pay willingly.'

He motioned Gavin forwards towards the table. 'Let me tell you something about the area you are in, Comrade.' He indicated a point on the map some twenty kilometres northwest of Saigon. 'This is Cu Chi district.' He circled an area of small villages clustered astride Route One. 'Here are the villages of An Nhon Tay and Phu My Hung, referred to by the Americans as the Ho Bo Woods. Phu My Hung is our area command post.' To the north of the area Gavin could see a faint blue line indicating the Saigon River. 'It is a district that was important to us in our war with the French, and that is important to us now, in our war with the Americans.'

'Because of its strategic significance?' Gavin interposed, trying hard to sound intelligent enough to warrant the confidence being placed in him.

Dinh nodded. 'Yes. As you see, the main road linking Phnom Penh and Saigon runs through Cu Chi, as does the Saigon River. We need to control these routes in order to bring supplies in from Cambodia.' He paused, and something that could have been a hint of a smile touched the hard line of his mouth. 'When I was a boy, this area was very green, very lush.'

Gavin knew that most of it was anything but green and lush now. A huge American army base had been built in the area, and in January a large-scale American military operation, code-named CRIMP had poured hundreds of troops into the countryside around Cu Chi in an effort to clear it of Viet Cong, and to secure it. In case they overlooked any Viet Cong, B-52s had then pounded the area with thirty-ton loads of high explosives.

'Were the tunnels here in January, when the area was bombed?' he asked, forgetting his claustrophobia as his reporter's intense interest in the story took over.

Again Gavin saw a faint glimmer of a smile. 'The tunnels have been here ever since the days when we fought the French. Every hamlet and village in the area built its own underground network where guerrilla fighters could hide, and from where they could launch surprise attacks upon the French Army. Now the tunnels have been repaired and extended. They cover an area from the Cambodian border to the outskirts of Saigon.'

If there had been a chair handy, Gavin would have gratefully sat down upon it. All the time he had been studying about Vietnam, preparing himself to come to Vietnam, he had never read a word referring to the enemy's use of tunnels. Paul hadn't mentioned the tunnels, nor had Jimmy or Lestor, which meant that they did not know about them. He felt like whooping with elation. When Paul read his story about Cu Chi, he wouldn't give a damn about the way he had disappeared without so much as a by-your-leave. He certainly wouldn't get the sack. He would get the press bureau's equivalent of a Pulitzer Prize!

'Let me give you some idea of the sophistication of our tunnel network, and then I will tell you why it is that I asked you to come to Cu Chi, and what it is that North Vietnam would like from you,' Dinh said, leading the way out of the chamber.

Gavin took a deep breath and followed him. He was beginning to feel slightly more acclimatized now and his interest superseded his fear.

For sixty yards or so at a time they would wriggle on their bellies like giant underground moles, and then they would scramble upright in a large chamber that served as a dormitory or an ammunition dump or a first-aid station. There was even a kitchen.

'Where does the smoke go?' Gavin asked, perplexed.

'It is ducted through several channels and finally escapes, greatly diffused, through ground-level chimneys a good distance from any tunnel entrance. Though most of our food is eaten cold,' Dinh said, a note of regret in his voice.

The strenuously physical tour continued. There were ventilation shafts and wells. There were false tunnels near some entrances, leading nowhere. There were dead ends. There were booby traps for any American soldier so enterprising as to discover an entrance and see through the false trails.

The booby traps were nearly Gavin's undoing. He was just congratulating himself on the way he had adjusted to the dark and the bodily stenches that poisoned the air, when there was a strange scuffling sound and Dinh wriggled into one of the hollows carved out of the tunnel's side that served as both a hiding place and a passing place.

'We will go no farther in this direction,' Dinh said, lighting a small candle to give light. 'It leads to a booby-trapped entrance. Can you see?'

In the flickering light of the candle, Gavin saw ahead of him, a mere three or four feet away, three huge rats reared on their haunches, teeth bared.

'*Jesus God!*'

He forgot all about making a favourable impression, about gaining Dinh's esteem. He jettisoned backwards, his terror overwhelming. He was unable to turn around in the narrow tunnel, unable to move fast, fast, fast enough, and there was a gurgling animal sound coming from his throat as he tried to put distance between himself and the creatures of nightmare in front of him.

'They cannot harm you, Comrade,' Dinh said, chuckling. 'They are tethered by the neck.'

Gavin did not care. He continued to scramble backwards, throwing the Vietnamese who had been accompanying them on their tour into noisy retreat. Not until he was again in one of the large chambers, the red clay walls civilizingly covered in looted US parachute nylon, did he come to a sweat-soaked, shivering halt.

'You were right to give our unpleasant friends a wide berth,' Dinh said to him when he rejoined him. 'They have been infected with bubonic plague. If anyone should discover that particular entrance, a trapdoor can be lowered, sealing that part of the tunnel from the rest of the complex. The leash tethering the rats can be severed from this side of the trapdoor, and the rats let loose. Once greeted in such a manner, we do not expect to be troubled further.'

Gavin tried to say that he was certain they would never be troubled, ever again, but he was still incapable of speech.

'We will eat now,' Dinh said, saving him from disgracing himself further. 'And then I will tell you what it is that we want from you.'

All six of them ate together, the two Vietnamese who had initially escorted him through the tunnels, and the two middle-aged but exceedingly tough-looking North Vietnamese officers who had been closeted with Dinh when he had first arrived. From the lack of comment about the food, Gavin assumed that it must be their normal fare: cold rice supplemented by the merest sliver of chicken, and accompanied by water in tin mugs.

Gavin had never been so thirsty in his life, and his initial instinct was to gulp the water down. Then it occurred to him that there was no way that the water would have been boiled. He crossed his fingers. He had to drink, and he had to hope for the best.

When the food had been eaten, Dinh settled himself on a rough wooden chair behind the desk. 'Perhaps you have heard of a journalist by the name of Wilfred Burchett, Comrade?'

Gavin nodded. Wilfred Burchett was world-famous as being the journalist who, in the days of Dien Bien Phu, had interviewed and become a friend of Ho Chi Minh. He was Australian, no longer young, and because of his fiercely held political sympathies, was regarded by fellow journalists as something of a maverick.

'There are very few foreign journalists of the calibre of Mr Burchett,' Dinh was saying. 'Journalists who report to the West the truth of what is happening in our country. Too many of them are misled by the false proclamations of victory coming from the American imperialists and their Saigon puppets.'

He paused, and Gavin felt a tingle run down his spine. Was Dinh going to ask him to assume the role of Burchett to his Ho Chi Minh? And if so, how could he possibly accept? He wasn't a freelance journalist able to write what he liked, when he liked. He was a news agency reporter. Whatever he wrote, even if it passed Paul Dulles's critical eye, it would be edited again in the Paris head office. When it reached the newspaper offices it was destined for, it would be edited again by a subeditor, who would put a headline on the story, place it in the paper, and cut it to fit. And the interference with the original story didn't end there. With agency stories it was customary for editors to merge the story with one on the same subject by their own correspondent.

To write stories covering Viet Cong activities, and to expect that they would be published in a form acceptable to the North Vietnamese, would be impossible for anyone but a freelance journalist with an established reputation.

'The Hanoi government has requested that you stay with us as our guest, Comrade,' Dinh said, confirming his suspicions. 'Like Mr Burchett, you will record our fight for freedom, and you will record the crimes of the American imperialists.'

Adrenaline began to pump along Gavin's veins. If he understood Dinh correctly, he was being offered the chance to go out on active operations with the Viet Cong. It was the kind of scoop that any journalist would sell his soul for. If the bureau refused to accept the story, on the grounds that there was no corroboration of it from any other source, then he would resign as a member of the staff and chance his luck as a freelancer.

'I am very honoured to accept your invitation,' he said, wondering how long he was going to be their guest, and if, now that he had accepted their invitation, he would be allowed to communicate with Paul.

'That is very good, Comrade,' Dinh said unexpressively. 'The people of Vietnam are waiting for a historic moment, a moment when the whole nation will rise up in revolt. The revolutionary forces of Vietnam will very soon show the rest of the world what they can do, and you will have the great privilege of being with them when they are victorious.'

Gavin frowned slightly. They had been speaking sometimes in French, sometimes in Vietnamese, and though Dinh spoke in the same regional accent as Vanh, obviously he had misunderstood something. However optimistic the North Vietnamese were of eventually attaining their aims, no one could imagine that those aims were going to be attained in the next few days or weeks.

'When I return here, will I be met and brought by car in the same manner as I was this morning?' he asked, assuming that his assignment was to be an ongoing one.

'I am afraid you have not quite comprehended, Comrade,' Dinh said, a note of genuine regret in his voice. 'You will not be returning here because you will not be leaving here, at least you will not be leaving here for Saigon. My mission in the South is completed, and in five days time I shall begin the journey north, up the Ho Chi Minh Trail. When I do so, you will accompany me.'

Gavin stared at him. Of course. He should have known from the beginning. He hadn't been blindfolded on his journey to Cu Chi. Secrets that the Americans would have given a ransom for had been carelessly revealed to him. And they had been so because all along his hosts had known that he would never be able to communicate what he had seen, not unless they wanted him to communicate it. He wasn't their guest. For reasons that he still didn't fully comprehend, he was their prisoner.

'Can I choose to change my mind and refuse your invitation?' he asked quietly.

Dinh shook his head. 'No, Comrade. You have no choice. You have had no choice ever since the moment when you stepped into the car outside the bureau office.'

He wondered if Nhu had known Dinh's intentions, and was sure that she had not. His only consolation was that she did at least know who it was he had gone to meet, and she would be able to tell Gabrielle.

Gabrielle. He closed his eyes, knowing with dreadful certainty that he was not going to see her again for a very long time, that he was not going to see her again for years.

# CHAPTER TWENTY

It was two-thirty on a Wednesday afternoon when the official-looking black sedan drove up and stopped outside Abbra's home. She had spent the morning writing, and her chapter was going well. At twelve o'clock she had taken a coffee break and had decided to go for a short walk before resuming work. She had driven across to Golden Gate Park and had strolled by the edge of the lake, mentally plotting out the end of her chapter. Satisfied that all she now had to do was to transfer the words in her head on to paper, she had driven back home, not thinking about Lewis, thinking only of the imaginary world that had become so real to her. And then, as she turned into the driveway, she saw the sedan.

The occupants didn't wait for her to turn off the Oldsmobile's engine before they stepped from the car, slamming the doors behind them. She froze, her hands tight on the wheel. Both men were in army uniform. Both were officers. And one of them was a chaplain.

They returned, beginning to walk towards her, and the instant she saw the expression on their faces she knew that Lewis was either dead or captured.

'Mrs Ellis?' the unordained officer asked her as she forced her hands numbly from the wheel and clumsily opened her car door.

She stumbled out on to the drive, facing him. 'Yes. I'm Mrs Ellis.' The sun, which only a few minutes before had been so pleasurable, was now sickeningly hot, so searingly bright that she had difficulty in focusing on the man's face.

'Could we speak to you inside for a few minutes, Mrs Ellis?'

She nodded, her throat dry, her heart pounding. *Please don't let him be dead!* she was screaming silently. *Please, dear God, don't let Lewis be dead! Don't let him be dead!*

She walked across the drive and slipped her key into the lock. She couldn't ask. If she asked, and if he were dead, there would be no going back. Every second that they didn't speak was a second longer of hope, a second longer of being able to pretend that everything was still all right, that perhaps it was a welfare visit. That perhaps Lewis had been injured and was being flown home, that perhaps . . .

'Your husband has been taken prisoner, Mrs Ellis,' the chaplain was saying to her gently.

They were in the living-room. Lewis's photograph was in a small silver frame on one of the side tables. She had planned to write to him that evening. It would have been one of her last letters, for in another four weeks he would be coming home to her.

'He and his companions were ambushed on one of the canals after they had searched a village for North Vietnamese forces.' It was the other officer speaking now. He was mature and grizzle-haired and his voice was full of regret. 'One of your husband's fellow officers managed to escape. He saw your husband taken prisoner. As he was captured in the South, it may be impossible to receive official confirmation for some time—'

'Was he hurt?' she interrupted harshly. Her hands were balled into fists. He was alive. He was alive and that had to mean that he would come home to her again eventually.

'It is the opinion of the officer who witnessed the incident that he was not seriously injured.'

'Thank God.' She was crying. The tears were streaming down her face. She tried to stop them. She tried to be as courageous and as dignified as she knew Lewis would want her to be, as befitted an army wife, but no matter how hard she tried she couldn't stop the tears.

'You will receive an official telegram tomorrow, Mrs Ellis,' the middle-aged and fatherly officer was saying to her, 'and if there is anything that the army can do . . .'

He handed her a card. She didn't even look down at the piece of paper. There was only one thing she wanted the army to do. 'Just bring my husband back to me,' she said, her tears splashing on to her dress and the card in her hand. 'Just bring Lewis home.'

They wanted to stay with her until her parents returned home from the art exhibition they were visiting, or until a friend or a neighbour could be telephoned to come and sit with her. She vehemently refused all such offers.

'No. I want to be alone for a while.' It was the truth. She didn't want solicitous comfort. She wanted to be alone with her thoughts of Lewis.

Reluctantly, sensing that it might be best, they took their leave. Slowly she crossed the sun-filled room, picking up his photograph from the table.

'Where are you?' she whispered brokenly, and then, to her horror, she was drowned by another emotion as well as grief. She was overcome with anger, anger that he should have promised her he would be home within a few short weeks, and now wouldn't be home with her for perhaps years and years, anger at the awful, terrible loneliness that she knew lay ahead.

'*Oh, Lewis!*' she howled in agony to the empty room. '*Where are you? When are you going to come back to me?*'

By the time her parents returned, her face was still wet and streaked with tears, but her voice was steady.

'If he's a prisoner of war, then you'll be able to write to him, communicate with him,' her father said gruffly when he had recovered from the worst of the shock.

'But I thought only pilots who were shot down over the North were prisoners of war?' her mother asked bewildered. 'Lewis was in the South, wasn't he? How could he possibly have been captured by North Vietnamese forces?

It doesn't make any kind of sense. We are *winning* the war, aren't we. . . . '

'It isn't as cut and dried as you seem to think,' Abbra's father responded sombrely. 'It isn't a game between the Rams and the Redskins. It's far more complicated than that.'

When her father mentioned the Rams, Abbra said quietly, 'The army will break the news to Lewis's father, but they won't contact Scott. I'll have to do that.'

'Nonsense!' her mother retorted despite her distress. As far as she knew, for the last month there had been no contact between Abbra and Scott Ellis, and she didn't want contact to be resumed. 'His father will telephone him. There's absolutely no reason for you to do so. You are far too upset.'

'No. Abbra is right,' her husband interrupted. 'Abbra should call him. It would be awful if he heard about it on the news or read it in the papers.'

'Colonel Ellis will contact him!' her mother insisted.

'I'd rather he heard the news from me,' Abbra said in a quiet, inflexible voice, and as her mother broke out into further protests she walked out of the room. The telephone in the hall was too public, and she went past it, crossing the hall and entering her father's study, closing the door behind her.

She hadn't seen or spoken to Scott for four weeks, ever since the day when she had last lunched with Patti Maine. Since then she had told the household help that if Scott telephoned, she was not at home.

A week before she had received an affectionate letter from him. He was assuming she was away on another research trip, but as he hadn't received so much as a postcard from her he was getting worried. Would she please telephone him the instant she returned home?

She had put the letter to one side, not knowing how to reply. The more she had thought about what Patti had said, the more she had realized the kernel of truth behind

375

it. She and Scott had been spending too much time together. People were beginning to speculate about the nature of their relationship. And Abbra had been too self-absorbed to notice. A tiny piece in a gossip column a week after her lunch with Patti showed her how very visible they had become as a couple.

Rams star Scott Ellis attended a charity game at La Jolla High School on Wednesday evening, and was *not* accompanied by his sister-in-law, the pretty and vivacious Mrs. Lewis Ellis. Could this sudden rift in family relations stem from Scott's involvements in antiwar demonstrations? His brother, Captain Lewis Ellis, is at present on a year's tour of duty in 'Nam. It could be that sister-in-law Abbra isn't the only one to have taken offence at Scott's antiwar stance. His father, Colonel Thomas Ellis, a highly decorated Second World War veteran, is also likely to be displeased.

It was an unpleasant little piece, but Abbra knew that if she had read it before she had lunched with Patti, she would have focused on the references to a possible rift between Scott and his father. She certainly would have missed the sexual insinuations completely. But they were there. She could see that now. Even worse, she knew that there were seeds of truth in the insinuation. She admitted it. She *was* physically attracted to Scott. He was so magnificently Adonis-like, so tall and powerfully built and golden-haired, she didn't see how any woman could fail to be. Yet until Patti had pointed it out to her, she had not realized how dangerous the situation was, how dependent she was on him emotionally, and how dependent he might be on her . . .

She knew that she needed him now. Her parents could commiserate with her, her friends and neighbours would be sympathetic, but she didn't need commiseration or sympathy. She needed someone who understood her, someone who would understand her anger as well as her grief. She needed someone who would realize just how monstrously obscene the prospect of not seeing Lewis again for years and years was.

After she had dialled his number, the telephone in his apartment rang for so long that she thought he must be out. Just as she was about to hang up, he answered, and at the sound of his familiar, zest-filled voice, her hard-won composure abandoned her.

'It's Abbra,' she said, her voice breaking. 'Oh, Scott! Lewis has been taken prisoner by the North Vietnamese!'

There was a second's stunned silence, and then he said, 'Hang in there, sweetheart. I'm on my way.'

She put the telephone back on its rest and leaned back against the wall, her eyes closed, her tears falling fast and free. It was what she had wanted to hear. He hadn't asked any of the questions anyone else would have asked, questions which she could not possibly answer. He had simply said that he would come to her. And when he did, she knew that he would give her the strength to be able to face the next few days, and the days that would follow those.

She didn't want to talk to him in the house. Despite the dreadful circumstances, she knew that her mother's attitude towards him had not changed. So as the time approached when she expected him, she waited in the hall, prepared to run out to his car the second she heard its engine.

'Do you think you should leave the house?' her father asked, a worried frown furrowing his brow. 'What if there is a telephone call from the army? What if there is further news of Lewis?'

'I have to talk to Scott, Daddy. And I have to do it away from the house.'

He nodded unhappily, understanding her reasons. There would be plenty of time for her to sit waiting for the telephone to ring. Too much time. 'I think I hear a car turning into the drive,' he said gruffly, wondering how long it would be before they heard any further news, until they learned exactly where Lewis was being held. And under what conditions.

She ran out of the house towards Scott's approaching Chevrolet. He drew to a halt, leaning over and opening the door for her, and then, as she tumbled into the passenger seat, he turned the car around, driving back down the drive and out into the wide, tree-lined street.

He drove to the Botanical Gardens on South Drive and parked in a quiet corner. Not until he had done so, and the Chevrolet's engine was switched off, did he speak.

'Who came to tell you?' he asked gently, turning to face her. 'What did they say?'

Her news had already marked his face. The lines around his mouth had deepened, and his eyes, usually so full of laughter, were dark.

'Two officers, one was a chaplain.' Her voice was unsteady but her tears were drying on her cheeks. She had been crying since she had called him, and now she could cry no more. She was exhausted both emotionally and physically, drained with shock. 'They said that Lewis and his companions had been ambushed on a canal after they had been searching a village for North Vietnamese forces. One of Lewis's fellow officers managed to escape and he saw Lewis being taken prisoner.'

'North Vietnamese? Not Viet Cong?'

'No. They definitely said that he had been captured by North Vietnamese.' She pushed the dark fall of her hair away from her face, asking, 'Do you think that means they will take him north, to Hanoi?'

He shook his head. 'I don't think so. I think the North Vietnamese who captured him probably came from Cambodia. It's much closer.'

'Would your father know?' Her voice was beginning to break again. 'I can't bear not knowing where he is. What if the North Vietnamese weren't taking Lewis prisoner? What if they simply took him away and shot him?' Her voice cracked.

He clenched his hands in order to physically prevent himself from reaching out and taking hold of her. He wanted to rock her against his chest. To soothe and comfort her. To lie to her if necessary. Instead, he said, his knuckles white, 'If the army thought that was likely, they would have told you that Lewis was missing in action, not that he had been taken prisoner. They've probably had other incidents exactly like this one. Maybe it's the policy of the NVA to take prisoners. Did they say anything else to you?'

'Yes.' His words were helping her put aside her worst fear – that Lewis had simply been led away and shot. She was beginning to feel a little better, a little stronger. 'They said that since Lewis had been captured in the South, it might be some time before there is official confirmation that he has been taken prisoner.'

'Which has to mean that this has happened before and that confirmation is usually forthcoming,' he said, trying to reassure her further.

She nodded, and then said with great hesitation, 'There's something else, Scott. Something that no one knows.'

He looked down at her, puzzled, wondering if the strain was already beginning to prove to be too much for her.

Her face was ivory pale, her eyes tortured with anxiety. 'Lewis isn't as fit as everyone thinks he is.' She had promised Lewis she would never tell anyone about his petit mal attacks. But it was a promise she could no longer keep. She had to be able to tell Scott. If she did not do so, he would never understand how terrible were her fears for Lewis's physical and mental health.

'Lewis is as strong as a horse,' Scott said gently. 'He's always been proud of his physical fitness.'

She shook her head, tears glittering on her eyelashes. 'No,' she said, praying that Lewis would forgive her. 'He suffers from petit mal. A mild form of epilepsy.'

If she had said that Lewis suffered from St Vitus' dance, he couldn't have looked more sceptical.

'*Epilepsy?* That's crazy, Abbra! Lewis is an army officer! He's never had a fit of any kind, ever, in his entire life!'

'Not the kind of fit that you are referring to. No, he hasn't, and I pray that he never will.' Her voice was choked with tears. 'But he suffered a head injury shortly before we were married, and ever since he has suffered from moments of disorientation.'

'Maybe, but it couldn't be called *epilepsy*,' Scott persisted.

'Lewis went to a private neurologist in Los Angeles. The form of petit mal he suffers from is so mild that in the majority of people it would not be worth mentioning. But Lewis is in the army. He couldn't risk having the words on his medical record. And so the army doesn't know. No one knows.'

Scott's face was nearly as white as her own. 'Are you telling me that this thing could develop? That imprisonment could make it worse? Could he develop the types of fits where people thrash on the floor?'

'I don't know. But I'm so afraid for him, Scott, so terribly afraid.' Her voice broke completely. After a few minutes, when she had regained control of herself, she said, 'My father says that as a prisoner of war Lewis will be able to write to me and receive letters from me. If that happens, then I will be able to bear it. I just need to know that he's still alive, Scott, that he will be coming back to me. Eventually.'

They had gone for a short walk through the rock garden and then he had driven her back home, promising to call her the following evening to see if there was any further news, and saying that he would drive up to see her again at the weekend.

'Tom telephoned,' her father said as she re-entered the house. 'I think he has taken the news quite badly, but is trying not to show it.'

'I'll phone him back.' Abbra desperately wanted to talk to him. As a military man, her father-in-law would be able to tell her what was likely to happen next, what steps would

380

be taken for Lewis's release and when she might be able to expect word from him.

' – we don't have much information about Americans who are being held prisoner in the South,' he told her, destroying her hope that he would know the location and name of the prison camp that Lewis might be sent to.

'But what about the Red Cross?' she asked. 'Surely if they arrange for letters and parcels to be delivered to prisoners, they must have details of where prisoners are held.'

There was a small, uncomfortable pause on the other end of the line, and then her father-in-law said gently, 'You mustn't raise your hopes that there will be contact with Lewis through the Red Cross, Abbra. It's true that there is some contact with Americans being held in Hoa Lo, but—'

'Where is Hoa Lo?' she interrupted. She prayed it was in the South. If it was in the South, she could still hope.

'It's an old French colonial prison in the centre of Hanoi.'

She closed her eyes, leaning against the wall, a feeling of dread rising. He didn't know any more than the officers who had visited her with news of Lewis's capture.

'I'm very sorry, my dear,' he said awkwardly, 'but I'm afraid there is nothing we can do but wait.'

The official telegram notifying her of Lewis's capture came the next day. She read it over and over, searching for any clues that she might have missed as to his whereabouts or his physical condition. There were no clues to be found.

The brief description of Lewis's capture was identical with the account she had already been given. The telegram then went on to say:

*In view of the above information your husband will be carried in a captured status pending receipt and review of a full report of the circumstances. You may be certain that you will be informed of any information received regarding your husband or any action taken regarding his status. Your great anxiety in this situation is*

381

*understood and I wish to assure you of every possible assistance together with heartfelt sympathy at this time of heartache and uncertainty.*

The last line read:

*Inasmuch as your husband is presently being carried on a captured status it is suggested for his safety that you reveal only his name, rank, file number, and date of birth to inquiries from sources outside your immediate family.*

She stared at the curt, brief words. *Why?* Why was she being instructed to be careful about who she spoke to and what she said? What possible difference could it make to Lewis's safety? The words puzzled her.

She put the telegram away in her bureau drawer, wondering when the army would be in touch with her again, when she would be told what was being done to effect Lewis's release.

That weekend Scott drove up to San Francisco and they drove together out to Lake Tahoe, walking for miles through the forest north of the lake. The mountain air was crisp and clean and she found the mindless exertion of placing one foot ceaselessly in front of the other hypnotically soothing. For the most part they walked in silence. She had no new information for him, and his own thoughts were too dark and too troubled to be shared.

Ever since she had called him with the news, he had been agonizingly reliving his first dreadful instinctive reaction. He had wished he could have Abbra to himself. Maybe for good.

He had murdered the feeling at its birth, overcome with horror and self-loathing so crushing in intensity that he had been scarcely able to breathe. Even if it meant never seeing Abbra again, he didn't want his brother dead and he didn't want him to be imprisoned in a filthy, godforsaken Vietnamese prison. He could not forgive himself that his reaction, however fleeting, had been so obscene.

Almost as difficult was the knowledge that just when Abbra needed him most, self-preservation demanded that he see very little of her.

'Did I tell you about the trip I'm taking to Mexico next week?' he asked, not looking across at her as he spoke, but riveting his eyes on a distant peak of the High Sierras.

She gave a small shocked gasp, swinging her head towards him. 'No . . . I . . . will you be away long?'

'Until the season starts,' he lied, self-hatred making his voice curt.

She stumbled slightly and he dug his clenched hands deeper into the pockets of his jeans, his fists clenched. He couldn't reach out for her now. If he reached out for her now, he would be lost.

'I'm sorry, Abbra,' he said, his eyes still fixed firmly ahead of him. 'I know it couldn't have come at a worse time . . .'

'No.' Her face was set and pale, her jawline firm. 'Perhaps it's better that you are going away, Scott.'

He was so certain that at last she had realized the true nature of his feelings, he halted in his long, loping stride, his eyes meeting hers. There was no new agony in her expression, no terrible understanding, only fierce determination.

'I must get used to being on my own,' she said quietly. 'And the longer you are with me, giving me companionship and comfort, the harder it will be for me eventually.'

They had stopped walking, and as they stood in the shade of the redwoods, looking across the glittering lake towards the High Sierras, it seemed to Scott that everything unspoken between them was being silently acknowledged. He had been wrong to assume that she didn't know how he felt about her. She did. Probably had known for a long time.

He replied thickly, knowing that they would meet only seldom in the future, and that their easy, happy-go-lucky camaraderie was over. 'I love you, Abbra.'

She was standing a yard or so away from him, her dark hair blowing softly around her face, the white silk shirt she wore tucked loosely into the waistband of her jeans.

'I know,' she said huskily, not trusting herself to say anything more.

She didn't turn to face him. She couldn't. She was too terrified of what might happen.

He was silent for a long time and then he said, his voice taut and strained, 'I think it's time I took you home, don't you?'

She nodded, turning away from the lake and the mountains, walking with him, ravage-faced, back towards the Chevrolet.

The loneliness that followed was crushing. She knew no other army wives, no other women who could identify with what she was suffering. She waited daily, expecting a communication from the army, some information about what was being done to effect his release, or even get in touch with him, but nothing came. At the end of the month, feeling as isolated as if she were alone on another planet, she called the telephone number on the card that she had been given.

The voice on the other end of the line was sympathetic and understanding and regretted that Abbra had not realized she had been assigned a personal casualty assistance officer who would keep her abreast of whatever development affected her or her prisoner husband.

It was the first time she had heard the expression 'prisoner husband' and she hated it. 'My husband's name is Lewis,' she said stiltedly. 'Lewis Ellis.'

She was transferred to her personal casualty officer, who said he was sorry that he had not previously been in touch with her, and who also referred to Lewis as her 'prisoner husband'. There was no news regarding Lewis. It was too soon, he said.

Her novel became her life support system. She withdrew into a world of imagination, writing from early morning to late at night, deriving a certain wry amusement from anticipating Patti's amazement when she received, so quickly, a novel she was not expecting for several months.

She didn't tell Patti that Lewis had been taken prisoner. She didn't want to have to endure more well-meant sympathy that would inevitably fail to comfort. The only person who could have given her comfort was Scott, and after his terrible admission to her at Lake Tahoe, she knew that she could never turn to him for comfort again.

Sometimes, at night in troubled sleep, Lewis and Scott seemed to merge into one person, and when she woke, the sense of loss and loneliness that she felt for both of them was indistinguishable. As the weeks passed, she found that she could fight her loneliness for Lewis a little by writing an ongoing letter to him in the form of a daily diary. The simple act of writing down his name, telling him of the way she was spending her day, what she was doing, what she was thinking, how she was missing him, seemed to bring him a little closer to her.

Where Scott was concerned there was no such comfort. She couldn't think about Scott. She dared not think about Scott. The football season had begun again, and according to the media, he was playing brilliantly.

He did not write to her, and he did not telephone her, nor did she expect him to. His three words in the depths of the Tahoe forest had made it impossible for him to do so. She knew that he was thinking of her, and that he shared her suffering as she waited for news of Lewis.

She started paying attention to the news.

At the beginning of October it was reported that US planes had attacked the city of Phu Ly, thirty-five miles south of Hanoi, and that all homes and buildings there had been destroyed.

Abbra wondered what the military objective had been at Phu Ly. The brief news reports gave no indication. That afternoon she went out and bought herself a large map of

Vietnam and a copy of Bernard Fall's *Street Without Joy*. Scott had once told her that if she wanted to understand what had led up to the US presence in Vietnam, and the rights and wrongs of US involvement, then Fall's was the book she should read. Over the last few weeks she had become acutely aware of how little she knew about the place her husband had been sent. She was also becoming angry and disillusioned at the army's seeming complacency over Lewis's capture.

The casualty officer who had been assigned to her continued to be sympathetic, but he never had any new information. He seemed more concerned in reminding her that if interviewed by the press, she was to give no information over and above Lewis's name, rank, serial number, and date of birth, than he was about the complete silence about Lewis's whereabouts. In January she finished her novel. She had put everything she had into it, adding all the pain and uncertainty of her past few weeks, but whether it was what Patti was expecting, she had no way of knowing. She was too close to what she had written to be able to judge it herself. She knew only that finishing it had given her a sense of achievement so great, it had been almost orgasmic. She telephoned Patti's office, intending to tell her that the novel was finished and that she was putting it in the mail, only to be told by Patti's secretary that Patti was on vacation and wouldn't be back until the end of the month.

She sent it off anyway, almost relieved that it would be at least another three weeks before Patti could read it, and before she would be coming back to her with an opinion.

A week later, in his State of the Union address, President Johnson announced sombrely: 'Although America faces more cost, more loss, and more agony in Southeast Asia, we will stand firm in Vietnam.'

Abbra was filled with an overwhelming sense of despair. The war would continue. But for how long? How long would it be before prisoners were exchanged? Before there were true negotiations?

On 2 February, just as she was beginning to wonder if Patti had returned yet from vacation, her telephone rang. She lifted the receiver, not imagining for a moment that it would be Patti, and Patti's husky voice said ebulliently, 'Congratulations! I came back from Argentina yesterday morning and spent all last evening reading *A Woman Alone*. It's even better than I had hoped it would be, and I'm sure that both the British and American publishers are going to love it. They took quite a gamble with you, and it's a gamble that will, in my opinion, pay off handsomely.'

Abbra was flooded with relief. She still had to wait to hear from the publishers, but if Patti was pleased about the book, then it meant she had succeeded in what she had set out to do. She had written a full-length novel with commercial possibilities. And if she had written one, then she could write another, and another. She was so ecstatic that she had nearly finished dialling Scott's number before she realized what it was she was doing.

She replaced the telephone receiver with a shaking hand. It had seemed so natural. He had given her so much encouragement; he had given her confidence. He had believed in her. Without him she doubted if she would ever have had the temerity to write more than the first page. And now she couldn't pick up the telephone and tell him that Patti thought the book was wonderful. They couldn't meet in the Polo Lounge to celebrate the news, laughing and talking as they had laughed and talked so often in the past. He couldn't read the manuscript.

'I wish you hadn't said it, Scott,' she said to the empty room, feeling as if her heart were breaking with longing. 'Oh, how I *wish* that you had never said it!'

Four weeks later, at the beginning of March, Patti telephoned her to say that the American publisher had already responded to her about *A Woman Alone* and that he was delighted with it.

'You'll be getting a long letter from the person who has been assigned as your editor, detailing what revisions they think are necessary. From what they say, no major surgery on the manuscript is needed, so don't worry. It's all very normal. I hope to be hearing from the British publisher by the end of the week, and I have absolutely no worries as to what *his* response is going to be. He's going to be thrilled! All you have to think about now is what you're going to write about next!'

In April she visited her father-in-law for a few days. Lewis's capture had done nothing to diminish Colonel Ellis's conviction that the only thing wrong with American military intervention in Vietnam was that it wasn't hard-nosed enough.

'We shouldn't only be bombing the North; we should be fighting on the ground in the North, where *everyone* is the enemy,' he said fiercely. 'Not pussyfooting around, worrying whether or not we're shooting so-called friendly civilians! If we invaded the North, no holds barred, Ho and his cronies would be grovelling for peace within days!'

He was equally emphatic in his views on the antiwar activists who were demonstrating in increasingly larger and larger numbers.

'They should be shot as traitors,' he said vehemently. 'They're not fit to call themselves Americans!'

Abbra disagreed. Some of the antiwar activists were veterans, men who had fought in Vietnam and who had been so appalled by their experiences that on their return they had publicly burned their uniforms and tossed their war medals into the garbage.

Instinctively she had always felt it was wrong for Americans to be in Vietnam, but out of loyalty to Lewis she had tried to view American intervention in a different light. To see it as necessary for world peace. She no longer held that belief. The reading she had done in the past few months had convinced her that her initial instincts had been correct and that she should have held to them. As far as the antiwar activists were concerned, she was in total sympathy, and the days she spent with her father-in-law, fond as she was of him, were a terrible strain.

In May she began work on a new book, and even though there was still no shred of information regarding Lewis and where he was being held, or even if he was still alive, she continued to write her daily journal to him.

In June she was contacted by the army, but not with the news that she had been praying for.

In light of the circumstances of Lewis's capture, and the dearth of information since, his status had been reviewed. He was no longer being classified as a prisoner of war, but as being missing in action.

She didn't leave her room for three days. She knew what the army was trying to say to her. They were trying to tell her that Lewis was dead, but she didn't believe it. He was alive. She *knew* he was alive. She couldn't have lived through the past months believing him to be alive if he had been dead. It wasn't possible.

Two days later Scott telephoned her. 'I'm sorry,' he said simply. 'But you shouldn't fear the worst, Abbra. Just because there's no hard information about the men who have been taken prisoner in the South doesn't mean they aren't still alive.'

'I know,' she said brokenly. 'And Lewis *is* alive, Scott! I know he is!'

He hesitated awkwardly. It was the first time they had been in contact for over ten months. 'Would it help if I came up to see you?' he asked, not knowing what he wanted her answer to be.

If he saw her again, he knew that nothing would have changed, that he would still want her as fiercely and hungrily as he always had. And nothing could come of it. Nothing could ever come of it. She loved Lewis, and as long as there was the faintest hope that Lewis was alive, she would never love anyone else.

And if Lewis were dead?

His jaw clenched, white lines edging his mouth. He didn't want Lewis to be dead. No matter what the price, he didn't want Lewis to be dead.

'No,' she said huskily, her voice sounding as if it were choked with tears. 'No, I don't think so, Scott.'

His disappointment was so devastating that he had to lean against the wall behind him for support. Of course he had known what he wanted her answer to be. And she had not given it.

'Bye, sweetheart,' he said thickly, wondering how she was managing without friends who could understand her position, without a supportive family, without anyone to lean upon or confide in.

All through the summer she worked on her new idea. There was still no news of Lewis, still no real reason for her to believe he was alive apart from her own unshakable conviction.

In September she decided that she had been a compliant army wife for quite long enough. She had done everything that the army had advised her to do. She hadn't spoken about Lewis to the press or to casual friends. She hadn't involved herself in the antiwar movement. She hadn't made a nuisance of herself, or been an embarrassment, in any way whatsoever. And her passivity had gained her nothing. She still didn't know if Lewis was dead or alive. If he were alive, she still didn't know where he was being held. In over a year she still hadn't met, or spoken to, another woman in the same situation. She had had a bellyful of passivity, and she was going to be passive no longer.

In October, when the antiwar movement announced it would be holding an enormous rally in Washington, its aim being the closing down of the Pentagon, Abbra locked her manuscript away in her desk and bought herself a plane ticket.

She was going to abandon her compliant-wife role and become a fierce antiwar activist. Helping to close down the Pentagon seemed as good a way as any in which to start.

# CHAPTER TWENTY-ONE

Serena turned off the main road into the cobbled mews at suicidally high speed, tyres screeching as she came to a stop. She was late. She had less than half an hour to bathe and change before Rupert arrived. They were going to have dinner at Quaglinos and then go on to the Colony in Berkeley Square. She slammed the front door behind her, wondering whether to wear her new Mary Quant dress, or her Louis Feraud.

As she slipped her key in the lock she could hear the telephone begin to ring. 'Damn,' she said beneath her breath, pausing for a moment to enjoy the fragrance of begonias and fuchsias spilling from a hanging basket. 'If that's Toby, he can jolly well wait.'

Despite her open involvement with Rupert, Toby was as persistent as ever. Because she was fond of him in a completely asexual way, and because she had known him for what seemed to be forever, and because all his friends were also her friends, she still continued to see him. Whenever there was a function where all her old cronies would be gathered, and where the behaviour was likely to be infantile, such as a hunt ball, where champagne could be expected to be sprayed with gleeful abandon over ball gowns and dinner jackets, or a debutante party where guests were likely to be thrown into a swimming pool, then she spared Rupert's dignity and was to be seen, instead, with Toby.

She stepped into the tiny hall and picked up the ringing telephone. 'I'm sorry, Toby my sweet,' she said, not sounding remotely sorry. 'But tonight is an impossibility, I'm . . .'

'It isn't Toby. It's Daddy.' Her father's voice was heavy and strained. 'I'm afraid it's bad news, darling. Sorry to break it to you like this, over the phone, but thought it was better you heard it from me than from anyone else.'

'Lance?' she said immediately, her voice cracking. 'It's Lance, isn't it? What's happened to him? Has he been arrested? Is he hurt? Where is he?'

Wherever he was, she would go to him. She would leave a note for Rupert. He would understand. Her hands tightened around her car key. 'Where *is* he, Daddy?'

Her father's voice sounded weary. 'It isn't Lance, darling . . .'

She leaned back against the wall, ashamed of the relief she felt. It was her mother. Her mother had been taken ill. She would drive to Bedingham early in the morning and stay there as long as necessary.

Her father cleared his throat. 'I'm afraid that it's Kyle. His father telephoned me a few minutes ago. He's been shot down. A colleague says he saw him alive on the ground after the crash, but it was in a heavily infested Viet Cong area and there's been no news of him since.' He paused uncomfortably and then said, 'He's been officially listed as missing in action. I'm sorry, my dear, I'm most dreadfully sorry.'

For a second she didn't feel anything at all. She couldn't. She was beyond feeling.

Her father's voice sharpened. 'Serena? Are you there? Can you hear me?'

'Yes,' she said at last with a great struggle. 'Yes, I can hear you, Daddy.' She couldn't think of anything to say, anything to ask. Incredibly, all the time Kyle had been in Vietnam, it had never occurred to her that he would be killed or injured or listed as missing. Other men might be, were being every day, but other men weren't Kyle. Kyle was too exuberantly alive, too fiendishly lucky, too arrogantly *sure* of himself, to come to grief. It was unthinkable to think of him as a loser. Inconceivable.

393

'Would you like to come home for a few days?' her father was asking. 'Bedingham is at its best, the walls are half drowned in roses and honeysuckle.'

Her eyes closed, she thought of Bedingham. The roses had been out on their wedding day; pale Ophelias and dark purple Reine des Violettes. What would have happened if Lance hadn't returned that day? There would have been no hideous scene for Kyle to walk in on, no need for him to have sped away from Bedingham and back to America. In all probability he would never have enroled at helicopter school, never have been sent to Vietnam.

'No, Daddy,' she said thickly. 'No, I don't think I'll come back to Bedingham. Not just now.'

If Lance hadn't returned that day, she and Kyle might have been at Bedingham now, together. To be there without him would be unbearable. Slowly she hung up the phone. She remembered someone, somewhere, saying 'if' was the smallest, most terrible word in the English language. Whoever had said it was right. *If* only she hadn't left Kyle's side and hurried to the nursery to meet Lance. *If* only Kyle hadn't grown impatient and followed her. *If. If. If.*

Rupert arrived twenty minutes later, looking elegant in a grey silk suit and with a carnation in his buttonhole. He took one look at her white, ravaged face and said, 'My God! What on earth is the matter, Serena? What's happened?'

She was holding a large vodka and tonic tightly in both hands. She made no move to put it down or to walk towards him. Her eyes met his, their smoke-grey depths so dark they seemed almost black. 'Kyle has been shot down,' she said with devastating simplicity. 'He's missing in action.'

He stood without moving for a moment, realizing instantly the changes and strains that were about to be put on their relationship, and then he walked across to her, gently taking the glass from her hand. 'Tell me,' he said with exquisite tenderness, drawing her towards him. 'Tell me everything you have been told.'

Dry-eyed and still in shock, she haltingly repeated what her father had said to her. He was appalled at the scant amount of information.

'When did it happen? How long ago? Why didn't the army contact you as Kyle's next of kin?'

'Presumably because Kyle never gave them my name as next of kin,' she said with unflinching candour. 'When he joined the army, he believed we were going to divorce. We were reconciled only hours before he left for Vietnam. I suppose it's only natural that he should have given the army his father's name as his next of kin, and not mine.'

'And have you spoken to his father yet?'

'No.' A tremor ran through her.

'Don't you think you should?' he persisted. 'You need to know whether Kyle was shot down in the North or in the South. If he was seen alive on the ground after he crashed, you need to know why he has been listed as missing in action when he could very possibly have been taken prisoner.'

'I need something else first,' she said unsteadily. 'I need to be able to believe that it's true, that it has really happened. I need to be able to cry.'

Even after she had spoken to her father-in-law the tears refused to come.

'*It's all your fault!*' he had shouted at her savagely. '*If it weren't for you, Kyle would never have joined the army! He would never have gone to 'Nam!*'

She believed him. She had known it the instant her father had told her what had happened. She was responsible. No one else.

For the next few days she still went into the antique shop, but she did so out of robot-like habit. She was no longer the ebullient, kooky personality that had so fascinated customers and gossip columnists alike. She was pale and withdrawn, and though she responded gratefully to Rupert's sympathy and support, she did not sleep with him. And she did not sleep with anyone else either.

She broke the news to Lance in his Chelsea *pied à terre*, standing with her back towards him, staring out over the grey, rolling expanse of the Thames.

'He was shot down near the Cambodian border,' she said bleakly. 'He was trying to pick up a reconnaissance squad that had been cut off and who were surrounded by Viet Cong. One of the other pilots, a friend of his, swears that he saw him scramble out of the helicopter alive, but the Viet Cong were everywhere and—'

She turned, about to tell him how Kyle's buddy had flown under suicidal fire time and again in an effort to land beside Kyle's blazing Huey.

He had been silent while she had been talking, and she had taken for granted that despite his virulent dislike of Kyle, and his fierce opposition to the war, he would be as shocked and as horrified as Rupert had been. No doubt if she hadn't turned around so unexpectedly, he would have made a hypocritical effort to sound, and seem, suitably sympathetic. She was never to know. She swung around, catching him unaware, and saw the expression on his face.

He was smiling, sheer pleasure written clearly on every feature. It was then that the frozen dam within her broke. '*You bastard!*' she howled, springing forward and raking at his face with her nails, the tears pouring down her cheeks. '*You miserable, mean-minded, pitiful, bastard!*'

It had been Rupert who had hauled her off him. He had been waiting for her in the street, in his Lagonda, and had heard her howl of rage. By the time he had sprinted into the block of flats and up the stairs, Lance had half fallen across a sofa and Serena was raining blows on him, sobbing hysterically, calling him names that would have made a stevedore blanch.

'*For Christ's sake!*' he had said, striding across the room and physically separating them, relieved to see that Lance had made no effort at retaliation. 'What's the matter with

396

the pair of you? Can't you behave like reasonable human beings?'

Serena was still sobbing, the tears spilling down her face and on to her minidress, her hair streaming wildly over her shoulders and down her back. She tried to speak and couldn't. Now that she had at last begun to cry, she was unable to stop. She was crying because she felt so wretchedly guilty, crying because Lance had been so stupidly insensitive and because things had once more gone wrong between them, and above all she was crying, at last, for Kyle.

Lance slithered into a sitting position on the sofa, his tie pulled halfway around his neck, a button torn from his shirt. 'It was my fault,' he said tersely to Rupert, dabbing at the scratches on his face with a handkerchief. 'Serry thought I was pleased about Anderson being declared an MIA.'

'You *were!*' Serena gasped convulsively. 'And he isn't *Anderson*, he's *Kyle!*'

'Were you?' Rupert asked him tightly.

Lance looked up. From where he was sitting, Rupert seemed very tall indeed. And very threatening.

'Yes. No,' he said undecidedly, springing to his feet so that he wouldn't feel at a disadvantage. 'Hell! I wasn't pleased in the way Serry thinks I was pleased! I wasn't pleased just because it was her husband who was missing!' He began to pace the room furiously. '*If* I was pleased, then I was pleased because the Americans have to learn they can't win in Vietnam, and it seems to me they're going to learn that only when the great American public finds the loss of American life in Vietnam unacceptable. As far as I'm concerned, the sooner they do *that*, the better!'

Serena had finally stopped crying. She pushed her hair away from her face, wiping her cheeks with her fingers, saying in a flat, tired voice, 'I should have known better than to have come here with such news. Will you take me home please, Rupert?'

Lance stopped pacing abruptly, his eyes flying to hers. He didn't want her to go. He didn't want there to be another rift between them, but he was damned if he was going to apologize to her in front of Rupert. He said instead, 'If Kyle is alive and if he's been taken prisoner, then you'd better start looking at things from my point of view, Serry. You'd better start getting involved and demonstrating for an end to the war, because until it ends, no one outside Vietnam is going to see Kyle Anderson again.'

She hadn't replied. She, too, had wanted to make things right between them, but somehow she felt that to do so would be disloyal to Kyle. And loyalty to Kyle suddenly seemed very important. It was all that she could give him, all that she could do for him.

Over the next few days she read everything that she could about the war. She read about the way Americans were treated by the Viet Cong if they fell into their hands, how they had been found with steel rods rammed up their penis and anus, of how some had even been skinned alive.

The war was no longer an event of no concern to her, and the more she read, the more she began to think that perhaps Lance's point of view wasn't so extreme after all. Three weeks later she received a letter, via her father-in-law, from Charles Wilson.

'. . . Kyle is alive, I'm sure of it,' he had written. 'I saw him scramble from the Huey, but there was no way anyone could land and pick him up. The ground fire was unbelievable'. He gave her the exact position where Kyle had gone down and then wrote, 'He was my best buddy, the best I've ever had, and I'm going to do my damnedest to try to have his status changed from MIA to POW.' He had signed the letter Chuck, not Charles.

She read and reread the letter and then put it down thoughtfully. It hadn't occurred to her that there was such a vital difference in status between MIA and POW. Until Kyle's disappearance, she had hardly been aware that there *was* a difference. She had thought there was nothing she could do for Kyle, but she had been wrong. She could campaign for his status to be changed. And to do that, she would first have to inform the United States Army that she was an army wife.

It was a decision she had almost made before she had read Chuck's letter. Although her father-in-law had forwarded that particular piece of mail to her, she couldn't rely on him. If she wanted to be sure of receiving every bit of possible information about Kyle, then she had to inform the correct authorities that she was his wife, and that she was entitled to receive it.

Two weeks after she had written to the army, enclosing her birth certificate and her wedding certificate, she received an official reply. For the first time she was given an official account of Kyle's last mission and the way in which he had been shot down. And she was told of how Chuck Wilson had flown through enemy fire repeatedly in an effort to land beside Kyle's blazing Huey, and of how, in doing so, he had sustained near fatal injuries.

She had reread Chuck Wilson's letter again. He had written merely that 'the ground fire was unbelievable'. There was no mention that he had been injured in his attempt to rescue Kyle. No mention that he had, apparently, been writing to her from a hospital bed.

The letter from the army also apologized that Kyle's personal belongings had been sent to his father and not to her, but assured her that there had been no personal mail among the items. It finished by asking her to treat all information regarding her husband as confidential.

'What information?' she had said aloud, bewildered. She had written back asking why, if her husband had been seen scrambling from his Huey alive, he was being listed as MIA and not as a possible prisoner of war. She also asked for the name of the hospital where Charles Wilson was being treated so that she could write to him and thank him for his brave rescue attempt.

399

At the beginning of October, she received her next official communication from the United States Army. She opened the buff-coloured envelope without any premonition that it might contain news other than the information she had asked for.

'—your husband's name has been included in a list of names recently released by Hanoi. It is believed that he is being held in Hoa Lo prison, Hanoi. In view of this information, your husband's status has been changed from MIA to POW. You may be certain that you will be informed of any further information received regarding your husband. Inasmuch as your husband is now being carried in a captured status, it is suggested, for his safety, that you reveal only his name, rank, file number, and date of birth to inquiries outside your immediate family—'

He was alive. She began to tremble, and then to laugh and cry at the same time. He was in some ghastly prison, but at least he was alive.

'I *knew* you wouldn't be dead!' she exulted aloud, as if he were in the room with her. 'You're too damned *hip* to be dead!'

Rupert was intensely relieved by her news. He knew how guilty she felt, and though he believed her guilt to be irrational, he had been unable to convince her.

'Nothing you did was responsible for Kyle haring back to the States and becoming a pilot,' he had said gently when she had told him why she felt so guilty. 'You can't imagine for a moment that if *I* had been in Kyle's shoes, and if I had walked in on that odious little scene in the nursery, that I would have imagined you were a willing party to what was taking place. The fact that Kyle did so only proves to me how little he knows about you.' Or loves you, he had been tempted to add, but hadn't.

Looking across at her as they sat on the sofa in his elegant Knightsbridge home and she finished telling him about Kyle's official change of status, he hoped that the news would enable her to shed some of her guilt, and that their relationship would at last return to normal.

His arm was around her shoulders, and he pulled her closer to him, sliding his free hand up a long, slender, smoothly naked leg. 'I've missed you in my bed, lady,' he said, his voice thickening. 'Welcome back.'

Despite the brisk weather, beneath her minuscule skirt she was wearing only the briefest of panties. He pulled them low, her honey-gold pubic hair brushing springily against the palm of his hand as he began to caressingly separate the lips of her labia, sliding his fingers into her hot moistness.

She gave a deep moan, stiffening and contracting against him. It had been nearly two months since she had made love. And Kyle was now no longer missing in action, feared dead, but a prisoner in Hanoi. She closed her eyes as Rupert lowered his mouth to hers, his thumb circling arousingly over her clitoris, his fingers continuing to move and probe. She had not made love and Kyle was safe. Very gently she pushed her hands up against Rupert's chest, pushing him away from her.

He looked down at her queryingly, his hand still moving rhythmically, loving the slippery, excited feel of her.

'No,' she said, her eyes apologetic. 'I'm sorry, Rupert. I can't.'

He frowned slightly, his penis so engorged it was straining painfully against his trousers. 'Don't be silly,' he said, his voice dark with need. 'There's no reason in the world for us not to make love now.'

'There is.' She was so excited she was nearly screaming, but she stilled his moving hand with hers. 'I didn't make love and Kyle is no longer missing in action but a prisoner of war. If I continue not to make love, then he'll be released, I know it.'

He stared at her. 'You are joking, aren't you?' he asked at last.

Smoke-grey eyes, wide-set and dark-lashed, held his. 'No,' she said, wriggling slightly and freeing herself from his hand. 'I know it isn't very logical, but . . .'

'It isn't logical at all!' Rupert said, thwarted desire trying his patience to the limit. 'It's sheer primitive superstitious nonsense! How on earth can your making or not making love affect what happens to Kyle in Hanoi? And when you talk of not making love until he's released, how long have you got in mind? The war has been going on for years already. It's hardly likely to come to a sudden halt just because you've taken a vow of celibacy! Kyle could be in Hanoi for years!'

She stood up, smoothing her miniskirt down over her thighs, her hand trembling slightly. 'Kyle couldn't endure captivity for years,' she said unsteadily. 'It would kill him.'

He rose to his feet slowly, facing her, bitterly regretting his ill-chosen words. 'Maybe he won't be there for years,' he said quietly. 'A war doesn't have to end for prisoners to be exchanged.'

'No,' she agreed, slipping on her shoes. 'It doesn't.'

She was going, and he knew that she would not be coming back. He regarded her with loving affection, and pity, and regret.

'If he *is* exchanged, it won't be because you have been behaving like a nun,' he said, resigned.

Despite the hideous images his words had conjured up, of Kyle being immured in Hoa Lo prison for years on end, an amused smile quirked the corners of her mouth. 'I don't see why not,' she said with a return of her old jauntiness. 'After all, going without sex is the greatest sacrifice I could possibly make!'

At the end of October her father telephoned her to say that he and her mother were going to Barbados for the winter. Although his domestic staff was quite capable of looking after his aging spaniels, he said the dogs would prefer it if a member of the family was also there and would she kindly oblige?

She obliged quickly. Bedingham was at its best in the autumn, and she had been away from it for far too long. She drove north out of London, beneath a pale apricot sky, feeling as if a physical burden were being lifted from her shoulders with each mile she travelled. At Bedingham she would be able to see the future more clearly. Her affair with Rupert was over, although he was still the first person she turned to if she needed advice, or sympathy or support. He had offered her a partnership in the antique shop in an effort to both retain her services in the shop and to ensure that contact was maintained between them, but she had turned it down.

She didn't want any encumbrances, however pleasurable. Kyle's capture had changed her life. Though she couldn't imagine what the future held, she was certain it was going to be something far different from anything she had experienced in her past. And when it came she wanted to be ready for it.

Lance had left several messages on her answering machine, but she had not contacted him. It was as if denying herself the relief of a reconciliation with him was yet another of her voluntary penances.

In November, during his weekly telephone call, Rupert rather ruefully informed Serena that he had become the regular escort of Lady Sarah Mellbury, the seventeen-year-old daughter of an old school friend.

Serena had been vaguely amused and not the slightest regretful. If she had wanted to resume her old relationship with Rupert, she knew that Lady Sarah would have been no obstacle. But she didn't want to resume their old relationship, at least not yet. She wanted to remain at Bedingham, tramping the grounds and the beech woods with the dogs and returning to drink Earl Grey and to eat piles of buttered crumpets before a roaring log fire.

The army had forwarded her the name of the military hospital in Japan where Chuck Wilson was being treated and she had written to him, thanking him for his brave attempt to rescue Kyle.

Just before Christmas she received a reply. It was an odd letter, brief and curt and indicating that he saw no reason why they should enter into further correspondence with each other. She wondered why. As a buddy of Kyle's, it was impossible to imagine him as being anything other than outgoing and extrovert, and his first letter to her, though full of pain, had been sympathetic and friendly.

He had been transferred to a hospital in the States and she decided not to be deterred by his almost formal reply. She wrote again, asking him when he expected to be discharged, saying that she would like to meet him, so that she could thank him personally.

When the New Year arrived, Serena was convinced that Lance was, for once, correct. Antiwar demonstrations were necessary if the war was ever to be brought to an end. She drove up to London to take part in a demonstration.

It was bitterly cold, and there was snow and ice underfoot as she merged with an amazingly large group of stalwart marchers, tramping with placards held high from Trafalgar Square to the American Embassy in Grosvenor Square.

She marched along near the front of the procession, linking arms with a bearded hippie carrying a banner with the words I HATE WAR on it, and a fierce-looking girl who said she was a student at the London School of Economics.

As they entered Grosvenor Square, chanting 'Ho-Ho-Ho Chi Minh, Americans *out*! Ho-Ho-Ho-Chi Minh, Americans *out*! Americans *out*!' they joined an advance group of protestors already in the square. A number of mounted police were gathering in the adjoining side streets. A grin touched her mouth as she saw Lance's distinctive silky-gold shoulder-length hair. It had been over four months since he had reacted so horribly to the news that Kyle had been shot down, and she had long ago forgiven him. She had also decided that after such a long time, a reconciliation would no longer be an act of disloyalty towards Kyle.

In an effort to negate the effeminacy of his hair, Lance had grown a Che Guevara style moustache. He was smoothing it with his forefinger, casting an assessing eye over the numbers entering the square, when he saw her. At first there was only blank amazement on his face and then, as her grin deepened and she waved exuberantly in his direction, relief flooded his eyes and he began to shoulder his way through the crowd towards her.

'Serry! What the devil are *you* doing here?' he shouted to her as the chanting around them became louder and more vitriolic and the police horses began to edge their way into the square.

'I thought I'd come and give you a little sisterly support!' she yelled back, hugging him tight, insanely happy to be back on the old footing with him again.

'Then stick with me and keep away from the horses! Christ alone knows why they're being used for crowd control when it's so slippy underfoot. One of them is sure to go down!'

'I hope not,' Serena said passionately, 'We're not such a large crowd. They don't need to use horses to keep us in control.'

Lance gave a snort of derision. 'You've a lot to learn,' he said darkly, grateful that she was making it unnecessary for him to apologize to her, that she knew that he was sorry, that his hideous little display of glee need never be mentioned between them again.

He took hold of her arm, forcing a way through towards the front of the crowd. 'What have you been doing with yourself all winter? Did you know that the parents have fled to Barbados?'

She nodded, squeezing after him, narrowly avoiding being hit in the eye by a placard declaring BRING THE TROOPS HOME. 'Yes, Daddy phoned me before they went and asked me if I would look after the dogs. I've been at Bedingham ever since.'

'Alone?' The words were out, and the implication that if he had known he would have joined her there, before he could stop them.

She tactfully avoided his eyes. 'Yes,' she said as a scuffle broke out on the edge of the crowd between one of the demonstrators and a foot policeman. 'I've been doing some reading, and thinking, and I've been bombarding the United States Army with letters.' She kept her eyes firmly averted from his. 'Kyle's status has been changed from MIA to POW. He's in Hoa Lo prison, in Hanoi. What I want to know from the army is what the hell they're going to do to get him out.'

'And have you had much success?' he asked, knowing damn well that she couldn't possibly have.

'No,' she said grimly. 'But they haven't heard the last from me. Not by a long shot.'

In March her parents returned from Barbados to Bedingham and she reluctantly returned to her mother's *pied à terre* in London. She began to be seen at parties and discos again, but she felt as if she were attending them merely out of force of habit. The more fun everyone around her was having, the more acutely she was aware of what Kyle must be suffering. When she went out to dinner with Rupert, and he sent back the wine because it wasn't chilled enough, she wondered whether Kyle was receiving clean water to drink, whether water was there for him when he needed it. If he was manacled and shackled for large parts of the day. If he ever thought of her, and of the precious hours they had spent together at Bedingham.

In April she received another letter from Chuck Wilson. He had been discharged from the hospital and was going to stay on an uncle's ranch in Wyoming for the summer, to recuperate. He still made no mention of his injuries, and he barely mentioned Kyle or his incarceration in Hoa Lo. The letter seemed hardly worth the bother of writing, unless, as there was no mention of his Wyoming address, it had been written to let her know that he would not be contactable for several months and to dissuade her from corresponding with him further.

'But I will, Mr Wilson,' she said to herself. The paper was stamped with what she presumed was his home address in Atlantic City, and she put it away carefully in a bureau drawer. She was beginning to have a shrewd suspicion as to why his letters were so out of character for a man who had been Kyle's best buddy, and she had every intention of finding out if her suspicions were correct. She would make contact with him when he returned from Wyoming, and it wouldn't be by letter. It would be in person.

All through the summer, her letters to the United States Army, and to the casualty assistance officer who had been assigned to her, continued. She asked if she could be given the addresses of other wives with husbands imprisoned in Hoa Lo, so that she could write to them, and introduce herself to them, but no addresses were ever forwarded. By the end of the summer her patience was wearing thin.

'They won't release any information to me,' she said exasperatedly to Lance as they shared a punt on the upper reaches of the Thames. 'I don't even know how many other men are being held in Hoa Lo. If I had the names and addresses of some of the other wives, I could at least write to them. They are probably just as frustrated by the American government's policy of discouraging inter-POW-family relationships as I am. We could form a pressure group of sorts. Hell, we have to do *something*. Some men have been held prisoner since 1965!'

'Write an open letter to *The Washington Post*, appealing for any other wives in the same situation to contact you,' Lance said practically, punting around the low-lying tendrils of a willow tree. 'And go to the States. There's a massive demonstration being planned for October in Washington. Dr Benjamin Spock is going to speak and a vigil is going to be held at the Pentagon. It's supposed to be the biggest antiwar demo yet held.'

'And it's at the end of the summer,' Serena said cryptically.

'What does that remark mean?'

Serena lay back against the punt cushions, a white silk shirt open at her throat, her long legs encased in a pair of pale blue jeans. 'It means that someone who has spent the summer in Wyoming will no longer be there,' she teased.

Lance didn't rise to the bait. Instead of asking her who the devil she knew in Wyoming, he said instead, 'Are you going to go to Washington for the Pentagon demo?'

She nodded, her eyes gleaming with fierce determination. 'Yes. And I'm not going to come back until I've made contact with other women whose husbands are being held in Hanoi. I can't be the only wife frustrated by the American government's attitude towards the prisoner issue. There must be other rebellious waiting wives. And I'm going to find them.'

# CHAPTER TWENTY-TWO

After the dizzying success of the open-air concert, life had been so hectic that Gabrielle scarcely had time to draw breath. The group had been inundated with offers from agents, all wanting to assume dictatorial control of their affairs. Radford had rebuffed all the offers no matter how extravagant the promises.

'Hell,' he had said to her with his crooked grin. 'I ain't come so far to hand myself over body and soul to some motherfucker who doesn't really give a shit. When the right agent comes along, I'll *know* it!'

The right agent finally came along in the shape of Marty Dennison, an Englishman with a formidable reputation where black music was concerned.

'And despite having a white lead singer and two white guitarists, your music *is* black,' he had said when Radford had introduced him to the band. 'That's its main strength. Your other strength is your singer. Anyone that sexy could take an audience by storm without your even having to play a note!'

Contracts had been drawn up, record contracts had been signed, a tour of England in November had been planned, new songs had been endlessly discussed and even more endlessly practised. By the time she realized that Gavin's last letter had not been followed by any others, it was the end of August.

At first she did not worry too much. The mail delivery to and from Vietnam had always been erratic, as she knew from years of correspondence with her aunt. And probably Gavin was not in a position to write to her. The newspapers were full of reports that United States air force jets had mistakenly attacked two South Vietnamese villages eighty miles south of Saigon, killing 63 and wounding over 100 civilians. It was likely that Gavin was down there, covering the story.

At the beginning of September, just as they were embarking on the first of their gigs, one of their pianists was found dead from a drug overdose.

Radford was almost beside himself with fury. 'That *son* of a bitch!' he raged. 'Why *now*, for Christ's sake? Why did the stupid bastard have to *spoil* everything right *now*!'

They had another pianist, and they could still make music, but their unique sound came from their ability to sound like an inflated studio band – three guitars, two basses, and not one piano, but two.

'Let Michel stand in,' Gabrielle had suggested, and because Michel knew backwards every number they had ever practised, and because he had very little choice, Radford had bad-temperedly agreed.

His bad temper had faded the moment he heard Michel play. 'Jeez! Why didn't you *tell* me he was this good?' he berated Gabrielle. 'He may not look the part, but that boy has *soul*!'

By the second week in September, Gabrielle's thoughts were no longer centred on her new singing style but on the lack of mail from Saigon. By the end of the month, when there was still no letter from Gavin, she was concerned. Then, on the first day of November, two letters, neither from Gavin, arrived simultaneously.

One envelope was postmarked Saigon and was in Nhu's handwriting. The other envelope was franked with the name of Gavin's press agency.

She picked them up from the mat slowly, sensing disaster. In his last letter he had not said what his next assignment was to be. He had been ragingly angry about the human cost of the Americans' free fire zone policy, and enthusiastic about his meeting with Nhu, saying that he was 'looking forward to meeting the rest of her family quite soon.' Was

410

that what had happened? Had he met Dinh? And if so, why hadn't he written since?

She opened Nhu's letter, her hand trembling as she smoothed out the wafer-thin paper. It was written in the manner of all Nhu's letters. No names were mentioned. Dinh was merely an 'uncle'. Gavin was a 'mutual friend'. The real content of the letter had to be guessed at from seemingly innocuous information.

*—your uncle was insistent, and as it was what our mutual friend wanted too, I thought there could be no possible harm . . .*

*. . . I think your uncle wants to show off his skill as a craftsman, and certainly our mutual friend seems eager to learn. . .*

*. . . so they are travelling together at the moment but I unfortunately have no address for them . . .*

He was with Dinh. She didn't know whether to feel jubilant or appalled. Dinh had once again come south and had asked to meet Gavin. And they were now 'travelling' together, and Dinh was 'showing off his skill as a craftsman' to him, which meant that Dinh had taken Gavin deep into Viet Cong territory and was showing him the war from a Viet Cong point of view.

Her first recognizable reaction was relief. If Gavin was with Dinh, then he was safe. She tried to remember everything her mother had ever told her about him. 'He was fiercely intelligent, even as a little boy,' she had said once, 'and because he was the only son he had a very, very strong sense of family.' Her voice had trembled slightly. 'And even though we have all been separated for so long, I know his sense of family is something that he has never lost. When he came south on his undercover mission for General Giap, he risked his life by entering Saigon and making contact with Nhu. He is still our brother. Still the head of our family.'

Remembering her mother's words reassured Gabrielle. Even though she had never met Dinh, even though there had never been any communication between them, he *was* her uncle. Gavin was his nephew by marriage, and, despite his nationality, would be treated as family.

411

Taking a deep breath, she opened the letter from Gavin's employers. At least it didn't contain any new or shocking information. Gavin wasn't dead or injured. He had gone off on an assignment of his own, no one knew where, and he had not returned. Enormous efforts had been made to trace him. He had been seen leaving the bureau with a Vietnamese woman and had then entered a shabby Renault, alone. The driver, a Vietnamese, had driven off in the direction of Cholon.

That was the last anyone had seen of him. Because of the nature of the note he had left behind, a copy of which was enclosed, no immediate alarm had been raised. Although absenting himself from Saigon without first conferring with his bureau chief, Paul Dulles, was highly irregular, it had been assumed that he was working on a story which had warranted the action he had taken.

His continuing silence, however, had given the agency no other option but to presume him missing. His salary would continue to be paid into her account for the next six months, after which, if there was still no news of him, the situation would be reassessed. They were very regretful and hoped most sincerely that their fears for Gavin's safety would prove to be false. If they could be of any further help she had only to telephone.

She walked into the kitchen with both letters and sat at the scrubbed wooden table, looking down at them thoughtfully. The Vietnamese woman who had been seen talking to Gavin in the bureau only minutes before he disappeared was obviously Nhu. Had the Vietnamese driving the car been Dinh? She had no way of knowing. Whether or not it had been, Gavin was most certainly with Dinh now. Her problem was whether to reveal her information to the press agency.

She reread both letters. If Gavin had wanted to reveal the identity of his informant, and the identity of the person he was going to meet, he could, presumably, have done so. And he hadn't. He had said merely that 'something

412

huge had come up' and that he would 'explain all' when he returned. But he hadn't returned, and the only person who could explain, even in part, was herself.

And if she did so? She rose from the table and put the kettle on in order to make some coffee, grateful that her mother was out visiting Madame Garine. Nhu would be questioned, possibly by the Americans, possibly by the South Vietnamese police, maybe by both. She would be clearly marked as having links with the Viet Cong, and it was more than likely that she would be arrested, which was precisely why Gavin had not revealed her name to his superiors. And why she could not do so either.

She poured the boiling water on top of the freshly ground beans. There were no decisions to make. Gavin had made them all for her. All she could do was wait patiently until he resurfaced in Saigon with what she knew was going to be the biggest news scoop of the war.

Despite the grimness of the weather, England in November was frenetic and fun. The band began their tour in the North, working the plush, giant-size, workingmen's clubs that attracted entertainers of the stature of Tom Jones, the Righteous Brothers and Georgie Fame and the Blue Flames. As their tour progressed and they moved further south, the traditional clubs gave way to a string of enormous, recently opened Mecca nightclubs. At both types of clubs they received thunderous ovations, and by the time they reached London, all of them, including Michel, were riding on a permanent high.

'Baby, this is one buzz that isn't going to die away!' Radford had said to her with his wide, lazy grin. 'We are really *going* places this time around!'

When they reached London they made their first ever studio television performance.

'What is the programme called again?' Gabrielle asked Michel as they piled into a black taxicab that was to take them to the studios.

'Ready, Steady, Go,' Michel said in execrable English, and then, reverting to French, 'It's networked all over the country and this is the first time, ever, that a group without a hit record has been asked to appear. God alone knows how Marty managed it.'

'He managed it because clips from the open air concert have been televised over here and because everyone in the country wants to know who the hell we are,' Radford said, holding one leg by the ankle across his knee, his free arm flung out across the top of the rear seat, brushing the back of Gabrielle's shoulders. 'And because when we *do* cut a record, it's going to go *straight* to the top, like a *rocket*, baby!'

Michel squeezed himself on to the jump seat with angular clumsiness, resenting the easy, careless manner in which Radford had made bodily contact with Gabrielle. His initial enthusiasm for the American had cooled the instant he had become aware of the almost palpable sexual attraction that existed between him and Gabrielle. He knew very well that Gabrielle had not physically capitulated to the attraction, but he was always painfully conscious of Radford's apparently innocent touchings, both on- and off-stage, and as the tour had progressed and they had all been thrown into one another's company for at least eighteen hours out of every twenty-four, his disquiet had increased.

'When *do* we cut the record?' he asked tersely, staring out the window at the dark wet London streets so that he wouldn't have to see Gabrielle's fiery red hair brushing against Radford's leather-jacketed arm.

'The morning after we arrive back in Paris,' Radford replied, his eyes dancing in amusement. He knew damn well what was bugging Michel and he wondered, not for the first time, just what Gabrielle saw in him that she valued his friendship so much.

Michel fell silent. There had been many discussions between Radford, Marty Dennison, and their record company about the song they were to launch with. The deal was that they would cut a single, which would be released quickly, and that they would then immediately begin work on an album. It had been agreed early on that the album would include at least one song written by Gabrielle. With a backing arranged by Radford, it was the best song in their repertoire, and Michel knew that there was a good chance that it might also be the choice for the single.

If it was, then he knew that in the future Radford would be working even more closely with Gabrielle, and that musically she would have less and less need of him. He wished that Gavin would return from Vietnam. At least his jealousy of Gavin wasn't touched by fear for her. With Gavin he knew that her happiness and the happiness of *le petit* Gavin were secure. Their happiness would certainly not be secure if she had an affair with Radford James.

Michel's large, ungainly hands hung impotently between his knees as the taxi drew up outside the television studio. He had known right from the very beginning that she would never turn to him as a lover, but at least he was her friend. And if Gavin Ryan didn't return soon from his mysterious assignment, then he had a dreadful feeling that, as a friend, he was going to have to give her some serious advice, advice which he was terrified she might not take.

Except for Christmas Day, the entire month of December was spent in a recording studio. After her long absence from *le petit* Gavin while she had been in England, Gabrielle hated that she could not take him to the studio with her, as she had taken him to rehearsals. He was growing into such an interesting little person, holding his head quite steady and following her around the room with his eyes, gurgling with delight whenever she approached him to pick him up. She wanted to be with him when he said his first word and took his first step. *She* wanted to be with him, and she was determined that once the mammoth recording session was over and they were back on the road again, wherever she went, *le petit* Gavin would go too.

She knew her relationship with Radford intrigued the rest of the band. The feeling of *rapprochement* between them was so total that it was impossible for anyone not to notice. Onstage, instead of merely backing her with guitar and vocals, he had begun moving forwards to share centre stage with her, turning several numbers into such highly charged, erotic duos that audiences had been brought stamping to their feet, howling for more.

But the sexual attraction was given rein only onstage. She wasn't in love with Radford. She was in love with Gavin. And although she was well aware that it was within her nature for her to enjoy sleeping with someone she wasn't in love with, she knew that it wasn't in Gavin's nature. Wherever Gavin was, she was certain that he was being faithful. And so for his sake, and because she knew that it mattered to him, so was she.

Wherever Radford was, there were girls. He treated them all with insolent carelessness, barely even remembering their various names. When she had teasingly chided him about his cavalier attitude, he had simply given her his dazzling gypsy smile and had said, 'Honey, if you would only come across, like you *know* you should, and be my old lady, I wouldn't have no *need* of anybody else!'

She had been standing and he had been sitting down, drinking a beer, and she had laughed and run her hand tightly over his tight, crinkly hair before turning and walking away from him. Despite his smile, his eyes had been hotly serious and a flush of heat had surged down into her vagina, so ragingly insistent that it had taken her nearly all her power to have been able to laugh and walk away.

All through January and February there was no word from Gavin. He had now been officially listed as MIA. He wasn't the only journalist to be so. Members of the press corps who eschewed the news briefings at the Follies and instead hitched lifts on whatever air transport was available to far-flung battle sights risked their lives just as much as the soldiers in the field.

Gavin's salary was no longer paid directly into their joint account. Instead, she had received a sympathetic letter from the Paris office and an ex gratia payment to cover her immediate needs. She had also received a letter from Paul Dulles and had agonized about how to reply to it.

She knew so much more than his employers did. She knew the identity of the woman who had visited Gavin at the bureau office. She knew who he had been going to meet. She was nearly one hundred percent sure of what had happened after that meeting, of the proposition that Dinh must have put to Gavin and that Gavin had been unable to turn down. She knew that he wasn't dead, that at any moment he was likely to emerge from the jungle several pounds lighter but triumphant. He would be able to give the agency a story that no other Western reporter could give, a story of the war as seen through Viet Cong eyes by a man who had lived with them for months.

But she couldn't tell Paul Dulles what she knew. If she did he would immediately seek Nhu out and question her rigorously. She would be unable to answer his questions, and this contact would bring her to the attention of the South Vietnamese authorities. So Gabrielle had replied to his awkward letter of sympathy by saying that she was confident Gavin was still alive and that fear for his safety was groundless.

Sometimes, in the long, dark hours of the night, doubt would assail her. If he were alive, surely he would have managed to get word to her via Nhu? She would toss and turn, trying to imagine circumstances under which such action was impossible. Even if Gavin couldn't make contact with Nhu, surely her uncle could do so.

She remembered the long years in which Nhu had heard nothing from Dinh. For men who had gone north to join the NVA, or who had stayed south and joined the Viet Cong, lack of contact with their families was normal. Gavin had been out of contact with his family for only seven months. Her uncle would regard that period of time as unimportant. But what if he weren't with Dinh? What if her aunt Nhu's assumptions were wrong? What if Gavin had been killed months before, on the day that he left Saigon?

It was then that she would slip out of bed and pad softly across to the crib that held her sleeping son. Gently, so as not to wake him, she would lift him up in her arms, holding him tight, tears glittering on the long, curling sweep of her eyelashes.

All through spring and early summer, letters continued to arrive from Nhu, but they contained no further information. Nhu's distress at being a party to Gavin's disappearance was obvious, though carefully concealed in her wording in case eyes other than theirs should read the contents.

In the bright light of day, Gabrielle continued to be fiercely optimistic. Gavin couldn't be dead. If he were dead she would *know*. Every instinct she possessed would be telling her so. 'He isn't dead,' she said repeatedly to Michel. 'But oh! I wish that he would get word to Nhu! Just one little word and I would be able to live on it until he returned!'

Workwise, her life was frenetic. The single had been released, and though not shooting to the top of the charts, it had entered them at a position that had pleased even Radford. Marty Dennison had asked for more songs from her, eager to capitalize on the success of the record and their British tour. He had arranged gigs for them all through the summer in places as far away as Stockholm and Dublin.

'You can't possibly take *le petit* Gavin with you!' her mother had declared, aghast, when Gabrielle had announced her intention of doing so.

'Yes I can,' Gabrielle had said stubbornly. 'Michel will help me look after him.'

'But what about when you are onstage? Who will look after him then?'

418

'I will find someone,' Gabrielle had said with immovable firmness. 'I'm sorry, *Maman*, but he's coming with me. It's hard enough living without Gavin. I'm not going to live without my baby as well.'

It had not been easy. Maids, in the hotels they had stayed in, had looked after him for her whenever they could, as had some of the fans she attracted, but baby-sitters on such an ad hoc basis were not an ideal solution. When she was in Dublin, the young Irish girl who had offered to care for him while she was onstage was so likable and so enamoured with *le petit* Gavin that Gabrielle asked her if she would like to become his nanny, travelling with them wherever they went.

She had accepted immediately and Radford, who had been left on more than one occasion literally holding the baby, was extremely grateful. 'Every band should have a nanny,' he had said laconically when she had asked if Maura could be put on the payroll. 'Man, it's what *this* band has needed all along!'

When the LP was released it was even more successful than the single had been.

'America next stop,' Radford had said triumphantly. 'Marty is fixing up a tour for the fall. From now on there ain't going to be no stopping us. This time we're *really* on our way!'

It was the end of the summer when the crucial letter from Nhu arrived. Gabrielle was in Paris because they were rehearsing for the autumn tour and her mother brought it into the kitchen with a troubled face.

'It is much heavier than usual, *ma chère*,' she said as *le petit* Gavin tried to walk towards her on chubby legs, holding on to the edge of a chair. 'Do you think there is news?'

Her eyes flickered over the envelope; Gabrielle knew that there was news, and that it wasn't good. She tore open the letter, reading slowly, her heart racing.

'I am very distressed to have to tell you that a visitor came to see me yesterday in order to inform me that we can expect no further news of your uncle, or of the friend who is travelling with him. Nor should we seek for such news. I am terribly sorry, dear niece, but it seems that at the moment nothing further can be done . . .'

She passed the letter silently across to her mother. Vanh read it slowly and then raised her eyes to Gabrielle. 'Perhaps . . .' she began quaveringly.

Gabrielle shook her head. She knew that her mother was beginning to believe that both Dinh and Gavin were dead. But *she* didn't believe that they were dead. They couldn't be dead. 'No,' she said fiercely, her hands balling into fists. 'Don't say it, *Maman*. They are alive. I *know* they are!'

Gabrielle had never really spoken to Radford about Gavin, but he knew the brief outline. Her husband was in Vietnam and was officially listed as missing. Now she told him about Nhu's dispiriting letter.

'That's pretty bleak news, baby,' he said sympathetically.

'My mother thinks that both he and Dinh are dead—'

He put his arm around her shoulders, hugging her tight. 'Hey steady there. No news is good news, isn't that what they say? And this letter from your aunt is a no-news letter. All it's saying is don't hound them. They'll get in touch in their own good time. Don't say one damn thing about either of them being dead.'

She had been grateful for his reassurance. She didn't want him as her lover because she didn't want anyone as her lover, only Gavin. But she did want him as a friend.

His eyes sharpened as he looked down at her. 'You're not going to do anything silly, are you?' he asked with sudden, terrible intuitiveness.

Her eyes were blank. 'I don't know what you mean,' she said truthfully.

420

He gave an inward sigh of relief. For once he was way ahead of her. She hadn't yet taken it into her head to hotfoot it to 'Nam herself. He hoped to God she never did. The band would certainly not survive without her. Thinking of the American tour that was soon to start, he said, 'I'm going to take time off when we're in Washington to march with the brothers. Why don't you join me? You might even meet up with other chicks in the same position as yourself.'

'I'm sorry,' she said, wondering how on earth she was going to survive the American tour when her mind would focus on nothing but Gavin. 'I don't understand.'

He tossed a foreign edition of the *Washington Post* across to her.

'A pretty uptight-sounding English chick isn't too pleased at the line the American government is taking toward POWs. Her husband is a chopper jock being held in Hanoi.'

Gabrielle took hold of the newspaper, reading the letter that had caught his attention. 'I'm going to write to her,' she said immediately. 'I'm going to write to her today.'

'And the march on the Pentagon?' he asked. 'The Black Muslims are taking part in a march on the Pentagon in a couple of weeks time.' He grinned and gave a black clenched fist power salute, raised high. 'I thought my old friend Malcolm X might like a little support from me.'

'Are they going to protest the war?'

'They sure as hell ain't going there to enlist!' he said, laughing down at her.

Despite her fearful anxieties for Gavin's safety, a small smile touched her mouth. An antiwar demonstration in the heart of Washington would be an event Gavin would certainly not want her to miss. And the English girl who had written so angrily to The *Washington Post* might also be going.

'I'll come with you,' she said decisively. 'The brothers won't mind, will they?'

# CHAPTER TWENTY-THREE

The pain in Lewis's shoulder was excruciating, and blood was pouring down his arm and his chest. To evade being captured he knew he had to act. Immediately. Before he even left the water.

'*Duoc!*' The North Vietnamese screamed at him. '*Di di!*'

His left arm was useless. It was a heavy blood-soaked weight that felt as if it had been ripped from its socket. He had to hurl himself at the North Vietnamese; he had to knock the Kalashnikov from his grasp. From far behind him, from the other bank, there came a high-pitched scream and then a silencing blast of machine-gun fire. He staggered in the waist-high water. It wasn't Duxbery. Duxbery had been killed in the first barrage of shots to hit the boat. It was Drayton. They'd killed Drayton and now they were going to kill him.

The water around him was carmine with blood. He steadied himself on the mud and slime of the canal bed and then, as the North Vietnamese, losing patience, moved angrily towards him, he summoned up all his strength and hurled himself forwards.

He knew as he moved that he stood no chance of escaping. Even if he disarmed and killed his potential captor, there were swarms of other North Vietnamese on both banks who would immediately open fire. He couldn't escape, and he knew it, but he sure as hell wasn't going to flounder to dry land at the point of a gun only to be shot like an animal at his captor's leisure.

The grin of triumph on the North Vietnamese's face vanished as Lewis dived upon him. At the same instant as Lewis's right arm made contact with the Kalashnikov, knocking it upward, it blasted into life, bullets plowing into the air. There would be other bullets soon, bullets far more lethally directed, but Lewis didn't care. His right hand was on his victim's throat as they fell together, rolling and tumbling under the surface of the filthy water.

He never knew why he wasn't shot there and then. His initial advantage, that of taking his enemy by surprise, was lost almost immediately. Blood was still pumping from the wound in his shoulder, pain was still searing through him, and his left arm was as useless as a piece of dead meat. It was only seconds before his opponent had the upper hand, and only a fraction of a second longer before other hands laid hold of him, dragging him half drowned and semiconscious towards the bank.

He expected to be shot. Never for one minute did he imagine that he was going to be taken prisoner. He was thrown facedown, a half a dozen Kalashnikovs pointing at his head.

The officer in charge gave a brusque order, and instead of the expected blast of automatic fire smashing him from this world and into the next, hands were laid on him once again and his sodden clothes, right down to his khaki shorts, were savagely stripped off him. His boots were next, yanked from his feet and handed over, the spoils of war, to the officer in charge.

Still with the Kalashnikovs aimed at his head, coughing and spluttering up fetid canal water, he rolled himself on to his knees. The wound in his shoulder was now clearly visible, and he saw with relief that it was a flesh wound and that though nerves and tendons to his arm had been severed, no bones had been smashed.

The officer nodded to one of the soldiers standing guard over him, and the next minute his right arm and his injured left arm were yanked behind his back. He cried out in agony, falling and blacking out. When consciousness returned, he was still on his knees and still in excruciating pain. His arms had been tied behind him with vine rope, and a pad made from the shirt they had stripped him of had been tied across the gaping wound in his shoulder.

It was the first hopeful thing that had happened to him since he had hit the water. Their action made no sense unless they intended to keep him alive. And if they were going to keep him alive, then he would be able, at some point, to make an escape.

He was gestured to his feet, and he rose with difficulty, towering over the smaller Vietnamese soldiers like a captured Gulliver over the inhabitants of Lilliput.

There was no noise from the river behind him, no sign of life. The bodies of the men who had travelled out from Van Binh with him floated facedown on the water, or lay sprawled on the far bank. He saw no sign of Duxbery or Drayton.

He was almost grateful for the pain. At least it dulled the rage he felt at being herded along like a tethered bull. They didn't make for the village he and his men had so recently searched. Instead, they forged a path westward, through the bush. With no boots, Lewis's feet were soon as bloody as his shoulder. He tried not to think about snakes, about red ants. Instead, he tried to recreate a map of the area in his head, to anticipate where they might be heading, and for how long the hideous march would last.

It seemed to take forever. At one point the North Vietnamese came to a halt, and water from a plastic bottle was poured into a tin pannikin and passed around, but he was given none and he would have roasted in the fires of hell before he would have lowered himself to ask. He wondered why he'd been selected to be a prisoner. Perhaps they were a regular unit of the North Vietnamese Army, and they were trying to emphasize the difference between themselves and the local Viet Cong. Perhaps they had a tradeoff in mind. Perhaps they thought he was a colonel or a bigwig in the CIA. Perhaps they wanted information from him.

He winced as he stumbled in the wake of the soldiers. He'd always believed he was mentally prepared for torture, but he had imagined himself facing it in the peak of physical fitness, not with a half-severed arm. He was burning up with the beginnings of a fever, and though his feet never stopped moving forwards, he knew that he was slipping in and out of semiconsciousness.

At the next halt he was given water. His near-naked body was tormented by feeding mosquitoes and leeches. He tried to distract himself by thinking of Abbra, of how the news that he was missing in action would be conveyed to her, and failed. He couldn't think of Abbra. He would fall apart. Think about Tam. Pretty Tam, who had begged him not to leave on the morning's mission. Tam who had so devastated him by telling him that she was in love with him.

He plodded on, pain from his injured arm and shoulder raging through him, the fever intensifying. What would Tam do when she heard the news? Who would tell her the news? Presumably the bodies on the riverbank would be found. Duxbery and Drayton would be verified as being killed in action. What about him? Would it be believed that he was dead as well? Somehow he had to escape. He had to inform someone that he was alive, that there was no need for Abbra to be contacted, no need for her to worry.

When they finally came to a permanent halt it wasn't in a village. It was a campsite deep in the bush. Half a dozen thatched bamboo and straw huts circled blackened rice pots and a mud-baked oven. Green and black nylon sleeping hammocks were slung between the surrounding trees. The soldiers immediately in front of him rounded on him, yelling at him to squat, Vietnamese fashion. He did so with relief, swaying dizzily, and then, unable to balance himself for his bound arms, toppling over. As he struggled back into a crouching position the wound in his shoulder began to bleed profusely again.

'*Ten yi?*' the officer demanded, standing over him. 'What is your name?'

His name at least he could give them. His name, his rank, his service number, and his date of birth. But nothing else. Section five of the Code of Conduct for Members of the Armed Forces of the United States, the oath he had sworn when he first joined the army, was categorical. 'When questioned, should I become a prisoner of war, I am bound to give name and rank, service number, and date of birth. I will evade answering further questions to the utmost of my ability. I will make no oral or written statements disloyal to my country and its allies or harmful to their cause.'

If his captors had not shot him because they thought he would give them information, then they had made a grave error of judgement. Section six, the final part of the Code of Conduct, was in his blood and his bones. 'I will never forget that I am an American fighting man, responsible for my actions, and dedicated to the principles which made my country free. I will trust in God and in the United States of America.'

'Captain Lewis Ellis,' he replied curtly, wishing to God that he didn't feel so faint, that the blood streaming hotly down over his chest and arm would once more begin to congeal. He gave his service number and his birth date and then felt himself beginning to lose consciousness.

There was a sharply rapped order from the officer, and two of the soldiers who had trekked behind him all the way from the canal ran forward and physically supported him, hauling him to his feet. Still bound, with leeches feeding on his blood-soaked body, he was dragged towards one of the huts and thrown inside. Seconds later a young boy entered. He was in uniform and over his shoulder he carried a small box. He put the box down, regarded the wound in Lewis's shoulder without moving forward to physically examine it, and then turned abruptly on his heel, leaving the box behind him.

Lewis struggled into a half-sitting position, leaning against the wall of the hut. He tried to focus on the box that the young boy had left behind. Was it a first aid kit? Was

427

the boy a paramedic? He summoned up all his remaining strength and began to edge himself towards it. He was saved having to attempt near-impossible contortions by the return of the boy. This time he carried an aluminium bowl of steaming water. Lewis began to tremble with relief, then was suddenly consumed by fury at the thought that his trembling would be seen as a sign of weakness.

His face impassive, the boy put the water down while two other soldiers remained at the doorway of the hut, rifles in their hands. The vine thongs tethering his arms were released.

With cloths that had obviously been used many times before but which had been boiled clean, the boy began to swab his arm and shoulder. Looking down, Lewis could see the wound clearly and he knew he had been lucky. The bullet, no doubt aimed at his heart, had scored a near miss, hitting no vital organs. But the way his arms had been wrenched behind him and tethered had caused the real damage to the severed nerves and tendons.

With a pair of stainless steel tweezers the boy began to dig into the wound for the bullet. With his jaw clenched tight, and his teeth clamped together to prevent himself from crying out, Lewis stared with fierce concentration through the open door of the hut, fixing his gaze on the mud-baked oven. Food was being prepared. Rice was being cooked in one of the large blackened pots. He fixed his eyes firmly on the pot as the boy prodded deeper. Once the bullet was out and the wound was cleaned, it would heal. And then he would be able to think of escape.

The bullet was retrieved and the boy began to swab his shoulder with a ball of cotton soaked in alcohol. The sooner he made an escape attempt, the better. Statistically, early escapes were the most successful. And he wanted to put a quick end to the mental agony – for him and Abbra.

The boy began to work the alcohol-soaked swab into the wound, and a nerve ticked convulsively at the corner of Lewis's jaw. Finally, just when he thought he could bear it no longer, the swab was withdrawn and discarded and fresh swabs, soaked in a solution he could not identify, were plugged into the gaping hole. His upper arm and shoulder were then bandaged with strips of green cloth.

'Thank you,' he said automatically when the boy had finished.

The boy picked up the aluminium bowl and the medical box and looked at Lewis directly for the first time. There was a faint gleam of surprise in his eyes but nothing more. He still did not speak. He merely gave a slight shrug of his shoulders and then turned, walking out of the hut, past the soldiers who were still standing guard.

Now that he was no longer in danger of dying from loss of blood, Lewis became aware of how ravenously hungry he was. He could smell the rice that was being cooked and hoped fervently that he would be offered some.

That he had been captured by a small group of North Vietnamese Army troops instead of Viet Cong was surely to his advantage. If he had been captured by the Viet Cong, he knew he would have been a short timer indeed.

The general pattern of Viet Cong captures was for the prisoner to be tethered by the neck and then hauled around Viet Cong sympathetic villages in order that the peasantry could observe how inferior and animal-like the Americans were. When the fun and games of baiting the helpless American were over, he would be shot, preferably by one bullet and by a very young boy just to emphasize to the onlookers how easy it was to kill a large, apparently invincible, *khi dot*. A big monkey.

Americans who were captured by the NVA were generally pilots shot down over North Vietnam. There, after being paraded through the streets like circus animals, they were imprisoned either in the huge Hoa Lo prison complex in Hanoi, or a smaller prison known to the Americans as the 'zoo', at Cu Loc.

But he wasn't in North Vietnam, he was in South Vietnam, and here there were no prison camps. He would just have to put his trust in the fact that the NVA were disciplined soldiers, soldiers that he, and the majority of his colleagues, had always regarded with respect.

The boy who had treated his shoulder, though no more than sixteen, had been competent. He wondered why they were so far south. It was possible that they were a splinter group from the large contingent who had been attempting to ferry supplies in from Cambodia, the group he and his men had engaged earlier in the month. But if they were, why hadn't they headed immediately back to their Cambodian sanctuaries?

The two soldiers on guard moved towards him, one of them bending down to pick up the vine rope. As he approached with it, obviously about to re-tether him, Lewis said abruptly in Vietnamese, 'If you wrench my arms behind me again, tying them at the elbows, I will lose my injured arm. It will die. Drop off.'

For a second both men hesitated. They knew that many Americans knew some Vietnamese words. Words for 'go' or 'come', or words that were blasphemous. But they had never encountered an American who spoke their language.

Their hesitation was minimal. His arms were seized and yanked behind him, and Lewis knew, through a sea of pain, that in the next few seconds blood would once more begin to trickle stickily down his chest. He was protesting vociferously when the young paramedic walked quickly into the hut.

'No,' he ordered his comrades. 'Tie him by the neck and feet. Not the arms!'

The vine rope was put around his feet, anchored on his right wrist and then looped around his neck. It was then run up to the bamboo rafters. If he tried to move more than an inch or two in any direction, the rope tightened around his neck, threatening to strangle him. While he was being tied like a hog, the paramedic was placing his left arm in a makeshift sling, which looked like a piece of dried banana leaf. Whatever it was, it served its purpose. He immediately felt better.

Outside the hut the soldiers were beginning to gather, bowls in their hands, around the huge rice pot.

If he were given a share of the rice, it would be a fair indication of the kind of treatment that lay ahead of him. He waited tensely. He needed food. The fever that had washed over him in waves on the trek to the camp was now subsiding, though he was damned sure it wouldn't have done so if his shoulder hadn't been so thoroughly cleaned.

At the first opportunity he intended making his escape, and the fitter he was, when that moment came, the better it would be for him. He wasn't daunted by the forests and swamps he would have to negotiate. He had been trained in jungle survival, and he had lived long enough in Van Binh to have come to terms with the water-logged, leech- and snake-infested terrain.

The officer who had appropriated his boots entered the hut. Looking at the small size of his feet compared to his own, Lewis wondered how he would ever find them comfortable to march in.

'You will come with me,' he said brusquely. 'You will answer questions.'

The two guards at either side of the doorway moved forward, releasing the vine rope that tethered him from the rafters.

Lewis abandoned all hope of a share in the rice. He certainly wouldn't be fed immediately before an interrogation, and sure as hell wouldn't be afterwards, when he had refused to tell them whatever it was they wanted to know.

It was dark now, and he was led across to a table shielded by a protective awning of green camouflage parachute silk. On the table was a tiny oil lamp made of a small glass bottle with a wick stub sticking out the top.

The officer sat behind the table, the two soldiers flanked Lewis, who stood before it, and the interrogation began.

'Your name?' he was asked again. 'Your rank?'

Lewis told him. He was still half naked and the evening chill struck through him, bringing goose flesh out on his arms and his legs.

'Your company?'

'Under the Code of Conduct for Members of the Armed Forces of the United States I am required to give only my name, rank, service number, and date of birth!'

The officer's face tightened. 'You will answer all questions or you will be given correctional period.'

Lewis had no need to ask what he meant. Correctional period was a euphemism for torture.

He repeated obdurately, 'I am required to give only my name, rank, service number, and date of birth.'

Some of the questions he was asked, and which he refused to answer, were oddly personal ones. Was he married? Did he have children? Whereabouts did he live in imperialist America?

Despite everything he could do to prevent it, he began to sway on his feet as he repeated, time and time again, his name, rank, service number and date of birth. His arm and shoulder were hurting like hell. He was freezing. He was hungry. And his cut and bloody feet were attracting the attention of ants and land leeches and God only knew what else.

Before he disgraced himself by fainting, the interrogation came to an abrupt end, and with no violence. He was marched back to the hut and then, before he was re-tethered, one of his guards threw a pair of black pyjamas and a sleeping mat towards him. As he struggled one-handed into the pyjamas, another soldier entered and placed a bowl of rice and a bowl of leaf tea down on the floor beside him. The rice was flavoured with salt pork soup and was surprisingly appetizing. He wolfed it down, uncertain whether to expect such treatment in the future, or if it was merely the calm before the storm.

He was re-tethered, a loop of the rope again going around his neck, making it nearly impossible for him to sleep. As he lay on the sleeping mat, shivering violently in the thin cotton pyjamas and with mosquitoes clustering on his unprotected feet, he wondered why the officer had accepted his noncooperation with comparative good grace. It had been almost as if he had not been really interested. And if that were the case, why on earth had he taken him prisoner?

He was in torment from the mosquitoes, and he tried to think about Abbra. Abbra, who had so naively wanted him to tell her all about his life in Vietnam so that she could feel a part of it. It suddenly occurred to him that he didn't know if Abbra had ever travelled out of the United States. If she had, it would have been only to Canada or to one of the more sophisticated Mexican beach resorts. Nothing she had ever experienced could possibly give her any idea of what Vietnam was like. It was beyond anyone's imagination.

He found himself thinking of Tam. Tam would know exactly what he was suffering. He hoped to God whoever was sent out to Van Binh to replace him would keep Tam on as cleaning girl. If she returned to her father, she would inevitably face beatings.

Despite his agony a smile touched the corner of his mouth. He recalled how hostile and defiant she had been when he had first met her. She had hated him so passionately she had fairly sparked with animosity. Later she had cared for him with all the diligence of a devoted wife, laundering his clothes, cooking, cleaning. He was going to miss Tam. She had brightened up the last few months immeasurably.

He had slept intermittently, waking at dawn to the sound of men drilling. The NVA's reputation for rigid discipline was obviously one that was well deserved. About ten minutes later the paramedic entered the hut, two guards in attendance. He didn't remove the dressing from Lewis's wound but bent his head towards it, sniffing it. It smelled clean, no sign of gangrene, and he gave Lewis an imperceptible nod before turning and walking away.

Later, a dish of leaf tea was brought to him and held for him to drink.

'I need exercise,' he said to the guard who held the dish to his mouth. 'I need to move or my blood will stop circulating.'

His body felt as if his blood had stopped long ago. The method by which he was tied was fiendish, the slightest movement causing pressure of his neck. The guard didn't respond by releasing his bonds, but to Lewis's even greater surprise, he took out a packet of Ruby Queens from his shirt pocket, lit one, and then gave it to him to inhale. It was the best cigarette he had ever tasted and one he knew he would never forget.

When the drilling was finished, the officer who had interrogated him the previous evening entered the hut. 'Good morning, imperialist American,' he said almost affably. 'You are to prepare to meet your new escorts.' As he was speaking to him, the guards were freeing his bonds.

Lewis stretched his cramped muscles gingerly. Escorts? Then he wasn't just being held prisoner. He was being taken somewhere. But where? Cambodia?

When he was led out into the morning sunlight, he groaned inwardly. Twenty or so black-clad Viet Cong were milling with the small group of NVA troops. He was going to be handed over. And in the hands of the less-disciplined Viet Cong there was no telling what might happen to him.

He tried to follow the conversations taking place around him. The NVA troops were continuing westward, back to their Cambodian sanctuaries after apparently bringing in a convoy of supplies. He was unable to discover where the VC were heading, though it was obvious from their behaviour that they were in transit and that they were not going to remain long in the makeshift camp.

In an agonizingly short space of time he was rebound though this time his arm was allowed to remain in its sling. His right arm was wrenched behind him, and tied to vine

434

rope that was threaded through over his bent left elbow. His left wrist, lying flat against his chest, was also tied so that he could not slip his arm out of the sling and ease the pressure of the rope. Then, as before, the rope was passed around his neck and down and under the right arm rope. It was an ingenious method of bondage, making his neck answerable to nearly every movement that he made.

There were no formal farewells as the troops divided and went in two different directions. The NVA westward, the VC heading towards the densest part of the U Minh forest. The ground was so waterlogged that it became impossible to follow any land trails, and a kilometre or so from the camp Lewis was ordered at gunpoint into one of a half dozen waiting sampans.

Travelling on a web of narrow canals, hemmed in by dense vegetation, they penetrated deeper and deeper into the U Minh. It was hideous, swamp-infested terrain, thick with snakes and poisonous spiders. Escaping, without a weapon of any kind, would be no picnic.

Lewis wondered again why he was being kept alive. Presumably it was believed he would give them information. And even when they found he wouldn't, he would still retain a certain value. Prisoners were highly prized commodities at peace negotiations, though not all prisoners were given their freedom when negotiations were complete. He remembered being told at West Point that thirteen French prisoners captured at Dien Bien Phu were not released by Hanoi until sixteen years later.

As the late afternoon merged into dusk a flight of B-52 bombers screamed overhead. They were probably from Guam. He wondered what their mission was, where they were heading.

Homesickness, strong and pungent, caught him by the throat. He'd been trained in jungle survival techniques and had been prepared both mentally and physically for captivity. But the reality was far worse than anything he had anticipated. The loss of dignity affronted him the most. He couldn't go for a pee or a shit without having a VC standing over him with a loaded AK-47, and the salt pork soup had affected his bowels adversely.

It was dark when their journey at last came to an end. He could discern small huts on stilts, their numbers indicating that this camp, unlike the previous one, was semi-permanent. He was given a half coconut shell of sickly-sweet palm sugar juice to drink and a minute portion of rice to eat. Then he was tied for sleep as he had been tied by the NVA.

The pain in his shoulder had begun to ease slightly, but his left arm had swollen to alarming proportions. He wondered if infection had set in and hoped to God that it hadn't. If it had, a couple of penicillin shots would be an easy cure, but he wasn't going to be given any penicillin shots, and he had a suspicion that the VC answer to the problem would be swift, and amateur, amputation.

He had been given a mosquito net for protection, and despite the numerous bugs that managed to circumnavigate it, he slept, lightly and restlessly. At dawn he was awakened by having the muzzle of an AK-47 prodded against his chest. He was taken to a latrine trench to relieve himself, and then marched back to the hut.

During the short journey he was able to verify his suspicions – the camp had been in existence for some time. He wondered how often US aircraft flew over it. Or if they did? If helicopters flew that way, he might be able to attract their attention. Even as the thought came to him, he knew that any such chance was minimal. The camp would not have survived as long as it apparently had without being skilfully camouflaged. He knew there wasn't a hope in hell of foot troops penetrating so deep in to the U Minh. It was an area that the Saigon military left alone. So as rescue seemed to be out of the question, the only alternative was escape.

He pondered how escape in such a hellish region might be achieved, when the two Viet Cong who had been standing guard at the door of the hut ordered him abruptly to his feet. He was led out into the heat of early morning and marched to the centre of the compound, where a Viet Cong officer, the black material of his pyjamas of much better quality than those of the guards, stood waiting.

Lewis took a deep breath. It looked as if he was about to suffer his first interrogation at the hands of the Viet Cong. And he doubted if it would bear much relation to his brief interrogation with the NVA.

He was right. All the information demanded of him was military. No one in the U Minh was interested in whether he was married or not, or where he was born.

He replied to the questions as he had to the previous ones. He gave his name, rank, service number, and date of birth and claimed that under Article 17 of the Geneva Conventions, no other information could be demanded of him.

The Viet Cong officer disagreed. 'You will be punished,' he said, and his eyes flicked towards the banana-leaf sling.

Lewis felt his stomach muscles contract. It was what he had expected from the first moment he had been captured. From the number of Viet Cong standing in a semicircle around the edge of the compound, everyone else had expected it too. The officer nodded towards two of the guards, and they approached Lewis, lengths of nylon cargo strapping in their hands. Lewis gritted his teeth. Damn his injured shoulder. Damn, damn, dammit!

'Have you changed your mind?' the officer asked him in Vietnamese. 'Do you wish to cooperate?'

Lewis swallowed hard and repeated his name, his rank, his service number, and his date of birth.

'And that is all?' the officer said when he had finished.

'Under Article 17 of the Geneva Conventions and under the Code of Conduct for Members of the Armed Forces of the United States, that is all.'

The officer did not seem disappointed. He merely nodded towards the guards and then stepped back a yard or two. In the few seconds before the guards laid hold of him, Lewis realized the officer had moved so that he would be well clear of any splattering blood. And then the banana-leaf string was ripped away and he didn't think of anything else except agonizing pain for a very long time.

Before the torture began he had been determined not to let even a groan of pain pass his lips for the onlookers' enjoyment. He didn't groan. He screamed. His shoulders were lifting out of their sockets, his chest was exploding, his ribs projecting like drawn bowstrings. Unconsciousness was a black pit he hurtled into gratefully, only to be wrenched back into agonizing consciousness by having cold water thrown over him.

The pressure was relieved. He was asked if he would answer the questions put to him. With his jaw clenched so tight that it felt permanently locked, he gasped out his name, rank, service number, and date of birth. And then he remained silent.

The pressure not only resumed, it intensified. He began to vomit and choke on his vomit. He lost control of his bowels and his bladder. He was no longer Lewis Ellis, West Point graduate, captain, husband of Abbra. He was an animal. A thing. A creature with no control over his bodily functions.

Each time he was asked a question he gaspingly told his questioner to go to hell. He told him in English, in French, and in every Vietnamese dialect he knew. And his suffering continued.

He didn't know whether the officer in charge finally ordered him to be released from the straps because of the possibility that he would die, and never be of any use, or because he had grown bored with the proceedings. Either way, the end finally came. Lewis couldn't walk back to the hut. He had to be dragged, leaving a trail of blood, bile, and faeces in his wake.

438

He knew it would happen again. It would happen again and again until he was broken and until he not only gave them all the military information he possessed, but until he also agreed to sign statements admitting that he was a war criminal, and that his country had perpetrated war crimes against the Vietnamese people.

He had to escape. Even if he just crawled away to die in the swamps. He had to escape and he couldn't even move.

All through the rest of the day he lay on the floor of the hut. At one point someone brought him water and a bowl of rice. He tried desperately to eat, but he only gagged and brought back every mouthful that he succeeded in swallowing. The wound in his shoulder had crusted over with dried blood. His left arm was useless. Unlike the rest of his body, he couldn't feel pain in it. He sniffed at it, wondering when signs of gangrene would begin to show, wondering what would happen to him when they did.

The guards at the door of his hut had changed. Dusk fell. He heard a radio. Over a roar of static, Radio Hanoi's 'Hanoi Hannah' was describing how massive US forces had been 'decimated', how innumerable US ships had been sunk and aircraft shot down.

As Lewis listened to the two obligatory American pop songs that followed the news item, included in the hope of persuading American servicemen to tune in to Hanoi, Lewis became aware that the new guards had moved some distance from the door of the hut, presumably to listen to the radio better, and that he was unmanacled. He was being given his chance, and even though his limbs were swollen and racked with pain, he had to take it.

He forced himself on to his knees and inched towards the door of the hut. As far as the Viet Cong were concerned, it was obviously recreation hour. They were all gathered around the radio, listening intently. The men who had been standing guard over him were only a few yards away, but their backs were to him. Could he do it? Could he simply crawl away? Even if he wasn't spotted, it would be only a matter of five or ten minutes before his disappearance was discovered. They would know almost immediately. But it was dark. And the forest was dense. It might be possible. And he had nothing to lose.

Stealthily, hardly able to believe that he could have even got to the door of the hut without attracting attention, he lay flat on the ground and wriggled outside. Every movement was unspeakable agony. It was impossible for him to lift his right arm above his head in an effort to haul himself onwards. He had to be content with clawing at the ground, one-handed, and digging his toes into the earth for leverage. But he was moving. He was heading away from the hut, away from the compound and the gathered, listening men, and towards the pitch-black immensity of the forest.

Over the radio's static Elvis Presley gave way to Joan Baez. 'Christ Almighty,' he said to himself as he cleared the beaten earth of the camp and burrowed into waist-high vegetation. 'Don't they know she's singing an antiwar song!'

The ground beneath him was becoming less firm. Moisture oozed through his fingers. Cautiously he raised himself to his knees, and then to his feet. He could no longer see the camp; he could no longer be seen. He headed off in a northeasterly direction, his feet sinking ankle depth into mud at every step. A snake that he could not see, but only sense, slithered across his feet. And then he heard commotion behind him.

He began to run, his left arm hanging uselessly at his side, his swollen ankle and knee and elbow joints screaming out in protest. He was sinking deep into the mire with every step. The ground was pulling him downward, drawing him back. He could hear the Viet Cong bursting into the forest behind him and he forced himself to go on, knowing that he had a lead of about fifty yards maximum. Water gleamed dully in the darkness. He headed towards it, floundering into its depths. If he could submerge himself, breathe through reeds, then he still might escape.

The water was a mere sheen covering swampland. Something hideous and nameless coiled itself around his legs and began to tighten its hold, dragging him downwards. He twisted and turned to free himself, and as he did so he began to sink down into the morass. He was embroiled up to his waist, and then his armpits. 'No!' he yelled out hoarsely, knowing that the creature wrapped about his legs was about to be the victor. 'For Christ's sake, no!'

The Viet Cong surged from between the trees. Hands grasped hold of him. He was being torn apart at the waist. One of the black-pyjama-clad figures leaned towards him and then thrust his AK-47 beneath the surface of the water and fired. The threshing, unseen weight around his legs was stilled. Like a beached whale he was dragged, bleeding and broken, on to firm ground.

Early the next morning he was transferred from the hut to a bamboo punishment cage. It measured a bare four feet by six feet and was just high enough for him to sit up in it.

And there he stayed. He wasn't taken out for exercise. He wasn't taken out to go to the latrine. There was no shade from the sun by day, and no shelter from the cold by night. His wound stank with putrefaction, but to his everlasting amazement the arm did not turn gangrenous and did not have to be amputated.

Day followed day, and week followed week, and month followed month. When he was taken out of the cage, a little while before Christmas, it was so that he could once more be questioned. And tortured. That was the first time he broke. Not outwardly but inwardly. They tied up his elbows again until they touched; they ruptured an eardrum; they beat him with bamboo rods. And when at last they threw him, more dead than alive, back into the cage, he closed his fingers around the bars and he thought of Christmas in California. He thought of turkey and hot showers and soft beds. And he thought of Abbra, and how it was going to be years before he'd see her again. If he ever saw her again. And he lowered his head to his hands, and wept.

441

# CHAPTER TWENTY-FOUR

The Huey never made it to the ground. It smashed into the jungle canopy, hanging vertically, a bomb just waiting to detonate. Kyle pushed himself bloodily away from the control panel and yelled at his copilot to get the hell out. There was no reply. One of the bullets had smashed the Huey's Plexiglas bubble and hit him between the eyes.

Kyle didn't hang around. He had only seconds to escape before the Huey exploded and he did not waste one of the them. He was out of his harness, out of the crippled ship, falling and tumbling through the thick foliage to the ground.

When the Huey blew the blast rocketed him for thirty yards. His helmet had been torn off and his hair and his flak jacket were on fire, he felt as if he had broken every bone in his body, and as he rolled in hellish agony on the ground he was aware that half a dozen North Vietnamese Army regulars were running forwards towards him. He struggled to reach for his pistol and failed.

His hand wouldn't move. His arm wouldn't move. He didn't know if it had been broken, or if it had been shot off or ripped off. He knew only that the flames were no longer picturesque and that he was in danger of becoming the barbecue dish of the day.

He rolled on the ground, struggling to reach for his pistol with his left hand, but where his pistol should have been there was nothing. Blaspheming viciously, expecting a round of machine-gun fire to blast him into eternity at any moment, he beat at the flames engulfing his head with his good arm.

No machine-gun blast came. He was surrounded. The flames leaping from his flight suit were extinguished. His scalp felt as if it were leaving the top of his head, but his hair was no longer on fire. High above him, coming under a slaughtering barrage of artillery fire, a Huey circled desperately. He knew who was at the controls. Chuck, risking his own neck in a suicidal attempt at rescue. He could see the Huey take fire, veer and dip.

'*Get the hell out, you dumb bastard!*' he yelled skywards as his boots were yanked from his feet and he was searched for weapons.

For the first time since he had hurled himself from his ship he could take mental stock of his injuries. His right arm was still attached to his body but was broken, the bone projecting unnaturally at the elbow. His back was burned, but he had no way of knowing how badly, and his scalp and face were also burned.

He was alive though. He clenched his teeth as he was ordered to his feet, wondering how the hell he was going to survive the pain of his burns without proper medication. He was alive, but he was also injured – God only knew where on the Cambodian-Laos-'Nam border – and a prisoner. He was, in short, in the biggest crock of shit he'd ever been in in his entire life.

The ground was littered with the bodies of the reconnaissance party, shot down as they had tried to board the Hueys. Kyle could see a couple of ARVN soldiers being herded away from the site at gunpoint, but he could see no other American survivors.

'You're on your own, baby,' he told himself grimly, fighting against waves of pain and faintness and nausea. And in Saigon, Trinh would be on her own too.

Long before they had cleared the scene of carnage he collapsed. When he fleetingly floated back to consciousness he was aware of being carried on a stretcher. For a crazy moment he thought it was a regulation US army stretcher and that he was on his way to a blissfully civilized, sanitized

US army hospital. And then he saw the khaki-uniformed pith-helmeted Asians carrying him and he wondered why they were going to such lengths to keep him alive, and what it was they intended doing with him.

The burns on his back were unbearable and for nearly two weeks he was able to think of nothing else. The NVA treated him by coating the burns with a mixture of leaves and gunge. When he weakly protested that the leaves would cause infection, he was told that the leaves possessed a special healing quality. What was in the gunge he never found out, and looking at the sickly mess, he thought it better that he didn't know.

His arm was bound tight against his chest and though awkward was the least of his troubles. His main concern, once his flesh began to heal, were the puckered scars on his forehead and temples. Would Trinh find them physically repulsive? He thought not. Serry would, but then, he wasn't in love with Serry anymore. He wondered how she would react to the news that he had been shot down. Her asshole of a brother would probably leap so high for joy he'd hit the fucking moon.

Since his capture, they'd rested only at night. The NVA kept on moving, travelling north. They were in a high mountainous area, and he suspected that they were in Laos, not 'Nam. Wherever they were, there were no US troops on the ground and the further they travelled, the less chance there was of them running into any, and of him being rescued by them. Occasionally planes would fly over, but the Viet Cong had ears like dogs and were always in deep cover before aircraft were directly overhead.

'For Christ's sake!' he said exasperatedly as they plowed on through another long, hot, insect-ridden day. 'Where the hell are we *going*?'

It was a question he had asked a hundred times before. For the first time he received a reply. 'Hanoi,' the Vietnamese at his side said succinctly. 'We go to Hanoi.'

Kyle stumbled and nearly fell. 'We're *walking* there?'

The Vietnamese grinned. 'We walk from north of Viet-nam to south, and from south to north many times,' he said in commendable English. 'Walking to Hanoi on Ho Chi Minh trail is holiday. Vacation.'

'Not for me it isn't,' Kyle muttered grimly. He knew now where he was being taken. To Hoa Lo prison, North Vietnam's main penitentiary.

The ARVN troops who had been taken prisoner with him had been left in one of the Montagnard villages that they had passed through. Now he knew why. Their status didn't warrant the long march to a prison used primarily for shot-down and captured US fighter pilots.

'And how long is it going to take us to walk to Hanoi?' he asked, sweat pouring down his face as they threaded their way through terrain thick with rotting vegetation.

'Twelve weeks, thirteen weeks,' the Vietnamese replied. He had a Soviet Kalashnikov AK-47 slung around his neck, and Kyle knew that if he made one false move he would be in the rifle's sights and it would be good-bye world forever.

All of the soldiers were Russian armed. The AK-47 was their basic weapon, but there was also a scattering of Type 56 assault rifles and one man even carried an RPG-7 antitank missile launcher.

Kyle thought constantly about overpowering one of the North Vietnamese and fighting his way free with a captured weapon. So far he'd had no chance, but he was constantly on the watch for one. He certainly didn't want to find himself incarcerated in Hoa Lo. Once in there, he might never see the light of day again.

Although the trail ran through rugged, mountainous country, they quite frequently met with parties of soldiers and peasants ferrying supplies south. The sacks of rice and crates of military hardware were strapped to bicycles, some of them modified with a length of bamboo attached to the handlebar and seat column, enabling the bicycle to be controlled by a man walking alongside it, even over the roughest ground.

Whenever such a party was sighted, his captors would slip a rope around Kyle's neck and lead him, animal-like. 'Why the hell is this necessary?' he fumed, hating the humiliation of if. 'You have AK-47s and Type 56 assault rifles levelled at my head all the time! You don't need to tether me as well!' He was never answered, but he knew why the rope was considered necessary. It wasn't enough for him merely to be their prisoner. He had also to be cowed and subjugated, and though he felt very far from being either, the rope around his neck gave him the appearance of being so.

As they climbed higher the terrain changed, the vegetation thinned, the dense foliage giving way to forests of pines. Their only food, apart from fruit and berries gathered as they trekked, was rice. Every soldier carried his own supply in a cotton tube slung over one shoulder and under the opposite arm. At night they slept on hammocks slung between the trees. They passed through no more villages, but the traffic on the trail grew heavier. There were carts and trucks as well as bicycles, as bombing raids by US aircraft became frequent.

He had been exultant when the first F-4 Phantoms screamed overhead, raining down orange-sized incendiary bombs. The bomblets were packed inside a canister and burst open immediately after release from the aircraft, seeding a large area. They were impossible to hide from, the only defence against them being to pray like the devil that they wouldn't drop on his patch of ground.

After he had spent a half dozen heart-stopping occasions waiting for a raid to come to a conclusion, his reaction became far less enthusiastic. Apart from human victims, the damage they caused was minimal. The trail was still roadworthy. Trucks, even if they were hit, were always miraculously repaired. Traffic on the trail continued with a dogged persistence that Kyle could only reluctantly admire.

Intermittently, as the altitude began to decrease and as they crossed the border into North Vietnam, there were anti-aircraft units and supply dumps and maintenance depots by the side of what had now become a recognizable road.

'Soon there will be anti-aircraft units and maintenance depots all the way into the South,' one of his guards told him proudly. 'Soon Ho Chi Minh Trail become a three-lane highway, just like you have in America.'

They began to travel only at night, though even then US planes flew overhead. Sometimes the planes were Phantoms, but more often they were air force gunships, converted transport aircraft fitted with low-light-level television, infrared sensors, ignition detectors, night observation scopes, and other electronic detection devices. But despite all their technological hardware, the traffic on the trail continued, ammunition, guns, and rice travelling in a near continuous flow from north to south.

'What is going to happen to me when we get to Hanoi?' Kyle asked the most talkative of his guards. He had a pretty good idea, but conversation of any sort was a relief to the constant monotony of walking, walking, walking.

'In Hanoi you will be very well treated,' the guard said with a confidence that Kyle didn't share. 'Vietnamese people realize you are not vicious imperialist aggressor but only a dupe of the imperialist American government. You will be educated to understand better.'

'And then?' Kyle asked, mildly amused.

'And then you will be given your freedom. You will be able to tell other American soldiers of how they, too, are dupes of imperialist American government.'

Kyle groaned. He had heard rumours, about pilots tortured in Hanoi until they made confessions of 'war crimes' that could be used by the North Vietnamese for propaganda. He needed to escape before he reached Hoa Lo prison, and his time was running out fast.

Night-time would be best, he plotted as he plodded on under his captor's watchful eyes. The greatest handicap to a successful escape was the impossibility of merging among

447

members of the local population. If he had been in France or Italy in the last war, then once he had initially escaped there would at least have been a chance of his staying free because, suitably dressed, he would have been indistinguishable from the natives. There was no such cover in Vietnam. In Vietnam, no matter how he dressed, he was immediately recognizable as a big white American. In daylight he would not be able to move twenty yards before the alarm was given and he was recaptured.

The risks were colossal but Kyle was determined to take them. He planned to make an attempt that very night. He would wait until the rest period, until he was taken into the vegetation at the side of the road to relieve himself. Then he would take his guard by surprise and overpower him, grabbing his weapon. What he would do after that, whether he would shoot it out with the remaining dozen or so soldiers or whether he would be able to steal off into the undergrowth undetected, he didn't know. He would play it by ear.

He was never given the chance. They had been on the trail only for an hour or two that night when two trucks, travelling south to north, drew up beside them. Seconds later he was being ordered at gunpoint into the rear of one of them. Some of the soldiers clambered aboard with him, grinning euphorically, while others boarded the second truck.

Kyle could have wept. There would be no more rest stops in the dark and at the side of the road. No more crazy, virtually impossible chances of escape. From now on escape was hopeless. He was travelling at high speed towards Hoa Lo, and there wasn't a damn thing in the world that he could do about it.

He closed his eyes and leaned his head back against the tarpaulin, wondering how he could get a message to Trinh, how he was going to survive incarceration, how long it would be before he was once again free.

Although the tarpaulin covers were still down early the next morning, he knew that they were now driving over asphalt instead of the rough road surface. Obviously they were very close to Hanoi, possibly even in Hanoi. At what he took to be a roadblock, they stopped for a few minutes. A uniformed figure flicked back the tarpaulin and gazed at Kyle in hostile curiosity. Then the tarpaulin was replaced and the journey continued. He could hear the sound of other motor vehicles. Jeeps and motorcycles.

They halted again, and this time the soldiers who had escorted him all the way from the Laos-Cambodia-'Nam border were gestured out into the road and two impassive-faced soldiers he had never seen before took their place, their rifles cocked. Kyle felt a pang of regret at his abrupt separation from his erstwhile companions. At least he had come to know what to expect from them. He didn't know what the hell to expect from his new guards, or the guards who awaited him Hoa Lo.

The tarpaulin hadn't been securely replaced, and he glimpsed the embankment of a large river and the houses and streets of a city. The truck began to slow down. There were trees and then a high concrete wall topped with shards of broken glass and a triple strand of barbed wire. The truck came to a halt. He had arrived. He was at Hoa Lo. And in another few minutes he would be inside. Perhaps for years. Perhaps forever.

The truck halted for a second and there was the sound of massive gates creaking open. Slowly the truck rumbled forwards again for a few yards and then came to a halt. Behind them the gates grated and slammed shut.

It was the most terrible sound that Kyle had ever heard.

Minutes passed and then the tarpaulin was lifted back by a Vietnamese wearing the uniform and insignia of an officer. He spoke sharply to the two soldiers in the truck, and they leapt to their feet, prodding Kyle out of the truck at rifle point.

His first impression was of how cold it was. Ever since he had arrived in Vietnam he had sweltered in almost unbearable heat. Now, in Hoa Lo, he shivered in the damp, chill air. He was at the entrance of what looked to be a long tunnel. The officer turned, leading the way into it, and Kyle saw that it was an underpass running beneath part of the great, gaunt building that stood above it.

At the end of the underpass were yet more gates. They were double gates made of heavy iron. Kyle had never heard of any captured Americans escaping from Hoa Lo, and the reason was obvious. Hoa Lo was escape-proof.

Beyond the gates was a bare courtyard about a hundred feet long and sixty or seventy feet wide, paved with worn cement. The buildings surrounding the courtyard were of grimy white stucco and the windows were few and high. Looking upward, Kyle could see that they were glassless and barred with double steel grating. He clenched his jaw. Being imprisoned in Hoa Lo would be awful, but he had to survive it. He had to think of Trinh and of what she would be suffering, not knowing what had happened to him or where he was.

He was marched to the far end of the courtyard, where there was yet another high double gate. It remained shut. Instead, he was led into the right-hand cell block, down a concrete-floored corridor, and through two sets of steel doors. There was no sign of other inmates, no noise except for the echoing resonance of the guards' booted feet. A cell door was thrown open and he was shoved inside.

It was then that his heart really sank, then that he experienced his first real wave of panic. The cell was barely seven feet by seven feet, and it was totally empty except for a sleeping pallet and a slop bucket. Ever since he had figured out where he was being taken, he had anticipated at least being with other Americans. He knew what his own strengths and weaknesses were. He could fly into the jaws of hell if necessary, with crazy, daredevil defiance, but he couldn't face the thought of being locked away alone.

He gritted his teeth, knowing damn well that if the bastards suspected how much he hated solitary they would keep him in it permanently. As it was, he would be alone only until after he had been questioned. Such a tactic was routine. A nerve began to tick at the corner of his jaw. What might not be so routine was the method of questioning. He had been captive now for over three months and he had suffered nothing worse than shouted insults and the prods of rifle butts. He had been lucky. Unless he was very much mistaken, his luck was fast beginning to run out.

He was ordered to strip out of the remnants of his uniform and was given two pairs of well-worn and well-washed shirts, two pairs of khaki trousers, two pairs of athletic shorts, two sets of underwear, and a belt. He sat on the edge of the low pallet, looking at the clothes in mild surprise. It was better than he had anticipated. At least the clothes were clean and the spare set indicated that they would be kept laundered.

He wondered if there was anyone in the adjoining cells and tapped experimentally on the wall behind him. Immediately a guard screamed at him through the inspection grate in the cell door. Kyle shrugged, seemingly unconcerned. He had achieved his object. His tap had sounded hollow and he was sure that the cells on either side of him were empty, which meant that the many pilots who had been shot down over the North, and imprisoned in Hoa Lo, were in another section of the prison, probably in the section beyond the double gates at the far end of the courtyard. The area he was in, then, was merely a reception area. His spirits lifted slightly – perhaps his eventual cell might not be quite so small or so spartan – and then immediately fell at the realization that he would find out only after he had been interrogated.

The questioning began the next morning, shortly after dawn. He was taken out of his cell and down the flaking whitewashed-walled corridor to a nearby room. In the centre there was a table, behind which sat the officer who had led him from the truck into the prison. There were steel hooks in the ceiling of the room and ominous dark brown stains on the walls and on the concrete floor. Kyle tried not to imagine what the hooks might be for and what the stains had been caused by, and concentrated instead on feeling nothing but contempt for the diminutive Vietnamese who had him so totally in his power.

'Your name?' the officer asked curtly in heavily accented English.

'Anderson.'

'Your full name?'

'Kyle Royd Anderson.'

'Your rank, service number, and date of birth?'

Kyle answered equally curtly. There was a moment's silence. He had given all the information that the Code of Conduct allowed and his interrogator was obviously well aware that he had done so. When he spoke again there was a more menacing tone in his voice.

'The name of your division?'

'I'm not obliged to answer that question.'

'I ask you again, the name of your division?'

Kyle eyeballed him. 'Under the American Code of Conduct I'm not obliged to answer that question.'

There wasn't a flicker of emotion on the officer's impassive face. 'The American Code of Conduct is not recognized in the Democratic Republic of Vietnam,' he said stonily. 'Please answer the questions you are asked. The name of your division?'

For a fleeting second Kyle was tempted to avoid what was obviously going to happen and to tell him. After all, he wasn't a duty, honour and country West Point grad. He hadn't been flying helicopters out of patriotism. He had been flying them for kicks, for the sheer hell of it. What difference would it make if the obnoxious bastard questioning him learned the name of his division? It was hardly information that would enable Hanoi to win the war. If he had been a fighter pilot with a knowledge of future targets, then he could understand the importance of keeping what he knew to himself. But he wasn't a fighter pilot. He was a chopper jock, and nothing he knew could be of the slightest

452

help to the North Vietnamese war effort. The temptation came and went. He was also an American and he had never yet been shit scared of anyone or anything.

'The name of your division?' the officer repeated.

'I'm not obliged to answer that question,' Kyle said again.

'But you will answer my question. You will answer all my questions,' the officer said, rising to his feet. For a disbelieving moment Kyle thought the interview had come to an end, and then the officer continued. 'Many Americans before you have stood where you stand now. They, too, have always said that they would not answer my questions.' He paused and gave a shadow of a smile. 'They always have. Eventually.' He began to walk towards the door. 'I am going to let you think about what I have just said. When I come back I will ask the same question again. It will be in your best interests for you to give me an answer.'

The door closed behind him, the guards remaining in the room. Despite the cool dampness of the walls a bead of sweat trickled down the nape of Kyle's neck. He had never been a coward, but he could think of better ways of spending his time than sitting in a room where blood had obviously been spilled, waiting for the moment when his own blood would, in all likelihood, mingle with the stains on the walls and the floor.

His interrogator was gone for what Kyle judged to be thirty or thirty-five minutes. When he returned he sat once more behind the table, resting his clasped hands lightly in front of him. 'You have now had time to think,' he said, his voice bereft of any inflection whatsoever. 'I will ask you again. What is the name of your division?'

Kyle knew that if he told him, it wouldn't end there. There would be other questions, hundreds of them. 'I'm not obliged to answer that question.' Contempt and defiance oozed from his every pore.

The officer smiled thinly. 'You are very foolish,' he said and nodded towards the guards at the door.

Behind him Kyle heard the door open and two sets of footsteps approach. He clenched his knuckles until they were white. The bastards could do whatever they wanted, but he wouldn't give them the satisfaction of seeing him break. He would die before allowing them to gloat over him.

His arms were wrenched behind him and his mouth tightened. His broken arm had mended while he had been on the trail north, but he was still protective of it. His elbows were strapped together and then his wrists. He gritted his teeth against the pain as his chest was forced outward. He had expected something different. He had expected them to make play of the barely healed skin on his back and head. Shackles were fastened around his ankles and then his legs were splayed out and a bar was run through the shackles to keep them that way.

*Trinh*, he thought. *I must think of Trinh.*

The strap was brought down and beneath the bar and then pulled, yanking the bar upward and forcing him into a contorted ball. He closed his eyes, fighting the cries that rose in his throat. He thought of Trinh, gentle-eyed and tender; he thought of her mischievous sense of fun, her beguiling naïveté.

His bones were being wrenched from their sockets, his muscles and tendons were being torn apart. He couldn't think of Trinh any longer. He thought only of wanting the excruciating agony to end.

It didn't end. It grew worse. Time no longer had any meaning. Periodically the straps would be released and his circulation would start to flow again, the pain as it did so almost as intense as that of the torture. He would be asked if he would now answer the questions put to him. Each time he refused, his interrogator would take another cigarette from the packet on the table and nod to his henchmen to restrap and shackle him and the agony would begin again.

At one time he thought the room was getting darker, as if night were approaching. Perhaps it was. Perhaps he had

454

been in hell the whole day. Or perhaps the room seemed dark because his eyes were full of blood.

He had vowed that he would die before allowing his torturers to gloat over his capitulation. He knew now that they weren't going to allow him the luxury of death. The agony he was suffering would not kill him, it would simply continue for ever and ever and ever. And he couldn't endure it. No one could. Now, when he was restrapped, eyeball to eyeball with his ass, he was also beaten. Bamboo clubs rained on his shins and elbows and knees. Rubber-strip whips cut into the barely healed flesh of his back. Fists smashed into his face. He vomited and kept vomiting and when he could croak out a sound other than a scream of pain, he pleaded with them for the pain to stop. And he promised to tell them anything that they wanted to know.

Afterwards, alone in his cell, he wept. The bastards had broken him. The information he had been able to give them had been minimal. But it would have made no difference if it had been top secret. He would still have given it. And the knowledge filled him with self-loathing.

For a week he was virtually ignored by his guards, and in that week something cold and rocklike entered into him. He had given into the bastards once, but he would not do so a second time. And there would be a second time, he was sure of it. It wasn't only military information that the North Vietnamese wanted from their prisoners. It was propaganda. The day would come when a uniformed figure would enter his cell and demand that he make a tape recording proclaiming how he repented of his war 'crimes', and admitting to being a 'Yankee imperialist aggressor'. At the thought of his father, or Serry, listening to any such babblings, his resolve became obsessional. He wouldn't do it. He had sunk as low as he was going to sink, and he would be damned to hell for all eternity before he would sink any lower.

At the end of seven days he was removed from his cell and taken once more down the corridor and out into the courtyard. The double gates at the inner end of the courtyard were opened and he was led through them into yet another underpass. This time it wasn't a tunnel, but a roof between two one-storey buildings. There was a further courtyard, slightly smaller than the first one, and to his intense relief he could see hands at the bars of the windows that looked out on to it.

He was marched across the courtyard and into the right-hand cell block. He could physically sense the nearness of other Americans and nearly sobbed with disappointment when he was led into another empty cell. Within minutes of his being left alone there, there came a tapping on the wall. He answered it eagerly, euphoric at making contact. Was it a fellow G.I.? The tapping continued in carefully spaced out rhythms. Kyle listened intently. Was it Morse? Was the guy in the cell next to him tapping out the Morse code? Whenever a guard was in the vicinity the tapping stopped, only to be continued later, in the same insistent rhythms.

Over the next few days tapping came from the cell on the other side of him as well. It wasn't Morse, he had worked that out nearly immediately, but it was obviously a similar code by which his fellow prisoners were communicating with each other. An alphabet code. And in order to participate, all he had to do was crack it.

He was still trying to fathom it out when he was moved from his cell and put in with another prisoner. His initial delight was slightly tempered by the fact that his fellow prisoner, a radar intercept officer who had been shot down in an F-4 Phantom, was sullen and uncommunicative and obviously suffering from some kind of mental breakdown. He had been a prisoner for eighteen months, and though Kyle could not get him to talk about himself, he did manage to get from him the key to the wall-tapping code.

The code was called the Smithy Harris code, and was named after the prisoner who had devised it. It was based on a crossword puzzle of letters, five lines down and five across. The first line across was A-B-C-D-E. To spell out a word containing one of these letters you made a tap on the wall to indicate that it was in the first line across, then paused and quickly tapped out one for A, two for B, and so on. The second line was F-G-H-I-J. Two taps indicated that the letter was in the second line, and then the taps followed the same pattern as for the first line. The letter K was not used at all, the letter C being used as a substitute in order to keep the letters to twenty-five, and not twenty-six.

The code transformed Kyle's life. Information could be passed and received around the prison. Conversations could be conducted via the walls. He discovered that as a helicopter jock he was a rarity in Hoa Lo, but that he wasn't alone in having capitulated to torture. The knowledge came as a kind of relief, but did not alter his fierce determination to withstand anything in the future rather than become a propaganda tool.

Tapping messages out, and receiving them, took painstaking time. Y-O-U A-R-E N-O-W I-N H-E-A-R-T-B-R-E-A-C H-O-T-E-L, his neighbour in the next cell tapped out to him when he first understood and began to use the code. T-H-E P-R-I-S-O-N A-S A W-H-O-L-E I-S C-N-O-W-N A-S T-H-E H-A-N-O-I H-I-L-T-O-N. T-H-E S-E-C-T-I-O-N W-H-E-R-E Y-O-U W-E-R-E I-N-T-E-R-R-O-G-A-T-E-D I-S N-E-W G-U-Y V-I-L-L-A-G-E. T-H-E-R-E A-R-E T-W-O M-O-R-E M-A-I-N S-E-C-T-I-O-N-S T-O T-H-E P-R-I-S-O-N. O-N-E O-F T-H-E-M I-S F-O-R W-H-E-N W-E M-O-V-E O-U-T O-F H-E-A-R-T-B-R-E-A-C, W-H-I-C-H I-S U-S-E-D A-S A R-E-C-E-I-V-I-N-G S-T-A-T-I-O-N. T-H-E O-T-H-E-R I-S L-A-S V-E-G-A-S A-R-E-A.

W-H-A-T I-S L-A-S V-E-G-A-S A-R-E-A? he tapped back, none too happy at the thought that if he was still in the receiving area, there were still, presumably, question sessions to undergo.

L-A-S V-E-G-A-S I-S A C-I-L-L-E-R came back through the wall. I-T I-S U-S-E-D F-O-R P-E-R-I-O-D-S O-F L-O-N-G-A-N-D B-R-U-T-A-L I-N-C-A-R-C-E-R-A-T-I-O-N. Y-O-U A-R-E B-E-T-T-E-R O-F-F H-E-R-E O-R I-N N-E-W G-U-Y T-H-A-N I-N V-E-G-A-S.

Kyle found it hard to believe that treatment anywhere in the Hilton could be worse than what he had received in New Guy Village. A chill ran down his spine. His decision not to cooperate if asked to make statements that could be used by the North Vietnamese for propaganda purposes would very likely lead him, eventually, into Las Vegas. It wasn't a prospect to look forward to, and he tried hard not to think about it, concentrating instead on culling every little bit of information he could via the wall taps.

He was asked to memorize the names of every man known to be imprisoned, so that if he were sent to another camp he could pass on all the names that he knew, and add new ones to the list. That way, if anyone escaped or was unexpectedly released, he could carry the names back to the States. There were over three hundred names and he memorized them all, in alphabetical order.

It came as a surprise to him to learn that somewhere on the route north Christmas had come and gone without him being aware of it. He wondered how Trinh had celebrated it, and remembering the family ancestral altar he had seen in her home, with candles flickering beside it, he wondered if she was perhaps more Buddhist than Catholic, and if she would have celebrated it at all.

Serry would have celebrated it. Serry would have been at Bedingham. He only had to close his eyes to imagine every aspect of Serry's Christmas. There would be a huge, decorated tree in the yellow and white formal living room. There would be log fires, holly and mistletoe, mince pies and mulled wine and carol singers. And if it hadn't been for her brother's stupidity on their wedding day, he would probably have been there, sharing it all with her. And he would never have met Trinh.

Despite his physical discomfort a smile tugged at the corner of his mouth. Trinh. God, but he loved her. When the present nightmare was over, he would track her down, wherever she might be. He would take her back to the States with him. Trinh was the only good thing to have come out of his time in Vietnam. Trinh, and his friendship with Chuck.

He sat on the low pallet in the cell, smoking one of the three cigarettes a day that were given them in Heartbreak. Chuck would tell Trinh that he had been shot down, and that he had not simply abandoned her. Chuck knew how serious they were about each other. He knew that their affair was not just the usual easy-come-easy-go arrangement enjoyed by the vast majority of Americans in 'Nam. He would have contrived a two-day pass to Saigon and would have gone straight to the International to tell her what had happened.

She would be waiting for him. She wasn't Serry, who he couldn't imagine waiting faithfully for anyone for even twenty-four hours. She was loyal and steadfast, and he was certain that she would wait years for him if necessary.

His body never recovered from the severity of the torture he had undergone on his arrival, and all through the long, tedious, pain-filled days of spring, the knowledge that Trinh was waiting for him sustained him.

He wasn't taken for questioning again for a long time. He knew the reason. New prisoners were being processed through New Guy Village and into Heartbreak thick and fast. America was obviously escalating the air war and the information to be obtained from shot-down B-52 and F-4 Phantom pilots was far superior to any that could be extracted from a mere helicopter pilot.

When they came for him again, it wasn't to try to extract further military information. It was to force him to make a written 'confession' that Hanoi could use for the purpose of anti-American propaganda.

It was just the beginning of the end for him, and he knew it. J-U-S-T D-O Y-O-U-R B-E-S-T fellow prisoners had tapped through the walls to him. T-H-E B-A-S-T-A-R-D-S W-I-L-L B-R-E-A-C Y-O-U. T-H-E-Y B-R-E-A-C E-V-E-R-Y-O-N-E E-V-E-N-T-U-A-L-L-Y. J-U-S-T D-O-N-T G-I-V-E I-N T-O T-H-E-M R-I-G-H-T A-W-A-Y. T-A-C-E A-S M-U-C-H A-S Y-O-U C-A-N F-I-R-S-T.

Kyle had no intention of giving in to them at all. He was taken to Room 19. It had been christened the Knobby Room by men unfortunate enough to have been questioned there. The nickname came from the fist-sized knobs of plaster on the walls designed to absorb the sound of screams.

The routine was exactly the same as it had been at his earlier interrogation. He was asked to write a statement confessing to war crimes. He refused. He was asked again, and at his second refusal his arms were once more yanked behind him and strapped tight and high at the elbows, almost separating his shoulder blades. His legs were forced into spurlike shackles, and a pipe and strong rope were used to lock his ankles into place.

As the pain intensified he struggled against it with mental strength. He would not write a statement that could be broadcast by Hanoi Radio. He would not. He would not. *He would not!*

When they returned him to his cell he was unconscious. His mute cellmate shook and shuddered, doing nothing to help him, terrified that he himself might be subjected to the same treatment.

The next day they came for him again. And the next. And the next.

T-H-R-O-W I-N T-H-E T-O-W-E-L C-I-D came the instructions via the tap code. Y-O-U H-A-V-E D-O-N-E Y-O-U-R B-E-S-T. D-O-N-T L-E-T T-H-E B-A-S-T-A-R-D-S C-I-L-L Y-O-U.

He couldn't throw the towel in. He was obsessed with shame at how easily he had capitulated when first under torture. He wouldn't give in to them again. He would endure all the fires of hell, but he vowed not to become a coward or a traitor.

Y-O-U C-A-N-T D-O A-N-Y M-O-R-E C-I-D the tap code repeated time and time again. N-O O-N-E I-S G-O-I-N-G T-O T-H-I-N-K A-N-Y L-E-S-S O-F Y-O-U F-O-R M-A-C-I-N-G P-R-O-P-A-G-A-N-D-A S-T-A-T-E-M-E-N-T-S F-O-R T-H-E-M. T-H-E W-H-O-L-E W-O-R-L-D W-I-L-L C-N-O-W I-T W-A-S O-B-T-A-I-N-E-D U-N-D-E-R T-O-R-T-U-R-E.

Kyle was no longer able to tap messages back. His fingers were broken, his nails wrenched from their beds. Somewhere in the part of his mind that was still functioning he knew he was being a fool. They were killing him by inches. He would never see Trinh again, never be able to take her to America. The knowledge made no difference. He was obsessed by his vow. Consumed by it. He would not be paraded before the world at large as a grovelling, humiliated traitor. He would die first. And he knew he was going to die soon.

They threw him in a cell in Vegas. He was deprived of sleep, deprived of food and water, and no comforting messages came through the walls. The scar tissue on his back had been sliced open by rubber whips and was festering and crawling with worms; he was covered in boils; every joint in his body was dislocated.

Then they took him into Room 18. The Meathook Room. He knew what they were going to do to him, and he knew he couldn't survive it. He thought of Trinh, of how her world would collapse when he did not return for her.

He was no longer screaming. He couldn't scream anymore. He could barely whimper. He thought of Serry as she had looked the day they had met at Bedingham, her pale gold hair falling water-straight to her waist. Serry, tall and high-breasted and magnificent, her crystal-grey eyes alight with joyous recklessness.

From a far distance he could hear the sound of Mick Jagger singing, and feel the warmth of the sun on his face as it filtered through the heavily laden branches of the beech trees. Then there was nothing. No music. No sunlight. He was flying. Flying higher than he had every flown before.

# CHAPTER TWENTY-FIVE

Gavin's emotions were in turmoil the five days that he spent with Dinh in the tunnels of Cu Chi. His main worry was Gabrielle. Somehow he had to let her know that he was alive and safe, yet he had no reliable means of doing so. Nhu would certainly write Gaby that he had been going to meet Dinh, but he was convinced that Nhu did not know Dinh planned to abduct him, and that she would be as alarmed and perplexed by his continuing absence as Gaby.

Dinh promised him that Nhu had been told about the mission, and that he was alive and well. Gavin hoped and prayed that he was speaking the truth.

'Because of the urgency with which my report is being awaited in Hanoi, our trek north will not be as arduous as it has been for me in the past,' Dinh said to him in a moment of rare confidence. 'Once we leave the Iron Triangle we will travel most of the way by jeep.'

Tingles prickled down Gavin's spine. He had heard the phrase 'Iron Triangle' before, on American lips. The area was rumoured to cover sixty square miles, and ever since the Second World War it had been a refuge for antigovernment forces. The area was cut by marshes and swamps and open rice paddies, and huge stretches of forest so thick that only foot trails could penetrate them, making penetration by American and South Vietnamese forces nearly impossible. It was in this area, to the northwest of Saigon and bordering the Cambodian border, that the Office of South Vietnam was rumoured to have its headquarters. Was that where they were going? To COSVN? To Viet Cong headquarters?

He knew better than to ask. Vietnamese were secretive by nature, and asking would end Dinh's quite extraordinary candour. The mystery of the COSVN's location obsessed the Americans. Jimmy Giddings had spoken of it as if it were a miniature Pentagon buried deep in the jungle, though when he had done so, Paul Dulles had corrected him, saying that in his opinion COSVN wasn't a place or a building, but that it was people.

Whatever it was, the Americans had gone to enormous lengths to find it and to bomb it into oblivion. So far, unsuccessfully. And now Gavin was probably going to walk right into it. If he had to wait a year before he could file his story, it would be worthwhile. He would have the scoop of a lifetime.

In the five days he spent in the tunnels, the area came under American surveillance three times. The first time, as US troops swarmed over the ground above them, they were so near that Gavin could smell their aftershave lotion.

'How can they not sense our presence?' he whispered to Dinh as the troops moved away, oblivious that they had been within feet of a North Vietnamese Army platoon, and an entire regiment of Viet Cong.

A slight smile touched Dinh's hard, straight mouth. 'Americans are not attuned to the earth as we Vietnamese. They look for the obvious. Even when they do stumble on to a tunnel entrance, it does not occur to them that it is anything but a short, underground bolt-hole. The trapdoors leading into the main complex are rarely discovered.' He paused, his eyes gleaming in the light from the makeshift oil lamp. 'And when they are, the discoverer does not usually live to tell the tale.'

Two days later Gavin saw first-hand what happened when a tunnel entrance was discovered. He and Dinh, and the handful of NVA men who were with Dinh, had been moving steadily through the tunnels in a northwesterly direction. The other occupants of the labyrinthine tunnel system were all Viet Cong. Their numbers staggered Gavin. Entire platoons were moving with ease beneath ground that was rigorously patrolled by South Vietnamese and American forces.

At one point they rested near a conference chamber where a small group of black-clad figures were in urgent conversation. On seeing Dinh, the leader of the group immediately approached him with slightly awed deference. Gavin could hear words that sounded like the name of a village, and then the Vietnamese name for Americans, but very little else. When the man had returned to his waiting companions, Dinh turned towards Gavin with a slight shrug of irritation.

'We are going to be delayed. The man who just spoke to me is the political commissar of the local defence force. The Americans swooped on his village a little less than an hour ago and in their search they found a tunnel entrance. They have blown the trapdoor away and are at the moment waiting for reinforcements before attempting to explore it further.'

'What will happen when they do? Will they simply lob dynamite down here?' Gavin asked, trying to sound casual about the prospect of being blasted into eternity.

'Our tunnels are too cleverly made for them to be able to cause much damage to the main complex from an entrance,' Dinh replied, a glimmer of amusement in his voice. 'We will go a little nearer and I will explain to you the steps that are being taken in order to turn events to our advantage.'

They were back to wriggling, bellydown, through the narrow communication tunnels. Above him, vibrating through the dark red earth, Gavin could hear the *whump-whump-whump* of helicopter rotor blades. They went up a three-foot shaft and into another communication tunnel and then Dinh motioned for him to crawl into a side alcove. Ahead of them Gavin could dimly discern the dark shape of another figure, a Viet Cong with his back towards them, crouched and waiting.

Ten minutes passed and then, as the sweat began to run into Gavin's eyes, there came the vibration of voices and

465

feet above them. No matter how many Americans had been brought in by helicopter, only one could enter the tunnel at a time. And when he did, the waiting Viet Cong would kill him.

Gavin began to shake. The situation was pure nightmare. He had to remain hunched and silent as an American slid into the tunnel to his death. If he called out he would probably be able to save him, but his own life would be forfeit.

There was the sound of a small earth fall, and Gavin knew the American was beginning his descent into the entrance shaft. All entrance shafts were shallow, little more than three feet in depth, and now Gavin saw why. The American had entered feet first, and as his feet touched the bottom of the shaft, and while his head and torso were still above ground, the Viet Cong several yards ahead of them fired at point-blank range into his undefended lower body.

Gavin clenched his nails so tight into his palms that he drew blood. At that moment he knew he had lost any innocence remaining to him. From now on he would feel, and be, old beyond his years.

There were cries of terror and agony from the wounded man, shouts of alarm from his comrades as they struggled to pull him free.

The Viet Cong in front of them had now turned towards them and was wriggling rapidly back down the tunnel towards the shaft leading into the lower communication tunnel. He paused, his hand flying once again to his pistol as he neared the side alcoves and he saw Gavin's pale, distinctly western face.

'*De ve nha,*' Dinh said softly. The Viet Cong stared hard at him for a moment and then continued his rapid retreat.

Gavin and Dinh followed hard on his heels. Behind him Gavin could hear the wounded American yelling desperately, '*For Christ's sake get me the hell outta here before that goddammed gook cuts off my balls!*'

Gavin knew damn well that when they did get him out, a barrage of firepower would be directed down the tunnel at their rear, and he propelled himself at top speed down the next, slightly deeper shaft, and into the second communications tunnel.

The Viet Cong had inserted himself into an alcove near the trapdoor above the shaft, and Gavin and Dinh wriggled past him like eels, not pausing until they had reached the trapdoor leading down into the main tunnel network.

'What happens now?' Gavin spat at him.

'If we are unlucky, they will throw gas canisters into the entrance shaft. The zigzag of the tunnels and the ventilation system will prevent the gas from poisoning the central complex, but there is not much chance that we would escape the fumes. If we are lucky, the Americans will do what they usually do. They will enter the first tunnel with the intention of rooting out whoever it was who injured their comrade.'

From Dinh's words Gavin realized with shock that it was possible the Americans still had no idea the tunnel could be anything other than a small, localized hiding place big enough to give shelter to one or two guerrillas.

In the darkness he could sense rather than see Dinh's rare smile. 'You will see that though we are now at a trapdoor leading down into the main tunnel system, this particular tunnel does not stop here. It continues on for another twenty-five yards.'

'Where does it lead?' Gavin whispered, listening fearfully for sounds of action from the first shaft.

'It leads nowhere. And if my comrades' plans are successful, it is all the Americans will ever find.'

There came the sound of first one pair of booted feet dropping cautiously to the floor of the first shaft, and then another.

'We must retreat to the main tunnel network to give my comrade room to manoeuvre. I will tell you what it is he is doing as he is doing it,' Dinh said, opening the trapdoor and slithering down into the black hole beyond.

Gavin followed quickly. As far as he was concerned, Dinh could have explained the entire exercise verbally, without having risked both their lives by bringing him along to watch.

Gunfire reverberated from the first communications tunnel down into the tunnel in which they were lying. Earth showered over them and Gavin was gripped by a new fear, a fear so terrible it almost made him lose control of his bowels. What if hand grenades and dynamite were thrown into the tunnel? What if the earth fell down in a wall both behind and in front of them? What if they were buried alive?

'The Americans are now entering,' Dinh whispered unnecessarily. 'My comrade will have removed the trapdoor to the second shaft and will be crouched in it, waiting for them.'

'And the gunfire?' Gavin whispered back, the blood pounding in his ears, his heart hammering so fast he thought it was going to give out.

'The Americans, firing down the tunnel ahead of them.'

Gavin wiped dry red clay from his face. The bullets would not find their mark. Their target was not hiding in the darkness ahead of them, but was concealed in a shaft leading downwards.

'What happens when the Americans crawl so far along the tunnel that they come to the shaft?'

'Wait,' Dinh said, his voice tense. 'And you will find out.'

A split second later the roar of an AK-47 blasted Gavin's eardrums. The whole earth shook around them as first one clip was let off and then another. Screams tore through the dank, enclosed darkness, and Gavin could feel his self-control galloping away from him. He didn't know if the screams were from the Viet Cong or the Americans, and he didn't care. He was bathed in pure terror. He wanted out. He wanted out as he had never wanted out before.

Dinh had begun to move again, wriggling fast and furiously deeper and deeper into the main tunnel network. When at last he reached an alcove and paused, he gasped out, 'That moment, as the Americans approach the second shaft, is the most dangerous moment of all. If they had rolled a hand grenade ahead of them and it had fallen into the shaft, then our comrade would have been killed. As it was, he waited until they were nearly on top of him and then he jackknifed out of the shaft in front of them, taking them by surprise.'

There came the sound of someone wriggling with practiced ease towards them, away from the hell of the continuing screams.

'It will be a long time before the Americans are able to remove their dead and wounded,' Dinh said comfortably. 'When they do, and when they pluck up the nerve to investigate again they will find the tunnel empty. The trapdoor to the second shaft will have been replaced, and will be indiscernible to them. They will simply crawl along the tunnel and into the decoy tunnel. At the far end of it they will find an escape hatch, assume that the guerrilla who inflicted the damage on them has escaped by it, and very thankfully regard their mission as complete. The dummy tunnel they have found will be dynamited and destroyed, and there will be no damage to the main network.'

The guerrilla who had, single-handed, inflicted such horrendous damage on the Americans slithered abreast of them.

'*Khong xau,*' Dinh said to him warmly.

Behind them, beyond the closed trapdoor, dull cries could still be heard. As Dinh and his comrade began to wriggle back towards the main complex of conference chamber and kitchen and sleeping chambers, Gavin followed them, consumed by horror and relief. He no longer felt like a journalist. He felt like a traitor. Not until he experienced an American bombing raid on Phu Hoa village some five days later did his sense of balance return.

They had left the tunnels behind them and their small party, consisting of himself and Dinh and two of Dinh's aides, had been travelling northwest at night, by bicycle.

'We will be able to replenish our supplies and rest at Phu Hoa,' Dinh said to him as the night sky began to pearl to grey, presaging dawn. 'I will also be able to renew some family contacts. A second cousin of mine is married to the local village chief and I have not seen her since we were children.'

Gavin was trying to work out what the relationship between Gaby and the village chief's wife must be, when dawn broke in a blazing crack of yellow and orange and crimson-rose, and the planes came.

There was no warning. There had been no sounds of gun-fire, no indication that any engagement was taking place in the vicinity between Viet Cong and ARVN or US troops. In the early dawn light the countryside looked spectacularly beautiful and peaceful.

They were bicycling through a plantation of banana and mango trees and there was very little low vegetation to hamper their progress. After the claustrophobia of the tunnels, the long night ride with humid air blowing soft against his face had been paradisiacal. In the light of the rising sun, Gavin could see a cluster of straw-thatched houses ahead. There would be breakfast of sorts. Eggs, if they were lucky, and almost certainly fruit. He was happy. He had survived what had to be the worst part of the ordeal, the tunnels at Cu Chi. He had established an amazingly close rapport with Dinh. And he had a news story that, when it was told, would establish his reputation as a war reporter.

It was Dinh who heard the planes first. '*B-52s!*' he yelled, throwing himself from his bicycle headlong on to the ground, his hands over his ears. Almost simultaneously the two young NVA officers riding with him followed suit. Gavin crashed to the ground a mere split second behind them. The planes never broke the early morning cloud cover. They could have been B-52s as Dinh averred. They could also have been Phantoms or F-105s. Whatever they were, they were unloading everything that they carried on to the unsuspecting village.

Even with his hands pressed tight over his ears, Gavin could hear the whistling of the bombs as they fell. '*Jesus, Mary and Joseph,*' he whispered beneath his breath, and then he was rocked almost senseless by the sound of the explosions. The ground heaved and kicked beneath him, giant fissures cracking wide. He dug his elbows and feet into the earth to gain some kind of purchase, but it was impossible. His body wouldn't adhere to the ground. He was plucked from it as if he were a dry leaf and carried amid a maelstrom of felled trees and gouged earth. When at last his body slammed back on to the ground he was fifty yards from where he had dived from his bicycle. There was no sign now of the bicycle. There was no sign of Dinh or the accompanying NVA officers. There was only a choking cloud of thick dust, the crackle of leaping flames, and the terrified screams of women and children.

He tried to crawl to his feet, but his legs wouldn't support him. Twice he stumbled and fell before managing to stay upright and run swaying towards the village and the flames and the screams. Through the dust and still-falling debris he saw Dinh and veered pantingly towards him.

'*Why?*' he shouted to him, unable to hear his own voice. Unable to hear anything. '*What was the provocation? The reason?*'

Dinh was shouting back at him, and like a lip-reader he read the words, 'No reason! There doesn't have to be a reason! Perhaps a US platoon is held down some miles from here and called in air support! Perhaps it is a matter of confused targeting! Perhaps it is a matter of the pilots merely off-loading their bombs! This, Comrade, is the war as suffered by the peasants. This is why you are here. To see and experience it.'

While Dinh had been shouting across at him, they had been running in the direction of the village. The two young

471

NVA officers were also on their feet and running. Their small party had miraculously sustained no injuries, but then, they had been on the periphery of the attack. It was the village that had sustained the full blast of the bombs.

They ran past the dead and dying buffalo, past terrified children running out into the banana and mango plantations away from the engulfing flames.

'Christ! What do we do when we *get* there!' Gavin yelled desperately. 'We have no medical kits! No plasma! We can't get these people to a hospital!'

Dinh turned his head towards him and smiled. It was a terrible smile. 'War is a different game without dust offs and quick evacuation to a military hospital, eh, Comrade?'

Gavin did not reply. They were among the injured who had managed to escape from the flames. A girl of about ten years old was laid on the ground, hideous gurgling noises coming from her throat. Her chest had been stoved in, the skin burnt and withered. One arm had been blown off just above the elbow joint, and though the upper portion of her face was still recognizable, the lower half was a nightmare of charred flesh.

Gavin fell on his knees beside her. He had nothing with which to ease her agony. There was not one damned thing that he could do for her. '*Oh God, oh Jesus!*' he sobbed as Dinh grabbed hold of his arm, pulling him away, dragging him onward.

The dead and dying lay scattered over a wide area. Although dawn had only just broken, several of the men had already been making their way towards their rice paddies. A small boy whose task was to care for the family buffalo lay dead beside it in a dyke, the rope with which the animal had been tethered still held tightly in his hand.

A Vietnamese wearing only a loose pair of cotton trousers ran through the mayhem towards them.

'See what they have done?' he cried to Dinh. 'See what they have done to my village!'

He was weeping, beating his bony chest with his fists. 'They have killed Sang! They have murdered the mother of my children!'

Dinh had his arms around him, hugging him tight, and then he was saying, 'Where is she? Take me to her.'

Gavin stumbled after them, aware that the distraught Vietnamese was obviously the village chief and that Sang must be the second cousin Dinh was so looking forward to seeing again.

She had been dragged clear of the flames engulfing the straw-thatched houses and lay on her back on the dusty ground, two small children clinging to her lifeless hand, sobbing fiercely.

Dinh knelt down beside her, his face a carved wooden mask. He felt for a pulse, a heartbeat, and then, his shoulders slumped, he slowly rose once more to his feet.

Gavin looked down at the dead woman. She had been no longer young and had the old, worn look of every peasant woman who was no longer in her early twenties. But her hair was still beautiful. Long and glossy-black, it lay spread around her like a fan.

Gavin felt his throat tighten. Somewhere, however distant, there had been a blood link between this woman and Gaby. Crazily, as he stood in the middle of the bombed and burning, obliterated Vietnamese village, the words of the seventeenth-century English poet and churchman John Donne came into his mind. 'No mind is an Island, entire of itself; every man is a piece of the Continent, a part of the main; if a *clod* be washed away by the sea, Europe is the less, as well as if a promontory were, as well as if a manor of thy friends or of thine own were; any man's death diminishes me, because I am involved in Mankind; And therefore never send to know for whom the bell tolls. It tolls for thee.'

There was nothing more that could be done for Sang, but there were scores of other villagers who needed whatever primitive treatment could be given them.

For the rest of the morning he worked with Dinh, bathing wounds with freshly boiled water, bandaging with makeshift lengths of torn cloth, fixing splints with sawn-off lengths of bamboo. It had been countless hours since he had last slept, and as he wearily helped the villagers to bury their dead, Dinh said to him again, 'This is why you are here, Comrade. To see and to report.'

Gavin nodded and wiped the sweat from his eyes. The question Dinh would never answer was when would he be allowed to file his report.

They worked all through the long, hot day and then rested briefly with the still-dazed survivors. No one showed surprise that the attack had taken place. No one offered a reason for it. It was possible that the village had been destroyed by criminal accident, and it was equally possible that it had been destroyed because it was reported to be a Viet Cong stronghold. Gavin had no way of knowing which was the truth. He knew only that where the village had existed there was now only a charred crater. And that Sang and dozens of her neighbours had died a hideous and violent death.

At night he, Dinh and the two accompanying NVA officers set off once more, their bicycles freakishly unscathed, heading northwest, towards the Cambodian border and the Ho Chi Minh Trail.

During the following arduous days and nights his rapport with Dinh deepened. Dinh told him why he had decided to go north, and what life had been like for him in the first painful years away from his family.

'I am a southerner, Comrade. A Saigonese. Even after all these years of living in the North, I am still a Saigonese.'

'Then what made you leave?' Gavin asked, excitement gripping his stomach muscles. Dinh's conversation was almost always conducted in official Communist jargon. The words *comrade*, *imperialist*, and *puppet regime* peppered his every sentence. His present friendly simplicity indicated that confidences might be about to be shared.

'I left in order to be able to fight the French under the only man who appeared to me to be capable of doing so. That man was Vo Nguyen Giap. At Dien Bien Phu we achieved our success. When we raised our flag over the shattered French command post, all of us who had fought so hard to rid our land of foreign domination were euphoric. We thought that Vietnam would now be governed by officials of our choosing. But then came the Geneva agreement.'

He paused for a long moment. They were sitting around a small campfire after a hard day's travelling. The two NVA officers had gone down to a nearby lake to try their luck at catching fish, and the only sound was that of insects in the surrounding undergrowth.

Gavin remained silent, waiting. At last Dinh said heavily, 'Vietnam was to receive independence, but she was also to be temporarily partitioned at the seventeenth parallel until elections were held. The prime minister in the South, Ngo Dinh Diem, reneged on his promise to hold elections, knowing full well that if elections were held, Ho would be in and he would be out.'

The flames crackled and spat. A small lizard ran across Gavin's booted foot. 'Under Diem the government in the South became increasingly oppressive. Men who had valiantly fought to free Vietnam of the French were regarded by Diem as rivals for power. They were hunted down and murdered. And it wasn't only those who actively fought the French who suffered. Very soon even his mildest supporters were herded into prison camps.'

Gavin remembered the countless US statesmen who had declared that South Vietnam was the model of a 'free world democracy' which America was committed to defend against the 'Communist threat'. Had they known the truth? When President Kennedy had made his inaugural address and charismatically stated 'Let every nation know, whether it wishes us well or ill, that we shall pay any price, bear any burden, meet any hardship, support any friend, oppose any foe to assure the survival and the success of liberty,' had

475

he known what kind of government he was supporting in South Vietnam? Had he known the kind of 'democracy' it was that he was calling on his countrymen to defend and to perhaps lay down their lives for? Gavin hoped passionately that he had not.

'It was then I knew that I could not return to Saigon,' Dinh continued, staring broodingly into the flames. 'As I had been active in fighting the French, it was only a matter of time before I would have been rounded up and killed. And so I gave my loyalty to the only man worthy of it, Ho Chi Minh.'

There came a sound of leaves being crushed underfoot as the two NVA officers returned from their fishing trip.

'It must have been very lonely for you,' Gavin said quietly, knowing how important family was to him.

Dinh nodded, but the two officers were now within earshot and he said merely, 'From that time on my overriding aim has been the reunification of Vietnam under Communist control. To that end I have relinquished family, personal ambition, and personal happiness.'

The two NVA officers were sitting down beside them, triumphantly displaying their catch. Before he congratulated them, and before he began to help in skewering the fish in order to roast them, Dinh turned his head. His eyes met Gavin's. 'And I have no regrets,' he said simply. 'None at all.'


For the next two weeks they continued northwest towards Cambodia, travelling only at night. They were heading towards the Fishhook area, where Cambodian territory bulged down into Vietnam like a gigantic teat.

The trail ended on the enormous Mimot rubber plantation. A wooden gate barred the way across the trail and there was a control point manned by half a dozen guards. As Dinh spoke with the guards, discussing him Gavin was sure, he felt dizzy with relief and euphoria. He was at COSVN, the famous Central Office of South Vietnam. No reporter had ever gained entry before him, and he doubted if any would after him. He had scored a momentous first and he burned with the longing to file his story.

'Come,' Dinh said to him. The heavy gate was lifted and they were escorted down the trail beyond by two of the guards.

The jungle vegetation on either side of them was thick and lush. Wild orchids ran riot, their wax-white cups stark against the dark green foliage; vines and creepers covered the trees so thick overhead that the sunlight fell through them in bright, slanting bars. Away from the trail, half hidden under the jungle canopy, were houses built peasant-style, and half a dozen long, low buildings with entrances to a tunnel system clearly visible.

They were taken to one of the houses nearest to the trail, and it became clear that only Gavin, under guard, was to be left there.

'Take this opportunity to rest, Comrade,' Dinh said as a look of unease flashed across Gavin's face. 'I and my companions must make our reports to our superior officers. There is much for us to discuss, and it may be some time before I see you again.'

It was three days. He was fed sparingly on boiled rice, a small hunk of salt, and dried fish. It was a diet he was becoming accustomed to. Looking down at a frame that was becoming increasingly gaunt, he wondered what Gaby would say when she saw him. In the loneliness of his temporary isolation he could almost hear her husky, unchained laughter.

His throat tightened and he clenched his fists. He must not allow his thoughts to dwell longingly on Gaby. If he did, he could become completely unstrung. The only way of surviving the tremendous opportunity that he had been given was by suppressing all thoughts of normality. Like an alcoholic, he had to live one day at a time.

However impressive Dinh's rank had been at Cu Chi, at COSVN it was dwarfed by the men of real power.

Later, when they were in the jeep travelling north again, he learned that not only was General Tran Nam Trung, the commander-in-chief of the National Liberation Forces, one of the senior officers that Dinh had to report to, but that he had also had to make his report to Pham Hung, a Politburo member and first party secretary, and General Hoang Van Thai, commander-in-chief of all northern forces in the South. It was a thunderingly impressive lineup.

'And now it's straight ahead for the North,' Dinh said to him with satisfaction as they vaulted into the jeep that had been provided for them. 'And think yourself lucky, Comrade, that you are travelling now and not ten years ago when I first made the journey. Then it was nothing but a near-impassable foot track snaking down from the North over the Truong Son mountain range.'

'Is the route still the same as the original?' Gavin asked curiously, deeply thankful to be exchanging the discomfort of his bicycle for the relative comfort of the jeep.

Dinh nodded as one of the NVA officers took the wheel. 'Yes, though now it is not just one single track but a network of routes running roughly parallel with cross-links at strategic intervals.'

'And for the moment we travel through Cambodia?'

'For the moment,' Dinh said, flashing one of his rare smiles.

There were times, in the nights that followed as they bumped and swayed over crated tracks, when Gavin almost longed to be back on a bicycle. Without a map he had only a hazy idea of where they were, and sometimes he was not even sure which country they were in, Cambodia, Vietnam, or Laos.

One night they only narrowly avoided being spotted by enemy planes as they crossed wide fields of thatch near Pleiku. For a little while after that he was able to judge where they were because Pleiku was a name that meant something to him. In February 1965 the Viet Cong had attacked the US base at Pleiku and he remembered it being referred to as a traditional market town in the central highlands.

From then on the route became increasingly mountainous and the amount of heavily camouflaged traffic on the trail continued to amaze him. After crossing the Ben Hai River they had descended into the foothills of the Truong Son. The massive mountain range ran like a backbone through North and South, but now there were no more perilous passes to negotiate. Instead, they were soon in thick forest and it was then, when for the first time attack seemed unlikely, that invisible B-52s bombarded the stretch of trail on which they were travelling.

As before, there was no warning. The world simply erupted around them in an apocalyptic frenzy. Although Gavin learned afterwards that the centre of the bombing had been over a mile away, the sonic roar of explosions tore at his eardrums, reducing him once again to total deafness. The jeep was lifted in the air by the blast and thrown yards off the trail, landing on its side. A blow to his head left him with no memory of how he crawled from the wreckage. He could only remember, as the attack continued, pressing himself into the earth and losing control of both his bladder and his bowels.

When at last it was over, he couldn't believe that he was alive. He forced himself to his knees, and then to stumble to his feet. 'Dinh!' he shouted into a ringing silence. 'Dinh!'

Fifty yards away two figures moved slowly, lifting themselves cautiously from the ground. Neither of them was Dinh. A new fear gripped Gavin, even worse than the mind-bending fear he had just experienced. 'Dinh!' he shouted, his voice cracking. 'DINH!'

'I am here, Comrade,' a voice said from behind him.

Gavin spun around, nearly sick with relief. 'Christ! I thought you were dead. I thought we were *all* dead!'

Dinh flashed him one of his rare grins, brushing debris from his uniform. 'Fear is debilitating, Comrade. You will have to learn not to capitulate to it so easily.' There was no censure in his voice, only amusement. 'Let us see if the jeep is still roadworthy. If it isn't, we have a long trek ahead of us.'

Together the four of them managed to rock the jeep back on to its wheels.

'The petrol tank is still intact,' one of the NVA officers said optimistically. 'I don't think we're going to have a problem.'

They didn't. Ten minutes later, with freshly hacked saplings camouflaging the hood, they were trundling north again.

'In another few minutes we shall be on a very safe section of the trail,' Dinh said to Gavin in confidence.

Gavin looked across at him suspiciously. 'We're not going underground again, are we?'

Dinh grinned again. He was beginning to enjoy Gavin's company. 'No, Comrade. For the next few miles we are going to travel by stream.'

They didn't take sampans. Instead, the NVA officer at the wheel simply drove into the shallow water, using the bed of the stream as if it were a road, constantly changing gear as he moved from sandy stretches to pebbled beds or to deeper portions.

'These sections of the trail are difficult to spot from the air,' Dinh said, visibly relaxing. 'The bushes on either bank give natural camouflage and the water erases all traces of movement immediately. Deeper streams are used to good account as well. Supplies are packed into waterproof containers and floated downstream from one supply post to another.'

Gavin believed him. He was beginning to think that there was nothing that he now wouldn't believe about NVA ingenuity.

The next day, at a busy supply post, they exchanged their battered jeep for a six-wheel-drive ZIL army truck.

'In which we will drive into Hanoi,' Dinh said, highly satisfied at the progress they were making. 'There is no more

480

jungle to negotiate. From here on we should experience no more delays.'

He was overly optimistic. Within an hour they came under attack again, this time from three F-4s. They survived the attack unscathed, but those travelling in trucks ahead of them were not so lucky.

It was dusk the next day when Dinh prodded him lightly in the side and said, 'You've been asleep for the last hour, Comrade. If you sleep any longer, you will miss our entry into Hanoi.'

Gavin shot upright in his seat, his heart beginning to beat in thick, short strokes. Hanoi! Whatever he had envisaged when he had left Paris for Saigon, it had not been this. To be riding in a Russian truck, accompanied by three NVA officers, into *Hanoi*! It was incredible! Unbelievable!

The shanty houses of the suburbs gave way to gracious stone-built mansions. On their right-hand side the broad, deep waters of the Lake of the Restored Sword gleamed dully. On their left-hand side, as more houses came into view, Gavin could see that despite their original grandeur, their façades were now crumbling, their paintwork peeling.

'Your first night in Hanoi will be one of comfort,' Dinh said, watching Gavin's reactions to everything with interest. 'The French built a splendid hotel in the city centre, the Metropole. A room has been booked there for us. You will excuse me this evening if I leave you almost immediately. I have to report to my superiors.'

Gavin nodded, unable to drag his gaze from the sombre streets. They drew up outside a huge, grandiose building that looked unutterably drab. But still Gavin was overwhelmed at his good fortune. He was in Hanoi. *Hanoi*. With luck he would soon be interviewing General Giap. Possibly even Ho himself.

# CHAPTER TWENTY-SIX

As she sat on the plane, flying from San Francisco to Washington, Abbra knew that she was on the verge of permanently alienating herself from her father-in-law. He regarded all antiwar demonstrators as traitors, and she knew that when he discovered she'd been involved in the march on the Pentagon, he would be both bewildered and outraged.

She gazed out of the window at banks of cloud and an autumn sun and wondered what Lewis's reaction would be. He had always believed implicitly that American involvement in Indochina was both a moral and a political necessity. Would he still think so? She had no way of knowing.

The plane began to descend through the clouds towards Washington's National Airport. She had no friends in the city; she knew no one who would be participating in the march. Scott would have come with her if it weren't football season but she was no longer able to ask Scott to accompany her anywhere. Their days of easygoing camaraderie were over.

She clenched her hands tightly in her lap. She would not think of Scott. Thinking of Scott was almost as painful as thinking of Lewis. Instead, she would think of the days ahead of her in Washington. She would need to check into a hotel, to find out where the meeting point for the beginning of the march was to be, and she would need to keep an eye out for other women who were in the same position as herself, women whose husbands were also either prisoners of war or missing in action in Vietnam.

In the first class cabin of a Boeing 707, Serena slipped on eyeshades and stretched her long, suntanned legs out in front

482

of her. There were another six hours before the plane was due to land at Washington's Dulles International Airport, and she intended spending the time asleep.

A stewardess asked her quietly if she would like a blanket and she nodded. It was 19 October. As the planned march on the Pentagon was to take place on the twenty-first, it meant that she would have to wait until the twenty-second before travelling on to Atlantic City and visiting Chuck Wilson.

She had not communicated with him since April, when he had written to say that he had been discharged from the hospital and was going to his uncle's ranch for the summer to recuperate. For all she knew, he could still be in Wyoming. If he was, she had no address for him, and if his uncle's last name wasn't Wilson, tracking him down would be impossible.

She began to drift off to sleep, wondering why his letters had been so curt and odd in tone, wondering if the antiwar demonstration in Washington was going to be similar to the one she had participated in in London, wondering what the French girl would be like who had written to her in response to her *Washington Post* letter, and wondering if they would manage to meet, as they had arranged, at the Lincoln Memorial before the march began.

Gabrielle drove into Washington on Route 46 with the same nonchalant expertise with which she drove in Paris. Their gig the night before had been in Baltimore, and though Radford still planned on making the march, there had been problems with the sound system and he had been forced to stay behind, ironing out the kinks.

It was a year and one month since Gavin had dropped so precipitately from sight. Since then there had been not a word about him, not even a rumour. Nhu's letters still arrived, strained and distressed, but she never mentioned him. Gabrielle did not believe he was dead. Why was she so *certain* that he was still alive?

483

However hard she tried, she could find no logical reason. Her conviction was based on instinct, nothing more. Her hands tightened fractionally on the wheel. Instinct was something that had never failed her, and she was willing to stake her life that it was not failing her now. Gavin was alive. All she could do was live through the time until he returned home.

She turned left, heading towards the Lincoln Memorial. Was that true? Was passively living through the intervening time all that she could do? She was half Vietnamese. Saigon had been her home, was, in her heart of hearts, still her home.

'*Mon Dieu*,' she whispered softly under her breath. She began to slow down, no longer able to concentrate on her driving, her heart racing.

Why hadn't she thought of it before? Merciful heaven, how could she have been so *stupid* as to not have thought of the obvious months earlier? She would go to Vietnam. She would make contact with whoever it was who had told Nhu that there would be no further news of Dinh and Gavin. She would follow the route that they had taken, and she would find Gavin herself!

The crowds were enormous. Abbra had never seen so many people all gathering together with one purpose in mind. The crush had been so dense that it had taken her over an hour to walk from her hotel in N Street, close by the White House, to the rallying point of the march, the Lincoln Memorial, a little over a mile away. The lawns around the memorial were black with people camping out. The majority of them were long-haired, and outlandishly dressed in Afghan coats and love beads, but a surprising number were no longer young.

There were middle-aged and middle-class protesters among the throng. The angular, silver-haired figure of Dr Benjamin Spock, the baby expert, was clearly visible, as were other notable personalities. Abbra caught a fleeting glimpse of both Arthur Miller and Norman Mailer before the throng

484

closed around them and they were lost to view amid a sea of waving placards.

Some of the placards had pictures of President Johnson on them, and were headed with the words WAR CRIMINAL in scarlet print. Others bore the words OHIO STATE, GET US OUT OF VIETNAM, BRING OUR BOYS HOME, MAKE LOVE NOT WAR, and STOP KILLING, STOP IT NOW.

A large contingent jostling near her was carrying red and white flags with yellow stars on them. She stared at the flags for a moment, puzzled, and then understanding dawned. They were Viet Cong flags. Horrified, she began to push through the crowd away from them. She was against the war, and didn't care who knew it, but that didn't mean that she had become a Viet Cong supporter, and she didn't want to be mistaken for one.

As the crowd began to move off, heading towards the Arlington Memorial Bridge, Abbra saw a girl who looked as bemused as she herself felt. Elegant and willowy, with pale blond hair falling straight down her back, she stood nearly a full head taller than most of those milling around her. A sumptuous wolf-fur coat protected her from the October chill, and because she wore it negligently thrown open, with her hands thrust deep in her pockets, Abbra could see that the dress beneath the coat was white and ravishingly short, barely skimming her thighs. Knee-high snakeskin boots and a distinctive silk Union Jack scarf completed the ensemble, and looking at her, Abbra wondered if the day would ever come when she, too, would be as stunningly, as effortlessly, sophisticated.

As the chant 'Hell no, we won't go' was taken up by the thousands around her, Abbra began to squeeze her way across to the girl who, despite the very British scarf, she was sure was Scandinavian.

'It's amazing, isn't it?' she said when she at last reached her. 'I never imagined so many people would be here. There must be 40 or 50,000 at least.'

485

'More, probably,' the girl said with a grin. Her voice was low and attractive, the accent not Scandinavian but decidedly English.

'Do you mind if I walk with you?' Abbra asked a little shyly. 'I was nearly swallowed up a few moments ago by a group carrying Viet Cong flags, and though I'm against the war, I don't want to be seen as a Viet Cong supporter.'

'Oh?' the girl queried, falling into step beside her. 'Why not?'

Abbra paused for a second. She very rarely spoke of Lewis, and never to strangers. Now she heard herself saying with surprising ease, 'My husband is an MIA.'

Eyes the colour of smoked quartz held hers. 'And mine is a POW,' Serena said, holding out her hand. 'My name is Serena Anderson, and I'm very pleased to meet you.'

Abbra shook her hand tightly. For an insane moment she wanted to cry.

'I'm Abbra, Abbra Ellis,' she said thickly, knowing that at last she had found someone who understood her suffering, someone with whom she could share her grief and her hopes. 'Have you been at antiwar demos before?'

Serena nodded. 'In London. Outside the American Embassy.' She flashed Abbra her wide, dazzling smile. 'I thought the numbers there were enormous, but this is incredible! I was supposed to be meeting another POW wife here. A French girl whom I've never met before. If you see anyone wearing a silk scarf replica of the French flag, let me know. It will be Gabrielle.'

They had reached the bridge and a crisp, chill wind was blowing off the waters of the Potomac. Abbra was wearing a bright red jacket over a dove-grey turtleneck sweater and dark grey trousers, and she pulled the collar of the jacket up high around her throat.

Serena plunged her hands even deeper into the pockets of her coat. 'My husband, Kyle, is being held in Hanoi. In Hoa Lo prison.'

486

All around them the chant 'Peace now, peace now' had been taken up and Abbra had to shout as she replied, 'My husband's name is Lewis. He's a captain and was serving with a four-man mobile advisory team deep in the Delta. He and his men were ambushed on one of the canals shortly after searching a village that was suspected of harbouring North Vietnamese troops. A survivor said that he saw Lewis being taken prisoner by North Vietnamese who had attacked them. That was a little over a year ago.' Her eyes were suddenly overbright, 'There's been no news of him since,' she finished tightly.

'Jesus,' Serena said. For a moment she didn't say anything else. She couldn't. In coming to the march she had hoped that she would meet another woman in the same situation as herself, and she had met one whose situation was worse. At least she knew where Kyle was. There was even the faint hope that he was receiving her letters. Abbra had no such hopes. At last she said simply, 'I'm sorry, that's really tough.'

The words were trite and inadequate, but as their eyes met, she knew that Abbra understood the depth of feeling that was behind them.

'Do you think there's going to be any trouble?' she shouted across to Abbra as she caught her first sight of the thousands of US army troops and state marshals and national guardsmen who surrounded the Department of Defense.

Abbra had no previous experience of antiwar demonstrations, but she shook her head. 'No. David Dellinger is the main organizer of the march, and he's a lifelong pacifist. The purpose is simply to seal off the Pentagon through sheer numbers so that no one can get in or out. Because of the scores of different groups of people taking part – women's groups and church groups and war veterans and civil rights pacifists, as well as students and black militants and left-wing intellectuals – Dellinger figures that the government will *have* to recognize how widespread opposition to the war is.'

487

They were near enough now to see the rifle barrels being held at half guard by the soldiers, and Serena, remembering the violence that had taken place at the much smaller demonstration outside the American Embassy in London, hoped that her conviction was well founded.

'What would your husband think of all this?' she asked curiously over the roars of chants of 'Johnson *out*! Johnson *out*!'

Abbra hesitated for a telltale second, and her cheeks coloured slightly. 'I guess he wouldn't like it, but when he comes home, I think that he will understand why I did it.'

They were no longer moving forward, and the crowd around them were so tightly packed that it was impossible to move more than a few inches to either the left or right.

'The enemy, we believe, is Lyndon Johnson!' one of the organizers of the march declared ringingly from the Pentagon's main entrance as the vigil began. 'He was elected to the presidency as a peace candidate and within three months he has betrayed us!'

'Do you think those things are loaded?' Serena asked Abbra, her eyes once more focusing on the half-raised rifles.

Abbra shook her head, a smile of amusement quirking the corners of her mouth. 'No. How could they be? This is America, Serena. Not some third world dictatorship!'

As Serena saw some of the young women at the front of the crowd flirting with the soldiers and placing flowers in the rifle barrels, she laughed at her idiocy. 'Sorry, I have a brother who always suspects the worst where authority is concerned, and some of his paranoia must have rubbed off on me.'

A wave of singing rippled through the vast throng. 'All we are saying, is give peace a chance,' thousands of voices sang in unison. Serena and Abbra sang with them, Abbra deeply grateful that she had not asked how her parents and her father-in-law would react when they knew of her participation in the march, and Serena far more moved than she had expected to be by the sight of so many Americans demonstrating against a war that their country was committed to.

'*Can't we go any further forward?*' Serena shouted across the roar of voices. '*Can't we get inside the building?*'

Abbra shook her head, blue-black hair swinging silkily against the upturned collar of her jacket. '*No. The permit for the demonstration allows us to assemble on the blacktop parking plaza outside the Pentagon's main entrance, and on the nearby lawns, but though public visitors are allowed into parts of the Pentagon, none are being allowed in today.*'

Serena was disappointed. Even Lance would have been impressed if she'd been able to enter the American government's military headquarters.

An Indian summer sun had broken through the clouds, and all around them coats were being shed. The unmistakable sweet-sweet odour of pot drifted over their heads and, looking around her, Abbra realized for the first time that they were no longer amongst a mixed section of the crowd – women's groups and church groups and middle-aged intellectuals – but that they were deep in a crush of hippies and left-wing activists.

She was just about to suggest to Serena that they edge their way back into a more moderate flank, when scuffles broke out a few yards away from them.

As the singing around them changed to shouting and the crowd began to sway disruptively she shouted, '*What's happening, Serena? Can you see?*'

'*Dellinger!*' a long-haired student in front of her yelled back before Serena could reply. '*He's been arrested for sitting in front of troops who ordered him to move on!*'

From that moment the tone of the demonstration changed. The left-wing activists surrounding them began to taunt and jeer the military police who were standing on the wall that separated the lawns from the parking plaza.

To the left of Abbra a youth wearing a Viet Cong flag tucked into his headband, picked up a stone and threw it

489

at the nearest MP. Other left-wing demonstrators began to follow suit.

'I think it's time we made a discreet retreat,' Serena shouted. 'If Dellinger is the pacifist you say he is, this is the very last thing he would want to have happen.'

Abbra agreed wholeheartedly. The left-wing activists carrying Viet Cong flags were only a tiny fraction of the crowd, but they were an ugly minority and were obviously eager to cause trouble.

The trouble came quickly. As she and Serena tried to force their way towards a women's group who were carrying a twenty-foot banner with the words SUPPORT OUR GI's. BRING THEM HOME! emblazoned on it, full-scale fighting and arrests broke out.

It seemed to Abbra afterwards that none of the activists who had actually caused the disturbance were the ones being hit on the head with federal marshals' nightsticks. As the marshals launched into the sea of protesters, it was students and hippies who bore the full brunt of the attack.

She was aware of Serena grasping her hand tightly to prevent herself from falling, of the blinding sting of tear gas, and then, as she fell against him, the long-haired student who had shouted to her that Dellinger had been arrested, was seized by a federal marshal. In horrified disbelief she saw the marshal raise his club, saw the student cover his head with his arms and his hair fly as the club made contact with his head and he sank down on to his knees.

'No!' she screamed, wrenching herself away from Serena's grasp, throwing herself on to the marshal, dragging hold of his arm as he raised the club again. '*No! No! No!*'

The marshal threw her off as if she were an irritating fly. His club came down again, and this time the force of the blow knocked the student's black loafers from his feet. As Abbra scrambled hysterically to her knees, she could see the blood pouring down from his hair on to the cement surface of the plaza. 'Bastard!' she screamed at the marshal, using a word she had never used in anger ever before in her life. 'You pathetic, cowardly, *bastard!*'

The marshal turned towards her, his arm rising again. All around them fellow demonstrators, male and female, were being clubbed and hauled off to police vans. Serena grabbed hold of a discarded coat that was being trampled underfoot and hurled it over the marshal's head. '*Quick!*' she shouted to Abbra. '*For Christ's sake, run!*'

Abbra tried to, but the crush was too dense. With Serena once more grasping tight hold of her, she pushed and shoved in Serena's wake, away from the marshals and their crucifying billy clubs. As tears from the gas poured down her face she was aware with surprise that she was not remotely frightened. She was angry, angry at the troublemakers who had betrayed the demonstration organizers and turned what had been a peaceful, dignified antiwar protest into a bloody brawl, and furiously, blazingly angry at the brutality of the federal marshals.

As arrest after arrest took place, a voice in the crowd began singing *The Battle Hymn of the Republic*, and more and more voices joined in. Singing lustily, almost resigned to the fact that they, too, would eventually be grabbed hold of and dragged off into one of the waiting police vans, Abbra and Serena tried to remain on their feet and to push through to the rear of the crush. As they did so, fresh localized spots of fighting between troops and demonstrators erupted.

'Oh, God,' Serena said resignedly. 'Here they come again.'

They had reached the fringes of a large contingent of black demonstrators. Abbra could see one placard with the words OLD SOLDIERS NEVER DIE . . . YOUNG ONES DO being carried by a uniformed black army veteran. Another placard bore the words NOT WITH MY LIFE YOU DON'T.

From somewhere in the distance Abbra was aware that *The Battle Hymn of the Republic* had ended and that *America the Beautiful* was now being sung defiantly. As she lustily launched into the second line, a half dozen of the black demonstrators were knocked to the ground by nightstick blows. Shielding her head with her arm in an attempt to avoid a similar fate, she suddenly saw a petite, red-headed girl go sprawling down amid the melee.

Serena had seen her, too, and together they instinctively rushed forwards to drag her clear of the danger.

Their action brought them in front of the military police. As Abbra caught hold of one of the girl's wrists, hauling her to her feet, a stunning blow hit her head. Dazed, she could hear Serena screaming her name, but she couldn't see her; she couldn't see anything but scarlet flashes scoring dense blackness.

'I'm all right!' she gasped, lying. 'I'm all right!' Blood, hot and sticky, was trickling down the side of her face and on to her neck. Incredibly, she still had hold of the girl's wrist, was still on her feet helping Serena pull the girl free of the demonstrators who had fallen on top of her.

Slowly, as the three of them staggered back into the main body of the crowd, her vision cleared. She could see Serena's face, white with anxiety, could see the face of the girl they had pulled clear of the military police nightsticks, her green eyes full of indignant outrage, a silk tricolour tied around her throat.

'We need to sit down,' Serena was saying. 'We need to bandage your head.'

Dizzily Abbra nodded and allowed herself to be led to the fringe of the crowd and the grassy lawns of the mall.

'*Mon Dieu!*' the girl they had rescued was saying as she staunched the flow of blood with a handkerchief. 'I thought things were more civilized in America! No one told me I should have come with a crash helmet and a baton!'

For no reason at all Abbra began to giggle. 'No one told me either,' she said, grateful that the pain in her head was beginning to ease.

'Are you okay?' Serena asked her tightly.

Abbra didn't venture to nod her head. To do so would have brought a roar of fresh pain. Instead, she said, her voice sounding strangely thick, 'I think so. I don't think I've got a concussion.'

The redheaded girl suddenly saw Serena's scarf and her eyes widened. '*Alors!* Are you Serena Anderson? Are you the girl I was to have met at the Lincoln Memorial?'

Serena nodded. She had noticed Gabrielle's scarf, but had been too concerned by Abbra's wound to take time to introduce herself.

Gabrielle, too, returned her attention immediately to Abbra. '*Je regrette,*' she said, distressed. 'It would not have happened if you had not stayed to pull me free.'

'It wouldn't have happened if we hadn't had trouble-makers at the front of the crowd, and unnecessary thuggery from the federal marshals and the military police,' Serena responded tightly. She took a close look at Abbra's head and said with relief, 'You're right, Abbra. I think you're going to be fine. The bleeding has stopped, but you're going to have a God almighty bump there for a few days.'

'And a God almighty headache,' Abbra said ruefully.

Serena looked around her. At the parking plaza and the grassy triangle of lawn beyond it, running battles were still taking place. Above the shouting could be heard a valiant rendering of *We Shall Overcome*.

'Let's get away from here,' she said. 'This thing is going to go on all night, and you're in no condition to risk another run-in with the troops. If we make it back as far as the traffic circle at the Virginia end of the bridge, we should be able to pick up a cab.'

'And go where?' Abbra asked weakly as the French girl slipped her arm supportingly around her waist.

'My hotel would be the best bet. We can call a doctor up to put some stitches in your head. It's no use going to any of the hospitals. They're going to be overrun.'

Abbra felt too weak to protest. Serena was obviously eminently capable, and she was quite happy to go along with anything that she said. As they began to edge their way through crowds both arriving in the vicinity and attempting

493

to leave, Serena said to her, 'Sorry, I haven't introduced you, Abbra. Gabrielle, Abbra Ellis. Abbra's husband is an army captain being held somewhere in South Vietnam. Abbra, Gabrielle Ryan. Gabrielle wrote to me after seeing a letter I wrote to the *Washington Post*. Her husband is Australian, and a journalist. He's been missing for just over a year.' She raised a hand, flagging down a taxi. 'We'll talk more when we get to my hotel, and after you've been seen by a doctor.'

Abbra willingly allowed herself to be helped into the taxi, smiling despite her violent headache when she heard Serena direct the cab driver to the Jefferson Hotel.

The Jefferson. Of course. Where else had she expected Serena to be staying? The Jefferson was one of the most prestigious hotels in town. Situated only four blocks away from the White House, its rooms were decorated with fine antiques, the laundry was hand ironed and delivered in wicker baskets, and the manager personally greeted guests at the front door. And with the Jefferson as an address, any doctor called would most certainly come. Knowing that she had nothing further to worry about, Abbra leaned back and closed her eyes for the duration of the short cab ride.

When the doctor had duly stitched the wound in her scalp and had given her a pain reliever, Abbra began to feel a great deal better.

'What are you doing in America?' she asked Gabrielle as a bellboy wheeled a trolley of food and drink into the room. 'Are you here just to see Serena?'

Gabrielle sat in a deep-buttoned armchair, her legs curled beneath her. 'No. I am a singer,' she said as Serena poured coffee for Abbra and two glasses of Château Latour, Grand Cru for herself and Gabrielle.

Serena handed Abbra the cup of coffee and Gabrielle her glass of wine. 'What kind of a singer?' she asked, interested.

Gabrielle grinned, her eyes full of mischievous laughter. 'At this moment in time, a rock singer.'

494

'Oh, God! I wish I'd known you when Bedingham had its pop festival! You would have been a sensation!'

'Bedingham?' Gabrielle had written to Serena at her London address. 'What is Bedingham?'

'Bedingham is my family home,' Serena said, a new note entering her voice. She put her wineglass down and, sitting on the end of the canopied bed, she began to tell Abbra and Gabrielle all about Bedingham.

Abbra lay back against the pillows. Serena had insisted that she go to bed the minute they had entered the room, and she had reluctantly obeyed. Now she was glad that she had. The pain reliever had made her feel slightly woozy and as Serena spoke of Bedingham she felt so relaxed that she was almost asleep.

'And you, Abbra?' Serena said at last, when she had told the story of the pop festival and how she had met Kyle. 'What do you do? Where do you live?'

'San Francisco,' Abbra replied, easing herself up against the pillows. And she told them of how her mother had asked Lewis to pick her up from a party, and of how they had fallen in love, and then she told them about her novel, and of how it was soon to be published, and of how she had already started on a second book.

Outside in the darkness, police sirens could still be faintly heard, but none of them paid any heed to them.

'And so what happens to us now?' Serena asked when Abbra had finished telling her story. 'Do you return to San Francisco, Abbra? To finish your novel? And do you finish your tour of America, and then return to France, Gabrielle? If so, when are we going to meet again? Because we *have* to meet again, that is obvious.'

'I am not returning to France,' Gabrielle said quietly. 'Or at least not for more than a few days.' She paused and they waited expectantly. 'I am going to Vietnam,' she said with devastating simplicity. 'I am going to look for Gavin.'

For a long moment even Serena was rendered speechless. It was Abbra who spoke first, her voice incredulous. 'But you can't! The country is at war! Where will you go? Where will you stay? How can you possibly find out any more than the Australian and the American authorities can find out?'

Gabrielle's kittenlike features were determined. 'I can go, Abbra, because Vietnam is as much my country as France is. My mother is Vietnamese. I lived in Saigon until I was eight years old.'

There was a sigh of understanding from Serena. It had been obvious to her almost from the first that Gabrielle was of mixed blood. Why hadn't she realized she was half Vietnamese?

'I speak Vietnamese,' Gabrielle was saying. 'I have family in Saigon.' She paused again, opened her mouth to say more, and then changed her mind.

'What is it?' Serena demanded, sensing her discomfort. 'What is it that you don't want to tell us?'

Gabrielle said awkwardly, 'This is difficult for me. Your husband is a prisoner in the North, and Abbra's husband is probably being held in terrible conditions by the Viet Cong in the South, and . . .'

'And?' Abbra prompted her gently.

Gabrielle gave a helpless Gallic shrug of her shoulders. 'And my uncle is a colonel in the North Vietnamese Army. Gavin wanted to meet him. To find out what the war was like from an NVA point of view. My aunt in Saigon arranged the meeting. Gavin went off with my uncle and nothing has been heard of them since. That was over a year ago. If he could have got in touch with me, I know that he would have. But he hasn't, and so . . .' Her voice faltered a little. The admission she was about to make was one she had never before put into words. 'And so I think that perhaps he is a prisoner. As Lewis and Kyle are prisoners.'

For a long time no one spoke, and then Serena shook her head slowly, as if to clear it to be able to think clearly. 'Jesus,' she said in a stunned voice. 'That is one *hell* of a story!'

Gabrielle rose to her feet in the lamplit room. 'You see why I hesitated before telling you. Perhaps now that you know about the loyalties of some members of my family, you would prefer it if I had never contacted you? If I now left?'

'Nonsense!' Before Serena could respond, Abbra sprang from the bed, ignoring the fresh waves of pain that her action occasioned. 'Your husband is missing just as mine is missing,' she said fiercely, taking both of Gabrielle's hands in hers. 'And I know that I am speaking for Serena as well as myself when I say that all that matters is that the three of us are friends, and that we are all suffering the same kind of agony.'

'She's right,' Serena said. 'She is speaking for me.'

'*Ça va*,' Gabrielle said, her eyes suspiciously bright.

Reassured that Gabrielle was no longer going to take flight, Abbra let go of her hands and returned a trifle unsteadily to the bed, sitting down on it Indian-fashion and saying with a smile, 'So that's it, Gabrielle. There is no more to be said.'

'Oh, but there is,' Serena corrected her. While Abbra had been talking so passionately to Gabrielle, she had walked across the room to the window and had stood, looking down into the neon-lit darkness of 16th Street. Now she turned around, her eyes holding Gabrielle's. 'There's something very important still to be said. I want to come with you to Vietnam, Gabrielle. Can I?'

If it had been anyone else, even Abbra, Gabrielle was sure that she would have said no. But Serena was different. She could sense a recklessness beneath the English girl's capably cool exterior that matched the recklessness in her own nature.

'Yes,' she said unhesitatingly. 'Of course you can come.'

'I have something to do first,' Serena said, adrenaline racing through her veins. 'I have someone to see in Atlantic City. Chuck Wilson. He was Kyle's buddy and he was seriously injured trying to rescue Kyle.'

'And I have something to do as well,' Gabrielle said, not looking forward to the scene that lay ahead of her. 'I have to tell Radford, the leader of the group that I sing with, that I'm

497

taking off for Saigon. After doing *that*, anything that happens to me in Vietnam will be a walkover!'

'What about me?' Abbra exclaimed indignantly. 'You surely don't expect me to return to San Francisco while you two fly off to Saigon! If you're going, I'm going too!'

'No,' Serena said emphatically. 'No, you're not, Abbra. Listen to me for a moment. Gabrielle's situation and my situation are very different from yours. You are an army wife in a way that I, for instance, am not. Your husband is a professional soldier. When he returns home he will return to a career in the army. And he won't thank you if you ruin his future prospects by upsetting the military.'

'But . . .' Abbra began stubbornly.

'But nothing,' Serena said gently but firmly. 'You have your book to promote, your second novel to write, and your father-in-law to appease. From what you've told us, if he thought for one minute you were going to fly to Vietnam, he would have a cardiac arrest!'

Abbra felt her throat tighten. Serena was right. Abbra knew it, but she didn't *want* her to be right. She wanted to go to Vietnam. She wanted to do something positive to find Lewis. And she couldn't. Lewis's career in the army was his life. She couldn't jeopardize it, no matter what the cost.

'Okay,' she said thickly. 'But write to me. Write to me every damned week.'

Serena grinned, relieved Abbra had been practical. 'We will,' she promised, and turned towards Gabrielle. 'So when do we leave?'

'Our American tour ends in two weeks. I'll return to Paris with the band and speak to my parents, and I'll meet you there. Don't bother about a hotel. As long as you don't mind sleeping on a sofa, you will be very welcome in Montmartre.'

'That's it, then. It's all settled,' Serena's satisfaction was bone-deep. 'But if you don't mind, Gabrielle, I won't accept your very kind offer of hospitality. I'll book into my usual haunt whenever I'm in Paris, the George V. I might as well enjoy what comfort I can while I can!'

A second bottle of Château Latour Grand Cru stood uncorked on the trolley, and she picked it up, topping up both her own glass and Gabrielle's, and pouring a glass for Abbra.

'Here's to us,' she said exuberantly as they raised their glasses high. 'And to our husbands; and to the day when we shall all meet again!'

# CHAPTER TWENTY-SEVEN

The next day, on the flight back to San Francisco, Abbra planned her immediate future. Although, as a loyal army wife, she knew she couldn't accompany Serena and Gabrielle to Vietnam, she had no intention of continuing with her present life-style. The advances from her book, though not enormous, had given her financial independence and she was determined to do at last what she had longed to do for months. She was going to move out of her parents' home and rent a small house of her own.

Not in San Francisco. Not anywhere where there would be distractions. She wanted a beach house on a lonely part of the coast where she could write without interruption, and where her surroundings would give her mental solace as she continued in her long, agonizing wait for Lewis's return.

Remembering the weekend, she felt a glow of comfort. Talking to Serena and Gabrielle about Lewis, knowing that they understood implicitly everything that she was suffering, had been the best kind of therapy she could possibly have undergone. And in talking about Lewis, he had seemed closer than ever to her. Optimism, fierce and strong, surged through her veins. She knew he was alive. All she had to do was wait for him.

Serena rented a car for the trip to Atlantic City. She had no idea what to expect when she arrived there. The address she was driving to was the one that had headed Chuck Wilson's last letter to her, the letter in which he had said only that he was going to Wyoming for the summer to recuperate, and the letter in which he had implied that there was no need for them to correspond further. The address could be his family's home or his personal one, or even, if the stationery had been borrowed, that of a friend.

As she approached the coastline and caught her first glimpse of grey, surging, Atlantic breakers, she hoped that her suspicions were not correct. If they were, then she did not know how she would react, what she would say.

She turned off the highway, driving through the suburbs into a quiet residential area. In another few moments she would be able to do what she had wanted to do for so long. She would be able to thank the man who had risked his own life in an effort to save Kyle from capture.

The house was an old white wooden-framed house with clapboard siding, set in a large plot thick with shrubs and bushes. She parked the car and picked up her full-length wolf coat from the rear seat, then, slipping the coat on, she walked up the pathway towards the front door.

She rang the bell and heard it jangle, but there was no response. She rang again, a slight frown creasing her brow. She couldn't possibly leave without making contact with either Chuck or with someone who knew where he was. There was no sign of life from the front of the house, and so she dug her hands into the pockets of her coat and began to walk around to the rear.

Flowers edged the pathway, asters and chrysanthemums and black-eyed susans, calendulas and marigolds. In the distance were more unexpected delights: bayberry and sumac and wild beach rose. She wondered bemusedly who the imaginative gardener was, and then turned the corner.

Dominating the rear was a big glass-enclosed porch furnished with a wooden table, presumably for summer meals, and several upholstered, cane-framed chairs. There was also another chair there, facing away from her, with an occupant in it. A wheelchair.

'Oh, God,' she whispered beneath her breath, her worst fears confirmed, and then as the figure in the wheelchair remained oblivious of her presence, staring broodingly out over the carefully tended lawns and shrubbery, she stepped resolutely forward and into the porch.

'Hello,' she said, her hands clenching in the depths of her pockets, the nails digging deep into her palms. 'I'm sorry to disturb you like this, but there didn't seem to be anyone in the house to answer the bell and . . .'

The wheelchair spun to face her.

'And so I thought I'd walk around and see if I could find anyone,' she finished inadequately.

He was about twenty-three or twenty-four, but his eyes were ages old. They were so old that she felt chilled just looking into them. And they were blazingly angry.

'Now that you've done that, would you kindly leave!' His voice was a whiplash in the mild autumn air.

'No,' Serena said, regaining her usual cool self-possession with difficulty. 'I'm Serena Anderson, and I presume that you are Chuck Wilson.' She stepped towards him and held out her hand. 'I've wanted to meet you for a long time, Chuck.'

He ignored her outstretched hand. He knew who she was. He had known the instant he had set eyes on her. 'I don't encourage visitors, Mrs Anderson, and I would prefer it if you left!'

She regarded him long and intently. He had light brown hair worn a trifle long, high cheekbones, a slightly aquiline nose, grey eyes, and a finely chiselled mouth. There was something about him that reminded her very strongly of Kyle. He was Kyle's build, tall and lean, and even though he was in a wheelchair, she could sense the same restless, reckless energy.

'I've no intention of leaving,' she said unperturbedly, her decision made.

She walked over to the nearest of the cane chairs and sat down. 'Now,' she said, swivelling her long legs in their over-the-knee derring-do boots to one side and crossing them at the ankle, her fur open to reveal her lemon minidress, 'Why don't you stop behaving like an embittered child and tell me all about it?'

He drew in his breath between clenched teeth, his knuckles white on the wheels of the chair. She opened her shoulder bag, taking out a couple of joints and a cigarette lighter. 'Keep me company,' she said, passing one across to him.

He hesitated for a long moment and then at last one hand uncurled and he accepted the proffered joint.

'What exactly is it you want to know?' he asked curtly when they had both lit up and inhaled.

She didn't ask any of the questions he had been expecting, questions about Kyle's shooting-down and capture. Instead, she said matter-of-factly and with a stunning lack of pity in her voice, 'Are you going to be in that obscenity for a lifetime, or is the day going to come when you can throw it away?'

A ripple of shock ran through him, and then he blew a plume of sweet smoke into the air, saying a trifle unsteadily, 'Kyle told me you could be a pretty surprising lady. You are. And the answer to your question is that I'm probably stuck here for life.'

She didn't say she was sorry. She didn't say any of the trite, banal, meaningless phrases that he was sick to the gut of hearing. Instead, she said with almost casual brutality, 'Then you had better start getting used to it, hadn't you?'

Before he could recover his power of speech she rose to her feet. 'If you point me in the direction of the kitchen, I'll make some coffee. Or perhaps wine and a few beers would be a better idea. Do you have any in, or shall I drive down to the local store?'

'You're staying, then?' he asked with what he intended to be cutting sarcasm, knowing even as he spoke that he wanted her to stay. She was doing what no woman had done since his Huey had been riddled with tracer fire. She was treating him without pity. And she was making him feel as if he still retained a shred of masculinity.

'Oh, yes,' she said with a lazy smile, her perfectly smooth blond hair swinging glossily straight almost to her waist. 'I never pass up a party. Of course I'm staying.'

A little later she made omelettes for them both. They ate them at the table on the porch, remaining there, talking and drinking until it was dark and then, when it became too chilly, they retreated into a room that Chuck described as his 'den', taking their third bottle of wine with them.

His mother had returned home from a family visit at the end of the afternoon and had been at first surprised, and then delighted, and finally disconcerted by Serena's presence. Now, as they settled themselves in the den, Serena curling up in a battered armchair, and Chuck propelling his wheelchair so that he was within arm's reach of the coffee table and his glass, she knocked on the door and hesitantly entered.

'Is there anything I can get either of you?' she asked a trifle awkwardly. 'I know that Mrs Anderson has already cooked a light supper, but if the two of you would like something a little more substantial . . .'

'We're fine,' Chuck said sharply, and at his graceless response Serena saw a spasm of pain cross his mother's face.

She could well imagine the hell it must be, living with a son so embittered, and she also knew how deeply shocked Mrs Wilson must be by her own behaviour. A POW wife, drinking heavily with her husband's crippled buddy, a buddy crippled because he had tried to save that self-same husband.

She smiled warmly at her, saying with all her considerable charm, 'Thank you so much, Mrs Wilson, but we really don't want to put you to any bother. Perhaps later we could all have some coffee and sandwiches together?'

'I'll do some chicken and ham,' Mrs Wilson said gratefully and then, remembering the omelettes and Serena's obvious unconventionality, added hurriedly, 'but perhaps you are a vegetarian? If so, I could . . .'

'I'm not a vegetarian,' Serena said firmly, aware of Chuck's glowering countenance, 'and chicken and ham would be fine.'

Appeased, Mrs Wilson thankfully withdrew and Chuck said tightly, 'There's no need for you to endure supper with my mother.'

Serena tilted her head slightly to one side and regarded him quizzically. 'Were you always such an obnoxious bastard towards her, or is it something you've worked hard at cultivating since 'Nam?'

He said obliquely, 'You'd be damn obnoxious, too, if you were trapped in someone's company twenty-four hours a fucking day.'

'But you're not,' Serena said. 'Cars can be adapted so that you can drive. I don't know what pension you get from the army, but it must be enough for you to hire whatever nursing help you need and to live independently if you want to.'

She made everything sound so easy that at that moment he hated her. He thought of the last letter Kyle had written to her, the letter in which he had told her about Trinh and of how he wanted a divorce. The letter which he had not handed over to be given to her along with Kyle's other personal effects. The letter was still in his possession, and for one vicious moment he was tempted to spin his wheelchair towards his desk, get the letter and hurl it into her lap. The moment came and went and he didn't move. He didn't want to hurt her. He didn't want to shatter all her illusions.

He said tersely, 'Let's change the bloody subject. Tell me what happened yesterday in Washington. The headlines in this morning's *Post* said, "55,000 Rally Against War; GIs Repel Pentagon Charge".'

She told him about the demonstration, about the peaceful gathering that had taken place at the Lincoln Memorial and that had been attended by at least 50,000 people, and she told him about the march and the peaceful way the demonstration had begun at the Pentagon, and how it had disintegrated and broken up into a series of vicious battles between troops and demonstrators.

She had no idea whether he would sympathize with antiwar demonstrators, as so many other war veterans did, or whether he would resent them. Even after she had finished telling him about the demonstration she was no wiser. He merely grunted, turning the conversation back to her again, asking her about her life in England, about Bedingham.

Her face took on an inner radiance as she began to tell him about her home. He watched her, tormented by so many conflicting emotions that he could barely contain them.

When Kyle had first told him about the blond-haired, long-legged, sophisticated, wild and reckless English aristocrat that he had married, he had been intrigued. And envious. She had sounded like a girl in a million. A girl out of a storybook. And she was. She was incredible. Her hair was so pale in the lamplight that it looked almost silver; her features were a perfectly carved cameo, her eyes crystal-grey, her mouth wide and full-lipped and passionate. It was a face he could look at for a lifetime and never grow tired of. And he couldn't contemplate making even the slightest sexual overture to her. To do so would be to risk seeing pity in her eyes. Even horror.

Rage and frustration and bitterness roared through him. He wished he were dead. He wished he had died in his Huey, not been whisked by his terrified copilot to the nearest aid station and then flown on to a superbly equipped military hospital.

Kyle had been luckier than he. Wherever Kyle was, he still had the use of his legs. When freedom came for him, he would still be able to flirt and screw and stagger with his buddies from bar to bar on all-night drinking sessions. A paraplegic didn't have drinking buddies. He would be only waist-high as they crowded round a bar. Conversation would flow over his head. He could imagine the bartender asking them if he, the cripple, would like something to drink. But he wouldn't ask him directly. People never spoke to cripples in wheelchairs directly. They always addressed their questions and comments to whoever else was there, as though the person in the wheelchair were handicapped mentally as well as physically.

It was a scenario he had assiduously avoided. He had contacted no old friends, no fellow veterans, no fellow war maimed. He had hidden himself away, first at his uncle's ranch in Wyoming, and then in his mother's house. And though she did not know it, Serena was the first person to have broken through.

He found his mouth crooking into a smile as she described her father's horrified reactions to Bedingham's pop festival.

Serena saw the smile and knew that she could give herself a small congratulatory pat on the back. The man she had encountered earlier that afternoon had quite obviously not smiled for a long, long time. She said quietly, knowing that now it was safe to talk about it, 'Tell me about Kyle. Tell me about your time together in 'Nam. Tell me of how he was shot down, and of what happened immediately afterwards.'

His smile died, but the rapport between them remained unbroken. 'Kyle was one hell of a buddy,' he began, his eyes clouding with reminiscence.

He didn't tell her about their mutual whoring. He didn't tell her about Trinh. He told her about the good times. How the two of them had flown their Hueys as if they were souped-up Mustangs, flaring their birds into hot landing zones through clouds of pink smoke, loading on wounded, kicking out some answering ammo, and then half an hour later coming back and doing it all over again. How, when they were contour flying, they had flown so low they had been practically skiing over the treetops and tall grass. And then he told her about their last mission. Of how Kyle had been shot down. Of how he had seen Kyle hurl himself from

507

the blazing ship to the ground and how he had flown into dense fire in an attempt to pluck him to safety.

'What happened?' she asked gently as he paused, unable to continue.

He looked away from her, his face suddenly closed and shuttered. 'First of all we took a burst through the cockpit. I was temporarily blinded by the debris. Then we were hit again, and this time a bullet hit below my chest protector and went right through to my spine. End of story.'

The bitterness was back in his voice, and this time she didn't try to jolt him out of it. She said instead, regretfully, 'I'd better tell your mother we're ready for supper now. In another half hour I shall have to leave.'

He kept his face averted from hers so that she could not see the sudden panic that had filled his eyes. 'It's too late for you to drive back to New York. Why don't you stay here the night?'

It was an invitation she had known that he would make. 'No,' she said, wishing that things were different, wishing that she could stay. 'Sitting smoking pot and drinking wine with you all afternoon and evening is reprehensible enough behaviour for a POW wife. I can't ruin my reputation completely by suggesting to your mother that I stay the night.'

He turned his head, his eyes meeting hers, and a new emotion flooded through her. 'Kyle told me you were a girl who didn't give a damn about what people thought of you, and as far as your reputation is concerned, it's more than safe enough with me. Now.'

She ignored the last savage barb and forcing a smile, rose to her feet. 'Nevertheless, I can't stay,' she said, her voice a little unsteady. 'I'll go and tell your mother that we're ready to join her for supper.'

'Then where will you stay?' he persisted, his eyes holding hers unrelentingly.

'I have a hotel room booked,' she lied, and appalled

at the realization that had so suddenly hit her, she walked quickly out into the hall and across into the living room.

Jesus! Why hadn't she been prepared for such a reaction the instant she had realized how similar he and Kyle were? When he had turned his head, his eyes meeting hers in the lamplit room, the emotion that had flooded through her had been one of overpowering physical attraction. And he was confined to a wheelchair, for God's sake! He probably couldn't even function in bed. Even if he could, he was Kyle's best buddy. And she had vowed to remain celibate until Kyle was freed from Hoa Lo.

Her hand was trembling as she knocked on the living room door and entered. The whole thing was too farcical to be true. She was probably just feeling gratitude towards him for what he had done for Kyle. Or she was overcome with admiration for his bravery. Another alternative came to her, this time repellent. Perhaps she was one of those sick freaks who was sexually turned on by deformity. She dismissed the possibility almost as soon as it occurred to her. She knew herself better than that. The simple truth was that wheelchair or no wheelchair, Chuck Wilson was a damned attractive man with whom she had felt an immediate rapport.

'We're ready to join you for supper now, Mrs Wilson,' she said with all the graciousness she was capable of. 'Chuck has told me all that he can about my husband, and I'm very grateful to him. And for what he did for Kyle.' She paused and then said, knowing how inadequate the words were, and knowing that there were no words adequate enough, 'I'm terribly sorry about the injuries Chuck sustained on Kyle's behalf. If there is anything I or my family can do . . .'

'There is nothing anyone can do,' Chuck's mother said bleakly, her eyes harrowed.

Serena hesitated. What she was going to say next could, if it were misinterpreted, sound appalling, but it had to be said. 'I don't want you to take offence, Mrs Wilson, but my family is reasonably wealthy and . . .'

To her intense relief she saw that no offence had been taken.

'I understand what you are saying, Mrs Anderson,' Mrs Wilson said with exquisite dignity, 'and I am appreciative of your offer. But it isn't a question of money. It is a question of Chuck's own attitude about what has happened to him. He has never, ever, said that he regretted what he did and he has never blamed your husband for what happened to him. But he can't accept what happened; he can't even begin to learn to live with it.'

There came the sound of the wheelchair speeding out of the den. There was nothing more that they could say to each other. At least nothing that mattered.

'I'll serve supper, then,' Mrs Wilson said as her son propelled himself into the room. 'It's so nice to have company for a change. Perhaps you'll call on us again, Mrs Anderson?'

Radford stared at Gabrielle as if she had taken leave of her senses, 'Do I hear you *right*, baby? You're walking *out*? You're giving up everything we've sweated for to go to *Vietnam*? You're going to make *me* and the *rest* of the band give up everything we've sweated and bled for just when everything is good?'

She nodded, her eyes holding his unflinchingly. She had known what it was going to be like. She had known that she wasn't only turning her own back on fame and fortune, but that by her defection, leaving them without a lead singer, she was in all probability forcing the entire band to turn its back on it too.

'Yes. *Je regrette*, Radford. I know how crazy this must seem to you. I know what terrible timing it is, just when the band is on the verge of the really big time and the new recording contract has been signed, but it is something I *have* to do, *mon ami*. You will be able to find another singer, someone far better than me . . .'

They were standing backstage amid a tangle of electric cables and amplification wires. Up front, on the piano,

Michel was experimenting with a new arrangement. The notes tinkled softly, stopped, began again, this time slightly differently.

In the dull light Radford's skin had a sheen to it. Beads of pure rage clustered on his brow. He had been checking the readjusted lighting system, still convinced that the physics were all wrong, the beams' focusing eyes away from Gabrielle's spot and not on her. He was wearing a T-shirt, hip-hugging jeans, and sneakers, and he was mad enough to murder.

'You walk in here. You tell me you're going to fuck up everything I've worked for since I was knee-high to a grasshopper, and you tell me you're *sorry*! What kind of a dude do you think I am? Do you think I'm going to say, "Oh, that's all right, Miss Anne. Sure ain't no bother for me", because I ain't going to *do* that, baby!'

Everything that had always smouldered between them was rising to the surface, seeking its outlet in frustrated anger.

'You *are* this band!' he spat out at her, 'just as much as *I* am. There ain't no way you going to walk out on everything now. No *way*, baby!'

The piano had ceased to tinkle. From somewhere a long way away Gabrielle could hear the faint sound of *le petit* Gavin squalling lustily. Maura would be with him. Maura would pacify him.

She could see the blinding, white-hot fury in his eyes and she knew it was completely justified. She was fucking him up, fucking the entire band up. She said a little unsteadily, 'I said I was sorry, Radford, because I know of no other word to use. I *am* sorry. I know exactly how damaging my action is going to be for everyone, but it is something that I *must* do. I must try to find Gavin. I can't remain, waiting impotently, any longer.'

'*Jesus Christ!*' He covered the distance between them in one stride, grasping her shoulders so hard that she cried out in pain. 'Forget about him! He's dead! Gone!

511

Finished!' Passionate fury had merged into other feelings too long suppressed. 'This shit has been going on for too long, Gabrielle! You want what I want. You want to be the number one attraction in the *world*! And we can be that! We can be that *together*. Do you understand what I'm saying to you? Not only together onstage, but *together*, baby! *You* and *me*! An *item*!'

The skin was taut across his cheekbones. She could smell the perspiration sticking to his body and the faint lemon tang of his cologne. She could feel his hardness as he pressed her against him and sexual longing screamed through her, demanding satisfaction.

'You want what I want,' he said again, no longer shouting at her, his voice harsh and full of need. 'I want *you*, baby. And you want me. You always have. You always will.'

Through the thin silk of her blouse his touch was scorching her skin. She couldn't move. A sob of shame and despair rose in her throat, and then Michel was saying tautly, '*Le petit* Gavin has fallen and grazed his knees. I think you had better come and comfort him.'

The sob turned to one of gratitude, and she pushed herself away from Radford, not looking at him, not daring to look at him. '*Merci*, Michel. Where is he? Take me to him.'

It was a long time before she felt calm again. She had been on the verge of betraying Gavin's trust in her and only Michel had saved her. The knowledge left her feeling drained and sick at heart.

When she next faced Radford, both of them knew that the personal Rubicon they had reached would not, now, be crossed.

'I will fly back to Paris the morning after our last American concert,' she said to him, deep circles carved beneath her eyes, her kittenish face, usually so full of impishness and laughter, white and grave.

512

He had known that nothing he could do or say would persuade her to stay. 'I'll get another singer,' he said raspingly, a nerve ticking convulsively at the corner of his jaw. 'But she'll only be a temporary. You're still a member of the band.' Knowing another moment of her nearness would unstring him completely, he pivoted on his heel and strode away.

She watched him, slim and supple in his blue jeans, his strong shoulder muscles rippling beneath his cotton T-shirt, and she hated herself for the regret knifing through her.


She was still feeling quite subdued two weeks later when she walked into the lobby of the George V to meet Serena.

Serena had arrived in Paris the day before. She had telephoned, announcing her arrival and saying that she was in possession of a Vietnamese visa, a fact that didn't surprise Gabrielle. She had known that a 'minor' difficulty such as obtaining a visa for a country at war would pose no problem for a girl who obviously had friends in high places.

She smiled to herself as she crossed the sumptuous lobby. If Serena had told her that her father was Britain's Home Secretary, she wouldn't have been surprised.

'Gabrielle!' Serena called out, striding to meet her, head-turningly stunning in a raspberry-pink, miniskirted wool suit.

They hugged in the centre of the lobby, oblivious to the masculine attention they were attracting. Serena suddenly pulled away from Gabrielle, regarding her still-strained face quizzically, 'My God, Gabrielle. What on earth has happened to you since we last met? You look as if you've been through the wringer!'

'I have,' Gabrielle responded with a grin, suddenly feeling her old, bubbly, bouncy self again. 'And you? You are looking a little strained too, *n'est-ce pas?*'

# CHAPTER TWENTY-EIGHT

The house Abbra rented looked out over the beach a half mile or so north of La Jolla. Her parents had been appalled when she told them she was moving, but she had been adamant.

'I need isolation in order to work, Mom,' she had said, slipping her arm through her mother's and giving it a loving squeeze, willing her to understand.

'You have all the isolation you need here! Why, you spend *hours* in your room writing. I'm sure it can't be natural for anyone to spend so many hours cooped up all alone . . .'

'All writers spend hours cooped up alone, Mom,' Abbra said, laughing. 'If they didn't, they would never get any work done.'

'You won't be able to spend hours cooped up alone when Lewis returns,' her mother retorted tartly. 'All this writing nonsense will have to stop then.'

Even though Lewis was MIA and not a POW, Abbra insisted that he be spoken of as though his eventual safe return were a certainty.

She sighed, knowing that now that her mother had brought her resentment of her writing into the conversation, there was absolutely no point in continuing.

Her mother had thought her writing a harmless occupation until the day that her book had been published. Then, seeing it in the bookstores, faced with tangible evidence of an achievement she didn't understand, she had regarded it as harmless no longer.

Though Abbra had been thrilled when she first saw her finished book, and was elated each time she saw it in the store her name boldly printed across the jacket, she was aware of her mother's consternation over her daughter's new stature. Now she said, not wanting to get into a futile discussion with her mother over Lewis's approval or disapproval, 'I'm going shopping for some sheets and tablecloths this morning. Why don't you come with me? We can lunch together and then stroll around an art gallery or a museum.'

Her mother had been slightly mollified. The conversation had changed course. And a week later, with her car packed to capacity with clothes and household items and books, and her typewriter safely wedged in the front seat beside her, Abbra had driven south to the new home she had chosen for herself, by herself.

Abbra's life soon took on a routine. In the morning she reread her previous day's work, and then wrote a minimum of twelve hundred words. The novel she was now working on was far more ambitious than her first novel had been and totally different in style. 'A novel about North Beach in the fifties and the burgeoning beat generation!' Patti had said doubtfully when she had first spoken to her about it. 'It doesn't sound commercial, Abbra.'

Abbra doubted that it was commercial too, but her first novel wasn't selling as many copies as she, Patti, or her publishers had hoped, so she didn't see that she had anything to lose by attempting something more ambitious.

In the afternoon she would walk on the beach, and when she returned she would write her daily diary, the diary that she mailed each week to Lewis, care of the North Vietnamese government.

There was never any reply. There was never any news of him. His name never appeared on any official list of prisoners being held. There were times, when she was overtired, or when it all seemed too much for her to bear, when she wondered if there was any point in continuing with the letters. They seemed to merely disappear into a black hole, a limitless void. The despair would pass, and the following week's letter would be sent, but the loneliness and the longing remained, and were never eased.

In the third week of December she returned to San Francisco for a few days to spend Christmas with her parents. There was a card for her from Scott, but there was no letter enclosed, only his signature, big and bold and achingly familiar.

She put the card back in its envelope quickly, aware of her mother looking speculatively in her direction. Although nothing had ever been said, it was almost as if her mother had guessed at the reason he no longer visited her or telephoned. She had put no letter in her Christmas card to him, either, and she had not told him that she had moved. If there were news of Lewis, then she would contact him. Until then, she had to stay out of his life.

There were cards and letters from both Gabrielle and Serena, and she drew enormous strength from them. They were both in Saigon. Gabrielle was making as many contacts as she could with people who had known her uncle, and Serena was working as a volunteer in one of the local orphanages. Abbra had been amused by the last revelation. It was hard to imagine Serena, so carelessly soignée, feeding and changing tiny babies and clearing up the kind of mess that tiny babies were apt to make.

On the first of February she turned on the television to listen to the morning news as she made her breakfast, and was stunned to hear the news of the Viet Cong's Tet offensive. It was the Vietnamese New Year and all across South Vietnam hundreds of towns and cities and US bases had come under simultaneous attack. In Saigon, Viet Cong guerrillas had blown a hole in the embassy wall and entered the grounds. There were reports that the embassy had been seized and was under Viet Cong control, that the war in all its fury had finally reached the heart of Saigon.

All day she listened to every newscast, fearful for Gabrielle and Serena, wondering if they were safe. The evening news programmes had live coverage of the events. At the embassy four GIs had been killed and another had been critically injured. The initial news flash, that the embassy had been seized, was denied, but the situation was still one of terrifying confusion. Dead Viet Cong lay sprawled on the embassy grounds as heavy automatic gunfire continued. Six and a half hours after the attack, the embassy was declared secure again, the last of the assailants being shot by a senior embassy official as he crept up a flight of inner stairs.

The American Embassy wasn't the only 'secure' building to come under attack. A small group of Viet Cong, a woman among them, had tried to break into the Presidential Palace. There were live pictures of American and South Vietnamese troops engaged in a pitched battle with the attackers, their dead still lying in the street where they had fallen.

Saigon's main radio station was seized. Roads were blocked to prevent American and South Vietnamese reinforcements from entering the city. General Westmoreland's headquarters were attacked. There were reports from outlying towns of foreign doctors, nurses, missionaries, and schoolteachers being slaughtered by the insurgents, and Abbra's fears for Serena and Gabrielle increased.

For a week, newscasts reported running battles in Saigon between the Viet Cong and American and South Vietnamese forces.

Abbra knew that she could expect no news of Serena and Gabrielle until order was restored. The often sunless February days passed with agonizing slowness. As normality returned to Saigon, there were horrific news reports of the fighting further north, in the old imperial capital of Hue.

The fighting in Hue continued for twenty-four murderous days, and at the end of the fighting, when the recently raised Viet Cong flag was ripped from the flagpole of the ancient fortress that dominated the town and the South

Vietnamese red and yellow banner rose again, one hundred and fifty US marines lay dead. Four hundred South Vietnamese troops also died in the often hand-to-hand fighting, and it was estimated that thousands of civilians, some victims of Communist death squads, others victims of American air and artillery strikes, had also died. The city itself, the most historical and the most beautiful in the whole of Vietnam, was devastated.

It was while she was reading a newspaper report in which an American officer was describing paradoxically how 'we had to destroy the city in order to save it', that a telegram arrived for her from Gabrielle. She and Serena were safe. Tet had been '*très grisant*', very exhilarating. Rocket and mortar explosions had trapped them in their hotel room for three days, but now they were okay. She would write soon. And she sent much, much love.

Abbra's relief was colossal. She was able to concentrate on her novel again. She had promised Patti that it would be finished by Easter, and she wanted to be professional and meet her self-imposed deadline.

For the next few weeks, television news coverage was all of the fighting at Khe Sanh, a marine base in the northwest corner of South Vietnam. The marines' mission was to cover North Vietnamese infiltration routes from Laos, eight kilometres away from them, to the west.

At the end of January they had found themselves besieged by two crack North Vietnamese divisions, one of them the same division that had, fourteen years before, led the assault on Dien Bien Phu. All through February and March the newspapers were full of harrowing reports of the fighting. Day after day, eighteen-, nineteen- and twenty-year-olds were being slaughtered. Looking at the photographs, Abbra's antiwar convictions solidified.

On 31 March, tired and looking ill, President Johnson went on nationwide television to announce that he would not be seeking re-election. Abbra felt a surge of hope. A new presidency would mean new political decisions. Both

Eugene McCarthy and Robert Kennedy, the two men seeking nomination as Democratic candidate, were antiwar. If either man became president, then the war would surely end. She began to root for Kennedy.

On 1 April, she finished her novel and on the third she delivered it to Patti, and they went for a celebratory lunch. On the fourth she felt as if she would never be able to celebrate anything again. Dr Martin Luther King was shot dead in Memphis. The assassination of a man who had always advocated peaceful resistance no matter how violent the provocation was so monstrous that Abbra felt as if a member of her own family had been murdered. There was worse to come.

On 6 June Robert Kennedy, the man she had hoped would be the next president, was gunned down in the Hotel Ambassador in Los Angeles minutes after triumphantly winning the California primary.

Two weeks later, when the black limousine slid to a halt outside her pastel-painted house, she knew that the saying 'Death comes in threes' held true. She never remembered going to the door or opening it. She only remembered facing the army officer and the accompanying chaplain, and the army officer saying gently, 'Do you have a friend we could call, Mrs Ellis?'

She shook her head, overcome by a dizzying sense of déjà vu. She had been here before. Another army officer had asked her if she could call a friend before breaking his news to her, and that news had not been news of Lewis's death. She clung to a remnant of hope. There was no reason why the news this time should be of Lewis's death. It couldn't be. She would have known if he had died. She wouldn't have to be told. She would have *known*.

Looking around him and realizing that there was no neighbour within easy reach who could be called on to sit with her, the officer said unhappily, 'May we come in, Mrs Ellis?'

She tried to say yes, but no words would come. Her throat was so tight that she felt as if she were being strangled. Mutely she opened the door wide and led the way into her little sitting room. Her typewriter was on the desk. She had been trying to get the synopsis for a new book down on to paper, and several discarded pages lay crumpled in the wastebasket.

'Please sit down, Mrs Ellis.' It was the chaplain speaking. His eyes were compassionate. She swung her eyes away from him, facing the officer, saying, 'It's Lewis, isn't it? There's news?'

Taking her lightly by the arm, the officer led her to the nearest chair. Numbly she sat. 'Yes,' he said at last. 'I'm afraid the news isn't good, Mrs Ellis.'

She waited. It was a gloriously hot day, and through the wide window of the room she could see the dazzle of sunlight on the distant surf. A half-finished page was still wound in the typewriter. She wondered what her last sentence had been and couldn't remember. She wondered if she would ever write another sentence.

'We have confirmation from a fellow prisoner, recently released, that your husband died in a jungle camp in the Ca Mau Peninsula sometime during October of last year.'

*October*. When she had flown to Washington for the antiwar demonstration. When she had met Serena and Gabrielle and been so full of renewed hope. October. Before her first novel had been published. Before her second novel had been completed. Eight months ago. Lewis had died eight long months ago, and she hadn't known. It was impossible. Inconceivable.

She said in a cracked, harsh voice that she didn't recognize as her own, 'I don't believe it.'

'It's a first-hand account, Mrs Ellis,' the chaplain said gently. 'There can be no mistake.'

She looked into his face, and saw that he was speaking the truth. Lewis was dead. He was dead and she was going to have to live the rest of her life without him.

521

She rose unsteadily to her feet. 'I'd like to be alone please.'

'I don't think that is a very good idea, Mrs Ellis.' It was the chaplain. He was in late middle age and he looked tired and drawn. She wondered how many other wives he had broken the same news to. How he could bear to wake up each day, knowing what his work entailed.

She repeated immovably, 'I would like to be alone, please.'

In the end, unhappily, they left. As their limousine pulled away, churning up a cloud of dust and the fine sand that always thinly layered her driveway, she stood in the centre of her sitting room. Lewis would never see it now. He would never live there with her. He would never know about the novels. Never touch her again. Never hold her and kiss her.

She was still dry-eyed. She couldn't cry. Her grief was too deep for tears. Despite the summer heat there was goose flesh on her arms and legs. 'Oh, God,' she whispered, wondering how she was going to survive. *'Oh, Lewis, Lewis, Lewis!'*

Her father-in-law came to see her; her parents came, insistent that she move back to San Francisco. She refused, knowing that she could never live there again. From now on her home was the home she had made for herself when she had thought Lewis was still alive.

Scott had sent her a telegram. He was in Rome on a summer vacation. He had told her to be brave, and from Scott the words had not seemed trite.

The hardest thing of all was in believing that it was true. If there had been a body to bury, it would have been easier. But there was no body. There was no coffin, no wreaths of flowers, no funeral service, no grave to visit. There was no tangible evidence of his death at all. It was as if Lewis, and the brief days of their marriage that they had spent together, had never been.

There were so few memories. Only the platonically affectionate dates that they had enjoyed together in Carmel and San Francisco; their one-night honeymoon and their week in Hawaii. That was all the time that they had had. The paucity of it broke her heart.

She had written to Serena and Gabrielle and had received long, commiserative, supportive letters back from them. And she had told Patti, who had been exquisitely sympathetic and who had immediately driven down from Los Angeles to see her. There had been no one else to tell. Their marriage had not been long enough for them to have formed any mutual friendships. Her grief could not be truly shared with anyone. Not until Scott returned from Italy.

His father had told her that he was vacationing in Europe until the end of July, and she had reconciled herself to not seeing him until then. Without a funeral to attend there was, after all, no reason for him to return.

A week after her official visitors had arrived in their black limousine, she slipped out of the house early, just as the sun was rising, and went for a long walk on the beach. She wanted to think about the future as well as the past. A future without Lewis. What would she do? Where would she go? How would she manage to exist through the half life that lay ahead of her?

It was too early even for pre-breakfast beachcombers and she was alone. A sea gull swept inland, below eye level, the rising sun glinting rosy on its back. She would write. That much was obvious. Whatever happened, she would always write. But what else? What else could there possibly be now that she no longer had Lewis?

In the distance she saw another person on the sand. She turned and began to walk slowly back in the direction of the house. Perhaps she should think about buying the house or, if that wasn't possible, buying another house close by. After all, she would need a home, and there was never going to be a home for her on an army base with Lewis.

Wry sadness flooded through her. She was an army widow who had never experienced army life. She would never know, now, whether or not she would have adapted successfully to such a change in her life-style. She was wearing dark grey slacks and a white silk shirt, a black cashmere sweater around her shoulders. She slipped her hands into the pockets of her slacks, looking broodingly out over the pearl-grey ocean as she walked.

She didn't look towards the house until it was twenty yards away. Then, turning away from the ocean to walk across the beach to the steps that led towards it, she looked up and saw him.

He looked as if he had been standing there for a long time, watching her. He had allowed his hair to grow indecently long. Beneath the early morning sun it gleamed the colour of ripening barley. She couldn't see the expression on his face or in his eyes; she didn't need to. Her heart began to beat in sharp, slamming strokes that she could feel even in her fingertips. He had come back.

'Scott!' she cried, taking her hands out of her pockets and breaking into a run. 'Scott!'

She hurtled into his arms, and as they closed around her, and as she clung to him, safe in the harbour of his strength and his love for her, the frozen waste inside her thawed, and tears came in a grieving torrent.

'He died, and I didn't know,' she gasped, her breath coming in great, shuddering sobs. 'Oh, Scott, how could I not have known? How could I not have been able to tell?'

He had no answer for her. He merely held her tight, stroking her hair, soothing her as best he could.

She wept as though she would never stop, and then at last she said thickly, 'I loved him so much. I thought I was going to have him to love for the rest of my life.'

'I know, baby. I know,' he said gently, and with his arm around her shoulders, he began to lead her back into the house.

\* \* \*

'Are you going to be able to talk to this guy who says he was in the same camp as Lewis?' he asked her as he cooked breakfast for them both.

She had cried until she could cry no longer. Now she sat with her legs curled beneath her on the window seat in the kitchen, watching him as he grilled bacon and fried eggs.

'No,' she said, her eyes so dark they were almost black, her face ivory pale. 'I wanted to, but in the official letter I received, I was told that the soldier in question was an Australian serving with the First Battalion, Royal Australian Regiment. He has been honourably discharged and his present whereabouts aren't known.'

Scott's jawline hardened. He didn't believe what she had been told for one moment. The army was simply trying not to cause waves, and perhaps trying to save her from further distress. He said, 'There's a Marlon Brando film showing in La Jolla tonight. Would you like to see it with me?'

The movies. It had been months since she had been to the movies, or anywhere else for that matter.

For an instant she was too shocked by the suggestion to reply and then she said, with no doubt at all in her voice, 'I'd love to.'

She needed distraction. She needed to go through the motions of living until the motions once again became natural. And she needed company, Scott's company.

For four months she told no one that he had reentered her life, and she didn't attend his games. But when he was in town he drove down from Los Angeles to take her out to dinner, to take her to the movies and the occasional concert, to discuss her work with her and to walk with her on the beach. She didn't tell her father-in-law; she didn't tell her parents; she didn't even tell Patti.

In all those months he never once referred to the words he had spoken to her in the forest above Lake Tahoe, and he never touched her, except chastely when helping her in and out of the car, or slipping her coat around her shoulders.

525

In October, as he was about to drive back to Los Angeles, and she was walking him from the house to his Chevrolet, he turned to her and said suddenly, his voice oddly abrupt, 'Has enough time passed, Abbra? Can I ask you now?'

It was early evening and behind him the ocean lay in indigo shadow, the surging surf milky-pale.

'Ask me what?' she said, smiling up at him with no intimation of what was to come.

There was no answering smile on his face. Every line of his body was taut with tension. 'Will you marry me?' he said simply.

Time wavered and halted. She couldn't speak, couldn't move. Somewhere deep in her subconscious she had always known that this moment would come, and she had refused to think about it, had refused to think of what her reply might be.

'I love you, Abbra,' he said, still not touching her, still not reaching out for her. 'I always have. I want you to be my wife.'

He was wearing a turtleneck sweater and jeans. Beneath the thick, sun-bleached tumble of his hair his eyes were onyx-dark. She could see white lines of strain edging his mouth and a pulse begin to beat at the corner of his jaw.

Still she couldn't speak or move. He had been her brother-in-law and for a long time, longer than she had cared to admit he had been the most important person in her life. He was also a professional football player, a pin-up, a man who could have his pick of hundreds of women. And he was in love with her. He had been in love with her for a long time.

Her heart was beating fast and light, high in her throat. Though she had known of Lewis's death for only four months, he had, in reality, been dead for a year. That was why Scott was asking her to marry him now. Because it had been a year. And because he loved her.

Suddenly it was as if a great dam inside her was at last breaking free. Loving Scott would not diminish her memories of Lewis. Nothing would ever do that. Lewis would be a part of her life always. But in a moment of stunning, dizzying revelation, she knew that she loved Scott. She was deeply, irrevocably, deliriously in love with the man who was asking her to marry him.

'Oh, yes!' she said, opening her arms and stepping towards him, so sure of the rightness of her answer that nothing in the world could have swerved her from it. 'Oh, yes, I *will* marry you, Scott! I want to marry you more than anything else in the world!'

His return trip to Los Angeles was forgotten. Lifting her up in his arms, he turned back with her to the house, striding through the sun-filled, book-filled room in which she worked, carrying her up the narrow stairs to the bedroom he had never entered.

There had never been any physical intimacy between them beyond hugs and an occasional chaste kiss. Now he was going to make love to her, and neither of them could wait. She unbuttoned her blouse with trembling fingers, slipping her skirt down over her hips, leaving it where it fell. She stood still in her bra and panties, filled with crippling shyness. Scott was so much more experienced than she was. The models and actresses that he had dated had all, surely, been knowledgeable and unimaginably abandoned. Was he going to be disappointed in her? Was he assuming qualities about her that she did not possess?

He had thrown his turtleneck sweater to the far side of the room. Now he kicked off his jeans, looking across at her, aware for the first time of her sudden hesitancy. He didn't need to ask her what was the matter. The reason for her apprehension was blatant in her eyes. Slowly he stretched his hand out across the bed towards her.

'I love you,' he said thickly. 'I've never been in love with anyone before, ever.' Her hand slipped trustingly into his. 'I've never been to bed with a woman I love. This is my first time, Abbra. You have as much to teach me as I have to teach you.'

She gave a little cry, overcome with love for him, and with gratitude for his understanding. Gently he pulled her on to the bed and into his arms. He had waited so long for her, he wasn't going to spoil everything by rushing now. 'I love you, Abbra,' he said again, pushing her silk-black hair away from her face, kissing her temples, her eyes, the corners of her mouth. 'I love you, lady. I'm always going to love you. All the days of my life.'

When he unhooked her bra and cupped her breasts in his large, strong hands, she shivered in delight. Slowly his thumbs brushed her nipples, slowly he lowered his head, kissing and gently sucking.

She had not waited for him to slide her panties down. She was so damp, and hot and eager for him, she had wriggled out of them herself, kicking them away, spreading her legs wide and pulling him down on top of her.

It had been as wonderful as he had known it would be. It had been more than wonderful. It had been the most cataclysmic, exquisite, joy-filled experience of his life. There was no ghost in the room with them. No doubt. No guilt. Only love, complete, and satisfying, and boundless.


When they broke the news that they were going to marry, her parents were so shocked they were almost catatonic. They refused point-blank to come to the wedding. They refused to meet Scott. They said that unless she came to her senses and called the wedding off, they would never have anything to do with her again.

Tom Ellis's reaction had been equally intense. At first he refused to believe it. And when they had lovingly and patiently assured him that they were telling him the truth, his rage had been terrifying. They were defiling Lewis's memory. They were shameless. Adulterous. He wished they were both dead, as Lewis was dead.

Abbra had been so distressed that it had taken nearly all her courage to break the news to Patti. What if Patti's reaction, too, was one of stunned horror? If it was, there would be no one at their wedding. They would have to pull strangers in off the street to act as witnesses.

'You couldn't have called at a better time,' Patti said cheerily from the sophisticated depths of her Los Angeles office. 'I was just about to call to tell you Book of the Month Club has bought the book! Publication date, by the way, is *definitely* February '69, and your editor tells me that the jacket is going to be *sensational*!'

'That's great, Patti,' Abbra said, barely registering it. 'I have some news for you too.' She took a deep, steadying breath. 'I'm marrying Scott, and I would like you to be my maid of honour.'

There wasn't even a fraction of a second pause. Patti let out a whoop of glee that must have been audible in the next block. 'That's *wonderful* news, Abbra! I'd *love* to be your maid of honour! When is the wedding? What shall I wear? What are you going to wear? Oh, my God, I haven't been so thrilled by a piece of news in years!'

'She's pleased?' Scott asked unnecessarily when she put the telephone receiver back on its rest.

Abbra grinned. 'She's pleased. And she's going to be my maid of honour.'

'And a buddy from the team is going to be my best man,' Scott said, pulling her lovingly down next to him on the sofa and drawing her into his arms. 'So all our troubles are over, and our guest list is complete.'

Despite the fact that there were going to be only two guests, they had decided on a church wedding.

It was a small, white-walled church, Spanish in style, and on the evening before their marriage she decorated it herself with small-budded pink roses and stephanotis and clouds of orange blossom.

Her dress was of pale ice-blue silk with huge puff sleeves,

a tiny waist, and a softly flowing full skirt. Her bouquet was made up of the same flowers that she had decorated the church with, and although she had transferred Lewis's wedding ring to the third finger of her right hand, with Scott's blessing she still wore his engagement ring on her left hand. Instead of an engagement ring Scott had bought her a pair of delicate, antique pearl-and-diamond earrings. Apart from these, and her ring, she wore no other jewellery.

Patti was exquisite in a pale pink dress the exact colour of the roses in her and Abbra's bouquets. She stood on tiptoe to kiss Scott warmly, flirted happily with the best man, and presented the bride and groom with a magnificent Lalique vase as a wedding present.

When the simple ceremony had been completed, they drove to the Hotel Valencia, overlooking La Jolla Cove, and celebrated with champagne and a lavish wedding breakfast.

They were flying to New Orleans for their honeymoon, because Abbra had never seen it before and it was a city that she had always wanted to visit.

The best man and maid of honour, by now comfortably holding hands, drove them to San Diego International Airport. At the departure lounge doors Abbra turned, her black hair swinging glossily as she tossed her bouquet towards Patti.

Patti caught it neatly with a wide smile and a naughty wink, and Scott's buddy, who was standing beside her, blushed sheepishly.

As the departure lounge doors closed behind Scott and herself, Abbra's heart was full to overflowing. She had a future again. She had someone she loved, who loved her in return.

# CHAPTER TWENTY-NINE

Gabrielle's return to Saigon was the most traumatic experience of her life. Everything had changed. She remembered the city as being languorous and exotically sophisticated.

Apart from a few disturbingly young flower sellers, none of the sights and sounds of her childhood remained. There was nothing remotely languorous or sophisticated about the city she had returned to. It had become as tawdry and as corrupt and dishevelled as an old whore. Instead of white-suited Malacca-cane-holding Frenchmen, the streets were thronged with GIs, some drunk, some stoned on drugs, nearly all of them rowdy and out for a good time.

Bicycles and pedal-cabs still thronged the streets, but they had to vie for road space with thousands of souped-up scooters and Honda 50s. Trucks and taxicabs and jeeps hurtled incessantly down the main thoroughfare. When Gabrielle had been a child it had been called rue Catinat; now it was known as Tu Do Street and all down its length, where there had once been elegant shops and boutiques and sidewalk cafés, there were girlie bars and clubs and brothels. She wasn't shocked. It wasn't in her nature. And she didn't regret the passing of the days when French colonialists dominated the city, and native-born Saigonese catered deferentially for their comforts.

Nhu had said in her letters that the American Army had simply replaced the French as an occupying force, and that the Saigonese were still second-class citizens whose primary function was to provide labour. Gabrielle could see why she thought so, but even though the main service industry was prostitution, she thought the status quo between Americans and Saigonese more equal and healthier than the unhappy status quo that had existed between the colonial French and Saigonese.

There were some things in Saigon that hadn't changed though. The stinging brilliance of the light was still the same, as was the heavy humidity and the rank aroma that rose from the Saigon River. And the Saigonese were still the same. Slim and dark and fragile-boned, they were as sassily streetwise and as quick-witted and as quick to laughter as she had remembered them to be. The years fell away and she was stunned by the realization that the Vietnamese side of her nature was far more dominant than the French. She felt as if she had never left the city, as if it were truly her home.

For Serena, adjusting to Saigon took much longer. Although it was November and there were often days when the city was awash beneath autumn rain, she found the underlying heat and humidity unrelenting and oppressive.

The first thing they had done after landing at Tan Son Nhut airport had been to drive to Gabrielle's aunt's house. The reunion between Nhu and Gabrielle had been joyfully tearful, and Serena had happily kept a low profile as the two of them caught up on family news, talking themselves hoarse. Nhu had invited them to stay with her, but Gabrielle had reluctantly declined.

'No, Aunt Nhu. We would excite the wrong kind of attention. We will stay at the Continental Palace or the Caravelle, where we will be less noticeable.'

'The Continental Palace,' Serena said firmly when they had said their good-byes to Nhu. 'Somerset Maugham is said to have stayed there, Graham Greene *definitely* stayed there, and if it was good enough for him, it must surely be good enough for us.'

Gabrielle hadn't argued. She did not care which hotel they used as a base, and as Serena was used to the comfort of hotels such as the Jefferson in Washington, and the George V in Paris, to expose her to anything less than the Continental in Saigon would have been an act of gross cruelty.

The standard of comfort and cuisine at the Continental

came as a monumental shock to Serena. The meat served at dinner was almost always buffalo meat, and *always* served with rice.

'The country is at war,' Gabrielle had said to her, amused. 'There is very little food, and anything other than buffalo meat and rice would be too expensive for the hotel to serve.'

For a long moment Serena's beautifully sculpted face had been void of all expression. Gabrielle wondered if she was reconsidering the venture and planning to return to the luxury of her jet-set lifestyle in London, but she grinned suddenly, pushing a long fall of pale blond hair away from her face, saying resolutely, 'I'll adapt. It's a family virtue.'

She had been true to her word. By the end of the first week she had accepted the ubiquitous military presence, the armed guards in front of nearly every public building, the lethal coils of barbed wire that barricaded certain streets. She had even learned not to flinch at the sound of distant gunfire. But what she could not accept, and could not ignore, was the sight of the children, some only four or five years old, wandering the streets in misery, begging for piastres.

'Don't they have any homes to go to?' she had asked Gabrielle as they crossed the central square in front of the old French Opera House.

Gabrielle hated the sight as much as Serena, but because of her streak of Eastern fatalism, she was better able to cope with it. 'No,' she said, her eyes darkening. 'They are war orphans. There are hundreds of them in the city. Probably thousands.'

Serena was more than deeply shocked. She was horrified. Nothing in her experience had prepared her for the reality of such abject deprivation. 'But why aren't they *cared* for?' she demanded incredulously. 'Why aren't they in orphanages?'

Gabrielle ignored the lascivious leer of a passing GI. 'I imagine that the majority of them are, but I suspect that the local orphanages leave an awful lot to be desired.'

'Jesus! Do you mean that the orphanages are so badly run

that these kids prefer to take their chances on the streets?'
Serena asked, stunned.

'*Alors*. I do not know, Serena,' she said, her cat-green eyes
still dark with anguish as she thought of the plight of the street
children. 'I do not even know who runs the orphanages in the
city. I am simply making what I think is called in English,
"an educated guess".'

They were on their way to meet Nhu, and an acquaint-
ance of hers, a Vietnamese journalist who had been born
in the South and had always lived in the South, but
whose father had chosen to go north in 1954. He worked
for a German news magazine, and was ostensibly loyal to
the Saigon government. But he had also been a friend of
Dinh's, and Nhu suspected that his true loyalties lay with
the Communist North. He was certainly a man that it was
necessary Gabrielle should meet, and it was important that
he should be convinced, at the outset, of Gabrielle's utter
trustworthiness.

Gabrielle, thinking about the meeting, lapsed into
thoughtful silence. Serena dug her hands deep into the
pockets of her stone-coloured Burberry, her forehead
puckering in a frown. No one could ever have accused her of
having a social conscience. All her life she had lived a
cosseted and privileged existence, and it had never occurred
to her to feel a sense of responsibility to those who were less
fortunate than herself. She was wilful, headstrong, and
selfish, and happy to be so. Charity work and good causes
were a bore she had always avoided, and she had had no
intention of changing the habit of a lifetime merely because
she was now living in a war zone.

Her frown deepened. She still had no intention of turning
into a ministering angel, rounding up the children on the
streets and establishing some sort of care for them. That kind
of thing wasn't her scene at all. Yet she had to do something.
The question was, what?

Her frown cleared as she came to a decision. She
would check out the orphanages in the city and see if

Gabrielle's assumptions about them were correct. Even though Gabrielle had insisted that she accompany her to see the journalist, Serena knew that she would be a handicap. She was English, married to an American POW, not half Vietnamese and related to Dinh. Her very presence at the meeting would be enough to insure that no information of any value would be divulged.

She stopped suddenly, saying, 'My going with you really isn't a good idea, Gabrielle. And I have something to do of my own. I'll meet you later this afternoon, back at the Continental.'

'Are you sure, *chérie*?' Gabrielle was wearing tight black cotton trousers and high-heeled mules. Because of the threat of rain, a short black leather jacket was slung around her shoulders, her spicy red curls brushing incandescently against the upturned collar.

Serena grinned. It was no wonder that they couldn't walk a yard down the street without being lewdly accosted. Gabrielle, quite innocently, looked every inch a pert and naughty high-class hooker. 'I'm positive,' she said, suddenly itching to be off on her personal investigation. 'I hope this guy you are meeting proves to be the genuine article.'

'*Moi aussi*,' Gabrielle said with heartfelt sincerity. '*Au 'voir, chérie*.'

As Gabrielle walked away from her, her provocatively tight-fitting trousers leaving very little to the imagination, Serena turned her attention to the task of flagging down a taxi or a pedal-cab.

'My God! Will you look at *that*!' a drunken GI called out to his buddies as his eyes focused upon her. 'Am I dreaming? Am I in heaven? Has Sweden suddenly entered the war and sent some women out here as a bridgehead?'

'Never mind a bridgehead, does she *give* head?' another riposted, swaying meaningfully across the pavement towards Serena, his buddies hooting with mirth at his wit and crowding in behind him.

'Hey, lady, is it true what they say about Swedish girls? Do they do it for free?'

Serena turned her head a mere fraction of an inch in his direction and looked at him with icy contempt, 'You'd be lucky if your wife would do it with you for free,' she said witheringly in her cut-glass English accent.

The GI flushed scarlet, and his buddies almost fell on the floor, laughing. Serena ignored them, turning back to her task of attracting the attention of a taxi driver. Drunken, opportunistic GIs were a constant nuisance, and both she and Gabrielle had become expert in dealing with their unwelcome attentions.

A Renault 4 taxicab swerved to a halt, and she opened the rear door, stepping inside and saying, 'An orphanage, please.'

The Vietnamese driver looked at her through the mirror, his eyes startled.

'An orphanage,' she repeated impatiently. 'A place where they take care of parentless children. It doesn't matter which one. Any will do.'

The driver lifted his thin shoulders expressively, '*Không xáu*,' he said agreeably. 'Okay. No sweat.'

They swerved away from the pavement and the still-whistling and appreciative GIs, and into the hurly-burly of Saigon's horrendous traffic system. A jeep blasted past them, the driver's hand firmly and permanently on the horn as he forged a way for an official Ford sedan. The taxi driver swore, swerved, regained his road space, and struggled to maintain it against a fleet of army trucks and a convoy of tanks. As they approached Cholon, the Chinese quarter, they ground to a halt as southbound vehicles plowed determinedly down both sides of a two-way street. Serena raised her eyes to heaven and fought for patience. It all seemed so senseless, and the white-helmeted Saigon police, known universally as 'white mice', seemed absolutely indifferent to the chaos around them.

After an interminable length of time, and amid much verbal abuse, the traffic jam unravelled itself. Minutes later the taxi careered to a halt outside an unpromising-looking stone-grey building.

'Orphanage,' the taxi driver said briefly. 'You pay me in dollars, please.'

Serena obliged, wondering why South Vietnam bothered with a currency of its own when the only acceptable form of payment for anything was American dollars.

She stepped out of the Renault and looked up at the building in front of her. For the first time she wondered how she was going to gain permission to wander around it at will. She didn't have a child to deliver there, and she didn't have a child to pick up, and she certainly didn't know the name of any child who was a resident. If she said she was a reporter, and if the orphanage was not well run, the staff would be immediately on their guard.

A cigarette seller approached her and she shook her head at him, pondering her problem. She could always say that she wished to make a donation. Donations, surely, were always acceptable. And if the orphanage proved Gabrielle wrong, and was admirably well run, then she would most certainly give a donation.

Her plan of action determined, she rang the bell. A young Vietnamese girl opened the door to her, looking at her apprehensively.

'Chào bà,' Serena said brightly, having culled from Gabrielle a minimum vocabulary so that she could at least say please and thank you in Vietnamese, and wish people good day and good-bye. 'May I see your administrator, please?'

The girl's apprehension deepened into unhappy bewilderment.

'Can I see the person in charge?' Serena repeated, and then, as the girl didn't seem to understand English, she tried French. '*Je peux parler à la directrice?*'

The girl's face registered understanding, but she still made no attempt to open the door wide and to invite Serena inside.

In the shadowed hallway behind the girl Serena saw an elderly nun approaching briskly. She set a smile on her face, stepped purposefully past the unwelcoming acolyte at the door, and said genially, '*Good morning*, Sister. It was very kind of you to say that I could visit this morning. I shan't take up very much of your time, I know how terribly busy and overworked you all are . . .'

The nun was stern-faced, and beneath her starched white wimple her eyes were implacable. 'We are expecting no visitors this morning, Madame,' she said frostily. 'There has been an error . . .'

Serena knew that if she hesitated now, all would be lost. She strode past the nun, ignoring her cries of protest, saying brightly and breezily, 'I am so pleased that you are happy to accept my donation to the orphanage, Sister. The British ambassador assured me that such an amount would be most welcome and put to extremely good use.'

The nun was hard at her heels, panting with the effort of trying to keep pace with her. At the mention of a donation and the British ambassador, she checked slightly. 'The message to say that you would be visiting obviously went astray,' she said breathlessly. 'If you would be so kind as to tell me your name . . .'

'Lady Serena Blyth-Templeton,' Serena said, reverting to her maiden name for maximum effect, 'and now, if I could see the children, please . . .'

She could smell them long before she saw them. The whole building was heavy with an aroma of urine and faeces and other substances that she could not place. She had never been in an orphanage before, never even been in a nursery, and she had not the slightest idea what to expect. As she strode into the nearest room and looked around her, the sight that met her eyes was worse than anything she could possibly have imagined.

There was row after row of white-painted metal cots, and the occupants, some of them old enough to be attending primary school, lay docilely two and three to a bed. Nearly all of them had disfiguring skin complaints, nearly all were lying on wet bedding. Serena gagged and fought down an overwhelming tide of fury. The nun now leading the way for her obviously saw nothing reprehensible in the conditions in which the children were being kept, and to give vent to her outrage would only result in her tour being precipitately terminated.

As she slowly walked the length of the room she saw that one dark head after another was thick with lice eggs. The children stared at her dully, with no sign of animation, and she knew that what she had initially taken to be docility was apathy. God alone knew when they had last been allowed to play. Or even when they had last been spoken to. Just as they were leaving the room, one of them began to cry. A Vietnamese nurse hurried forwards, giving the child a sharp smack. As Serena sucked in her breath sharply, the elderly nun at her side said quickly, 'That child is always crying. He cries out of naughtiness.'

'My God! How can he be naughty? He's caged in his crib like a small animal!'

The nun's face tightened. 'I think that is all I can show you of our highly esteemed orphanage. In the next room the babies are being fed. A visitor would be disturbing to them.'

'Don't worry, Sister. I've seen enough,' Serena said grimly. 'Can you give me a list of the other orphanages in the city, please?'

'And your donation?'

'A list please, Sister.'

The nun didn't move and Serena said, a hint of menace in her voice, 'The ambassador specifically asked me to ask for a list from you. The British Embassy's list is not as up-to-date as he would like.'

'I have no written list.'

'Then if you would tell me the names of the other orphanages, I will make a note of them.'

'And the donation?'

'The names please, Sister.'

The nun's nostrils flared and then she said curtly, 'Phu My, Go Vap, Dêm Hè, Cam Hoài, St Paul's, Ngo Thuy.'

As she continued with her list, Serena wrote the names rapidly in her pocket diary.

'And now the donation, if you please,' the nun finished impatiently.

Serena looked around her. No matter how large a donation she gave, she could not imagine it being spent constructively, or changing the conditions for the better.

'An appropriate donation will be sent when I have seen the conditions in the other orphanages,' she said, slipping her diary into her raincoat pocket. She had every intention of giving money. A lot of money. But hopefully it would be to an orphanage that would make good use of it.

Ignoring the nun's exclamations of indignation, she strode out of the evil-smelling building and into Cholon's crowded streets. It was 1967. Vietnam was on the conscience of the world. Where was all the money being collected by European and American charities going to? How could orphanages like the one she had just visited possibly be tolerated?

She flagged down a pedicab, and beginning with the first name that the nun had so reluctantly given her, she began a day-long tour of Saigon's orphanages.

It was a day that changed her life. Not all of the orphanages were as bad as the first one. Many of them were making desperate attempts to care adequately for children in almost impossible conditions. At Phu My, older children helped look after younger children. At the orphanage run by the Sisters of St Paul de Chartres, though there was over-crowding and the orphanage was desperately understaffed, at least it was obvious that the sisters cared for the children, and were deeply committed to their welfare. However, not every orphanage was run by the Sisters of St Paul.

At Go Vap, a state-run orphanage, the conditions were horrendous. Food was simply put out for the children to help themselves to, and in the mad scramble, the smallest and the weakest received nothing. Serena tried to count the number of dark heads in one courtyard alone and gave the task up in despair after she had reached three hundred and twenty. There was no laughter in the orphanage, no toys, no personal care for any child. Physical chastisement seemed to be the only way that any sort of order was enforced and, as at the first orphanage she had visited, the air was redolent with the smell of soured milk and sodden bedding.

As she wearily left the misery of Go Vap behind her and told her taxi driver to take her to the last-named orphanage on her list, she felt physically sick. The scale of the problem was stupefying. There weren't simply hundreds of children in Saigon's orphanages, there were thousands.

The next orphanage was situated in a rat-infested alley not far from Tu Do Street. Serena took a deep breath, prepared for the worst, and entered.

It was like entering another world. The attendant who opened the door to her was not a nun, but neither was she an untrained peasant girl, as many of the assistants at the other orphanages had been.

'Can I help you?' she asked in a pleasant New Zealand accent.

Serena didn't stoop to the lies she had felt necessary previously. 'Yes,' she said, looking beyond the girl to a small courtyard where dozens of tiny babies were lying kicking their legs in the sunshine. 'I'm British and I'm going to be in Saigon for quite a while. I've been trying to find an orphanage that would appreciate whatever help I could give it.'

The girl's face broke into a broad smile. She was in her early twenties with a mass of thick dark hair held away from her face in a ponytail. 'Then you've come to the right place,' she said zestfully. 'My name is Lucy Roberts. Step right inside.'

Within minutes Serena was aware that her initial instincts had been correct. The nursery was small, packed to capacity, and lovingly and efficiently run. Some of the staff were young Vietnamese girls and not trained nurses, but their attitude to the children in their care was heartening. Apart from Lucy, the girl who had welcomed her inside, there were four other trained members of staff, another New Zealand girl, an American, and a German.

'And who has overall responsibility?' Serena asked as Lucy handed her a baby to hold and feed while she began to feed another.

'Dr Daniels. He's a New Zealander too. He isn't here at the moment, as it's his day for taking a clinic at Grall, the former French military hospital. He's an eye specialist,' she added.

Serena awkwardly adjusted the tiny baby in her arms. She had never bottle-fed a baby before, and it was proving to be a far more difficult operation than she imagined.

'Why are the majority of the other orphanages in the city so badly run? Why is this orphanage, and to a lesser extent the orphanages run by the Sisters of St Paul, the only exceptions?'

Lucy sighed, deposited the baby she had been holding back on to the rug, and picked up another little mite who was noisily demanding to be fed.

'The main problem is that there are far too many abandoned and orphaned children needing to be looked after. The orphanages can't cope, and the majority of people employed in them are untrained. Hence the conditions that you have seen today.'

The baby Serena was holding finished its bottle and copying Lucy, Serena lifted the baby and laid it against her shoulder, rubbing his back to encourage a burp.

'What do you mean by abandoned? Do you mean that some of these children do have parents?'

As the noise of crying babies demanding to be fed increased, Lucy had to raise her voice.

'Probably fifty percent of them.'

Serena nearly dropped the child she was holding '*Fifty percent*? Then why are they in orphanages? I don't understand.'

'That's because you haven't been in Vietnam for very long,' Lucy said gently. 'The poverty that exists here is something nearly impossible to comprehend if you have only lived in the West. Many women abandon their children because they cannot feed them. Others are abandoned because they are deformed and will be an economic liability. Others are unwanted because they are of mixed race. Many are the children of prostitutes who simply want to be free of the child so that they can return to work. And in Vietnam it is easy to be free of a child. There is no documentation of birth. The charity wards of the maternity hospitals have two and three women to a bed. It is the easiest thing in the world for a woman to walk out, leaving her baby behind her.'

'And the others?' Serena asked, aware of a dizzying, fundamental change taking place deep within her.

'The others are casualties of the war. Thousands of civilians are being killed in the fighting. These pathetic scraps of humanity are the result. Babies and children without parents or grandparents. We do the best we can, here at Cây Thông. We are funded entirely by voluntary subscriptions. Mainly from the western embassies and from various military units based in Saigon. It's a very hit-and-miss affair, and we need all the help we can get.'

Serena laid the baby that she had been holding back on to the rug and picked up another one. She had taken off her Burberry, and where she had been holding the baby, her lime-green Mary Quant minidress was damp with regurgitated milk stains. She did not care. For the first time in her life she was seized by a sense of mission.

'I can help you financially,' Serena said, thinking of the money she had been left by her grandparents and which had always enabled her to live in comfortable ease. 'But I would also like to help practically.'

'Then you need to speak to Dr Daniels. He'll be here in half an hour. Don't be put off by his abrupt manner. It comes from having a crucifying workload and working eighteen and nineteen hours out of every twenty-four.'

Mike Daniels regarded her unenthusiastically. 'Are you a trained nurse?'

543

'No.'

'Are you a trained child-care attendant?'

'No.'

He didn't look like a doctor. He was a strongly built man of about thirty, carelessly dressed in slacks and a sleeveless Sea Island shirt that exposed a chest and arms that might have belonged to a professional weight lifter. His hair was thick and unruly and very dark, as were his eyes. Her first impression was that he was a purely physical personality, and then she noted the sensuality and the sensitivity in the lines of his mouth. Aggressive he may be, but it would be rash for her to make any hasty judgements.

'Then you can't possibly be of the slightest use to us here.'

Serena gasped in indignation. 'Why not? I'm intelligent. I can certainly look after children a damn sight better than most of the people I've seen looking after children today.'

'Those children were not in Cây Thông.' Mike Daniels's eyes flickered over the waist-length fall of silver-blond hair, the exquisitely cut and ridiculously short minidress, the beautifully shaped and vibrantly pink-lacquered fingernails. 'I'm well aware of your motivation in offering us your help, Miss . . . ?'

'Mrs Kyle Anderson,' Serena said frostily, aware that her title and maiden name would cut no ice with Mike Daniels and would probably only antagonize him further.

'You see yourself swanning around the nursery, being an angel of mercy, though not, of course, soiling your expensively manicured hands in the process. Vietnam, to you, is a romantic adventure. Well, I'm sorry, Mrs Anderson, but I can't accommodate you. If time is hanging heavy on your hands, as I'm sure it is, then you'll have to find some other way of occupying yourself.'

Serena's right hand itched to slap his face. She controlled the impulse with great difficulty, saying through clenched teeth, her eyes blazing, 'Has anyone ever told you that you are an arrogant, insufferable, ignorant, *prejudiced* bastard?

I want to work at Cây Thông because there is a sea of human misery around me and I want to do something, *anything*, to help relieve it! I'm quite capable of feeding babies, and changing nappies, and washing laundry and sitting up with sick children. I've seen the children here and I know the sort of ailments they're suffering from. If I am shown, I am more than capable of simple medical tasks such as giving injections and treating skin eruptions. I have a far more realistic idea of what is involved than you seem to think I have, Dr Daniels! And I have every intention of being here at seven in the morning and helping out with whatever task you wish to give me, even if the task is cleaning the floors!'

Before he could reply, she spun on her heel, marching from the courtyard, terrified that even a second's delay would enable him to say scathingly that if she came, she would not be admitted.

When she reached the Continental she was still seethingly angry. How *dare* Mike Daniels suggest that she would be less than useless, and that her motives were selfishly suspect! Even if he did not need her, his nursery and the children did. She had had to sidestep a rat as she had left the alley outside the nursery. She shuddered, wishing to God that she could round up every abandoned and unloved child she had seen and miraculously transport them to the open spaces and green lawns of Bedingham.

Another thought occurred to her, so startling that it took her breath away. There was no reason why at least *one* of those children shouldn't have the benefit of growing up at Bedingham. After all, they were orphans. And it was customary, where possible, for orphans to be adopted. She began to giggle to herself, imagining her father's reaction and Lance's reaction. But she didn't dismiss the idea. It was far too obvious and sensible.

'*Mon Dieu!* You're going to do *what*?' Gabrielle exclaimed incredulously as they drank Manhattans in the Continental's cocktail lounge.

'I'm going to do voluntary work at the Cây Thông orphanage, and I'm going to see if, when I return to England, I can take one of the children with me.'

'You mean *adopt* one of them?'

Serena grinned. 'Well, I don't think they would let me take one home under any other condition.'

'I think that is a very good idea, *chérie*,' Gabrielle said when she realized that Serena was serious. Her pert face was unexpectedly sombre. She was missing *le petit* Gavin more and more each day and was seriously considering whether or not she should fly him out to Saigon. Only the night-time sounds of distant gun and rocket fire deterred her. If the Viet Cong attacked the city and *le petit* Gavin were harmed, she would never be able to forgive herself.

'How did your meeting with the Vietnamese journalist go?' Serena asked, well aware that the sombre expression on Gabrielle's face meant that she was thinking longingly of her son.

Gabrielle took a sip of her drink and with great difficulty turned her thoughts away from *le petit* Gavin. 'I think he is going to be a very important contact,' she said, lowering her voice so that no one could overhear them. 'He admitted having been in contact with Dinh when Dinh was last in Saigon, and he said that he had heard rumours that a round-eye was travelling north with Dinh when Dinh left the city.'

'Did he know where they were heading? Was he able to tell you why you had been told that there would be no further information about them?'

Gabrielle shook her head, her sumptuous red hair gleaming beneath the soft lighting. 'No. He did not know who the source was. But he said that he would make what inquiries he could. And he trusts me, that is the important thing, *n'est-ce pas?*'

'It is indeed,' Serena agreed.

The last of Gabrielle's gravity disappeared. 'You have not yet told me about this doctor who made you so angry,' she said, her eyes dancing with mischief. 'Is he very handsome?

Is that why you are prepared to be a Cinderella and to sweep floors?'

'He is not *remotely* handsome,' Serena said emphatically, conveniently forgetting Mike Daniels's hard-muscled body, and his dark eyes and dark mop of unruly hair. 'He is pig-headed, obstructive, and the most *annoying* man I have ever met.'

'*Alors*, to have aroused such a passionate response, I think he must be very handsome,' Gabrielle said complacently. 'Which is more than can be said for the men that I am at present meeting. The Vietnamese journalist was pock-marked, and Paul Dulles, Gavin's bureau chief, though he is pleasant, is certainly not the kind of man one would suicide oneself for.'

Almost the first thing Gabrielle had done on arriving in Saigon had been to visit Paul Dulles. She had made up her mind before she went that, hard though it would be, she would not tell him of Gavin's disappearance. Dulles was a professional newsman and would be incapable of keeping such information to himself. All she had told him was that she was confident that Gavin was still alive, and that, as she had relations in Saigon, she intended staying in the city for an indefinite period of time.

At the thought of a man handsome enough to suicide one-self for, Serena sighed. Right from the start she and Gabrielle had realized that where the opposite sex was concerned, they both had similar naturally adventurous appetites.

'Unlike Abbra,' Serena had said not unkindly when she and Gabrielle had been alone for a few moments after the three of them had met at the Washington peace march. 'Abbra would never even be tempted to indulge in an extra-marital affair. It's impossible, in a million years, to imagine her sleeping with anyone for the sheer fun of it. She would have to be totally and irrevocably in love with someone before she would go to bed with him.'

Now she said to Gabrielle, 'I can hardly believe it, but I'm actually living a celibate life. It's killing me.'

547

Gabrielle gave a grin of sympathy. She knew all about Serena's superstitious belief that if she wasn't unfaithful, Kyle would be released alive.

Gabrielle, thinking of the times she had been tempted to seek physical comfort in Radford's bed, said sympathetically, 'Me too. But whenever I think of Gavin, I know that it is worth it. And even if it wasn't, who is there we could have an affair with? All the available men in Saigon are either pot-bellied journalists or clap-ridden GIs!'

They both collapsed into laughter, and then strolled into the Continental's dining room for yet another meal of impossibly tough buffalo meat and fried rice.

Their lives soon settled into a regular routine. Despite Mike Daniels's continuing low opinion of her, Serena continued to spend all day, every day, at the orphanage. She filed her nails short and removed her nail polish. She fastened her hair at the nape of her neck with a narrow ribbon. She forsook her stylish minidresses and high-heeled boots and sandals and began to wear serviceable jeans and T-shirts and flat-soled sneakers.

Gabrielle's days were spent in cultivating contacts with people who were Viet Cong, or whose sympathies were Viet Cong, in the hope that she would eventually find someone who would be able to give her hard information about Dinh. It wasn't an easy task. For a Vietnamese to admit to being a member of the Viet Cong or to being a Viet Cong sympathizer was to risk arrest and possibly death. However, slowly but surely, once it became known that Dinh had been her uncle, some trust was extended to her. But no one could tell her where Dinh or his companion were, or even if they were still alive.

At Christmas both she and Serena received a card and a long letter from Abbra. At the end of January, just as Gabrielle had decided that she could survive no longer without *le petit* Gavin, and was going to put arrangements in hand to have him flown out to join her, the Viet Cong launched their Tet offensive.

She and Serena were asleep in their room at the Continental where they were awakened by explosions and gunfire.

'Hell! That's near!' Serena said, sitting bolt upright in bed and turning on her bedside light. 'It sounds like it's right outside, in the square.'

'Impossible,' Gabrielle said sleepily. 'What time is it?'

Serena looked at her little travelling clock. 'Two-thirty.'

There was more gunfire and then an explosion that shook the windows. Gabrielle's eyes widened. *'Tiens!* I think you are right. It *is* in the square!'

They both flung their bedcovers to one side, running to the window. In the darkened square below them men with guns were emerging from manholes and racing towards the top end of Tu Do Street in the direction of the American Embassy. As they watched, US troops began to pour into the square from the south side, firing as they came. Bullets began ricocheting off the Continental's walls, and both she and Serena ducked hurriedly back into the room.

'What the hell is happening?' Serena gasped, struggling out of her nightdress and pulling on her jeans and a T-shirt.

'It's the Viet Cong,' Gabrielle said, searching frantically for briefs and a bra. 'They are inside the city and trying to take it.'

For the next three days, as raging battles took place between the Viet Cong and American and South Vietnamese Army troops, Serena and Gabrielle were unable to leave the Continental. Several times Serena tried, desperate to reach the orphanage and to ensure that the staff and the children were safe, but each time she was beaten back by sniper fire.

On 3 February she finally succeeded. There was still heavy sniper fire and the sound of rocket and mortar attacks, but she ran from building to building, reaching the orphanage dishevelled and breathless.

There was no tap water, and the electricity had been cut off. 'God knows how we're going to survive if the fighting continues for much longer,' Lucy said to her, ashen-faced with fatigue. 'We're down to quinine water and whatever supplies Dr Daniels can bring in. And every time he leaves the orphanage for water, he takes his life in his hands.'

The next time Mike Daniels left the orphanage on a foraging trip, Serena accompanied him. He didn't thank her for her assistance, but afterwards a grudging respect crept into his attitude toward her.

'He's no longer abominably rude to me,' Serena said in amusement to Gabrielle. 'Only deplorably rude.'

Once the worst of the Tet offensive was over there were letters for both of them from Abbra, letters from Radford and Michel for Gabrielle, and a letter from Chuck for Serena.

'I thought you said Chuck Wilson had discouraged you from keeping in contact with him,' Gabrielle said curiously.

'He did. But that was before we met.' Serena slipped the letter into her lingerie drawer. Chuck Wilson was an ongoing dilemma for her. Whenever she thought of him, it was with sexual undertones. There were times when she wished she had the nerve to write to him, asking him outright if his injuries precluded him from making love. And if they didn't? What would she do then? It was a question she could never satisfactorily answer. She knew only that she couldn't shake him from her mind, and that she was glad that he had written to her.

Gabrielle was bemused by Michel's letter, and unsettled by Radford's. Michel's letter was full of details of the success of one of their songs. It was a lyric she had written in the Black Cat days, and that he had put music to, and that the band, with the singer who had replaced her, had recorded. It had reached number thirty-five in the British pop charts and had been covered almost immediately by a well-known British singer. *It's going to earn us a fortune*, Michel had written ecstatically. *Three more of our songs have already been sold to well-established singers and are due to be recorded within the next few months. You may have walked out on fame as a singer, Gabrielle, but it looks as if you're going to make it as a songwriter!*

Radford's letter had been short to the point of terseness. He simply wanted to know when the hell she was coming back.

On 31 March, when President Johnson went on American television to tell the people he would not be running for re-election, Gabrielle was near the demilitarized zone. Nhu's journalist friend had told her of a man who had served beneath Dinh in the North Vietnamese Army, and was now disabled with a war injury and living in his home village a few miles south of the 17th parallel. Accompanied by one of the many Vietnamese friends she had made, Gabrielle had immediately set off through the war-torn countryside in search of him.

She returned to Saigon on 6 June, the day that Robert Kennedy was assassinated in the kitchens of the Ambassador Hotel, Los Angeles.

'Dear heaven,' Serena said devoutly as Gabrielle entered their room at the Continental. 'Where have you *been*?'

Gabrielle, looking a good eight pounds lighter than when she had started out in March, grinned wearily. She was wearing a black cotton jacket and a pair of loose black trousers with a drawstring waist. Despite their shapelessness, the trousers fitted lightly on her hips, so that even dressed as a peasant, with rough, rubber-soled sandals on her feet, she still managed to look provocative and sexy.

'Don't ask, *chérie*,' she said, collapsing into a softly upholstered cane-framed chair. 'Not until you have poured me a Pernod. A very *large* Pernod.'

When the ice-cold drink was safely in her hand she said, 'I reached the village just south of the demilitarized zone, and I spoke to the man who had served in Dinh's unit. He said that it was common knowledge that for a long period of time, Colonel Duong Quynh Dinh was accompanied nearly everywhere by a fair-haired round-eye.'

551

'And?' Serena prompted tensely.

Gabrielle shook her head. 'And that was the only reliable information he was able to give me. He was posted to another unit and has not seen or heard of Dinh for many months. He doesn't know where Dinh now is, or if Gavin is still with him.'

She paused and pushed a scratched and cut hand tiredly through her mop of fiery hair. 'The good news is that I know that Gavin definitely *is* with Dinh, and that he remained with him after they left Saigon. The bad news is that I still don't know where they are, or how I can contact them, or why Gavin has been unable to contact me.'

Serena was silent for a while and then she said awkwardly, 'Did the man you spoke to give any indication as to whether Gavin was being held against his will or not?'

'No.' Gabrielle's eyes were suddenly very brilliant. 'But he must be, *chérie*.' Two large tears began to trickle down her cheeks. 'There can be no other explanation for his silence and his long absence.'

Abbra's letter telling them that Lewis had died the previous October plunged them into even deeper despondency. Though they had not seen Abbra since the Washington peace march, the bond that they felt with her was as strong as ever.

'*Merde*,' Gabrielle said. '*La pauvre petite*. What will she do now, I wonder?'

What Abbra proceeded to do stunned both of them so much that for several seconds neither of them could speak.

'She did *what*?' Gabrielle spluttered. She had just given *le petit* Gavin his morning cereal. He had arrived in Saigon two months previously, cared for on his flight from Paris by an Air France stewardess. Ever since his arrival Gabrielle's spirits had lifted and she was again dauntlessly confident that eventually one of the many contacts she was nurturing would bear fruit, and she would learn exactly where Gavin was being held.

Serena looked down at the letter in her hand and began to grin. 'She married her brother-in-law,' she said again.

'*C'est impossible!*' Gabrielle forgot all about the mess her son was making with his food. 'The quiet, so-well-behaved Abbra? She has married her *brother-in-law*? A professional *football* player? It is unbelievable, *n'est-ce pas? Incroyable!*'

Serena's grin deepened. 'It may be *incroyable*, Gabrielle, but that's what she has done. Still waters run deep, as my father always used to say. What shall we send her as a wedding present?'

They had sent an exquisitely carved, traditional Vietnamese wedding box decorated in mother-of-pearl. And they had sent her all their love and all their sincerest best wishes for her future happiness.

From the day that Serena had entered the doors of the Cây Thông orphanage, it had never occurred to her to leave Saigon and to return to London. With Mike Daniels's reluctant help she had obtained a residence permit, her profession listed as charity relief worker. She existed on her own private income, receiving no money for the long, arduous hours that she worked. Under Mike Daniels's grudging guidance she had learned to give medication and shots and to put in IV infusions. When she wasn't tending the children, she helped out in the kitchen, making vast amounts of fresh yogurt each day, and killing giant-size spiders and cockroaches and ants.

A few days after she had received Abbra's letter she was sitting in the office, trying to catch up on some paperwork for Mike, when Lucy came in hurriedly, saying, 'There's a Vietnamese girl here, asking if we will care for her baby. Little Huong has haemorraghic fever and I must get him down to the Children's Hospital as soon as possible. Interview her for me, will you? She doesn't look the usual type. I don't think she's trying to abandon the child. I'll send her in to you.'

She dashed away and Serena put her pen down and pushed the report she had been working on to one side. A second or two later a rather hesitant young Vietnamese woman entered the office, a child of about eighteen months in her arms. Serena's interest quickened. The child, a little girl, was obviously Amerasian. Though the hair was glossily black and poker straight, her eyes were blue, her skin so pale she could easily have been mistaken for a Celt.

Lucy had been right about the mother too. All too often they were approached by prostitutes wishing to permanently relinquish their inconvenient babies. It was a task that no member of the orphanage staff liked to undertake. Mike Daniels insisted that every mother be counselled against abandoning her child, and that they were all told that they would be given whatever help they needed if they would only change their mind and keep their babies.

The woman standing in front of her was obviously no prostitute. She was twenty-one or twenty-two and was dressed in a traditional silk *ao dai*. Her hair hung waist-length down her back, glossily sleek. Her face showed signs of strain but she was still stunningly pretty, and when she spoke it was in carefully phrased English.

'Excuse me,' Trinh said a little uncertainly. 'I was told that I must come and speak to you if I wish to leave my daughter in your care.'

Serena shook her head gently. 'I am sorry, but it is not our policy to care for children who have mothers able to care for them . . .' she began.

Trinh flushed rosily. 'I do not want to leave my daughter with you permanently. I was told that you sometimes took in children of working mothers on a daily basis. You see, I have no mother, and my sister cannot help me, as she also is working. As a secretary,' she added quickly, in case the phrase should be misunderstood and it should be thought that Mai was a bar girl or a prostitute. 'I am a hotel receptionist, but I need someone to look after Kylie for me through the day . . .'

'Kylie?' It suddenly seemed very quiet. Serena could hear no street noise, no noise from the nearby creche. She looked at the child and the child looked back at her with a confident, curious, blue-eyed stare, her hair tumbling forwards over her forehead in a familiar manner.

'Kylie is my daughter's name.'

Serena sat very still. She had seen eyes like that before. And hair that fell the same way. The more she looked at the child, the more certain she became. There wasn't only American and Vietnamese blood running in the little girl's veins, there was a dash of Irish blood as well.

'Kylie is an unusual name,' she said, dragging her eyes away from the child and back to the mother with difficulty. 'Is it her full name?'

'No,' Trinh said, slightly overawed by Serena's elegantly cool, gold-haired beauty. 'Her full name is Huyen Anderson Kylie.'

Serena let out a long sigh. Why, knowing Kyle as well as she did, had the prospect of such an eventuality never occurred to her?

'And your name?' she asked, wondering if Kyle had known about the child before he had left on his last mission, wondering which of the emotions she was feeling was uppermost, grief, or rage, or wounded pride, or disillusionment.

'Trinh,' Trinh said, wondering why the English girl's manner had suddenly become so taut.

Serena drew in a deep, steadying breath. The next few minutes were not going to be pleasant ones for either of them. 'We need to talk, Trinh,' she said, and all the conflicting emotions that had initially assailed her faded, and in their place she felt only stoic resignation. 'We need to talk about Kylie's father.'

# CHAPTER THIRTY

Gavin found Hanoi fascinating. If the price he had to pay for being there was temporary loss of his freedom, then it was a price he was happy to pay. Hanoi seemed like the real Vietnam to him, the Vietnam he had not found in Saigon. Beneath the shabbiness and the poverty it was still a beautiful city. The wide, ponderous splendour of the Red River curved protectively around it in a giant arc, and nearer to the city, some of them even in its heart, was lake after lake.

By daylight the Lake of the Restored Sword was even more beautiful than it had been at dusk. On a small verdant island a pagoda rose, drowned in magnolia blossom and honeysuckle. Gavin stood looking at it, Dinh at his side. When he had first stepped out into the crowded streets he had been afraid that he would be regarded as an enemy, an American. He had been pleasantly surprised. On their walk through the crowded city streets he had met with no hostility, only curiosity.

'There is a story about the pagoda,' Dinh said as a pair of young lovers strolled past them, the girl with her head resting on the boy's shoulder, their hands tightly clasped. 'It is built on the spot where a turtle arose from the water, carrying a sword with which an ancient Vietnamese hero drove out Chinese invaders.'

Gavin smiled. Dinh was no longer so stiff and formal with him. They were becoming companions, friends.

'And now we will go to the school,' Dinh said, turning away from the lake, walking past a bench full of old men resting and gossiping. 'You will see how well prepared we are for imperialist bombing attacks.'

When Dinh and Gavin entered the classroom, the girls showed the same interest and the curiosity that he had met with on the streets, though this time politely masked. Beside every desk was a trapdoor leading to an underground shelter.

'My entire class of fifty children can disappear within seconds,' the teacher told them with pride.

The same meticulous protection against attack was visible in the streets. The French-built centre of the city was laid out on a craft basis, entire streets devoted to ivory carving or wood carving or leatherwork. Here there were no trapdoors, but every few yards they had to sidestep a manhole cover.

Dinh removed one of the covers to reveal an underground dugout just large enough for one man. 'And it is not only Hanoi that is well prepared against attack,' he said as he replaced the cover. 'Every village creche is similarly protected. Deep shelters have been dug beneath the cribs and the little ones can be lowered into them at a moment's notice, en masse, on slings.'

'I'd like to go out to one of the villages,' Gavin said as they began to cross a road thick with cyclo-pousses and handcarts. 'It's the villagers who have been suffering most from the bombing, isn't it?'

Dinh nodded grimly. 'I will take you, Comrade. You are going to learn more about life in the North than any western journalist has ever learned.'

For the next few months Gavin was high on sheer adrenaline. When he returned to Europe he would be seen as an expert on North Vietnamese affairs. He would be able to write a book, several books. He still missed Gabrielle desperately, just as he would have missed her if he had remained in Saigon. When they had parted they had known that it would be at least a year before they would be together again. His being in the North instead of the South made no difference to their separation,

557

now that he had learned she knew where he was, and who he was with.

'And she does,' Dinh had assured him. 'There is no need to worry anymore, Comrade. She will be with you in spirit and her heart and her mind will be at peace.'

At Tet he shared in the celebrations as if he were a native-born Vietnamese. The streets were vivid with red flags, the air thick with the sound and smell of firecrackers. He and Dinh shared rice cakes and then mingled with the crowds in the street, slowly but surely making their way to Lake Hoan Kiem and the Ngoc Son temple. As they crossed the Huc Bridge, surrounded by peasants dressed in their festive best, Gavin knew that if Gabrielle had been beside him, it would have the been the happiest, most memorable moment in his life.

Two weeks later they set off for Thai Binh, a northern town near the coast which had suffered a heavy bombing attack.

'When we return I am afraid that we will not see each other quite so often,' Dinh said regretfully. 'I am to undertake active duty again and this time in a place and on a mission that you are not to be informed of.'

The jeep they were travelling in rocked and bumped over a potholed road.

'How long will you be away?' There was apprehension in Gavin's voice. Whenever Dinh was away he was replaced by an impassive-faced NVA officer whom Gavin cordially disliked. And also, his year in North Vietnam was coming to an end. He had enough copy to keep him at his typewriter for a lifetime, and his longing for Gabrielle and le petit Gavin was becoming unbearable.

'I cannot say, Comrade. It could be . . .'

His sentence was never completed. Death came out of the air as it had come to so many thousands of others. One minute they were driving along the road leading to Haiphong with other army vehicles a few hundred yards in front of them, the next they were bombed into oblivion.

558

Gavin could feel himself being sucked into the air, his eardrums bursting, his heart bursting, his only thought, '*Not now! Jesus, not now! Not when I'm so close to seeing Gaby again!*'

He was slammed bodily into a tree, losing consciousness. When he regained it, blood was streaming down his face, and the air was thick and acrid with smoke and debris.

'Dinh!' he shouted, pushing himself to his knees, experiencing the same terrible fear that had seized him when they had been bombed on the Ho Chi Minh Trail. '*Dinh!*'

This time there was no answer. Dinh's body was still in the burning jeep, the head at an improbable angle.

'*Oh, God, no!*' he sobbed, staggering to his feet. 'Dinh! *Dinh!*'

He began to run towards the leaping flames. Army officers from one of the vehicles that had been in front of them reached it first. Dinh was dragged from the jeep and laid at the side of the road.

Gavin ran stumblingly towards it, half blinded by pain and blood. 'He's dead,' one of the army officers said cursorily, and then, turning, saw Gavin clearly for the first time.

Gavin was oblivious of the sudden change of expression on the officer's face. He stared down at Dinh, tears mixing with the blood on his cheek. He had been a good friend in North Vietnam, he had been his only friend.

The army officer who had spoken to him was joined by another. They flanked Gavin, AK-47s at the ready.

'I am Australian, not American,' Gavin said, his first, old fear returning. 'I am a guest in North Vietnam. A journalist.'

'Come,' one of the officers said, motioning him towards an undamaged vehicle.

Gavin felt cold fingers beginning to close around his heart. They would, he supposed, take him back to Hanoi. In Hanoi he would be taken before Dinh's military superiors, the superiors who had authorized his presence in North

Vietnam. What would happen then? Would the impassive-faced NVA officer be assigned to him on a permanent basis? Would he be told that his mission was over and would he then be escorted back down the Ho Chi Minh Trail into the South? He had no way of knowing. All he could do was climb obligingly into the army truck and hope for the best.

They did not take him to Hanoi. They continued north-wards to an army camp.

'I should be taken back to Hanoi,' Gavin said patiently when he was first officially questioned. 'The authorities in Hanoi know who I am. They have given me authorization to be in North Vietnam.'

'Where are your papers?' his interrogator demanded. 'Where is your authorization?'

'I am a nephew by marriage of Colonel Duong Quynh Dinh, the North Vietnamese Army officer who was killed in the bombing raid,' Gavin repeated, trying to keep his growing fear under control. 'I am on a mission to the North to see and to report on the sufferings of the Vietnamese people.'

His interrogator eyed him disbelievingly and then put a telephone call through to Hanoi. There was no quick reply from Hanoi, and Gavin was taken away and held in a cell.

'Don't panic,' he told himself repeatedly, as first one hour went by and then another. 'The authorities in Hanoi know who I am. They will authorize the officer here to return me to Hanoi. In Hanoi my troubles will be over.'

The door of his cell opened. 'Come,' an unsmiling officer commanded.

He went. He was not met with a smile and an apology. 'The authorities in Hanoi have ordered that you be placed under arrest,' his interrogator said curtly. 'You are to be taken further north, where you will be held with other enemies of our country.'

It was the nightmare he had feared ever since the moment on the Ho Chi Minh Trail when he had thought that Dinh was dead. 'No!' he said forcefully. 'You are making a mistake! I was *invited* to the Democratic Republic of Vietnam! I am a *friend* of the Democratic Republic of Vietnam!'

'You are an Australian,' his interrogator said flatly. 'You have no papers, no authorization.'

'I am a *journalist!*' Gavin protested, 'I am here to *serve* the Democratic Republic of Vietnam!'

None of it was any use. He was taken away, bundled into a truck, and driven north.

The camp he was taken to was small. Any hopes he had entertained of finding American pilots there were soon dashed. All the other inmates were Vietnamese. His cell was furnished with a sleeping pallet, a slop bucket, and nothing else. He tried to keep control of himself. It wouldn't be for long. There had been some confusion. When the authorities in Hanoi realized who he was, orders would be very swiftly given for his release.

No such order came. The hours merged into days, and the days into weeks. For twelve hours out of every twenty-four he was taken from his cell and put to work alongside the other inmates in nearby fields. Unlike them, he was never ill-treated, and his conviction that his captors knew perfectly well who he was, and what his status had been in Hanoi, grew. No one ever interrogated him. It was as if they knew all they needed to know about him.

The daily diet was rice and a minuscule sliver of dried fish. When rice and chicken and a flat round of dough with a candle pressed into the centre were brought to him one day, he stared in amazement.

'It is Christmas,' his guard said beamingly. 'At Christmas there is celebration, yes?'

He wondered where Gaby and *le petit* Gavin were celebrating Christmas. Would she have been told of his arrest? Would she know that he was still alive?

Time no longer had any meaning. He had no means of keeping track of the date by writing it down, and he began to scrape a small notch on the wall for every day that passed.

561

Occasionally he would overhear snatches of conversation between the guards, but their conversation was almost always centred on when they could next expect leave, and very rarely on world events.

On one memorable day he overheard the guards talking of huge antiwar demonstrations that were taking place in America, on another day he even heard Joan Baez singing an antiwar song on a distant radio.

In between there was nothing. Only the stifling heat or the freezing cold of his cell, depending on the season, and backbreaking daily toil in the fields.

At the beginning of 1969 he contracted malaria and most of the year was spent in delirious spells. He was unable to faithfully notch each day that passed on his cell wall, and in periods of lucidity he panicked, unable to remember if *le petit* Gavin was two years old or three years old.

He no longer believed that Gaby still thought he was alive. How could she? How could anyone? Sometimes, late at night, he wondered if she was still singing at the Black Cat, and he conjured up her image, imagining the song she was singing, the dress she was wearing.

Towards the end of the year he was given his first piece of official news. Ho Chi Minh was dead. Formal truce negotiations had begun in Paris.

There were times when he wondered if he was living in an extended dream, if any of what was happening to him was real. And then there were other times when he wondered if it was the life he had lived before Vietnam that was the dream. If Paris, and Gaby, and *le petit* Gavin were nothing more than the products of malarial hallucination.

The notches on the wall ran the entire length and breadth of his cell. Year followed year. His guards were no longer coldly polite, but were his friends, friends who did not allow him to leave the compound.

When he was told that all American troops had been withdrawn from Vietnam, he did not believe them. How could they be? How could the war be over? There were still Vietnamese prisoners in the camp. *He* was still being held prisoner. Nothing had changed and he could no longer imagine anything ever changing.

When the camp commandant came to him and told him that he was being moved from the camp to another prison camp nearer to Hanoi, he was distraught. He didn't want to leave his possessions behind. His sleeping pallet, the tin bowl from which he ate, the conical hat he had been given to shade him from the sun when he worked in the fields.

He cried when they bundled him into the back of the truck that was to take him away from everything that was familiar. Gaby. He had to think of Gaby. He always thought of Gaby whenever things became too much to bear.

He no longer knew if in the flesh the titian-haired, emerald-eyed, kitten-faced, huskily laughing image that brought so much comfort even remembered him. It was something he tried not to think about. He remembered her. He loved her now as he had always loved her. As he would always love her, until the day he died.

'Gaby,' he said brokenly, passing his emaciated hand across his eyes. 'Oh Gaby, Gaby, *Gaby!*'

# CHAPTER THIRTY-ONE

As Christmas approached, Gabrielle found her despondency returning. She had made no new contacts, discovered no new information about Gavin's whereabouts, and it seemed very unlikely that any new information was going to be forthcoming.

It was two and a half years since she had last seen him. Sometimes she would wake in the middle of the night filled with panic, unable to remember how his face looked when he laughed, unable to recall the exact timbre of his voice. Her body ached to be held, to be made love to. Only Serena's companionship had made the last year bearable, but now it was bearable no longer. She yearned for male company; to be able to flirt a little; to be made to feel womanly and sexy and desirable.

'It's two and a half years, Gavin,' she would whisper heartbrokenly into the darkness. 'Would you mind so much, *mon amour*? Would it be so very great a betrayal?'

No answer ever came. She knew that if the situation were reversed, he would never be unfaithful to her. Not in any way. It wasn't in his nature. Why, then, was it in hers? Not to be totally unfaithful. Not to fall in love with someone else and out of love with Gavin. That she would never do, it would be impossible. But surely an affair would not be so very terrible? She would toss and turn and eventually fall into a restless sleep, the dilemma unresolved.

With the coming of Christmas and the approach of the Vietnamese New Year, the American and European community in Saigon became increasingly edgy. Memories of that year's Tet, and the Viet Cong offensive that had accompanied it, were still fresh in everyone's mind, and though it was unlikely that the Viet Cong would have the resources to launch another, similar attack in Tet '69, it could not be completely ruled out.

'Perhaps you should take *le petit* Gavin home to France for Christmas and the New Year,' Serena suggested tentatively. 'Just in case there is another attack on the city.'

'I will think about it, *chérie*,' Gabrielle had said non-committally.

The thought of leaving Saigon terrified her. In Saigon she was able to fight the temptation to take a lover. In Saigon there was no Radford.

Serena had looked across at her, puzzled. Gabrielle was a fiercely protective mother, and she had expected the mention of another possible Tet attack to have sent Gabrielle scurrying to the nearest Air France office in order to fly *le petit* Gavin out of the country until the sensitive few weeks of Tet were safely over.

Deeply ashamed of her motive for doing so, Gabrielle had decided to risk staying on in Saigon. Two events, both on the same day, changed her mind for her.

On 21 December a grenade was thrown into a street café full of American soldiers. Gabrielle and *le petit* Gavin had been walking back from the park that lay just behind and to the left of the Roman Catholic cathedral. Though they were thirty yards away from the café, they were spattered with shards of glass and a piece struck *le petit* Gavin on the forehead, terrifying him and making a deep and ugly gash.

When they returned to the Continental, there was a letter from her mother. Her father had suffered a heart attack. It had only been mild and his condition was not serious, but her mother suggested that it might be best if she and *le petit* Gavin were to return home. At least for a little while.

'Will you able to get seats on a flight so near Christmas?' Serena asked, a worried frown creasing her brow.

'I do not know, *chérie*,' Gabrielle said with a Gallic shrug of her shoulders. 'All I can do is to try.'

For several hours it looked as if she was going to be unsuccessful, and then Air France called her back, saying they had two seat cancellations on a Christmas Eve flight, leaving at eight in the morning.

'And you?' Gabrielle said to Serena. 'I do not know how long I will be away. It may be for quite a while. Will you be all right in Saigon by yourself? Will you stay on here?'

Serena thought of Bedingham at Christmas. Of the huge log fire that would be burning in the Adams fireplace in the yellow living room; of the enormous, gaily decorated fir tree that would be standing in the grand entrance hall; of walks over crisply frozen ground, her father's ancient spaniels at her heels; of mince pies and traditional turkey and carol singing in the little local church that was almost as old as Bedingham itself. And then she thought of the children in the orphanage. Of those whose parents had died in B-52 attacks; of the malformed who had been abandoned because they were an economic liability; of the mixed-race children whose mothers were prostitutes, and who had voluntarily relinquished them.

'Yes,' she said, pushing all thoughts of Bedingham to the farthest recess of her brain. 'I shall stay on. And I shall be okay. Maybe I'll move in with Lucy. She has an apartment on Phan Van Dat.' But she knew she would not.

Gabrielle had packed two bags, one for herself and one for *le petit* Gavin. He was two and a half years old now and full of ebullient energy and curiosity. She couldn't imagine how he was going to endure the long, tedious flight, and she put several nursery rhyme books and a notepad and crayons into her shoulder bag hoping that they would help to keep him amused.

'I would not hurry back to Saigon,' Nhu said to her sombrely when she went to say good-bye to her. 'I do not think there is anyone who can tell you anything further about Gavin's whereabouts. All we can do now is to wait.'

It had been a dispiriting note on which to leave the city.

As the Air France Boeing climbed into the sky, Gabrielle looked down on the rose-red rooftops and wondered how long the wait would be before she would do so with Gavin at her side.

When she arrived home, not only were her parents there to welcome her, but Michel as well.

'*Alors!* How on earth did you know that I was coming home?' she asked delightedly, hugging him tight.

'Your mother telephoned me,' he said sheepishly.

He hadn't changed. He was still as thin and gangling and awkwardly clumsy. His bony wrists projected a good inch from beneath the bottoms of his shirt cuffs, and his tortoise-shell glasses ensured that he looked more like a schoolmaster than a musician. He was laden with gifts. There were handmade Belgian chocolates for her mother, a box of Hoyo de Monterroy cigars for her father, a giant bottle of Chanel No 5 for herself, and an armful of toys for *le petit* Gavin.

'I was afraid he would have forgotten me,' Michel said, hunkering down and opening his arms wide to catch *le petit* Gavin, as Gavin gave a joyous crow of recognition and began to toddle eagerly towards him.

'He is like his mama,' Gabrielle said with a happy chuckle, 'He does not forget his friends.'

It felt amazingly good to be back in Michel's undemanding company. Already she was thinking about songs again. In order to pass the time on the long flight from Saigon she had occupied herself by writing a lyric. It was the first one she had written in over a year and she had found the exercise deeply satisfying.

'Are you too busy writing arrangements for other people to write any arrangements for me?' she asked, knowing very well that he would never be too busy to write arrangements for her. Not ever.

He stood upright, *le petit* Gavin in his arms, saying heavily, 'Gabrielle, you have no idea how *desperate* I have been for you to return to Europe so that we can write some more songs together. Radford and the band have now recorded six of your songs that I arranged. The song that made it into the top thirty has now been covered by *three* other singers and is currently at number twelve in the American charts. You have a lot of money coming to you, and an accountant who is going demented because he says you never reply to any of his letters.'

Gabrielle had the grace to look a little abashed. The accountant had written to her with monotonous regularity over the last few months but somehow, in Saigon, it had seemed an intrusion, a reminder of a way of life that she had temporarily left far behind her.

'I will go and see him,' she promised, picking up the cuddly toy elephant that *le petit* Gavin had dropped in order that he could secure his hold on a wooden train set more firmly.

As her mother set a place for Michel at the table, and began to bring in dishes of hot spicy food from the tiny kitchen, Gabrielle said with studied casualness, 'How has the band been doing? I understand Radford soon found a singer to replace me. Is she very good?'

Michel blushed slightly. 'Yes. Though not as good as you,' he added hastily.

Gabrielle tilted her head to one side and waited, intrigued by Michel's embarrassed reaction.

'Her name is Rosie Devlin and she is an Irish girl. Very petite and vivacious, like you. And full of incredible energy, also like you.'

'And?' Gabrielle prompted him, wondering if he was embarrassed because Rosie was having an affair with Radford and, if she was, wondering how she was going to react to the news.

'And I am in love with her,' he finished bashfully.

Gabrielle was aware of an incredible feeling of relief. 'And is she in love with you?' she asked without giving herself time to analyse the reason for her response.

568

Michel's blush deepened, 'Yes,' he said with a happy grin. 'Incredible though it may seem, and she is *very* cute and sexy, she is in love with me.'

Gabrielle laughed delightedly. 'And are there going to be wedding bells, *chéri*?'

'I haven't asked her yet, but I want to. I was hoping that perhaps you would have a word with her first. You know, see if a marriage proposal would be welcome . . .'

Gabrielle shook her head in mock despair. 'I can't do that, Michel. I have never even met her!'

'But you will be meeting her,' Michel said, and at his next innocent words her smile faded and all her old anxieties returned in full measure. 'You will meet her tomorrow at the rehearsal room the band is using. Radford and the boys are throwing a welcome home party for you.'

It was a party impossible not to attend. The rehearsal room was over a café in the rue de Charenton, not very far from the original rehearsal room where she and Radford had first met. The band hadn't changed. There had always been a great bond of affection and musical respect between herself and them, and she was touched to discover that the affection had survived her thirteen-month absence. There was a loud cheer and a cacophony of whistles the instant she and Michel entered the room.

'Welcome back to Paris. Gabrielle!'

'Great to see you, baby!'

'You been away too long, honey!'

Only Radford was silent. He stood at the far end of the room, slim and supple in hip-hugging faded denims and a T-shirt with the words BLACK LOVERS ARE BEST immodestly emblazoned across his chest.

They looked across at each other, neither of them attempting to make the first move, and as the whistles and shouts of welcome began to die down and as attention began to be focused upon them, Michel saved the moment by saying guilelessly, 'Gabrielle, you must meet Rosie. Where *is* Rosie? *Rosie!*'

A vivacious, merry-eyed girl, her dark hair scooped up and secured on top of her head, a frizz of curls cascading forwards forties-style over her forehead, stepped forwards from behind the bass player.

'I'm very pleased to meet you,' she said perkily to Gabrielle.

Her French was heavily accented with a beguiling Irish brogue, and despite teeteringly high-heeled white boots she was no taller than Gabrielle.

'I'm pleased to meet you too,' Gabrielle said sincerely, warming to her immediately.

Out of the corner of her eye she was aware of Radford moving lazily forwards towards her.

'Don't be worried that I may be resentful about you coming back into the band,' Rosie was saying, 'I've always known what the deal was, right from the beginning. However, Radford thinks there will be room enough for both of us.' She began to giggle. 'He says we're so similar in build and personality that we will complement each other onstage, not detract from each other.'

'It's very sweet of you to take that attitude,' Gabrielle said, aware that Radford was now at her side. She could no longer put off the moment she had been both dreading and looking forward to, the moment when their eyes would meet. 'But I have no intention of returning to the band. Rock singing was fun for a while, but it's not really what I do best . . .'

'And what is it that you do best, baby?' Radford asked, and there was no mistaking the sexual innuendo in the rich dark timbre of his voice.

She turned towards him, lifting her eyes slowly up to his. She was wearing a short-skirted white cotton-piqué suit and a black cotton Italian turtleneck sweater that she had bought in Baltimore on their American tour. The jacket was thrown casually around her shoulders, and at her neck was knotted a long black and white crepe scarf, the ends falling freely down her back. A black and white leather belt with a gilt buckle cinched her waist, and on her left wrist were black and white twisted bracelets that Serena had bought her for her last birthday. She looked as coolly sophisticated as Serena at her best. Incredibly Parisian. Incredibly chic.

'I'm a nightclub singer,' she said, her voice betraying none of her inner perturbation.

He was as handsome, as sensually aware, as mocking, and as confident as ever. Beneath the tight crinkle of his close-cropped hair, his eyes were hot with an expression that sent a flood tide of desire racing through her veins.

'That may be what you *think* you are,' he said, one corner of his mouth curling into a crooked smile, 'but what I *know* you are is one of the best female rock singers in the business. And to prove my point, I want you and Rosie to duet on the Martha and the Vandellas number *Dancing in the Street.*'

'I'm not coming back to the band,' she said, grateful that there was at least one decision she was not in doubt about. 'You're doing just fine as you are, without me. And I want to go back to what I feel most comfortable doing.'

'Singing love songs in dime-a-dozen clubs?' he said, the humour leaving his voice, his eyes narrowing.

'The clubs don't have to be dime-a-dozen,' she said, returning his gaze unflinchingly. 'And they won't. Not if I have half the talent you insist I have.'

'You're crazy.' His nostrils flared and she knew that despite his careless dismissiveness, he was furiously, blazingly angry.

'Come on, Gabrielle,' the leading guitarist said encouragingly. 'We've been looking forward to this for days. Let's enjoy ourselves.'

There were glasses and bottles of champagne on the lid of the nearby piano. The bass player played the opening riff of *Dancing in the Street* and grinned across at her. 'It's a song just made for the two of you,' he said. 'Why don't you give it a blast?'

She looked across at Rosie, who was looking at her in slight consternation. Gabrielle understood why. Her refusal to sing could be interpreted as pique at being asked to share centre stage with another singer. If Radford took it into his head that that was her reason for refusing to come back as a member of the band, then he might very well ask Rosie to leave it.

She gave a sudden grin. '*Ça va*,' she said, knowing that to continue to refuse was impossible, and knowing also that an informal session with the band would make not the slightest difference to the decision she had made.

Rosie's pert little face cleared with relief, champagne corks flew, Michel took his place at the piano, and Radford said to her with a smile, sure that she had changed her mind about preferring the clubs to the rock circuit, 'Give it all you've got, honey,' his voice thickened to a caress, 'It's been too long a time without you.'

This time she kept her eyes steadfastly averted from his. The undercurrents between them were so raw and live that it seemed impossible to her that the other members of the band, and Michel and Rosie, should be oblivious to them. With her fingers trembling slightly, she slipped her jacket off her shoulders, laying it on a chair, and followed Rosie. What was going to happen when the session was over? How was she going to retain self-control and self-respect? Michel began to play the first few bars experimentally, and with monumental effort she tried to think of the song she was about to sing.

'How are we going to do it?' she asked Rosie. 'I'm not even sure that I know all the words.'

Rosie's elfinlike face split into a grin. 'We're going to do it just as it comes,' she said exuberantly. 'We are going to enjoy ourselves!'

From the first few bars they jelled together as if they had been singing duos for years. Even though Gabrielle had no intention of changing her mind about the decision she had made, not to return to the band, she had to admit that Radford had been right and that they would have been a sensation together onstage.

After *Dancing in the Street* they went into the Gladys Knight and the Pips number, *I Heard It Through the Grapevine*, and then the Supremes' *You Can't Hurry Love* and *You Keep Me Hangin' On*.

'And now I want to hear you sing one of your own songs,' Rosie said, panting for breath, perspiration sheening her face. 'The kind of song that you say you prefer to sing.'

Before Gabrielle could even reply to her, Michel played the first few bars of a song that had been her favourite in the Black Cat days. The rest of the band stayed silent. Radford didn't move, but every line of his body was suddenly taut.

She stood for a few moments, breathing deeply after the exertion of the dancing that had accompanied the last few numbers and then, as Michel played her in again, she took hold of the mike, and closing her eyes she began to sing.

Apart from her voice, low now in register and deeply sensual, there wasn't a sound in the large, drafty rehearsal room. Watching her, Michel knew that the decision she had made was the decision that was right for her. When she sang like this, when she was totally herself, she possessed an erotic presence that was electrifying. When the last note had died away there was a pause before the band broke out into wild applause. It was a pause by her peers, acknowledging a rare talent, a stage quality so mysteriously and implacably egocentric that there was no possible name for it.

Only Radford did not join in the storm of hand-clapping and whistles and foot-stamping.

'She is superb!' Rosie said to Michel. 'When she releases herself in a song she is not only a singer, she is a great dramatic artist as well.'

'She has the one essential ingredient of international star-dom,' the bass player said in a low aside to Radford. 'Every man who sees her onstage will want to make love to her.'

A pulse had begun to beat at the corner of Radford's jaw. He didn't like what he was seeing and hearing because he knew damn well what it meant. She really wasn't going to come back to the band. Musically she was going to go down her own road, even if that road never led to fame and riches.

'Another!' Rosie was calling out.

'What about *Fever*?' one of the guitarists shouted across to her.

Gabrielle shook her head. 'No, not *Fever*. Let's do *Stormy Weather*.'

This time every musician in the room reached for his instrument. The drummer did an experimental riff on the rim of his drum, and then, after a moment's pause, Gabrielle once more began to sing.

There was such deep pain in her husky, broken-edged voice that the simple words of the song became heart-wrenching.

The café proprietor had come upstairs to listen more clearly. 'Now, that,' he said when the song came to an end and applause burst around Gabrielle's ears like foam, 'is my kind of song.' He gave Radford a knowing wink and a leer. 'And my kind of woman. Where the hell have you been hiding her all this time?'

Despite insistent requests from the band that they continue the session, Gabrielle walked away from the microphone and over to the chair where she had left her jacket. She was drenched in perspiration, and the intensity of emotion that had been behind the words of her last song had left her feeling emotionally drained.

Michel walked quickly after her, slipping her jacket around her shoulders, saying, 'If you're not careful, you're going to catch a chill. This is Paris, not Saigon, and you don't even have a coat with you.'

Radford had picked up a black leather jacket, and with his thumb hooked beneath the collar, had swung it over one shoulder.

'You and me have to talk, baby,' he said, ignoring Michel.

'Yes.' It would have been infantile to have refused. She knew they had to talk. They had to talk about the decision she had made about her musical future, and they had to talk about other things as well, things that she was terrified of putting into words.

In retrospect, she knew that the instant she left the rehearsal room with him the decision she had agonized for so long over had been made. There was going to be no going back. She was in utter subjection to her body and her physical needs, and she wanted one thing only. To lay naked beneath Radford's hard-muscled body, to feel herself exploding with a passion that had been kept in check for too long, to kiss and to bite, to lick and to suck and to yield.

There was a crazily ostentatious sports car parked outside the café. An Aston-Martin DB Mark 3. Radford opened the door for her and then strode quickly around to the driver's side.

'Thank Christ you've come to your senses at last,' he said harshly, gunning the powerful engine into life.

She knew that he wasn't talking about music or her career or her return to Paris. There had always been a primitive telepathy between them. She didn't have to tell him by word or gesture that she had inwardly sexually capitulated to him. He already knew.

He rounded the corner of the street with a screech of the tyres, not speaking to her again, not even looking at her. They raced down the rue de Charenton and across the place de la Bastille, nearly mowing down a bicyclist and narrowly avoiding a collision with a truck.

She had never been to his place, never had the remotest idea of where he lived. They swerved to a halt outside a typically grim-looking Parisian apartment block. The concierge eyed them indifferently as, still not touching, they began to run up the steep flight of uncarpeted stairs.

In the apartment she was aware of stark white walls, of several colourful rugs, of a minimum of furniture, a record player and recording equipment, and literally hundreds of records stacked along the entire length of one wall.

They didn't make it to the bed. His T-shirt was off the instant he entered the room. By the time the door slammed behind them his shoes and his socks were off and his jeans were unzipped.

She scrambled out of her panties, kicking off her shoes, lost to reason and conscience and self-respect.

'*Mon Dieu!*' she moaned as he bent her in towards him, lowering her to the floor, pushing up her skirt, 'Be quick! Please, *mon amour*, be quick!'

It was like the coupling of two savage animals. Both of them had waited to sexually gratify themselves with each other for too long. There was no tenderness, not even the pretence of love. She lifted her legs up and over his shoulders, her nails scoring his flesh, drowning in a release that nearly rendered her senseless. Only later, when he carried her to the bed, did they take time to savour each other, to touch with sensuality, and to explore.

She had always been aware of his almost-pagan handsomeness. Naked, he was beautiful. His dark body gleamed the colour of rich mahogany. There was a light mat of tightly curling hair on his powerfully muscled chest, and a much denser bush of hair between his thighs. As she lay beside him, running her fingertips lightly up the length of his thigh and on over the flatness of his stomach, skirting his prick, which had fallen sideways and lay large and flaccid and still throbbing on his belly, she said with devastating honesty, 'I don't love you, *chéri*. I find you stunningly exciting, unbearably desirable, and I think that I must be a little *in* love with you. But I don't *love* you. There is a difference, *comprends-tu*?'

He understood all right. His eyes narrowed, his face suddenly expressionless. For a long moment he didn't speak, and when he did, it was to say with casual brutality, 'Your husband may not be alive. He may be dead. He may have been dead for months.'

She winced, and he knew a moment of harsh satisfaction.

'*Non*,' she said, her voice slightly unsteady. 'Gavin is alive. I know that he is.'

Her fingertips were still on his flesh. His sex stirred and began to harden again. He didn't want to talk about her husband. He didn't want to do anything but make love to her again and again and again, until she forgot about Gavin Ryan, until she forgot about every other man she had ever had or had ever wanted, until she forgot about everything but him.

When they made love again he refused to allow her to rush him. He took his time, teasing and tormenting her, using every trick he knew to give her the kind of pleasure that would have her on her hands and knees begging for more. Whenever she came to the brink of orgasm he denied her, turning his attention to another part of her body, crucifyingly in control of himself.

'*Mon Dieu*,' she whispered brokenly, 'I can't survive much more of this, *chéri*! I am going to die!'

He was kneeling between her thighs, and she felt utterly vulnerable, utterly dominated. His tongue was hot and rough, moving in a long, agonizingly slow journey from her anus to her vagina, pushing deep inside and then, when she thought she could endure not another second, withdrawing and flicking lightly over her clitoris, sucking and nibbling and pulling with his lips at the velvety soft folds of her flesh.

'Now, oh, please, now,' she gasped. She had been too long without a lover. She could not delay her climax as he was delaying his.

At the desperate plea in her voice he raised his head momentarily, a smile of triumph touching his lips, and then he thrust his tongue deep inside her. Seconds before she came he slipped a moistened finger inside her anus, and as the most intense orgasm of her life rocked through her she arched her back, giving a long, ululating cry of shock and ecstasy and total abandonment.

He resisted the almost overwhelming temptation to ask her if her husband had ever made love to her with the same shameless expertise. He doubted it. Where bed was concerned, he immodestly figured he was far better equipped and far more skilful than any Australian could possibly be.

Their affair lasted all through the spring and summer. Never once did she say that she loved him, and out of pride, never once did he say that he loved her. In bed they satisfied each other totally, and out of bed they struck the same kinds of sparks off each other that they had always struck. His fury at her refusal to come back as a member of the band was white hot, but nothing that he could do or say would make her change her mind.

She began to sing at the Chez Duprée, in the Latin Quarter. It was run by Inez Duprée, a singer who specialized in fried chicken and jazz, and Gabrielle soon established a name for herself there. She wasn't cutting records and doing tours as Radford and the band were, but she was doing what pleased her best. She was singing the songs that she wanted to sing, many of them her own, in the way that she wanted to sing them.

It was early autumn when Nhu's letter arrived, informing her of Dinh's death.

*I am very grieved to be writing to you with the news that your uncle has been killed up-country in a farming accident. I believe that the accident took place some time ago, but exactly when I still do not know. There is no news of the friend who was with him.*

No news. There had never been any news. And now Dinh was dead. She wondered what the words *farming accident* really meant. Dinh was a soldier, not a farmer. He had never been a farmer. Was Nhu trying to tell her that Dinh had died fighting? If so, had Gavin been involved in the fighting as well? And where was he now? She put the letter down unsteadily. Wherever Gavin was, without Dinh to protect him, he would be a prisoner. As Lewis had been a prisoner. As Kyle still was. There would be no news now until the war was over.

'Oh, my love, stay alive for me!' she whispered fiercely through her tears. 'Stay strong and stay alive!'

The formal truce negotiations between America and the Saigon government and Viet Cong representatives continued in Paris. Gabrielle received a letter from Abbra in which Abbra expressed the hope that perhaps the end of the war was now in sight, that perhaps soon there would be news of Gavin's whereabouts.

At the time of Tet, Communist forces carried out massive rocket and mortar attacks against 115 bases, towns, and cities in South Vietnam, and Gabrielle, intensely relieved that she had not remained in Saigon with *le petit* Gavin, waited anxiously to hear from Serena.

A letter came from her within days. The attacks in Saigon had been nothing like as bad as last year's Tet attacks, and there was good news regarding some of the children at the orphanage. In the past two months six of them had been successfully placed for adoption with families in Belgium and Luxembourg and Serena was hopeful that more would be placed in other European countries.

In June came the first piece of optimistic news since the peace talks had begun. At a meeting at Midway Island with President Thieu, President Nixon announced the planned withdrawal of 25,000 American combat troops from Vietnam.

It really was beginning to seem as if the end could be in sight. Gabrielle had written to Nhu, asking if she thought any purpose could be served by her returning to Saigon, but Nhu's reply had been disappointingly negative.

Then, in September, Radio Hanoi announced the death of Ho Chi Minh.

'I don't see why you think Ho's death is such a big deal,' Radford had said to her, irritated as he always was by any

579

mention of Vietnam and any reference to Gavin, however oblique.

'It could make all the difference in the world,' Gabrielle had said, deeply thoughtful. 'It could change the attitude of the North Vietnamese.'

'Well, if it does, no doubt President Nixon will tell us so,' he responded sarcastically.

Gabrielle did not rise to the sarcasm. They were in his apartment and had just made love. She swung her legs from the bed, beginning to dress. He raised himself up on one arm, saying bewilderedly, 'Where the hell are you going, baby? You don't have to be at the club for another three hours.'

She slipped on her shoes and picked up her clutch bag, her face fiercely determined. 'I cannot wait for President Nixon to discover whether Ho's death is going to make any difference to the North Vietnamese stance at the peace talks. I'm going to go there myself to find out.'

'You're going to *what?*' Radford yelled, sexually satisfied lethargy vanishing as he shot upright in the bed. 'You're going *where?*'

'To the peace talks,' Gabrielle said composedly. 'I'm going to speak to Xuan Thuy, the chief North Vietnamese delegate, and I'm going to ask him where Gavin is being held.'

# CHAPTER THIRTY-TWO

In Los Angeles, Abbra, too, wondered what political changes would result now that Ho was dead.

'That's why the North Vietnamese Army and the Viet Cong made such an all-out attempt to take the South last year at Tet,' Scott said to her wryly. 'It must have been obvious to them that Ho was an ill man who only had a year or so to live. I guess they wanted a decisive victory that would enable him to die happy.'

The war still played a large part in both their lives. Abbra kept in regular communication with both Gabrielle and Serena, and in November, two months after Ho's death, when another massive antiwar demonstration took place in Washington, both she and Scott were among the quarter of a million participants.

'What are we going to do about this latest idea of yours?' he said to her as they flew back home to Los Angeles. 'Are we going to go ahead with it?'

Her hand tightened in his. Serena had written to her, telling her of how some Cây Thông orphans had been adopted by European families. *The bureaucratic difficulties involved in the arrangements were horrendous*, she had written in her large distinctive handwriting, *but when I finally waved the children good-bye, knowing that they were going to homes where they would be loved and cherished, the satisfaction I felt was the deepest I have ever experienced.*

The letter had profoundly affected Abbra. She and Scott had been married for over a year now and though they had both been united in their desire to have a baby as quickly as possible, no baby had as yet put in an appearance.

'There is no medical reason why you shouldn't conceive,'

the gynaecologist she had consulted had told her. 'You must be patient, Mrs Ellis. Nature often takes her time about these things.'

She still hadn't despaired of having a baby of her own, but Serena's letter opened up other possibilities. Why didn't she and Scott adopt a Vietnamese baby who had been abandoned or orphaned? If they had a baby of their own afterwards, it wouldn't matter. The child they had adopted would simply be a ready-made older brother or sister for it.

She hadn't been afraid of suggesting such an unconventional idea to Scott as she would have been of suggesting it to Lewis. There had been times, in her short marriage to Lewis, when she knew that she had made very wrong assumptions about the way he was thinking or feeling. She still remembered her bewilderment and horror when he had revealed that there were some aspects of battle that he actually enjoyed. She had felt as if they were each on opposite sides of a deep chasm, a chasm that had been bridged only by her very idealistic love for him.

No such chasm had ever sprung open at her feet while she had been married to Scott, and it was unthinkable that it would ever do so. They were as mentally in tune as they had become physically in tune. On their first night in bed together he had overcome her momentary nervousness with passionate ease, making her laugh as well as arousing desire so intense that it almost bordered on pain.

Lewis had always made love to her with slow, tender deliberation. Scott's lovemaking was stunningly uninhibited. He taught her that in bed, between two people who loved each other, nothing was wrong or offensive or out of bounds if it gave mutual pleasure.

Their marriage, when it became public knowledge, gave rise to a lot of prurient speculation and gossip, but between the two of them there was never the slightest problem. Lewis's name was mentioned freely and often. His photograph stood on her desk as it had always, only now it stood alongside a photograph of herself and Scott.

On their first wedding anniversary her father-in-law had telephoned them, his voice abrupt with embarrassed awkwardness as he wished them well. Despite repeated attempts at reconciliation on their part, it was the first time he had spoken to either of them since the day they had told him of their decision to marry.

There was no such overture from Abbra's parents. The marriage was one they were totally incapable of accepting. What made things even worse, for them, was that Scott was such a public figure. There were regular articles in football magazines about him. His name was mentioned with zestful enthusiasm by television sports commentators. His photograph, with Abbra at his side, appeared regularly in the gossip columns of nationwide newspapers. It seemed to them that everyone in the country knew that their daughter had been widowed and had, within months, married her playboy football-star brother-in-law.

Abbra knew very well that her parents would be violently opposed to her adopting a Vietnamese orphan, but she was determined she and Scott would live as they wished to.

As the stewardess moved deftly through the first class cabin, removing empty glasses and serving fresh drinks, Abbra lifted her face away from Scott's shoulder, where it had been resting, and said softly, 'Do you want to, darling?'

He nodded, smiling down at her, his eyes so full of love for her that her heart seemed physically to turn within her chest. 'You know I do,' he said, and at the husky undertone in his voice she knew that he was thinking about their previous night's lovemaking.

She smiled, a deeply happy woman, and with her hand still clasped in his, laid her head once more against his shoulder. 'I'll write to Serena the minute that we reach home,' she said, wondering how long it would take for all the necessary documentation to be completed. She wondered, also, how old the child that would be sent to them

583

would be and if it would be a boy or a girl, and not caring an iota either way.

As they walked through the arrivals lounge at the Los Angeles airport, they were spotted by photographers almost immediately. Over the last year or so they had become a well-known media couple. The public liked to be reminded that some of their hard-muscled, handsome heart-throbs were also genuine Mr Nice-Guys, and since his marriage Scott had fallen most definitely into the Mr Nice-Guy category.

Abbra, too, had become worthy of media attention in her own right. Her novel about North Beach, and the burgeoning Beat Generation, had won a prestigious literary prize, and had established her very firmly as a young writer of great promise.

Flashbulbs popped and a journalist who was hanging around the arrival area for any story that might come his way called out, 'Hey, Scott! I understand you've just flown in from attending the antiwar demonstration in Washington. How do you think your brother would have felt about that? Didn't he pick up a handful of medals before he was blown away in 'Nam?'

It was the kind of tasteless, brutal question that was regularly thrown at him by some members of the press, and though he was filled with an overwhelming desire to punch the journalist in the nose, he merely said with practised ease, 'I make it a rule not to talk about my brother in airport lounges, I find it disrespectful. What do you think about the Broncos' performance this week? That new head coach of theirs is certainly hurling them from the backwoods into the twentieth century. They're a team really going places.'

They were outside the arrivals lounge now, but the journalist was still hard on their heels. Suddenly there came a distant cry of 'I tell you, Brigitte Bardot is aboard the New York flight that has just landed! She's travelling as Mrs Evelyn Watson!' Their tormentor spun on his heel, almost falling over himself in his haste to run back inside the building.

'Thank goodness for that,' Abbra said with a sigh of relief as they walked over to the car park. 'Another minute and we would have been in "how does it feel to sleep with your brother's widow" country.'

Scott grinned. 'One of these days I'm going to tell them that it feels just fine and they can make of it what they want!'

They didn't have far to drive to reach the sanctuary of their home. Although one of the first things they had done after their marriage was to buy the little beach house that Abbra had been renting, they also had a home in Westwood, less than twelve miles from the airport.

It was an elegant house, in an elegant district, and Abbra had decorated and furnished it with warmth and love. The floors were of polished beech, the rugs Oriental in soft colours of dusty rose and muted green. There were plants everywhere and comfortable sofas and chairs. On the walls were the paintings they had bought for each other over the past two years: a La Jolla beach scene that had been Abbra's first Christmas gift to him, a watercolour of the Spanish Steps that he had bought for her in Rome, an oil painting depicting a rainy evening beside the Seine, a stunning charcoal sketch of Lincoln Cathedral.

There were shelves of books, and books piled up on the glass-topped coffee tables. Poetry, and English and American classics for Abbra, biographies and spy thrillers for Scott. Beneath a long, chintz-covered window seat were hundreds of LPs. Oscar Peterson and Sarah Vaughan companionably piled against the Rolling Stones and the Beatles and Chopin and Mozart.

In the kitchen there were copper pans on the walls and jugfuls of fresh flowers and in the bedroom there was a brass-headed bed covered with a white damask French counterpane. The walls were pale yellow, the carpet was creamy-beige and ankle deep, and the windows looked out over their flower-filled garden towards Santa Monica and the sea.

There was a blue and white decorated guest room that Patti had often occupied, and another room that had stood empty for too long.

That evening Abbra opened the door on to it, and stood looking at it thoughtfully. It had been decorated as a nursery. Hand-painted nursery-rhyme figures decorated the white walls. The bassinet was a French antique that they had bought on a visit to Gabrielle in Paris. Stuffed toy teddy bears and tigers and elephants were crammed on to the seat of a low-legged, Victorian carved-rosewood chair which she had reupholstered herself. Soon she would be sitting in the chair, telling bedtime stories to her adopted son or daughter. A warm tingle of excitement surged through her veins. She would need to buy a small bed in case the child that they were sent was no longer a baby. If the child was a girl, then she would pretty up the room a little more. If it was a boy, then she would ask Scott's advice as to the kind of toys she should buy, toys to supplement the waiting teddies and tigers and elephants.

It was February the following year before Serena was at last able to write to them and confirm that all the necessary documentation had been processed and that now all that was necessary was the exit visa for Fam, the five-month-old baby girl whom they were to adopt.

*She was brought in to us from a village some twenty miles north of the city. Her parents both died when the village was caught in cross fire between American forces and Viet Cong. She was severely malnourished when we received her and even now is not very robust. The sooner she leaves Saigon the happier I shall be. We are suffering from a measles epidemic at the moment and several children have already died.*

586

March came and went and still little Fam's exit visa was not processed.

*Believe me, I am doing everything that I can,* Serena had written in angry frustration.

> *Fam's travel documentation is with the Vietnamese authorities and every day I inquire I am told that the documentation will be finalized 'tomorrow'. I keep thinking of a few lines from Kipling:*
> *And the end of the fight is a tombstone white with the name of the late deceased,*
> *And the epitaph drear: 'A Fool lies here who tried to hustle the East.'*
> *If I should meet an unexpected end, it will be the most apt epitaph in the world for me!*

Two weeks later there was another letter, full of rage and despair.

> Dearest Abbra,
> I don't know how to break the news to you, but little Fam has died. She caught measles three days ago and was totally unable to withstand the disease. If only the authorities had processed her travel documentation with even partial efficiency she would be alive and well and with you in Los Angeles. As it was, we received her exit visa just two hours after burying her.

For days Abbra felt numb. She had never held Fam, had never even seen her, but for weeks she had regarded her as her daughter. And now she was dead and the little room that she had made so pretty for her would never be hers.

'It doesn't mean the end of our plan to adopt, sweetheart,' Scott had said to her gently. 'The one thing Vietnam has, God help her, is an abundance of orphans.'

'I know,' she had said quietly, 'but I need to grieve for the child I thought was going to be ours. If I don't, who else will?'

He had given her a sad smile. 'Me,' he said, pulling her lovingly into the circle of his arms and holding her close.

Towards the end of her letter, Serena had written bitterly:

Fam isn't the only victim of crass inefficiency. Do you remember Sanh? He is the little boy who was taken so very ill with haemorrhagic fever within his first few days of coming to us. He nearly died then because he was left unattended and uncared for in an overcrowded hospital ward. Shortly afterwards he contracted polio. He is nine years old now and in leg irons but the most cheerful, lovable child imaginable. Last Wednesday he came down with what seemed to be a sudden toxicosis.

Unfortunately, neither Mike, Lucy, or I were there at the time. A large bomb had gone off in Cholon, killing dozens of people and injuring scores more, and we had been asked to go down there and give what assistance we could. In our absence, the Australian girl who had been left in charge took Sanh to the hospital, the same one he had previously been taken to. The minute I knew what had happened I rushed down there to see him. Once again he had been left alone and unattended, this time in a passageway full of decaying food and medical refuse. He had a temperature of 105 and was delirious. Mike came down to the hospital in a taxi and we took him immediately back to Cây Thông, where I have been nursing him night and day for the past three days. This morning, thank God, his temperature has begun to drop. I truly believe that if we hadn't removed him from the hospital, he, too, like Fam, would be dead by now.

\* \* \*

Abbra reread the entire letter before sitting down to write back to Serena. Sanh was nine years old. She and Scott had imagined adopting a small child. A baby, or possibly a toddler. It would be strange to become overnight the parents of a nine-year-old boy, and a boy who was also crippled.

She sat for a long time, the letter in her hand, thinking. Then she pushed her chair away from her desk and went in search of Scott.

He was in the large basement room that had been converted into a gymnasium, working out. For a brief moment, as she watched him lifting weights, his arm and shoulder muscles bulging, his magnificent body gleaming with perspiration, she wondered if what she was going to suggest to him was fair. He was an athlete. Physical fitness was essential to him. If he had a son, he would surely want a son who would be able to follow in his footsteps, a son he would be able to play football and baseball with. To run and to swim and to go off on camping weekends with.

He looked across at her and grinned, putting the weights down. 'What is it, sweetheart? News from Patti?'

Patti had telephoned earlier in the week to say that French translation rights were pending on Abbra's newly finished novel and that she would be in touch immediately after the deal was finalized.

Abbra shook her head. Incredibly, over the last few days she hadn't written a word and hadn't given her work a thought. 'No. It's something else.'

At the hesitancy in her voice he rose to his feet, throwing a towel around his neck and walking towards her. She was wearing a pair of faded denim jeans and a gentian blue, open-necked cotton shirt. Her dark, jaw-length hair fell forwards softly at either side of her face; and her feet, with their pearly-pink painted toenails, were bare. He was filled with the sudden urge to make love to her, to slide her down beneath him then and there on the polished pine floor. Her eyes met his, clouded with uncertainty, and he suppressed the desire with difficulty, saying gently, realizing that something was troubling her, 'Is it Fam? Are you brooding about her and unable to work?'

She looked up at him, loving him so much that her chest seemed to ache. 'No, it's not Fam. I've accepted what happened to Fam. Or accepted it as much as I will ever.'

Beneath the electric lights of the basement his shaggy mop of undisciplined hair was the colour of old gold. A trickle of perspiration was running down his throat, and she wanted to stand on tiptoe and lick it away. As his eyes held hers, she knew with a surge of relief and shame that by doubting what his reaction to her suggestion was going to be, she was doing him a great disservice.

'I've been rereading Serena's letter. Do you remember her references to Sanh, the nine-year-old boy who is crippled by polio and who has just been so ill?'

Scott nodded, wiping his neck slowly with the towel, a slight frown touching his brow.

'Serena hasn't said so, but I imagine that a crippled nine-year-old will be far less likely to be adopted than small, healthy babies, and so . . .'

'And so you wondered if we might adopt him,' he finished for her, his frown clearing. He had been apprehensive that she had been mentioning Sanh because the child's plight was causing her even further distress. Now that he knew what was on her mind, he slipped his arm around her shoulders, saying, 'It's a good idea, sweetheart. I don't know why we didn't think of it when we first read Serena's letter.'

'And you don't mind . . . about his disability?'

He gave her a mock punch against her jaw. 'A child of our own could be born with a physical handicap. You wouldn't expect it to make any difference to me then, would you? Besides, with the right kind of medical treatment and the right kind of care, who is to say that he will have to remain in leg irons? I don't know a damn thing about polio and its after effects, but while the adoption

590

documentation is going through I'm going to find out all I can.'

In May, when an estimated 100,000 demonstrators gathered in Washington to oppose the bombing of Communist base camps in Cambodia, Abbra and Scott were in Paris, visiting Gabrielle.

Feelings at the Washington demonstration were higher and more intense than ever before. Four days earlier, at an antiwar demonstration at Kent State University in Ohio, in an act that stunned America, the National Guard opened fire on the students. Four of them, two of them girls, were killed. Eleven others were injured. With the television scenes from Kent State still searing their minds, Abbra and Scott were in an unusually sombre frame of mind when they met Gabrielle at the nightclub where she sang.

'It is terrible, *mes amis*,' Gabrielle said as they sat at a small table in an alcove, toying with the sole Normandie that all three of them had ordered. 'At the beginning of the year I thought that perhaps there would be a negotiated peace before the year was out. Now . . .' She gave a despairing shrug of her shoulders. 'Now I am not so sure. There are times when I think that it will never end. That *mon petit fils* is going to be a man before Gavin sees him again.'

Her voice had broken slightly at the mention of Gavin. Abbra felt pain shoot through her, so intense she could hardly breathe. She could only imagine what Gabrielle must be suffering. What she herself would have been suffering if there had been no confirmation of Lewis's death and if she had still been living every day, waiting for news.

'What is happening at the peace talks?' Scott asked quietly after they had sat in silence for several minutes.

'*Merde alors!*' Gabrielle said graphically, raising her eyes to heaven. 'The peace talks! They are beyond belief, *mon ami*. You know, do you not, that it took seven months for them merely to reach agreement on

591

the seating arrangements? Neither the Saigon delegate nor the National Liberation Front of South Vietnam delegates would sit opposite each other. Nothing productive is being discussed. All that is happening is that both sides spend hours each day verbally maligning each other.'

'And have you managed to speak with Xuan Thuy yet?' Abbra asked, ignoring the large Neapolitan ice that had followed the sole Normandie.

Gabrielle's cat-green eyes glinted beneath the long sweep of her eyelashes. 'No, not yet. But I have not given up hope. It is in the nature of a Vietnamese to be able to sit out eternity if necessary. And I am half Vietnamese. I can be just as stubborn as the embassy, just as determined. And in the end I will have my answer.' She pushed her Neapolitan ice away from her, untouched. 'That is what the Americans do not understand about the Vietnamese,' she said with stark frankness. 'They do not understand that we see time differently. And that is why they will lose the war. Americans will not endure a war that continues for ten, fifteen, twenty years. The Vietnamese will do so, *have* done so, when you consider how long it is since they first began to fight the French.'

Scott nodded in agreement. An immediate rapport had sprung up between himself and Gabrielle, just as it had sprung up between the two women. When Abbra had first introduced them, Gabrielle had looked up at Scott's magnificent physique and six-foot-four-inch stature and with a naughty twinkle in her eyes had said with a husky, unchained laugh, '*Félicitations*, Abbra. *Il est magnifique!*'

Scott, in his turn, thought the petite Gabrielle an absolute delight. He admired the way she was bringing up her son by herself, the way she had turned her back on easy fame with the rock band she had once sung with in order to sing in a style true to herself, and he admired her steadfast efforts to discover news of her husband and the fierce love that was in her voice whenever she spoke of him, even though it was now four years since he had disappeared.

He knew of her affair with Radford, though Gabrielle took care that neither he nor Abbra ever met Radford. Gavin was the love of her life, and when she was with them, she wanted to talk only of him. Her tortured guilt at not being strong enough to live without physical love in Gavin's absence was often apparent, and both Scott and Abbra deeply sympathized with the terrible limbo in which she was living, and the means she had taken in order to endure it.

'I have visited the North Vietnamese Embassy every morning for the last eight months,' she continued as the untouched ices were removed from the table and Scott ordered a round of martinis. 'And every morning the routine is the same. I ring the doorbell and a Frenchwoman of about forty-five, very efficient-looking in a black skirt and a white blouse, opens the door. I ask if I may speak with Xuan Thuy. I am refused. I ask if I may speak with anyone who can give me information about my husband, and I am told that there is no one there who can give me any information. And the door is closed in my face.'

'Do you think things are ever going to change?' Abbra asked as the musical trio who had been playing dance music came to the end of their number. 'Do you think you ever will gain entrance?'

Gabrielle's eyes were bright with determination, 'Oh, yes,' she said dauntlessly. 'Yesterday I saw one of the Vietnamese officials in the street and he was unable to escape me. For the first time I was able to impress upon someone in authority just who I am. Who my uncle was. He repeated only the familiar "Madame, I am sorry. We have no information about your husband" routine, but I could see that his attitude towards me had changed.' The pianist began to play the lead-in to Gabrielle's first song, and she rose from the table, saying with a wide, gamin-like smile and unquenchable optimism, 'There will be news soon, *chérie*, I am sure of it.'

★ ★ ★

Sanh wasn't the only Vietnamese child arriving in the country that day. A woman named Lucy Roberts had escorted seven children from Saigon, six of them babies. How she had managed, single-handedly, to feed and change and care for them on the long flight, Abbra couldn't even begin to imagine. But her attention wasn't focused on the babies. It was focused on the bright-eyed little boy who, his withered legs encased in braces, was propelling himself forwards with difficulty in Lucy's wake.

'This is Sanh,' Lucy said with a tired smile as they all met in the middle of the airport waiting room. 'How I would have managed without his help on the plane I do not know.'

'Hello, Sanh,' Scott said, slipping his arm lightly around Sanh's shoulders. 'Welcome to America.'

Abbra's heart was beating so hard that she thought even Lucy and Sanh must be able to hear it. 'Hello, Sanh,' she said, stepping towards him and holding out her hand to him. 'Welcome to your new home.'

His hand slipped into hers, and as he looked up at her and grinned, saying in heavily accented English, 'I am very glad to be here, *Maman*-Abbra,' she knew that all her panic-stricken fears were groundless.

'Who told you my name?' she asked, love for him flooding through her, knowing that it was going to be all right, knowing that from now on they were going to be a family.

'*Cô* Serena,' he said, his hand remaining trustingly in hers.

Abbra smiled, grateful for Serena's thoughtful foresightedness. Although Sanh's first language was Vietnamese, his second was French, not English. It was only natural that he should, at first, refer to her as *Maman*. And *Maman*-Abbra was an ideal appellation for the first few days, when they were getting to know each other and when anything else would be touched with artificiality. Soon, she knew, the Abbra would be dropped. And soon, also, *Maman* would change quite naturally to Mom.

\* \* \*

In April President Nixon announced that 100,000 American troops were to leave South Vietnam by the end of the year. Abbra listened to the television newscast with relief. Perhaps this time it really was the beginning of the end. She wondered if Scott had heard the news over the car radio. He and Sanh had gone to watch a basketball game and were then going on to Musso & Frank's Grill on Hollywood Boulevard. It was the only chophouse Scott knew where they served adequately burned onions with grilled liver, and he and Sanh often ate there after attending a basketball or a baseball game.

When the news programme came to an end, she turned the television off, impatient for Scott and Sanh to return home. It was Sanh's tenth birthday the next day, and though Sanh did not know it, they were going to take him to a kennel that evening in order that he could choose a puppy for his birthday present.

As she turned away from the television set she saw a car enter the drive. A sleek, black, official-looking car. She stood very still, ice seeping down her spine, transported back in time to the occasions when she had been first brought the news that Lewis was missing in action, and then the news that he was dead.

What on earth was the reason for today's visit? Had they found Lewis's body? Were they coming to tell her that Lewis's body was being returned home?

The doorbell rang and with a heavy heart she forced herself to move, to walk across the room and into the hallway. She had been so happy a minute before, waiting for Scott and Sanh to return home, looking forward to Sanh's delight when they told him that he could choose a puppy for his very own. Now, if her visitors were bringing her the news that she suspected they were bringing, Sanh's birthday would be permanently marred. Instead of being a day of joyous thanksgiving, it would be a day on which she would always remember the news that came immediately prior to it.

The doorbell rang again and she put her hand on the catch. Perhaps it wasn't what she feared. Perhaps her visitors were calling about some innocuous bureaucratic matter that would be explained and over in a mere few seconds.

She opened the door wide, and the instant she saw their faces she knew that the matter they had come about was anything but innocuous.

'Mrs Ellis? May we speak with you, please?'

She nodded, her throat dry, leading the way into the living room.

'Is your husband at home? I'm afraid that this is a matter that concerns you both.'

She shook her head. They weren't the same men who had called on her on either of the two previous occasions, but they were so similar in manner and looks as to be virtually indistinguishable.

'No. Please tell me whatever it is you have to say to me.'

'I'm afraid I can't do that, Mrs Ellis, not without your husband here with you.'

The officer who had so far done all the speaking looked ashen-faced. She wondered if his previous assignment had been to tell some poor woman that she was now a widow.

She was suddenly filled with a passionate desire to be rid of both him and the chaplain who was standing sombrely silent at his side before Scott and Sanh returned home.

'I've received two such visits previously,' she said with cool composure. 'On both occasions I was informed that information couldn't be given to me unless someone was with me, and on both occasions, eventually, the information was given while I was unaccompanied. That is the way I prefer to hear difficult news, Major. By myself.'

The major was beginning to look physically ill and the chaplain cleared his throat, saying placatingly, 'I am afraid this time, because of the nature of the circumstances, we really must insist that your husband be present. Where is he at the moment, Mrs Ellis? Will he be long?'

'He's away for the weekend,' she lied, shocking herself at the lengths she was prepared to go in order to insure that they leave before Scott and Sanh returned home.

'Then I think we will have to call again on Monday,' the chaplain responded unhappily.

'No!' Her voice was so adamant that both men blinked. 'I've received, alone, the worst news that any woman can receive. Nothing you can tell me today can be any more shocking than the news that has been broken to me in the past. Whatever it is, I insist upon hearing it.'

She wasn't speaking to the chaplain, she was speaking to the major. His eyes held hers and then he said at last, slowly, 'Okay, Mrs Ellis. I guess there's never going to be an easy way of doing this. Will you sit down, please?'

She didn't want to sit, but it seemed pointless to prolong the proceedings by making trivial protests.

She sat. She wondered where Lewis's body had been found. How it had been found. The possibilities sickened her. But at least now he could have a proper burial.

'Mrs Ellis.' The major had seated himself in a chair opposite her, and he was leaning towards her, his eyes very grave, his hands clasped tightly and held between his knees. 'Mrs Ellis. I want you to listen to me very carefully. A month ago, as part of the negotiations that have been taking place in Paris, the North Vietnamese agreed to release three prisoners of war. No names of the men to be released were given until three days ago.' He paused, and she waited patiently for him to tell her of the dead who were also, obviously, to be returned as well.

'Mrs Ellis, when we received the names of the three men who are to be released to us, your husband's name was the first of the three.'

She continued to stare at him, waiting for him to continue, to explain.

He didn't do so. She said at last, with a little helpless gesture of her hands, 'I'm sorry, I don't understand. My husband' – she corrected herself – 'my first husband is dead.

He has been dead for four and a half years now. There was a witness to his death. Has his body been found? Are the North Vietnamese releasing it along with two prisoners of war? Is that what you are trying to tell me?'

The major shook his head. 'No, Mrs Ellis. What I am trying to tell you is that your husband, Captain Lewis Ellis, is alive. On receiving his name, we checked immediately with the North Vietnamese authorities. There is no doubt whatsoever. Your husband was held for three years in a jungle camp in the Ca Mau peninsula and moved north eighteen months ago. He is to be released, with two other prisoners, in a week's time.'

'Lewis is alive?' the words were a stunned whisper. For a brief second of time her whole being was filled with such intense joy that she thought her heart would burst. And then, through the window, she saw Scott's car enter the drive. Lewis was alive, and her marriage to Scott was bigamous. Or illegal. Or invalid. He wasn't really her husband. He had never been her husband.

The car came to a halt and he opened the driver's door, stepping out on to the gravel. His shaggy mop of wheat-gold hair gleamed in the late afternoon sunshine. He strode round to the passenger seat door, opening it, helping Sanh to step out of the car. They were both laughing. Through the open window she could hear their laughter and she knew that she would never, ever, forget it.

'Tonight, Papa? Are we going for the puppy tonight?' Sanh was saying eagerly.

He had been with them for four months now, and already she could not imagine life without him. If her marriage to Scott was now invalid, what about Sanh's adoption? Was that invalid too? How could she live without him? How could she possibly live without Scott?

'Oh, God,' she whispered as the front door opened and they came noisily and laughingly into the house. 'Oh, sweet Jesus! What is going to happen to us? What are we going to *do*?'

# CHAPTER THIRTY-THREE

Serena rose to her feet. It was impossible to keep on talking to Trinh from behind a desk. Their conversation was no longer official. It was highly personal and couldn't be conducted as if she were a person in authority and Trinh a supplicant. At this moment in time they were equals. Two women in love with the same man.

She looked out the window before beginning to speak. *Were* they both in love with the same man? Was *she* still in love with the daredevil, roustabout Irish-American that she had married in such reckless haste three years earlier? Amazingly, it was a question she had never thought to ask herself. She had simply assumed that she was. Certainly his being returned to America safe and well was one of her goals. It was concern for Kyle that had brought her to Saigon. Because of her superstitious fear that unfaithfulness on her part would affect his eventual fate, she had lived as chastely as a nun for what had begun to feel like a lifetime. So surely she was still in love with him?

Outside in a small courtyard a dozen babies lay on blankets, kicking their legs and gurgling contentedly. She stared at them unseeingly, wondering if the exquisite-looking Vietnamese girl was also in love with him. Certainly she must have been at one time. She most obviously wasn't a prostitute or a bar girl. What had Kyle told her? That he would get a divorce and marry her? And what did the girl know of Kyle's whereabouts? Did she believe that he was dead? Did she think that he had simply abandoned her? Or did she know that he was in Hoa Lo, and if so, who had told her?

She turned slowly away from the window. 'What I have to say is very difficult,' she began, and to her horror her voice sounded tight and brittle. She paused, trying to control it, to sound reasonable and calm. When she spoke again her voice was only slightly unsteady. 'I know Kyle Anderson, the father of your little girl.'

She kept her eyes resolutely away from the child. There would be time enough to look at Kyle's child. For the moment she couldn't cope with the emotions that the child was arousing in her.

Trinh's whole expression and demeanour changed. 'You do?' She stepped towards Serena eagerly, her eyes bright with fierce love and desperate anxiety. 'You are a friend of his? A relative? Do you have news of him?'

Serena's throat hurt. She had her answer to one of her questions. The girl was still in love with him. At that moment she hated Kyle. She hated him for his irresponsibility. She had never, in a million years, expected that he would be faithful to her while he was in Vietnam. That would have been out of character. But why couldn't he have contented himself with the willing bar girls of Tu Do Street? Why, instead, had he seduced a nice, respectable girl and probably ruined her whole life?

She said simply, knowing no other way of phrasing the words so that they sounded even remotely acceptable, 'I'm his wife.'

Trinh merely stared at her. For a second Serena wondered if she had overestimated the girl's seemingly excellent English.

'Do you understand me?' she said gently, wondering why she was feeling so much compassion for a girl who should, instead, be arousing in her feelings of outrage and jealous fury. 'I am Kyle's wife. That is why I came to Saigon. To perhaps gain news of him, to be able to feel a little closer to him.'

'No,' Trinh whispered, stepping back uncertainly, her free hand stretched out as if feeling for some form of support. 'No, I do not believe you. You are mistaken. You are talking of another American. Another Kyle Anderson.'

On the floor near the desk was Serena's shoulder bag. Serena picked it up and opened it, taking out a dark green Gucci wallet. Silently she withdrew a photograph of Kyle. It had been taken in Scotland, only hours after their Gretna Green marriage. Kyle was laughing, his dark hair tumbling low over his brow. He was holding a can of lager in one hand and was wearing a pair of hip-hugging jeans and an open-neck shirt. Behind him were moors and the gleam of a distant loch. Serena didn't remember where they had been when she had taken the photograph. She could only remember their laughter, their crazy elation at having pulled off a prank that was going to shock all four parents to the core. It all seemed so long ago now. A different lifetime, a different world.

She held the photograph out towards Trinh. The girl didn't take hold of it. She simply stared at it, the blood draining from her face. 'No,' she whispered again, her hands tightening around the child in her arms. 'No, I do not believe it! I cannot believe it!'

'It's true,' Serena said starkly. She withdrew a pack of cigarettes from her bag. 'Would you like one?' she asked, offering the pack to Trinh.

Trinh shook her head, tears rolling mercilessly down her cheeks. 'He never told me that he was married. I had no idea. I did not know. I am sorry, Madame. I do not know what to say. How to apologize to you . . .' Her voice broke completely, and she could not continue. Her tears were falling on to her *ao dai*, on to the bewildered child in her arms.

'Sit down,' Serena said practically, moving a chair towards her.

Trinh didn't move, didn't seem capable of moving, and Serena took her lightly by the arm, pressing her down into the chair.

'It isn't up to you to apologize,' she said, amazed at the maturity she was displaying and which she genuinely felt. 'I believe you didn't know that Kyle was married. Do you know where he is now? Do you know that he is imprisoned in Hoa Lo?'

Trinh's head shot upright, relief replacing shocked distress in her eyes. 'He is alive? Do you know for sure that he is alive? His friend wrote to me and told me that he was alive after his helicopter crashed, but that there was no news of him afterwards.'

'His friend?'

Tears still coursed their way down Trinh's face. 'Mr Chuck Wilson,' she said thickly. 'That is the name of Kyle's friend. In Saigon, they were always together.'

Serena's nostrils flared. So Chuck had known about Trinh; he had probably known about Kylie, but he kept his knowledge to himself. She didn't know how she felt about his deceit. It was something she would have to think about later. She could not possibly start to assess it at the moment.

Kylie had begun to squirm in Trinh's arms and to vocally protest at being held for so long, so tightly. Trinh set her down on the floor, her eyes still holding Serena's as she waited tensely for whatever information Serena could give her.

'I know that after he was shot down he was taken to Hanoi,' Serena said, feeling so overwrought that she could quite easily have burst into tears herself. 'In October of the year he was shot down, the North Vietnamese released a list of names of men being held in Hoa Lo. Kyle's name was on the list. There has been no communication from him, but there has been no communication from the vast majority of POWs being held. Only a very small percentage has been allowed to write to their families. Kyle hasn't been one of them, but that doesn't mean that he isn't still alive.'

'Oh, *Choi oui!*' Trinh gasped softly. Oh, my God!

She began to sob and Serena, feeling equally emotionally spent, walked slowly back to her desk and sat down behind it, weak-kneed.

The child, sitting happily on the floor, regarded her with a steadfast, curious gaze. Serena returned it. Every Amerasian child she had ever seen had been stunningly attractive and Kyle's child was no exception. She was ravishingly beautiful, with the kind of bone structure that indicated a beauty that would last lifelong.

Serena was tempted to rise to her feet again and to pick the child up and sit her on her knee. She resisted the temptation, unsure of how Trinh would react if she were to do so.

Trinh's sobs of relief had begun to subside, and when she was able to speak she said awkwardly, 'You have been very kind to me, Madame, under the . . . the circumstances.' She paused, remembering that though Kyle was alive and in Hoa Lo, he was also married. He had lied to her. He had not been going to marry her. He had never intended to marry her. Her heart was breaking and she didn't know how she was going to bear the pain. She said stiffly, 'I will go now. You will not want my daughter here, at Cây Thông.'

She rose from the chair, bending down and scooping Kylie into her arms.

Serena regarded the pair of them thoughtfully. She, too, had thought of the difficulties attendant on taking Kylie into Cây Thông. And she had also thought of the alternatives – the other orphanages in the city, crammed and dirty and loveless. It was unthinkable that she should allow Kyle's child to suffer in some such institution.

She said, choosing her words carefully, 'I would very much like Kylie to be cared for at Cây Thông. She would be as well cared for here as she could possibly be anywhere, and no one but us would know of the rather peculiar relationship that exists between us.'

Trinh stared at her, her face troubled, and then said hesitantly, 'Forgive me asking, Madame, but do you and

'. . . and' – she swallowed, continuing only with the greatest difficulty – 'and Kyle have children of your own?'

Serena shook her head, 'No, we were married a year before Kyle came to Vietnam, but during that year we were together for only a few days.'

For a moment Trinh was too stunned by Serena's frankness to be able to react, and then relief flashed through her eyes, followed by a look of triumph that she couldn't quite hide.

Serena waited, knowing why Trinh had asked her if she had children of her own, knowing what was troubling her.

'Some of the children at Cây Thông have been adopted by British and American families,' Trinh continued. Serena's display of frankness encouraged her to be equally frank. 'You have no children of your own, Madame. Perhaps if I left Kylie here, with you, because she's your husband's child, you would take her from me?'

'No,' Serena said quietly. 'I will not take Kylie from you. I do not want her for myself. I simply want to ensure that as she is my husband's child, she is suitably cared for.'

She knew it was useless to say anything more. Trinh would either believe her or not. For the child's sake, she hoped very much that Trinh was going to believe her.

From outside the open window the babies could be heard, beginning to noisily demand feeding. Trinh stood silently, Kylie in her arms, struggling to come to a decision.

There was a brief knock on the rattan door, and a New Zealand girl opened it, saying, 'Sorry to interrupt, Serena, but the babies are ready to be fed. As Lucy is still at the hospital, could you possibly give me a hand?'

'I'll be right with you,' Serena said, rising to her feet.

When the door had closed and they were once more by themselves, Trinh said unhappily, 'I do not think I have any choice. I will bring Kylie to Cây Thông to be looked after through the day while I work. And I will return for her every evening.'

Serena nodded, relieved. They were not a day nursery, and the arrangement was not a usual one, but she knew that she would be able to square it with Mike Daniels.

'And nothing will be said to anyone?' Trinh asked again anxiously. 'No one will know that she is your husband's child?'

'No,' Serena affirmed. Christ. It was the last thing in the world that she wanted. She could just imagine Mike Daniels's reaction. Lucy's reaction. She rose from behind the desk and crossed the small room, opening the door for Trinh and Kylie.

In the doorway Trinh paused. 'Thank you,' she said simply. For a moment they were only a heartbeat away from friendship, and then Trinh said formally. 'Chào bà, Madame.' Good-bye. And the moment was lost.

Serena stood in the doorway, watching as Trinh walked gracefully away down the corridor, her hyacinth-blue *ao dai* fluttering softly around her legs. Kylie was in her arms, facing back over her shoulder. Her eyes met Serena's and suddenly, beneath the dark mop of hair, her face broke into a wide, mischievous smile.

At that moment she reminded Serena so much of Kyle that the blood pounded in her ears. She had encouraged Trinh to use Cây Thông as a nursery for Kylie because any other alternative had been unthinkable. But she still had no idea how she was going to come to terms with having Kyle's illegitimate daughter at Cây Thông, or of how she was going to come to terms with seeing Trinh every day, as she deposited and collected Kylie.

'When you're eventually released from Hoa Lo, you're going to have one hell of a lot of explaining to do, Kyle Anderson!' she said grimly under her breath as the hyacinth-blue *ao dai* disappeared around a corner and then, more emotionally confused than she had ever been before in her life, she hurried out into the courtyard to help feed the now-crying babies.

★ ★ ★

Kylie soon became a favourite at Cây Thông. She was the only child who was neither an orphan nor abandoned, and though some members of staff had been mildly curious about the arrangement, none of them ever suspected the truth about her paternity.

For her own mental well-being Serena took great care not to establish any sort of special relationship with Kylie. It wasn't easy. Kylie was by nature an affectionate and gregarious little girl, and Serena's gentle but firm rebuffs left her obviously hurt and bewildered. Serena steeled her heart. She could not allow mutual affection to spring between herself and Kylie. It would lead to all sorts of complications and, possibly, to untold misery. And so the rebuffs continued and eventually Kylie no longer approached Serena. But she would often stare at her, her dark blue eyes uncomprehending and miserable.

Whenever she brought Kylie to the orphanage, or picked her up, Trinh avoided Serena as assiduously as Serena avoided Kylie. The situation was one that Trinh didn't know how to handle. Kyle had lied to her, but she still loved him and she was living in the hope that despite the strangeness of their last meeting he still loved her. His wife had said herself that she and Kyle had lived together only a few days. Perhaps that was why Kyle had not mentioned his marriage to her, because it was not truly a marriage at all. The thought had cheered her, but left her perplexed about Serena's presence in Saigon. She could imagine a woman doing such a thing only if she were very much in love. And if Kyle's wife was very much in love with him, then perhaps she would be able to persuade him to return to her when the war was over, and when he was released from Hoa Lo.

For the next year Serena rarely moved beyond the suburbs of Saigon. Mike Daniels made regular trips to the provinces, visiting regions as far apart as Da Nang and Hue in the north of the country, and Soc Trang and Can Tho in the Delta. He always returned with more orphans and more abandoned waifs, and Serena's work, trying to find loving homes for them in Europe and in America, never ceased.

Serena often thought that her relationship with Mike Daniels was very like her relationship with Trinh. It was a relationship that was going nowhere, a relationship that neither developed nor regressed. Although occasionally she thought she caught a look of interest in his eyes, his manner never changed. He tolerated her, and that seemed to be all. It was a masculine reaction that Serena had never encountered before, and it was one that infuriated her beyond bearing.

It wasn't that she lusted after him. Not the way she had with Chuck. If he had propositioned her, she would have turned him down flat. But she did admire him. He was dedicated to the task of improving the lot of the sick and the destitute. As an eye specialist, his workload at the local hospital was enormous, and he took other clinics as well, clinics at the refugee camps in the city's suburbs, clinics in Cholon, clinics in the outlying villages around Saigon. And every penny he earned went into the running of Cây Thông.

Without Mike at the helm organizing the funding, and bullying and brow-beating the government and the military for whatever provisions he could get from them, Cây Thông would have been unable to survive. The children that were tended with such loving care in clean, sanitary surroundings would instead have had to fight for their survival in the unspeakably overcrowded and often rat-infested city orphanages.

But though she admired him unreservedly, he often seemed to be barely aware of her existence. Only rarely did he suggest they have a drink together at the end of the day, and when they did so their conversation was always impersonal. He knew nothing whatsoever about her private life, about her initial reason for being in Saigon. And she knew nothing at all about him. Not even if he was married, or had been married.

\* \* \*

In 1970, at about the time she was arranging for Sanh to be adopted by Abbra and Scott, Serena told Mike of her intention to adopt not just one child, but several children.

'Ridiculous,' he said shortly, not looking up from the paperwork on his desk. 'I haven't taken children in from the streets and from unbelievably bad provincial orphanages in order for them to run wild with drunken journalists at the Continental.'

'They wouldn't be running wild with drunken journalists at the Continental,' she retorted with acerbity. 'They'll run wild in acres of glorious English countryside.'

He put his pen down and looked up at her. 'Just what the hell,' he said heavily, 'are you talking about?'

For once she had his attention, and she felt a stab of satisfaction. She pulled a battered cane chair near the corner of his desk and sat down. She had been nursing a sick child all night and her long pale-gold hair was scooped into a loose knot at the nape of her neck. There was no makeup on her face, and her amethyst-grey eyes were dark with tiredness. Even so, she was still the most beautiful woman he had ever seen.

'With Ho dead, and the peace talks under way, the war must be coming to an end,' she said practically. 'When it does, I shall return to England, to Bedingham.'

'Bedingham?' he queried, his winged brows drawing together perplexedly.

'My home.'

He pushed his chair away from his desk a little, leaning back in it. The sun was behind him, and she couldn't see the expression in his eyes.

'Tell me,' he said briefly, his interest quickening. Serena didn't receive a piastre for her work at Cây Thông, and yet she lived permanently, and with obvious financial ease, at the Continental. Her family home had to be more than a grandiosely named semi-detached villa in a London suburb.

608

Serena stretched out her long legs and crossed them at the ankles. They'd never been so relaxed together before. For once he was obviously prepared to give her some time and to listen to her.

'Bedingham,' she said, her voice warm with love as she spoke its name, 'is my ancestral home. It is in Cambridgeshire and was originally an abbey. Henry VIII put an end to its clerical life and gave it to one of my ancestors, Matthew Blyth, as a reward for services rendered.'

She told him of how Bedingham had survived under Mary Tudor's reign, and then under Elizabeth's. She told him of how, in the reign of the roustabout Charles II, Bedingham had reached its apotheosis, playing host to the king and his Portuguese queen, and being lavishly extended, with west and east wings added, and elaborately formal gardens conceived and executed.

'Only in the last two hundred years or so did Bedingham run into any real problems,' she finished. 'And as these were financial, my grandfather very sensibly solved them by marrying the only daughter of an American railway king.'

He was grinning, the first time she had ever been aware of him doing so to her.

'And when I adopt my children, Bedingham, with its lake and its lawns and woods, is where I am going to take them and where I am going to make a home for them.'

He had moved slightly in his chair and the sun was no longer behind him. The expression in his eyes was one of frank curiosity.

'Is Bedingham yours? Have you inherited it?'

She shook her head. 'No, my parents are still alive. But I've written to both my father and to my twin brother about my plans. My father says as long as his study and his library are sacrosanct, I can do what I like with the remainder of the house.' A small smile played at the corner of her mouth. 'Bar holding a pop concert, that is. Lance, my twin brother, is a left-wing Socialist. He says he can think of no better use for Bedingham than its becoming a home for Vietnamese war orphans. So you see, there are no objectors.'

His eyes were suddenly devoid of expression. 'What about Mr Anderson?' he asked, his voice studiedly neutral. 'You never mention him, but I assume that he exists. What is his opinion?'

'I haven't been able to ask him,' she said, rising to her feet. 'For the last four years he's been held in Hoa Lo prison, Hanoi.'

The shock on his face was naked. Before he could recover from it she turned on her heel, and with an odd sense of satisfaction, swept out of his office.

Lucy had always been the person delegated to escort groups of children leaving for adoptive homes in Europe and in America, but at the beginning of 1971 Serena asked Mike if she could act as escort for the next group of children due to leave for the US

'Sure,' he said easily. 'Any particular reason?'

Since their tête-à-tête re Bedingham and her long-term plans, and about Kyle, their relationship had slowly changed until it had reached a point where they could be safely described as being on friendly terms with each other.

She shifted the baby girl she was holding from one arm to the other. It had entered the orphanage only two days previously, and its hair had been infested with lice. She had got rid of the insects by powdering them with DDT, and had spent hours picking out the eggs by hand. Even now she was unsure as to whether the baby was lice-free or not.

'I have friends to see. Abbra Ellis for one. She and her husband adopted Sanh a couple of months ago and Abbra wants me to visit, to see for myself how quickly the three of them have become a family, and how happy they are.'

'And two?' Mike prompted. 'You said friends, plural.'

Her eyes slipped away from his. 'I also want to see Chuck Wilson. He was my husband's best buddy and was seriously injured trying to rescue Kyle. When I last saw him he was crippled . . . confined to a wheelchair. Since then he's been undergoing intensive physiotherapy at Walter Reed Army Hospital. I'd like to see him again. To see how he is doing. And to ask him a few questions.'

Chuck's letters had been maddeningly unenlightening. He had written to her late in 1969, saying that he was moving to Washington so that he could be treated long-term at Walter Reed. He was still there, still receiving treatment, but he had never specifically said whether he had recovered the use of his legs or not.

In her own letters to him she had also evaded certain important issues. She hadn't told him about her meeting with Trinh. She hadn't asked if he knew about Kylie. And she hadn't asked the question she most wanted an answer to. Had Kyle's affair with Trinh been serious, or had it been a casual fling?

She didn't want a handwritten reply to her last question. She wanted a face-to-face situation in which he would not be able to avoid telling her the truth. And so, after months of prevaricating, she was going to see him.

'How long will you be away?'

It was a Thursday, and he had just returned from his clinic at Grall. His office had a door screen made of thick inch-square wire meshing, in order to deter any grenades that might be thrown at it, and he was leaning against it, his arms folded across his broad chest. He was wearing one of his crazily coloured Sea Island shirts and a pair of faded shorts, and with his dark hair and eyes and hard tan, he looked more like a Greek navvy than a highly skilled and deeply dedicated doctor.

'Two weeks, that's all. Maybe three.' She could hear tanks rumbling down the nearby street. It was such a familiar sound that neither of them took any notice of it. 'Why?' she asked mischievously, 'Are you going to miss me?'

A slight grin crooked the corner of his mouth. 'Stranger things have happened,' he said, easing himself away from the door. 'I'm going up to Qui Nhon while you're away. The situation there is god-awful. A camp with six thousand refugees and no facilities at all beyond a fly-infested shack used as a clinic. You'd better rest up as much as you can while you're in the States. When you come back, we're likely to have a lot of new inmates, all of them in a bad medical condition.'

The children she was escorting were going to homes in the New York area and so, after a one-day stopover, she flew directly from there to Washington. She would visit Abbra later. After she had seen Chuck.

Once again she visited him without giving him any forewarning. The house he had rented was similar in style to his family home in Atlantic City, only instead of being built of clapboard, the Washington house was built of red brick. She rang the doorbell and her sense of *déjà vu* increased. There was no reply, but she was certain that he was home.

At the side of the house was a doorway leading through into the rear garden. She unlatched it, walking along the pathway hoared with frost, reflecting that February had not been a very sensible time of year in which to make a visit. After the heat of Saigon, the bitter cold of Washington was almost unbearable. She pulled the collar of her hastily acquired wool coat higher around her ears and turned the corner of the house.

He sat in his wheelchair, looking out over the lawn, just as he had been the first time she had seen him. Only the flowers that were in bloom were different. Instead of a vivid blaze of black-eyed susans and chrysanthemums and calendulas and marigolds, there were snowdrops and crocuses and early-flowering Lenten roses.

She stood very still, the cold knifing through her. He was still in his chair. He was still crippled. Nothing had changed. She cleared her throat and stepped forwards, and the wheelchair spun to face her.

'Goddammit!' he exploded, 'Can't you pick up a telephone and warn people you intend to visit? Do you always have to appear like a genie from a lamp?'

Not only had the scenario not changed, his physical appearance hadn't changed either. He was still as heart-stoppingly handsome as she remembered. Long-lashed grey eyes; well-cut thick hair growing a trifle long; faint hollows beneath his cheekbones; a mouth finely chiselled, slightly arrogant, wholly exciting.

She stepped forwards with a grin, knowing that his wrath was only pretence and that he was as pleased to see her again as she was to see him.

'If I had warned you, you might very well have run out on me.'

His mouth twitched into an answering grin. 'No one but you would suggest to a man in a wheelchair that he might run away!'

The empathy that had sprung up so instantly between them when they had first met was there again, easy and effortless.

They began to laugh, and she said, 'What the hell are you doing out here? It's freezing! Take me inside, for God's sake, and thaw me out!'

The inside of the house was decorated in early American, the rather stern decor warmed by an open fireplace and crackling log fire. 'Is the decor your choice,' she asked, sitting down in a deep, red leather couch, 'or did you inherit it?'

He had steered his chair towards a cocktail cabinet and was busy pouring two stiff martinis. 'My choice,' he said briefly.

'So Washington is permanent?' she asked, avoiding his eyes as he turned towards her with her drink.

'Yes.'

He was giving nothing away. The house was obviously superbly cared for, and she wanted to ask who looked after it for him. Who looked after him. How much longer he expected to be undergoing treatment at Walter Reed. When he would be able to expect to see some results from it.

She said instead, with no preamble, 'I've met Trinh, the Vietnamese girl Kyle was having an affair with.'

He had positioned his chair so that it was opposite the couch on which she was sitting. He tilted his head a little to one side, nursing his martini, saying, 'And you want to know if I knew about it, and if I did, why the hell I didn't tell you.'

'I know that you knew about it,' she said, and there was an edge to her voice that hadn't been there a moment before. 'She told me that you had written to her, telling her that you saw Kyle alive on the ground after he crashed. But you're right about your second question. Yes, I do want to know why the hell you didn't tell me about it.'

He looked away from her, staring into the fire. Slowly he drank his martini and then he put his glass down and turned towards her again. 'To be honest, I'm not sure what my motives were. It may have been out of a sense of loyalty to Kyle, though I doubt it. After all, any dues I might have owed Kyle are more than fully paid. It may have been because of the way I felt about you. I didn't want to cause you any further hurt. And it may have been because I thought it was unimportant. Hell, she was only a Vietnamese. It was no mammoth, earth-shattering affair.'

All the time he had been speaking she had been watching him very closely. Now she said quietly, 'I think you're lying to me, Chuck. I think it *was* an earth-shattering affair. For him as well as for her.'

Her coat lay over the arm of the couch. She was wearing a lavender-grey cashmere dress that clung provocatively in all the right places and accentuated the smoke-crystal colour of her eyes. Her hair was swept into a French knot, making her look very elegant, very sophisticated. He wanted her so much that his cock hurt.

He said tautly, 'Come to bed with me and then I'll tell you all about it.'

Shock flared through her eyes, and then something else, something that she couldn't hide, however hard she tried. 'Okay,' she said, her breath so tight in her throat that she could hardly speak, 'I will.'

It wasn't why she had visited him. Not consciously. She had come because she wanted to ask him about Trinh and Kyle, because she wanted to know if the treatment he had been undergoing at Walter Reed had been effective. Or so she had thought. She knew now that she had been wrong. She had visited him because he was like Kyle, and she couldn't get him out her mind. She had wanted to know if he was sexually capable. Well, she now had her answer. He wouldn't be asking her to go to bed with him if he weren't.

He said thickly, 'Come on. Into the bedroom. I no longer favour rugs in front of fires.'

She didn't argue. She didn't care where they did it. It had been five years since she had last made love, and she was so sexually hungry, and so horny, that when she rose from the couch she could barely stand.

He propelled his wheelchair swiftly out of the room, and across a hallway into another ground floor room. A bedroom. She followed, so possessed by physical need that she almost fell against the bed. It was higher than most beds, specially adapted so that he could transfer himself from bed to wheelchair with maximum ease.

She unzipped her dress with trembling fingers, stepping out of it, leaving it where it had fallen on the floor. He was already lying on the crisply made-up bed and his shirt was off. She didn't know how he had managed to move so quickly. She had thought she would have had to help him. Although he was as leanly built as Kyle, his shoulder and arm muscles had become powerfully developed by his

615

having to rely on them so much. Semi-naked, he didn't look like a cripple. He looked wonderful.

She peeled off her stockings in desperate haste. She had kept her self-imposed vow of celibacy for five years, but she was totally incapable of keeping it for a moment longer. It had been a romantic, ridiculous vow that could not possibly have any effect on what was happening to Kyle in Hoa Lo. When she told him about it, she knew he would shout with laughter. She wondered if she would tell him about Chuck and didn't know.

She scrambled on to the bed beside him, hurtling into his arms. For a second she wondered if, because of his partial paralysis, she would have to be the one to take the initiative, to perhaps straddle him in order that he could enter her. He rid her of the notion within seconds.

'God, if you only knew how many years I've longed for this!' he breathed harshly, rolling her forcefully beneath him. 'I've wanted you for years, lady! For years before I even met you!'

His lips were hard and hungry on her mouth, his fingertips moving down over her neck, her shoulders, her breasts. He was still wearing his jeans, and she unzipped his fly and reached inside, taking hold of him. There was nothing crippled or semi-paralysed about his erection, and she whimpered in longing.

'Quickly!' she said urgently, pressing herself up against him, not wanting him to be tender, not wanting him to take his time. 'Quickly!'

He didn't disappoint her. She ground her hips beneath his, moaning with pleasure. It had been so long since she had been made love to. Far, far too long.

'Oh, God, that feels good,' she panted, glorying in his size and hardness, not wanting it to come to an end, wanting it to last forever.

He raised himself up on his arms, grinning down at her, revelling in the knowledge that at that precise moment in time, she was completely at his mercy. And then his grin died away and his eyes darkened. He, too, was no longer in control. A look almost of agony crossed his face as he thrust deeper and faster.

Her hands tightened in his hair, dragging his head down to hers. His tongue drove past hers and the blood roared in her ears. She was coming and the relief was so colossal that she thought her heart was going to burst. It went on and on and she thrashed beneath him, her words and exhortations so basic and explicit that they tipped him over the edge. His own climax came, terrible in its intensity, and he arched his back, lifting his head, crying out like a wild animal.

For a long time afterwards she simply lay limply beneath him, drenched in sweat, utterly satisfied, wonderfully replete.

At last she said, 'Were you always capable of making love? Even before you began treatment at Walter Reed?'

He nodded, rolling his weight away from her, lying companionably at her side.

She raised herself up on one elbow and her hair tumbled free of its chignon, sliding silkily and glossily down over her shoulders and breasts. 'You mean you were perfectly capable of making love when we first met?'

'Mmm mmm,' he said corroboratively.

She thought of all the wasted years, the regular trips she could have made from Saigon to Washington.

'Then why the hell,' she demanded indignantly, '*didn't* you?'

He began to laugh, pulling her down towards him so that her face was buried against his neck and his arms were tight around her waist. 'Has anyone ever told you that you're a very fast, forward lady?'

'Not for a long time,' she said wryly, thinking of the chasteness of her Saigon life-style. She ran her fingertips over his chest and said, 'Have there been many ladies in the last few years, since you were injured?'

Her hand slid lower and she began to caress his limp cock.

'A few.' He watched her speculatively. 'There are some women who are disabled freaks. They really get off making it with cripples.'

She pushed herself up again on one arm, looking down at him. 'And you think that I fall into that category?'

He was stiffening again in her hand. He grinned. 'No,' he said. 'I think you're far too way out to merely get turned on by a wheelchair!'

She giggled and lowered her head, kissing his chest and then his belly. 'Tell me about the ladies you've had while I've been in Saigon,' she whispered, her lips brushing his skin.

He folded his hands behind his head. 'There's only been one who mattered. Things were fine until she became pregnant. Then she couldn't get an abortion quick enough.' His voice had become bitter, and she paused in her ministrations, raising her head, her eyes fixed on his face. 'I told her that as I was crippled in an air crash, it was hardly a condition that could be passed on hereditarily, but she obviously chose not to believe me. Or maybe she did believe me, but figured that though frolicking in bed with a cripple was okay, having one as the father of her child was definitely not as attractive a proposition.' His eyes met hers, and a shadow of a smile quirked the corner of his mouth. 'She's history,' he said briefly. 'Don't stop what you're doing.'

She didn't. Desire was already stirring in her again, and this time he satisfied it as she did his, with mouth and tongue and hands.

When at last he said huskily, 'I think it's time we regained some energy with another martini,' she didn't disagree.

'Make mine *very* dry,' she said, stretching out in satiated languor against the tumbled pillows.

He grinned and swung his legs to the floor. His shoulder and arm muscles were still sheened in sweat, and she eyed them appreciatively. 'Shaken, not stirred,' he said, and rose to his feet and walked a trifle unsteadily from the room.

For a second she didn't register what had happened, and then she realized and shock hit her so hard in her chest that she gasped for breath.

'Chuck! *Chuck!*' She was out of the bed, running after him. 'You didn't *tell* me! You *knew* I didn't know! When did it happen? How long ago? Why were you sitting in your wheelchair, you crazy bastard?' They were in the living room, and she was in his arms again, laughing and crying at the same time. 'How could you let me go on thinking you were crippled when you can *walk*, goddammit!'

'I guess I figured you might be one of those ladies who are turned on only by disablement,' he said with a grin. 'And anyhow, I like surprising people.'

'You've certainly done *that*,' she said as he released his hold of her in order to make the martinis. 'When did it happen and *why* were you in the wheelchair when I arrived?'

'To answer your first question, it's happened over a long period of time, very slowly, and to answer your second question, I was in it because I still sometimes need it, and I was reminding myself of how much I hate it and brooding about how long it would be before I could throw it on the scrap heap.' He splashed vermouth into generous measures of gin.

'And when will you be able to throw it on the scrap heap?' she asked, taking the glass he was proffering, enjoying being naked, enjoying the sight of his nakedness.

'Soon,' he said noncommittally. While he had been talking he had crossed to a writing desk. 'Do you want to know about Kyle and Trinh now?' he asked.

She nodded, her mood instantly changing. When she had left Saigon she had believed that this was the real purpose of her trip. Now it no longer seemed important.

He opened a drawer in the desk and took out a creased envelope. 'Kyle was in the middle of writing this to you when we were called out on our last mission. A lot of his personal possessions were put in with mine, either accidentally or intentionally, I'm not sure. I sent everything else I had of his on to his folks in Boston. This I kept.'

She took it from him.

*Dearest Serry*, Kyle had written. *This really is going to be a hell of a letter to write, but it has to be done, and I know that you will understand. I've fallen in love with a Vietnamese girl. Her name is Trinh, and she is very beautiful . . .* Serena's vision was suddenly so blurred that the next few lines were indecipherable. *I shall always be glad that you flew to Alabama before I left for 'Nam*, he had written in large scrawls very reminiscent of her own. *What we've had between us is something I wouldn't have missed for the world, and something I will never forget. But I have to be able to marry Trinh. I have to be able to protect her. If you knew what life was like out here, Serry, you would understand.*

She lifted her eyes from the notepaper and stared unseeingly out of the living room window. When he had written those words he couldn't have remotely imagined that when she read them, she would know exactly what it was like in Saigon.

She waited to feel betrayal, bitterness, hurt, grief. Nothing happened. She only felt sad. Sad for Kyle, in Hoa Lo; sad for Trinh; sad for Kylie.

When she finished reading it, she said quietly, 'I'm glad you didn't show me it when we first met. If you had, I don't suppose I would ever have gone to Saigon. I would never have found a purpose in life, never have discovered what it is that I can do, and do well.'

'And that is?' he asked.

She looked across at him and smiled. 'Let's go back to bed,' she said, 'and I'll tell you.'

'And so Bedingham is going to get a whole new lease on life,' she said contentedly when they had made love again. 'It's near enough to London for you to continue to receive the kind of treatment you've been receiving at Walter Reed, and it's deep enough in the countryside to be an absolute paradise for the children.'

She didn't notice how very still he had become.

'What children?' he asked, and this time it was he who lay propped up on one arm, looking down at her.

'As many Vietnamese orphans as the authorities will allow me to adopt. Money isn't a problem, or at least, it's not an acute problem. I'm hoping to be able to leave Saigon with at least ten children, maybe more.'

He sat upright, swinging his legs from the bed. For a long moment he remained with his back towards her, and then he twisted around, saying in an oddly offhand voice, 'And you expect me to shack up with a houseful of Viets?'

She stared at him for a moment, nonplussed. 'It won't be a crush,' she said, uncertain as to whether he was teasing her or not. 'Bedingham could house fifty children quite easily.'

It was his turn to stare at her. His eyes were dark, almost expressionless, as if he were carefully beating down whatever emotion he was feeling. 'You really don't understand, do you?' he said, and this time the tone of his voice left her in no doubt at all that the conversation had turned suddenly and deeply serious.

She pushed herself up against the pillows. 'No. No I don't,' she said in genuine bewilderment. 'Tell me.'

He reached across to the bedside table for his cigarettes and lighter, so obviously delaying the moment before he spoke that she no longer felt bewildered, only crazily, irrationally, afraid.

He lit a cigarette, inhaling deeply, still not speaking. It was very, very quiet. A clock could be heard ticking, but that was all. She was seized with the passionate desire to silence the clock. To halt time. A few seconds before they had been joyously happy. She wanted to go back to that moment. She didn't want him to speak. She didn't want her terrible premonition of dread to be realized.

He blew a thin plume of smoke upwards and said in the tone of voice in which he might have asked her if she wanted her drink freshened, or milk in her coffee, 'I never want to see another Viet as long as I live.'

She closed her eyes for a moment, knowing that it was a reaction she should have anticipated, should have been prepared for. When she opened them again he was looking at her steadily, waiting for her response. There was a gleam of perspiration on his shoulders and slight scratch marks where her nails had dug deep into his flesh. The faint, polleny odour of semen still clung to their bodies and the rumpled sheets.

She said carefully, knowing that their whole future was at stake, 'You feel like that only because of what happened to you in 'Nam. But there's no need to feel like that. The children didn't cause the war and the atrocities. They are not responsible. They have suffered terribly because of it, just as you have. When you see them, when you meet them, you will feel different.'

His eyes held hers for a long moment. From somewhere unseen the clock continued to tick. 'No,' he said at last, turning away from her, reaching out for his jeans. 'No. It isn't so simple. It goes too deep.'

She pushed the sheets aside, kneeling towards him, saying urgently, 'You don't feel hatred or revulsion toward Trinh. Why should you feel any different about the children? Why should . . .'

'It's no good.' There wasn't the slightest trace of doubt in his voice. It was flat. Unequivocal. All emotion carefully excluded. He began to pull on his jeans. 'Trinh is one of a kind. When I met her I had no feelings about the Vietnamese one way or another. And afterwards, after Kyle was shot down, after I was injured' – he shrugged dismissively – 'she was Kyle's girl. That was how I thought of her. It's how I still think of her. I don't think of her as being a Viet. I think of her simply as being Kyle's girl.'

She said eagerly, 'And when you meet the children you will see them as being just children, children who need love and stability and a home. . .'

'Then give them love and stability and a home,' he said with a slight, careless shrug of his shoulders, 'but don't expect me to play the role of papa-san. I don't want to live with any reminders of 'Nam. Not now. Not ever.'

She swung her feet shakily to the floor and stood up, facing him across the disarrayed bed. 'We could make it work,' she said, her voice trembling slightly, 'I know we could.'

He shook his head, and with terrible finality she knew that she had been living in a dream world. There was going to be no future for her with him at Bedingham, just as there was going to be no future for her with Kyle.

'No,' he said again. 'You have a choice. The children or me.'

'There is no choice,' she said, and though her eyes were full of pain, her voice was as free of doubt as his had been. 'It's the children. It will always be the children.'

His face tightened. An expression she couldn't decipher flashed into his eyes, to be instantly suppressed. 'Then it's over,' he said, and walked from the room.

He didn't speak to her again. There was nothing more for him to say. She had paused at the doorway, her wool coat tightly belted, the collar already raised against the chill she would meet when she stepped outside. 'I'm sorry,' she had said simply. 'It could have been so good between us.'

His thumbs were hooked into the pockets of his jeans. He had given a slight, almost imperceptible shrug of his shoulders, his eyes telling her that it still could be if only she would give up the children.

She turned away from him, unable to make the sacrifice he was demanding, and without saying good-bye, closed the door behind her.           ★   ★   ★

623

In the sanctuary of her motel room she retrieved a couple of Earl Grey teabags from the bottom of her handbag and made herself a cup of tea. Then she called Gabrielle.

'Where are you telephoning from, *chérie?*' The line was bad and Serena did not hear the urgent anxiety in Gabrielle's familiarly husky voice.

'Washington. I visited Chuck,' she said succinctly.

'Oh!' There was a slight pause at the other end of the line, as if Gabrielle was having difficulty in marshalling her thoughts.

Serena glanced down at her wristwatch, trying to estimate what the time was in Paris. Her brain wouldn't function and she couldn't do it, but she knew that it must be the middle of the night, which would account for Gabrielle sounding so unlike her usual exuberant self.

'I still don't know exactly what kind of treatment he's been receiving at Walter Reed,' she continued, 'but it has been successful. He can walk.'

Gabrielle knew all about Chuck. Even though it was two years since they had lived together in Saigon, Gabrielle was still her friend and confidante. It was a role that Lance had once fulfilled, but though they exchanged occasional letters, she hadn't seen Lance for a long time. And it had been even longer since he had been the most important person in her life.

She said now, knowing that she had no need to expressly tell Gabrielle that she had broken her vow of celibacy and had made love with Chuck, knowing that Gabrielle would realize that without having to be told, 'Everything was better than I could ever have hoped – until I told him about my plans for Bedingham.' She paused for a moment, aware that her voice was about to crack. When she had regained her self-control, she continued, 'He said there was no way he could live with such a permanent reminder of Vietnam. He was absolutely adamant. I could have him or the children. I couldn't have both. So it's over. End of story.'

'Oh, *chérie*, I am so sorry . . .'

'So am I,' Serena said wryly. 'However, onward and upward. I'm flying to Los Angeles in the morning to see Abbra and Scott and Sanh . . .'

'No, *chérie*,' Gabrielle interrupted her, her voice cracked and raw. 'I have just received a telegram from Abbra. She will not want to see you. Not just now. She will not want to see anyone.'

Serena's heart began to thud erratically, 'Is it Sanh? Is he ill? Has there been an accident? For God's sake, Gabrielle, what's happened?'

'No, it is not Sanh. It is Lewis.'

'Lewis? I don't understand. Lewis is dead . . .'

'No, he is not, *chérie*,' Gabrielle said, a catch in her voice. 'He is alive and he is being released by the North Vietnamese. He is on his way home right at this very moment.'

Like Abbra, and like Gabrielle, Serena's first reaction was one of dizzying relief that a man believed to be dead was alive. And then, in the same split second, came stupefying horror as she realized the nightmare of the situation.

'Jesus,' she whispered, sitting down slowly on the edge of the bed, 'what on earth is going to happen? What in the world is Abbra going to do?'

She didn't stay in Washington. She left next morning for Saigon, aboard a Pan Am Boeing.

'Nice to have you back,' Mike said to her laconically when she walked into the orphanage two days later. 'But why so soon?' His eyebrow quirked quizzically. 'I thought you were going to stay awhile and visit friends?'

'I was,' she said briefly. Later, as they sat in the Caravelle Hotel's rooftop bar, she told him about Abbra and Lewis. And about Abbra and Scott and Sanh.

He had whistled softly through his teeth, his eyes dark with compassion. For a moment she had been tempted to tell him about Chuck. She remembered the utter finality in Chuck's voice when he had said that he would never live with Vietnamese children, would never be cast in the role of a papa-san, and the temptation faded. She couldn't tell Mike about Chuck. They were a breed of men so different from one another that each would find the other totally incomprehensible.

In April President Nixon announced that 100,000 American troops would leave South Vietnam by the end of the year. Serena no longer felt that such news was an indication that the end of the war was in sight. There were more refugees streaming into Saigon than ever. South Vietnamese troops, assisted by US artillery, air and helicopter support, had invaded Laos in an effort to cut the Ho Chi Minh Trail once and for all. The result was official figures of 1,146 South Vietnamese troops killed in action, and 4,245 wounded. US air-crew losses were lighter, with 176 dead and 1,042 wounded. The war was continuing and Serena could see no likelihood of it coming to an early end.

She spent the rest of 1971 and the first half of 1972 hitchhiking lifts on military planes and jeeps in an almost incessant round of visiting provincial orphanages with Mike. The conditions were appalling. Too many children. Too few people to care for them. Not enough food. No medical facilities. Sometimes they were able to make their trips on the Lambrettas that they both used for quick and easy movement in Saigon, but tiny babies and sick children could not be transported in that way, and endless hours were spent cajoling lifts from sympathetic army personnel.

In March 120,000 North Vietnamese troops swept across the partition line and into South Vietnam.

'This is it,' Mike said to her prophetically. 'This, at last, is the beginning of the end.'

The invasion did not penetrate very far, but the North Vietnamese were not repulsed. Despite savage battles with South Vietnamese and US troops, they remained on South Vietnamese soil. Cities fell and were retaken and fell again, and hundreds of thousands of refugees streamed pathetically southwards, towards Saigon.

In April President Nixon announced that American troop strength in South Vietnam would fall to 49,000 by 1 July.

'He's obviously made up his mind that he's going to come to an agreement with Hanoi,' Mike said, swabbing the wound of a child who had been injured in a grenade attack on a café. 'Let's just hope he gets the hell on with it!'

It took another nine months. On 27 January, 1973, the Paris peace accords were signed and the Vietnam War officially ended. President Thieu was to remain in power in South Vietnam. All American prisoners of war were to be released and returned home.

'And as far as I can see, that's all that has been achieved,' Mike said bitterly. 'Years of bloodshed and suffering and for what? For an agreement that could have been reached at any time. And it's the end only for America. It isn't the end for Vietnam. It won't be the end for Vietnam until she is reunited into one country again.'

Serena was acting as Mike's nurse while he took a clinic in a makeshift shack in a refugee camp. Flies were clinging to her sweat-soaked hair and the child that she was holding, and that Mike was examining, was whimpering. She soothed the pain-racked child as best she could, trying to come to terms with the enormity of what had taken place in Paris.

Kyle was going to be released. He would soon be flying home. She would have to be there when he did so. Even if their marriage was over and it was Trinh he was really returning to, she would have to be there when he stepped off the plane.

Mike finished treating the child, and she carried it outside, handing it back to its anxious mother. An army helicopter was due to pick her and Mike up in ten minutes. Despite the horrific number of women and children still needing attention, they had done all they could for that day.

She stepped back inside the shack. Mike was repacking his medical bag and as she entered he paused, looking across at her, saying in a voice that was oddly abrupt, 'I suppose this is the end for you as well?'

'You mean because of the POWs being returned?'

He nodded. Although it was January, it was very hot in the shack. Heat beat through the tin roof in waves. A column of red ants were narrowly skirting their feet. She thought of London and of Boston. Of Bedingham.

'No,' she said slowly, 'it isn't the end for me. I shall not leave Saigon, at least not for good, until I absolutely have to.'

Very faintly they could hear the *whump-whump-whump* of rotor blades as the helicopter approached.

He put his bag down, saying bluntly, 'I don't understand. Your husband is being released after six years of God only knows what kind of hell. And you say you won't be leaving Saigon. It doesn't make any sense.'

'It does when you know the facts.'

'And they are?'

The helicopter was coming in to land and she had to raise her voice. 'He isn't in love with me anymore. He wrote asking for a divorce shortly before he was shot down.'

'And you *still* came here?'

At the incredulity in his voice she grinned. 'I didn't know when I came. I didn't see the letter until a long time afterwards.'

'And are you still in love with him?'

She shook her head. 'No. I probably never was. Not in the way that you mean. We were just kids and fellow free spirits. We never had a marriage in the real sense of the word. Just a crazy elopement followed by an impossibly grand wedding. Within hours he was winging his way thousands of miles away from me and we didn't meet again until a few days before he was due to leave the States for Vietnam.'

Outside the shack, the down-draft of the helicopter's rotor blades was whipping the treetops into a frenzy.

'Then *why*?' he demanded, his eyes and voice light with relief.

'Why did I come here?' She shrugged dismissively. 'A guilty conscience, I suppose. For reasons too complicated to go into at the moment, I felt responsible for Kyle's decision to join the army, and consequently I felt responsible for what happened to him out here.'

'That's crazy,' he said, ignoring the shouts from outside demanding that they board the waiting Huey.

She began to laugh, suddenly ridiculously happy. Within days Kyle would be free again. And after she had welcomed him home she would return to Saigon and Mike. And that was what she wanted, what, without realizing it, she had wanted for a long, long time.

'I know it's crazy, but that's how I felt then. I don't feel like that now. I know now that you can't shoulder the responsibility for other people's actions so easily.'

'I didn't mean that your guilt was crazy,' he yelled across to her as the Huey's copilot raced across the mud-baked earth towards them. 'I meant it was crazy that your husband could possibly have fallen out of love with you!'

Her eyes danced with mischief. Her next few words were going to stupefy him. 'Not really,' she shouted back. 'He fell in love with a Vietnamese girl. Kylie's mother.'

The running copilot was within yards of the shack's open door. 'Will you two numbnuts get a *move on*?' he yelled at them. 'We're wasting *time* here!'

Mike ignored him. He looked like a man who had been poleaxed. 'Kylie is your husband's child?'

'*We're going*!' the copilot was yelling. '*With or without you, we're going!*' He spun on his heel, sprinting back towards the Huey, ducking low as he approached it in order to avoid the spinning rotor blades.

Serena nodded, so obviously untroubled by the fact Mike found his stupefaction dissolving into dizzying relief. She hadn't been sitting out the years waiting for her husband to return to her. She wasn't going to leave Saigon now that the war was over.

'*Come on,*' he shouted, grabbing hold of her hand. '*That guy meant it when he said he would leave without us.*' And with her hand tightly holding his, he began to run with her towards the Huey.

In Saigon, Serena reminded the military of her existence and her status as a POW wife. She was told that on 12 February the first group of prisoners were being released. Kyle's name was not among the names they had been given.

'But the list isn't comprehensive, Mrs Anderson,' her casualty assistance officer said reassuringly. 'Not all the POWs are being released at once. It's going to be some weeks before all the men are returned home.'

By the end of the month there was still no news, though it was reported that another large batch of prisoners was going to be released in the first or second week of March.

'I'm going to do the rest of my waiting in the States,' she said decisively to Mike. 'He could be released at any time and without any warning. The casualty officer says that all the men are being flown via Clark Air Base in the Philippines to Travis Air Force Base in California. I want to be there when he lands.'

She was in her room at the Continental, packing her suitcase, when the telephone rang and reception informed her that an army officer was on his way up to her room to see her.

Gleefully she replaced the receiver on its rest. If he was coming with the news that Kyle was among the men being released in the next week or two, then she would be in the States in plenty of time to greet him. She had a seat booked on a flight leaving Tan Son Nhut in ten hours' time. She slipped a photograph of Kylie into her valise, unable to imagine how Kyle must be feeling. He had been a prisoner for nearly six years. One of the men who had been among the first batch of prisoners to be released had been a prisoner for seven years.

There was a short knock at her door, and she ran across the room to open it. 'There's no need to tell me I need to pack my bags,' she said with a wide smile to the thick-set army officer facing her. 'I'm already in the middle of doing so.'

He gave her no answering smile. Instead, he said stiffly, 'May I come in, Mrs Anderson? I'm afraid I have bad news for you.'

She stepped back into the room, her heart beginning to beat fast and light, her throat tightening. He took off his cap, holding it in the crook of his arm, saying unhappily, 'Perhaps you would like to sit down, Mrs Anderson.'

'Oh, God,' she whispered softly, 'Kyle is dead. That is what you have come to tell me, isn't it? He's dead.'

The officer nodded. 'I'm afraid so, Mrs Anderson. It happened in late 1966. He died under torture in Hoa Lo.' He hesitated, and then added with deep sincerity, 'I'm sorry, Mrs Anderson. Intensely sorry.'

Nineteen sixty-six. It was so long ago that she could barely comprehend it. She doubted if Kylie had even been born by then. She said with difficulty, 'And his body? Is that being returned to the States for burial?'

The officer nodded. 'I have all the details.' She looked so pale that he was terrified she was going to faint. 'Before I give them to you, could I get you a drink? A whiskey, perhaps? Or a brandy?'

When he had gone she had telephoned Mike at the orphanage with the news. 'Kyle's father has asked that Kyle be buried near their home, in a local cemetery in Boston. I'm going to fly there on tomorrow's flight as arranged. I don't know exactly when the funeral is going to take place and so I don't know when I'll be back. Trinh doesn't have a telephone, and there's no way I can get in touch with her before I leave. Will you tell her for me?'

'Yes,' he said gently, wishing that she didn't have to fly to the States alone, wishing that he could be with her. 'And,

Serena . . .' It was a hell of a time to choose to tell her, but he couldn't help it. He had to tell her. He had been crazy never to have told her before. 'I love you.'

There was a long pause at the other end of the line, and then she said, so softly that he had to strain to catch the words. 'I know, Mike. I love you too.' And with tears for Kyle streaming down her face, she had replaced the telephone receiver on its rest.

It was snowing when she arrived in Boston. She knew that Kyle's parents would want nothing to do with her, and she had no intention of forcing her presence on them. She spoke to Kyle's father on the telephone, telling him that she would be attending the funeral service, but would not be coming to the house first to leave for the church and the cemetery with other family mourners. Neither would she be returning to it after the service. Royd Anderson had barely been able to bring himself to speak to her. 'It's your fault,' he had said harshly, his bitterness as raw as it had been on her wedding day. 'It's all your fault. Goddamn you!'

She arrived at the church in a taxicab, her wool coat tightly belted against the harsh wind and still-falling snow. The church was full of mourners, and as she entered she was aware of heads swinging in her direction; of a sea of whispers; of countless hostile stares. She ignored them all, walking with self-composed dignity down to the front of the small church. Kyle's mother and father were seated in the left-hand front pew, their eyes fixed on the flag-draped coffin that lay before the altar. Neither of them looked towards her as she took her place in the right-hand pew.

The army chaplain conducting the service gave her a slight nod of his head, acknowledging her presence and her status as Kyle's widow, and then asked everyone to join with him in singing *Rock of Ages*.

Serena was aware of nothing but the coffin. She knew that immediately after his death in Hoa Lo, Kyle's body had been buried in a weedy plot across the Red River from

Hanoi. Now, beneath the American flag, it lay encased in bronze. There were still flecks of snow on her hair, and her face was stinging with cold. It was impossible to think that it was Kyle lying only a few feet away from her. Even after all this time, it was impossible to think of Kyle as being dead.

As the last notes of the hymn died away, the chaplain began to read the twenty-third Psalm. 'Yea, though I walk through the valley of the shadow of death, I will fear no evil . . .'

She remembered seeing a young marine in Saigon sporting a flak jacket emblazoned with the words 'Yea, though I walk through the valley of the shadow of death, I will fear no evil, for I am the meanest son of a bitch in the valley.'

'. . . Surely goodness and mercy shall follow me all the days of my life: and I will dwell in the house of the Lord forever,' finished the chaplain.

There was another hymn, and then the chaplain spoke of Kyle, of how he had been a fine, upstanding young man, a son of whom, since infancy, his parents had been nothing but proud; of how patriotism and love of his country had led him to his terrible death.

It wasn't the Kyle that Serena recognized nor, she was sure, was it one that Kyle himself would have recognized.

Pallbearers in army uniform moved forwards and lifted the casket, carrying it out of the church and on to a waiting hearse. Serena and Kyle's parents followed immediately in its wake, the rest of the mourners walking behind them.

The trip from the church to the cemetery was short. Serena wished that she could reach out and take hold of Mrs Anderson's hand, but the elder woman was gripping her black handbag tightly, her body rigid, her red-rimmed eyes steadfastly refusing to acknowledge Serena's presence.

The snow was still falling as they stood at either side of the open grave. Serena wondered where Chuck was, why he wasn't there, and was ashamed at the relief she felt at his absence.

She joined mechanically in the Lord's prayer, snow and tears mixing saltily on her cheeks. Then a bugler played taps and a uniformed officer took the flag off the coffin, folding it reverently and handing it to her. She was aware of Mrs Anderson's grief-stricken, harrowed face, of Royd Anderson glowering at her with unconcealed loathing.

Her tears continued to fall. She and Kyle had been such heedless children when they had met and eloped. For her, life had taken shape and substance and she could barely recognize the headstrong, thoughtless girl she had once been. If Kyle had lived, no doubt, he, too, would have changed and matured. But he had not lived. He had died an early, agonizing, unspeakable death in Hoa Lo, and her heart hurt with grief.

Slowly she raised the flag to her lips and kissed it. It was not a patriotic gesture, as it would have been if she had been an American. It was, quite simply, her last good-bye to Kyle. Then she walked to where Kyle's mother was standing, and with heart-touching dignity, she handed the flag to her.

'Thank you,' his mother said quietly.

Royd didn't say anything. His face was as harsh and taut as if it had been carved from stone.

Serena turned away from them, the snow lying heavy on her hair, and on the shoulders and upturned collar of her coat. It was over. All that remained was for her to return to Saigon, where Trinh would be waiting for her.

# CHAPTER THIRTY-FOUR

When the peace treaty was signed in Paris, Gabrielle immediately made contact with the North Vietnamese official who had been feeding her tiny scraps of information ever since the summer of 1970.

'Will my husband be released with the Americans?' she demanded, her red-gold curls incandescent against the sleek, night-black mink coat that had been her Christmas present to herself.

The official's face and tone of voice was as expressionless as always. 'Your husband is not an American, neither is he being held as a prisoner of war—'

'But he is a prisoner!' Gabrielle interrupted fiercely.

'He is not an American and he is not officially a prisoner of war,' the North Vietnamese repeated implacably. 'Because of your family connection to Comrade Duong Quynh Dinh, and because of the respect in which his memory is held, you have been given information that would normally have been forbidden. You know that your husband is alive. You know that he is being held with captured puppet troops. That is all that I can tell you, Comrade. When there is new information, then you will be informed of it.'

There was no new information. On 12 February several hundred haggard but jubilant Americans were flown out of Hanoi to the Philippines and then on to Travis Air Base, California. In March the last American troops left South Vietnam and more prisoners were released from Hanoi. A handful of civilians, some of them journalists, who had also been held prisoner by the North Vietnamese were also released. Gavin was not among them.

Gabrielle returned to the North Vietnamese Embassy. Her contact there was as immovable as ever. 'I have told you everything that I can, Comrade,' he said, repeating verbatim what he had told her previously. 'Your husband is alive. He is being held with captured puppet troops—'

'The Peace Accords state that all South Vietnamese POWs are to be released, as well as American POWs,' Gabrielle interrupted tautly. 'Have they all been released yet? If not, when they are released and returned to the South, will Gavin be among them?'

'I cannot tell you, Comrade,' the official said heavily. 'When I have information I will give it to you. Until then, *chào bà*.'

Bitterly disappointed, Gabrielle walked away from the embassy and headed back towards Montmartre, wondering for the thousandth time where it was exactly that Gavin was being held. Over the years she had managed to glean that the prison he was being held in was small, and that it was in a rural area. That was all. No matter how hard she had pleaded, no further information had been forthcoming. The Americans who had been released had come not only from Hoa Lo, but from three other prisons in Hanoi, from six prisons within a fifty-mile radius of Hanoi, and from a prison camp situated in the northern mountains, five miles from the Chinese border.

As she reached the place Blanche and the Moulin Rouge, she wondered if the northern camp could possibly be the camp where Gavin was being held. It was known to the Americans merely by the nickname Dogpatch, and though it was quite possible that it was both small and rural, for Gavin to be imprisoned there he would have had to be marched or transported by the North Vietnamese nearly the entire length of North Vietnam. She couldn't imagine them going to so much trouble when there were other prison camps nearer the point where he had been arrested. And her contact at the North Vietnamese Embassy had been adamant that Gavin was not sharing his imprisonment with captured Americans, but with captured South Vietnamese troops.

She crossed the place Blanche and began walking briskly up the steeply winding rue Lepic. She and her parents and *le petit* Gavin no longer lived in the tiny, cramped apartment in the rue Rodier. In the past few years her reputation as a nightclub singer par excellence had soared, and to her delight her bank balance had soared accordingly.

If she had wanted to, she could easily have bought an apartment in a smart residential area, but when it had come to buying an apartment of her own, which she could share with her family, she had chosen to remain in Montmartre. Although she never felt a true Montmartroise in the way that when she was in Saigon she felt a true Saigonese, when she was in Paris, Montmartre was her home and she could not conceive of living anywhere else.

She loved the village atmosphere of the hill, the magnificent plane trees in the place Émile Goudeau, the green benches on the sidewalks, the small shops and the constant beehive of activity. She loved the translucent light that never seemed to be any different no matter what the season. The spacious apartment that she had bought was situated in a small street not far from the place du Tertre, on the crown of the hill. From the bedroom and living room windows was a magnificent view down to the boulevards of Pigalle and across the city. It was an apartment that her mother loved and that they were all exceedingly comfortable in.

She wondered how she was going to break the news to her parents and to *le petit* Gavin that for the next few weeks, possibly even the next few months, they would be living there without her. If Gavin was not being released with the Americans, then he would eventually be returned to Saigon. And she was going to be there when he was.

She walked quickly upwards towards Sacré-Coeur, her high-heeled black leather boots beating a tattoo on the cobbles, her mink coat fastened high and snug around her throat. She had stayed away from Saigon far too long.

First her affair with Radford had ensured that she remain in Paris, and then her escalating career had ensured that she stay. Now her career was established, and Radford was no longer her lover.

The shops and frenzied activity of the lower reaches of the street were behind her, and the atmosphere was now that of a French provincial village. She turned the corner towards the church, a small frown creasing her brows.

The decision to end the affair had been hers, but she had not found it an easy decision to make nor an easy decision to live with. Between herself and Radford there was a rapport and a physical attraction so strong that she had needed all her considerable emotional strength in order to be able to tell him that it was over. And she had found the strength because she had known that she was on the verge of betraying Gavin irrevocably. She was on the verge of falling in love.

Radford had refused outright to allow her to escape from him totally, and they still saw each other frequently, but no longer as lovers. Now she had to decide whether or not she would say a final good-bye to him before leaving for Saigon.

In the place du Tertre winter tourists strolled from souvenir stall to souvenir stall and admired the work of the only artist hardy enough to have set up an easel. One of the stalls had a display of T-shirts, and with a surge of amusement she saw that one of them was decorated with Radford's picture. Over the last two years her success as a singer had been dazzling, but Radford's success, coupled with that of the band, far exceeded hers.

He had become a cult figure, a sex symbol on par with Mick Jagger and Jimi Hendrix, and he revelled in the female adulation and hysteria that he excited. His Aston-Martin DB Mark 3 had given way to the latest Ferrari. He had bought a magnificent 18th-century house at Neuilly, as well as a London flat and a New York apartment. He had everything in the world that he wanted except one thing. And that was she.

Common sense told her that she shouldn't get in touch with him before leaving Paris, but common sense had never played a large part in their relationship. She would see him again, to say a final good-bye. After all, when she returned to Paris, she would be returning with Gavin. It would be too late for good-byes then. Radford would be in her past, where he would belong.

'. . . and so it is time for me to go back to Saigon,' she said at the family dining table that evening.

Her father, who took less and less interest in anything other than his daily game of boules, grunted noncommittally.

Her mother's eyes flew wide open with alarm. She knew, as they all did, that just because American involvement in Vietnam was at an end, it did not mean that a long-term peaceful solution to the conflict there had been found. The present truce between North and South would not last long. Fighting would break out again as the North sought to unite Vietnam into one country. And when the fighting did break out again, it would be as fierce and as terrible as anything that had gone on before.

'Oh, *chérie*, is that necessary?' Vanh began, and was interrupted by her grandson.

'I think that is a *magnificent* idea, *Maman!*' he said, forgetting all about the food on his plate as he looked across at her, his face radiant. 'When can we leave? Can we leave before the next school term starts? Can we leave *this week?*'

Gabrielle suppressed a grin as her eyes met his. He was six and a half years old now and gave her so much happiness that she found it impossible to look at him without smiling. Now she said, hoping that she looked and sounded like a responsible, stern mama, 'School is very important, Gavin.

And Saigon is not a very pleasant place in late March. It will be humid and smelly and—'

'And I want to go with you, *Maman*,' he finished simply, his eyes, so like his father's, burning hers. 'A little part of me is Vietnamese, is it not? And I, too, want to be there when Papa returns.'

Looking at his mop of tousled hair and his snub nose with its scattering of freckles, and the gap in the middle of his front teeth that made his grin so winning and mischievous, Gabrielle felt her throat constrict. 'Of course you do, *mon petit*,' she said thickly, ignoring her mother's silent plea that she say nothing further. 'And of course you will come with me.'

Vanh gave a small, inarticulate cry of protest and Gabrielle said gently, 'It is right that he should see the city in which his mother was born, and it is also right that he is there when his papa is released from captivity.'

'But the conditions!' Vanh said in distress. 'Nhu says that the city is choked with refugees! That on the streets air-conditioner and refrigerator packing boxes house up to ten children at a time! Those are not the kind of sights that a little six-year-old boy should be seeing!'

'No, they are not,' Gabrielle said gravely. 'Neither are they the kind of conditions that six-year-old boys should be enduring. It will not harm *le petit* Gavin to be made aware of the dreadful suffering that war entails. Such awareness is far more preferable to his playing at war, thinking it glamorous and manly.'

The subject had come to a close. She was leaving for Saigon just as soon as she could arrange the flight details. And *le petit* Gavin was going to accompany her.

Breaking the news to Radford proved to be a far more highly charged affair. She had known it would be, and though he had asked her to drive to his mansion in Neuilly where, after just returning from a major tour of the States, he was supervising the building of a recording studio in the basement, she had declined.

'Meet me at La Coupole,' she had suggested, and he had agreed. At La Coupole in Montparnasse it was unlikely that their sophisticated fellow diners would pester them for autographed menus.

When she entered, her mink slung carelessly around her shoulders, he was already seated, sipping a bourbon.

'*Bonjour, chéri*,' she said, kissing him lightly on the temple, '*Ça va?*'

'That depends on why you want to see me,' he said darkly as a waiter removed the mink from her shoulders and discreetly withdrew.

She grinned, slipping into the high-back seat across the table from him. Another waiter had approached, and she ordered a kir, saying, when they were alone again, 'It is because I have something to tell you, *chéri*.'

Despite the subdued lighting, he had been wearing a pair of sunglasses. He removed them with the panther-wary grace that characterized his every action, saying, 'Unless it's to say that you've come to your senses and that you're going to move your bags and possessions down to Neuilly, I don't want to *know*, baby.'

She didn't reply to him immediately. Whenever they met, it always took her a few minutes before she was able to come to terms with his dangerous, overpowering masculinity. She steadied her breathing, looking around the art-nouveau-decorated dining room, recognizing several of the other diners.

'You've been so *unavailable* lately,' Radford was saying, not taking his disturbing gaze from her face, 'that I've been wondering if you'd make it today. You keep so *busy* all the time.'

Her mouth twitched in the beginnings of a grin. She had herself in control again, and Radford being provokingly sarcastic was a Radford that she could easily handle.

'You're not the only cat in this town with a career to think of,' she said affectionately, turning to face him. 'I've been singing at a new club in Saint-Germain-des-Prés. The mix there is very exciting. Jazz, African, Brazilian.'

'And you?'

'And me.'

'As you say, baby, quite a mix!' His voice was lazily mocking, and he flashed her a sudden smile, his teeth very white against the dark, arrogant, almost Arabic planes of his face. 'But that isn't why you invited me into town, to tell me about the new club.'

'No.' She paused again. She was dressed starkly in a beautiful cut black wool dress. Her legs were sheathed in sheer black stockings and her shoes were black suede, ridiculously high, ridiculously insubstantial. She wore a large baroque, carved ivory bangle on one wrist, and apart from her wedding ring, no other jewellery. In the subdued lighting her short springing curls were fox-gold, her wide-spaced, tip-titled eyes as green as a cat's. She looked sexy, and stunning, and he wanted her now as he had always wanted her.

He said with sudden harshness, 'Let's *cut* all this crap, Gabrielle. We're wasting time and both of us know it. The dude you've been seeing at the embassy is stringing you a line. Gavin isn't alive. Not after all this time. Even if he *was* alive, the two of you would have *nothing* going for each other. It's been too long.'

She shook her head, pushing her untouched drink away from her. 'You are wrong, *chéri*. He is alive. I know it in my heart and in my blood and in my bones. That is why I wanted to see you today. To tell you good-bye. I am going to Saigon with *le petit* Gavin, and I am not returning until Gavin returns with me.'

His hands tightened into fists. Ever since he had heard that the American POWs were to be released, he had known what it was that she would do. He was losing her. And to a man she hadn't seen for nearly seven years. It was crazy. So dumb he could hardly believe it.

He leaned forwards across the table, saying fiercely, 'I'm *wild* about you, lady! Doesn't that *mean* anything? Christ! At this particular moment in time I could probably have most any woman I want. And I want *you*! I want you so much that if marriage is what you want, then we'll get married. What else can I *say* to you? What more can I do to show you that I love you just as much as your husband ever loved you, that I love you *more*, that I love you more than *anyone* else is ever going to love you!'

She knew that heads were turning in their direction, that if they weren't careful an enterprising photographer would soon be on the scene. She didn't care. She reached out, taking hold of his tightly balled fist, prising the fingers apart, interlocking her fingers with his, saying in her touching, broken-edged voice, 'I am sorry, *chéri*. Truly sorry. I, too, have loved you. I have loved you too much, and that is why I have to say good-bye. Gavin came into my life first, and when I told him that I had given him my heart, I was speaking the truth. He still has my heart, just as I believe that I still have his.'

As she had been speaking, his face had drained of expression, hardening into an impenetrable mask. He was not going to allow them to part as friends. She had been foolish to have ever imagined that he would do so. Gently she disentangled her fingers from his and rose to her feet.

He watched her, tight-lipped and cobra-eyed. A waiter slipped her coat around her shoulders and she was grateful for its warmth. The restaurant had become suddenly cold. Almost Arctic.

'Good-bye,' she said, and before he could say a word in reply, before temptation became too much for her to overcome, she turned away from him, walking quickly between white-naperied tables and out on to the boulevard du Montparnasse. ★ ★ ★

At the end of March, as another batch of haggard American POWs flew jubilantly out of Hanoi, Gabrielle and *le petit* Gavin flew into Saigon.

Serena was at Tan Son Nhut to greet them.

'Gavin! My goodness! I wouldn't have recognized you!' she exclaimed laughingly as Gavin hurtled towards her. She hugged him tight, delighted that after so many years he still remembered her.

'And me?' Gabrielle asked teasingly. 'Would you not have recognized me, *chérie*?'

She was wearing a shocking-pink crossover sweater with a deep décolletage, skin-tight; three-quarter-length black pedal pushers, and high-heeled, backless patent sandals.

'Gabrielle, I would recognize you *anywhere*,' Serena said truthfully, hugging her even tighter than she had hugged *le petit* Gavin.

'That is good, *chérie*, I would hate to think that I had become inconspicuous!'

They grinned at each other. Even though she had driven straight from her work at the orphanage and was wearing a T-shirt and jeans, Serena still managed to look elegant. A Christian Dior scarf covered her hair and was tied at the nape of her neck. Her short, unlacquered nails were exquisitely manicured and buffed a pearly pink.

'How is Saigon?' Gabrielle asked as they walked across to Serena's jeep. 'Do the Saigonese think that the truce will last?'

'No,' Serena replied briefly. 'Everyone knows that it won't. The South is going to last only as long as President Thieu's ammunition lasts.'

'I thought that under the terms of the peace treaty, it had been agreed that America would replace weapons and ammunition as they were expended?'

Serena slammed the jeep into gear and began to speed towards the airport's exit. 'That's what the small print says, but only a fool would put any trust in it. More to the point is Article Four of the peace agreement: "The United States

644

will not continue its military involvement or intervene in any way in the internal affairs of South Vietnam." America wanted out. She's now got out. No matter what happens in the future you can bet your life that she's going to stay out!'

They drove straight to Nhu's, where *le petit* Gavin received such a fierce embrace that he was almost smothered. From Nhu's, leaving a happily chattering Gavin behind them, Serena and Gabrielle drove to the centre of the city.

'Where do you want to go first?' Serena asked as she crossed Nguyen Hue, the street of the flower sellers. 'To the Continental, to check in? To the orphanage? Or to Givral for coffee and croissants?'

Givral was a little air-conditioned restaurant on the corner of Le Loi and Tu Do, across from the Continental. It baked its own croissants and baguettes, and when they had first begun living in Saigon, Gabrielle and Serena had quickly realized that breakfast at Givral was far preferable to breakfast at the Continental.

'Givral,' Gabrielle said unhesitatingly. 'I want to go back to all our old haunts and reorient myself as quickly as possible.' She began to chuckle. 'When we first arrived in Saigon, *I* was the one who showed *you* around. Now it's you who are the old hand and I am the one feeling a little like a tourist!'

'You won't feel like a tourist for long,' Serena said soothingly. 'Not only are all the old haunts still here, so are a lot of old faces. The debonair Paul Dulles has been recalled to Paris, but one of Gavin's old colleagues, Lestor McDermott, is still in town, and you have missed Jimmy Giddings only by inches. He left for the Philippines at the beginning of February in order to cover the POWs' arrival and from there he was sent on to the Middle East.'

They were both silent for a moment, thinking of the American POWs who had returned home alive, and those who hadn't. Thinking of Kyle.

645

At last Gabrielle said quietly, 'Was the funeral very difficult for you, *chérie*?'

Serena thought of the imposing bronze casket; the waiting frost-hard ground; Kyle's mother's face, harrowed and tear-streaked; the hatred emanating from Royd Anderson and directed solely towards herself; the terrible feeling that the funeral had nothing to do with Kyle.

'Yes,' she said truthfully. 'It was difficult. But it was more difficult to break the news to Trinh. Mike had already told her for me that Kyle was dead, but she had refused to believe it. She was certain that I would return from the States with the news that it was all a mistake and that he was alive. Even now I'm not sure if she truly believes that he is dead.'

'What will she do?'

They had parked the car and were walking across the square towards the restaurant. 'I don't know. She has a family home in the city which she shares with her sister. Perhaps life will continue for her just as it has for the past six and half years. She will continue with her job, Kylie will be looked after at the orphanage, and one day, God willing, she'll meet a man she loves and who loves her, and they will get married.'

Gabrielle hesitated slightly and then said a little cautiously, 'And Kylie? How do you feel about Kylie, Serena?'

They sat down and ordered coffee, and it wasn't until they had done so that Serena said, 'I try not to think too much about Kylie. I've tried never to have too much to do with her.'

'Because you haven't wanted to become too fond of her?'

'Because I *am* too fond of her,' Serena said with stark truthfulness. 'It was the moment I set eyes on her. She's far more American than she is Vietnamese. She has Kyle's hair and eyes and mouth and charm. And she has other qualities of his as well. Where Kyle was recklessly devil-may-care, Kylie is impishly mischievous. She is a loving, intelligent, exuberant little girl who is very, very hard to resist.'

'And will it cause any problems for you if she and *le petit* Gavin should become friends?'

Serena's sombreness vanished, and she flashed Gabrielle her wide, dazzling smile. 'Idiot,' she said affectionately. 'Of course it won't. Is that what you intend doing? Spending time with *le petit* Gavin at the orphanage?'

'I shall have to occupy myself somehow,' Gabrielle said with an answering grin. 'Do you think I shall make a good nurse? Or will the fearsome Dr Daniels be as rudely and as unjustly disapproving of me as he has always been of you?'

Serena's smile widened. 'You have just reminded me that there are some pieces of news that I haven't quite brought you up-to-date on. Come on, finish your coffee and we'll drive to the orphanage. The fearsome Dr Daniels is waiting to greet you.'

Gabrielle was ecstatic when she realized what the situation was between Serena and Mike.

'I knew it,' she said complacently to them both as they stood holding hands in one of the orphanage's sun-filled and child-filled courtyards. 'The minute that Serena told me you were not *remotely* handsome, and that you were pigheaded and obstructive and the most *annoying* man that she had ever met, I knew that she must be falling in love with you!'

Mike shouted with laughter and the playing children turned to look at him, intrigued.

'Is *that* what she said about me?' he asked, still chuckling and not looking a bit put out by the revelation.

Serena didn't give Gabrielle time to answer. 'There are times, Mike Daniels, when I *still* feel like that,' she said teasingly, 'and you haven't given Gabrielle an answer as to whether or not she can come to Cây Thông as a volunteer nurse.'

Mike looked across at Gabrielle. At her riotous mop of flame-gold curls, her sizzling pink sweater and skin-tight

647

# CHAPTER THIRTY-FIVE

After the official notification of Lewis's imminent release, Abbra was inundated with advice from both the military and from her father-in-law. The overriding question was when, and by whom, Lewis should be told of her now-invalid marriage to Scott. As far as Abbra was concerned, there was no decision to make. The task of breaking the news to Lewis had to be hers. The main problem was going to be the publicity. Both she and Scott were well-known media figures. The gossip columnists were going to go crazy with delight when news of their predicament became public.

'We'll do everything possible to ensure that your husband sees no newspaper or magazine and is not approached by any reporter until after he has been apprised of the situation by yourself,' her casualty assistance officer said to her.

No one from the military plucked up the nerve to ask the question that was uppermost in everyone's mind. Was she going to leave Scott and return to Lewis? Or was she going to remain with the man she had, for the past two and a half years, believed to be her husband?

If they had asked her, Abbra would have been unable to give them an answer. She looked like a wraith, her face bloodless, deep circles carved beneath her eyes. She was in a private hell where no one, not even Scott, could reach her. She felt as if she were suspended in time, impaled by her memories of the past, paralysed by the dilemma of the present, and totally unable to conceive of what the future might hold.

Her father-in-law had insisted that *he* should be the family member to first meet Lewis and to inform him of the marriage that he had always disapproved of.

'And I've been proved right!' he stormed over the telephone to Scott. 'It was a disgraceful thing to do, marrying a woman who had been, who *is*, married to your brother. I knew no good would come of it! I told you both so at the time!'

Only the intervention of Abbra's casualty assistance officer ensured that, because of the abnormal circumstances, Abbra would be the only family member to immediately greet Lewis on his return to the United States.

It was Scott who came to a decision about their far greater dilemma.

'I'll go away with Sanh for a few weeks. Take him down to Mexico and the Sea of Cortez. I'll arrange with the military that similar arrangements, elsewhere, are made for you and Lewis. You can't possibly stay anywhere where the two of you are known and where you will be hounded by newsmen. He's bound to have to be hospitalized for a little while, and his debriefing could take anything from a few days to a couple of weeks, but all that can take place in a protected environment. Once it's over, I suggest you go off to a small hotel at Yosemite or Yellowstone. Somewhere miles from anywhere. Then you can tell him.' His voice, so strong until then, cracked and broke as his arms tightened around her. 'And then you are going to have to make your own decision, sweetheart . . . Lewis or me.'

She began to weep, and she wept and wept, her heart breaking, hugging her breast as though holding herself together against an inner disintegration. How could she make such a decision? It was impossible. She loved Scott. She loved Scott more than anything else in the world. Yet once she had loved Lewis. She was married to Lewis. He had survived five years of terrible captivity believing that she was waiting for him. How could she let him down? It would destroy him. And living without Scott would destroy her.

'Let's take it step by step,' he said gently, stroking her hair, his own eyes full of tears that she could not see. 'Lewis needs to be told of our marriage. And you need to discover just how you feel about Lewis after all this time. Only then can any decisions be made.'

She had nodded and clung to him and he had said huskily, 'But whatever decision you make, remember that I love you, Abbra. Only you, forever.'

If it hadn't been for her casualty assistance officer saying to her, 'Lewis has seniority and so will be the first to disembark,' Abbra would not have known who he was.

He was in full uniform, but he looked old, and stooped, and gaunt. She suppressed a cry of anguish, and then Lewis was being officially greeted. Flags were flying. Her legs began to shake as she became aware of the large number of photographers and newsmen covering the event.

'Don't worry,' her casualty officer said, sensing her distress. 'There are going to be no questions allowed.'

There were none, but Lewis was given the opportunity to say a few words.

'The three of us who have been released, stand here today, proud to be American. We are American fighting men and in all the years of our captivity we have never, for one moment, forgotten it. We have kept our trust in God, our trust in our fellow countrymen, and our trust in America. Now we want to join with the rest of America in striving to obtain the release of the hundreds of men we left behind us.'

There were cheers and a storm of applause and then Lewis and his two companions were swiftly led away into waiting limousines.

His speech was exactly the kind of speech that she would, once, have expected Lewis to make. But she had forgotten so much about him. She had forgotten how utterly he was a professional soldier. She wondered what he would say when he learned of her participation in the antiwar marches, and

651

her nails dug deep into her palms. What he would say when he learned of her antiwar activities was the very least of her problems.

From the air base Lewis and his companions were brought immediately to the hospital. In a very short time they would be reunited. She would see him in the flesh. She tried to remember Hawaii and their passionate last night together before he had flown back to Vietnam. She couldn't do it. She could see only Scott's anguished face as he had said good-bye to her. The hands she remembered, hot and ardent on her body, were Scott's hands.

She began to tremble, praying for the strength to survive the next few hours. The military chaplain who had counselled her had told her that God never gave a person a burden heavier than they could bear. She clung to that thought, knowing that she had to be strong. She had to be strong for all their sakes. For Scott, for Sanh, and for Lewis – Lewis who had suffered so much, and who she had once loved so very, very, desperately.

The casualty officer had left the room to talk to the many officials milling around in the corridor. Now she returned, saying quietly, 'The men have arrived and are in the building.'

'Will Lewis be coming here? To this room?' Abbra's voice was stilted, the words forced through dry lips.

'No, he's waiting for you in a room across the corridor,' the officer said. 'Are you ready?'

Abbra shook her head. She was going to greet Lewis exactly as she would have if she had never married Scott. After his five years of captivity, and of believing that she was faithfully waiting for him, it was the very least she could do. When his medical examinations and debriefing were completed, she was going to take him away to a small hotel in Yosemite National Park. Then, and only then, would she tell him about her and Scott.

The only thing she had asked the military to do was tell

Lewis that everyone believed he was dead. Once he knew she thought he was lost to her forever, he would be a little prepared for the news that had to be broken to him.

'Then if you are ready . . .' the casualty assistance officer said, opening the door wide.

'Yes,' she said, the blood drumming in her ears, 'Yes, I'm ready.'

It was only a short walk out of the room and across a corridor and into another, yet she knew that it was the longest walk she would ever take. The tension was so great that Abbra was convinced she wouldn't survive it. She felt as if she were going to faint, or have a heart attack, or die.

There were military officials in the room, and doctors. She was scarcely aware of them. She had eyes only for Lewis. His skin had taken on an unhealthy greyish-yellow cast. His hair was no longer a thick and curly brown, but grizzled, clipped short to his skull. He looked older in the flesh than he had on the television screen. Only his eyes were the same. Dark, and brown, and full of both overwhelming relief and with love – love for her.

'Lewis,' she said softly, taking a step towards him. 'Oh, Lewis. What did they do to you? How did you bear it?'

He covered the distance between them in two limping strides, and her arms opened wide.

'Abbra!' He crushed her to him, burying his face in her neck, his tears of thankfulness and joy hot upon her flesh. 'Oh, dear Christ! *Abbra!*'

At that moment, all that mattered was that he was alive, and that he was home. She clung to him, returning his kisses. He had endured, and he had survived, and she thanked God for it, from the bottom of her heart.

Lewis's commanding officer cleared his throat. 'I know this must seem very heartless, Mrs Ellis, but your husband still has to be medically examined. Your real reunion will have to take place a little later in the day. Perhaps even tomorrow.'

Abbra tried hard not to let her relief show in her eyes. 'That's all right,' she said, holding Lewis's hand tightly in hers. 'We've waited so long to be together again, a few more hours won't make any difference.' She raised the back of Lewis's hand to her mouth and kissed it. 'Good-bye for a little while, Lewis. I've been given a room in the hospital. I won't be far away.'

Her voice was as smokily-soft as he had remembered it, her hair still as silk-dark, still as glossy; but there was something different about her, something he couldn't at first fathom. Then it came to him. There was an air of sophistication about her that the Abbra he remembered had not possessed. He reminded himself that she was six years older than when he had last seen her, that she was no longer a teenager, but a young woman. And however much she had changed, it wasn't an iota compared to the changes that had taken place in him.

For the next few days, though they met together for a little time each day, they were never alone. First of all came intensive medical checks. He was suffering from exhaustion, malnutrition, a glucose problem, an enlarged prostate gland. And epilepsy. He was told not to worry about the epilepsy. It could be fully controlled with drugs. He was certainly not made to feel any shame about it, rather, the reverse. As far as the medics were concerned, it indicated the very great suffering that he had undergone under torture.

After the medicals came the debriefing sessions. What other Americans had been imprisoned in the U Minh with him? Had he overheard his captors mention any American names? Any other southern camps where men who were MIA might be being held? Exactly how had he been captured? And interrogated? And treated? What information, if any, had he given to the enemy? What were the names of the men who had been his captors? Where exactly in the U Minh had his prison been located?

The questions went on and on until he was dizzy with them. He was seen by army psychiatrists, who reluctantly pronounced him stable enough to take a five-day vacation with his wife. The medical staff knew what the purpose of the vacation was and were deeply unhappy that this was the way Abbra wanted to break her news to Lewis.

'It would be far better for such emotionally traumatic news to be broken to your husband while he is under medical supervision,' Lewis's psychiatrist had said to her sombrely.

She had thanked him for his advice and had ignored it. She didn't want to break the news to Lewis in such clinical surroundings. She needed to be alone with him. Really alone with him. Their short periods of time together at the hospital, with medical and military staff always close by, were a nightmare that didn't grow any easier.

He was a total stranger to her, and that moment when they had first met and she had looked into his eyes and thought she had seen the old Lewis had not come again. He was a middle-aged man, deeply fatigued and physically changed almost beyond recognition. Although the physical changes had shocked her, she had been prepared for them. After such long captivity, in such horrendous conditions, it would have been ridiculous to have imagined that he would return looking no different from when they had last said good-bye.

Other changes she found harder to adjust to. His brooding sombreness, his almost manic patriotism, and his stubborn belief that the war he had fought had been a just war.

'We should be fighting in the North, where everyone is the enemy, where you don't have to worry whether or not you are shooting friendly civilians,' he had said to her passionately one day. 'Our biggest, most basic mistake is in the way we focus on chasing Viet Cong guerrillas. Those guerrillas have been deployed to grind down our forces until big North Vietnamese units are

655

ready to launch major operations as at Khe Sanh and at Tet in '68.'

She had wanted to cover her ears with her hands and scream. She didn't want to hear him talking about the war and about strategy and about how great a president Nixon was. She couldn't understand how he could even bear to dwell on such subjects. Surely his debriefing was bad enough. The hideous reliving of years of days and nights of sheer hell.

Apart from the physical changes, Lewis hadn't changed, she suddenly realized. She had changed. Even if she hadn't fallen in love with Scott, even if she had known that Lewis was alive, now that they were reunited she would still be having problems relating to him. She didn't know whether the realization was a shred of comfort or an added agony. She knew only that the necessity of staying within the confines of the hospital was giving her claustrophobia, that she needed Scott, needed him with all her heart and mind and body.

The small sports car she had bought when her third novel had been published had been brought to the hospital for her and left in the underground staff parking garage. Lewis knew of her plans that they take a short vacation together in Yosemite and had said enthusiastically that he thought it was the best idea anyone had come up with since he had set foot again on American soil.

He was waiting for her now, dressed in civilian clothes, his bag packed. They were going to have to leave the building by a rear service exit to avoid the newsmen who still thronged the main entrance, and she hoped that he wouldn't question their method of leaving, or begin to think there was anything odd about the way he was being kept from contact with the press.

He looked slightly more familiar to Abbra in civilian clothes. He was wearing a maroon-checked open-neck cotton shirt with a matching maroon V-neck sweater on top of the shirt, cream-coloured chinos, and a pair of white leather loafers. She had bought the clothes herself and was relieved to see that though the chinos and sweater hung loosely on him, they were not grossly the wrong size.

'You look nice,' she said sincerely.

He glanced at himself in the mirror. At his grizzled hair and still greyish-yellow pallor. 'I look a wreck,' he said truthfully, but there was also a refreshing hint of humour in his voice. 'Come on. Let's leave before someone decides they want yet another goddamned urine test or blood sample.'

He picked up his bag and she led the way out of the room and along the corridor and down the rear service stairs to the parking area.

He stared at the sports car in bemusement. 'Whose is this? Have you borrowed it?'

She shook her head, smiling. 'No. It's mine. A present to myself.'

A slight frown creased his brow. 'On an army pension? Wasn't that a little wasteful?'

'No,' she said equably, stowing his bag in the trunk. 'Because that isn't how I paid for it.'

She was already behind the steering wheel, and he opened the passenger door, seating himself next to her.

'Explain,' he said, his face as stern as the psychiatrist's had been when he had said he wanted them both back at the hospital in five days.

She turned the key in the ignition and slipped the car into drive. 'You remember my writing? Well, I've been doing a lot of it over the last few years.'

'You mean that you were able to buy this car by writing stories for women's magazines?'

For the first time since they had been reunited, she giggled. 'No. I write books. I bought the car with the payment I received when my third novel was published.'

His frown didn't disappear. In the rearview mirror she saw it deepen. She didn't say anything more. He had never been enthusiastic about her writing, and it would probably take him a little time to adjust to the fact that she was now a full-fledged novelist.

She drove up the ramp, speeding away quickly before any reporters or photographers should spot them. Then he said wryly, 'Your driving hasn't improved with time.'

'No.' She managed a grin, grateful that there was humour in his voice again. They were both trying so hard to be normal with each other and it was so hellishly difficult. For him, as well as for her.

In a silence that was almost companionable they drove east towards the wild grandeur of Yosemite. At dusk, dramatically sculptured rocks and 200-foot-high giant sequoia trees came into view and she said unnecessarily, 'We're nearly there.'

He merely nodded, his eyes turned away from her, feasting on the wonderful views as if he could never get enough of them.

She knew why he was being so silent. He was almost as nervous as she was. She turned into the parking lot at the side of the hotel, needing Scott so badly that she didn't know how she prevented herself from crying out his name.

What was she going to do? In the name of God, how could she possibly make a choice between them? Lewis needed her in a way that Scott never would. He needed her in order to reaffirm his manhood and to help him adjust to freedom after years of unbelievably brutal captivity. Yet it was Scott who was her friend and lover, Scott whom she truly felt married to.

'You look tired,' Lewis said to her as he lifted his bag from the trunk. 'This whole thing must have been as big a strain for you as it has been for me.'

A light evening breeze lifted her hair, blowing it softly against her face. 'They told me you were dead,' she said simply, and at the memory of that terrible moment her eyes became overbright and tears glittered on her eyelashes. 'For three years I believed it to be the truth.'

He put his bag down and drew her into his arms. 'I know, my love. I know,' he said comfortingly. 'But it's all over now.' He tilted her chin upwards with his forefinger, smiling down at her with the crooked smile that she remembered so well. 'We're together again, Abbra, and we have our whole future before us.'

'Lewis . . .'

'Come on.' He picked up his bag and put his free arm around her shoulder. 'Let's check in and shower and eat. We can do all the talking we have to do afterwards. I want to know everything that you've been doing. What the books you have been writing are about, where you've been living, if you've seen much of my family over the years.' He lowered his voice as they entered the hotel lobby. 'And I want to do more than talk.' In his dark brown eyes she saw again the old Lewis, the Lewis she had fallen so much in love with. 'I want to make love to you,' he said softly as they walked across to the reception desk. 'Oh God, Abbra! How I want to make love to you!'

They ate dinner at a candlelit table in the hotel's small dining room. Abbra was never able to remember what it was that they ate, or if there were many other diners.

Lewis tried to keep the conversation light and innocuous, but nearly every subject that he touched upon was traumatic for her.

'I understand Scott is still with the Rams?' he said as her almost-untouched sirloin steak was removed.

'Yes.' She was reduced to monosyllables, terrified of saying anything further for fear of where a conversation might lead.

Dessert came, and then coffee. He stretched a hand across the table towards her. 'Let's leave the coffee,' he said, and though his voice was carefully casual, there was a plea in his eyes that tore at her heart.

She nodded, rising to her feet, accompanying him from the room.

Where were Scott and Sanh now? How was Scott enduring their separation? How was he surviving not knowing what was taking place between her and Lewis, whether they had begun to sleep together or not? Whether she was going to return to him or not.

Their room was decorated in tones of pale yellow. The bedstead was of polished brass, and there were a half dozen goose-down pillows on it and crisp sheets and thick blankets and a yellow-hued patchwork bedspread.

She had made her decision not to tell him about Scott until the morning, but with every passing minute it was a decision that was becoming harder and harder to abide by.

As he began to undress he said awkwardly, 'I want you to be patient with me, Abbra. It's been so long . . . and I feel so damn shy!'

His touchingly honest admission gave her the inner strength she needed. He was her husband, and even though they were now, in so many ways, complete strangers to each other, she still did love him. Not as she loved Scott, but then, Scott was different. Scott was lighthearted and fun-loving and made her laugh. She refused to think about Scott. She couldn't think about him. If she did, she would collapse.

She stepped out of her dress, saying truthfully, 'I feel shy as well, Lewis. We're going to have to be patient with each other.'

She had seen him semi-naked at the hospital, when he had been undergoing some of his medical tests, but the sight of the scars that he bore still shocked her inexpressibly.

There was a puckered scar high on his left arm where a bullet had been removed. That scar was the least terrible of all that he bore. His back was criss-crossed with the healed lacerations of repeated and prolonged whippings, and there were burn marks on his chest.

'I'm not a very pretty sight,' he said, his eyes dark with anxiety as he saw her look at him and look quickly away. 'I'm sorry, Abbra. If it offends you I'll . . .'

She didn't wait to hear what it was that he was going to suggest. Her head spun towards him, her eyes anguished.

'*Offends* me?' Her voice was choked with tears. 'Oh, Lewis! How can you possibly imagine that it *offends* me? If I look away as I did then, it's only because I can't bear to think of what they did to you . . . what you suffered.'

She crossed the room to him quickly, hugging him close. 'I love you,' she said thickly, and it was the truth. She *did* love him. She had always loved him. Even after she had fallen so very much in love with Scott, Lewis had still retained a place in her heart. And now for the next few hours, for his sake, she had to forget the terrible dilemma that she was in. She had to think only of Lewis and of his very great need.

He was gentle with her, and she remembered that he always had been. Slowly, with tender deliberation, he removed her bra and her panties.

'It's been so long, my love,' he murmured as he drew her close to him. 'I can't tell you how often I've dreamed of this moment, longed for it with every fibre of my being.'

Her arms closed around him, and the intervening years slid away. As she closed her eyes she could almost imagine herself back in Hawaii.

'I thought I would never see you again,' she whispered as his hands travelled caressingly down from her breasts to her thighs. 'Oh, Lewis! When they told me you were dead, I thought I was going to die too!'

His lovemaking had always been conventional, and as he rolled her over on to her back and covered her body with his, she was grateful for it. She didn't want to be brought to screaming pitch by his tongue and his fingers. She didn't want the fevered intensity that erupted so easily and so often between her and Scott. She merely wanted to hold him close, to feel his heart beating next to hers, to savour the incredible knowledge that it was Lewis who was

661

gaining physical release and pleasure from her body, Lewis, who she had thought was dead, and who was alive.

Afterwards, still in each other's arms, they were quiet for a long time. Abbra felt a deep sense of calm and well-being. No matter what would happen between them in the morning when she told him about Scott, the lovemaking they had just experienced could not be taken away from them. Lewis would know that he was sexually capable.

She ran her hands gently over the ugly weals on his back. She had been terrified that when they went to bed she would feel as if she were committing adultery. It hadn't been like that at all. She didn't feel as if she had been unfaithful to Scott, even though she still felt far more married to him than she did to Lewis. As his weight remained comfortably on top of her and his breathing subsided, she wondered if it was because, despite all his care and tenderness, she had not been brought remotely close to orgasm. It was as if, for her, physical delight and Scott were so inextricably bound together, her subconscious mind would not allow her to respond in the same manner to other hands, no matter how familiar those hands had once been. Or how much loved.

At the thought of Scott a pang of grief stabbed through her. Scott . . . She needed him so much. He always knew exactly what she was thinking; he was always so supportive to her, always so loving, always able to make her laugh and see things in perspective.

Lewis moved his head and brushed his lips against her cheek. She stirred, and though he did not read it as such, it was a movement of protest. He merely thought that his weight had become too much for her and he rolled off her and on to his back, sliding his arm beneath her shoulders.

'I love you,' he said, his voice heavy with physical satisfaction and with overwhelming tiredness. 'And tomorrow will be even better, my love. I promise.'

She didn't say anything in return. She couldn't. She simply lay close beside him until he fell asleep and then turned on her side, waiting for the morning.

When he awoke he lay utterly rigid, sweat breaking out on his forehead, his eyes darting from one corner of the ceiling to another as he tried desperately to reorientate himself.

'It's all right,' she said gently, reassuring him. 'You're in America and we're at a hotel at Yosemite, remember?'

Slowly he relaxed. 'Yes,' he said, his voice slightly unsteady. 'Of course we are. I'm sorry, Abbra, but just for a moment . . .'

'I know.' His doctors had told her about the nightmares, of how, even if he didn't wake in the night screaming, he woke in the morning bathed in perspiration, certain he was still in Vietnam, his changed surroundings were simply a change of prison.

He shuddered and wiped a hand across his eyes and then said with a great effort at normality, 'What is it we're going to do today. Visit Yosemite Valley? Or drive up and visit Glacier Point?'

She sat up and swung her legs to the carpeted floor. 'I need to talk to you a little while, Lewis,' she said, uncomfortably aware of her nakedness in a way she had not the previous night. She reached for her negligee and slipped her arms into the batwing sleeves. 'So much has happened since you were captured. For me as well as for you.'

She rose to her feet, tying the ribbons on her negligee into a bow at her throat before turning to face him.

He had pushed himself up against the pillows. He was still naked, and in the early morning sunshine she could see that his chest and shoulders were already beginning to build up the muscle they had lost. In another few months he would be nearly as broad-chested and as toughly built as he had been when she had first met him.

She thought she saw a look of panic dart through his eyes, and then he had himself perfectly in control. 'You

663

mean about what happened after you had thought I was dead,' he said sombrely.

She nodded. She had been wrong in assuming that it had not occurred to him that there might have been other men in the years when she had believed herself to be a widow.

'Yes.' Her lips were so dry that she could hardly force the words past them, but she had to continue. 'I thought you were dead,' she said quietly. 'However you feel about what I am going to tell you, you must remember that, Lewis. I never even looked at another man all the months that I believed you to be alive.'

His eyes held hers, so dark that it was almost impossible to read any emotion in their gold-flecked depths. 'You had an affair?' he said briefly.

She nodded and he abruptly swung his legs from the bed, sitting with his terribly mutilated back towards her, not moving.

After a long moment he said, 'When they told me I'd been listed as KIA, I knew . . . I realized there was such a possibility.' He rose slowly to his feet and faced her, as oblivious of his nakedness as she had been conscious of hers. 'It doesn't matter to me, Abbra. I understand. Christ, how could I *not* understand. What is in the past is in the past. It doesn't need to affect us anymore . . .'

'But it does!' He was moving towards her and she knew that she had to tell him before he touched her, before he held her close in his arms. 'I . . . we . . .' The tears were spilling down her face now, and she couldn't stop them. 'We married, Lewis! I thought you were dead and . . . oh, God, I can't bear it! I can't bear hurting you like this! If only I hadn't been told that you were dead! If only I hadn't believed that I would never see you again, not ever!'

He had stopped moving. He had begun to pant, to hyperventilate. His lips had gone white, and she thought he was going to faint.

'Lewis!' She rushed towards him, seizing hold of him, knowing that she had been a fool to have believed that she could handle such a nightmare situation by herself. 'Lewis, please don't be ill! I've told you like this, myself, because I didn't want a stranger to tell you! Because I still love you! I still care for you!'

He rocked slightly on his heels and then his breathing began to steady as he inhaled deeply through flared nostrils.

'You love me? You married him only because you thought I was dead?'

'Yes! Yes!' Surely it was true. She couldn't possibly have married Scott if she had believed Lewis was still alive. And she *did* love him. She had always loved him.

With slow deliberation he removed her hands from his arms and walked a little way towards the window, looking out over a landscape of mountains and forest. When at last he turned to her, it seemed that the lines on his face furrowing his brow and running from nose to mouth were etched a little deeper. He was looking nearly as haggard as he had the day he had landed at Travis Air Force Base.

He forced a small, comforting smile. 'Then that's all that matters. The marriage can't be valid. You're still my wife, not his.'

She knew that he meant to be comforting. He believed that he had heard the worst news possible and had survived it. At the thought of what was still to come, tears rained down her face, spilling on to her hands, on to her negligee.

'Lewis, I . . .'

At her continuing distress his eyes darkened in concern. 'What is it? Is the guy threatening you? Insisting that you return to him?'

She shook her head, struggling for the right words and failing to find them.

'Where is he now? Hasn't someone spoken with him and explained the situation? Hell, who is he? Is he someone you met through your writing?'

She shook her head again, knowing that the most terrible moment of her life was upon her. 'No,' she said, and she was no longer crying. She was far, far beyond tears. 'No, it isn't someone you don't know, Lewis.' Her eyes held his, filled with unspeakable pain, and his eyes returned her gaze, bewildered and perplexed. With a slight, almost inconsequential motion of her hand, she said simply, 'It's Scott. I fell in love with Scott.'

His legs buckled, and as she rushed towards him, he thrust her violently away, staggering towards the bed.

'*Jesus Christ!*' That was all she could hear him say '*Jesus Christ! Jesus Christ! Jesus Christ!*'

He had pushed her with such force that she stumbled and fell, sprawling on the floor. She crawled to her feet, her breath coming in harsh gasps.

'*Lewis! Please! Lewis!*'

She reached a hand up towards him, and he grasped hold of it, pulling her up on the bed beside him, burying his face in her neck.

'Oh, my sweet Jesus, Abbra!' He was sobbing as she was now sobbing. 'Did you think you could stay married to me through Scott? Is that how much you grieved?'

His words were incoherent, and she could barely grasp the sense of them. She knew only that his reaction was not remotely the reaction she had expected, and she was almost senseless with relief. Only slowly, as he continued to talk to her, rocking her against his chest, did she realize what it was he had chosen to believe.

'Poor Scott! Christ, what he must be going through! Is that why he and Dad weren't allowed to visit? Was the virus they were both supposed to have just a lie to keep us apart until you had broken the news to me?'

She nodded, wishing that it hadn't been so easy, wishing he had realized that she had married Scott because she had fallen in love with him, that the possibility that she might still be in love with Scott had also occurred to him.

She put her hands against his chest, pushing herself gently away from him. 'When I went through a marriage ceremony with Scott, I went through it because I had fallen

666

in love with him,' she said, choosing her words with great care so that he should not misunderstand her.

He rose to his feet and shrugged on a dark blue terry-cloth bathrobe. Then he lit a cigarette and walked with it over to the window, leaning against the window frame, staring out over the golden beauty of the mountains.

'The North Vietnamese had a favourite way of conducting their interrogation sessions,' he said, his tone of voice as unemotional as if he were asking her if they should breakfast in their room or downstairs in the hotel restaurant. 'They would strap vine rope around my injured arm, just above the elbow, then the bite end would be passed over and around my right arm. When that was done they would throw me to the ground and roll me on my side, and then the vine rope would be pulled higher and tighter, drawing my elbows together behind my back. Within only seconds the pressure would be so great that my shoulders would lift out of their sockets . . .'

She cried out in anguish, but he did not pause or look towards her.

'My chest would feel as if it were exploding and my ribs would project like drawn bowstrings. Then, if I were lucky, I would pass out. After I had passed out, water would be thrown on me to bring me back to consciousness. They would put their questions to me again, and I would refuse to answer them again, and then straps would be put around my ankles and knees and the loop from the arm straps would be passed around my neck. The loop from the leg straps was then pulled high, drawing my heels up towards my buttocks. And then the two straps were tied together.'

She was crying softly, but he still ignored her, saying conversationally, 'At this point I would begin to vomit, and to choke on my vomit. I would lose control of my bladder and my bowels. I would no longer be Captain Lewis Ellis, I would be an animal. A thing. And do you know what kept me going through all those numberless sessions of torture? Through all the years of being kept for long periods in a cage

667

measuring barely four feet by six and just high enough for me to sit in?'

He turned towards her, and in his eyes was a desperate unspoken plea. She understood then why he was telling her about what had happened to him, even though he knew that she had already been told by the doctors. It was his way of asking her to stay with him. To choose him and not Scott. It was his way of telling her how very desperately he needed her.

'You did, Abbra,' he said, and his voice had lost its indifference and was raw and hoarse. 'They ruptured my eardrum, they beat me with bamboo rods, and through it all only one thing kept me sane. Knowing that you were here, in America, waiting for me. I lived because I knew that if I lived, I would have you to return to. You kept me alive, Abbra. No one and nothing else. Only you.'

As their eyes met and held, she felt her heart break. There was no decision for her to make. A decision could be made only if there was a choice of actions, and she saw now that there was no choice. There never had been a choice. Her duty and her loyalty lay with Lewis.

She crossed the space between them and slid her arms around him, knowing that by doing so she was saying good-bye to Scott and to Sanh and their loving, laughter-filled, joy-filled life together.

'You did have me to return to, Lewis,' she said thickly, laying her head against his chest so that he should not see the agony that was in her eyes. 'You always will have me.'

# CHAPTER THIRTY-SIX

Although Scott had said she would have to make a decision, Lewis or himself, Abbra knew that deep down Scott had been sure there was only one decision she could possibly make. Their life together had a shape and substance to it that her life with Lewis had never possessed. They had believed themselves to be married for two and a half years, and with their adoption of Sanh they had become not merely a couple, but a family.

Fresh pain knifed through her. Sanh would have to remain with Scott. The adoption would probably have to be amended so that only Scott remained as his legal guardian. She was losing not only Scott, but the little boy who had become her son as well.

For the next four days she made a superhuman effort to overcome her anguish and to help Lewis adjust to the strangeness of being both free and a tourist. They rented horses at White Wolf and trekked the back trails of the High Sierra country at an easy pace. They fished for trout, and they drove up to Glacier Point.

When the time came for them to check out of their hotel and head back for the hospital, Lewis was reluctant.

'It's the same questions time and time again. What kind of military information had my captors sought from me? What kind of military information was already in their possession? Christ, it goes on and on!'

'It won't be for much longer,' Abbra said, knowing that when his debriefing and his medical checks were complete, the real difficulties would start.

They wouldn't be able to live in California. She wouldn't

be able to survive knowing that Scott and Sanh were only a car ride away from her. And once Lewis was released from the hospital, he would no longer be protected from the publicity, publicity that would centre, not around his curiosity value as a POW who had been released in a propaganda gesture by the North Vietnamese, but around the mistaken notification of his death and his wife's subsequent marriage to his football superstar younger brother.

'You're crazy! I don't believe you! I *won't* believe you!' Scott shouted through the telephone to her. 'Jesus God! I *knew* I shouldn't have let you break the news to him alone!'

'My decision has nothing to do with my having broken the news to him by myself,' she said, gripping the telephone receiver so tightly that her knuckles were white. 'It is simply that it is the only decision that *can* be made. If you knew what he has suffered, Scott . . .'

'Christ, I've every sympathy with what he's suffered, but it doesn't mean that you have to return to him! Not when you are no longer in love with him, and you *aren't* in love with him, are you?'

It was a question she had known that he was going to throw at her. 'I still love him . . .' she began steadfastly.

'That doesn't answer my question.' His voice was remorseless. 'Loving someone and being *in* love with them are two very different things. *I* love Lewis. He's my brother. And that's how I believe you love him now. As a brother. But you're not *in* love with him anymore. You can't be, because you're in love with me.'

There wasn't a shred of doubt in his voice, and she knew that there was no reason for any. Everything he had said was true. But she wasn't going to change her mind about staying with Lewis. She couldn't. If she did, she would never be able to live with herself.

'I've made up my mind,' she said, and in her soft, smoky voice was the stubbornness that was characteristic of her.

Hearing it, his own voice took on a note of desperation. 'You have to change it, Abbra! You can't leave Sanh and me. We're a *family*, for God's sake! You were never a family with Lewis. You had a total of eight days together as man and wife. Christ, Abbra! You barely *know* Lewis!'

She closed her eyes, wondering how it was possible to have cried so much and to still be able to cry more. 'I'm sorry, Scott,' she said brokenly, 'I love you with all my heart. Good-bye, my darling.'

As she lowered the telephone receiver she heard him shout, '*I'm coming to get you! I was a fool ever to have let you out of my sight!*'

She covered her eyes with her hands. She would have to inform Lewis's doctors of what had happened. They would make sure Scott wasn't allowed into the building. And when Lewis was released? She lifted her head up, her jawline strong and firm.

Lewis and his superiors had agreed that he should take a year's sabbatical before deciding whether or not to continue his career in the army. They would be able to go away somewhere together. Perhaps to the East Coast, to be nearer his father. Perhaps even farther, to London or to Paris. Wherever they went she would be able to write, that was some comfort at least. It was the one thing that no one would be able to take away from her. Not ever.

Lewis's doctors had been unified in their opinion that a meeting between Lewis and Scott would simply subject Lewis to unnecessary stress.

Despite trying to physically storm down the doors, Scott had been refused all access. Abbra remained inside the building, grateful for the privacy of the single room

671

that she had been allocated while Lewis underwent what was described as a 'reorientation' process.

Six years of his life had been lost. The world he had left behind him in 1966 was no longer the same. China was no longer regarded as an arch enemy, but as a friend. Friendly overtures were being made by the American government to the Soviet Union. Everything was upside down, and he and his fellow prisoners had to be brought up-to-date on all the world events that had taken place during the years of their imprisonment.

There were times when it was almost too much for him. The changes inside America were the hardest for him to come to terms with. Hours and hours of newsreels took him step by step through the development of the antiwar movement. He leapt to his feet, blaspheming viciously and storming out of the room when he was shown scenes of long-haired college students burning their draft cards. The details of Watergate dumbfounded him. In his book Richard Nixon was a hero, the guy to whom he owed his freedom. And then there were the hippies, and the amazing way homosexuality had become an accepted alternative life-style.

For hour after hour, day after day, he sat through films, read a six-year backlog of magazines and newspapers, sat in on lectures that varied in content from America's new relations with China and the Soviet Union to the change in fashion and morals to details of new military hardware.

It was dizzying and sometimes overwhelming. How could politics, fashion, morals, music, technology, even speech, change so drastically? How come the seventies were so radically different from the sixties? He watched reruns of popular television shows, episode after episode of the Waltons.

'I don't intend to watch television ever again,' he said firmly to Abbra when his reorientation was over. 'Nor will I ever willingly listen to today's pop music. The

sixties were bad enough, but this new stuff is horrendous.'

She had laughed and hugged his arm as they went out
of the building by the staff exit, glad to be leaving the
hospital behind them for good. At Lewis's request they
were going to spend the next few days with his father in
New York. The hospital authorities, eager to prevent an
unpleasant confrontation between Lewis and Scott, had
agreed to press announcements over the next few days
indicating Lewis was still a patient and his release couldn't
be expected before the end of the following week, by which
time, if Lewis was agreeable, Abbra intended to be half a
world away, in London.

Over the next few days, and weeks, and months, things
did not grow easier. They grew more difficult. Despite the
slow and steady improvement in his physical health, Lewis
continued to have hideous nightmares. On their first night
in London he had woken at 3:00 a.m. drenched in sweat,
calling out in terror, *'Tam! Tam!'*

The next day he had shut himself broodingly away
in the parlour of their hotel suite, refusing to go out
with her, refusing even to have breakfast or lunch
with her.

His psychiatrist had told her that there would frequently
be periods when Lewis would need to be alone, and that
she would have to come to terms with that need, no matter
how difficult it might be for her.

On that day, their first in London, she had breakfasted alone and spent the morning wandering around
the National Gallery and the National Portrait Gallery.
She had telephoned him before lunch to see if he wanted
to eat with her, and when he had said that he didn't, she
had lunched alone at Fortnum & Mason. Afterwards she
had walked along Piccadilly and into Hatchards, where she
had the satisfaction of seeing her latest novel prominently
displayed.

Back at their hotel she had knelt beside his chair, saying concernedly, 'Tell me what it is that is troubling you, Lewis. Is it your nightmare? Was the name you called out the name of one of your guards?'

He hadn't had to ask her what the name had been. 'No,' he said, running his hand through his hair, which was growing thick and curly again. 'I was dreaming about Tam, the cleaning girl that we had at Van Binh. Do you remember me writing to you and telling you about her?'

She rested her weight back on her heels. It was so long ago, but she did remember him telling her about the village girl who had been badly mistreated by her father, and of how he had removed her from her father's care by engaging her as a general all-purpose maid.

'Was Tam the girl who asked you to teach her English?'

He nodded, the hard line of his mouth softening slightly as he remembered their teacher-pupil relationship.

Abbra looked at him, perplexed. 'But when you called out her name it was because you were terrified. You were drenched in sweat. Shaking. Why? I don't understand.'

His mouth hardened again as he rose to his feet and paced across to the window. 'There's going to be no American victory in Vietnam, Abbra,' he said, staring down into the rainwashed London street. 'There's going to be a negotiated settlement that will enable America to withdraw her troops. After that, depending on what agreement is reached and how it is supervised, there may be relative stability for a little while, but it won't last. And when the North invades the South, as they will, then everyone who has ever worked for Americans, as Tam did, will be in danger.'

'And that was why you had the nightmare?'

674

'Yes,' he said, 'that was why.'

'The press wouldn't be interested in us if you hadn't written any novels,' Lewis said tightly the first time he saw a magazine article about him, Abbra, and Scott. 'Christ, have you read this stuff? It's absolute filth!'

She had read so many more articles about them than he had that she was well prepared for whatever was in this one.

'It isn't so bad,' she said comfortingly, dropping the magazine into a wastebasket. 'It's simply what is known in the trade as a human interest story, and it's the sort of thing we have to expect.'

He rounded on her savagely. '*I* don't have to expect it!' he said explosively. 'Just because you and Scott lived your lives in a blaze of publicity doesn't mean that I have to become part of the circus as well!'

The blood had drained from her face. She knew that she dare not stay in the room with him. If she did, she would say things that would destroy everything they were trying to build together.

'I'm going out,' she said tersely, and without waiting for him to reply she spun on her heel and walked swiftly from the room.

There were other difficulties as well. Although sexually he desired her as much as ever, he was a conventional lover. His caresses were always the same: tender, deliberate, and unexciting. She yearned for Scott's passionate, imaginative lovemaking, for the laughter that they had shared in bed, for the sense of total togetherness that had always existed between them.

Sometimes her loneliness seemed so encompassing that she wondered if she would be able to survive it. Even London was no distraction. Before Lewis had left the States, his superiors had given him introductions to several US Embassy officials. To Abbra's surprise he had followed the introductions up almost immediately and had quickly become a part of a social circle that she felt alien in.

Instead of partying with the wives of the friends that Lewis had made, she spent long hours wandering around art galleries and museums, her thoughts not on paintings or ancient artifacts, but on Scott and Sanh. Often, regardless of where she was, tears would stream down her face. One morning she began to cry in the middle of Piccadilly Circus, another day she began to weep while shopping in Harrods. She knew what was happening to her, knew that she was heading full steam towards a nervous breakdown, and all her strength and determination were directed at staving it off.

The only person who knew her address in London, apart from her lawyer, was Patti. All through the year her letters came thick and fast, the questions in them remorseless. Why wasn't she writing? She was under contract to her publisher to deliver another book by next May. Had she forgotten? Had she made contact with her London publisher yet? How was Lewis? Were the two of them happy in London? Were they unhappy? Was that why Abbra wasn't writing? Was it why she wasn't even writing letters? Did she want to meet and talk? If so, she would fly immediately to London.

Even worse than the questions was the information. Scott had brought Sanh to visit her. Sanh was well and happy but Scott had looked taut and strained. He was still demanding her and Lewis's London address, and she was still adamantly refusing to give it to him. It wasn't easy. On a previous visit when she had refused, his frustration had been so great that he had become violent and had smashed a door through with his fist.

Abbra had put the letter down, unable to read any further. There was no way in the world that she could see Scott again and remain with Lewis. But Sanh. Surely she could see Sanh?

'*No*,' Serena had written to her firmly.

It wouldn't be fair to him to see him for a few hours or a few days and then to disappear from his life again. The traumatic relationships between you and Lewis and Scott would be beyond his understanding. Scott still writes regularly so I know that he is giving Sanh one hundred percent of his time. With Scott, Sanh is receiving all the emotional stability he needs. For you to remain in contact with Sanh, when Sanh knows that you are not in contact with Scott, would be far too difficult a situation for him to handle.

And so, because she loved him so much, and because she would have died rather than have caused him distress, she lived without her adopted son, as she lived without Scott.

The only person who did not seem to be suffering was Lewis. When they arrived in London she thought they might be there for a few weeks, perhaps even a month. But Lewis had fallen in love with the city.

He bore very few physical reminders of his imprisonment. He had always been toughly and compactly built, and through rigorous exercise his body was as hard and as muscular as it had been previously. As his hair had regrown, the grey in it no longer appeared so jarring. Instead, it merely flecked his hair, seeming to add to his physical attractiveness instead of detracting from it.

That he was still very physically attractive was obvious from the way embassy wives discreetly flirted with him. He was certainly far more popular, socially, than she was.

'Every time those women look at me, it's so obvious what they are thinking, what they are remembering,' she had said after a dinner party where she had barely been spoken to by anyone other than her hostess.

Lewis had removed his dinner jacket and begun to take the cuff links out of his evening shirt. 'I'm afraid that is the price you have to pay, Abbra,' he had said casually, and had continued to undress, oblivious to her stunned look of disbelief.

She had known exactly what he had meant. Near social ostracism was the price she had to pay for having married Scott when she thought herself a widow. At least it was the price she was going to have to pay as long as she remained in *his* world and among his friends.

At the beginning of 1972, as his sabbatical year drew to a close, her feeling that they were growing more and more estranged increased.

'It's time we moved out of the flat and bought a house,' he said to her one morning as they shared a prebreakfast cup of coffee. 'I've been offered a position as an adviser at the embassy and I have decided to take it.'

She put her coffee cup down a trifle unsteadily. 'What sort of adviser? Why haven't you spoken to me about it? I thought you were still trying to decide whether or not to continue your career in the military?'

'Well, I've decided,' he said, and smoothly changed the subject by asking if she had remembered that they were going to the theatre that evening.

There were times, as 1972 dragged itself into 1973, when she wondered wildly if his new position as an adviser was actually a position with the CIA. He never spoke about what he was advising on. He never told her anything about the work that he was doing. She had not made the deadline on her book, and though Abbra was afraid the publisher might cancel the contract, she could not write.

Letters still came to her, via her lawyer, from Scott. They were always the same, demanding, reasoning, pleading with her to leave Lewis and to return to him. He enclosed photographs of him and Sanh, and whenever she withdrew them from the envelope she thought that her heart would break. She loved them both so much. But she couldn't return to them, not after the solemn promise

678

that she had given to Lewis. When the Peace Accords were signed in Paris, she had expected that Lewis's still-frequent nightmares would grow fewer and fewer. Instead, they increased, and they seemed to centre more and more on the Vietnamese girl he had befriended.

His psychiatrist had warned her that some POW returnees centred all their bitterness on to one often trivial image. She wondered if that was what Lewis was doing now, of if he was deeply concerned about Tam because there had been far more to his relationship with her than he had ever admitted.

It was an intriguing supposition, but one she couldn't quite imagine. There was a puritanical streak in Lewis where sex was concerned. Despite the approaches that admiring women must have made to him, she was certain he hadn't responded to any of them. And she was equally sure that he had never been unfaithful to her while he had been in Vietnam.

Within weeks it became quite obvious that Lewis was correct and that the truce between North and South was not going to be adhered to. Almost the first people to die were nine members of an international peacekeeping commission whose helicopter was blasted out of the sky by Viet Cong guerrillas.

By autumn, small-scale Communist attacks were taking place throughout the South. In the early months of 1974 the attacks escalated in both frequency and scale. Serena's monthly letter to her from Saigon was full of the difficult-ies she and Mike were experiencing in arranging for the adoption of the scores of children still in their care. *We have to make the arrangements quickly*, Serena had written. *Everyone in Saigon realizes that there is very little time. That the end cannot be very far away now.*

She was still receiving letters from Scott, via her lawyer, but their tone had changed. *I love you, and I still want you back, but I'm not living like a monk anymore*, he had written in his last letter to her,

It isn't in my nature, as I'm sure you realize! But I hate it, Abbra. I don't want other women. I want you. Surely you know by now what a colossal mistake you have made. Pity isn't any reason to live with anyone. If Lewis knew that pity was your motive in choosing to remain with him, he wouldn't thank you for it. I know that you believe that what you are doing is the right and honourable thing, but you are wrong, sweetheart. It isn't. The right and honourable thing is to return to the people who love you and you love in return. Come home, sweetheart. Please.

At Christmas Patti had written to her, telling her that one of her writers, a girl Abbra had met a couple of times in Los Angeles, was going to London.

Her husband is a diplomat so you're bound to meet on the embassy circuit. I think you last met her at one of my parties. Scott remembers her, anyway. He says you liked her when you did meet, so I hope you are not going to take offence at my suggesting she keep an eye out for you . . .

Abbra had decided the previous year that she hated Christmas. It reminded her too strongly of children and of Sanh, and made her agonizingly aware of all the things that might have been.

'I know you don't like parties,' Lewis said to her as she dressed reluctantly for a cocktail party that was being held at the French ambassador's residence, 'but tonight is rather special. There'll be a lot of gossip about the deteriorating situation in Vietnam and I want to be privy to it all.'

As always happened at such functions, they became almost immediately separated and swept off into different champagne-sipping groups.

'. . . And so in my opinion, the Communists are now ready to launch an all-out attack on the South,' the Englishman she was standing next to was saying.

She looked across the room and saw Lewis talking to a fair-haired girl who looked vaguely familiar. A small smile quirked the corner of her mouth. It was the novelist who was also agented by Patti. She wondered what on earth they were finding to say to each other.

'I'm sorry I didn't catch your name when we were introduced,' the girl was saying breathlessly. 'There's such a crowd in here that you can hardly hear yourself speak.' She glanced around, looking for a familiar face and said, 'Oh goodness, is that Abbra Ellis over there? We share the same agent. I can't imagine why she hasn't written anything recently. Do you think she's ill? She certainly looks it. The last time I saw her she was with her second husband, or the man she *thought* was her second husband. She simply *glowed* with happiness. I have never in my life seen two people so much in love . . .'

Lewis was no longer listening to her. He was looking across the room at Abbra.

'. . . and so Patti said to me, if you get a chance, *do* track her down, because she's become a positive recluse . . .'

'Excuse me,' Lewis said curtly.

He weaved his way through the crowded room, and as he approached her, Abbra smiled at him. For the first time he was aware of how pale and strained she had become, how very much she had changed.

'Let's go home,' he said briefly, taking hold of her by the arm.

'But why? I thought you wanted to find out what the general feeling was about what's happening in Vietnam . . .'

'I think I've been very foolish,' he said, steering her through the throng and towards the door, 'and I need to talk to you.'

He drove her home through the darkened streets in silence. Once in the luxurious warmth of their flat, he poured her a sherry and handed it to her, lighting himself a cigar.

'What is it?' she asked, bewildered. 'Have you accepted a position somewhere else? Someplace you think I'm not going to like?'

She had seated herself in a chair near a small rosewood desk. He remained standing, looking at her. Despite the shadows beneath her eyes and her ivory paleness, she was very beautiful. Just as she had always been. Her dress was a narrow sheaf of black wool crepe, exquisitely and expensively cut.

He said without prevaricating, 'The woman I was talking to said that she had met you in California. You were with Scott.'

Abbra's fingers tightened around the stem of her sherry glass. 'Yes, we met at Patti's.'

His eyes held hers, their gold-flecked depths sombre. 'She said that you were glowing, that she had never seen a woman so much in love.'

She held his gaze and said nothing. There was nothing for her to say. The time for pretence between them was long past.

'Were you in love with Scott? Have I been a fool to have believed all this time that you had married him simply because you saw in him an extension of myself?'

She rose to her feet and set the sherry glass down on the desk. 'I was very much in love with Scott,' she said steadily. 'I told you so at Yosemite. You chose not to ask me about it.'

'Christ!' he said softly, crushing the barely touched cigar out in an ashtray. 'And all this time you've remained in love with Scott?'

They looked at each other across the lamplit room. 'Yes,' she said quietly, knowing that she could lie no more, that she would never lie again. Ever.

They remained standing, yards apart, staring at each other. At last he said incredulously, 'I can't believe that I've been such a fool. Because of my ego I've nearly destroyed you. And the crazy thing is, it's all been unnecessary. I *did* need you those first few weeks. But afterwards, when we were in London, I realized that we barely knew each other. My interests were not yours, and your interests could never be mine. We were strangers, tied together out of deep affection and a mutual sense of duty.'

The relief she felt was so dizzying, she thought she was going to faint. 'You mean that . . . that you realized you were no longer in love with me?'

'I'm in love with Tam,' he said, his eyes tortured. 'After the way you had stood by me, I didn't see how I could possibly tell you. Or how I could possibly go back to Vietnam for her.'

'But you can now.'

'Yes.'

Suddenly the terrible tension between them broke. They stepped towards each other simultaneously.

'Go back for her now, quickly!' she said, hugging him tight. 'Serena says that there isn't much time.'

'And you? What will you do?' he asked, his voice thick with emotion.

She was laughing and crying at the same time, 'I'm going to fly back to California on the first available flight. This time tomorrow, if they will have me back, I will be with Scott and Sanh!'

# CHAPTER THIRTY-SEVEN

All through 1974, in Saigon, the unease increased. There were repeated clashes near the demilitarized zone between government soldiers and Communist troops. The truce agreed to in Paris was a truce in name only. Although no American combat troops were now on Vietnamese soil, the killing continued.

Mike and Serena, terrified of what would happen to the children in their care if and when Saigon fell and they were no longer able to look after them, worked eighteen hours a day, ceaselessly battling with bureaucratic red tape as they endeavoured to finalize adoptions in America and Europe, and to obtain the necessary exit visas.

Gabrielle's bouncy vitality and infectious sense of fun had made her a favourite among the children. They were fascinated by her flaming red hair and by her ability to speak their language fluently. To both her and Serena's bemusement, although they had made no effort to encourage a special friendship between them, Kylie and *le petit* Gavin had naturally gravitated towards each other. Perhaps it was because they both looked a little different from the majority of the other children. There was a hint of Vietnamese in *le petit* Gavin, yet his hair was a cross between Gabrielle's fiery tones and his father's blondness, and freckles still sprinkled the bridge of his nose. Kylie was quite obviously Amerasian, but her vivid blue eyes and creamy skin and black hair made her look more Irish than Vietnamese.

It was a friendship that neither Gabrielle nor Serena discouraged. Now that Kyle was dead, Serena's complex emotions about Kylie were no longer so traumatic. She found herself able to spend time with her, and to make friends with her, as she had long wanted to. Her relationship with Trinh, too, had improved. They were not bosom friends, nor ever would be, but she had had the photograph of Kyle reproduced and had given it to Trinh, together with a photograph of his flower-bedecked grave which Kyle's mother had forwarded to her some weeks after the funeral. In return, when Trinh brought Kylie to the orphanage she would often bring a small bunch of flowers with her, or some homemade *chao tom*, little sticks of shrimp paste, and give them to Serena.

'Have you spoken to Trinh about her and Kylie leaving Saigon?' Mike asked Serena shortly after they had received the news that North Vietnamese forces had captured Phuoc Binh, a city that was a mere eighty miles north of Saigon.

Serena was cleaning the wound of a child who had been hit by flying glass when a bomb had exploded in a café in Cholon.

She glanced up briefly from her task. 'No, but there won't be any problem about it, will there? Kylie is obviously Amerasian, and I understood that the Vietnamese wives and children of American servicemen would be given priority if it came to an evacuation.'

'Trinh wasn't a wife,' Mike pointed out, beginning to stitch the wound in the child's arm.

'We can testify that she was his common-law wife.'

'True. But I still think you should talk it over with her. She may not even want to be evacuated. Vietnamese love their country deeply. You need to point out to her that anyone who obviously consorted with Americans is not going to be too kindly treated under a Communist regime. And that Kylie is so obviously of mixed blood that she's never going to be wholly accepted into whatever society evolves in Vietnam once it is reunited.'

Trinh had shaken her head stubbornly when Serena had broached the subject. 'No. Where would I go? Where would I live?'

'You would go to America, Trinh. You would be looked after, I would see to that. You speak English fluently, so that isn't a problem.'

'But Vietnam is my country. Saigon is my home.'

'The Communists have captured the capital of Phuoc Long province. America has done nothing to intervene, except to make a statement denouncing the action, nor will it. After Phuoc Long other provinces will fall into Communist hands. Within months, possibly weeks, the North Vietnamese Army is going to be poised to strike at Saigon.'

Trinh's eyes were frightened, but she again shook her head. 'No, I cannot believe it. There have been bomb attacks in Saigon, and the fighting at the Presidential Palace and at the American Embassy in 1968. But North Vietnamese troops marching down Tu Do Street? No. America would never let it happen. It is impossible.'

'It *is* possible,' Serena said grimly. 'For Kylie's sake the two of you will have to leave, and you will need the necessary papers. I can't get them for you without your cooperation, Trinh.'

'Later,' Trinh said unhappily. 'I cannot think about it now. It is too big a decision. Later I will give you my answer.'

There was nothing more that Serena could do. Phuoc Binh had fallen to the Communists in January. By March they had attacked Ban Me Thuot, the capital of Dar Lac province, the city falling to them within a day. President Thieu panicked. In a vain attempt to secure the provinces immediately around Saigon, he ordered his troops to retreat south. With that one order, half of South Vietnam was ceded to the Communists. Hundreds of thousands of refugees began to flee south, vying for space on the roads with the retreating troops.

On the twenty-first, the North Vietnamese began to assault Hue, the old imperial capital. For three days heavy artillery fire bombarded the city's outskirts and then the South Vietnamese area commander gave the order to abandon the city, fleeing with his troops by sea to Da Nang and leaving Hue's inhabitants to their fate.

Mike strode into Cây Thông's crowded nursery and said briefly to Serena, 'There's an American here, asking for you. Apparently you know his wife.'

Serena finished inserting an IV tube into a baby's arm, strapping it firmly so that it couldn't be dislodged.

'He must have got me confused with someone else.'

'No, he hasn't. His name is Lewis Ellis. He intends to go down into the Delta to Van Binh, to find a girl who used to work for him in '66. He wants to know if we can give him any help.'

'Lewis?' Her voice was incredulous. 'Abbra's Lewis?'

'The very same,' Mike said with an exhausted grin. 'Though I have a feeling, judging by his desperation to find this girl, that he's Abbra's Lewis no longer.'

Stunned, Serena hurried to where Lewis was waiting. Her first impression was that he was older than she had imagined, and then she remembered the time he had spent as a prisoner in a jungle camp. He had a face she immediately liked. Strong and uncompromising, but with a warmth in the eyes that belied the straight firmness of his mouth.

'Hello,' she said, stretching her hand out towards him, 'I'm Serena Anderson.'

His handshake was like everything else about him, strong and firm. 'I'm very pleased to meet you.' His voice was deep and rich and she understood why Abbra, at eighteen, had fallen so much in love with him. 'Abbra has told me a lot about you.'

It was no time for small talk. She said without prevaricating, 'Mike tells me you want to go down into the Delta?'

'I'm going. Tomorrow. Since you and Mike know the situation here as well as anybody, I thought I'd ask your advice about the best way of doing it.'

'The best way of doing it is not to do it,' Mike said dryly. 'There are God knows how many North Vietnamese battalions converging on Saigon. Your chances of reaching Van Binh are so slim as to be extinct.'

'Nevertheless I'm going,' Lewis said without the least hint of doubt in his voice. 'I need to find a girl down there, Nguyen Van Tam. Once I've found her I'm bringing her back to Saigon and then taking her to the States with me.'

'It's been nine years,' Serena said gently, inwardly rejoicing that Abbra must now be reunited with Scott. 'Whatever understanding you had with Tam, you can't possibly imagine that she will be still waiting for you?'

Lewis's eyes were very dark. 'No, I can't. But I can at least see her again, and give her the opportunity to leave with me if she wishes to do so.'

'There's a small orphanage near Van Binh run by a small group of Catholic nuns,' Mike said. 'The children there are in desperate need of being brought into Saigon. There's still a chance that places can be found for them on the adoption programme.'

'You mean that you will come with me?' Lewis asked abruptly.

Mike nodded, knowing very well that Lewis's chances of making and surviving the trip alone were slim. He knew all about Lewis's long imprisonment in the U Minh, and as far as he was concerned, the guy had suffered enough. If the girl he was looking for was so important to him, then he was only too happy to help him in his search for her.

Within hours of their leaving the city, Gabrielle ran into the orphanage, her face radiant.

688

'At last, *chérie*! I have news! Real news! A journalist in Saigon who works for a Western newspaper but who is, in reality, a Communist undercover agent, has contacted Nhu. He has told her that the Communists intend to take Saigon within the next few weeks and that when they do so, Gavin will be brought south with the conquering forces!'

'Oh, Gaby,' Serena hugged her tight. 'But how can you know that the man is genuine? That he is speaking the truth? *Why* should the army be bringing Gavin south with them?'

'Out of respect for Dinh. Because that is what Dinh intended. That, as a journalist sympathetic to the North, Gavin would be an ideal person to chronicle the historic taking of the South.'

'He might have been an ideal person nine years ago, but they surely can't believe that he is sympathetic to them now? Not after they have kept him in the North so long against his will?'

Gabrielle gave a helpless shrug of her shoulders, her eyes still shining. 'It may not seem to make much sense, Serena. But Vietnamese minds are not Western minds. We do not know what Gavin has said to them, or what he has agreed to. What is important is that Nhu's contact says his information is utterly reliable. When the North Vietnamese Army takes Saigon, Gavin will be with them!'

On Easter Sunday the coastal town of Da Nang fell. The chaos there was even worse than the chaos that had taken place in Hue. The city was choked with refugees who had fled from towns already captured, and hundreds of thousands, terrified of Communist reprisals, tried to escape by sea. Soldiers fought civilians in the effort to commandeer boats. Children were separated from parents and crushed and drowned in the stampede.

On that day, in Da Nang, the South Vietnamese Army reached its nadir. Leaderless and uncontrolled, they

689

stripped themselves of their uniforms and subjected the local population to a reign of terror that could not have been exceeded by the Communists themselves.

'You cannot wait any longer, *chérie*,' Gabrielle said glumly to Serena when news of the surrender of Da Nang reached them. 'The adoption papers and exit visas of all the remaining children must be processed immediately, no matter what the bureaucratic difficulties. And you must speak to Trinh again. Arrangements must be put in hand for her and Kylie to fly to America.'

'What about *le petit* Gavin?' Serena asked. Ever since the news that Gavin would be entering Saigon with the North Vietnamese Army, it had been patently obvious that no matter what happened, Gabrielle would not be leaving the city.

'I want you to take him with you when you and Mike leave.'

Serena nodded. Neither she nor Mike wanted to leave, but their respective embassies had left them in no doubt that when the time came for a full-scale evacuation of all non-Vietnamese personnel, they would have to be among those airlifted out of the city.

That evening she spoke to Trinh again, this time with desperate urgency. 'You must realize by now that nothing is going to stop the Communist advance, Trinh. Do you want Kylie to grow up under a Communist regime? Do you want her to risk victimization because she is so obviously half American?'

Trinh had wrung her hands, her black-sloe eyes anguished. 'No, of course I do not. But I have family in Saigon. My sister . . .'

'I will make arrangements for your sister too,' Serena said, wondering how the hell she was going to be able to keep her promise. 'Pack a bag and keep it ready, and leave everything else to me.'

After leaving Trinh she went straight to the American Embassy. The official she spoke to there looked at her first appreciatively, and then, when she told him what she wanted from him, pityingly.

'Lady,' he said wearily, 'have you any idea how many Vietnamese want to get the hell out of this city? There are one hundred and forty thousand names on our "endangered" list, and that's just the tip of the iceberg.'

'This woman was the common-law wife of Kyle Anderson, a helicopter pilot with the first Cav who died under torture in Hoa Lo,' Serena said icily. 'She has a child by him. Kyle died in his country's service. The least America can do is to ensure that the woman he loved, and his child, are flown to safety.'

The official looked at her with interest. 'How come you know so much about it?'

'Because she may have been his common-law wife, but I was married to him,' she said coolly. 'He wrote asking me for a divorce before he was killed. There is no doubt at all that it was a serious relationship and that Trinh and her daughter are as deserving to be evacuated as any other Vietnamese dependents of Americans.'

'Phew!' the official said, regarding her with deepening interest. 'I've heard quite a few stories across this desk, but this is the first time I've had a wife in here, pleading for a plane seat for her husband's mistress. It takes some believing, but as I *do* believe you, bring the necessary documents in and I'll make sure that she and her daughter are put on the list of evacuees.'

'And another family member,' Serena said ruthlessly. 'Trinh's sister.' With a wide, dazzling smile, she blew him a kiss of thanks and disappeared out of the room before he had a chance to refuse her.

It was when she returned from the embassy to the orphanage that she heard what was for her the worst news of the entire war.

Shortly after 3 p.m. a US military C-5A had departed from Tan Son Nhut crammed to capacity with orphan children bound for new homes in the States. The flight had been organized by Rosemary Taylor, a young Australian adoption-agency director both Serena and Mike had great respect for.

There were 243 children loaded on to the plane, with escorts to care for them on the long flight. Within minutes of takeoff the rear cargo doors blew out and the plane began to lose height. It skidded over the Saigon River, and then crashed into rice fields, breaking in half, the tail section erupting into flames, the nose section continuing to plow over the ground for another quarter of a mile or so.

One hundred and thirty-five of the three hundred and twenty-seven people aboard the plane died. Seventy-eight of the dead were children.

'Oh, God! I can't bear to think of it!' Serena sobbed when Gabrielle broke the news to her. 'Those children had so much to look forward to! A whole new life!'

Gabrielle put her arms around her, comforting her, her face ashen. It could so easily have been Cây Thông children aboard the C-5A. It could so easily have been Kylie and *le petit* Gavin.

It was now nearly three weeks since Mike and Lewis had set off in a requisitioned army truck for the Delta. No one who knew of the expedition, apart from Gabrielle and Serena, believed that they would ever be seen again. As the first week of April drew to a close, and the noose that the Communists had thrown around Saigon tightened, even Gabrielle and Serena began to lose hope.

'Even if they successfully reached Van Binh, how could they possibly evade the NVA on their return trip?' Gabrielle said despairingly. 'It is not possible, *chérie*.'

'It has to be possible!' Serena said fiercely. 'I couldn't survive if Mike died! I wouldn't know how to go on living!'

Gabrielle said nothing, instead she walked to the nearby Catholic cathedral and, for the first time in years, prayed.

On the morning of 8 April nearly everyone in Saigon thought the end had come. A fighter-bomber flew in from the South, bombing the Presidential Palace and the giant fuel dumps west of the city. As anti-aircraft fire blasted in retaliation, Gabrielle and Serena ran out of the orphanage and into the street, certain that a full-scale attack was about to take place. Instead, all they saw was the lone bomber banking steeply and flying away from the city, and a battered truck, enormous red crosses painted on the roof of the cab and the sides, crawling towards them.

'It's Mike!' Serena shrieked. 'Oh, dear God! It's *Mike*!'

She flew down the street, and the truck coughed and spluttered to a halt. Mike jumped down from the cab, grimy and weary and scarcely recognizable beneath a heavy growth of beard. She hurtled into his arms uncaringly. 'I thought you were dead!' she sobbed, hugging him so tight that she nearly knocked him off his feet. 'Never do this to me again! Never! Never! Never!'

As well as Lewis and a remarkably composed Tam, there were also thirteen children in the truck. All of them were tired to the point of collapse, and hungry and dehydrated.

'Let us get the children inside,' Gabrielle was saying, hugging Lewis, hugging Tam, so relieved at seeing them that she didn't know whether to laugh or cry.

'We're flying out on a scheduled flight,' Lewis said later that evening to Mike. 'I've been to the embassy and I've got clearance for Tam. Rules are being bent now, thank God.'

Mike didn't say anything, but he couldn't help wryly wondering if the fact that Lewis was West Point, an ex-POW, and an adviser at the American Embassy in London might not have had a little something to do with the ease with which the rules were, for him, being bent.

The next morning he drove Lewis and Tam out to Tan Son Nhut. The route was so packed with the cars of fleeing rich Vietnamese that the normally short drive took them nearly two hours.

'You're sure you've got seats reserved?' he asked Lewis anxiously. 'These people are going to be willing to pay bribes of thousands in order to get on a flight out.'

'Don't worry,' Lewis said grimly, his arm around Tam's shoulders. 'I've got everything that is necessary, and nothing on God's earth is going to prevent us flying out and putting Vietnam behind us forever!'

Tam had said very little to Mike on their arduous journey from Van Binh, but he was a good judge of people and he wasn't worried about her. She would find America strange at first, but she was a very special girl who allowed nothing to faze her. And she obviously thought that Lewis was the sun and the moon and the stars. Taking into account Abbra's marriage ceremony to Scott, a divorce between Lewis and Abbra would be quickly and easily obtained. Within months, maybe even weeks, Tam would be Mrs Lewis Ellis. Mike thought that when she was, she would be the kind of wife that any man would envy.

As they approached the airport gates they could see barbed-wire barricades being erected. A heavy police presence was vetting every car and possibly, Mike thought, demanding bribes. When Lewis showed the pass he had been given by the embassy, there were no such demands. They were waved through without harassment, and the same treatment was accorded them once they were inside the airport building. Despite the horrendous lines and the crush at the check-in desks, Lewis's pass insured that they were swept straight through towards the exit for departures.

'I don't know what the hell is on that pass of yours,' Mike said admiringly, 'but I wouldn't mind having a half dozen like it!'

It was time to say good-bye. A genuine friendship, born of mutual like and respect, had sprung up between them on the perilous journey to and from Van Binh, and they shook hands warmly, clasping each other on the back.

'Make sure Serena and *le petit* Gavin get out safely,' Lewis said urgently. 'There's not much time left, Mike. Perhaps only days.'

'I know,' Mike squeezed Lewis's hand hard one last time, kissed Tam on the cheek, and then stood back as they turned and walked out through the departure exit towards their waiting plane.

The adoption work at Cây Thông was facilitated by the Australian government's decision to take an unlimited number of children, providing that they were going to Australian parents. Australian planes were available to fly the children out. Air France and Pan Am flights were still taking children whose adoption had been processed to their new homes in America and Europe. For Mike and Serena, their days were a treadmill of caring for the children, of obtaining exit visas and travel documentation for those about to leave, arranging escorts for them and transporting them out to Tan Son Nhut.

On 17 April, Mike and Serena and Gabrielle were officially warned by their respective embassies that they should plan to leave the country while commercial aircraft were still operating.

'I'm not leaving yet,' Serena had said fiercely, 'not while there's a remote chance of getting more children out.'

'What about Trinh?' Gabrielle asked. 'Does she know what it is she has to do?'

The official Serena had spoken to at the American Embassy had agreed that Trinh and her sister and Kylie would leave the city when the order came for a final evacuation. Buses would pick up Americans and Vietnamese designated for departure at appointed places around the city and deliver them to various helicopter pads. From there they would be flown out to American ships, which would be waiting offshore.

Serena nodded. 'Yes, she's been given documentation and the address she has to go to immediately after the signal for the evacuation is broadcast over American armed forces radio.'

'And what is the signal?' Gabrielle asked curiously. As yet it was still a secret, but she knew that Lewis had informed Serena and Mike of it.

'When time has finally run out, and the North Vietnamese are only hours away, the armed forces radio will broadcast this announcement every fifteen minutes: "The temperature in Saigon is one hundred five degrees and rising" and the announcement will be followed by Bing Crosby singing *White Christmas*.'

Gabrielle giggled. 'A white Christmas in Saigon is not possible, *chérie*. Especially in April!'

On Friday 24 April, the last of the children for whom Mike and Serena had been able to arrange adoptions left for America. It was Serena who drove them to the airport. A report over Radio Hanoi had announced that all Vietnamese who had worked in any capacity for the adoption of orphans would be treated as war criminals. Mike had asked every one of the Vietnamese who had worked for them either as child-care helpers or as domestics if they wanted to leave the country. All those who had said they did want to leave had been officially listed as escorts for the departing children.

The flight they were leaving on was Pan Am's last flight from Saigon. The simple task of escorting the children through the necessary security checks and into the departure lounge took on nightmare proportions. There was a panic-stricken crush of people pleading vainly for tickets, and even those who possessed tickets were pushing their way through into the departure lounge as if, at any moment, the tickets would be ripped from their hands and their departure foiled.

With admirable British coolness Serena shepherded her flock through the chaos. The majority of those who were also cramming into the departure lounge were Vietnamese who possessed French citizenship and French passports. They were the elite. The lucky ones.

As Serena said a last good-bye to the children and to the Vietnamese escorts who were leaving with them, fighter jets flew in low and fast, strafing the perimeter of the airfield.

'Oh, what is happening?' one of the Vietnamese women said tearfully, grasping hold of Serena's hand. 'Are we not going to be able to leave? Is our plane going to be bombed?'

Over the sound of artillery and mortar fire, Serena assured her that the plane was going to leave and that it was going to leave safely.

Minutes later, as the fighters disappeared, the call came for all departing passengers to make their way towards their waiting plane.

Serena watched them file away, her heart in her mouth. But the fighters did not return. The giant plane taxied down the runway, lifting smoothly into the air, taking with it the last remaining orphans for whom it had been possible to arrange adoptions. They, at least, had a future to look forward to. They were going to families who would love and cherish them. The war would mar their lives no longer. She turned away, suddenly so tired she could barely stand. Almost semiconscious with weariness, she drove back through the refugee-thronged streets towards the Continental. There, in the room that had been her home for so many years, she tumbled into bed fully dressed, asleep within seconds.

Two days later, on 26 April, it was officially announced that General Duong Van Minh would take over as president of South Vietnam. There were very few foreigners left in the city now. The British Ambassador had departed, the New Zealand Embassy was empty and deserted; even a large majority of newsmen had left.

Free of the burden of ensuring that every child with an adoptive home to go to had all the necessary documentation and a flight seat, Mike had become a full-time doctor again, spending all his time trying to alleviate the suffering of the sick and often dying refugees who were still streaming into the city.

Serena spent the entire following day with Trinh. She had already spoken to Abbra on the telephone, telling her exactly what the situation was, and asking Abbra to meet Trinh and Mai and Kylie on their arrival in the United States. The happiness in Abbra's voice as she readily agreed, and as she told Serena of how she and Sanh and Scott were all reunited and living together as a family, was radiant. Now Serena wanted to make sure that Trinh understood who Abbra was, and how to get in touch with her if there was any difficulty.

'This is a photograph of Abbra,' she said, handing a group photograph of Abbra and Scott and Sanh to Trinh.

Trinh looked down at it and then up again at Serena. 'Her little boy. Is he Vietnamese?'

'Yes, Abbra and Scott have adopted him. I'm sure he'll love having visitors who are also Vietnamese, and I am sure that Kylie will make friends with him just as quickly as she did with little Gavin.'

'Little Gavin is not so very little anymore,' Trinh said with a rare, mischievous smile. 'Madame Ryan will soon have to think of another name so as not to confuse him with his father.'

No matter how many times Gabrielle and Serena had requested that Trinh cease to speak to them so formally, and to address them instead by their Christian names, she had refused.

'This may be the last time we shall see each other in Vietnam,' Serena said, rising to leave, suddenly serious. 'Big Minh is to be inaugurated as president tomorrow and I think that once he is president, the end will come very quickly.'

'But I will see you in America?' Trinh's dark eyes were anxious. If Kyle had been alive, America would have held

698

no terrors for her. But Kyle wasn't alive, and America seemed a very strange and frightening prospect.

'Yes,' Serena said unequivocally. 'I shall see you in America. *Chào*, Trinh.'

'*Chào*, Serena,' Trinh said a trifle shyly.

Serena grinned. It had taken a long time, almost too long, but at last she had broken through Trinh's doubts and reserve and gained her friendship. Kyle would have been pleased.

The next day the sky was grey and ominous, heavy clouds threatening to unleash the first monsoon of the season. The swearing-in ceremony of General Minh took place at five o'clock. It was a televised ceremony, and Gabrielle and Serena and Mike watched it together in Gabrielle and Serena's room at the Continental.

As the general began to speak, the heavens opened, rain pouring down on the city's roofs and pavements.

'The situation is very critical,' Minh said, trying to make himself heard over the sound of rolling thunder. 'I feel a responsibility now to seek a ceasefire and bring peace on the basis of the Paris Agreements . . .'

Lightning cracked over the hotel, followed by a long volley of thunder. At the same time, other rumblings could be heard. Serena looked across at Mike apprehensively. 'Artillery fire?' she asked.

Mike shook his head, striding to the window, no longer listening to the man who was now South Vietnam's president. 'Yes, but there are planes as well. Their target seems to be Tan Son Nhut.'

Before he had finished speaking they were aware of firing very near to them, coming from the direction of the Presidential Palace, and then Mike swung away from the window, saying tersely, 'Get down! The planes are coming this way, strafing as they come!'

From outside they could hear screaming in the street, and then anti-aircraft fire deafened them as they threw themselves to the floor.

When the brief attack was over, Serena ran for the phone, dialling Trinh's number. The lines were dead. 'I must go to her! Make sure she's okay!' she said frantically.

Mike walked across to her and removed the telephone receiver from her hand. 'You will do no such thing,' he said firmly. 'The streets aren't safe, there's still tracer fire. Trinh knows exactly what she must do. She has her radio, she has her documentation, and she has her bags packed. You can't achieve anything by going over to her.'

Serena leaned against him, knowing that he was right, hoping that now that there was no more hope for the city, the end would come swiftly.

That night Mike stayed with Serena and Gabrielle in their room at the Continental. None of them got any sleep. Tan Son Nhut was repeatedly bombed. Rocket fire lit up the night sky, and as dawn finally broke, Serena and Mike knew that the coming day was going to be the last they would spend in Saigon.

As artillery fire bombarded the outskirts of the city, Mike hurried through the now nearly deserted street, to the orphanage. There were no children there, for they had taken no more in since the last group had left for the States. He went into his office, rifling through files, selecting those that were vital, destroying those that weren't. Then he quickly packed a small bag of personal possessions and headed back towards the Continental.

As he entered the room, Serena said to him, 'The evacuation signal has been broadcast. It's being broadcast every fifteen minutes. Listen.'

She turned the volume up on her radio. Music was playing. After a few minutes it came to an end and a calm, unruffled voice announced, 'The temperature is one hundred and five degrees and rising' and then there came the soft, dulcet tones of Bing Crosby singing 'I'm dreaming of a white Christmas'.

'That's it then,' Mike said. 'Let's go.'

He turned towards Gabrielle. 'Are you sure you're doing the right thing staying, Gabrielle? Are you sure you will be safe?'

'*Oui*,' she replied with a big smile. 'In another few hours Gavin may be in Saigon. Already he is probably on the outskirts with the army. Nothing in the world would make me leave Saigon now.'

Looking down at her, so petite and so heartbreakingly optimistic, Mike felt his throat tighten. 'How long has it been, Gabrielle?' he asked. 'How long have you and Gavin been apart?'

Her eyes met his, overly bright. '*Neuf Noëls*,' she said huskily. Nine Christmases. She looked down at her son, who had been staring at the window, gazing down into the square with rapt attention. 'It is time for us to say *au 'voir* for a little while, *chéri*,' she said lovingly. 'Stay with Serena and Mike. Keep very tight hold of Serena's hand and do not let go of it, do you promise me?'

Gavin nodded. He had already spent long days trying to persuade his mother to allow him to stay with her, but it had been hopeless. She had been adamant that he leave with Serena and Mike. Now, knowing that to argue any further was useless, and looking forward to the promised helicopter ride from the roof of the embassy to a ship of the US 7th fleet far out in the China Sea, he merely said, 'I promise, *Maman*,' and then, as he had done when he was younger, he flung himself against her and hugged her tightly saying, 'I love you, *Maman*!'

'I love you too, *chéri*,' Gabrielle fought back an upsurge of tears. '*Au ' voir*, take care.'

The streets that had been deserted all morning were suddenly no longer deserted. Army buses and private cars and taxis began speeding through them as the remaining Americans in Saigon heeded the message that had just been broadcast to them and began heading hell-for-leather towards their prearranged pick up points.

As they did so, the Saigonese teemed out from wherever they had been sheltering, converging like lemmings on the American Embassy, determined to have one last, valiant try at hitching a helicopter ride out of their doomed city.

Mike and Serena and *le petit* Gavin didn't need transportation to reach the embassy. It was only a few blocks away. Carrying one bag of hand luggage each, they hurried up Tu Do, past the twin-spired red-brick cathedral and on to Thong Nhut Boulevard, where the embassy was situated.

Mike took one look at the crowds of desperate Vietnamese besieging the gates and walls and said grimly, 'We're never going to get through. Not at this entrance anyway.'

Barbed wire had been rolled along the tops of the nine-foot-high walls, and marines, M-16s at the ready, were standing behind the barbed wire, preventing anyone from scrambling over or swinging across from the nearby lamp stanchions.

'What shall we do?' Serena yelled, gripping hold of *le petit* Gavin's hand tightly. 'Try the Mac Dinh Chi gate entrance?'

Mike nodded, and they battled their way through a mass of desperate humanity. Many of those haranguing the soldiers on the wall were waving pieces of paper, shouting out that they were the employees of Americans, that they had been promised evacuation. Because of their loyalty to Americans the North Vietnamese would shoot them. The marines were deaf to all solicitations, she saw one marine kick his booted foot into the face of one youth who had managed to scale the wall, and another marine bring the butt of his M-16 down hard on a hand searching frantically for leverage.

As they fought their way towards the Mac Dinh Chi entrance gate her bag was wrenched from her hand. She was almost grateful to be relieved of it. There was nothing in it of great value, and without it, it was easier to forge a way in Mike's wake.

At the Mac Dinh Chi gate a marine spotted them in the crowd and yelled, 'Push to the front! I'll haul you over!'

It was easier said than done. At the knowledge that a couple of privileged Americans were about to be dragged to safety while they were left behind, the crowd went wild. Serena felt blows raining down on her as Mike physically fought to make a passageway through for them.

'Gavin!' Serena gasped. 'Get him to take Gavin first!'

Mike took hold of Gavin, lifting him shoulder high. The marine bent forwards, took hold of Gavin's hands, and hauled him upwards. As he did so, Mike tossed his bag, and Gavin's, high over the wall.

'I have passport! I have passport!' a Vietnamese woman was yelling frantically to Serena. 'Tell them to let me in too! Tell them my husband, my son, both work for Americans! Both now in Bangkok! I cannot be left here alone! Tell them, Madame! Tell them!'

'I'm going to inch open the gate!' the marine yelled down to Mike. 'Slip through fast. You won't get a second chance.'

The gate inched open and from the pressure of the crowd around her, Serena felt as if the breath were being squeezed out of her body. Mike had pushed her in front of him and as the crowd surged forwards she literally fell into the embassy compound.

'There's a woman out there with a passport! Her husband and son both worked for Americans! You have to let her in!' she yelled up to the marine. But it was too late. Mike was panting for breath, the gate firmly closed behind him, and the desperate hands clenching on to the gate's bars went ignored.

'Jesus! This is worse than anything I'd ever imagined,' Serena sobbed, hugging a terrified Gavin close. 'Those poor people! What on earth is going to become of them? I thought everyone who had worked for the Americans had been promised a safe passage out?'

'They had, it's a promise that's going to be impossible for the Americans to keep,' Mike said, putting his arm around her shoulder and picking up his bag and *le petit* Gavin's. 'Time has run out. Tan Son Nhut is unusable, and so there'll be no evacuations from there. This whole process should have been started weeks ago, not left to the last minute.'

The embassy compound was thronged with Americans and third-party nationals like themselves, and with high-ranking Vietnamese. A landing zone in the embassy's parking lot had been cleared in order that helicopters could land, but so far none had arrived.

'There must be over two thousand people here,' Mike said, wiping beads of perspiration from his forehead. 'How many can a Huey hold? Fourteen? Sixteen?'

It was obvious that they were going to be in for a long wait before they were flown out, and they edged their way through crowds that were now orderly to find room in which they could all sit down.

As Serena was reflecting that she had been foolish not to have had the forethought to have brought some food and drink with her, she heard an American close by saying, 'Christ! I thought I wasn't going to make it at all! My evacuation station was in Hūu Ngoc Street, and then we were told that no one was going to show there, that we had to make our way here. If it hadn't been that they sent a bus for us, we'd never have made it. The atmosphere out there is definitely ugly!'

Serena spun towards him. 'Hūu Ngoc Street? Did you say Hūu Ngoc Street?'

The American nodded. Panic seized hold of Serena's heart. 'Were there any Vietnamese with you? Did the Vietnamese leave with you on the bus?'

The American shook his head. 'There weren't any Vietnamese that I remember. Hell, why would there be? The house in Hūu Ngoc was a strictly American pickup.'

Serena had known that. But the official at the embassy had assured her that with the documentation that Trinh possessed, it would make no difference.

And if the helicopter pickup from Hũu Ngọc Street had gone as planned, it wouldn't have made any difference. But would Trinh and Mai and Kylie have been able to make it into the embassy compound? She remembered the desperate Vietnamese outside, waving passports, waving letters, waving all the pathetic pieces of documentation that they had believed would see them out of the country.

She turned to Mike, gripping hold of his arm. 'You heard all that, didn't you? She couldn't have made it, Mike. I *know* that she couldn't have made it!'

Mike looked around at the crush in the compound. To search it, looking for Trinh and Mai and Kylie was practically an impossibility. It would take far too long. Especially if she wasn't there, because by then it would be too late to go in search of her.

He said briefly, 'I'll go back outside and see if I can see her. She may even have returned home if she thinks it's truly hopeless. Or she may have had the forethought to go to Gabrielle at the Continental.'

'Oh, God!' Serena whispered hoarsely. 'Be careful, Mike! Please be careful!'

He kissed her long and hard and then, without another word, he spun on his heel, striding towards the nearest exit, aware that at that precise moment in time, he was the only man in the entire city of Saigon that wanted to leave the American Embassy compound and not enter it.


The next few hours were the longest of Serena's life. At five o'clock the first of the helicopters arrived and marines began to organize the two-thousand-strong crowd into some sort of order.

At dusk Mike still hadn't returned, and her British coolness was fast beginning to desert her. She and Gavin had searched the compound time and time again, and had found no trace of Trinh, or of Mai and Kylie.

705

The clamour outside the gates had intensified to nightmarish proportions, and combined with it was the sound of heavy shelling in the city's outskirts.

'They're not going to be able to get us all out before the city is taken,' an elegantly dressed American woman said quietly to Serena. 'If I were you, I would take your place in line, otherwise you and your little boy might be left behind.'

Serena didn't care if she was left behind, not if Mike was too, but she couldn't risk *le petit* Gavin being left behind. Very reluctantly she edged a way into the line that was moving slowly forwards towards the foot of the stairs leading to the embassy's roof.

At about eight o'clock there was a loud explosion from the front of the embassy. Someone said that it was a hand grenade exploding, someone else said that it sounded as if a match had been dropped into the petrol tank of a car. No one knew.

Serena and Gavin were nearing the top of the six flights of stairs, and she knew that if she stayed with him any longer, she was going to find herself on a helicopter, winging her way across the South China Sea, and not knowing where Mike was, or what had happened to him.

She bent down so that she was eye to eye with Gavin. 'Listen, my love. I'm going back into the compound to see if I can find Mike. Whatever happens, you are not to move from here. You are to continue in the line, and if your turn comes to board a helicopter and I have not come back, you are to board it by yourself. Do you understand?'

He nodded. Although he was only nine, he already possessed his mother's unwavering common sense, and Serena knew that she could rely on him.

'These are your papers,' she said, slipping his passport and identity documents into his inside jacket pocket. 'Look after them very, very carefully.' She kissed him lightly on the forehead. 'I will see you soon. Either back here, or on an American ship far out at sea!'

706

He grinned. He didn't really mind being left alone. It made everything even more exciting. And he couldn't wait to board one of the helicopters and fly out into the darkness.

Serena squeezed her way back down the stairs and out into the compound. She satisfied herself that Mike and Trinh were not among those still waiting for a place in the line and then pushed her way towards the main gate. More marines than ever were now manning the walls, and the shouts and pleas from those outside were deafening.

'Have you seen a New Zealander out there?' she yelled up to the marine nearest to her. 'A big, broadly built man?'

The crowd outside the walls was turning very nasty and the marine didn't take his eyes away from it to look at her, but he shook his head.

Overhead in the purple-deep sky the *whump-whump-whump* of helicopter rotor blades battled against the sound of artillery and rocket fire. Serena wondered how many people there were waiting to be flown out, how many more flights would be able to be made, how many would be left behind when the last flight had departed.

Suddenly, scanning the faces of the throng in the street beyond the barred gate, she caught a glimpse of Mike.

'*That's him!*' she yelled to the marine. '*Can you see him? Has he someone with him?*'

Despite the scores of hands gripping the bars of the gate from the outside, her own fingers found a place on them.

'*Mike!*' she yelled with all her strength. '*Mike!*'

He heard her, saw her. He was carrying Kylie in his arms, and Trinh was at his side, but she could see no sign of Mai.

The marines were yelling at him, leaning over as far as they dared, hitting out at the crowd with the butts of their M-16s in order to make a way through for him. She saw him reach the gate, saw Trinh's terrified face,

707

and then, before they could be hauled inside, the crowd turned on him. She saw one youth raise a club and bring it hard down on Mike's head, saw Mike falter, drop Kylie, and fall.

She was screaming at the marines to open the gates so that she could get to him, but their attention was centred on the mob in front of them. Trinh was sobbing, grabbing hold of Kylie.

Serena seized hold of the person nearest to her, not knowing if it was a man or a woman, a Vietnamese or an American. '*Lift me up!*' she screamed at them. '*For Christ's sake, lift me up!*'

Whoever it was obeyed her, and blessedly strong arms hoisted her high. She could no longer see Mike, but she could see Trinh and Kylie, and she shouted out, '*Pass Kylie over to me, Trinh!*'

Out of the corner of her eye she was aware that Mike's unconscious body was being hauled up the side of the wall at rifle point by two marines. He was safe. There was only Kylie and Trinh to worry about now, and Trinh was already lifting Kylie up towards her.

The little girl was screaming in terror, but Serena had hold of her. With a strength she didn't know she possessed, she lifted Kylie clear of the gate, dropping her down to safety. Then, sobbing with relief, she turned to grasp hold of Trinh's upstretched hands. Their fingers touched, grasped hold. Stones were being thrown at them now, and one of them hit Serena's left temple. She cried out in pain, blood gushing into her eye, still holding on to Trinh. A marine stretched his hand down towards Trinh, about to haul her upwards and in utter rage a Vietnamese who had for hours been beseeching the marines to allow him to enter lifted a pistol high and fired at Trinh's head.

Blood spurted on to Serena's hands and arms. Shards of Trinh's skull flew upwards into the night air. She fell backwards and the crowd closed over her, baying for more blood. Baying for American blood.

Whoever it was who had been holding Serena lowered her exhaustedly to the ground. 'I'm sorry, lady,' he said awkwardly, handing her a handkerchief.

She pressed it against the cut on her face, looking at him for the first time. He was a big, burly Australian who looked as if he might be a construction worker.

'Yes,' she said numbly, and then, 'Thank you.'

She bent down, putting her arms around Kylie's shoulders, hugging her close, not knowing how much she had seen.

'It's time for us to go,' a dearly loved voice said gently.

She looked up, and Mike was standing unsteadily beside her, his face ashen.

'Yes.' She stood upright, her arm still around Kylie's shoulders. 'Where was Mai?' she asked. 'Wasn't she with you?'

Mike shook his head. 'She changed her mind at the last minute. Trinh and Kylie went to the evacuation point alone.'

Above them a CH-47 Chinook rose from the embassy roof, skimming over the garden of the French Embassy that was adjacent to the American Embassy, and climbing away eastwards.

'Let's go,' Mike said again, and heavy-hearted and sombre-eyed, he led the way back towards the line leading to the stairs.

It was two in the morning before they were finally evacuated. As they sat hunched in the helicopter, Kylie no longer sobbing, but whimpering softly as Mike held her gently in his arms, Serena looked down at the city below them. The roads converging on it were full of lights. The headlights of North Vietnamese army trucks. She wondered if Gavin Ryan was in one of them, if, in another few hours, he and Gabrielle would at last be reunited. She hoped so. She hoped some happiness would come out of Saigon's hideous death throes.

# CHAPTER THIRTY-EIGHT

Despite the mayhem in the streets and the deafening noise of artillery and mortar fire that was coming from the city's suburbs, the Continental Hotel was strangely silent. There were no more journalists there, or if there were, they were conspicuous only by their absence.

Gabrielle removed all her western clothing and donned the loose black pyjamas of a peasant. Then she covered her vivid red hair with a black kerchief and topped that with one of the conical straw hats that all the local girls wore. She looked at herself in the mirror and was satisfied. All the Vietnamese aspects of her features had been accentuated, and she doubted if anyone would mistake her for a Westerner.

She slipped out of the hotel, making her way to her aunt's house. Nhu, the sister of a man who had held the rank of colonel in the North Vietnamese Army, was waiting for the North Vietnamese Army's arrival without the least trace of fear.

'It will not be long now,' she said, pouring Gabrielle a glass of rice wine and then turning the lamp on the table down low so as not to attract any attention from the looters who were already rampaging the streets.

'No,' Gabrielle agreed, so tense with excitement that she could scarcely breathe.

They were talking of different things. Her aunt was referring to the final reunification of North and South Vietnam into one country. Gabrielle was thinking only of Gavin.

There was very little sleep for either of them. Every twenty minutes or so there would be the sound of helicopters flying in and landing in the parking lot at the embassy or on the rooftop. Then, after a short interval, they would hear them again, lifting into the night sky and wheeling eastwards over the city towards the South China Sea. In the early hours of the morning there came the sound of a loud explosion from the direction of the embassy. Neither of them could imagine what it could be.

The sound of helicopters beating overhead continued, and occasionally the sounds of shouting and screaming also reached them. 'It is those who worked for the Americans,' Nhu said quietly, 'those who are going to be left behind when the helicopters cease to come.'

The helicopters came and departed with less and less regularity. Shortly after seven-thirty a Chinook 46, escorted by six Cobra gunships, flew from the roof of the embassy. After that there were no more helicopters.

Nhu looked tiredly across at Gabrielle. 'They have gone,' she said simply. 'The Americans have finally left Vietnam.'

Gabrielle's hands tightened in her lap. *Le petit* Gavin would be aboard a US ship now with Mike and Serena. He would be safe, and when they were reunited, he would be reunited with Gavin also.

Nhu raised the blinds on a bright, sunny morning, clean and sweet-smelling after the previous day's downpour.

'I'm going out,' Gabrielle said, picking up her conical straw hat. 'I'll bring back some croissants for breakfast.'

'And I will stay by the radio,' Nhu said, tuning it to the BBC.

Gabrielle walked leisurely towards the central square. The city was transformed almost beyond recognition. There were no cyclos racing down the streets, no Hondas, no blue and yellow taxis, no traffic at all. And there were no policemen.

Even the pavement outside the Continental was deserted. No flower sellers, no cigarette peddlers, no prostitutes. It

712

was like walking on an empty stage set, waiting for the curtain to rise on the first act of a new play.

She bought some croissants, and then returned to Nhu's.

'There is nothing on the BBC,' Nhu said as she made coffee. 'Only news of the evacuation. Nothing about a surrender.'

'Let's try Radio Saigon,' Gabrielle said, adjusting the frequency. She was just in time to hear General Minh begin to speak.

'I believe firmly in reconciliation among all Vietnamese,' he began emotionally. 'To avoid needless bloodshed I ask the soldiers of the republic to put an end to all hostilities. Be calm and remain where you are now. To save the lives of the people, do not open fire. I also call on our brothers, the soldiers of the Provisional Revolutionary Government, not to open fire, because we are waiting here to meet with their representatives to discuss the orderly turnover of the reins of government, both civilian and military, without causing senseless bloodshed to the people.'

At the same time as the speech was being broadcast over the radio, Nhu and Gabrielle could also hear it being relayed over loudspeakers in the streets. Then, as General Minh finished speaking, there came the faint rumble of approaching tanks.

Despite Nhu's pleas, Gabrielle refused to stay indoors. Gavin might be with the very first soldiers to enter the city. She had to see the tanks arrive, had to be there.

Other Saigonese were also hesitantly gathering in the streets, fearful and apprehensive. Gabrielle began to walk in the direction of the Presidential Palace. The North Vietnamese would want to occupy key buildings first, and the first place they would want to fly their flag from would be the Presidential Palace.

At first there was only one tank. It rumbled majestically and undeterred down the street towards the palace and crashed through the palace gates. Small groups of bystanders gathered to see what would happen next.

Minutes later, on the palace balcony, the flag of the Provisional Revolutionary Government was raised over Saigon.

Other tanks soon followed the first one, and columns of soldiers followed the tanks, but there was no gunfire. Everything was very quiet, very orderly. Gabrielle stood for a moment watching the flag, realizing that at last, for better or for worse, Vietnam was again one country, and then she turned and began to make her way back towards the central square and the Continental.

That was where Gavin would head first. The Continental had always been the central meeting place in the city for all journalists and Europeans. He would go to the Continental in order to get his bearings, and she would be there, waiting for him.

The atmosphere in the streets was very strange. The North Vietnamese were neither being welcomed into the city as liberators, nor were they being repelled as invaders. It was as if they were simply being endured by a people who had endured much and would, no doubt, endure much more.

At the Continental Gabrielle went up to the room she had shared for so long with Serena. It looked out over the square and would give her a grandstand view of all arrivals.

Occasionally, as the long afternoon progressed, she would go back down into the street and across to Givralle where the proprietor was doing a roaring trade selling freshly baked rolls to North Vietnamese troops. With her face shaded beneath her conical straw hat, and in her black peasant pyjamas, Gabrielle attracted no attention, but she was shocked at how young the majority of the soldiers were.

She went back to her room and her vigil. She saw the western journalist she had seen earlier, this time he was talking to a South Vietnamese police colonel in front of the large statue of American marines that dominated the square. As she watched, the Vietnamese turned away from the journalist, saluted the statue, and then, before the journalist could stop him, raised the pistol to his head and fired.

Gabrielle covered her eyes. Despite the lack of house-to-house fighting, or bloodshed in the streets, it was obvious that retribution would be meted out by the North Vietnamese to men who had held high rank in South Vietnam's army or police force.

The man in the square below her had decided not to face such retribution, and she knew that there would be many others who would make the same choice.

Just as dusk was approaching, a fresh convoy of trucks chugged their way up Tu Do Street and into the square. They were crammed full of *bo dois*, North Vietnamese Army foot soldiers. All of them were dressed in baggy, dark green uniforms; all of them were wearing pith helmets. All but one. His hair was shaggy and tumbled and sun-gold.

She threw open the tall French windows, leaning perilously far out over the windowsill. '*Gavin!*' she cried, her heart full. '*Oh, mon amour! Gavin!*'

He stood in the back of the crowded truck looking around for the source of the cry. Then he looked upwards. Gabrielle saw a face that at first she scarcely recognized. There were deep lines furrowing his brow and running from nose to mouth, and then she saw his eyes, and they were Gavin's eyes, warm and grey and blessedly unchanged.

'Gavin, *mon amour!*' she shouted again hoarsely.

For a second he did not recognize her, and then she ripped the black kerchief from her hair, and her sizzling red curls tumbled free. With a cry rent from his very soul he vaulted from the truck, sprinting towards the Continental's entrance.

Gabrielle was already at the room of her door, running, running, running. She raced along the corridor, narrowly missing the elderly waiters who, with no customers to wait on, had taken to sleeping in the passageways on rush mats. She raced to the head of the stairs, her heart thundering,

715

the blood crashing in her ears. Down the stairs, running, running, running, taking them two and three at a time.

He was racing towards her. They were only yards away from each other. Only feet away.

'Oh, Gavin, *mon amour!*' she cried, hurtling into his arms, '*Tu m'es manqué*! How I have missed you!'

As soon as his lips touched hers, the long intervening years went whistling down the wind. Between them, nothing had changed. Between them, nothing ever would change.

'I love you, Gaby!' he said over and over again. 'Oh, sweet Christ! How I love you!'

She was laughing and crying at the same time, touching his face with her fingertips, running them over his eyebrows, his cheeks, his mouth. 'Is it really you, *mon amour*? Oh, after all this time, is it really you?'

Still kissing, still with their arms wrapped tightly around each other, they sat on the red carpeted steps of the Continental's grand staircase.

'I've never stopped missing you, never stopped loving you, Gaby,' he said huskily.

Her eyes held his, so full of love that he thought he would die with happiness. 'Nor me you,' she said softly and truthfully. 'Nor me you, *chéri*.'

A long time later they moved downstairs to the empty, grandiosely furnished main lounge.

'What happened?' she asked simply. 'What happened to you after Dinh was killed?'

With his arm around her shoulders, as Saigon prepared for its first night under Communist rule, Gavin told her of the life he had led for the last nine years, and which he had begun to think he would always lead.

'I was never treated badly. I was simply put to work in the fields, as were all the other prisoners in the camp I was in. There were no in-depth interrogation sessions, but whenever there was even the slightest contact between myself and any official, I always repeated that I was a friend of North Vietnam. That Comrade Duong Quynh Dinh, a hero of North Vietnam and a personal friend of General Giap, had invited me into the North to chronicle the historic battles that were taking place.

'And every official seemed completely indifferent to what I said. Then, a month ago, there was a change of attitude. I was told that North Vietnam was poised to take Saigon. And that at last I could fulfil the mission Colonel Duong had assigned to me.'

Gabrielle cuddled close against him. 'And so you travelled south, with the troops?'

'Yes.' He could still scarcely believe that it had happened, that he was no longer a prisoner, that he was free and with Gabrielle and in the Continental Palace Hotel in Saigon. 'And you?' he said gently, tilting her face upwards towards him. 'What have you been doing in the nine years that I have been away?'

She thought of Radford, and the rock band; of her return to the kind of singing that she loved the best, and of the heady success that she had achieved with it. She thought of the long months and years she had spent besieging the Vietnamese Embassy in Paris to get information about him, the years in Saigon with Nhu and Serena. And she thought of *le petit* Gavin. None of the other things mattered. She would tell him about them all, eventually. Even about Radford. For now she would tell him about his son.

When she had finished, and when it was completely dark outside, she said, 'What happens now, *mon amour*? Will we be allowed to leave the country?'

He nodded. 'I've been told to report to the French Embassy. It's the only embassy still functioning. It may be a long time until there are scheduled flights, but when there are, we'll be on board one of them.'

'And so it is all over,' she said, raising the back of his hand to her lips and kissing it. 'No more waiting. No more heartbreak.'

717

He grinned down at her. One of the aged waiters had thoughtfully lit the lamps in the room, and in the lamplight Gavin's shaggy mop of hair was a dull, burnished gold. Incredibly, at that moment he scarcely looked any older than he had the day she had met him. 'For you, and me, and for *le petit* Gavin, everything good and wonderful is just about to start,' he said huskily, and then he lowered his mouth to hers, and her arms slid around his neck.

# EPILOGUE

Abbra and Scott, with Sanh holding Abbra's hand tightly, stood in the arrivals hall at Orly Airport. Serena and Mike, and Kylie and *le petit* Gavin were with them. An Air France 707 from Bangkok had just landed, and Gabrielle and Gavin were aboard it.

'Oh, goodness, I wish they would hurry the passengers through passport and customs!' Abbra said impatiently. 'It's been on the ground for fifteen minutes now!'

Serena's mouth was so dry that she couldn't speak. Her arm was around *le petit* Gavin's shoulders, and the emotional drama of the scene that was about to be enacted was almost too much for her.

'They're beginning to come through now,' Scott said tensely as a handful of passengers filed out, pushing luggage-laden trolleys before them.

'Oh, God!' Abbra whispered beneath her breath, her eyes shining. 'They will be here in a minute! Oh, I can't believe it!'

An old woman came out of the swinging doors leading from the customs hall, and then a couple of teenagers. Serena felt as if she were going to die with nervous anticipation. They could be only minutes away now. Only seconds.

The doors swung open again, and this time no heavily laden luggage trolley was trundled through. Instead, Gavin and Gabrielle burst into the departure hall, holding hands.

Serena saw a fair-haired, surprisingly boyish-looking man in his early thirties, with warm grey eyes and a dazzlingly attractive smile.

'*Gabrielle!*' Abbra cried, racing forwards.

Serena was hard on her heels. For a few crazy seconds they hugged and kissed, three women who had shared the same brand of suffering, who were bound closer together as friends than they would ever be with anyone else, ever.

At the same moment, Serena and Abbra remembered *le petit* Gavin. They stood aside. *Le petit* Gavin's eyes were fixed on Gavin's. Suddenly they were all very still. If there was noise in the arrivals hall around them, none of them was aware of it.

Gavin smiled at his son. 'Hello, Gavin,' he said tenderly. 'We have a lot of time to make up for, don't we?' and he opened his arms wide.

*Le petit* Gavin uttered a strangled cry and then sprinted forwards into his father's arms, clasping him tight, tears falling down his face.

Gabrielle looked around at her friends, her smile radiant. 'I think some introductions are called for,' she said, her eyes dancing with laughter at the ridiculous realization that there they were, all such good friends, and yet not everyone had been introduced. 'Scott has not yet been introduced to Serena and Mike, Mike hasn't been introduced to Abbra, and Gavin has not yet been introduced to anybody!'

'Let's make all the introductions over champagne at La Closerie des Lilas,' Gavin said, setting his son back on the ground but keeping firmly hold of his hand.

'A good idea!' Abbra enthused as Scott slipped his arm around her shoulders.

'A *wonderful* idea,' Serena agreed in the cut-glass English accent that amused Gabrielle and Mike so much.

Mike took Serena's hand in his and Gavin's free hand encircled Gabrielle's waist. Abbra and Serena and Gabrielle looked across at each other and laughed with sheer joy. Then, their children at their side, they walked out of the arrivals hall into the Parisian May sunshine, three stunningly beautiful women, deeply and happily in love.

THE END